TWENTY THOUSAND ~~LEAGUES~~
UNDER THE SEAS

JULES VERNE was born in Nantes in 1828, the eldest of five children in a prosperous family of French, Breton, and Scottish extraction. His early years were happy apart from an unfulfilled passion for his cousin Caroline. Literature always attracted him and while taking a law degree in Paris he wrote a number of plays. His first two books, entitled *Journey to Scotland* and *Paris in the Twentieth Century*, were not published in his lifetime. However, *Five Weeks in a Balloon* was accepted by the publisher Hetzel in 1862, and became an immediate success. It was followed by *Journey to the Centre of the Earth*, *Twenty Thousand Leagues under the Seas*, *Around the World in Eighty Days*, and sixty other novels covering the whole world—and beyond. Verne himself travelled over three continents, before suddenly selling his yacht in 1886. Eight of the books appeared after his death in 1905—although in fact partly written by his son, Michel.

WILLIAM BUTCHER was formerly Head of the Language Centre at the Hong Kong Technical College. He has studied at Warwick, Lancaster, London, and the École Normale Supérieure, and has taught languages and pure mathematics in Malaysia, France, and Britain. As well as thirty articles on French literature, he has published *Mississippi Madness* (1990), *Verne's Journey to the Centre of the Self* (1990), and translations and critical editions of Verne's *Humbug* (1991), *Backwards to Britain* (1992), *Journey to the Centre of the Earth* (1992), and *Around the World in Eighty Days* (1995). Dr Butcher is at present working on a book on natural language processing.

OXFORD WORLD'S CLASSICS

*For over 100 years Oxford World's Classics have brought
readers closer to the world's great literature. Now with over 700
titles—from the 4,000-year-old myths of Mesopotamia to the
twentieth century's greatest novels—the series makes available
lesser-known as well as celebrated writing.*

*The pocket-sized hardbacks of the early years contained
introductions by Virginia Woolf, T. S. Eliot, Graham Greene,
and other literary figures which enriched the experience of reading.
Today the series is recognized for its fine scholarship and
reliability in texts that span world literature, drama and poetry,
religion, philosophy and politics. Each edition includes perceptive
commentary and essential background information to meet the
changing needs of readers.*

OXFORD WORLD'S CLASSICS

JULES VERNE

The Extraordinary Journeys

Twenty Thousand Leagues under the Seas

Translated with an Introduction and Notes by
WILLIAM BUTCHER

OXFORD
UNIVERSITY PRESS

OXFORD

UNIVERSITY PRESS

Great Clarendon Street, Oxford OX2 6DP

Oxford University Press is a department of the University of Oxford.
It furthers the University's objective of excellence in research, scholarship,
and education by publishing worldwide in

Oxford New York

Athens Auckland Bangkok Bogotá Buenos Aires Cape Town
Chennai Dar es Salaam Delhi Florence Hong Kong Istanbul Karachi
Kolkata Kuala Lumpur Madrid Melbourne Mexico City Mumbai Nairobi
Paris São Paulo Shanghai Singapore Taipei Tokyo Toronto Warsaw

with associated companies in Berlin Ibadan

Oxford is a registered trade mark of Oxford University Press
in the UK and in certain other countries

Published in the United States
by Oxford University Press Inc., New York

British Library Cataloguing in Publication Data

Data available

Library of Congress Cataloging in Publication Data

Verne, Jules, 1828–1905.
[Vingt mille lieues sous les mers. English]
Twenty thousand leagues under the seas / Jules Verne; translated
with an introduction and notes by William Butcher.
(Oxford world's classics) (The extraordinary journeys)
Includes bibliographical references.
1. Underwater exploration—Fiction. 2. Submarines (Ships)—
Fiction. I. Butcher, William, 1951– . II. Title. III. Series.
IV. Series: Verne, Jules, 1828–1905. Voyages extraordinaires. English.
PQ2469.V4E5 1998 843'.8—dc21 97–29726

ISBN–13: 978–0–19–282839–2
ISBN–10: 0–19–282839–8

11

Typeset by Best-set Typesetters Ltd., Hong Kong
Printed in Great Britain by
Clays Ltd, St Ives plc

CONTENTS

ACKNOWLEDGEMENTS

I would like to thank Greg Scott, Angela Brown, and Elizabeth Stewart for their tremendous help with the preparation of the manuscript, together with Priscilla Lee, Iris Yuen, Coty Leung, Art Evans, Laurence Price, Betty Harless, Henry Sharton, Cécile Compère, Cécile Hautière, the staff of the Centre de documentation Jules Verne d'Amiens, and Susie Casement. A special word of thanks should go to John Joseph for the friendship and support he gave at a crucial stage. Frederick Walter provided many invaluable suggestions. Angel Lui, finally, has given her help and affection unstintingly.

LIST OF ABBREVIATIONS

BSJV	*Bulletin de la société Jules Verne*
MD	Marcel Destombes, 'Le Manuscrit de *Vingt mille lieues sous les mers* de la Société de Géographie', *BSJV* 9: 3v16 (July–Dec. 1975)
MÉR	*Magasin d'Éducation et de Récréation*: without other reference, *MÉR* refers to the serial publication of *20TL* (1869–70)
MS1 (or MS1A or MS1B)	the earlier of the two manuscripts in the French National Library
MS2 (or MS2A or MS2B)	the later of the two manuscripts in the French National Library
PC	Peter Costello
20TL	*Twenty Thousand Leagues under the Seas*
WJM and FPW	Walter James Miller and Frederick Paul Walter

'1869' refers to the first book publication of *20TL* (1869–70).

'1871' refers to the definitive (illustrated) book publication of *20TL*, used for nearly all modern editions.

INTRODUCTION

IF you ask people for the name of the world's most translated writer, the best-seller of all time, the only popular writer to have increased in popularity over more than a century,[1] you will get some surprising answers. If you further enquire as to the identity of the only Frenchman to have achieved universal renown and which of his fictional heroes and vessels are often quoted without even naming the work, some odd looks may be forthcoming.

Verne, Nemo, and the *Nautilus* have entered the world's collective memory; but the three remain so far away from real recognition that they must be located in some deep, subconscious fold of it. The only signs of their existence, dragged up from the murky depths, are invariably confused or mistaken. These blinking apologies for a reputation need to be put out of their misery. Thus Verne is *not* a science-fiction writer: most of his books contain *no* innovative science. He did *not* write for children. The poor style often associated with his name is *not* his. And Nemo does *not* speak with a mid-Atlantic drawl.

In order to try to understand how these ideas came to life, and how such an outstanding literary figure could have acquired so poor a reputation in Britain and America, we should start by briefly disposing of the author's life and studying Verne's publishing history.

Jules Verne was born and brought up in Nantes, studied and worked in Paris, and then spent the rest of his life in Amiens. His first foreign visit was to Scotland in 1859, an experience which deeply marked his works. From about 1870 Verne displayed an increasing pessimism about many of his early enthusiasms, with the previous admiration for technology replaced by apprehensions on social and political issues, and with the British, the heroes of

---

[1] Unesco's *Index Translationum* lists the number of new editions of translations appearing worldwide each year. In Vol. 39, covering 1992, Verne had 215 publications, ahead of the Bible, and behind only Lenin (260) and Agatha Christie (290). However, in Vol. 8 for 1955, Verne had 94 for Christie's 45, and 1970 is similar. It is clear, then, that if total figures are calculated, and the Bible is excluded, Verne becomes the overall leader, on an estimated 6,000 to 8,000 volumes.

his first two novels, sometimes now the villains. The Franco-Prussian War and the Commune of 1870 seem to have been the most important external catalysts for the change. In terms of the individual works, *The Chancellor* (written in about 1870, but published in 1873) was the clear turning-point; but signs of uneasiness may already be visible in *Twenty Thousand Leagues under the Seas* (written in 1865–6 and 1868–70, and published in 1869–70).

From the beginning, recognition for the series of the *Extraordinary Journeys* was slow in coming in the English-speaking countries. The first novels of Verne's to be translated in book form came out after Verne had already written most of his best work. It must have been disappointing for the author of *The British at the North Pole* to see this book unavailable to the British themselves.[2] But when the works did begin to appear, it might have been better if they hadn't.

The books were generally chopped by about 20 per cent. The translators, frequently anonymous, often did not understand the French, and so mistranslated it. In the process, they produced some wonderful howlers. In the English Verne the hero visits the 'disagreeable territories of Nebraska' or 'jumps over' part of an island; reference is made to 'prunes' or 'Galilee'; and Napoleon dies broken-hearted in 'St Helen's'. Verne himself wrote of 'the Badlands of Nebraska', 'blowing up', 'plums', 'Galileo', and 'St Helena'! Nor is such abuse of the rights of the author yet over. A great majority of the current English editions of Verne continue to be of an unacceptable standard. And this, I would claim, is the main reason for his poor reputation.

If we examine *Twenty Thousand Leagues under the Seas* in particular, there have been hundreds of editions of this work, perhaps making the English version the most frequently published novel of all time. Lewis Mercier's 1872 translation was typical of the time: adequate on 'style' but extremely weak on details. Also, about 22 per cent of the novel is missing! Since then, over half of the editions have reproduced Mercier, many of them making further minor changes without, unfortunately, referring back to

---

[2] History was to repeat itself, for *Backwards to Britain* was published in six countries (with two different editions in Italy!) before belatedly appearing in Britain.

the French; and it is often the editions that protest the most about poor translation which are themselves the least faithful and the most Mercier-like!

There has also been a low level of critical commentary on the *Extraordinary Journeys* in the English-speaking world, frequently the result of monolinguals studying these truncated and inaccurate translations. Even Verne's most distinguished novel has not received the treatment that other works of the English or French literary canon get by right. Nor has the most basic textual work been done. The different original editions of *Vingt mille lieues sous les mers* have hardly been compared; there is no properly established text; and to date no one has studied the manuscript in detail.[3] These three omissions are all the more surprising when one considers the position this novel occupies in the history of ideas and the resonances it continues to produce on successive generations.

We need to proceed cautiously if we are to understand the work translated as *Twenty Thousand Leagues under the Seas*, and we should be wary of secondary sources, even of the published French text. As an introduction to the novel itself, we will start by examining the plot, before studying the origins of Verne's inspiration.

Twenty Thousand Leagues is Verne's most ambitious novel in terms of the breadth and diversity of its themes and psychology. It recounts a circumnavigation of the globe by submarine, with Captain Nemo ('nobody' in Latin) as the sombre hero. It includes many dramatic episodes: the underwater burial of a dead crewman; an attack by Papuan natives; a battle with giant squid; a passage under the Antarctic ice-cap; a farewell to the sun at the newly discovered South Pole; and a vision of the underwater ruins of Atlantis. But much of the interest comes from the intense if distant relationship between Nemo and his passengers, Dr Aronnax, Conseil, and Ned Land, and from the anguish gripping the captain. Nemo seems to have an unhealthy interest in

---

[3] Destombes is the only exception, but his excellent study looks at relatively small parts of the manuscripts.

In general, further information about the ideas in this Introduction will be found in the Note on the Text and Translation (p. xxxii) and the Explanatory Notes (p. 385).

shipping lanes and vessels in distress. On one occasion he demands that Aronnax be shut up in a cell. Further mysteries are the portraits in his room of patriotic heroes and of a woman and children, later revealed to be his murdered family. At the end of the novel the captain is attacked by an unidentified ship, and retaliates by sinking it. The three guests escape as the *Nautilus* sinks into the Maelstrom.

According to the author's grandson, Jean Jules-Verne, Verne's original idea was simply to write a 'poem' to the glory of the sea. Maurice Verne is reported to have said that, 'at bottom, my uncle Jules only had three passions: freedom, music, and the sea'. We also know that in 1865 the novelist George Sand suggested to Verne that the sea was the one area of the globe where his 'scientific knowledge and imagination' had not yet been put to use.

Much of the inspiration for *Twenty Thousand Leagues* came in fact from Verne's own experience. He was born on an island in a major whaling port; and while preparing the book he spoke to mariners in Nantes and Amiens, including his brother Paul, a retired naval officer. In 1865 he bought a fishing-boat of 8 or 10 tonnes and used it as a study while sailing along the Brittany and Normandy coasts. In 1868 it was refitted and baptized the *Saint-Michel*; in September he sailed to Gravesend on it, where he wrote: 'I'm just finishing the first volume of *Twenty Thousand Leagues* . . . How beautiful [the scenery] is and what fuel for the imagination!' His wife is meant to have sardonically commented: 'How can Jules write all those things [about the sea's marvels], when he turns his backside to them all the time?'

For two of the major scenes of *Twenty Thousand Leagues*, Nemo's elevated surveying of the ruins of Atlantis and his claiming of the new continent of Antarctica, it is no exaggeration to say that, *mutatis mutandis*, the author is drawing inspiration from Scotland, and in particular from the King's Park in Edinburgh. On Verne's second day outside France, the volcanic Arthur's Seat dominating the park was the first mountain he had ever visited. Imbued as he was with Scott and romanticism, immediately in love with this exotic land, he generated a sublime vision from the classical and marine view, one which was to be recycled endlessly in his novels. Equally surprisingly, Nemo's domestic arrangements in the heart of the raging depths are drawn from Verne's visit a couple of days later to the rain-swept but luxurious 'château' of 'Ockley' in Fife. This building can be identified here for the first time as Inzievar House in Oakley; a reading of chapters 27–9 of Verne's *Backwards to Britain* (written in about 1859, but published only in 1989), and the most cursory of visits to Inzievar House demonstrates that it must be the source of Nemo's plumbing, furnishings, artistic preferences, and general life-style. Verne indeed acknowledges the debt when he presents Nemo at the organ, 'us[ing] only the black keys, giving his melodies an essentially Scottish tonality'—in *Backwards to Britain* Verne's adored Amelia had similarly told his companion to 'play using only the black keys' (ch. 24).

Verne's other sources are wide-ranging, taken from literature, science, geography, and history, and are often acknowledged quite openly. Literary inspiration is undoubtedly the most important. While elements may perhaps be taken from Fenimore Cooper and Théophile Gautier, there is clear influence from the Bible, Homer, Plato, Hugo, Michelet, Scott, and Poe. *Moby-Dick* presents many affinities in details and in plot.

The most important non-literary sources are the scientists and popularizers Maury, Cuvier, Figuier, Mangin, Larousse, Agassiz, and Renard. A remarkable number of the naturalists *Twenty Thousand Leagues* quotes, including Buffon, Gratiolet, Lacépède, Milne-Edwards, d'Orbigny, Quatrefages, and Tournefort, were professors at the Museum of Natural History in Paris. Although the novel cites one nineteenth-century encounter with a giant squid (at the time dismissed by science), an unquoted source, Denys de Montfort, is surely the main origin of the captain's epic battle. And if the description of Nemo himself is taken from a Colonel Charras, exiled from 1852 until his death in 1865, his life must be based partly on Gustave Flourens, a scientist and freedom-fighter in several countries praised in *Paris in the Twentieth Century* (written about 1863, but published only in 1994).

Many commentaries have concentrated on the originality of the *Nautilus*, but it should be emphasized that Verne's technology was not at all innovative. Nemo's presentation of his vessel provides more than enough information about its length and girth, but his only explanation of its motive power is in terms of an electricity

which is 'not the commonly used sort', multiplied by 'a system of
levers'! Submarine craft had in any case been around for a long
time. Underwater vessels were used in the American War of
Independence and Civil War; Verne's own mathematics teacher
had built a working submarine; and even craft named *Nautilus*
were commonplace, including a vessel that the author saw during
his visit to the Paris Universal Exposition of 1867. Again, a piece
in the *Musée des familles* of 1857 ascribed to Verne, 'Submarine
Locomotives', humorously foresees that man might domesticate
whales and harness them to his underwater vessels. More than
three books with titles like *The Depths of the Sea*, *Submarine
Adventures*, and *The Submarine World* were published in France
in 1867–9 alone. So crowded, indeed, were the submarine deeps
that Verne was afraid of being accused of plagiarism.[4]

Verne himself was categorical: 'I am not in any way the inventor of submarine navigation.' He even claimed he was 'never
specifically interested in science', only in using it to create dramatic stories in exotic parts; and indeed his reputation as a
founding-father of science-fiction has led to a major obfuscation
of his literary merits.

Amongst the many tales of submarines, only Verne's has survived—undoubtedly because of the living nature of his text,
because he integrates both his own experience and his literary and
scientific reading. His originality does not lie in creating a vessel
or the idea of underwater exploration, but in his unbridled *literary* imagination.

Verne's correspondence is also important for an understanding of
the work. A succession of letters, predominantly to his publisher,
Hetzel, reveals his mounting excitement:

Chantenay, 10 August [1866] I am also preparing our *Journey under
the Waters*, and my brother and I are arranging all the mechanics

---

[4] From 10 October 1867, Aristide Roger (pseudonym of Dr Jules Rengade)
published a serial about a circumnavigation of the globe in a submarine called
the *Éclair* (published in book form as *Le Voyage sous les flots*, 1868). Verne
wrote: '28 October 1867. You have been publishing in *Le Petit journal* for some
time now a very interesting work by M. Aristide Roger entitled *Aventures extra-
ordinaires du savant Trinitus*. | A year ago I began a book whose title is *Voyage
sous les eaux*.'

needed for the expedition. I think we'll use electricity, but it's still not completely decided.

[1865?] It is certainly serious, very unexpected, and no one has ever done anything like it before.

[29 July 1867] I'm working hard, but as you say, my dear Hetzel, after 15 months of abstinence [while writing *Geography of France* (1867)], my brain greatly needs to burst: so much the better for the *Journey under the Waters*, there will be overabundance, and I promise I'll have myself a good time.

[28 March 1868] I'm working furiously. I've had a good idea that emerges nicely from the subject. This unknown man must no longer have any contact with humanity . . . He's not on earth any more, he manages without the earth . . . the sea must provide him with everything, clothing and food . . . Were the continents and islands to vanish in a new Flood, he'd live the same way, and I beg you to believe that his *ark* will be a bit better equipped than Noah's ever was. | I believe this 'absolute' situation will give much depth to the work. | Oh, my dear Hetzel, if I don't pull this book off, I'll be inconsolable. I've never held a better thing in my hands.

Paris, 10 March 1868. My dear father . . . I'm in the middle of . . . *Twenty Thousand Leagues under the Seas.* | I'm working on it with tremendous pleasure . . . In three or four months, when I have the proofs, I'll try to send you and Paul the first volume, so that you can hunt out the mistakes and imperfections. I very much want this machine to be as perfect as possible.

Crotoy, Thursday [1868] What is difficult is to make things that are very implausible seem very plausible, but I hope I've succeeded.

[June 1868] Yes, I'm slogging hard and the first volume will be finished by the end of July . . . But let's agree on one thing, I'll have to rewrite it from beginning to end. It'll be ready by the end of August and I hope we can begin publication with the new volume on 20 September. | Oh my dear friend, what a book if I've pulled it off! How many good things I've found in the sea while sailing on the *Saint-Michel.* The hardest job is to make all that seem so plausible that everyone will want to go there. Well, we'll see.

[Summer? 1868] As for the ending, the carrying off into unknown seas, the arrival at the Maelstrom without Aronnax or his companions having any inkling, their idea of remaining when they hear that sinister word, the boat carried away with them despite their efforts, it will be superb, yes superb! | Then the mystery, the eternal mystery of the *Nautilus* and its captain! | But I am heating up while writing to you! A little calm so as to embrace you. | Yours with all my heart.

[11 August 1868] Oh the perfect subject, my dear Hetzel, the perfect subject!

In addition to the novel as 'machine', we may note the sustained metaphor of what Verne heatedly holds in his hands and the 'abundance' of his textual production. The letters clearly show his excitement about the novel's depth and the idea of the 'unknown man', and his fears that the challenge of the 'absolute' subject might not be met. But we can also observe the emphasis on sea-based self-sufficiency, the biblical reference, and the uncertainty as to the captain's fate.

Turning now to the manuscripts of *Twenty Thousand Leagues* (MS1 and MS2), it is surprising these have received almost no attention to date for many parts of the novel are in fact quite different in them.

Thus the published daily phrase, 'Nautron respoc lorni virch', was originally 'Nautron *restoll loui* virch', perhaps even harder to decipher. The location of Nemo's home port, which he takes such pains to hide, is given away in MS1 as near 'Tenerife'. A debt to Dumas *fils*, Verne's friend and literary collaborator, is acknowledged in the manuscripts; and there is also a quotation from Scott. MS2 contains a different agreement with Nemo governing Dr Aronnax's life on board: it has three conditions rather than one and makes the passengers 'prisoners' rather than 'guests', with Aronnax formally undertaking never to try to escape. But in the final dialogue, Aronnax throws in Nemo's face his moral right to leave, and Nemo throws back: well, leave then! The ending is generally much fuller in MS2: we visit the seabed of the English Channel, and the narrator conjures up medieval visions from the shadows on the cliffs near Le Havre. The three escapees think of landing in Scotland, an irresistible idea for Verne; and the *Nautilus* forms part of a delightful scene of happy dawn and sunny tranquillity off Dover. Given that its existence has never before been suspected, it is worth quoting in full:

The sky was white, the air calm. Not a breath of wind. On the sea small regular ripples created intersecting diamond shapes. The sun picked them out in sparkling points. The water, like liquid emerald, heaved in broad waves that the *Nautilus* did not even feel. In the quivering haze, a few far-off fishing boats and two or three coasting luggers with flaccid sails faded indistinctly away. The smoke from a steamer traced a motionless cloud against the backdrop of the sky.

We see, above all, a different Nemo, more independent and more intransigent. In addition to being an engineer, naturalist, collector, writer, and freedom-fighter, the earlier Nemo is a composer as well; and the music he prefers to 'all the ancient and modern' is his own! The often incongruous Christian element in the published text is generally absent from his life, while the Virgin by Leonardo is here 'a half-dressed woman'. When scores of Papuans start to invade his ship, the captain simply electrocutes them, deliberately and without remorse. Nemo describes the all-important *Vengeur* as a 'Republican' ship: a red rag designed to enrage the publisher Hetzel, who did not allow his author to touch on potentially controversial matters. Whereas in the 1871 version Aronnax suggests that the captain should change his ways ('may hate die down in that wild heart', etc.), in the closing words of the first manuscript he is praised as 'the Man of the Waters, entirely free'.

Probably because of Hetzel, Verne excised all of the above ideas. In his letters he mentions further imposed alterations changing the sense of the novel, and in particular Nemo's mission. Thus on one occasion he reminds his publisher of his regret for what he calls the 'best' idea, namely the captain versus society at large. He also states his preference for a second idea with Nemo as a Polish patriot opposing Russian tyranny, whose wife has been murdered and daughters raped. He points out that both ideas were rejected for the wrong reasons; and he says how little he thinks of the publisher's suggestion that the captain should be attacking slave-transporting ships. To Hetzel's proposal that the *Nautilus* be trapped by a surface vessel in a cul-de-sac, Verne scathingly ripostes how implausible that would be. Unfortunately we do not have his response to his mentor's unhinged idea of placing a Chinese boy on board so as 'to cheer things up'!

Many of the changes can indeed be regretted. The image of Nemo as a creative artist is a striking one: playing his own compositions to console himself in his self-constructed submarine forms a powerful image of creative movement short-circuited back on to itself. Similarly, his original behaviour with regard to Aronnax, the Papuans, and his enemies' ships is striking. But it is not clear what Verne would have done on his own, nor whether Hetzel's interventions were harmful overall. We do not seem entitled, in sum, to argue that the stronger images are invariably what Nemo and the novel are 'really' like. Trying to produce an edition of *Twenty Thousand Leagues* to restore the author's intentions would be difficult, if only because of the knock-on effects of putting the deleted passages back in.

What is clear, however, is that the 1871 version contains echoes of nearly all of the ideas omitted, and that all the deletions help us to understand the novel. This work, which forms such an important part of the modern imagination, cannot be fully understood without assessing the original ideas from which it grew.

To pay too much attention to the early stages of Verne's imagination might obscure the power of that imagination itself, however. The letters show that he knew this novel would be exceptional. Verne's mastery of the genre is indeed demonstrated in the interlocking and superimposing literary devices and the many vibrant episodes presenting new settings. The number of themes is also impressive: technology, of course; biology; the study of the seas; exploration of unknown areas; life on desert islands; history; biblical themes; mythical ideas; even international politics. The characters, too, are more complex than in many of Verne's works.

The plot may in fact leave the reader confused on first reading. All information is filtered through Aronnax's first-person narration, and although his observations attempt to be scrupulously exact, his interpretations and forecasts are invariably wildly out. Many of the events of the novel are indeed beyond the ken of a naïve bachelor from a sheltered background. The episodes of Atlantis, the underwater burial, and the Maelstrom are typical of scores of others in being misinterpreted by him until nearly the end—when it is too late to study the evidence. The central enigma, above all, remains unsolved, for we never know Nemo's real name or nationality, his past life, or his reasons for going round sinking ships.

One initial way of coping with the complexity is simply to study the behaviour of the submarine itself. Its very freedom and power mean that, to create tension, it must encounter dangers of some sort. Most of the threats to its shiny self-containment fall into four categories: perforation, invasion, immobilization, or suffocation. (Mechanical problems are out of the question. That the hatch might let in water never seems to cross anybody's mind, either.)

Thus it risks rupture by man's most advanced ballistic technology or by massed sperm whales and intrusion by giant squid or hordes of people. The most frequent problem, however, is that the 'cigar-shape' has an uncontrollable desire to slip into passages for which 'it's too big', as Farragut's sailors put it. This enables it to reach its refuge via an underwater tunnel and to seek out the passage connecting the Red Sea to the Mediterranean, and hence visit the seven seas without retracing its path. But under the ice-cap its bold thrusting creates dangers, for the submarine manages to get into a tunnel which is not only closed at both ends but shrinking by the hour. In another incident, potentially involving all four dangers, it chooses to pass through the 'most dangerous strait on the globe', duly gets stuck on the rocks, and attracts hundreds of New Guinea natives.

Getting into so many scrapes does imply that something is going on. At the beginning, when the *Nautilus* keeps exposing itself to ships, rubbing up against them, or even penetrating them, the captain may indeed be drawing attention to his marvellous machine. But quite apart from the sexual subtext, Nemo has a secret agenda that will become clearer only at the end.

The *Nautilus* conditions the whole structure of the novel. Because of its hothouse atmosphere and Nemo's aversion to setting foot on land, those occasions when he does leave the submarine are all the more heightened. During such episodes, Aronnax has to be there as well to tell the tale; but Conseil and Ned are usually excluded. Typical is Nemo's sudden night-time invitation to visit the underwater realm wearing diving suits. This poetic experience helps us understand how individual scenes are put together, and is therefore worth studying in detail.

Aronnax is fidgety from the start. He jumps when he hears rain pattering on the surface and feels acutely conscious of his leaden feet crunching a 'bed of bones'. He wonders at the giant furrows on the ocean floor, the distant glow, and the clearings in the petrified forest. His over-excited mind starts imagining castles and cities—even seabed friends for the captain. His hyper-photographic vision sees everything in fine silhouette and his movements are light: leaping tree trunks, breaking creepers, flying over chasms. Aronnax's exaltation, Nemo's pace, and the imperfect tense produce a strange mood. A metaphor converts the sea back into land, the living into the man-made, tentacles into brush, and crabs and lobsters into suits of armour. After a climb up a volcano, after the vegetable and animal kingdoms have led up the Great Chain of Beings, Aronnax again imagines human works.

But an eruption suddenly steals the scene—and with it comes the revelation of a sunken city. In an elegiac vision and the longest sentence of the book, teasing glimpses appear of technology and religion, Greece and Tuscany, triremes and temples, even a sea within the sea. All this is an unusual chance for Nemo and Aronnax to communicate, for although they cannot talk, they do touch, speak through their eyes, and even use the intimate second-person singular form; above all, Nemo uses a convenient piece of chalk and rock-wall to write a message: 'ATLANTIS'.

Feverish as he is, Aronnax runs through the whole gamut of legends about the lost continent. He imagines, pell-mell, biblical and prehistoric scenes, a land bridge to America, the giant contemporaries of the first man. He conflates geological, biblical, and mythological time to return to the origins where, paradoxically, man was at his most evolved. But he is simultaneously careful to leave his mark on the living past, subtly altering the landscape so as to prove to himself that it is not all a dream. The transcendental scene closes with the spotlight on a rare relaxed Nemo. He is 'leaning on a mossy stele', as if on a reading desk in his library, contemplating time past, empathetically 'turned to stone' in 'his' landscape. 'Was it here that this strange being came to commune with history and relive ancient life—he who wanted nothing to do with modern times?'

And this is the Verne who has been argued to be a pure positivist, a scientific apologist, a blind technological anticipator! He is in fact a high romantic, with his poetic language, nostalgia, and yearning for significance. The grandeur of the novel comes not only from the many 'privileged' locations the submarine takes us to but also from its reference to a higher destiny.

The structure of *Twenty Thousand Leagues* is also marked by many long lists. Even the paroxysm of Atlantis is interrupted at the vital moment by the eruption of names of people who have written about the lost continent. The lists reportedly made the poet Apollinaire exclaim, half in admiration: 'What a style! Nothing but substantives!' There are indeed a bewildering number of common and proper nouns in the novel.

In the carefully crafted opening chapter about the 'monster' terrorizing the seas, ambiguity is already maximized between fact and fiction, persistent legend and documented reports, authorial information and narratorial misinformation. The lists are similarly a massive importation of real-world information, proof that Verne has done his homework, a guarantee of seriousness and plausibility. On one level, nevertheless, they are devoid of significance. A procession of obscure fish hardly advances the plot. Scientific knowledge does not consist merely of scientists' names, nor exploration of explorers'.

But many of the lists do provide an archaeology of knowledge. The substantives often come from Verne's sources, to which he adds adjectives, structure, and significance. One example is the suspension of Nemo's romantic, rebellious ecstasy at the South Pole by the quoting of the successive explorers who have got closer and closer to it. Complete with date, nationality, and longitude, they provide a structured history of Antarctica.

In other cases, the lists are a mine of information. Hidden amongst the names of the pro-Atlanteans are allusions to Bailly's notions of a tropical Atlantis at a North Pole heated by exhalations from the Earth's core; and to Malte-Brun, from whom Verne derived the phrase and very idea of going 'around the world in eighty days'.[5] His passing mention of George Sand indicates the writer who may have given him the original idea for the novel; his reference to Edom may point to a strong biblical influence, and thence to a brilliant short story called 'Edom' published in 1910 under his name. The citing of 'Hartz', finally, is an unmistakable pointer to a literary movement and to a particular scene in *Moby-Dick*. In sum, although Verne's lists may no longer have the resonances they had for a French reader, they often provide important pointers to the diffusion of ideas in nineteenth-century literature.

Another way of approaching *Twenty Thousand Leagues* is to study the characters themselves. Their number is severely curtailed: apart from the four main protagonists and Captain Farragut, no speaking part survives for more than a paragraph or so. Nor does a single woman feature in the work, apart from Nemo's dead and in any case nameless wife: the painter Rosa Bonheur and a picture of a 'courtesan' were both deleted at manuscript stage. Even the ships' names, and especially the submarine's, are in masculine mode.

As Roland Barthes has brilliantly noted, Verne's vehicles provide a near-absolute division of the world. On the exterior can be interstellar space, boiling water, or murderous savages, but within all is calm, security, food, and—in *Twenty Thousand Leagues*—humanity's 12,000 best books. Nemo, Aronnax, Conseil, and Ned inhabit a closed universe. As in a Pinter or Beckett play, the submarine is the *in camera* locus for the intensive interaction of four threesomes and five pairs: only Nemo and Conseil never communicate with each other.

Verne's first-person narrators seem shadowy sorts of people. They are generally middle-class and well off, the same age as the author, and long-term travellers without family. Most come from hard-nosed professions like journalism or science, with their work their publication. They exist to narrate, and narrate to exist.

Aronnax is no exception. He is practical, serious, cautious, uninvolved, unimaginative, characterized indeed by what he

---

[5] See my translation and critical edition of *Around the World in Eighty Days* (Oxford: OUP, 1995), 204.

himself calls his 'cowardice' and 'complete negativity'. Or, as Nemo tells him, 'you only see snags and obstacles'. Aronnax in fact mainly serves to organize knowledge, to ask naïve questions, to act generally as a foil, and to transcribe Conseil's classifications. Even his manservant is livelier, described as acrobatic in his ability to ascend and descend the taxonomic hierarchy; and he alerts his master when he is being unduly hypocritical or intellectually lazy.

If nothing else, Aronnax is systematic. He is an adept of Linnaeus's binomial taxonomy, with its 'phyla, divisions, classes, sub-classes, orders, families, genera, sub-genera, species, and varieties'. His deductions follow sequences of branching alternatives, dividing the known and unknown, order and chaos. He also studies many objects whose shape is a branching 'arborescence': spiders, squid, and especially coral, characterized by their multiple 'branches', 'ramifications', and 'arborizations'. His science, in other words, has the same positivistic structure as many of the objects it studies!

Just as Aronnax's lists attempt to cram everything in, so his classifications go down to the smallest detail. Everything inside is neatly labelled, as in Nemo's museum; but the unintelligible or uncontrollable are banished. His systems give up in panic when presented with the new. The good doctor exhaustively picks over the details of Nemo's visible life, often revising his perceptions, but cannot answer any of the essential questions about him. What he lacks is the ability to connect, to go beyond. Creativity is absent from his reproductive, convergent sort of mind-set. He is almost schizophrenic in his attempt to abolish the murky subconscious and to conceal his lack of invention. Perhaps his real problem is a fear of writer's block?

Aronnax invariably abuses his position as narrator. Thus he only notices the body being carried on the four crewmen's shoulders after more than two hours underwater; and he only spots the portraits of Nemo's heroes and family on his second and third views of his bedroom. In his discussion with Ned about the monster, the sailor is a model of scientific accuracy whilst virtually everything the scientist affirms is erroneous. Aronnax-the-character is unable to understand that a social inferior will not accord him intellectual deference—and Aronnax-the-narrator backs him up. The general problem is that the naturalist is conditioned by his immediate impressions, usually erroneous, which he does not make the effort to correct when he records his notes or writes them up. An unreliable narrator is an unusual feature in the popular literature of the nineteenth century. Most readers will give Aronnax the benefit of doubt for much of the novel—but will be forced to revise their views by the end.

Verne thus has the best of both worlds. Aronnax's lack of imagination lends credibility to his most fantastic descriptions. But his unreliability as soon as it comes to interpretation conceals the captain's nature right until the end. Nemo's express wish not to be 'judged' is ultimately respected, for we only see him tête-à-tête with Aronnax and so never have an objective basis on which to assess him.

What we do know about the captain is that he shares many of the characteristics of Verne's heroes, who emulate Renaissance man in the variety of their intellectual, physical, and cultural qualities. Evans neatly sums these up as: 'courage, aesthetic sensitivity, idealism, devotion to justice, humor, thirst for glory, compassion, love of freedom, and "grandeur" in general.'[6] But Nemo and the other heroes also have paranoid and self-destructive tendencies: withdrawal abruptly alternating with dramatic speeches or cold anger.

The captain's monogram translates as 'Mobile in the mobile element'; but the motto apparently at the origin of his name, 'Nemo me lacessit impune', is perhaps more revealing. 'No one assails me with impunity', the emblem of Edinburgh and of Scotland, must often have been seen by Verne on his formative visit. It is echoed in the novel, and defines Nemo's behaviour perfectly, for his driving force is revenge.

From the beginning, conflict is probable. Aronnax, Conseil, and Land arrive uninvited on the submarine, indeed as part of an attempt to destroy it. As Nemo explains, his only choices are to betray the secret of his life, throw them back in the sea, or take them in for ever. One reason for his decision is that he already knows Aronnax from his learned volumes, *The Mysteries of the*

---

[6] Arthur B. Evans, *Jules Verne Rediscovered: Didacticism and the Scientific Novel* (New York: Greenwood Press, 1988), 75.

Ocean Deeps. But he is visibly disappointed by the man behind the book. In any case, the two have opposing interests: Nemo's, to conceal information about his mission; Aronnax's, to glean as much as possible for his next book.

The Frenchman gets off on the wrong foot. Nemo intones: 'Our voyage of underwater exploration begins at this precise moment.' Aronnax (or perhaps the conventional Hetzel!) replies: 'May God protect us!' The remark is undignified, unflattering for the submarine, inappropriately religious—and results in the captain taking his leave. Nemo will repeat his sharp exit after his impassioned speech about an under-sea Utopia, and indeed whenever his guest is being tactless, unsympathetic, or lacking in understanding.

Aronnax apparently embodies Nemo's entire social life, for the captain virtually never goes out—and Conseil and Ned never come in. His only external contacts seem to be wordless signs to a diver, dreams of launching a message in a bottle, and violent interchanges with passing ships. Outside his submarine he is only too aware of humanity's depredations and unprovoked attacks; within his bedroom he appears anguished, lost either in mathematical calculations or in memories of his heroes or his murdered family. Even on the platform Nemo seems less than welcoming, perhaps because it is part of his workplace or because Conseil and Ned are often there. Although Aronnax once visits him in his room, with unfortunate results, the captain almost never goes to his and rarely seems to seek out the naturalist's company.

One exception is when Aronnax is just about to escape, having already put his coat on. On this occasion Nemo seems to take deliberate pleasure in spinning out the conversation, leading even the obtuse Aronnax to wonder whether his plans have been discovered. Nemo chooses this precise occasion not only to reveal his financial contributions to the 'oppressed races' and especially the Cretans, but also to invite him to visit Atlantis: things which persuade Aronnax that he does want to stay after all.

Stretching out on the sofa is in general Nemo's only relaxed posture. The library is indeed the only place where he and Aronnax can freely meet. Unlike later heroes, Nemo has none of Verne's books, despite his collection of 'the modern and ancient masters': indeed, there are virtually no nineteenth-century novel-ists at all. The huge ship's library—the true control room of the submarine—may contain hints of Verne senior's study, but also bears remarkable similarities to Hetzel's bookshop in the rue Jacob; in any case it seems to symbolize established authority. Hetzel was himself a well-known writer, older than Verne, and contributed to his works (although not free from suspicions of borrowings in the other direction). The presence within Nemo's library of Aronnax's volumes seems to reflect this complex rela-tionship. It is also the focus of two connected tensions: change and stasis; and reproduction and creativity.

The yellowing newspapers are a sign of the problem. Just like the prehistoric but nineteenth-century cavern in *Journey to the Centre of the Earth*, Nemo's library is both brand new and clas-sical, contemporary and *passé*. Aronnax deduces from a book in it that 'the fitting out of the *Nautilus* did not date from after' 1865. In fact he means the opposite, for time has got muddled for him. Nemo claims that the concept of 'modern artist' no longer exists for him: they are all either out-of-time or 'two or three thou-sand years old'. He is, in other words, an exile in time or a time-traveller (the two are equivalent). His decision to halt his world is a conscious one: 'I would like to believe that humanity has thought or written nothing since then.' The captain uses 'your' to mean things to do with Aronnax or France but also to do with 'terrestrial' or 'living'. Everything seems perfect in his library, for it is the perfection of death. His timeless existence means that he is 'dead', as he himself claims. And the tragedy of the living dead is that, although eternally young, they are prone, like Rider Haggard's She, to topple over into exponentially accelerating decay.

The library is stranded uneasily between the 1865 newspapers and an adolescent or artistic eternity. The only disruption to the sterile stasis, the only emergence of the new, would be if creative works were actually produced on board the *Nautilus*. Aronnax asks Nemo whether he is an 'artist'; he seems to reply in the affirmative, but then paraphrases it as being instead a collector: creation is tantamount to mere conservation and accumulation. But in fact Nemo does write. For a start, he produces annotations to Aronnax's book, but these were perhaps made long ago and in any case mostly revise or recycle the past. As in a Beckett endgame, however, the slightest sign of change must be sought, even the remotest route out of the temporal and ontological cul-de-sac. The notes may be a surreptitious sign of creativity: they may form an embryo of Nemo's story or even of Aronnax's planned book, for both men eventually admit to writing first-person sea tales rather than their previous scientific writings. Both authors look as though they might have no readers at all (except perhaps each other?); it is suggested that both books may indeed end up in the sea whence they came; and neither volume can admit to its title or its author's name. Writing is apparently a solitary, secretive, even shameful activity.

The library, in sum, is a pointer to Nemo's twin problems of time and creation. Other aspects of his character develop more slowly. Although most of the incidents initially puzzle Aronnax, many are in fact connected: hindsight (and a good memory) are required to put the plot back together again at the end.

More of Nemo's deeds are going to be influenced by Aronnax's presence than he will admit. One example is the decision to open the hatches when the submarine is grounded and covered with aggressive-looking Papuans. The result, predictably, is an invasion, soon repelled by administering an electric shock. But in fact Nemo can have no reason to open the hatches so soon before leaving—apart from a wish to impress the Frenchman. The scene is even more surprising when juxtaposed with Aronnax's pompous but humane remarks about merely retaliating against 'savages'. It anticipates the killing at the end of Part Two, which in turn echoes the incidents with the liners in the opening chapter. 'A pure accident,' says Nemo of the collision with the *Scotia*. Possibly, but he omits to account for those with the *Moravian* and the *Etna*. A more plausible explanation, therefore, is an attention-seeking ploy or the first signs of the later aggression.

Equally unclear is Nemo's attitude towards Aronnax. He sometimes seems to show disdain for that conventional person; he may on occasion be retaliating to perceived slights. He often ignores his presence; and at one stage knocks a telescope out of his hand. Aronnax decides that he is not the object of the hatred, on the basis that Nemo is not looking at him—but this does not neccessarily follow. Common sense will tell us that when confronted with an unwelcome guest, a man without friends or intellectual equals is likely to oscillate between extremes, and that any apparent indifference may be feigned. On the other hand, there are occasions when the captain does seem genuinely unaware of the naturalist; and his last words, 'God almighty! Enough! Enough!', sound sincere enough. But does Nemo dislike his guest enough to wish his death? If we think Nemo is aware of the various escape plans after all, we may surmise that the captain actually hopes his captives will go, but deliberately chooses for them the spot 'from which no ship has ever been able to escape'.

The ultimate mysteries in the novel, carefully built up in the episode when Aronnax is secretly drugged, are the motive for Nemo's sinkings and the nationalities of his victims. Revenge is clearly at work, but in the published version the rest of the evidence is inconclusive, for one of the ships attacked is called the *Florida*, a reference to a famous Confederate vessel, but in contrast, Nemo's beloved *Vengeur* is French. A whole series of different countries for both Nemo and his enemies is indeed hinted at at various points.

Nemo thus remains a mysterious figure—we do not even know who he normally eats with. His chosen crew reflect him in being anonymous, mute, and repressed. Only at the end do we discover that these blank, interchangeable ciphers actively support Nemo's campaign. But it is still not clear why so many different nationalities are represented amongst them.

MS2 actually names the captain 'Juan Nemo'—opening up fascinating avenues. Some of his characteristics, such as his pride or grandiloquence, do seem slightly Spanish—and his home port is on Spanish territory. But is the name perhaps an allusion to Don Juan, or rather to an anti-Don Juan (Nemo never sees a woman from one year to the next)?

In sum, we know very little about Nemo. In an interview in 1903 Verne described him as 'a misanthropist', and, in a letter in 1894, as 'confining himself in his [*Nautilus*]'; but this does not get us much further. What determines his overall route? Why has he not visited either Pole before? Does he avoid French and North American ships out of kindness for Aronnax and Ned? Why does he conceal one of his attacks, but show Aronnax the other two? Does he display the portraits of his heroes and family so as to seek understanding and approval? Does he try to influence his image in Aronnax's ongoing book?

Like the number of Lady Macbeth's children, questions as to Nemo's true nature and the ultimate meaning of the novel are virtually unanswerable, because of the narrator's very presence on board. As with a married couple, Aronnax's and Nemo's behaviour cannot be separated out: each action is modified by those of the other half, each factor in the interactive equation is fed back in, each conclusion seems undermined by its deliberately complementary opposite. Nemo-as-seen-by-Aronnax cannot be broken down. Narrator and narratee are in symbiosis.

Many of the enigmas of course serve to displace the author's unanswered questions on to the characters. Nemo in particular is caught between the devil of his creator's desires and the deep blue sea of what his publisher would allow. Verne systematically avoids France in his books. Just as Fogg flies over the entire country without it receiving so much as a mention,[7] so the submarine is spirited past first the South of France and then Verne's own beloved Brittany and Picardy without a single reference to either. Nemo himself is not allowed to be French, of course, or Polish either, or indeed anything at all. His rebellion is not permitted to strike at any established authority. It is not surprising, therefore, that he has an identity crisis and that he goes around looking for anonymous enemies to defend himself against.

What seems probable is that Verne himself feels torn between the captain and his guest. He identifies with Aronnax in his more logical and systematic aspects, but with Nemo for his imagination, energy, and freedom. Equally probable is that the clash of personalities reflects the slightly incestuous relationship between Verne and Hetzel. The intense but secretive writing activities on board the submarine ultimately result in an overabundance of manuscripts, proofs, and letters flying between the author and the publisher. Hetzel's blue pencil may be connected with Aronnax's

---

[7] This is done in a complex flashback that becomes an anticipation, and thus disguises its own existence for most readers.

uncomprehending literalness, narrowness, and 'realism', but Hetzel's principled exile in Belgium corresponds to Nemo's political idealism.

Exile, atemporality, intertextuality. The 'unknown man' yearns for both the future and the past, but not for his own period. The captain's technology is well in advance of its time, enabling him to discover a new continent. His social vision seems futuristic, his causes espouse the tide of history. He is anti-slavery, internationalist, individualist, rationalist, and against entrenched privilege and intellectual sloth. But if he is so much of a modern, why does a whiff of nostalgia still hang about him, an air of things we shall not see again? Part of the answer may lie in the all-embracing nature of his talents, but also in his unwillingness to use social means to effect change, his absolutism, his reluctance to get involved. Even at the time, his mysterious cause could probably be seen as a losing battle, his way of life a dead-end.

But part of the answer must also be in our own end-of-millennium perspective, our post-everything-ness. We no longer believe that an individual can change the world, or even defy humanity for long. The Asians would have reverse-engineered the *Nautilus*, the Americans turned it into a tourist attraction. Nemo is a prisoner of his historical circumstances. He has a romantic and classical soul, but we feel we have got past all that. We believe we have absorbed the repeated Byronic and '68 rebellions: we are all post-revolutionaries now, at least in stylistic externals.

Nemo's principled refusal to set foot on the inhabited continents embodies the *raison d'être* of the *Extraordinary Journeys*. The series can only prosper by visiting virgin territories; but the quicker they are deflowered, the sooner the subject will be exhausted. *Twenty Thousand Leagues under the Seas* therefore occupies the fatal point of no return: the dark continent and the North Pole have already been done, snapshots even taken of the dark side of the moon. The ocean deeps and the South Pole are the ultima Thule of a certain mode of being and of writing. The *Nautilus* can only be the end of the line.

Nemo is the last of the romantics, out of his time. He is in a geographico-historical cul-de-sac, and the absolutism of his fight cannot be permanent. He seems caught between George Stephenson and R. L. Stevenson, born too late or too early, post-romantic but pre-modern. Captain Nemo's oceanic freedom is a mortgage on things to come. Technologically inspired rebellion is a rapidly shrinking option for off-white males in the late nineteenth century. But his passion for music and the sea are surely destined to be eternal.

NOTE ON THE TEXT AND TRANSLATION

The Manuscripts

Two manuscript versions (MS1 and MS2) of *Twenty Thousand Leagues* (*20TL*) are known to exist, both kept in the French National Library. According to Destombes' excellent article (see Select Bibliography), MS1A (dating from the second quarter of 1868) corresponds to chapters 11 to the end of Part One and MS1B (first and second quarters of 1869) to the whole of Part Two. MS2A (third quarter 1868, in other words before MS1B), headed 'Twenty Thousand Leagues under the Oceans', contains the whole of Part One, MS2B (third and fourth quarters of 1869), the whole of Part Two. Each of the four documents is numbered separately.

A letter written by Verne's son, Michel, to Prince Roland Bonaparte in 1906 says that the manuscripts being sent to him 'seem' to include a third version of Part Two, but no trace of this has been found. C.-N. Martin states that Verne gave yet another version to the Comte de Paris in 1878; but this is far from certain.

In MS1, chapters I 12 and 13[1] form a single unit; I 14–16, only two chapters; and II 1 and 2, a single unit. Some of the titles are different in MS1: 'The Coalmines of Tenerife' for the published 'Underwater Coalmines' (II 10), 'Sawfish and Whales' for 'Sperm Whales and Baleen Whales' (II 12), 'An Attack' for 'A Massacre' (II 21), and 'Maelstrom' for 'Captain Nemo's Last Words' (II 22).

In the opening chapters of MS2, we read such variants from the published work as: 'the *Constitutionnel*' for 'the old *Constitutionnel*', 'throw [. . .]' for 'squeeze into my trunk', 'transshipped' for 'transported', 'a striped top-shell' for 'a whelk', 'la pier' for 'le *pier*', and 'an immense majority of disbelievers' in the truth of Aronnax's story for 'a few disbelievers'. Some phrases are

---

[1] References to *20TL* are of the form II 7 (i.e. Part Two, ch. 7).

absent: '*lowering and* raising the American flag', 'I can't believe *that* a whale, cachalot, or sea-unicorn *could manage such a thing*', and 'a naturally slow animal wouldn't have been given such a speed *if it didn't need it*', together with the episode of Ned killing the two whales 'in a single go'. But MS2 contains interesting details such as 'in the humid shadows' (1871: 'in the distance'), 'and not as I supposed [Ned] to be at the beginning of the expedition', or 'not [...] a single point unexplored [...] *between Hawaii and the Bering Strait*'.

Inception and Publication

In a letter to Verne dated 25 July 1865 the novelist George Sand suggested that he write an under-sea novel, although some critics doubt whether her suggestion was really the origin. Verne seems to have written an outline in August 1865, but stopped from 1867 to 1868 to finish the *Illustrated Geography of France and its Colonies*. In December 1868 he submitted a second manuscript, 'Twenty-Five Thousand Leagues under the Waters', which Hetzel did not accept; and then a final one in 1869 (presumably MS2).

The novel often changed title: *Journey under the Waters*, *Twenty Thousand Leagues under the Waters*, *Twenty-Five Thousand Leagues under the Waters*, *Twenty-Five Thousand Leagues under the Seas* (in Hetzel's sales catalogue of September 1868), and *Twenty Thousand Leagues under the Oceans*. The definitive title was apparently Hetzel's idea.

Twenty Thousand Leagues under the Seas appeared in fortnightly two-chapter instalments in the *Magasin d'Éducation et de Récréation* [*MÉR*] from 20 March 1869 to 20 June 1870, with the subtitle 'Submarine Tour of the World' ('Tour du monde sousmarin'). We know that Verne sometimes inserted topical references up to (or even after) the date of publication of the last serial instalment. Verne complained that his novel was 'fragmented' by serialization; and its structure does seem to reflect its initial publication. What is more, Hetzel seems to have used the pretext of the partly juvenile audience of the *MÉR* to suggest changes to the novel (Verne's letter of March/May 1869).

The first volume of the first edition, 18mo without illustrations, was placed on sale on 28 October 1869, but the second volume only on 13 June 1870. The large octavo edition, with 111 illustrations by Riou and de Neuville, was put on sale on 16 November 1871.

The 'MÉR' Edition

In the *MÉR* of 5 September 1867 it was announced that 'M. Jules Verne is putting the more or less final touches to a book which will be the most extraordinary of all, a *Journey under the Waters*. Six months spent beside the sea, in total retreat, have been necessary for the conscientious and dramatic writer to collect together ('rassembler') the materials for this curious book.'

The *MÉR* publication in 1869 had a dedication at the top of the first page, which was never reprinted. Although signed 'Jules Verne', it is rather patronizing, and may have been written by Hetzel:

TO THE READERS OF THE *MÉR* [. . .] I hope that this voyage under the seas will instruct and interest at least as much, if not more than the other journeys. Let [readers] fear nothing, for I am sure to bring them back in good health from this excursion of such a new type. Although we will be the first to discover the depths of the Ocean, going in all directions and to every depth, the deep will not be as terrible for us as it was for so many brave sailors who vanished without trace. [. . .] This curious, bizarre, almost unknown world, which had to be opened up at any cost, has rewarded me a hundredfold for all the difficulties and efforts its discovery has caused me.

The *MÉR* edition presents a large number of minor variants. Most of the 1871 amendments must be considered positive or neutral, with the possible exception of 'vous autres, Français' for 'vous autres Français'.

The stylistic variants include: the absence of 'surtout' and 'si puissant'; 'de toutes couleurs', 'réflexions'; 'réel et sérieux' for the later 'réel, sérieux', 'que [. . .] on accusa' for 'qui [. . .] fut accusé', 'la France' for 'France', 'En effet' for 'Comme vous dites', 'prendrait route' for 'ferait route', semicolons for commas, and commas for dashes. The *Abraham Lincoln* is described as a 'frigate *à éperon*' ('with a ram'); and the footnote explaining the English word 'pier' appears on the second occurrence of the term.

Later in the *MÉR* edition (I 21–2) we see the omission of a paragraph break, 'tecks' for 'teks', 'stype' for 'stipe', 'kakatuas' for 'kakatoes', 'kanguroos' for 'kangourous', and 'terre[s] Amélie' for 'terre[s] Adélie'.

The 1869 edition was apparently set from the *MÉR* edition. It again presents a large number of minor, mostly stylistic, variants from the definitive version. WJM and FPW note a number of significant differences, using, however, a second-hand source. But in any case, the 1869 variants probably form in general a subset of the *MÉR* ones, which in turn constitute only some of the many variants visible in MS2 and especially in MS1. It is urgent, in sum, to produce a full critical edition of *Twenty Thousand Leagues* which will systematically indicate the differences between the MS1, MS2, and 1871 versions.

The Present Translation

The text used here is the Presses Pocket one (1991), which seems to follow the 1871 edition. This translation is an entirely new one, benefiting from the most recent scholarship on Verne and following the original text very closely. However, indications of interlocutors, ellipses, and exclamation marks have been slightly reduced, and very long sentences broken up. All translations from the French cited in the critical material are my own.

Note on Mistakes

There are perhaps 2,000 rare words and proper names in the French edition, but more than 100 are incorrect. The policy here is to amend clear spelling mistakes in real-world names and words found in dictionaries, normally indicating such changes as a guide to future editions. However, substantive information will not be amended, even when clearly erroneous, but is generally identified in the notes.

Verne often Gallicizes proper names and words. Thus he (or his editor) writes 'the *Castillan*' for 'the *Castilian*', 'the *Albermale*' for 'the *Albermarle*', 'oaze' for 'ooze', or 'ice-blinck' for 'ice-blink'. Even some of the French terms he uses have not been located, such as 'déponté' ('with its cover off'); and others seem to be erroneous, such as 'nageoire thoracine' for 'thoracique' ('thoracic') or 'crécelles' ('screechings') for 'crécerelles' ('kestrels').

Geographical Information

Verne is not always consistent, using for example 'Bourbon' and 'Réunion' for the same island. In most cases old-fashioned names have been replaced here: 'Propontis' by 'the Sea of Marmara', 'the Asphaltite Sea' by 'the Dead Sea', 'the Sandwich Islands' by 'Hawaii', 'New Holland' by 'Australia', 'Viti' by 'Fiji', 'the New Hebrides' by 'Vanuatu', 'Lazarev Island' by 'Matahiva', 'Clermont-Tonnerre' by 'Reao', 'the Friendly Islands' by 'Tonga', 'Navigators Islands' by 'Samoa', 'Ceylon' by 'Sri Lanka', and 'Edo' by 'Tokyo'. However, a relatively traditional spelling system is used.

A number of Verne's names seem erroneous, like 'Liarrov' for 'Lyakhov', 'Hadramant' for 'Hadramaut', '*Paramatta*' for '*Parramatta*', 'Kittan' for 'Kiltan', or 'Arfalxs' for 'Arfak'. This is confirmed by variant spellings (both 'Tikipia' and 'Tikopia') and what must be total misreadings, such as 'Captain Bell on the *Minerve*' for 'Captain Bellingshausen on the *Mirny*'!

Despite emphasizing the political importance of the difference between the Paris and Greenwich meridians (I 14), Verne often uses one or the other indiscriminately. In any case many of the co-ordinates quoted are approximate or simply wrong, such as those for Fiji and Vanuatu (I 19). Other information is occasionally as unreliable. Thus a direction cannot be 'east-north-easterly' and then still 'north-north-east' (I 14–15); the distance from $45°37'$ N, $15°12'$ W to Cape Clear in fact exceeds '300 miles' (I 1); Mauna Kea, described as '5,000 metres' (I 18), is 4,205 m; the '476-fathom-high Mount Kapogo' (I 19) reaches at most 810 m; 'Mannar Island, whose rounded shape loomed to the south' (II 3) should probably read 'the north'; 'the eastern point of the Gulf of Carpentaria' (I 23) should read the 'western' (as WJM and FPW point out); and the crater above Nemo's home port is described as 'five or six hundred metres high' but then 'not [. . .] more than eight hundred feet' (II 10) (WJM and FPW).

Verne says 'The British foot is only 30.40 cm long' (I 1), but this is a slip for 30.48. (Perhaps as a result, the distance required to increase underwater pressure by 1 atmosphere is quoted as both '30 feet' and '32'.) In any case, he uses both French and British feet and miles. Verne uses leagues 'of four kilometres' (II 7)—

French land ones (whereas an English league is 3 miles, or 4.8 km). No adjustment has been made here to measures, since otherwise the title would have to become something like *Sixteen Thousand Six Hundred and Sixty-Seven Leagues under the Seas*! Nevertheless, nautical miles per hour have been changed to knots, and measures have occasionally been converted (e.g. decimetres to centimetres and thousands of pounds to tons).

Marine Terminology

Verne often uses the rather vague term of 'poulpe', corresponding to the obsolete English 'poulp' or 'polyp' and including both 'squid' and 'octopus'. However, the contextual information indicates that he is invariably thinking of squid. One exception is when he says that 'Bouyer's squid' has eight, rather than ten, tentacles (one of the two illustrations (II 18) also has eight—although the other has ten): an understandable slip, for the animal was not even recognized by scientists at the time. To maintain Verne's intentions, 'seiche' and 'encornet' have usually been translated as 'cuttlefish', and 'calmar' as 'squid' or 'calamar'.

The long lists of fish names in *20TL* are a translator's nightmare; the lists are occasionally mixed up without regard for habitat. Many of the marine names quoted are Latin ones, but Gallicized to some degree. They also contain some spelling mistakes.[2] Spelling occasionally even varies within the same passage, with both 'hyales' and 'hyalles' ('hyales'), 'pirapèdes' and 'pyrapèdes' ('pirapeds'), and 'coryphèmes' and 'coriphènes' ('coryphènes' or 'dolphinfish').

In other cases, Verne writes just half the binomial name, for instance 'parus' ('*Pomacanthus paru*' or 'French angelfish'). Sometimes hyphenated names are not really compound: Verne

---

[2] Thus Verne writes 'gymontes' for 'gymnotes', 'chrysotones' for 'chrysotomes', 'thétys' for 'Tethys', 'xhantes' for 'xanthes', 'molubars' for 'Mobula', 'albicores' for 'albacores', 'aulostones' for 'aulostomes', 'munérophis' for 'murénophis', 'melanopteron' for 'melanopterus', 'thasards' for 'thazards', 'spinorbis' for 'spirorbis', 'dauphinules' for 'dauphinelles', 'cacouannes' for 'caouannes', 'alariées' for 'araliées', 'Rhodoménie' for 'Rhodyménie', 'pantacrines' for 'pentacrines', 'dorripes' for 'dorippes', 'chrysaores' for '*Chrysaora*', '*Iamettosa*' for '*lamellosa*', '*Cyproea*' for '*Cypraea*', '*Laurentia primafetida*' for '*Laurencia pinnatifida*', 'apsiphoroïdes' for '*Aspiphoroides*', and 'phyctallines' and '*Phyctalis*' for '*Phyllactina*' and '*Phyllactis*'.

often conjuncts a French version with a learned or foreign variant of the same name, or attaches adjectives like 'American-' simply to mean 'found in America'.

Although about 99 per cent of the marine names have been identified, in a few instances no trace of the form has been found, and a reasoned choice has therefore had to be made. In cases like 'clystomores', 'axidies', 'aodons', 'spinimanes', '*Coenodulli*', or other classical-sounding words, the approximate form has been retained. In the remaining one or two instances, equivalents have been found using the context.

Implausibilities

The text of *20TL* contains a number of implausibilities, where the translator/editor has to be especially faithful so as not to obscure the situation further. A select list of textual mysteries might include the following. Why are the *Scotia*'s passengers having 'lunch' at 4.17 p.m.? How do you 'push' someone along when he is floating 'motionless on his back, with arms folded and legs extended'? Why don't Aronnax and his companions locate the platform during their first night on the submarine? How is Aronnax able to describe his own facial expressions? Where does the out breathing-tube on the diving apparatus go? How does the *Nautilus* manage to remain motionless in the depths using just its inclined planes and the thrust of its propeller? Why does lightning strike fish,· and not the much larger metal submarine? What happens to the fragile objects in the salon when the submarine lists dramatically or collides with objects? Why do Nemo's apartments take up so much space, when his twenty crew members have a living space of 5 m by 2 m?

Gagneux also poses a number of pertinent questions. How does the sun shine brightly at 100 m depth, and how does it produce a rainbow underwater? How does Aronnax hear rain 300 m down? If the diving helmet withstands the pressure in the depths, why isn't blood forced into the head from the unprotected body? How does Nemo extract sodium from salt water, given that this requires a temperature of 3,000°C? How does a compass work inside a metal hull? How does an 8-metre wide cylinder resist a pressure of 1,600 atmospheres? How do you reverse a submarine at 20 knots through a narrow ice-tunnel? Where does the *Nautilus* find the power required to do 50 knots? Does the 16,000-metre rise in four minutes not equal more than 120 knots? What about the bends? What happens to the inclined planes when the submarine goes clean through the ship? And finally, where are the toilets?

SELECT BIBLIOGRAPHY

Hachette, Michel de l'Ormeraie, and Rencontre (reprinted by Edito-Service) represent the only complete editions of the *Voyages extraordinaires* since the original Hetzel publication, although 44 of the books have also appeared in Livre de Poche. All these editions are, however, partly out of print.

The major scholarly books on Verne in English are Andrew Martin, *The Mask of the Prophet: The Extraordinary Fictions of Jules Verne* (Oxford: OUP, 1990) and William Butcher, *Verne's Journey to the Centre of the Self: Space and Time in the 'Voyages extraordinaires'* (Macmillan, 1990). Arthur B. Evans's *Jules Verne Rediscovered: Didacticism and the Scientific Novel* (New York: Greenwood Press, 1988) is also well worth consulting.[1]

Amongst the French critics, François Raymond and Daniel Compère's *Le Développement des études sur Jules Verne* (Minard (Archives des lettres modernes), 1976), although now showing its age, still remains the most readable introduction. There exist many stimulating collections of articles, notably: *L'Herne: Jules Verne*, ed. P.-A. Touttain (L'Herne, 1974), *Colloque de Cerisy: Jules Verne et les sciences humaines*, ed. François Raymond and Simone Vierne (Union générale d'éditions, 1979), *Modernités de Jules Verne*, ed. Jean Bessière (Presses Universitaires de France, 1988), and the seven volumes of the Minard (Lettres Modernes) series on Verne, especially *Machines et imaginaire* (1980) and *Texte, image, spectacle* (1983).

The following may also be useful: Jean Chesneaux, *Une Lecture politique de Jules Verne* (Maspero, 1971, 1982), translated as *The Political and Social Ideas of Jules Verne* (Thames and Hudson, 1972); Simone Vierne, *Jules Verne* (Balland (Phares), 1986); and Alain Froidefond, *Voyages au centre de l'horloge: Essai sur un texte-genèse, 'Maître Zacharius'* (Minard, 1988).

The best biographies are Jean Jules-Verne, *Jules Verne* (Hachette, 1973), translated and adapted by Roger Greaves as *Jules Verne: A Biography* (MacDonald and Jane's, 1976), and Charles-Noël Martin, *La Vie et l'œuvre de Jules Verne* (Michel de l'Ormeraie, 1978). But there are also Marc Soriano, *Jules Verne (le cas Verne)* (Julliard, 1978),

---

[1] All places of publication are London or Paris unless otherwise indicated. All dates of Verne's works are those of the beginning of their first publication, usually in serial form.

Olivier Dumas, *Jules Verne* (Lyon: La Manufacture, 1988), and Herbert R. Lottman, *Jules Verne: An Exploratory Biography* (New York: St Martin's Press, 1996).

The only comprehensive secondary bibliographies are: William Butcher, 'Jules and Michel Verne', in *Critical Bibliography of French Literature: The Nineteenth Century*, ed. David Baguley (New York: Syracuse University Press, 1994), and the listing in Jean-Michel Margot, *Bibliographie documentaire sur Jules Verne* (Amiens: Centre de documentation Jules Verne, 1989). Piero Gondolo della Riva, *Bibliographie analytique de toutes les œuvres de Jules Verne. I: œuvres romanesques publiées* (Société Jules Verne, 1977), provides authoritative information about the dates of Verne's novels.

In English, although the overwhelming majority of translations of Verne are of an unacceptable standard, a number of reliable editions have appeared recently. As well as *Humbug* (Edinburgh: Acadian, 1991), and, in Oxford World's Classics, *Journey to the Centre of the Earth* (Oxford: OUP, 1992) and *Around the World in Eighty Days* (Oxford: OUP, 1995), edited and translated by William Butcher, there are *The Tribulations of a Chinese Gentleman*, translated by Ellen E. Frewer (Hong Kong: OUP, 1991), *Backwards to Britain*, translated by Janice Valls-Russell and edited by William Butcher (Edinburgh: Chambers, 1992), *The Rat Family*, translated by Evelyn Copeland (New York: OUP, 1993), and *Paris in the Twentieth Century* (New York: Random House, 1996).

Many useful studies on *20TL* are in French. The following are a selection in both languages:

Asimov, Isaac, 'Father Jules', in *Twenty Thousand Leagues under the Sea* and *Around the Moon* (New York: Platt & Munk, 1965), 9–13 (disappointingly old-fashioned view of Verne as 'father of science fiction').

Bardin, Jacques, 'Nemo, héros vernien?', unpublished master's dissertation (Nice: University of Nice, 1986) (a survey of Nemo's characteristics).

Barthes, Roland, '*Nautilus* et Bateau ivre', in *Mythologies* (Paris: Seuil, 1957, 1970), 80–2 (brilliant but ultimately limited exploration of the psycho-physiology of Verne's ships and their closure, finitude, and appropriation of space).

Berge, François, 'Jules Verne, romancier de la navigation', *La Revue générale*, 62 (1929), 455–68 (sensitive early study of style and symbolism in the marine novels).

Bradbury, Ray, 'The Ardent Blasphemers', in *Twenty Thousand Leagues under the Sea*, translated by Anthony Bonner (Toronto, New York, London, Sydney: Bantam, 1962, 1981), 1–12 (accompanying a reasonable translation, a lyrical comparison, by a long-standing admirer, of the 'American' spirit of Nemo and Ahab, with Nemo representing more positive values of curiosity and belief in historical progress).

Buisine, Alain, 'Un Cas limite de la description: L'Énumeration', in *La Description: Nodier, Sue, Flaubert, Hugo, Verne, Zola, Alexis, Fénelon* (Lille: Université de Lille III and Editions universitaires, 1974), 81–102 (dense, academic, structuralist study of the rhetoric of description in *20TL*).

Chelebourg, Christian, Preface to *Vingt mille lieues sous les mers* (Livre de poche, 1990), pp. iii–xxviii (useful analysis of sources and background).

Costello, Peter ['PC'], Introduction and notes in *Twenty Thousand Leagues under the Sea*, 'translated by H. Frith' [this is an error: the translator is Lewis Mercier] (Everyman, 1993), pp. xix–xxvii and 275–304 (old-fashioned introduction; disastrous translation; some useful notes).

Curtis, Jean-Louis, Preface to *Vingt mille lieues sous les mers* (Gallimard, 1978), 7–20 (Verne's influence on subsequent writers).

Delabroy, Jean, Preface to *Vingt mille lieues sous les mers* (Presses Pocket, 1991), 5–17 (fluent general introduction).

Destombes, Marcel, 'Le Manuscrit de *Vingt mille lieues sous les mers* de la Société de Géographie', *BSJV* 9: 36 (July–Dec. 1975), 59–70 (highly informative and ground-breaking study of the two manuscripts).

Ellis, Richard, *Monsters of the Deep* (New York: Knopf, 1994), *passim* (harshly criticizes Verne for scientific 'errors', but itself contains a number of mistakes).

Gagneux, Jean, 'Le *Nautilus* pouvait naviguer', *La Nouvelle revue maritime*, 386 (May–June 1984), 99–111 (studies the *Nautilus* from the perspective of modern submarine technology, and finds a few slips).

Guermonprez, Jean-H., 'Le *Nautilus* est-il "Le Bateau ivre"?', *BSJV* 4: 13 (Jan.–Mar. 1970), 1–5 (convincingly proves Rimbaud's borrowing from Verne).

Helling, Cornélis, 'Le Capitaine Nemo, ce grand inconnu!', *BSJV* 5: 19 (July–Sept. 1971), 59–61 (the Nemo of *The Mysterious Island* is not authentic).

Huet, Marie-Hélène, 'L'Écrivain tératologue', *Jules Verne 3: Machines et imaginaire* (Minard, 1980), 53–66 (the role of monsters in Verne's imagination).

Martin, Andrew, *The Knowledge of Ignorance: From Genesis to Jules Verne* (Cambridge: CUP, 1985), 150–9 and *passim* (a brilliant and ironic account of the structural foundations of Verne's imagination; explores *20TL* as ark and archive).

Michaluk, Stephen, *et al.*, *The Jules Verne Encyclopedia* (Scarecrow, 1996), 208–14 and *passim* (list of English editions of *20TL*, hidden amongst generally irrelevant or pointless material that ignores the scholarly activities of the last twenty years).

Michel, Jacques, 'Le Scaphandre du capitaine Nemo', *La Nouvelle revue maritime*, 386 (May–June 1984), 112–15 (the Rouquayrol–Denayrouze apparatus).

Mickel, Emanuel, Introduction and notes in *Twenty Thousand Leagues under the Sea*, 'a new translation by Emanuel J. Mickel' [*sic*: the translation is by Lewis Mercier] (Bloomington: Indiana University Press, 1991), 3–63 (thin introduction, strongly criticizing Mercier, persuading one respected academic to describe the translation as 'truly professional in its scope and integrity'; but the translation is in fact generally Mercier's word-for-word, meaning that the ascribed authorship is dishonest; the 482 (computer-generated?) notes explain where Corsica is, but provide little interesting information).

Miller, Walter James, 'Jules Verne in America: A Translator's Preface', in *Twenty Thousand Leagues under the Sea*, translated by Walter James Miller, assisted by Judith Ann Tirsch (New York: Washington Square Press, 1966), 7–22 (useful introduction on problems of translation; although called 'New' and 'Definitive', and castigating previous editions, especially Mercier, the translation itself is very poor, omitting considerable portions of Verne's text).

——'A New Look at Jules Verne', 'Jules Verne, Rehabilitated', and notes in *Twenty Thousand Leagues under the Sea*, translated by Lewis Mercier (New York: Crowell, 1976), 7–22, 356–62 (analyses Verne's strange reputation in the USA, caused mainly by the atrocious quality of the translations; but himself reprints Mercier's unacceptable translation).

——and Frederick Paul Walter ['WJM and FPW'], Introduction and notes in *Twenty Thousand Leagues under the Sea* (Annapolis: Naval Institute Press, 1993), pp. vii–xxii (interesting introduction on the problems of translation; very good translation; informative notes, but marred by a piecemeal approach and by ignoring French scholarship, the correspondence, and the manuscripts). [References in this text to WJM and FPW's footnotes do not include page numbers.]

Pividal, Rafaël, *Le Capitaine Nemo et la science* (Grasset, 1972) (modern science is soulless, whereas Nemo's machine provides uninterrupted pleasure).

Porcq, Christian, 'NGORA, ou les images de la folie dans les *Voyages extraordinaires* de Jules Verne', unpublished doctoral thesis (University of Paris V, 1991), *passim* (imaginatively exposes the personal and psychoanalytic aspects of *20TL*, especially dreams and the subconscious).

Robin, Christian, 'Le Récit sauvé des eaux', *Jules Verne 2: L'Écriture vernienne* (Minard, 1978), 33–56 (important structuralist study of the theme of writing within *20TL*).

——'Verne et Michelet, chantres de l'océan', *La Nouvelle revue maritime*, 386 (May–June 1984), 59–65 (the borrowing from Michelet).

Sigaux, Gilbert, Preface to *Vingt mille lieues sous les mers* (Lausanne: Rencontre, 1966), 7–19 (Nemo in *20TL* and *The Mysterious Island*).

Verne, Jules, *Twenty Thousand Leagues under the Seas* (Sampson Low, Marston, Low, and Searle, Nov. 1872) (the first English-language version, translated by Lewis Mercier).

——and Adolphe d'Ennery, *Voyage à travers l'impossible* (J.-J. Pauvert, 1981) (this play, first performed in 1882, presents Atlantis and other fantastic settings, together with unrecognizable parodies of many of Verne's characters, including Nemo; probably mostly d'Ennery's doing).

Vierne, Simone, *Jules Verne, une vie, une œuvre, une époque* (Balland, 1986), 197–218 (readable survey of *20TL*, followed by extracts from the novel).

——Introduction and archives of the work in *Vingt mille lieues sous les mers* (Garnier-Flammarion, 1977), 5–48, 519–35 (entertaining and informative account of the background to the novel).

A CHRONOLOGY OF JULES VERNE

1828   8 February: birth of Jules Verne on the Île Feydeau in Nantes, to Pierre Verne, a lawyer and son and grandson of lawyers, and Sophie, née Allotte de la Fuÿe, from a military line.

1829   Birth of brother, Paul, later a naval officer, but retired in 1859 and became a stockbroker; followed by those of sisters Anna (1836), Mathilde (1839), and Marie (1842).

1834–8 Goes to school: the teacher, Mme Sambain, is apparently the widow of a sea-captain, whose return she is still waiting for.

1838–41 Collège Saint-Stanislas. Performs well in geography, translation from Greek and Latin, and singing.

1841–6 Goes to Petit Séminaire, then to Lycée Royal de Nantes. Above average; probably won a prize in geography. Passes *baccalauréat* without difficulty. Writes short prose pieces.

1847   Studies law in Paris; his cousin, Caroline Tronson, with whom he has been unhappily in love for several years, gets engaged. Writes a play called *Alexandre VI*.

1848   June: revolution in Paris. Verne is present at the July disturbances. He continues his law studies, sharing a room at 24 Rue de l'Ancienne-Comédie. His uncle Châteaubourg introduces him into literary salons. Meets novelists Alexandre Dumas *père* and *fils*. Writes plays, probably including *La Conspiration des poudres*.

1849   Passes law degree. Father allows him to stay on in Paris. Writes more plays.

1850   12 June: his one-act comedy *Les Pailles rompues* runs for twelve nights at Dumas's Théâtre historique, and is published.

1851   Publishes short stories 'Les Premiers navires de la Marine mexicaine' and 'Un Voyage en ballon'.

1852–5 Becomes secretary of Théâtre lyrique. Publishes 'Martin Paz', 'Maître Zacharius', 'Un Hivernage dans les glaces', and the play *Les Châteaux en Californie* in collaboration with Pitre-Chevalier. His operette *Le Colin-maillard*, written with Michel Carré, is performed to music by Hignard.

1856   20 May: goes to a wedding in Amiens, and meets a young widow with two children, Honorine de Viane.

1857   10 January: marries Honorine, becomes a stockbroker in Paris, and moves house several times.

1859–60   Visits Scotland with Hignard, and is greatly marked by the experience. Writes *Voyage en Angleterre et en Écosse*.

1861   3 August: birth of only child, Michel.

1862   Goes to Norway and Denmark with Hignard.

1863   31 January: *Cinq semaines en ballon* appears, three months after submission to publisher Jules Hetzel, and is an immediate success. Writes *Paris au XXᵉ siècle*.

1864   Publication of 'Edgar Poe et ses œuvres', *Aventures du capitaine Hatteras*, and *Voyage au centre de la Terre*. Gives up his unsuccessful stockbroker practice, and moves to Auteuil.

1865   *De la Terre à la Lune* and *Les Enfants du capitaine Grant*. Death of Mme Estelle Duchêne of Asnières, close friend of Verne's.

1867   16 March: goes with brother Paul to Liverpool, thence on *Great Eastern* to United States. First English translation of any of the novels, *From the Earth to the Moon*.

1868   Buys a boat, the *Saint-Michel*. Visits London.

1869   Rents a house in Amiens. *Vingt mille lieues sous les mers* and *Autour de la Lune*.

1870   Outbreak of Franco-Prussian War: Verne is a coastguard at Le Crotoy (Somme).

1871   3 November: father dies.

1872   Moves to 44 Boulevard Longueville, Amiens; becomes member of Académie d'Amiens. *Le Tour du monde en quatre-vingts jours*.

1873–4   *Le Docteur Ox*, *L'Île mystérieuse*, and *Le Chancellor*. Begins collaboration with Adolphe d'Ennery on stage adaptations of novels (*Le Tour du monde en 80 jours* (1874), *Les Enfants du capitaine Grant* (1878), *Michel Strogoff* (1880): all highly successful).

1876–7   *Michel Strogoff*, *Hector Servadac*, and *Les Indes noires*. Buys second, then third boat, the *Saint-Michel II* and *III*. Gives huge fancy-dress ball. Wife critically ill, but recovers.

1878   June–August: sails to Lisbon and Algiers.

1879–80   *Les Cinq cents millions de la Bégum*, *Les Tribulations d'un Chinois en Chine*, and *La Maison à vapeur*. Michel, who had caused problems throughout his childhood, marries an actress, despite the opposition of his father. Verne sails to Norway, Ireland, and Scotland, including Edinburgh and possibly the Hebrides.

1881   *La Jangada*. Sails to Rotterdam and Copenhagen.

1882   October: moves to a larger house at 2 Rue Charles-Dubois, Amiens. *Le Rayon vert*.

1883–4   *Kéraban-le-têtu*. Michel abducts a minor, Jeanne. Has two children by her within eleven months. Divorces, and marries her. Verne leaves with his wife on a grand tour of the Mediterranean, but cuts it short. On the way back, is received in private audience by Pope Leo XIII.

1885   *Mathias Sandorf*.

1886   *Robur-le-conquérant*. 15 February: sells *Saint-Michel III*. 9 March: his nephew Gaston, mentally ill, asks for money to travel to England. Verne refuses, and the nephew fires at him twice, laming him for life. 17 March: Hetzel dies.

1887   15 February: mother dies.

1888   Elected local councillor on a Republican list. For next fifteen years attends council meetings, administrates theatre and fairs, opens Municipal Circus (1889), and gives public talks.

1889   *Sans dessus dessous* and 'In the Year 2889' (published in New York: signed Jules Verne but written by Michel, and then probably translated into English).

1890   Stomach problems.

1892   *Le Château des Carpathes*. Pays debts for Michel.

1895   *L'Île à hélice*, the first novel written in a European language in the present tense and third person.

1896–7   *Face au drapeau* and *Le Sphinx des glaces*. Sued by chemist Turpin, inventor of melinite, who recognizes himself in *Face au drapeau*. Successfully defended by Raymond Poincaré, later president of France. Health deteriorates. Brother dies.

1899   Dreyfus Affair: Verne is initially anti-Dreyfusard, but approves of the case being reviewed.

1900   Moves back into 44 Boulevard Longueville. Sight weakens (cataracts).

1901   *Le Village aérien.*

1904   *Maître du monde.*

1905   17 March: falls seriously ill from diabetes. 24 March: dies,
        and is buried in Amiens.

1905–14 On Verne's death, *L'Invasion de la mer* and *Le Phare du bout
        du monde* are in the course of publication. Michel takes
        responsibility for the remaining manuscripts, and publishes
        Le Volcan d'or (1906), *L'Agence Thompson and Co.* (1907),
        La Chasse au météore (1908), *Le Pilote du Danube* (1908),
        Les Naufragés du 'Jonathan' (1909), *Le Secret de Wilhelm
        Storitz* (1910), *Hier et Demain* (short stories, including
        'L'Éternel Adam') (1910), and *L'Étonnante aventure de la
        mission Barsac* (1914). In 1978 Gondolo della Riva proved
        that Michel in fact wrote considerable sections of these
        works, and between 1985 and 1989 the original (i.e. Jules's)
        versions of most of them are published.

Twenty Thousand Leagues under the Seas

CONTENTS

PART ONE

PART TWO

PART ONE

I

A Shifting Reef

THE year 1866 was marked by a strange event, an unexplained and inexplicable occurrence that doubtless no one has yet forgotten. Without mentioning the rumours which agitated the denizens of the ports and whipped up the public's imagination on every continent, seafaring men felt particularly disturbed. The merchants, shipowners, sea-captains, skippers, and master-mariners of Europe and America, the naval officers of every country, and eventually the various national governments on both continents—all became extremely worried about this matter.

For some time already, sea-going ships had been encountering an 'enormous thing': a long, spindle-shaped object, which sometimes appeared phosphorescent and was infinitely larger and quicker than a whale.

The facts concerning this apparition, as noted in the various logbooks, agreed quite closely as to the structure of the said object or creature, its extraordinary speed of movement, its surprising ability to get from place to place, and the peculiar vitality with which it seemed endowed. If it was a cetacean, then the size of this whale surpassed all those classified by science until that date. Neither Cuvier, Lacépède, M. Duméril, nor M. de Quatrefages* would have accepted that such a monster existed unless they had seen it—really seen it, that is, with their own scientific eyes.

Taking the average of the observations made at the various junctures—rejecting both the timid evaluations assigning the object a length of 200 feet and the exaggerated opinions making it three miles long by a mile wide—it could be affirmed that this phenomenal being greatly exceeded all the dimensions the ichthyologists had admitted until then—if indeed it existed at all.

But it did exist, there was now no denying the fact; and given the inclination of the human mind to seek the fantastic, it is easy to understand the sensation that this supernatural apparition caused worldwide. As for dismissing it as a myth, it was no longer possible.

The reason was that on 20 July 1866 the steamship *Governor Higginson*, of the Calcutta and Burma Steam Navigation Company, had encountered this object moving five miles east of the Australian coastline.* At first Captain Baker had thought that he was facing an unknown reef; and he was even getting ready to calculate its exact position, when two columns of water* projected from the baffling object shot 150 feet into the air, whistling. Hence, unless the reef was subject to the intermittent gush of a geyser, the *Governor Higginson* was well and truly dealing with some aquatic mammal unknown until then, whose blowholes were spurting columns of water mixed with air and vapour.

A similar phenomenon was observed in the Pacific Ocean on 23 July of the same year by the *Cristóbal Colón* of the West India and Pacific Steamship Co. This extraordinary cetacean was thus able to move from one place to another with surprising speed, for the *Governor Higginson* and the *Cristóbal Colón* had observed it within three days of each other at two points on the chart separated by more than 700 nautical leagues.

A fortnight later and two thousand leagues further on, the *Helvetia* of the French Line and the *Shannon* of the Royal Mail,* sailing on opposite tacks on the Atlantic between the United States and Europe, signalled to each other a sighting of the monster at 42° 15′ N and 60° 35′ W of the Greenwich meridian. From these simultaneous observations, it was claimed that the mammal could reliably be estimated to be at least 350 British feet[1] long, since the *Shannon* and the *Helvetia* were both smaller than it, although measuring 100 metres from stem to stern. Now the biggest whales, the *kulammak* and the *umgullick** frequenting the waters around the Aleutian Islands, have never exceeded 56 metres—if indeed they have ever reached that length.

These reports arriving hot on the heels of one another, fresh observations made on board the transatlantic liner *Pereire*, a collision between the monster and the *Etna* of the Inman Line,* an

[1] About 106 m. The British foot is only 30.40 cm long.

official memorandum drawn up by the officers of the French frigate *Normandie*, a very serious declaration obtained from Commodore Fitzjames's senior staff on board the *Lord Clyde*— all this greatly thrilled public opinion. In countries with a light-hearted mentality the phenomenon was joked about; in the serious, practical countries of Britain, America, and Germany, it was a matter for serious concern.

The monster came into fashion in all the big cities: it was sung about in the cafés, jeered at in the newspapers, acted out in the theatres. The *canards* had a perfect chance to lay whoppers of every hue. Each imaginary gigantic creature resurfaced in the papers, admittedly short of good copy: from the white whale, that terrible 'Moby Dick'* of the polar regions, to the enormous Kraken,* whose tentacles can enlace a 500-ton ship and drag it down into the depths of the sea. People even reproduced the form-ally attested reports of olden times, the opinions of Aristotle and Pliny conceding the existence of such monsters, the Norwegian tales of Bishop Pontoppidan, and the account of Paul Egede.* So, lastly, were the reports by Captain Harrington,* whose good faith could not be put in doubt when he declared in 1857 that, while on board the *Castilian*, he had seen that enormous serpent which until then had only frequented the seas in the pages of the old *Constitutionnel*.*

There then broke out an interminable argument in the learned societies and scientific journals between the credulous and the incredulous. The 'monster subject' inflamed people's minds. Those journalists who professed science, at war with those who pro-fessed wit, spilled oceans of ink in this memorable campaign; and some of them even two or three drops of blood, for from the sea serpent they moved on to the most offensive personal remarks.

For six months the war raged back and forth. The weighty art-icles of the Geographical Institute of Brazil, the Berlin Royal Academy of Sciences, the British Association, and the Smithsonian Institute in Washington, the discussions in the *Indian Archipelago*, in Abbé Moigno's *Cosmos*, and in *Petermanns Mitteilungen*,* and the science sections of the quality press of France and elsewhere— all were driven back by the rest of the press with unfaltering repar-tee. These amusing writers, punning on a saying of Linnaeus's*

quoted by the monster's opponents, argued that 'Nature does not produce idiots',* and so adjured their contemporaries not to give the lie to nature by admitting the existence of Krakens, sea serpents, Moby Dicks, or other lucubrations of crazed sailors. The last straw was an article written for a much-feared satirical newspaper* by its most popular writer, who pushed his spurs in like Hippolytus* and delivered a deadly blow to the monster, putting it out of its misery amidst universal laughter. Wit had proved mightier than science.

During the first few months of 1867 the question did indeed seem dead and buried, without any hope of rising from the ashes, when some fresh information became known to the general public. There was now in fact a genuine and serious danger to be avoided, rather than simply a scientific question to be decided. The problem took on a different complexion. The monster became an islet, a rock, a reef; but a reef that was shifting, vague, and slippery.

During the night of 5 March 1867 the *Moravian* of the Montreal Ocean Company was sailing at 27° 30′ N, 72° 15′ W* when her starboard quarter struck a rock that was not marked on any chart. She was making 13 knots under the combined effect of the wind and her 400 horsepower. Without any doubt, had it not been for the superior quality of her hull, the *Moravian* would have sunk from the hole made by the collision, together with the 237 passengers she was bringing back from Canada.

The accident happened at about 5 a.m., just as day was breaking. The officers of the watch rushed to the stern of the vessel. They examined the sea with the closest attention. They saw nothing but a powerful swirl breaking at about three cables' distance, as if the surface strata of the water were being violently threshed. The position was carefully noted, and the *Moravian* continued on her way without visible damage. Had she hit a submerged rock, or else the enormous wreck of some half-sunken ship? There was no way of finding out; but when the hull was inspected in dry dock,* it was realized that part of the keel had been broken.

This occurrence, extremely serious on its own, would perhaps have been forgotten about like so many others, had it not happened again in identical circumstances three weeks later. This time the event had a tremendous impact because of the nationality of the ship involved in the collision and the reputation of the company operating the vessel.

The name of the celebrated British shipowner Cunard* is known to everyone. In 1840 this far-sighted industrialist set up a postal service from Liverpool to Halifax using three wooden paddle-steamers of 400 horsepower and a burden of 1,162 tons. Eight years later the company added four ships of 650 horsepower and 1,820 tons to its fleet, and two years after that, two further vessels of still greater power and tonnage. In 1853 the Cunard Line, which had just had its mail-carrying monopoly renewed, successively added to its fleet the *Arabia*, the *Persia*, the *China*, the *Scotia*, the *Java*, and the *Russia*, all amongst the fastest and the largest ships, after the *Great Eastern*,* ever to have sailed the high seas. In 1867 the company owned twelve vessels, eight being paddle- and four propeller-driven.

If I give these brief details, it is so that everyone realizes the importance of this shipping line, known worldwide for its intelligent management. No ocean-going company has been run with greater skill; no business crowned with greater success. During the past 26 years, Cunard ships have crossed the Atlantic 2,000 times, and never cancelled a journey, arrived behind schedule, or lost a letter, man, or vessel. That is why, in spite of the strong competition provided by France, passengers still choose the Cunard Line more than any other, as is apparent from reading the official registers of recent years. Consequently no one will be surprised at the stir produced by the accident to one of its finest steamships.

On 13 April 1867, in a fine sea and moderate wind, the *Scotia* was at 45°37′N, 15°12′W. Under the force of its 1,000 horse-power it was moving at 13.43 knots. Its paddlewheels were beating the sea with perfect regularity. Its draught was 6.70 m and its displacement 6,624 m³.

At seventeen minutes past four in the afternoon, while the passengers were in the main saloon taking their lunch, a blow, hardly perceptible in fact, was felt on the hull of the *Scotia*, on the quarter a little behind the port wheel.

The *Scotia* had not run into something: something had run into it, and a cutting or a perforating implement rather than a blunt one. The blow seemed so slight that nobody on board would have worried but for the shout of the hold-workers who rushed up on to the deck shouting:

'We're sinking! We're sinking!'

At first the passengers were quite frightened—but Captain Anderson* quickly reassured them. Actually the danger could not be imminent. The *Scotia*, divided into seven compartments by its watertight bulkheads, was guaranteed to resist any leak with impunity.

Captain Anderson headed immediately for the hold. He observed that the fifth compartment had flooded; and the speed of the flooding proved that the hole was a considerable one. Very fortunately, the boilers were not in this compartment, for the fires would have gone out immediately.

Captain Anderson had the engines stopped at once, while one of the sailors dived to assess the damage. Shortly afterwards, the existence of a two-metre hole in the hull was confirmed. Such damage could not be repaired and the *Scotia*, its wheels half underwater, had to continue its journey in the same state. It was 300 miles from Cape Clear, and was three days late when it sailed into the company docks, having greatly worried Liverpool.

The engineers then carried out an inspection of the *Scotia*, which was in dry dock. They couldn't believe their eyes. Two and a half metres below the water-line appeared a neat hole in the form of an isosceles triangle. The break in the plate was perfectly clean, and could not have been cut with greater precision by a punch. The perforating implement that had made it had therefore to be of an uncommon temper—and, having been propelled with prodigious strength to pierce the four-centimetre sheet metal in this way, it must then have withdrawn by itself in a reverse movement that was truly inexplicable.

Such was this most recent event, which resulted in public opinion being stirred up once more. Starting from that moment, maritime losses from unknown causes were simply attributed to the monster. This fantastic animal shouldered the blame for all such shipwrecks, which unfortunately occur in considerable numbers; for, out of the 3,000 ships whose losses are recorded each year by the Bureau Veritas,* the number of steam or sailing ships presumed lost with all hands through lack of news is as high as 200!

It was now 'the monster' which was being blamed for their disappearance, rightly or wrongly. Because of this, and because travel between the various continents was becoming increasingly dangerous, the public spoke its mind and categorically demanded that the oceans be finally rid of this formidable cetacean, whatever the cost.

2

Pros and Cons

AT the time these events were occurring, I was returning from a scientific exploration of the Badlands of Nebraska, in the United States. The French government had attached me to this expedition in my capacity as a lecturer* at the Museum of Natural History in Paris. After six months spent in Nebraska, I had arrived in New York towards the end of March, laden down with my precious collections. My departure for France was scheduled for the beginning of May. In the meantime, I was attending to the classification of my mineralogical, botanical, and zoological treasures—when the *Scotia* incident happened.

I was perfectly aware of the topic in the news, for how could it have been otherwise? I had read and reread the European and American newspapers without coming any closer to a solution. This mystery fascinated me. Unable to form an opinion about it, I had drifted from one extreme to the other. That there was *something*, there could be no question, for doubting Thomases could be invited to touch the wound in the *Scotia*'s side.

When I arrived in New York the question was a hot one. The theory of a floating island or elusive reef, put forward by a few unqualified individuals, had been totally discredited. And in truth, unless the reef had an engine in its belly, how could it move around with such awesome speed?

In the same way, the idea of a floating hulk, an enormous wreck, was rejected, and again because of the speed it moved at.

This left two possible answers to the problem, which in turn produced two highly distinct groups of supporters: on the one hand, those who swore by a monster of colossal strength; and on the other, those who argued for a 'submarine' vessel* of immense locomotive power.

Now the latter theory, admissible after all, was unable to survive the researches carried out in the Old and New Worlds. That a private individual had at his disposition a mechanical contrivance of this sort was improbable. When and where could he have had it built, and how could he have kept its construction secret?

Only a government could possess such a weapon of destruction, and in these disastrous times, when humanity endeavours to increase the power of its weapons of war, it could not be thought impossible that a country had tested this formidable device unbeknownst to the others. After the chassepot rifles came floating mines; after floating mines, underwater rams;* then . . . a reaction. At least, I hope there will be one.

But the idea of a war machine had to be abandoned all the same, in the light of what the governments declared. As it was a matter of the public interest, since intercontinental communications were suffering, the governments' truthfulness could not be doubted for one moment. In any case, how could it be imagined that this submarine vessel's construction had escaped public notice? Keeping a secret under such circumstances is very difficult for a private individual, and certainly impossible for states whose every act is continuously observed by rival powers.

Consequently, after research had been carried out in Great Britain, France, Russia, Prussia, Spain, Italy, America, and even in Turkey, the hypothesis of a submarine *Monitor** was rejected once and for all.

The monster therefore surfaced again, despite the constant witticisms that the popular press showered on it; and people's imaginations followed this path and soon allowed themselves to culminate in the most absurd dreams of fantastic ichthyology.

When I arrived in New York, several people had done me the honour of consulting me on the phenomenon in question. In France I had published a two-volume in-quarto work entitled *The Mysteries of the Ocean Deeps*. This book, particularly relished in scholarly circles, had made of me a specialist in that relatively obscure area of natural history. My views were sought. So long as I was able to deny the reality of the fact, I enveloped myself in complete negativity. But soon, with my back against the wall, I was forced to explain myself unequivocally. The *New York Herald* even challenged 'the honourable Pierre Aronnax,* lecturer at the Paris Museum', to formulate an opinion of some sort.

I complied. I spoke, since I was unable to remain silent. I analysed the question from every angle, both political and scientific; and will provide here an extract from a very full study that I published in the newspaper on 30 April:

As a result of the above, and having successively examined the various hypotheses, and since every other supposition is to be rejected, we are necessarily obliged to accept the existence of a marine animal of very great power.

The great depths of the ocean are totally unknown to us. Sounding lines have been unable to reach them. What transpires in those remote abysses? What beings live or can live twelve or fifteen miles below the surface of the sea? What is the make-up of these animals? We can scarcely even guess.

Nevertheless, the solution to the problem which has been submitted to me can be formulated as a two-pronged alternative.

Either we know all the varieties of beings which inhabit our planet, or we do not.

If we do not know them all, if Nature still holds secrets for us in ichthyology, it is quite acceptable to recognize the existence of fish or cetaceans of unknown species or even genera, of an essentially 'deep-based' composition, which inhabit the deeps inaccessible to the sounding line and which some event, a whim, a caprice as it were, brings up to the upper part of the sea at infrequent intervals.

If, on the contrary, we know all living species, we are necessarily compelled to seek the animal in question amongst marine beings that are already catalogued, and, in this case, I should be disposed to accept the existence of a Giant Narwhal.*

The common narwhal or sea-unicorn often attains a length of 60 feet. Multiply this dimension by five, by ten even, endow this cetacean with a strength proportional to its size, enlarge its offensive weapon, and you will obtain the required animal. It will have the dimensions ascertained by the officers of the *Shannon*, the instrument required to pierce the *Scotia*, and the force necessary to breach the hull of a steamship.

The narwhal is armed with a kind of ivory sword, a halberd in the terminology of certain naturalists. This is a principal tooth with the hardness of steel. Some of these teeth have been found embedded in the bodies of whales, which the narwhal always attacks with success. Others have been removed, not without difficulty, from the hulls of vessels that have been pierced through and through, like a drill through a barrel. The museum of the Faculty of Medicine in Paris possesses one of these tusks that is 2.25 m long and 48 cm wide at its base!

Now imagine a weapon ten times as big and an animal ten times as strong, launch it at a speed of 20 knots, multiply its mass by its velocity, and you obtain a shock capable of producing the required catastrophe.

Accordingly, until further information becomes available, I shall vote for a sea-unicorn of colossal dimensions, armed not with a halberd, but with a genuine spur like the ironclad frigates called war 'rams', whose weight and motive power it would also have.

Thus the inexplicable phenomenon would be explained—unless there is nothing there at all, which is always possible, in spite of what has been glimpsed, seen, felt, and experienced!

These last words were a piece of cowardice on my part; but I wished to a certain extent to protect my dignity as a scholar, and to avoid the danger of becoming a laughing-stock for the Americans, for they laugh wholeheartedly when they do laugh. I left myself a way out, but at bottom, I admitted that 'the monster' did exist.

My article was hotly debated, and produced quite a stir. It won over a number of supporters. But in any case, my proposed solution left full scope for the imagination. The human mind enjoys grandiose conceptions of supernatural beings. Now the sea is their best vehicle, for it is the only environment which can produce and develop such giants: beside them the land animals, the elephants or rhinoceroses, are mere dwarfs. The liquid masses carry the biggest known species of mammals, and perhaps harbour molluscs of extraordinary size, crustaceans terrifying to contemplate, lobsters a hundred metres long, or crabs weighing 200 tons! Why ever not? The land animals of long-gone geological eras, the quadrupeds, quadrumanes, reptiles, and birds, were formerly built to a gigantic template. The Creator cast them in a colossal mould which slowly reduced with time. Why could the unknown depths of the sea not have maintained these vast specimens from another age, that sea which never changes, unlike the terrestrial core which is almost continually being modified?* Why should she not conceal in her bosom the last varieties of those titanic species, whose years are as centuries and centuries as millennia?

But I am allowing myself to be carried away by these musings which I no longer have the right to mention! Enough of these chimeras which time has changed for me into terrible realities! I repeat: at that time people made up their minds on the nature of the phenomenon, and the public accepted without question the existence of a prodigious being that had nothing in common with the sea serpents of legend.

But if some people saw merely a purely scientific problem to be solved, others of a more positive nature, especially in America and Britain, agreed to purge the seas of this redoubtable monster, in order to safeguard cross-ocean communications once more. The industrial and commercial journals treated the question chiefly from this point of view. The *Shipping & Mercantile Gazette and Lloyd's List*, the *Paquebot*, and the *Revue maritime et coloniale*,* together with every newsletter devoted to the insurance companies, who were threatening to raise their premium rates—all were in agreement on this point.

Since public opinion had come to a decision, the States of the Union spoke out first. Preparations were made in New York for an expedition to hunt the narwhal. A fast frigate, the *Abraham Lincoln*, made ready to sail at almost no notice. The arsenals were opened for Captain Farragut,* who actively pushed on with arming his frigate.

But as it happened, as it always happens, once it had been decided to hunt it, the monster put in no further appearances. For two months it was not heard of at all. No ship came upon it. It seemed that the unicorn knew about the plots being hatched against it. It had been discussed so often, and even over the transatlantic cable! The wags claimed that this sharp customer had stopped some telegram on its way across* and was now turning it to its own advantage.

As a result, although the frigate was armed for a distant campaign and equipped with formidable hunting tackle, nobody knew where to send it to. Impatience was building up more and more, when, on 3 July, it was learned that a steamer of the San

Francisco–Shanghai line* had again seen the animal, three weeks previously in the seas of the northern Pacific.

The excitement caused by this piece of news was tremendous. Captain Farragut was given less than 24 hours' respite. His provisions were on board. His bunkers overflowed with coal. Not a man was missing from his crew's roll-call. He only had to light his furnaces, stoke up, and cast off! He wouldn't have been forgiven even half a day's delay! To get going was all Captain Farragut wanted to do in any case.

Three hours before the *Abraham Lincoln* left its Brooklyn pier,[1] I received a letter couched in these terms:

Dr Aronnax
Lecturer at the Natural History Museum of Paris
Fifth Avenue Hotel*
NEW YORK

Dear Sir,

If you would like to join the expedition on board the *Abraham Lincoln*, the government of the Union would greatly appreciate having you represent France in this enterprise. Captain Farragut holds a cabin at your disposal.

Very cordially yours
J. B. Hobson*
Secretary to the Navy

3

As Monsieur Pleases

THREE seconds before J. B. Hobson's letter arrived, I no more dreamed of hunting the unicorn than of seeking the Northwest Passage. Three seconds after reading the letter from the honourable Secretary to the Navy, I realized that my real vocation, my main aim in life, was to pursue this disturbing monster and rid the world of it.

[1] A sort of individual quay for each vessel.

However, I was returning from a difficult journey, tired and longing for rest. I pined only to see my country again, my friends, my small lodgings at the Jardin des Plantes, my dear and precious collections! But nothing could hold me back. I forgot everything, tiredness, friends, collections; and I accepted the American government's offer without further reflection.

'In any case,' I thought, 'all roads lead to Europe, and the unicorn will surely be so kind as to lure me towards the French coasts! This amiable creature will allow itself to be captured in European waters as a special favour to me; and I wish to bring back no less than half a metre of ivory halberd for the Museum of Natural History.'

But meanwhile I needed to search for this narwhal in the northern Pacific Ocean; which amounted to heading for France via the Antipodes.

'Conseil!'* I cried impatiently.

Conseil was my domestic servant. A devoted young man who accompanied me on all my journeyings; a good Fleming whom I liked a great deal and who reciprocated; a creature who was phlegmatic by nature, ordered by principle, and eager by habit: astonished by few of life's surprises, very good with his hands, suited for any service, and, despite his name, never giving counsel—even unasked.

By rubbing shoulders with the scholars of our little milieu at the Jardin des Plantes, Conseil had come to know a thing or two. I had in him a specialist, very well up on natural history classification, with an acrobat's dexterity at working his way through the whole hierarchy of phyla, divisions, classes, sub-classes, orders, families, genera, sub-genera, species, and varieties.* But his scientific knowledge ended there. Well versed in the theory of classification but little in its practice, he wouldn't, I think, have distinguished a sperm whale from an ordinary whale! And yet what a good and honest fellow!

For the past ten years, Conseil had followed me everywhere science had taken me. Never a comment from him on the length or fatigue of a journey. No objection to packing his suitcase for any country whatsoever, China or the Congo, however far away. He travelled anywhere, without expecting anything else. Moreover, his fine health thumbed its nose at every illness; and he had powerful muscles but no nerves, not even the appearance of them—mentally speaking, I mean.

The fellow was thirty years old, and his age was to his master's as fifteen is to twenty. May I be excused for saying in this way that I was forty.

Conseil had but one fault. A rabid formalist, he only ever spoke to me in the third person—to the point of becoming annoying.

'Conseil!' I repeated, while at the same time beginning my preparations for departure with a feverish hand.

Certainly, I felt sure of this fellow of such devotion. Normally I never asked whether or not it suited him to accompany me in my travels; but this time it was an expedition which could last indefinitely, a hazardous enterprise in pursuit of an animal capable of sinking a frigate as easily as a nutshell. There was food for thought in that, even for the most impassive man in the world. So what would Conseil say?

'Conseil!' I cried for the third time.

Conseil appeared.

'Did monsieur call?'

'Yes, my good fellow. Please get me and yourself ready. We're leaving in two hours' time.'

'As monsieur pleases,' Conseil replied calmly.

'Not a moment to lose. Squeeze into my trunk all my travel utensils, coats, shirts, and socks, without skimping and as much as you can, and hurry!'

'And monsieur's collections?' enquired Conseil.

'We'll deal with them later.'

'What! The Archaeotheria, Hyracotheria, Oreodons, Chaeropotami,* and monsieur's other carcasses?'

'The hotel will look after them.'

'And monsieur's live babirusa?'*

'They'll feed while we're away. In any case, I'll give instructions for our menagerie to be sent to us in France.'

'So we're not returning to Paris?' Conseil enquired.

'But of course . . . most definitely . . .' I replied evasively, 'but via a detour.'

'Whichever detour monsieur wishes.'

'Oh it hardly makes any difference! Not quite so direct a route, that's all. We're sailing on the *Abraham Lincoln*.'

'As monsieur requires,' replied Conseil calmly.

'You know, my friend, it's the monster ... the famous narwhal ... We're going to rid the seas of it! ... The author of the two-volume in-quarto *Mysteries of the Ocean Deeps* cannot decline to embark with Captain Farragut. A mission full of glory, but also ... dangerous. We don't know where we'll end up. Those creatures can be awfully flighty. But we're going all the same! We have a captain who's got guts!'

'Wherever monsieur goes, so will I.'

'Please do think it over. I don't want to hide anything from you. It's one of those journeys you don't always come back from!'

'As monsieur pleases.'

A quarter of an hour later, our trunks were ready. Conseil had packed them standing on his head, as it were. I could be sure that nothing was missing, for this fellow classified shirts and coats as skilfully as he did birds or mammals.

The hotel lift* dropped us at the mezzanine lounge. I descended the few steps leading to the ground floor. I settled my bill at the huge desk always besieged by a large crowd. I left instructions for my packages of stuffed animals and dried plants to be forwarded to Paris (France). Having opened a well-provisioned account for the babirusa, and with Conseil following, I jumped into a cab.

This vehicle, costing twenty francs a trip, went down Broadway as far as Union Square, followed Fourth Avenue as far as its junction with The Bowery, turned into Katrin Street, and stopped at Pier No. 34. There the Katrin Ferry took us, men, horses, and cab, to Brooklyn, New York's great extension on the left bank of the East River. A few minutes later we were standing on the quayside where the *Abraham Lincoln* was spewing out torrents of black smoke through its twin funnels.

Our bags were immediately transported on to the frigate's deck. I rushed on board and asked for Captain Farragut. One of the sailors took me to the poop deck, where I found myself in the presence of an officer of pleasant appearance, who stretched out his hand.

'Dr Pierre Aronnax?'

'Himself. Captain Farragut?'

'In person. Welcome aboard, Dr Aronnax. Your cabin is ready.'

I bowed and, leaving the captain to his task of getting under way, had myself shown to the designated cabin.

The *Abraham Lincoln* had been perfectly chosen and fitted out for its new task. It was a high-speed frigate, equipped with super-heating apparatus enabling its steam pressure to be raised to 7 atmospheres. At this pressure, the *Abraham Lincoln* typically reached 18.3 knots: a considerable speed but still insufficient to compete with the gigantic cetacean.

The accommodation of the frigate reflected its nautical nature. I was very satisfied with my cabin, situated at the stern and opening into the officers' wardroom.

'We'll be comfortable here,' I said to Conseil.

'With due respect, monsieur, as comfortable as a hermit-crab in a whelk's shell.'

I left Conseil to stow our trunks properly, and went back up on deck to watch the preparations for weighing anchor.

At that moment Captain Farragut was directing the casting off of the last ropes securing the *Abraham Lincoln* to the Brooklyn pier. A quarter of an hour's delay, less even, and the frigate would have left without me; and I would have missed out on that extra-ordinary, supernatural, implausible expedition, whose recounting may indeed find a few disbelievers.

Captain Farragut did not want to waste a day, nor even an hour, before heading for the seas where the animal had just been reported. He sent for his engineer.

'Are we under pressure?'

'Yes sir.'

'Go ahead!' cried Captain Farragut.

On this order, transmitted to the machine-room by means of compressed air, the engineers activated the starting-up wheel. The steam hissed as it rushed through the half-open slide valves.* The long horizontal pistons groaned and pushed the crank arms of the drive shaft. The blades of the propeller beat the waves with increasing speed as the *Abraham Lincoln* advanced majestically through the midst of a hundred ferry-boats and tenders[1] filled with a retinue of spectators.

The wharves of Brooklyn and the rest of New York lining the

---

[1] Small steam-driven boats that serve the great steamships.

East River were covered with bystanders. Three successive hoorays resounded from 500,000 chests. Thousands of handkerchiefs continued waving above the compact mass acclaiming the *Abraham Lincoln* until it arrived at the waters of the Hudson, encountered at the tip of the elongated peninsula that forms New York City.

Then the frigate followed the splendid right bank of the river, the New Jersey side crowded with villas, and passed between the forts,* which saluted it with their largest cannons. The *Abraham Lincoln* responded by lowering and raising the American flag three times, with the 39 stars* resplendent on the tip of the mizzenmast. Then, slowing down to take the buoys marking the channel which curves round the bay enclosed by Sandy Hook, it skirted past its sandy tongue, where thousands of spectators greeted it with more applause.

The escort of boats and tenders continued to follow the frigate, only leaving it when abeam of the lightship with two beacons that marks the entrance to New York Harbour.

Three o'clock was striking. The pilot climbed down into his boat and boarded the small schooner waiting for him to leeward. The boilers were stoked up, the propeller beat the waves faster, and the frigate skirted the low, yellow coast of Long Island. At eight o'clock, having left the lights of Fire Island to the northwest, it was heading at full steam over the dark waters of the Atlantic.

4

Ned Land

CAPTAIN FARRAGUT was a good sailor, and worthy of the frigate he commanded. His ship and he were one. He was its very soul. He did not allow the slightest doubt about the cetacean to enter his mind, nor did he allow any discussion on board about whether the animal existed. He believed in it as some good women believe in Leviathan,* through faith, not reason. The monster existed; and he had taken an oath to rid the seas of it. He was like a Knight of Rhodes,* a Dieudonné of Gozo,* marching out to face the serpent laying waste to his island. Either Captain Farragut would kill the narwhal or the narwhal would kill Captain Farragut. There could be no middle course.

The officers shared their captain's views. You could hear them chatter and debate and argue and calculate the chances of an encounter as they scanned the vast expanses of ocean. Quite a few of them voluntarily stood watch, climbing up to the fore-topmast crosstrees, when under any other circumstances they would have cursed such a duty as a terrible chore. Every moment that the sun spent describing its daily arc the rigging was full of people unable to remain in one place and who found the planks on deck too hot for their feet. And yet the *Abraham Lincoln*'s prow had not even started cutting the suspicious waters of the Pacific.

As for the ship's crew, they longed with all their hearts to meet the unicorn, in order to be able to harpoon him, hoist him on board, and carve him up. They watched the sea very closely. Captain Farragut had in fact mentioned a sum of $2,000 for the first person to spot the animal, whether cabin boy, able seaman, mate, or officer. So I leave to your imagination how much the men on board the *Abraham Lincoln* used their eyes.

For my own part, I was as absorbed as the others, and would not have let anyone take my share of the daily watch. The frigate could have had a hundred reasons to be called the *Argus*.* The only exception was Conseil; he displayed indifference to the question absorbing us, thus constituting a slight 'damper' to the enthusiasm on board.

I have already indicated that Captain Farragut had carefully equipped his ship with everything that was needed to catch the enormous cetacean. A whaling ship could not have been better armed. We possessed all known weapons, from the simple hand-harpoon, via a blunderbuss firing barbed arrows, to exploding bullets from a punt gun. On the fo'c'sle stood the latest model of breech-loading cannon* with a great thick barrel and narrow bore, identical to the one due to be exhibited at the 1867 Universal Exposition.* This valuable American-made weapon could send a conical four-kilogram shot a mean distance of 16 kilometres with the greatest of ease.

Thus every means of destruction was available on board the

Abraham Lincoln. But there was better than this. There was Ned Land,* the king of harpooners.

Ned was a Canadian of almost unbelievable manual dexterity, unrivalled in his perilous profession. He possessed skill and composure, bravery and cunning, to a remarkable degree, and it was an exceptionally devious whale or astute cachalot that could evade his harpoon.

Ned was about forty years old. He was of considerable size, more than six feet tall, strongly built, grave, silent, sometimes aggressive, and very bad-tempered when contradicted. He compelled attention through his appearance, especially the power of his gaze, which made his facial expression quite remarkable.

I believe that Captain Farragut had done well to engage this man. Because of his steadiness of eye and arm, he was worth the rest of the crew put together. I can only compare him to a powerful telescope combined with a cannon always ready to go off.

A Canadian is really a Frenchman, and however uncommunicative Ned Land was, I must admit that he developed a certain affection for me. My nationality attracted him no doubt. It was an opportunity for him to speak and for me to hear the old language of Rabelais, still in use in some of the Canadian provinces. The harpooner's family came from the town of Québec, and had already become a tribe of hardy fishermen when that town belonged to France.

Gradually Ned got used to chatting: I enjoyed listening to his tales of adventure on the Arctic seas. He showed much natural poetry of expression in recounting his fishing exploits and battles. His stories had an epic form, and I imagined I was listening to a Canadian Homer reciting some *Iliad* of the polar regions.

I am in fact describing this hardy companion as I now know him. We became old friends, united by an unshakable friendship that was initiated and sealed by the most terrible shared experiences. Oh good Ned, how I long to live another hundred years just to be able to remember you for longer!

So what was Land's opinion concerning the marine monster? I must admit that he scarcely credited the unicorn theory, being the only man on board not to share the general conviction. He even avoided the subject when I tried to engage him on it.

On the lovely evening of 30 July, three weeks after our

departure, the frigate was about thirty miles to leeward of Cape Blanco on the coast of Patagonia. We had crossed the tropic of Capricorn, and the Strait of Magellan was scarcely 700 miles southwards. Within a week the *Abraham Lincoln* would be sailing over the waters of the Pacific.

Sitting on the poop, Ned and I were chatting about this and that while watching the mysterious waves, whose depths are still hidden from human eyes.* I brought the conversation subtly round to the subject of the giant unicorn, and explored what chance of success our expedition had. Then, noticing that Ned was letting me talk without saying a word, I pressed him more directly:

'But how is it, Ned, that you are so unconvinced of the existence of the cetacean we are pursuing? Have you any particular reasons for being so sceptical?'

The harpooner looked at me for a few seconds without replying, struck his forehead with a gesture he often used, closed his eyes as if to collect his thoughts, and at last said:

'Perhaps I have, Dr Aronnax.'

'But Ned, a man like you, a professional whaler, familiar with the great marine animals, who must easily be able to accept the idea of enormous whales—under these circumstances you ought to be the last person to harbour any doubts!'

'It's just there that you're wrong monsieur. It's one thing for ordinary folk to choose to believe in incredible comets crossing space or prehistoric monsters living inside the Earth; but neither the astronomer nor the geologist accept such fantasies.* The same goes for the whaler. I've hunted hundreds of whales, harpooned masses, killed them by the dozen; but however strong and well armed they were, not one of their tails or tusks could have pierced the side of a metal steamer.'

'But Ned, there have been cases when a narwhal's tooth has pierced ships through and through!'

'Wooden ships perhaps,' replied the Canadian, 'although personally I've never seen any. But until I have proof to the contrary, I can't believe that a whale, cachalot, or sea-unicorn could manage such a thing.'

'Just listen to me, Ned . . .'

'No sir no. Anything you like except that. Perhaps a giant squid . . .?'

'Even less likely. The squid is only a mollusc; and its flesh is soft, as that very word implies. Even if it were 500 feet long, the squid wouldn't belong to the branch of vertebrates, and so remains perfectly harmless to ships like the *Scotia* or *Abraham Lincoln*. We must therefore relegate all feats of Krakens and such-like monsters to the realm of fable.'

'Then sir,' said Ned in rather a mocking tone, 'as a naturalist, are you sticking to your view about the existence of a huge cetacean?'

'Yes Ned, I repeat my view with a conviction based on the logic of facts. I believe in the existence of a large powerful mammal belonging to the vertebrates, like the whale, cachalot, or dolphin, and fitted with a tusk made of horn of very great penetrative power.'

'H'm,' said the harpooner, shaking his head in the manner of one refusing to be convinced.

'Just consider, my good Canadian, that if such an animal does exist, and inhabits the depths of the ocean a few miles down, it would have to have a body of unparalleled strength.'

'And why would it need such a powerful body?'

'Because it would require incredible strength to live so far below the surface and resist the pressure.'

'Really?' said Ned, looking at me and blinking.

'Yes, and a few statistics can easily prove it.'

'Oh statistics! You can do anything you want with statistics!'

'In business, Ned, but not in mathematics. Please listen. Let us assume that atmospheric pressure is equivalent to the pressure of a column of water 32 feet high. In reality the column would be shorter, since it would be sea water, which is denser than fresh water. Well, Ned, when you dive, your body undergoes a pressure equal to 1 atmosphere for every 32 feet of water you go down, that is 1 kilogram for each square centimetre of its surface. It follows that this pressure would be 10 atmospheres at 320 feet, 100 atmospheres at 3,200 feet, and 1,000 atmospheres at 32,000 feet, or about 2½ leagues. In other words, if you could reach this depth, each square centimetre on your body would be undergoing a pressure of 1,000 kilograms. Now, my good Ned, do you know how many square centimetres you have on your body?'

'No idea, Dr Aronnax.'

'About 17,000.'

'As many as that?'

'And since atmospheric pressure is in fact slightly more than 1 kilogram per square centimetre, your 17,000 square centimetres are at this very moment undergoing a pressure of 17,568 kilograms.'

'Without me realizing?'

'Without your realizing. And the only reason you are not crushed is the air entering your body with an equal force. The inward and outward pressures are in perfect equilibrium, they cancel each other out, and so you can bear them without discomfort. But it is not the same underwater.'

'Now I understand,' replied Ned, suddenly more attentive. 'Because the water is all round me, and isn't coming into my body.'

'Precisely Ned. So at 32 feet you would be subject to a pressure of 17,568 kilograms; at 320 feet ten times that pressure, namely 175,680 kilograms; at 3,200 feet 100 times that pressure, or 1,756,800 kilograms; and at 32,000 feet at least 1,000 times that pressure, or 17,568,000 kilograms. In other words you would be as flat as if between the plates of a hydraulic press.'

'How amazing!' exclaimed Ned.

'So my worthy harpooner, if vertebrates several hundred metres long and of corresponding girth inhabit such depths, their surface area is millions of square centimetres and the pressure on their bodies must be estimated to be billions of kilograms. Calculate now what the strength of their skeletons and resistance of their bodies must be to withstand such pressures.'

'They must be made of eight-inch metal plate, like ironclads.'

'Exactly Ned, and now think of the damage that such a mass would do if it hit the hull of a ship while moving at the speed of an express train.'

'Well . . . yes . . . perhaps,' said the Canadian, shaken by these figures but unwilling to concede.

'Are you convinced now?'

'You have convinced me of one thing, monsieur, which is that if such animals do live at the bottom of the seas, they must clearly be as strong as you say they are.'

'But if they do not exist, my obstinate harpooner, how can you possibly explain the accident to the *Scotia*?'

'Perhaps . . .' he began.

'Well go on!'

'. . . because it's not true,' he replied, unwittingly echoing a celebrated riposte of Arago's.*

But this reply simply proved the harpooner's obstinacy—nothing more. I pressed him no more on this occasion. The accident to the *Scotia* was undeniable. The hole existed to the extent that it had had to be stopped up, and I do not think that a hole's existence can be any more conclusively demonstrated. And as the hole did not get there on its own, and since it had not been produced by submarine rocks or weaponry, it must have been caused by the perforating tool of some animal.

Now in my view, and for the reasons already listed, this animal had to belong to the branch of vertebrates, class of mammalia, group of pisciforms, and order of Cetaceae. As for the family—i.e. whale, cachalot, or dolphin—and genus and species that it had to be put into, these could be determined later. To decide, we would have to dissect the unknown monster; to dissect it, catch it; to catch it, harpoon it, which was Ned Land's business; to harpoon it, see it, the ship's affair; and to see it, first encounter it—which was up to chance.

5

In Search of Adventure

FOR a while the voyage of the *Abraham Lincoln* continued without any particular incident. Nevertheless, something did occur which served to demonstrate Land's remarkable prowess, and to show what confidence one could have in him.

On 30 June,* off the Falklands, the frigate communicated with some American whalers, who told us that they had had no contact with the narwhal. But the captain of one of the ships, the *Monroe*, knew that Ned was on board the *Abraham Lincoln*, and asked for his help in hunting down a whale then in view. Captain Farragut wanted to see Ned Land in action, and therefore authorized him to go on board the *Monroe*. And luck so favoured the Canadian that he harpooned, not just one whale but two in a single go, striking one through the heart and catching another after a chase of only a few minutes.*

Decidedly, if ever the monster came to grips with Land, my bet would not be on the monster.

The frigate ran down the south-east coast of the Americas at a tremendous rate. On 3 July we sighted the Strait of Magellan near Virgin Cape. But Captain Farragut didn't want to enter such a tortuous strait, and directed our course round Cape Horn instead.

The crew supported him unanimously. After all, was it likely we would encounter the narwhal in such a narrow passage? A number of sailors declared that the monster couldn't get through, 'as it's too big for it!'

At about three p.m. on 6 July, keeping 15 kilometres to the south, the *Abraham Lincoln* rounded a solitary island, an isolated rock at the extreme tip of the American continent: Cape Horn as it was called by Dutch sailors after their native town. Our course now lay north-westwards; and next day the frigate's screws were finally beating the waves of the Pacific.

'Keep your eyes peeled,' the sailors kept saying to each other.

And they did keep them exceptionally peeled. There was not a minute's rest for eyes or for telescopes—both slightly dazzled, it must be admitted, by the prospect of the $2,000. The ocean was scanned day and night. Those with good night-vision had a fifty per cent better chance, and thus a very respectable prospect of winning the prize money.

As for me, although largely oblivious to the lure of the money, I was one of the most watchful on board. Wasting only a few minutes on meals and a few hours on sleep, careless of the sun and wind, I rarely left the deck. Sometimes I leaned on the fo'c'sle rail but sometimes over the poop-rail, my greedy eyes devouring the cotton-wool wake that whitened the ocean as far as the eye could see. And how often I shared the officers' and men's emotions when some whale capriciously raised its blackish back above the surface. The frigate's deck would be crowded in an instant. The hatchways would throw up a torrent of officers and men. Panting for breath, with restless eyes, all would watch the cetacean as it moved through the waves. I also looked, risking wearing out my eyeballs and so going blind—while Conseil, always phlegmatic, would calmly repeat:

'If monsieur would be so good as to open his eyes a little less, monsieur would see much better.'

But the excitement was invariably short-lived. The *Abraham Lincoln* would change its course towards the animal in question, a mere whale or common cachalot, which soon disappeared amidst a volley of curses.

For the moment the weather remained favourable. The voyage was taking place in perfect conditions. It was meant to be the stormy season, for July in southern latitudes corresponds to our January in Europe, but the sea remained calm and could be observed over vast distances.

Ned still displayed the most unwavering scepticism. Except during his watch, he pretended not to examine the sea, at least when there was no whale in view. Even though his wonderful eyesight would have rendered us great service, the stubborn Canadian spent eight out of every twelve hours reading or sleeping in his cabin. A hundred times I reproached him for his detachment.

'Bah!' he would reply. 'There's nothing there, Dr Aronnax, and even if there was, what chance would we have of seeing it? We're wandering at random, aren't we? People have seen this invisible beast on the high seas of the Pacific, or so they say, and I accept that; but two months have gone by since then, and to judge from your narwhal's temperament, it doesn't like hanging about the same area. It can move at preposterous speeds. Now you know as well as me, Dr Aronnax, that Nature doesn't do anything the wrong way round. So a naturally slow animal wouldn't have been given such a speed if it didn't need it. Consequently if the beast does exist, it'll be hundreds of miles away by now!'

I had no reply to this. We were evidently groping in the dark. But how else could we proceed? Our chances of success were very slim. However no one gave up hope, and there wasn't a single sailor on board who would have laid odds against the narwhal and its next appearance.

We crossed the tropic of Capricorn at 105°W on 20 July, and the equator at 110°W on the 27th. Having measured its position, the frigate now set a more westerly course, heading into the middle of the Pacific. Captain Farragut thought, quite sensibly, that the monster would be most likely to frequent deeper waters. It would keep away from landmasses or islands, which it seemed reluctant to approach, 'no doubt because there wasn't enough water for it,' as the boatswain opined. The frigate passed by Tuamotu, the Marquesas, and Hawaii, crossed the tropic of Cancer at 132°E, and then sailed on towards the China Seas.

We had at last reached the scene of the monster's latest antics. In fact we lived for nothing else. Our hearts palpitated fearfully, laying the foundation for incurable aneurisms in the future. The whole ship's company suffered from a nervous overexcitement that I cannot possibly describe. No one ate, no one slept. Twenty times a day an optical illusion or a mistake by some sailor perched on the yardarms gave rise to unbearable aches, and this emotion, repeated twenty times, kept us in a state of permanent erethism,* one too overwhelming not to produce a reaction, sooner or later.

And the reaction did eventually arrive. For three months—three months when each day lasted a century—the *Abraham Lincoln* had been sailing across every sea in the South Pacific, running up when a whale was signalled, making abrupt turns, sailing first on one tack then on the other, stopping suddenly, reversing then going ahead—all in rapid succession and in a manner designed to put the engine entirely out of joint. The ship did not leave a single point unexplored between the shores of Japan and the west coast of America. But there was nothing there, nothing except the vastness of the watery wilderness. No sign of a giant narwhal, nor of a submerged islet, shipwrecked hulk, or shifting reef, and no sign at all of anything remotely supernatural.

Then the reaction set in. First came discouragement, which permeated people's minds and opened the way to scepticism. A new mood arose, made up of three-tenths shame and seven-tenths anger. Everyone on board felt very foolish, and all the more annoyed because we had been taken in by a mirage. The mountains of arguments that had piled up for a year crumbled away immediately, and the only idea in everybody's head was to use the hours for eating and sleeping, and so make up for all the time so stupidly wasted.

With the fickleness of the human mind, we went from one extreme to the other. The keenest supporters of the enterprise inevitably became its most ardent detractors. There came a reaction, starting from the depths, moving from the stokers' hold to the officers' watchroom; and had it not been for the uncommon obstinacy of Captain Farragut, the frigate's prow would certainly have headed straight back south again.

In fact this useless search could not go on any longer. The *Abraham Lincoln* could have no reason to reproach itself, since it had done its utmost to ensure success. Never had an American Navy crew shown more patience or energy, and the failure could not be blamed on anyone. There now remained no choice but to go home.

A representation to this effect was addressed to the captain. He remained firm. The sailors did not conceal their discontent, and the service deteriorated. I do not mean that there was actually a mutiny, but after a reasonable period of perseverance Captain Farragut asked for three more days, like Columbus before him. If during that time the monster had still not appeared, the helmsman would receive orders to put about, and the *Abraham Lincoln* would head for the North Atlantic.

This promise was made on 2 November. Its first effect was to restore the crew's failing courage. The ocean was scanned with fresh zeal. Everyone wanted to take that one last look wherein memory lies. Telescopes were feverishly employed. This was the last challenge hurled at the giant narwhal: he couldn't now refuse to reply to this taunt to reveal himself!

Two days went by. The *Abraham Lincoln* stayed at low pressure. The crew employed a thousand ways of catching the attention or stirring the apathy of the animal, should he happen to be passing by. Enormous quantities of bacon were trailed from the stern—to the great satisfaction of the sharks, I may add. While the frigate lay hove to, the boats pulled in all directions round it, not leaving a single spot on the ocean unexplored. But the evening of 4 November arrived without any elucidation of the submarine mystery.

The grace period was due to expire at noon the following day. After determining his position, Captain Farragut, faithful to his promise, would have to give orders to head south-east and abandon the northern Pacific Ocean.

The frigate was at 31° 15′ N, 136° 42′ E. The landmass of Japan lay less than 200 miles to leeward. Night was coming down. Eight bells had just rung out. Heavy clouds veiled the moon, then in its first quarter. The sea was rising and falling calmly below the stern.

I was for'ard, leaning over the starboard rail. Conseil was beside me, staring ahead. The ship's crew, perched in the shrouds, were scanning the horizon, which was closing in as it got darker. The officers, equipped with their night glasses, peered into the increasing gloom. The sombre sea would at times scintillate in the moonlight darting between the edges of the clouds. Then all luminous trace would disappear into the darkness again.

Observing Conseil, I noticed that the good fellow was yielding ever so slightly to the general influence. Or at least I thought so. Perhaps, for the first time in his life, his nerves were vibrating with a feeling of curiosity.

'Well Conseil,' said I; 'here is our last chance to pocket the $2,000.'

'Monsieur must permit me to say that I have never counted on winning this sum; and the government of the Union might have promised $100,000 and been none the poorer.'

'You're right, Conseil. This has turned out to be a crazy business that we rushed into without thinking. Consider how much time we've wasted! Worrying about nothing! We could have been back in France a full six months ago.'

'In monsieur's little apartment, in monsieur's museum. I would already have classified monsieur's fossils, and the babirusa would be settled in his cage in the Jardin des Plantes, attracting all the inquisitive people of Paris.'

'Exactly Conseil, and no doubt they will all laugh at us.'

'Yes,' said Conseil quietly, 'I do think they may laugh at monsieur. And may I add . . .?'

'You may.'

'Well; monsieur will only be getting what monsieur deserves.'

'Indeed!'

'When one has the honour of being a scholar like monsieur, one does not expose oneself . . .'

But Conseil was never to finish his compliment. A voice had just rung out through the surrounding silence. It was Ned Land's, shouting:

'Ahoy! The thing itself, to leeward on the weather beam!'

6

Full Steam Ahead

AT this cry the whole crew ran towards the harpooner: captain, officers, mates, seamen, and cabin boys—even the engineers abandoned the engine-room, and the stokers the boilers. The order 'Stop her!' was heard, and now the frigate was gliding over the water under its own inertia.

It was very dark: however good the Canadian's eyes might be, I wondered exactly what he had seen and how he had been able to see it. My heart was pounding as if to burst.

But Land had not been mistaken, and we soon all spotted the object he was pointing at.

Not far away from the *Abraham Lincoln*, on the starboard quarter, the sea looked as if it was illuminated from below. There could be no mistake, for this was no ordinary phosphorescence. Several fathoms below the surface, the monster gave forth a very strong, inexplicable light, as described in the reports of several captains. This fantastic irradiation must have been produced by some tremendously powerful illuminating agent. The radiant area on the surface formed a huge, highly elongated ellipse, whose centre was a burning condensed focus of unbearable intensity, but which gradually faded further away from the centre.

'It's just a mass of phosphorescent organisms!' cried one of the officers.

'No sir,' I replied with conviction. 'Neither the common piddock nor the salpa produces such a powerful light. This brilliance is essentially electric . . . In any case look, *look!* It's moving, it's moving forward—going back—it's coming straight at us!'

A cry rose from the frigate.

'Quiet!' cried Captain Farragut. 'Put the helm up hard! Ship astern!'

The sailors rushed to the wheel; the engineers to the engine-room. The power was immediately put into reverse and the *Abraham Lincoln* paid off, describing a semi-circle to port.

'Helm straight . . . go ahead!' cried Farragut.

As these orders were executed, the frigate moved rapidly away from the luminous centre.

I am wrong. The frigate *attempted* to move away, but the supernatural animal closed in at twice our speed.

We could not breathe. Astonishment rather than fear kept us silent as if transfixed. The animal caught up with us with the greatest of ease. It swam round the frigate, which was making fourteen knots, and enclosed us in its electric beams like luminous dust. It then moved two or three miles off, leaving a phosphorescent trail behind it, like the spirals of steam behind the locomotive of an express train. All of a sudden, from the dark limits of the horizon, the monster accelerated and rushed towards the *Abraham Lincoln* at a frightening speed, then stopped abruptly only twenty feet away from the frigate's wales and extinguished its light—not by plunging beneath the surface, since the brilliance did not disappear gradually—but suddenly, as if the source of the brilliant discharge had instantly dried up! It then appeared on the other side, meaning it had gone either round or underneath. At every moment a collision seemed imminent: one which could easily have been fatal to us.

I was puzzled by the frigate's behaviour. It was running away and not attacking. It was being hunted when it was meant to be the hunter—and I said as m. ch to Captain Farragut. His normally impassive face betrayed an indefinable astonishment.

'Dr Aronnax,' he replied, 'I do not know what formidable creature I am dealing with—and I do not want to risk my ship needlessly in this darkness. In any case, how can one attack an unidentified object, or even defend oneself? Let's wait for daylight, when the tables will be turned.'

'So you have no doubts about the nature of the animal?'

'It's obviously a giant narwhal, but an electric one too.'

'Perhaps it is just as dangerous to approach as an electric eel or ray?'

'Quite possibly. And if it does have the ability to give out an electric shock, then it will be the most terrible beast ever to have sprung from the Creator's hand. That is why, sir, I must remain on my guard.'

The entire crew stayed at action stations that night. Nobody thought of going to bed. Unable to move faster than the creature, the *Abraham Lincoln* had first decreased its pace, and then stayed at easy steam. For its part, the narwhal lay rocking in the waves, just like the frigate: it seemed to have decided to remain on the scene of the battle.

At about midnight, however, it disappeared, or rather 'went out' like an enormous glow-worm. Had it left? This was to be feared, rather than hoped for. But then at 12.53 a deafening hissing sound was heard, like that produced by a head of water escaping with inordinate force.

Captain Farragut, Ned, and I were on the poop. We sedulously searched the deep darkness.

'Ned Land,' said the captain, 'have you often heard whales blowing?'

'Yes sir, but never whales that pay $2,000 when you sight them.'

'You have indeed earned the prize. But tell me, is this the same noise cetaceans make when they spout water from their blowholes?'

'It's the same sound, sir, but much, much louder. I'm certain. It's definitely a whale astern. With your permission sir, we'll have a word or two with him at first light.'

'If he is in a mood to listen, Master Land,' I said in a sceptical tone.

'If I get within four harpoons' distance of him,' riposted the Canadian, 'he'll have to listen!'

'But for you to get near must I give you a whaling-boat?' enquired the captain.

'Obviously sir.'

'And in so doing, risk the lives of my men?'

'And mine too,' replied Land, simply.

At about two in the morning, the light reappeared, just as bright but five miles to windward of the *Abraham Lincoln*. Despite the distance and the noise from the wind and waves, the formidable beating of the monster's tail could distinctly be heard, even its hoarse respiration. When the huge narwhal came to the surface to breathe,* the air rushing into its lungs was just like the steam in the massive pistons of a 2,000 horsepower engine.

'H'm,' I thought, 'a whale with the horsepower of a whole regiment of cavalry must be a fine specimen!'

Everyone remained active until daybreak, getting ready for battle. The fishing tackle was laid out along the rails. The first mate ordered the loading of the blunderbusses that could throw a harpoon a distance of a mile and of the long punt guns for firing exploding bullets which are fatal to the most powerful of animals. Ned Land merely sharpened his harpoon, a terrible weapon in his hands.

At six o'clock dawn began to break, and with the first gleams, the narwhal's electric light went out. At seven the sun was high enough, but visibility was reduced by a thick fog which the best glasses could not pierce. Hence considerable disappointment and exasperation.

I climbed up the mizzenmast. A few officers were already perched around the masthead.

At eight o'clock the fog began to roll heavily over the waves, as its thick spirals dissipated. The horizon gradually expanded as the mists cleared.

Suddenly Ned's voice rang out, just like the day before.

'The thing in question, port astern!'

Everyone looked in the direction indicated.

About a mile and a half from the frigate, a long black body emerged about three feet from the waves. Its tail was beating violently and produced a considerable swell in the water. Never had a tail hit the water with such force. An enormous wake of dazzling whiteness marked the course of the animal as it described a long curve.

The frigate approached the cetacean. I examined it as closely as I wished. The *Shannon* and *Helvetia*'s reports had slightly exaggerated its dimensions, for I estimated its length to be only 250 feet. As for its girth, this was difficult to evaluate, but the animal's dimensions appeared admirably proportioned.

While I was examining the phenomenal creature, two jets of water and vapour spurted from its blowholes and rose to a height of 120 feet—thus settling its method of respiration. I concluded once and for all that the animal belonged to the vertebrates, class of mammals, sub-class of monodelphians, group of pisciforms, order of cetaceans, family—but here I was unable to make up my mind. The order of Cetaceae comprises three families, whales, cachalots, and dolphins, and narwhals are classified amongst the last category. Each family is in turn divided into several genera, each genus into species, and each species into varieties. I did not yet know the creature's variety, species, genus, or family, but I felt confident about being able to complete my classification with the help of Heaven and Captain Farragut.

The crew were waiting impatiently for orders. The captain observed the creature carefully, and then called for the chief engineer, who quickly ran up.

'Have you plenty of steam?'

'Aye-aye sir.'

'Good. Fire up; and full steam ahead.'

Three cheers greeted this order. The time had come to fight. Soon the frigate's two funnels were belching forth waves of black smoke and the engines were making the deck shake and shudder.

Pushed on by its powerful propeller, the *Abraham Lincoln* headed for the animal. The creature allowed the frigate to get quite close, but then moved slightly away, keeping at the same distance but not bothering to dive.

This pursuit continued for about three-quarters of an hour without the frigate gaining three yards on the cetacean. It became obvious that if we carried on in this way we would never catch up.

Captain Farragut was angrily twisting the thick clump of hair sprouting below his chin.

'Land!'

The Canadian arrived.

'Well, Master Land,' said the captain, 'do you still think we should launch the boats?'

'No sir; for the creature will not let you take him unless he wants you to.'

'So what should we do then?'

'Keep maximum pressure, sir. With your permission, I'll wait under the bowsprit, and if we get within distance I'll harpoon him.'

'Fine, Ned!'

And to the engineer: 'Go ahead faster!'

Ned Land took up his position. The furnaces were stoked, the propeller turned at 43 revolutions a minute, and the steam roared through the valves. The log was heaved, and showed the frigate's speed to be 18½ knots.

But the cursed animal was also moving at 18½ knots.

For another hour the frigate continued at this pace without gaining a yard. This was rather humiliating for one of the fastest vessels in the United States Navy. A deep anger ran through the ship's crew. They swore at the monster, which did not, however, condescend to reply. Captain Farragut no longer twisted his goatee, he chewed it.

The engineer was summoned again.

'Are you at your absolute maximum pressure?'

'Yes sir!'

'What pressure?'

'Six and a half atmospheres.'

'Make it ten!'

This was truly an American order. It couldn't have been bettered in a Mississippi riverboat race, 'so as to leave the competition behind'.

'Conseil,' said I to my faithful servant standing nearby, 'do you realize that we may easily blow up?'

'Whatever monsieur says.'

But I had to admit I was glad that we were giving it a go.

The steam-gauge rose. The furnaces overflowed with coal. The ventilators sent torrents of air over the flames. The ship moved faster. The very steps of the masts shook, and the funnels hardly seemed big enough to let out all the whirlwinds of smoke.

The log was heaved again.

'Well helmsman?' enquired the captain.

'Nineteen point three sir.'

'Stoke the fires higher.'

The engineer obeyed. The steam-gauge showed ten atmospheres. But the narwhal had 'fired up' as well, for it was now also proceeding at 19.3 knots, effortlessly.

What a chase! I cannot describe the feelings that moved my whole being. Ned stood in position, harpoon in hand. Several times the animal allowed us to get nearer.

'We're gaining, we are!' cried the Canadian.

But just as he was getting ready to strike, the cetacean would shoot ahead at a speed I cannot estimate to be less than 30 knots. And even at the frigate's maximum speed, it played with us by going round us! Cries of fury came from each man's breast.

At noon we were no further on than at eight o'clock.

Captain Farragut decided to employ more direct measures.

'So', he said, 'the animal can move faster than the *Abraham Lincoln*. We will see if he can outrun a conical shell. Bosun, man the for'ard gun.'

The bow gun was immediately loaded and aimed. It went off, but the shot passed several feet above the cetacean, half a mile away.

'Somebody with a better aim!' shouted the captain. 'And there's $500 for the man who puts a shot into the infernal beast.'

An old gunner with a grey beard—I can still see him—came forward with a determined air and a steady eye. He pointed the gun and took careful aim. A loud detonation was heard amidst the crew's cheers.

The shot reached its target and hit the animal, but not at right angles: it glanced off its rounded flank, and fell into the sea two miles away.

'Humph!' angrily cried the old gunner. 'The cursed thing is covered in six-inch iron-plate!'

'Damnation!' shouted Captain Farragut.

The chase began again. The captain leaned towards me: 'I shall pursue that animal until my frigate blows up!'

'Good on you! You're right!'

Our only hope was that the creature would be more susceptible to fatigue than a steam-driven engine and would sooner or later become exhausted. But no such luck. The hours passed and still the animal showed no signs of feeling tired.

But I must say in support of the *Abraham Lincoln* that it fought with tireless determination. I estimated the distance it covered on that unfortunate 6 November to be at least 300 miles. But eventually night came down and cloaked the choppy sea in its shadows.

I imagined that our expedition was finished, that we had seen the last of the fantastic creature. But I was wrong.

At 10.50, roughly three miles to windward, the electric light appeared again, as clear and as bright as the night before.

The narwhal seemed to be motionless. Perhaps it felt tired after the day's exertions, and was sleeping in the rocking sway of the billows? This was an opportunity which Farragut decided to seize.

He gave a few orders. The frigate was put at easy speed, and proceeded cautiously so as not to wake its enemy. It is not rare to meet whales fast asleep in mid-ocean, and they are sometimes successfully attacked: Ned Land had frequently harpooned them in this way. He took up his position under the bowsprit.

The frigate moved towards the animal and stopped its engines not far away, quietly drifting on under its momentum. No one dared breathe. A profound silence reigned on deck. We were now less than a hundred feet from the bright centre, whose light began to blind us as we got closer.

I saw Land on the fo'c'sle below me, holding on to the martingale with one hand and brandishing his terrible harpoon in the other. We were scarcely twenty feet away from the motionless monster.

Suddenly Ned's arm moved violently, and the harpoon shot forward. I heard the sonorous blow as it hit its prey; it sounded as if it had come into contact with a hard substance.

The electric light went out abruptly. Two enormous columns of water fell over the frigate's deck, rushed fore and aft like a river, knocked the crew down, and broke the lashings on the spars.

There was an awesome impact and before I had time to take hold, I was thrown over the bulwark and into the sea.

7

An Unknown Species of Whale

ALTHOUGH I was surprised by my unexpected fall, I retained none the less a clear impression of my sensations.

At first I was plunged down to a depth of about twenty feet. I am a strong swimmer, although not claiming to be as good as Byron or Poe, who are masters;* and this nosedive caused me no panic. Two strong kicks and I was up on the surface again.

My first concern was to locate the frigate. Had the crew noticed my disappearance? Had the *Abraham Lincoln* put about? Was Captain Farragut launching a boat for me? Could I hope to be rescued?

It was very dark. I could see a black object disappearing in the east, its position lights dimmed by the distance. It was the frigate. I felt lost.

'Help! Help!' I cried, swimming despairingly in the direction of the *Abraham Lincoln*.

My clothes got in the way. The water made them stick to my body, paralysing my movements. I was sinking; I was suffocating.

'Help!'

This was the last cry I uttered. My mouth filled with water. I fought as I sank into the depths.

Suddenly my clothes were seized by a strong hand. I felt myself being pulled roughly back up to the surface, and I heard—yes, heard—some words in my ear: 'If monsieur will have the great kindness to lean on my shoulder, monsieur will swim more easily.'

I seized the arm of my faithful Conseil.

'Is it you?' I said. '*You!*'

'Indeed,' replied Conseil; 'awaiting monsieur's orders.'

'The collision threw you into the sea at the same time?'

'Not at all; but I followed monsieur since I am in monsieur's service.'

The worthy fellow could see nothing extraordinary in that!

'And the frigate?'

'The frigate,' replied Conseil turning on his back; 'I think monsieur would be better not to rely on it.'

'What do you mean?'

'I mean that as I jumped overboard, I heard the helmsman shout "The screw and rudder are broken!"'

'Broken?'

'Yes, by the tusk of the monster. It was apparently the only damage the *Abraham Lincoln* suffered. But unfortunately for us, it can no longer steer.'

'Then we are lost!'

'Perhaps so,' replied Conseil calmly. 'But we still have some hours ahead of us, and a great many things may be accomplished in such a time.'

The imperturbable composure of Conseil gave me new strength. I swam more energetically; but I was hindered by the clothes sticking to me like lead weights, and found it very difficult to keep afloat. Conseil noticed this.

'Will monsieur permit me to make a slight incision?'

And sliding a naked blade into my clothes, he slit them from top to bottom with a quick slash. Then he slowly took off my clothing, while I swam for us both.

I in turn rendered him the same service; and we continued to 'navigate' close together.

But the situation was still alarming. Our disappearance had possibly not been noticed, and even if it had, the rudderless frigate could not come back for us against the wind. Our only chance lay in the boats.

Conseil calmly reasoned out this hypothesis, and made plans accordingly. What an amazing character! The phlegmatic fellow was behaving as if at home!

It was thus concluded that being rescued by the frigate's boats constituted our only chance of being saved and that we needed to arrange matters so as to wait for them as long as possible. I decided that we should divide our forces in order not to exhaust us both; and this was how we managed it. While one lay motionless on his back, with arms folded and legs extended, the other would swim and push him along. The role of tugboat was to last for only ten minutes, and by taking it in turn, we might be able to swim for several hours, possibly even until dawn.

It was only a small chance, but hope is firmly rooted in the human heart. Also, there were two of us. Although I tried to destroy all hope, indeed to fall into the deepest despair, I declare that I was unable to do so, however improbable this may seem.

The collision between the frigate and the cetacean had happened at about 11 p.m. I counted on eight hours' swimming before sunrise: a perfectly feasible operation if we took it in turns. The sea was smooth, and did not tire us greatly. Sometimes I tried to penetrate the thick darkness, broken only by the phosphorescence from our movements. I looked at the luminous wavelets breaking over my hand, with their gleaming surface covered with pale patches. It was as if we were swimming in a bath of mercury.

At about one o'clock I suddenly felt very tired. My limbs stiffened with violent cramps. Conseil had to support me, and our survival now depended upon his unaided efforts. I soon heard the poor fellow panting. His breathing was coming short and hurriedly. I realized that he couldn't hold on much longer.

'Let me go!' I cried. 'Leave me behind!'

'Abandon monsieur? Never! I intend to drown before he does.'

At that moment the moon broke through the edge of a large cloud being driven eastwards by the wind. The surface of the sea shone with light. This kindly illumination brought our strength back. I raised my head again. I looked round at every point on the horizon. I spotted the frigate. It was about five miles away—a black and scarcely identifiable point. And there was no boat!

I tried to cry out; although what was the point at such a distance? My swollen mouth refused to utter a single sound. Conseil could speak a little, and I heard him shouting several times:

'Help! Help!'

Temporarily stopping our swimming, we listened out. Was that buzzing noise coming from congested blood pressure in my ear; or was it an answer to Conseil's cry?

'Did you hear that?' I murmured.

'Yes, yes!'

And Conseil sent another desperate cry into the air.

This time there could be no mistake. A human voice replied.

Was it the voice of some other unfortunate abandoned in the midst of the ocean—some other victim of that collision? Or was it a boat from the frigate hailing us through the darkness?

Conseil made a supreme effort and, leaning on my shoulder while I resisted in a final paroxysm, he half rose out of the water before falling back exhausted.

'What did you see?'

'I saw,' he murmured, 'I saw—but let's not talk, let's keep our strength up!'

What had he seen? For some reason, the monster came back to my mind for the first time. But there was the voice. The times are past for Jonahs to live in whales' bellies!

Conseil paddled me forward once more. At times he raised his head to look ahead, and uttered a cry of recognition, to which a voice replied, nearer each time. I could scarcely hear. My strength was spent; my fingers were no longer obeying me; my hands could no longer keep me up; my mouth, convulsively opening, was filling with salt water; and my limbs were being seized by cold. I raised my head one last time, and went under.

At that moment a hard body struck me. I clung to it. Then I felt someone pulling me upwards, bringing me back up to the surface, and with my chest collapsing, I fainted.

I must have come to very quickly thanks to the vigorous rubbing moving up and down my body. I half opened my eyes.

'Conseil!' I murmured.

'Did monsieur call?'

At the same moment, in the last light of the moon going down over the horizon, I caught sight of another face, not Conseil's, which I immediately recognized.

'Ned!' I exclaimed.

'In person, sir, looking for his prize money!'

'So you were thrown into the sea by the frigate's collision?'

'Yes,' he replied; 'but I was luckier than you were, and managed to set foot on a floating island straightaway.'

'An island?'

'Yes, or rather upon our giant narwhal . . .'

'Explain yourself, Ned.'

'Though I soon realized why my harpoon hadn't stuck in the creature's hide and why it was blunted.'

'But why, Ned, why?'

'Because this beast is made of steel plate!'

I now have to recover my composure, search my memory, and make sure my statements are really true.

The Canadian's last words produced a sea-change in my mind. I pulled myself up to the top of the half-sunken being or object on which we had taken refuge. I kicked it. It was certainly a hard body: impenetrable and not made of the yielding substance that constitutes the larger marine mammals.

But this hard substance might be a bony carapace, like that of some prehistoric animals; and I might be able to get away with classifying it amongst the amphibious reptiles such as the turtle or alligator.

But no! The blackish surface I was standing on was smooth and polished, and had no overlapping sections. It gave a metallic sound when struck and, incredible though this may seem, it appeared to be made of riveted metal plates.

Doubt was no longer possible. It had to be admitted that the creature, the monster, the natural occurrence which had puzzled the entire scientific world and baffled and troubled the minds of seamen in both hemispheres, constituted a still greater marvel—a man-made phenomenon.

I would not have been nearly so astonished to discover the most fabulous and mythological of creatures. That what is extraordinary could have come from the Creator, is easy to believe. But to discover all of a sudden a mysterious human construction of the impossible, to find it before your very eyes, was enough to unhinge your mind.

But there was no room for doubt. Here we were sitting on the back of a species of submarine boat, with the shape of a massive steel fish, in so far as I could judge. Such was Ned's firm opinion. Conseil and I had no choice but to agree with him.

'But', said I, 'this contrivance must contain some sort of machinery for moving from place to place, as well as a crew to operate it?'

'Yes, it has to,' replied the Canadian; 'but all the same, I've been in residence on this floating island for three hours, and it hasn't given a single sign of life during that time.'

'The boat hasn't moved?'*

'No, Dr Aronnax; it's been rocked by the waves, but it hasn't budged.'

'We know for a fact that it can move very fast. Now as it needs an engine to produce this velocity, and an engineer to operate the engine, I can conclude that we are saved.'

'H'm,' voiced Ned dubiously.

At this moment, and as if to prove my point, a disturbance came from the stern of the strange vessel, evidently screw-driven, and it began to move. We scarcely had time to seize hold of the top part, nearly a yard out of the water. Luckily the speed was not very great.

'As long as it goes over the waves, we're okay,' murmured Ned Land. 'But if it decides to dive, I wouldn't give two dollars for my hide!'

The Canadian might have made a still lower estimate. But in any case it was now essential to communicate with whatever beings were within the flanks of the machine. I searched for an opening on its surface: a hatch, or manhole to use the proper term; but the lines of rivets solidly fixed along the joints of the iron plates were firm and regular.

Also the moon disappeared, leaving us in total darkness. We would be forced to wait for daybreak before finding a way of getting inside the submarine vessel.

Our safety thus depended entirely upon the caprice of the mysterious helmsmen who piloted the machine: if they decided to dive, we were lost. But if they didn't, I was confident of being able to make contact with them. And indeed, if they didn't manufacture their air themselves, they had to come up to the surface sometimes to replenish their supply of breathable molecules. Hence the need for an aperture so that the interior of the boat could communicate with the outside air.

We had given up all hope of being rescued by Captain Farragut. We were being carried westwards; I estimated that we were going at the relatively moderate speed of 12 knots. The screw beat the waves with mathematical regularity, but sometimes emerged and spurted phosphorescent jets of water to a great height.

At about 4 a.m. the speed increased. We had some difficulty in coping with the giddy pace, since the waves washed freely over us. Fortunately Ned Land found a large ring set in the upper part of the iron back, and we managed to hold securely on to it.

The long night finally came to an end. My imperfect memory cannot recall all the impressions of those hours. But one small point comes to mind. During some of the lulls in the wind and the waves, I fancied I could vaguely hear some sort of elusive harmony produced by distant chords. What then was the nature of this submarine navigation which the whole world was seeking in vain to understand? What kind of beings lived in this strange vessel? By what means did they move at such a prodigious rate?

Daylight appeared. The morning mist wrapped us in its folds, but was then torn asunder. I was about to make a careful survey of the hull, whose upper part formed a kind of horizontal platform, when I realized that it was slowly sinking.

'Hey! What the hell!' cried Ned, loudly stamping on the hull. 'Open up, I say, you pirates!'

But it was difficult to produce a sound while the screw was beating vigorously. Fortunately the sinking stopped.

Suddenly a sound was heard from inside the boat of bars being pushed back. A plate was raised; a man appeared, uttered a strange cry, and immediately vanished.

A few seconds later, eight strong fellows with expressionless faces silently appeared and pulled us into their formidable machine.

8

Mobilis in Mobile*

THIS action, so roughly executed, was carried out with lightning speed. My companions and I had no time to look around. I do not know what Ned and Conseil felt as they entered the floating prison, but for my part I must say that a rapid shudder chilled my skin. Who were we dealing with? Doubtless pirates of a new sort, who were using the seas for their own purposes.

Scarcely was the narrow hatch closed than I was in complete

darkness. Coming in from the daylight so suddenly, my eyes could see nothing. I felt my bare feet on the rungs of an iron ladder. Land and Conseil, very tightly held, followed. At the foot of the ladder a door opened, and immediately shut behind us with a loud clang.

We were alone. Where, I could not say—scarcely even imagine. Everything was black, but of such an absolute blackness that even after several minutes my eyes had not seen any of those indeterminate scintillations that linger on, even on the darkest nights.

Ned Land was furious at such treatment and gave free vent to his indignation.

'What the devil!' he cried. 'Even the New Caledonians are more hospitable than these people. All we need now is for them to be cannibals. I wouldn't be at all surprised; but I will not be eaten without protesting!'

'Calm down, friend Ned, calm down,' Conseil said quietly. 'Don't get carried away too soon. We're not in the frying pan yet.'

'Frying pan no,' riposted Land, 'but we *are* in the oven. At any rate it's as dark. Luckily I've still got my bowie-knife on me,[1] and I can see well enough to use it. The first of these bandits that lays a finger on me . . .'

'Don't get angry, Ned,' I said, 'and don't make our position worse by useless violence. Maybe they can hear us.* Let's instead try to find out where we are.'

I advanced with hands outstretched. At five paces I reached a wall of riveted iron plates. Turning round, I collided with a wooden table, surrounded by a few stools. The floor of this prison was covered with a thick matting of New Zealand flax which deadened the sound of our footsteps. The bare walls didn't seem to have any doors or windows. Conseil, who had been working his way round in the opposite direction, bumped into me, and we came back to the middle of the cabin, which seemed to be about twenty feet long by ten across. Even Ned, tall as he was, could not find out how high the ceiling was.

The situation did not change for half an hour, but then our eyes

---

[1] A broad-bladed knife that an American always carries with him.

were abruptly exposed to a violently bright light. Our prison was suddenly filled with a luminous element of such brilliance that at first I couldn't bear it. From its whiteness and intensity I recognized the electric light which had produced the magnificent phosphorescence around the submarine vessel. After being instinctively forced to close my eyes, I opened them again and realized that the light came from a ground-glass half-globe in the ceiling of the chamber.

'At last we can see,' cried Ned Land, standing on the defensive, bowie-knife in hand.

'Yes,' I replied, and risked an antithesis: 'although the situation is no less obscure.'

'If monsieur will only be patient,' said the impassive Conseil.

The sudden illumination of the cabin gave us the opportunity to examine it minutely. It contained nothing but the table and five stools. The door was invisible but was clearly hermetically sealed, for no sound reached our ears. Everything seemed dead on board the vessel. I had no idea whether it was still moving over the surface of the ocean or plunging into its depths.

All the same, the lamp had not been lit without reason. I therefore hoped that the crew of the vessel would soon put in an appearance. When you wish to put people away for ever you do not illuminate their dungeon.

I was not mistaken; the sound came of bolts being withdrawn, the door opened, and two men came in.

One was rather short but with strong muscles; he had broad shoulders, robust arms and legs, a good head, thick black hair, a vigorous moustache, and alert piercing eyes: his whole body was stamped with that southern vivacity which marks the people of Provence. Diderot* has correctly maintained that man's gestures are metaphoric, and this diminutive man was living proof of it. One had the impression that his habitual speech had to be filled with prosopopoeia, metonymy, and hypallage.* But I was never in a position to discover whether this was true, since in my presence he always employed a peculiar and utterly incomprehensible idiom.

The second stranger deserves a more detailed description. A pupil of Gratiolet or Engel would have read his physiognomy like an open book.* I instantly recognized his dominant feature:

confidence in himself, for his head rose nobly from the curve formed by his shoulders and his dark eyes looked at you with a cool assurance. He was composed, since his skin, more pale than ruddy, indicated a calmness in the blood. Energy he possessed, as demonstrated by the rapid contraction of his eyebrow muscles. And courage also, since his deep breathing marked great vitality and expansiveness.

I should also say that this man was proud, that his steadfast, self-composed look seemed to reflect lofty thoughts, and that from all this and from the unity of expression in the movements of his body and face, there resulted an indisputable open-heartedness, in line with the observations of the physiognomists.

I felt myself 'involuntarily' reassured by his presence, which augured well for our conversation.

This individual might have been thirty-five or fifty, I couldn't tell. He was tall; he had a wide forehead, straight nose, clearly defined mouth, and magnificent teeth; his hands were long, thin, and eminently 'psychic', to use a word from palmistry: that is, adapted to a noble and passionate being. This man was certainly the most admirable specimen I had ever met. One particular detail: his eyes, set rather apart, could embrace nearly a quarter of the horizon. This faculty—as I later confirmed—was accompanied by an eyesight superior even to Land's. When this curious personage was looking intently at something, his eyebrows frowned and his broad eyelids contracted to circumscribe his pupils and thus restrict his visual field—and he *did* look. What a gaze! How he made distant objects larger, and how he penetrated your very soul! How he could pierce the liquid depths,* so opaque to our eyes, and how he could read to the bottom of the seas!

The two strangers wore sea-otter-skin caps, seal-skin sea-boots, and clothes of a peculiar material that sat loosely upon them, allowing them great freedom of movement.

The taller of the two—evidently the chief on board—regarded us with great concentration but without speaking. Then turning to his companion, he conversed with him in a tongue I could not understand. The language was ringing, harmonious, and supple, with the syllables seeming to receive very varied stresses.

The other replied with a movement of his head, adding two or three totally unintelligible words. Then he appeared to be questioning me personally with his regard.

I replied, in good French, that I did not know his language; but he did not appear to understand me, and the situation became somewhat embarrassing.

'Monsieur should try to relate our story,' said Conseil. 'Perhaps the gentlemen would understand a few words.'

I then began the story of our adventures, distinctly pronouncing all the syllables and not omitting a single detail. I announced our names and positions: I presented in due form Dr Aronnax, Conseil his manservant, and Master Ned, harpooner.

The individual with the calm and gentle eyes listened quietly, even politely, and with remarkable concentration. But his physiognomy showed no sign that he understood my story. When I had finished, he said not a single word.

There still remained the resort of using English. Perhaps we would be able to make ourselves understood in that almost universal language. I knew some, and some German as well: enough to read them fluently, but not to speak them accurately. Here, however, it was essential to be understood properly.

'Go on,' I said to the harpooner; 'it's your turn, Master Land. Draw from your bag the best English ever spoken by an Anglo-Saxon,* and try to be more successful than I was.'

Ned needed no prompting, and repeated my tale. I more or less understood him, for the contents were similar, if the form was quite different. The Canadian, carried away by his character, spoke with great passion. He complained bitterly about being imprisoned, which was against human rights, asked what law was being used to detain him in this way, invoked *habeas corpus*, threatened to take to court those who were unlawfully keeping us prisoners,* waved his arms, gesticulated, exclaimed, and finally, by a most expressive pantomime, gave to understand that we were dying of hunger.

This was true as a matter of fact, although we had more or less forgotten.

To his tremendous surprise, the harpooner did not appear to be more intelligible than I had been. Not a muscle moved on our visitors' faces. It was evident that they understood neither the language of Arago nor that of Faraday.* I was very perplexed, having exhausted our philological resources to no avail; and did not know what to do next, when Conseil intervened:

'If monsieur will permit me, I will tell the story in German.'

'What, you know German!'

'Like a Fleming,' he replied, 'if monsieur has no objection.'

'None at all—quite the contrary. Go ahead, my lad.'

And Conseil calmly recounted our various adventures for the third time. But notwithstanding the narrator's excellent accent and elegantly turned phrases, German was no more successful than before.

At last, and as a final resort, I summoned everything I could from my early studies, and undertook to relate our adventures in Latin. Cicero would have stopped his ears up at such dog Latin, but I did nevertheless make it to the end. With the same result, however.

Our last attempt having totally failed, the two strangers exchanged a few words in their incomprehensible idiom and then withdrew, not even giving us one of those reassuring signs understood in every country in the world. The door closed behind them again.

'It's a disgrace!' exclaimed Ned Land as he exploded for the twentieth time. 'Why, we have spoken to those scoundrels in French, in English, in German, and in Latin, and neither of them has had the courtesy to reply!'

'Calm yourself, Ned,' I said to the fiery harpooner; 'getting angry will not help.'

'But don't you realize, sir,' persisted our irascible companion, 'that we may easily die of hunger in this iron cage?'

'Bah,' said Conseil philosophically, 'we can hold on for a long time yet.'

'My friends,' I said, 'we must not despair. We have been in worse situations. Do me the favour of waiting a while before forming an opinion of the captain and crew of this vessel.'

'My opinion's already formed,' countered Ned. 'They are rogues.'

'All right; but from what country?'

'From the land of rogues.'

'My good Ned, that country is not yet indicated clearly enough on the world map; I must confess that the nationality of the two strangers is difficult to determine. That they are neither British nor French nor German is all we can say. I am tempted to think that the captain and his mate must have been born in the lower latitudes. There is a southern look about them; but their physical type does not allow me to decide whether they are Spaniards, Turks, Arabs, or Indians. As for their tongue, it is simply incomprehensible.'

'That is the drawback of not knowing every language,' commented Conseil, 'and the disadvantage of not having a universal one.'

'Which would not help us at all!' said Ned Land. 'Don't you see that those fellows have got a language of their own, invented so as to annoy anyone who asks for something to eat? If you open your mouth, move your jaws, and smack your lips and teeth, don't they understand what you mean in every country in the world, with room to spare? Wouldn't it indicate "I am hungry; give me something to eat" in Québec and Tuamotu, in Paris and the antipodes?'

'Oh?' said Conseil. 'There are some people so stupid . . .'

The door opened as he was speaking. A steward[1] entered. He brought us clothing:* jackets and sea trousers of a material I could not identify. I quickly put them on, with my companions following suit.

During this time the steward—dumb, and perhaps deaf as well—laid three places at the table.

'This is significant', said Conseil, 'and even most promising!'

'Bah!' replied the Canadian resentfully. 'What the devil do you expect to be able to eat here: turtle liver, fillet of shark, dogfish steak?'

'We shall see,' replied Conseil.

The dishes, with silver covers, were placed harmoniously on the cloth, and we took our places. We were decidedly dealing with civilized beings; and had it not been for the electric light flooding over us, I would have thought we were sitting at the Adelphi Hotel in Liverpool* or the Grand Hôtel in Paris. I should mention that there was no wine or bread. The water was pure and fresh; but

---

[1] A waiter on board a ship.

water it was, and so not to Ned's taste. Amongst the dishes served I recognized various kinds of fish, delicately prepared; but I could not reach an opinion on some of the dishes, albeit excellent, since I was unable to say whether they belonged to the animal or the vegetable kingdom. The table service was elegant, and in perfect taste. Every knife, fork, spoon, plate, and utensil was inscribed with a letter surrounded by a motto, of which the following is an exact facsimile:

MOBILIS IN MOBILE

N

Mobile in the mobile element! The device fitted the submarine vessel perfectly, provided that the Latin preposition 'in' was translated as 'in' rather than 'on'. The N was no doubt the initial of the enigmatic individual who commanded the depths of the ocean.

Ned and Conseil did not waste time in such reflection. They had begun to eat, and I quickly followed them. I felt in fact reassured as to our fate, for it seemed clear that our hosts did not want us to die of starvation.

Everything must have an end in this world, however, even the hunger of people who have not eaten for fifteen hours. Once our appetites were satisfied, the need for sleep began to make itself imperiously felt: a natural reaction after the interminable night in which we had fought with death.*

'My goodness, I could do with a sleep . . .' said Conseil.

'I'm off already,' from Land.

My companions lay down on the matting, and were soon sound asleep.

For my part I yielded less easily to the urgent need for slumber. Too many thoughts crowded into my brain, too many unanswerable questions pressed upon me, too many impressions kept my eyes half-open. Where were we? What strange force was taking us away? I felt, or rather believed I felt, the machine sinking down to the furthest depths of the ocean. Fearful waking nightmares tormented me. I glimpsed a whole world of unknown animals sheltering in mysterious refuges, with the submarine vessel as one of their congeners, living, moving, formidable like them. Then my brain calmed down slightly, my imagination dissolved into a vague somnolence, and I fell into a dull sleep.

9

Ned Land's Fits of Anger

How long we slept I do not know, but it must have been a long time, for we awoke completely refreshed. I was the first to wake up. My companions had not yet moved, stretched out in their corners like inert masses.

Scarcely had I got up from my rather hard bed, than I realized that my brain was clear and my mind invigorated. I began to examine the cell attentively.

Its internal arrangement had not changed at all. The gaol was still a gaol, the prisoners still prisoners. But the steward had cleared the table while we slept. There was no sign of any change in our situation and I seriously wondered whether our fate would be to live in this cell indefinitely.

This prospect was made more unpleasant by feeling a great weight on my chest, although my brain was clear. I could breathe only with difficulty. The heavy air was no longer sufficient for my lungs to function. Although the cell was very large, it was evident that we had consumed most of the oxygen in it. In an hour a man uses up the oxygen in 100 litres of air, and this air, filled with an almost identical quantity of carbon dioxide, becomes unbreathable.

It was therefore urgent to renew the air in our prison, and presumably in the rest of the submarine craft as well.

This was a question that taxed my mind. How did the captain of this floating habitation manage? Did he obtain air by chemical means, using heat to free the oxygen contained in potassium chlorate, and absorbing the carbon dioxide with caustic potash? In that case he would still have to maintain contact with dry land in order to obtain the necessary materials. Did he simply store air in high-pressure tanks, and then decompress it again as the crew needed it? Possibly. Or, using a method that was much more natural, economical, and therefore probable, did he simply come up to the surface to breathe like a whale, and thus renew his supply of air for the next 24 hours? Whatever the truth, whatever the method, it seemed sensible to me to employ it as soon as possible.

I was in fact already being forced to breathe in and out more quickly so as to extract what little oxygen the cell contained—when I was suddenly refreshed by a draught of pure air, full of a salty fragrance. It was a real sea breeze, vivifying and laden with iodine! I opened my mouth wide, and saturated my lungs with the fresh molecules. At the same time I was aware of a rocking or rolling motion that, although slight, was clearly perceptible. The boat, the metal monster, had obviously just come up to the surface to breathe, exactly as whales do. How the ship was ventilated was now perfectly clear.

When I had filled my lungs up with the pure air, I looked for the method by which it had come in, the 'aerifery'* which allowed this life-giving emission to reach us; and I did not take long to discover it. Over the door was an opening through which the fresh air entered and renewed the atmosphere in our cell.

I had got this far in my observation when Ned and Conseil woke up under the influence of the invigorating air, both almost at the same moment. After rubbing their eyes and stretching their arms, they were soon on their feet.

'Did monsieur sleep well?' enquired Conseil with his usual politeness.

'Very well,' I replied. 'And you, Master Land?'

'Very deeply. But—can it be true?—I seem to be breathing in a sea breeze!'

A sailor couldn't be wrong, and I told the Canadian what had happened while he was sleeping.

'That explains the roarings we heard when the so-called narwhal was near the *Abraham Lincoln*.'

'Quite so, Master Land, that was its breathing.'

'Dr Aronnax, I have no idea what time it is—unless it is dinner-time?'

'Dinner-time, my good harpooner? More likely breakfast, for it is certainly the day after yesterday.'

'Which means', said Conseil, 'that we have slept for 24 hours!'
'Indeed.'

'I won't argue,' said Ned Land. 'But I would be glad to see the steward again, whether for dinner or breakfast.'

'Both,' said Conseil.

'Good point,' replied the Canadian. 'We're entitled to two meals, and I personally will do justice to both.'

'Well Ned, let's wait,' said I. 'These people are obviously not planning to let us die of starvation, or yesterday's meal would have been wasted.'

'Unless they wanted to fatten us up a bit.'

'Don't be stupid. We have not fallen into the hands of cannibals.'

'They might make an exception,' replied the Canadian in all seriousness. 'Maybe these people have been starved of fresh meat for ages? And in that case, three healthy and well-built individuals like monsieur, his manservant, and myself . . .'

'Banish all such thoughts, Master Land, and above all do not use them as an excuse to get angry with our hosts. It would only make matters worse.'

'In any case,' said Ned, 'I'm as hungry as a thousand hunters. Dinner or breakfast, where is it?'

'We must fit in with the ship routine,' I replied. 'I imagine that our appetites are ahead of the chef's bell.'

'So we'll simply have to reset them to the right time,' said Conseil calmly.

'That is just like you, friend Conseil,' replied the impetuous Canadian. 'You don't ever worry or fuss, you're always calm. You're the kind to give thanks for what you have yet to receive, and to die of hunger rather than complain!'

'But what would be the point?' enquired Conseil.

'The point would be to complain! That would already be something. And if these pirates—I use the word with all due respect, and to avoid upsetting the professor who won't let us call them cannibals—if these pirates imagine that they are going to keep me prisoner in this suffocating cell without learning what swear words I use to spice up my fits of anger, then they are making a serious mistake. Look here, Dr Aronnax, and tell me frankly: do you think we'll be in this iron crate for long?'

'To tell the truth, I know no more than you, friend Land.'

'But what do you *think*?'

'I think that chance has made us privy to an important secret. Now if it is in the submarine crew's interest to keep the secret, and if this interest is more important than the lives of three men, then I believe we are in great danger. But if not, the monster that has swallowed us up will return us to the world of our fellow men at the first opportunity.'

'Unless he impresses us as crew,' said Conseil, 'and keeps us that way.'

'Until the day', replied Ned, 'that a frigate faster and more skilful than the *Abraham Lincoln* defeats this den of robbers, and hangs us and them on the yardarm.'

'A good point, Master Land,' said I, 'but it seems to me nobody has yet made us such a proposition. It is therefore pointless to discuss what to do in such a case. I repeat, let's wait and make our decisions depending on circumstances: let's do nothing, because there is nothing to be done.'

'On the contrary, sir,' replied the harpooner, who would not give in; 'we must do something.'

'Well what, Master Land?'

'Escape!'

'To escape from gaol is difficult enough on land, but to get out of a submarine prison appears to me quite impossible.'

'Now friend Ned,' said Conseil, 'what do you say to monsieur's argument? I cannot believe that an American is ever at a loss for words.'

The harpooner, visibly put out, did not say anything. In the circumstances that fate had dealt us, leaving was out of the question. But a Canadian is half French, as Master Land showed by his reply.

'So, Dr Aronnax,' he said after a moment's consideration, 'you don't know what people should do when they can't escape from prison?'

'No, my friend.'

'It's very simple: they ought to get used to staying . . .'

'Yes indeed,' said Conseil, 'we are better off inside than above or below!'

'. . . having thrown out the gaolers, turnkeys, and watchmen!'

'What Ned, are you seriously contemplating taking over the vessel?'

'Very seriously.'

'Impossible!'

'Why? A suitable opportunity may occur; and I don't see what should stop us taking it. If there are only about twenty men on board, they won't be able to stand up to two Frenchmen and a Canadian, will they?'

It was wiser to concur with such a view than to discuss it, so I merely said:

'Let's wait and see what events throw up. But until then please control your temper. We can only act by ruse, and you will not produce favourable opportunities by getting angry. So promise me you will take things as they come, without getting too annoyed.'

'I promise,' replied Ned, in a not very reassuring tone. 'I shall not say or do a single aggressive thing, even if the table isn't served with the required punctuality.'

'I have your word on it, Ned.'

Our conversation ended here, and each of us began to think his own thoughts. For my part, I must confess that I had few illusions, despite the harpooner's pledge. I didn't believe in the favourable opportunity Ned had mentioned. To be so well piloted, the submarine boat had to have a large crew, and if it came to a fight we would be on the losing side. Besides, we would need to be at liberty, which was not the case. I couldn't even see a way of escaping from this hermetically sealed cell of metal plates. And if the vessel's strange commander had any sort of secret to maintain—which was highly probable—he would not allow us to act freely on board. Might he not eliminate us by violent means, or one day cast us off on some remote piece of land? There was no way of telling. But all these conjectures appeared to me extremely plausible, and I reflected that you had to be a harpooner to hope to escape again.

I understood, moreover, that Ned's thoughts were becoming gloomier as he considered matters. I heard oaths beginning to growl in the depths of his throat, and I could see his movements growing threatening once more. He got up and began to pace around like a wild beast in a cage, and to hit and kick the walls.

As time went by, hunger began seriously to trouble us, and this time the steward did not appear. Our situation as castaways had been forgotten about for too long if they really did have good intentions towards us.

Ned Land, tormented by the gnawing pains of his capacious stomach, got more and more wound up; and I really was afraid that there would be an explosion if the crew arrived, whatever promises he had made.

For two hours Ned's anger grew fiercer. He shouted and shrieked in vain. The metal walls were deaf. I could not hear a single sound in the boat, which lay as if dead. It was not moving, for I would have felt the trembling of the hull from the throbbing of the screw. It was probably plunged into the depths of the waters, far from the earth. The deathly silence felt terrifying.

As for our abandonment, our isolation in this cell, I did not dare guess how long it might continue. The hopes I had had during our meeting with the commander faded by degrees. The kind expression of the person, the generosity of his physiognomy, the nobility of his bearing, all disappeared from my mind. I saw the enigmatic individual as essentially pitiless and cruel, as he was forced to be. I felt him as being beyond the pale of humanity, insensible to feelings of pity, the remorseless enemy of his fellow beings, against whom he must have sworn an undying hatred!

But was this man simply going to let us die of hunger, locked up in a cramped cell, exposed to those terrible temptations which assail men under the influence of extreme hunger? This fearful thought took on terrible power in my brain, and with my imagination at work, I felt myself becoming the prey of a mad terror. Conseil was quite calm. Ned was raging.

At this point in my thoughts a sound came from outside, and footsteps resounded on the metal plates; the bolts were shot back, the door opened, and the steward appeared again.

Before I could block or otherwise prevent him, the Canadian had flung himself on to the unfortunate man, thrown him to the ground, and taken hold of his throat. The steward was being strangled in a powerful grip.

Conseil was already attempting to loosen the harpooner's deadly grasp on his half suffocated victim, and I was just about to help, when I was suddenly fixed to the spot by these words in French:

'Calmez-vous, maître Land, et vous, monsieur le professeur, veuillez m'écouter!'*

10

The Man of the Sea

IT was the commander of the vessel.

Land got up quickly. The steward, almost strangled, staggered out at a sign from his master; but such was the captain's authority on board, that the man betrayed no sign of what was surely his resentment against the Canadian. Conseil was interested in spite of himself, and I, astonished: we awaited the dénouement of the scene without speaking.

The commander, leaning against the side of the table, his arms crossed, regarded us with very great attention. Was he hesitating before speaking, or did he regret addressing us in French? That might easily be the case.

After a few moments' silence, which none of us dreamed of breaking:

'Gentlemen,' he said in a calm and penetrating voice, 'I can speak French, English, German, and Latin with equal ease. I would have been quite able to reply to you at our first meeting, but I wished to learn first and reflect afterwards. Your fourfold account agreed in every particular, and assured me of your identity. I now know that fate has brought me Dr Pierre Aronnax, lecturer in natural history at the Museum of Paris, on a foreign scientific mission; Conseil, his manservant; and Ned, a Canadian by birth, harpooner on board the frigate *Abraham Lincoln* of the United States Navy.'

I nodded to indicate my acquiescence. The captain had not asked me a question, so no reply was necessary. He expressed himself with perfect ease, without any accent. His sentences were well phrased, his words well chosen, his fluency remarkable. Nevertheless, I had the impression he was not French.

He continued as follows:

'You doubtless thought that I took a long time to pay you a second visit. It was because, once your identity had been established, I wished to consider seriously how to treat you. I hesitated for a long time. The most unfortunate circumstances have brought you into contact with a man who has broken with humanity. You have come to disturb my existence . . .'

'Unintentionally,' I put in.

'Indeed?' repeated the stranger, raising his voice. 'Was it unintentionally that the *Abraham Lincoln* searched for me on every ocean? Was it unintentionally that you embarked on that ship? Was it unintentionally that your shells ricocheted off the hull of my vessel? Was it unintentionally that Master Land here struck me with his harpoon?'*

I perceived a hidden irritation in these words. But to all such recriminations I had a perfectly natural answer to make, and I made it.

'Monsieur,' said I, 'you are not aware of the discussions about you which have taken place in Europe and America. You do not know that the various accidents you have caused by the collisions with your submarine machine have stirred public opinion on both continents. I spare you the countless hypotheses which people have constructed to explain the inexplicable phenomenon of which you alone possessed the secret. But you must realize that in pursuing you even to the heart of the Pacific, the *Abraham Lincoln*'s crew were under the impression that they were pursuing some powerful marine monster, which it was necessary to rid the ocean of at any cost.'

A half smile parted the lips of the captain; then in a calmer voice:

'Dr Aronnax, dare you affirm that your frigate would not have followed and fired balls at a submarine vessel rather than a monster?'

This question caused me some embarrassment, for Captain Farragut would not have hesitated a single moment. He would have considered it his duty to destroy a device of that kind as much as a giant narwhal.

'So you appreciate, monsieur,' continued the stranger, 'that I have the right to treat you as enemies.'

I did not reply, and with good reason. What was the point of debating such a proposition, when force could overcome the strongest of arguments?

'I hesitated for a long time,' repeated the captain. 'Nothing obliged me to offer you my hospitality. Had I wanted to part company with you, I would not have wished to meet you again. I could have returned you to the platform of this ship on which you took refuge. I could have dived beneath the surface and forgotten that you ever existed. Did I not have this right?'

'Perhaps the right of a savage,' I replied, 'but not that of a civilized being.'

'Dr Aronnax,' answered the captain sharply, 'I am not what you call a civilized being! I have broken with society for reasons which I alone have the right to appreciate. So I do not obey its rules, and I ask you never to invoke them in my presence again!'

This was clearly articulated. A flash of anger and disdain had lit up the stranger's eyes, and I caught a glimpse of a frightening past in this man's life. Not only had he placed himself outside humanity's laws, but he had made himself independent, free in the strictest sense of the word, out of all reach! Who would dare pursue him to the bottom of the seas, given that he could foil any efforts made against him on the surface? What ship could resist a collision with his submarine monitor? What iron cladding, however thick, could resist an attack from his ram? No man alive could demand from him an account of his works. God, if he believed in Him, and his conscience, if he had one, were the only judges to whom he could answer. These thoughts rapidly crossed my mind, while the strange individual was silent, absorbed as if withdrawn into himself. I regarded him with a terror mixed with curiosity, in the same way as Oedipus must have looked at the Sphinx.*

After a longish silence the commander spoke again.

'So I hesitated,' he said, 'but I thought that my own interest might coincide with that natural clemency to which every human being has a right. You will remain on board, since fate has cast the three of you here. You will be free, and in exchange for this freedom, admittedly quite limited, I will impose only one condition. Your word of honour that you accept it will suffice.'

'Pray continue, sir,' I said. 'I presume that it is a condition that honourable men can accept.'

'Certainly, and it is as follows. It is possible that certain unforeseen circumstances may compel me to confine you to your cabins for a few hours, or days in some cases. As I never wish to use force, in such a case I expect passive obedience from you, even more than in other circumstances. In acting in this way, I will take all responsibility from your shoulders, I absolve you completely, for it will be my task to ensure that you do not see what should not be seen. Will you accept this condition?'

So things happened on board that were strange to say the least, and which were not fit to be seen by people who had not put themselves outside social laws! Amongst the surprises that the future held for me, this was not to be the least.

'We accept,' I replied. 'But I request your permission to ask one question—only one.'

'Pray continue, sir.'

'You have said that we will be free on board?'.

'Entirely.'

'I would like to enquire what you mean by such freedom.'

'I mean the freedom to come and go, and to study and observe all that takes place here, except in a few rare circumstances: in short, the same freedom my companions and I enjoy.'

It was clear that we were talking about different things.

'I beg your pardon,' I added, 'but that liberty is only the one granted every prisoner, to walk around his prison. That is not enough for us.'

'Well it must suffice, in any case.'

'What! You would have us renounce ever seeing our friends, relatives, or native lands again?'

'Yes, monsieur. But to give up the insupportable yoke of the land which men equate with freedom is perhaps not such a great sacrifice as you may imagine.'

'What an idea!' exclaimed Ned Land. 'I will never give my word not to try and escape!'

'I am not asking for your word, Master Land,' the captain replied coldly.

'Monsieur,' I replied, carried away in spite of myself, 'you are taking advantage of us. This is cruelty.'

'No monsieur, it is mercy. You are my prisoners after the battle. I am holding you when, with just a word, I could have you thrown back into the depths of the ocean. You attacked me. You came and discovered a secret that no man on earth must penetrate—the secret of my entire existence. And you imagine that I am going to send you back to shore, where nothing is known about me any longer? Never! By holding you, it is not you that I am protecting, but myself.'

The captain's words indicated a resolve against which no argument could prevail.

'So,' I continued, 'you are merely giving us the choice between life and death?'

'Yes, I am.'

'My friends,' I said, 'to a question asked in this way no reply is possible. But no promise binds us to the master of this ship.'*

'None sir,' replied the stranger.

And in a gentler voice:

'Now, let me finish what I have to say. I know you, Dr Aronnax. You, if not your companions, will have little to complain about the destiny that has tied you to my fate. Amongst the books which make up my favourite reading you will find the work you published on the great deeps of the sea. I have often studied it. Your book took you as far as earthbound science allowed. But you don't know everything, you still have things to see. So let me tell you that you will not regret the time spent on board my vessel. You are going to travel through a wonderland. Astonishment and stupefaction will probably be your normal state of mind. You will not easily become blasé about the sights continually offered to your eyes. I am going to embark on a new underwater tour of the world—who knows, perhaps the last?—and revisit everything I have studied on my many travels; and you will be my study companion. Starting today, you will enter a new element, you will see what no man has ever seen before (for my men and I no longer count); and our planet, through my efforts, will deliver up its last secrets.'

I cannot deny that these words of the captain's had a tremendous effect on me. He had touched me on my weak spot, and for a moment I forgot that the contemplation of such sublime things could not compensate for the loss of freedom. But in any case, I counted on the future to settle this important question. So I merely replied:

'Sir, if you have broken with humanity, I cannot believe that you have given up all human feeling. We are castaways, magnanimously taken on board, and we will not forget it. I personally recognize fully that if interest in science can overrule even the need for freedom, what is promised by our encounter will offer me a great deal of compensation.'

I thought the captain was going to offer me his hand to finalize our treaty. He did nothing of the sort. I thought he should have.

'One last question . . .' I said, just as the inexplicable being seemed about to withdraw.

'I'm listening.'

'How should I address you?'

'Monsieur,' replied the captain, 'I will merely be Captain Nemo for you;* and you and your companions will simply be for me the passengers of the *Nautilus*.'*

Captain Nemo called. A steward appeared. The captain gave him orders in that foreign tongue that I could not place. Then, turning to Ned and Conseil:

'A meal is waiting for you in your cabin. Please follow this man.'

'I won't say no!' said the harpooner.

And Conseil and he finally left the cell they had been imprisoned in for more than 30 hours.

'And now Dr Aronnax, our lunch is ready. Allow me to lead the way.'

'At your disposition, captain.'

I followed Captain Nemo, and immediately outside the door found myself in a sort of corridor lit by electricity, rather like the gangway on a ship. After about ten yards, another door opened in front of me.

I entered a dining-room, decorated and furnished with austere taste. Tall oak dressers, full of ebony ornaments, rose at both ends of the room, and on their scallop-edged shelves sparkled fine china, porcelain, and glassware of an inestimable value. The plates shone in the rays from the brilliant ceiling, whose glare was filtered and softened by fine paintings.

In the centre of the room stood a richly laid table. Captain Nemo indicated the place where I was to sit down.

'Please be seated,' he said, 'and eat as a man who must be dying of hunger.'

Lunch consisted of a number of dishes made of ingredients from the sea, as well as a few portions whose nature and origin I could not guess. I had to admit that they were good, with a peculiar flavour which I quickly got used to. All the different foods seemed to be rich in phosphorus and I decided that they had to come from the sea.

Captain Nemo was watching me. I did not say anything, but he read my thoughts and without prompting answered the questions I was dying to ask him.

'Most of the dishes are unknown to you,' he said. 'But you can eat them without fear. They are good and nourishing. I gave up food from the land a long time ago and my health is none the worse for it. My crew, who are fit and well, eat the same dishes as me.'

'So all this food is produced by the sea?'

'Yes, the sea provides for all my needs. Sometimes I let out my nets and draw them in full to breaking. Sometimes I go hunting in the midst of this element thought inaccessible to man, and pursue the game living in my underwater forests. My flocks, like those of Neptune's old shepherd,* graze without fear on the immense ocean plains. There I have a vast property which I alone farm and which is always replanted by the hand of the Creator of all things.'

I looked at Captain Nemo somewhat astonished and replied:

'I understand perfectly well, monsieur, that your nets provide excellent fish for your table; I comprehend less well how you can pursue aquatic game in your underwater forests; but I entirely fail to grasp how any meat, however small the quantity, can appear on your menu.'

'But I never make use of the flesh of earthbound animals.'

'Then what is this?' I said, pointing to a dish where a few scraps of fillet still remained.

'What you believe to be meat is simply fillet of turtle. Here are also a few dolphin livers that you would take for stewed pork.

My chef is skilful, and is very good at preserving the various products of the ocean. Taste all these dishes. Here is a sea slug jam that a Malay would declare without equal anywhere in the world; this is a cream made from milk provided by whales' breasts and sugar from the great wracks of the North Sea; and finally let me offer you some anemone jam which is the equal of the most savoury fruits.'

I tasted them, more out of curiosity than as a gourmet, while Captain Nemo enchanted me with his incredible tales.

'But the sea, Dr Aronnax, this prodigious, inexhaustible wet-nurse doesn't just feed me, it also clothes me. The materials you are wearing are woven from the byssus of certain shellfish; they are dyed with the purple used by the ancients or else the fine violet shades that I extract from the Mediterranean sea hare. The perfumes you will find on the wash-stand in your cabin were produced by distilling marine plants. Your bed is made of the softest wracks in the ocean. Your pen will be made from whalebone, your ink from the liquid secreted by a cuttlefish or squid.* Everything I use comes from the sea, as everything will one day return to it!'

'You love the sea, captain.'

'Yes I do love it! The sea is everything. It covers seven-tenths of the terrestrial globe. Its breath is healthy and pure. It is a spacious wilderness where man is never alone, for he can feel life throbbing all around him. The sea is the environment for a prodigious, supernatural existence; it is nothing but movement and love; it is a living infinity, as one of your poets has said.* And indeed, sir, nature is present there in its three kingdoms, animal, vegetable, and mineral. The animal kingdom is well represented by the four groups of zoophytes, three classes of articulates, five classes of molluscs, and three classes of vertebrates—mammals, reptiles, and countless legions of fish, which constitute an innumerable order of more than 13,000 species, of which only a tenth live in fresh water. The sea is nature's vast reserve. It was through the sea that the globe as it were began, and who knows if it will not end in the sea! Perfect peace abides there. The sea does not belong to despots. On its surface immoral rights can still be claimed, men can fight each other, devour each other, and carry out all the earth's atrocities. But thirty feet below the surface their power ceases, their influence fades, their authority disappears. Ah, sir, live, live in the heart of the sea! Independence is possible only here! Here I recognize no master! Here I am free!'

Captain Nemo suddenly fell silent in the midst of the enthusiasm welling out of him. Had he allowed himself to get carried away beyond his usual reserve? Had he said too much? For a few moments he paced agitatedly up and down. Then he calmed down, his physiognomy took on its customary coldness, and he turned to me.

'Now monsieur,' he said, 'if you wish to visit the *Nautilus*, I am at your disposition.'

11

The Nautilus

CAPTAIN NEMO got up. I followed him. A double door opened at the back of the room, and I discovered a room of the same size as the one I had just left.

It was a library.* Tall furniture, made of black rosewood and inset with brass, bore on its long shelves a large number of books with uniform bindings. The shelves followed the shape of the room, with vast settees below them, upholstered in brown leather and offering the most comfortable of curves. Light reading-desks, which could be moved around at will, provided support for books being read. In the centre stood a huge table covered with periodicals, including several newspapers that already seemed quite old. The harmonious setting was flooded with electric light falling from four frosted-glass globes recessed in the vaults of the ceiling. I looked with real admiration at this room, so carefully organized, and I could scarcely believe my eyes.

'Captain Nemo,' I said to my host, who had just stretched out on a sofa, 'this is a library that would do honour to more than one palace in the New or Old Worlds, and I am truly astonished when I think that it travels with you to the deepest parts of the ocean.'

'Where could one find more privacy or silence? Does your study in the Museum offer so complete a peace?'

'No sir, and I must add that it is very thin in comparison with yours.* You must have six or seven thousand volumes here . . .'

'Twelve thousand, Dr Aronnax. These are the only ties still connecting me to the land. The world finished for me on the day my *Nautilus* dived beneath the water for the first time. That day I bought my last books, my last magazines, my last newspapers, and I would like to believe that humanity has thought or written nothing since then. These books, Dr Aronnax, are at your disposal and you can make free use of them.'*

I thanked Captain Nemo, and approached the shelves. Books abounded on science, on ethics, and on literature, written in every language, but I could not see a single work of political economy: these seemed totally prohibited on board. Curiously enough, all these books were not classified according to their language; and this lack of system implied that the captain of the *Nautilus* had little trouble in reading any of the volumes he might select.

Amongst the works, I noticed the masterpieces of the modern and ancient masters, comprising everything that humanity has produced of greatest beauty in history, poetry, the novel, and science: from Homer to Victor Hugo, from Xenophon to Michelet, from Rabelais to Mme Sand.* But the focus of this library was more on science; books on mechanics, ballistics, hydrography, meteorology, geography, geology, etc., took up at least as much space as works on natural history, making me realize that they must form the captain's principal study. I saw there all of Humboldt and Arago, the works of Foucault, Henri Sainte-Claire Deville, Chasles, Milne-Edwards, Quatrefages, Tyndall, Faraday, Berthelot, Abbé Secchi, Petermann, Commander Maury, Agassiz,* etc., the reports of the Academy of Sciences, the bulletins of the various geographical societies, etc., and, in a prominent position, the two volumes which were perhaps the reason why Captain Nemo had given me a relatively warm welcome. Amongst the books of Joseph Bertrand, *Les Fondateurs de l'astronomie** even gave me a definite date: as I knew that it was published in 1865, I was able to conclude that the fitting out of the *Nautilus* did not date from after that.* Captain Nemo had accordingly begun his underwater existence not more than three years previously. I hoped, moreover, that still more recent works would let me determine the date even more closely; but I had plenty of time to carry out such research, and did not wish to hold up the tour of the *Nautilus*'s wonders.

'Sir,' I said, 'thank you for making this library available to me. It contains treasures of science that I will put to good use.'

'This room is not just a library,' responded Captain Nemo, 'it's also a smoking-room.'

'A smoking-room? Do people smoke on board?'

'They do.'

'Then I must conclude that you have maintained relations with Havana.'

'Not at all. Please accept this cigar, Dr Aronnax, and although it does not come from Havana, you will appreciate it if you are a connoisseur.'

I took the cigar offered. The shape reminded me of a Havana cigar, but the leaves seemed to be golden. I lit it using a small lighter on an elegant bronze stand, and I breathed the first mouthfuls in with all the delight of a smoker who has not indulged for two days.

'It is excellent, but it is not tobacco.'

'Correct; this tobacco does not come from Havana or the East. It is a sort of seaweed rich in nicotine that the sea provides me, rather sparingly in fact. Do you regret your Havanas, sir?'

'Captain, I shall disdain them from this day on.'

'Smoke, then, as much as you wish, and without wondering where the cigars came from. No state monopoly has licensed them; but I may presume they're none the worse for that?'

'On the contrary.'

While speaking, Captain Nemo opened the door opposite the one we had used to enter the library, and I passed into an enormous, magnificently lit salon.*

It was a vast rectangle cut off at the corners, 30 feet long, 18 feet wide, and 15 feet high. A luminous ceiling decorated with delicate arabesques provided a clear but soft light for all the wonders gathered together in this museum. For it *was* a museum, within whose walls an intelligent and prodigal hand had assembled every treasure of nature and art—but in the artistic disorder typical of a painter's studio.

About thirty identically framed paintings by masters, alternating with dazzling panoplies, hung on the walls, which were covered with tapestries of a severe design. I saw paintings of the very highest worth, most of which I had previously viewed in private European collections or in exhibitions. The various schools of the old masters were represented by a Madonna by Raphael, a Virgin by Leonardo da Vinci, a nymph by Correggio, a woman by Titian, an Adoration by Veronese, an Assumption by Murillo, a portrait by Holbein, a monk by Velázquez, a martyr by Ribera, a country fair by Rubens, two Flemish landscapes by Teniers, three small genre paintings by Gerrit Dou, Metsu, and Paul Potter, canvases by Géricault and Prud'hon, and a few seascapes by Backhuysen and Vernet.* The works of modern art included paintings signed Delacroix, Ingres, Decamps, Troyon, Meissonier, Daubigny,* etc.; and standing on pedestals in the corners of this magnificent museum were a few outstanding marble figures and bronze statues, reproductions of the finest models of antiquity. The condition of stupefaction that the captain of the *Nautilus* had predicted was beginning to invade my mind.

'Dr Aronnax,' said this strange being, 'please excuse the informality with which I receive you as well as the untidiness of the room.'

'Sir,' I replied, 'without trying to discover who you are, may I possibly recognize in you an artist?'

'At best an amateur. I used to enjoy assembling the finer works created by man's hand. I was an avid collector, an untiring visitor of antique shops, and I was able to pick up a few objects of value. These are my last memories of the world which is now dead for me. In my eyes, your modern artists are not to be distinguished from the ancients: they could be two or three thousand years old and I mix them all up in my mind. The great masters are ageless.'

'And these composers?' I said, pointing to scores by Weber, Rossini, Mozart, Beethoven, Haydn, Meyerbeer, Hérold, Wagner, Auber, Gounod,* and several others, scattered over a piano-organ of a famous make filling one of the side panels of the salon.

'These musicians are contemporaries of Orpheus,* for chronological differences are erased in the memory of departed musicians—and I am dead, sir, as dead as those of your friends reposing six feet below ground!'

Captain Nemo fell silent and seemed lost in a deep reverie.* I considered him with considerable emotion, silently analysing his strange features. Leaning on the corner of a precious mosaic table, he no longer saw me, he forgot that I was there.

I respected this meditation, and continued to examine the curiosities adorning this sitting-room.

Side by side with the works of art, natural rarities occupied a very important place. These were principally plants, shells, and other objects produced by the ocean, apparently Captain Nemo's own finds. In the middle of the drawing-room the water of a fountain, lit by electricity, rose and fell into a basin made of a single *Tridacna*. This shell, from the biggest of the acephalous molluscs, had a delicately festooned rim of a circumference of about twenty feet; it was therefore larger than the two fine *Tridacnae* given to François I by the Republic of Venice, from which the Church of Saint-Sulpice in Paris made gigantic fonts.

Around this fountain, in elegant display cabinets reinforced with copper, the most precious products of the sea ever to be made available to a naturalist's scrutiny were classified and labelled. One can imagine how happy the scientist in me felt.

The branch of the zoophytes offered very curious specimens from its two groups of polyps and echinoderms. In the first group appeared tubipores, fan-shaped gorgons, soft sponges from Syria, isis from the Moluccas, sea pens, an admirable virgularian from the seas of Norway, varied umbellulas, alcyonarians, and a whole series of the madrepores that my master Milne-Edwards has so judiciously classified into sections. Amongst them I noticed adorable flabelliforms, Oculinidae from Réunion, Neptune's chariots from the Caribbean, some superb varieties of corals, and lastly all the kinds of curious polyparies that cluster together to form whole islands and, eventually, continents. Among the echinoderms with their remarkable spiny covering, the whole collection of individuals of this group was represented by starfishes, sea stars, pentacrinoids, comatulids, asterophons, sea urchins, holothurians, etc.

A highly strung conchologist would certainly have fainted at the many display cases classifying specimens from the branch of molluscs. There I saw a collection of inestimable value, which time does not allow me to describe in full. Amongst the various products, I will cite for memory only: the elegant royal hammer-shell of the Indian Ocean, with regular white spots standing vividly out from a red and brown background; a brightly coloured imperial spondylus, all bristling with spikes, a specimen rarely seen in the museums of Europe, and worth, I thought, about 20,000 francs; a much-sought-after common hammer-shell from the seas of Australia; some exotic cockles from Senegal: fragile white shells with double valves, that a breath would have blown away like a soap bubble; several varieties of the watering-can shells of Java: sorts of chalky tubes edged with foliaceous folds, much desired by collectors; a whole series of top shells: some greenish-yellow ones found in the seas of America, some of a reddish-brown familiar in the waters off Australia, others remarkable for their complex shells from the Gulf of Mexico, yet other stellaria found in the Southern Seas, and finally the rarest of all, the magnificent spur-shell from New Zealand; then admirable sulphuret tellins, precious species of cytherea and venus-shells, the trellised solarium of the Tranquebar coasts, the turban shell veined with resplendent mother-of-pearl, the green parrot shell from the seas of China, the nearly unknown cone shell of the genus *Coenodulli*, all the varieties of cowries which serve as currency in India and Africa, the most precious shell in the East Indies, the Glory-of-the-Seas; and finally some periwinkles, delphiniums, screw shells, ianthines, ovules, volutes, olives, mitre shells, casques, murexes, whelks, harps, winkles, Triton's shells, cerites, spindle-shells, wing shells, scorpion shells, limpets, hyales, and *Cleodora*: all delicate and fragile shells that science has baptized with its most charming names.

Apart from them, in special compartments, lay pearl chaplets of the greatest beauty, picked out in fiery points by the electric light: pink pearls plucked from the marine pinna of the Red Sea, green pearls from the haliotis iris, yellow ones, blue ones, and black ones. These were the curious products of the varied molluscs of every ocean, of distinctive mussels from the northern rivers, and finally a few specimens of inestimable value distilled by the rarest of pearl oysters. A few of these pearls were bigger than a pigeon's egg. They were therefore worth more than the one that the traveller Tavernier* offered to the Shah of Persia for three million francs, and surpassed the pearl of the Imam of Muscat, which I had previously thought without rival anywhere in the world.

To ascribe a value to this collection was virtually impossible. Captain Nemo must have spent millions acquiring the different items, and I was just wondering what source he might use to satisfy his collector's whims, when I was interrupted:

'You are examining my shells, sir. They may indeed interest a scientist; but for me they have an additional charm as I collected them all myself. There is not a sea on the surface of the globe that I have not searched.'*

'Captain, I can understand the delight of strolling through such wealth. You are among those who have amassed their treasures by themselves. No museum in Europe possesses a comparable collection of marine products.* But if I exhaust all my admiration here, there will be none left for the ship bearing them! I do not want to penetrate secrets which are yours alone. However I must confess that the *Nautilus*, the propulsive force it holds, the mechanism allowing it to be steered, the powerful agent which gives life to it—all this arouses my curiosity to the highest degree. I can see instruments hanging on the walls of the salon, with functions I am unaware of. May I possibly know . . .?'

'Dr Aronnax,' replied Captain Nemo, 'I have said that you are free on board my ship, and consequently no part of the *Nautilus* is forbidden. You can visit any section of it, and it will be a great pleasure for me to act as your guide.'

'I do not know how to thank you, captain, but I will not abuse your kindness. I will simply ask what these scientific instruments are for . . .'

'These same instruments are to be found in my bedroom, and it is there that I will have the pleasure of explaining their use to you. But first come and visit the cabin reserved for you. You must see how your domestic arrangements are to be taken care of on board the *Nautilus*.'

I followed Captain Nemo through one of the doors in the two oblique angles in the sitting-room, and into the ship's gangways. He took me forward and there I found not a cabin but an elegant bedroom, complete with a bed, dressing table, and several other pieces of furniture.

I could only thank my host.

'Your bedroom is next to mine,' he said opening the door, 'and mine leads into the salon we have just left.'

I entered the captain's room. It had a severe, almost hermit-like appearance.* A small iron bedstead, a work table, a few pieces of furniture for his toilet. Everything illuminated by indirect light. No comfort. Only the barest of necessities.*

Captain Nemo indicated a chair.

'Please be seated.'

I sat down and he spoke as follows:

12

All by Electricity

'DR ARONNAX,' said Captain Nemo, pointing to the instruments hanging on the walls of his room, 'these are the instruments needed for sailing the *Nautilus*. Here, as in the salon, I have them always in view, telling me my position and exact direction in the middle of the ocean. Some of them you already know, such as the thermometer, which tells me the temperature inside the *Nautilus*; the barometer, which measures the weight of the air and hence forecasts changes in the weather; the hygrometer, which registers the amount of moisture in the air; the storm-glass, whose mixed-up contents separate out to herald the arrival of storms; the compass, which shows me the course to take; the sextant, which indicates my latitude by the altitude of the sun; the chronometers, which enable me to calculate my longitude; and lastly the telescopes, for day and night use, which I use to examine every point on the horizon when the *Nautilus* is on the surface.'*

'These are the usual navigational equipment, and I am aware of their functions. But I can see others which must correspond to the special requirements of the *Nautilus*. Isn't that dial with the moving needle a pressure-gauge?'

'Yes indeed. It is in contact with the water outside, and by telling me the pressure, indicates what depth my vessel is at.'

'And are these a new kind of sounding instrument?'

'They're thermometric sounding devices registering the temperature at various depths.'

'And these other instruments whose purpose I cannot begin to guess?'

'Before going any further, Dr Aronnax, I must explain a few things. So please pay attention to what I have to say.'

Captain Nemo paused briefly and then continued:

'There is one agent which is powerful, responsive, easy to use, suitable for all kinds of work, and which reigns supreme on board. It does everything. It provides me with heat and light; it is the soul of my machines. That agent is electricity.'*

'Electricity!' I exclaimed, somewhat surprised.

'Yes indeed.'

'But captain, the great speed you move at seems to have little to do with the power of electricity. Until now the dynamic capacity of electricity has remained very limited, only capable of producing small forces!'

'Dr Aronnax,' answered Captain Nemo, 'my electricity is not the commonly used sort, and that is all that I wish to say on the matter.'

'I will not press the point, monsieur, but merely remain astonished at the outcome. A single question, however, which needs no answer if it seems indiscreet. The elements that you use to produce this astonishing agent must be used up quickly. Zinc, for example: how do you replace it since you no longer have any contact with land?'

'Your question will be answered,' replied Captain Nemo. 'First let me tell you that there are zinc, iron, silver, and gold deposits on the bottom of the sea whose extraction would certainly be possible. But I decided to owe nothing to the metals of the earth and simply derive the means to produce my electricity from the sea itself.'

'From the sea?'

'Yes, sir, and I had plenty of choices. For example, I could have established a circuit between wires sunk at different depths, and hence obtained electricity from the difference in temperature between them;* but I decided to employ a more practical method.'

'Yes?'

'You are aware of the composition of sea water. In 1,000 grams, 96.5 per cent is water and about 2.66 per cent, sodium chloride, with small quantities of magnesium and potassium chloride, magnesium bromide, magnesium sulphate, lime sulphate, and lime carbonate. You will see that sodium chloride is found in considerable proportions. Now, it is this sodium which I extract from sea water to give me my constituents.'

'Sodium?'

'Yes. Mixed with mercury it forms an amalgam which replaces zinc in Bunsen* batteries. The mercury is never used up. Only the sodium is consumed, and the sea itself provides me with more. Also, sodium batteries must be regarded as producing the most energy, for their electro-motive power is double that of zinc ones.'

'I fully understand the suitability of sodium in your present circumstances. It is to be found in the sea. So far so good. But it must still be produced, or rather extracted. How do you do this? Clearly you could use your batteries; but if I am not mistaken, the sodium utilized by the electrical apparatus would be greater than the quantity extracted. You would be consuming more than you were producing!'

'Consequently I do not use batteries for extraction, but simply the heat from coal.'

'Coal or sea coal?' I persisted.

'Let's say sea coal if you like.'

'And you are able to work underwater coalmines?'

'Dr Aronnax, you will see me at work.* I will only ask for a little patience, since you have plenty of time to be patient. Just remember one thing. I owe everything to the sea: it produces electricity and electricity gives the *Nautilus* heat, light, and movement—in a word, life.'

'But not the air you breathe?'

'Oh, I could manufacture all the air I need for my consumption, but that would be pointless since I go back up to the surface whenever I want. But even if electricity does not provide me with air for breathing, it does work the powerful pumps that store air in special tanks, thus allowing me to remain at the deepest levels as long as I wish.'

'Captain, I can only admire this. You have evidently discovered the real dynamic power of electricity that people will undoubtedly discover one day.'

'I do not know whether they will,' replied Captain Nemo rather coldly. 'But in any case, you are already familiar with the first application that I have made of such an invaluable tool. It is this agent which gives us light more continuously than the sun could. Look at this clock: it is an electric one, and keeps time more accurately than the best chronometers. I have divided it into 24 hours, like Italian clocks, since for me there is neither night nor day, sun nor moon, but only the artificial light which I carry with me to the bottom of the seas. Look, it is now ten in the morning.'

'I see.'

'Another application of electricity: this dial before our eyes serves to indicate the speed of the *Nautilus*. An electric circuit connects it to the propeller of the log, and its needle shows me the actual speed of the engine. Look, at the moment we are moving at a moderate speed of 15 knots.'

'It's amazing, and I can see, captain, that you were right to use this agent which will one day replace wind, water, and steam.'*

'We haven't finished yet, Dr Aronnax,' said Captain Nemo getting up, 'and if you would like to follow me, we will visit the rear section of the *Nautilus*.'

I was already familiar with the entire forward section of the submarine craft, whose exact layout I will give here, going from the centre to the cutwater: the 15-foot dining-room, separated from the library by a sealed bulkhead preventing any water from penetrating; the 15-foot library; the 30-foot salon, separated from the captain's bedroom by a second watertight division; the bedroom itself, 15 feet long; mine, 8 feet; and finally a 24-foot air tank reaching to the bow. The total length was about 115 feet.* The bulkheads had doors let in them that closed hermetically by means of rubber seals, and these allowed total security on board should the *Nautilus* ever spring a leak.

I followed Captain Nemo through one of the gangways situated along the sides of the ship, and arrived at its centre. Here there was a sort of open shaft between two watertight compartments. An iron ladder, fixed firmly to the wall, led to the top of the stairwell.

I asked the captain what the ladder was for.

'It goes up to the dinghy.'

'What, you have a dinghy!' I replied in astonishment.

'But of course. An excellent craft, light and unsinkable, which we use for excursions and for fishing.'

'But then don't you have to go up to the surface, when you want to use the boat?'

'Not at all. The dinghy is fixed to the upper part of the *Nautilus*'s hull, in a recess designed for it. It is completely decked over and held in place by strong bolts. This ladder leads to a manhole in the *Nautilus*'s hull, which corresponds to a similar hole in the side of the dinghy. I enter the boat through this double opening. The hole on the *Nautilus* is then closed; I shut the one in the boat by means of a pressure screw; I release the bolts, and the lifeboat rises to the surface at a prodigious speed. I open the hatch on the deck, carefully fastened until then, and hoist the mast, raise my sail or use my oars, and so move as I wish.'

'But how do you come back on board?'

'I do not come back, Dr Aronnax, it is the *Nautilus* that comes back.'

'Following your instructions?'

'Following my instructions. I am connected to it by an electric wire. I send a telegram, and that's that.'

'Indeed,' I said, intoxicated by these miracles; 'what could be simpler!'

Having gone past the well of the staircase leading up to the platform, I saw a cabin 7 feet long; in it Conseil and Ned, delighted with their meal, were busy wolfing it down. Soon a door opened on to the 10-foot kitchen situated between the huge storerooms.

All the cooking was done with electricity, even more powerful and obedient than gas. The wires under the cookers evenly distributed and maintained the heat over the platinum plates. The electricity also heated distillation devices which used evaporation to provide excellent drinking water. Near the kitchen opened a bathroom, comfortably laid out, with taps providing hot or cold water at will.

After the kitchen came the crew room, 16 feet long. But its door was closed* and I could not see how it was arranged, which might have told me how many people were required to operate the *Nautilus*.

At the end was a fourth watertight division separating the crew room from the machine room. A door opened, and I found myself in the chamber where Captain Nemo—certainly an engineer of the first order—had installed his machinery for locomotion.

The engine room was brightly lit, and more than 20 metres long. It was divided into two clear parts. The first contained the devices for producing the electricity, and the other, the mechanism for transmitting the movement to the propeller.

Right from the start I was surprised by the unique smell filling the room.

Captain Nemo noticed my reaction.

'There are a few gas emanations because sodium is being used; but they are only a slight inconvenience. In any case, we ventilate the ship in the open air every morning.'

While he was talking, I examined the machinery of the *Nautilus* with an interest easy to understand.

'You can see that I use Bunsen batteries rather than Ruhmkorff* ones. Ruhmkorff batteries would not produce the same power. Being massive and powerful, not so many Bunsen ones are needed, and I have discovered they are the preferable solution. The electricity produced moves to the rear, where, via huge electromagnets, it acts on a special system of levers and gears which transmit their motion to the propeller shaft. The diameter of the propeller is 6 metres with a total pitch of $7\frac{1}{2}$ metres, which can produce up to 120 revolutions per second.'*

'Giving . . .?'

'A speed of 50 knots.'*

There was still a mystery here, but I did not insist on trying to solve it. How could electricity possibly act with such power? Where did this almost unlimited force come from? Was it obtained from a new variety of coils of extremely high voltage? Could the transmission be increased indefinitely through an unknown system of levers?[1] This was what I could not understand.

'Captain Nemo, I note the results and will not attempt to explain them. I saw the *Nautilus* manœuvring near the *Abraham Lincoln*, and I know what sort of speed we're talking about. But that is not everything. You need to know where you're going! And you need to be able to move right or left, up or down. How do you reach the great depths, where you must encounter an increasing resistance amounting to hundreds of atmospheres? How do you come back up to the surface? And how do you stay in one particular spot? Or am I being indiscreet in asking all these questions?'

'Not at all, sir,' replied the captain after a moment's hesitation, 'since you will never leave this submarine. Come into the sitting-room. It is our real study and there you will learn all you wish to know about the *Nautilus*.'

13

A Few Figures

A MOMENT later, we were sitting on a divan in the drawing-room, smoking cigars. The captain showed me a blueprint containing the floor plan, section, and elevation of the *Nautilus*. Then he began his description as follows:

'The various dimensions of the ship you are in are as follows. It is an elongated cylinder with conical ends.* Its shape is quite close to that of a cigar, a design already adopted in London for several constructions of the same sort. The cylinder measures exactly 70 metres from end to end, and its beam is 8 metres at its widest point. It is not therefore constructed on an exact ratio of one to ten like your fast steamships, but its lines are sufficiently

---

[1] In fact there is talk at the moment of a discovery of this sort in which a new set of levers produces considerable force. So has its inventor met Captain Nemo?

long and its run extensive enough for the displaced water to escape easily and to provide no obstacle to headway.

'These two measurements will allow you to calculate the surface area and volume of the *Nautilus*. Its surface area is 1,011.45 m², its volume 1,500.2 m³*—which is the same as saying that, when completely submerged, it displaces 1,500 m³ or weighs 1,500 tons.

'When I drew up the plans of this ship designed for submarine navigation, I wanted it to be nine-tenths submerged when in equilibrium in the water, with only a tenth above the surface. In other words, it had to displace nine-tenths of its volume, or 1,356.48 m³, and so had to weigh 1,356.48 tons. This weight was to be the maximum when I constructed the ship to the above dimensions.

'The *Nautilus* has two hulls, one inside the other, joined by T-shaped bars which give it very great strength. Thanks to this cellular construction, it has the same resistance as if it were a solid block. Its plating cannot give; it holds together by virtue of its construction and not through the tightness of the rivets; and its unified construction, due to the perfect assembly of the materials, allows it to defy the most violent seas.

'The two hulls are constructed from steel plates with a density 7.8 times that of water. The first hull is no less than 5 cm thick, and weighs 394.96 tons. The keel alone, which is 50 cm high by 25 cm wide, weighs 62 tons; and the total weight of the keel, the second envelope, the engine, the ballast, the various fixtures and fittings, and the bulkheads and internal braces is 961.62 tons, which, when added to the 394.96, gives the required total of 1,356.48 tons.* Am I clear?'

'Perfectly,' I replied.

'So when the *Nautilus* is floating in these conditions, a tenth of it emerges from the water. Now if I have arranged tanks of a capacity equal to this one-tenth, in other words holding 150.72 tons, and if I fill the tanks with water, the boat will then weigh and consequently displace 1,507 tons, and will be completely submerged. And this is what happens in actual practice. The tanks are placed very near the sides in the lower part of the *Nautilus*. I open the taps, the tanks fill, and the boat sinks until it is just below the surface of the water.'

'Fine, captain, but now we are approaching the real difficulty. I understand how you can be just touching the surface of the ocean. But when it dives below the surface, isn't your submarine craft going to encounter a pressure and consequently an upwards impulse of 1 atmosphere for each 30 feet of water it goes down, or about 1 kg/cm^2?'

'Absolutely sir.'

'So unless you fill the *Nautilus* entirely, I do not see how you can make it go down into the depths.'

'Dr Aronnax,' replied Captain Nemo, 'one must not confuse statics with dynamics, for that can lead to serious errors. Very little effort is required to reach the lower levels of the ocean, for bodies have a tendency to sink. Please follow my reasoning.'

'I'm listening, captain.'

'When I wanted to determine the increase in weight that the *Nautilus* would require to dive, I only had to worry about the progressive reduction in volume that sea water experiences as it becomes deeper.'

'Clearly.'

'Now although water is not completely incompressible, it *is* very hard to compress. Indeed, according to the most recent calculations, the reduction is only 436/10,000,000ths per atmosphere of pressure, or for each 30 feet down. If I wish to go to a depth of 1,000 metres, I need to take into account the reduction of volume due to a pressure equivalent to a column of water 1,000 metres high, that is at a pressure of 100 atmospheres.* This reduction will then be 436/100,000ths. I must therefore increase the weight so as to weigh 1,513.77 tons instead of 1,507.2. The increase will consequently be only 6.57 tons.'

'Is that all?'

'Yes, Dr Aronnax, and the calculation can easily be checked. Now I have auxiliary tanks with a capacity of 100 tons. I can therefore descend to considerable depths. When I want to come back up to the surface and stay there, all I have to do is expel the water and empty all the tanks if I want the *Nautilus* to have a tenth of its total volume out of the water again.'

Given these figures, I had no objections to make against his reasoning:

'I accept your calculations, captain, and would look foolish to contest them, since experience proves them daily. But I am now faced with one real difficulty . . .'

'Which is, sir?'

'When you are at a depth of 1,000 metres, the hull of the *Nautius* undergoes a pressure of 100 atmospheres. If you wish at this moment to empty the auxiliary tanks so as to lighten your boat and head back up to the surface, the pumps will need to overcome a pressure of 100 atmospheres, i.e. $100 \, \text{kg/cm}^2$. Hence a power . . .'

'That only electricity can give,' interjected Captain Nemo. 'I repeat, sir, that the dynamic power of my machines is almost infinite. The pumps of the *Nautilus* have a prodigious strength, as you must have seen when their jets of water fell like a river on the *Abraham Lincoln*. In any case, I use the extra tanks only to reach depths of about 1,500 or 2,000 metres, in order to economize on my engines. When the desire takes me to visit the depths of the ocean, perhaps 2 or 3 leagues beneath the surface, I use methods that take longer but are just as reliable.'

'Namely, captain?'

'This leads me naturally to explain how I steer the *Nautilus*.'

'I'm impatient to hear.'

'To direct the ship to starboard or to port, that is to steer it in the horizontal plane, I use an ordinary rudder with a wide blade attached to the back of the stern post, operated by a wheel and tackle. But I can also make the *Nautilus* move in the vertical direction by means of two inclined planes attached to the vessel's sides opposite its centre of flotation. These planes can be moved into any position, and they are operated from inside by means of powerful levers. If the planes are kept parallel to the vessel, it will move horizontally. If they are inclined, then, depending on their angle and the thrust of the propeller, the *Nautilus* dives or climbs at an angle for as long as I wish. But if I want to come up to the surface more quickly, I engage the propeller and the pressure of the water makes the *Nautilus* rise like a balloon filled with hydrogen climbing rapidly through the air.'

'Bravo, captain!' I exclaimed. 'But how does the pilot follow the course through the waters that you wish him to?'

'The pilot is placed in an enclosure jutting out from the top of the hull of the *Nautilus*, and with windows in the shape of lenses.'

'Capable of resisting such pressures?'

'Yes. Although crystal is fragile when subjected to shock, it generally offers considerable resistance. In experiments involving fishing with electric lights carried out in the middle of the northern seas in 1864, plates of glass only 7 millimetres thick were able to withstand a pressure of 16 atmospheres, while at the same time allowing the rays to pass through to dissipate the heat. Now the glass I use is never less than 21 centimetres thick at its centre, that is 30 times as thick.'

'All right, Captain Nemo, but to be able to see in the first place, there must be light to dispel the darkness, and I wonder how in the midst of the dark waters . . .'

'Behind the pilot-house is a powerful electric reflector, whose beams can illuminate the sea for half a mile.'

'Oh congratulations, captain, heartiest congratulations! Now I understand the phosphorescence from the supposed narwhal which so intrigued scientists! And while on the subject, could you possibly tell me whether the collision between the *Nautilus* and the *Scotia*, which caused such a stir, was the result of an accident?'

'A pure accident, sir. I was sailing 2 metres below the surface when the shock occurred. I saw in any case that no serious damage had been done.'

'None, sir. But as for your encounter with the *Abraham Lincoln* . . .?'

'Dr Aronnax, I am sorry this had to happen to one of the best ships of the fine American Navy, but I was being attacked and I had to defend myself! I was content, all the same, with putting the frigate in such a condition that it could no longer do me any damage—it will not be difficult to repair its damage at the nearest port.'

'Ah captain,' I exclaimed with conviction, 'your *Nautilus* is truly a magnificent ship!'

'Yes sir,' responded Captain Nemo with genuine emotion, 'and I love it like the flesh of my flesh!* If everything seems dangerous for one of your ships subject to the hazards of the ocean, if the first impression when *on* the sea is that of feeling the abyss below one, as the Dutchman Jansen* has so well put it, on board the submerged *Nautilus*, man's heart need no longer fear. There is no change in the shape of the ship to worry about, for the double hull of this boat is as strong as anything; no rigging to be strained by the rolling and pitching; no sails for the wind to carry off; no boilers for the steam to tear to pieces; no danger of fire, for this vessel is made of metal, not wood; no coal to run out, for it is powered by electricity; no collision to be feared, since it is the only craft to navigate these deep waters; and no storms to endure, since it is a few metres below the surface and hence in absolute tranquillity! Yes, it is the ultimate ship! And if the engineer has clearly more confidence in his ship than its constructor, and the constructor more than the captain, you can understand with what entire confidence I entrusted myself to the *Nautilus*, since I am at one and the same time the captain, the constructor, and the engineer!'

Captain Nemo was speaking with a captivating eloquence. The fire in his eyes and the passion in his gestures transformed him. He loved his ship like a father loves his child!

But one question, perhaps indiscreet, instinctively occurred to me, and I could not resist asking it.

'Are you an engineer then, Captain Nemo?'

'I am. I studied in London, Paris, and New York when I was an inhabitant of the continents.'

'But how did you construct this superb *Nautilus* in secret?'

'Each of its components, Dr Aronnax, was sent to me from a different point on the globe via a forwarding address. Its keel was forged by Le Creusot, its propeller shaft by Penn and Co. of London, the iron plates for its hull by Laird's of Liverpool, and its propeller by Scott & Co. of Glasgow. Its tanks were constructed by Cail and Co. of Paris, its engine by Krupp of Prussia, its cutwater by the workshops at Motala in Sweden, its precision instruments by Hart Brothers of New York,* and so on; with each of the suppliers receiving my plans under a different name.'

'But', I countered, 'once these pieces had been made, they still had to be assembled and adjusted?'

'I set up my workshops on a small desert island in the middle of the ocean. There with my workmen, that is my good companions whom I instructed and trained, I completed our *Nautilus*. Then once the work was over, fire destroyed any trace of our presence on the island, which I would have blown up had I been able to.'

'So one can deduce that the cost of the ship was extremely high?'

'Dr Aronnax, an iron ship costs 1,125 francs per ton. Now the *Nautilus* displaces 1,500 tons. Its price is therefore 1,687,000 francs,* about two million if you include its fitting out, or four or five million with the works of art and other collections it contains.'

'One last question, Captain Nemo.'

'Go on.'

'You must be very well off then?'

'Infinitely sir, and without undue difficulty I could pay off the ten billion francs of France's debts!'*

I stared at the bizarre person speaking to me in such a way. Was he insulting my credulity? Only time would tell.

14

The Black River

THE area of the terrestrial globe covered by water is estimated to be 383,255,800 square kilometres, or more than 38 million hectares.* This liquid mass occupies 2,250 million cubic miles and would form a sphere of sixty leagues in diameter, whose weight would be three quintillion tons. To understand this last number, it should be pointed out that a quintillion is to a billion as a billion is to one, i.e. a quintillion is a billion billion. This mass is approximately equivalent to the water that all the rivers on Earth would produce over 40,000 years.

During former geological eras, the period of fire was followed by the period of water. At first there was nothing but ocean. Then, in the Silurian Period, mountain tops began to appear, islands emerged and disappeared again under partial floods, surfaced again, then connected together and formed landmasses; and finally the land settled down in the geographical locations we are familiar with. The solid conquered 37,000,657 square miles from the liquid, that is 12,916,000,000 hectares.

The positions of the continents allow the water to be divided into five main areas: the Arctic, the Antarctic, the Indian, the Atlantic, and the Pacific Oceans.

The Pacific extends from north to south between the two polar circles, and west to east between Asia and America, over a distance of 145 degrees of longitude. It is the most tranquil of seas; its currents are broad and slow, its tides minimal, its rainfall abundant. Such was the ocean that destiny called me to travel over first in the strangest of circumstances.

'Sir,' Captain Nemo said to me, 'if you wish, we can determine our exact position and thus the starting-point of our voyage. It is a quarter to twelve. I am going to return to the surface.'

The captain rang an electric bell three times. The pumps began to expel water from the tanks; the needle of the pressure-gauge showed the changing pressure and hence the upward movement of the *Nautilus*, but then stopped.

'We're there,' said the captain.

I headed for the central staircase leading to the platform. I went up the metal steps, through the open hatch, and out on to the upper part of the *Nautilus*.

The platform was only 80 centimetres above the water. The bow and stern of the *Nautilus* were spindle-shaped, making it resemble a long cigar. I noticed that its metal plates overlapped slightly,* like the scales which cover the bodies of great land reptiles. I therefore perfectly understood how this boat had invariably been taken for a marine animal, in spite of the best telescopes.

At about the middle of the platform, the ship's boat formed a bulge where it was half recessed in the hull of the ship. Fore and aft were two structures with angled walls, of moderate height, partly covered by thick glass lenses: one of them was for the pilot who steered the *Nautilus*, the other for the powerful electric light to illuminate the route.

The sea was magnificent, the sky clear. The long vessel was hardly affected by the broad undulations of the ocean. A light easterly breeze ruffled the surface of the water. The horizon, free of mist, allowed for perfect observation.

There was nothing in sight. Not a reef, not the tiniest of islands. The *Abraham Lincoln* had disappeared. An immense desert.

Captain Nemo, equipped with his sextant, was about to measure the altitude of the sun in order to calculate the latitude. He waited a while for the sun to move and touch the edge of the apparent horizon in his sextant. While he watched not one of his muscles moved, and the instrument would not have been steadier in a hand of marble.

'Twelve noon,' he said. 'Dr Aronnax, whenever you wish . . .?'

I looked for the last time over the slightly yellowish seas off the Japanese coast, and went back down to the drawing-room.

There the captain calculated his position by comparing the chronometer with the longitude and checking it against his previous observations of the hour angles. Then he said to me:

'Dr Aronnax, we are at 137° 15′ W . . .'

'Of which meridian?' I asked quickly, hoping that the captain's reply might indicate his nationality.

'I have various chronometers, set respectively to the Paris, Greenwich, and Washington meridians. But, in your honour, I will use the Paris one.'

This reply taught me nothing. I bowed, and the captain continued:

'Longitude 37° 15′* west of the Paris meridian, and latitude 30° 7′ N, that is about 300 miles from the coast of Japan. Today is 8 November, it is twelve o'clock, and our voyage of underwater exploration begins at this precise moment.'

'May God protect us!'

'And now, Dr Aronnax,' added the captain, 'I will leave you to your studies. I have set an east-north-easterly course at 50 metres' depth. Here are large-scale maps where you can follow our movements. The salon is at your disposal, and with your permission I will now retire.'

Captain Nemo bowed to me. I remained alone, absorbed in my thoughts. They all focused on the master of the *Nautilus*. Would I ever know to what nation this strange man belonged, that boasted of belonging to none? Who had produced the hatred he had sworn for the whole of humanity, the hatred which might perhaps seek a terrible vengeance? Was he one of those unrecognized scientists, one of those geniuses 'who had been hurt' to use Conseil's expression, a modern Galileo;* or was he one of those scientists like the American Maury,* whose career was ruined by a political revolution? I could not yet say. He had received me coolly but courteously, as a person thrown by chance on board his ship, as a person whose life he held in his hands. The only thing was that he had not taken the hand I had held out to him. He had not offered me his.

For a whole hour I remained plunged in these reflections, seeking to pierce the mystery which so intrigued me. Then my eye fell on the vast planisphere spread out over the table, and I placed my finger on the precise point of intersection of our observed lines of longitude and latitude.

The sea has rivers like the continents. These are distinctive currents, recognizable by their temperature and colour; the most remarkable one being known as the Gulf Stream. Science has determined the direction of five main currents on the globe: one in the North and one in the South Atlantic, one in the North and one in the South Pacific, and a fifth in the southern Indian Ocean. It is even probable that a sixth current used to exist in the northern Indian Ocean, when the Caspian and Aral Seas were connected to the great lakes of Asia and formed a single expanse of water.

Now, one of the currents flowed past the point on the planisphere where we were: the Kuro-Scivo of the Japanese, the Black River, which leaves the Bay of Bengal* where it is heated by the vertical rays of the tropical sun, then traverses the Strait of Malacca, works its way up the coast of Asia and round to the North Pacific as far as the Aleutian Islands. It carries with it trunks of camphor trees and other indigenous products, and the pure indigo of its warm water contrasts with the ocean waves. It was this current that the *Nautilus* was going to cross. I followed it with my regard until I saw it vanish in the immensity of the Pacific, and I could feel myself being carried along with it, when Ned Land and Conseil appeared at the door of the sitting-room.

My two good companions stood as if turned to stone at the marvels displayed before their eyes.

'Where are we?' the Canadian kept exclaiming. 'In the Québec Museum?'

'If monsieur pleases', replied Conseil, 'it looks more like the Hôtel du Sommerard!'*

'My friends,' I replied, motioning them to come in, 'you are neither in Canada nor in France, but on board the *Nautilus*, 50 metres below sea-level.'

'If monsieur says so, it must be true,' replied Conseil, 'but to be frank, this room is enough to astonish even a Fleming like me.'

'Be astonished, my friend, and look, since there is work to be done by a classifier of your skill.'

I had no need to encourage Conseil. The good fellow, leaning over the display cases, was already murmuring words in the naturalists' language: class of Gastropods, family Buccinidae, genus cowrie, species *Cypraea madagascariensis*, etc.

During this time Land, who was not much of a conchologist, was asking about my discussion with Captain Nemo. Had I found out who he was, where he was from, where he was going, how deep he was going to take us—in sum, a thousand questions which I had no time to reply to.

I told him what I knew, or rather everything I did not know, and asked in turn what he had seen or heard.

'Seen nothing, heard nothing! I haven't even seen the crew of this boat. Are they also electric, do you think?'

'Electric?'

'You would certainly think so. But Dr Aronnax,' asked Ned, who tended to follow a single line of thought, 'can't you tell me how many men there are on board? Ten, twenty, fifty, or a hundred?'

'I cannot say, Master Land. In any case believe me, give up for the moment any idea of taking over the *Nautilus* and escaping. This boat is a masterpiece of modern technology, and I would regret not seeing it! Many people would willingly accept the situation we are now in, if only in order to stroll through its wonders. So please remain calm, and try to observe what is going on around us.'

'Observe!' exclaimed the harpooner. 'But we can't see anything, we will never see anything out of this metal prison! We are moving and sailing blind . . .'

Just as Ned Land pronounced these last words, it suddenly went dark, completely and utterly dark. The luminous ceiling went out so quickly that my eyes were hurt by the change, just as if the opposite had happened and it had gone from complete darkness to bright light.

We remained silent and motionless, not knowing what surprise was in store for us, whether pleasant or unpleasant. We heard a sliding sound. It sounded as though the panels on the side of the *Nautilus* were being opened or closed.

'This is the end!' said Ned Land.

'Order of the hydromedusas!' murmured Conseil.

But suddenly light appeared on both sides of the salon, coming in through two oval-shaped openings. The water was now brightly lit by the electric current. Two crystal panes separated us from the sea. I trembled at first at the thought that these fragile partitions might break, but strong copper frames reinforced them, giving them almost infinite resistance.

The sea was distinctly visible over a radius of a mile around the *Nautilus*. And what a sight! What pen could ever describe it? Who could ever depict the effects of the light on those transparent mantles, the gradualness of its progressive fading away into the upper and lower regions of the ocean!

The diaphanous quality of the sea is celebrated. It is known to be clearer than fresh water, for the mineral and organic substances it holds in suspension in fact increase its transparency. In certain parts of the West Indies, the sandy sea-bed can be seen with surprising clearness through 145 metres of water. The penetration of the sunlight seems to reach as much as 300 metres' depth. But in the environment the *Nautilus* was moving in, the electric brilliance was produced within the heart of the sea itself. It was no longer illuminated water, but liquid light.

If we accept the hypothesis of Ehrenberg,* who believes that the submarine depths are illuminated by phosphorescence, nature has certainly reserved one of her most spectacular sights for the inhabitants of the sea, as I could now judge from the thousand effects of the light. On each side I had a window on the unexplored abysses. The darkness in the salon made the light outside seem all the brighter, and we watched as if this pure crystal were the window of some enormous aquarium.

The *Nautilus* seemed to be motionless. The reason was that there is no point of reference. Sometimes, however, the lines of water, cut by its prow, shot past our eyes at tremendous speed.

In a state of wonder, we propped ourselves up before the display windows. None of us had yet broken our stupefied silence, when Conseil said:

'You wanted to see, friend Ned, well now you *can* see!'

'Amazing, amazing!' said the Canadian, who had become irresistibly engrossed and forgotten all about his anger and ideas of escape. 'You'd go a long way to see such a fanatastic sight!'

'Ah!' I exclaimed. 'Now I understand this man! He has built a world of his own which reveals its most astonishing marvels to him alone!'

'But where are all the fish?' asked the Canadian. 'I do not see any!'

'Why should you worry, dear Ned,' replied Conseil, 'since you do not know anything about them?'

'Me? But I'm a fisherman!'

And a discussion ensued between the two friends, for they both knew about fish, but each in a very different way.

As is well known, fish form the fourth and last class of the primary division of vertebrates. They have quite correctly been defined as 'vertebrates with double circulation, coldblooded, breathing through gills and designed for life in the water'. There are two distinct series: bony fish, whose spinal columns are made up of bony vertebrae, and cartilaginous fish, with spines made of cartilaginous vertebrae.

The Canadian was perhaps aware of this distinction, but Conseil knew more about it, and now that he had made friends with Ned, he could not admit that he was any less knowledgeable than him. So he said:

'Friend Ned, you are a killer of fish, a highly skilled fisherman. You have caught a large number of these fascinating animals, but I bet that you do not know how they are classified.'

'Yes I do,' replied the harpooner seriously. 'They are classified as fish that can be eaten and fish that can't!'

'That is a glutton's distinction,' responded Conseil. 'But tell me whether you know the difference between bony fish and cartilaginous fish?'

'Perhaps I do, Conseil.'

'And the subdivisions of the two main classes?'

'No idea,' said the Canadian.

'Well! friend Ned, listen and remember! The bony fish are divided into six orders. Primo, the acanthopterygians, whose upper jaw is complete and movable, and whose gills have the form of combs. This order contains 15 families, or three-quarters of all known fish. Type: the common perch.'

'Quite tasty,' replied Ned.

'Secundo,' continued Conseil, 'the abdominals, which have ventral fins under the abdomen and behind the pectorals but not attached to the shoulder bones—an order which contains the majority of freshwater fish. Types: the carp and the pike.'

'Pouah!' exclaimed the Canadian with some disdain. 'Freshwater fish!'

'Tertio,' said Conseil, 'the subbrachials, whose ventral fins are attached below the pectorals and directly hanging from the shoulder bones. This order contains four families. Types: plies, dabs, turbots, brills, soles, etc.'

'Excellent, excellent!' exclaimed the harpooner, who only liked to consider fish from the edible point of view.

'Quarto,' resumed Conseil, not at all put out, 'the apodals with elongated bodies, absence of ventral fins, and a thick and frequently sticky skin—an order which consists of only one family. Types: the eel and the electric eel.'

'Pathetic, pathetic!'

'Quinto, the lophobranchiates, which have complete and free jaws, but whose gills are formed of small crests arranged in pairs along the branchial arches. This order consists of only one family. Types: the seahorses and the pegasus dragons.'

'Rubbish, rubbish!'

'Sexto and finally,' said Conseil, 'the plectognaths, whose jawbone is attached firmly to the side of the intermaxillary forming the jaw, and whose palatine arch meshes with the cranium by means of sutures, thus rendering it immobile—an order which does not have genuine ventral fins and which is made up of two families. Types: the tetrodons and the sunfish.'

'Not worth spoiling the pot with!'

'Do you understand, friend Ned?'

'Not a single word. But carry on, it's all very interesting.'

'As for the cartilaginous fishes,' Conseil continued imperturbably, 'they only contain three orders.'

'So much the better.'

'Primo, the cyclostomes, whose jaws are welded into a movable ring, and whose gills lead to numerous openings—an order consisting of only one family. Type: the lamprey.'

'An acquired taste.'

'Secundo, the Selachii, with gills similar to those of the cyclostomes, but whose lower jaw is movable. This order, the biggest in the class, comprises two families. Types: the ray and the sharks.'

'What?' exclaimed Ned. 'Rays and sharks in the same order? Well, my friend, in the rays' interests, I don't recommend that you put them in the same receptacle together!'

'Tertio, the sturionians, whose gills, as is normal, open into a single slit adorned with gill covers—an order which contains four genera. Type: the sturgeon.'

'Ah, good Conseil, you've kept the best for the end—in my view anyway. And is that it?'

'Yes, my good Ned; and notice that when one knows all this, one still knows nothing, for families are subdivided into genera, sub-genera, species, varieties . . .'

'Well, my friend,' said the harpooner, leaning on the glass panel, 'we've certainly got lots of varieties passing.'

'Yes, so many fish! One would think one was in an aquarium!'

'Hardly,' I said, 'for an aquarium is just a cage, and these fish are as free as the birds in the air.'

'Well my good Conseil, name them, go on, name them!' said Land.

'I am unable to! That's my master's department.'

And indeed the worthy boy, although a fanatical classifier, was not a naturalist, and I do not know whether he could have distinguished a tuna from a bonito. He was, in short, the opposite of the Canadian, who named all fish without hesitating.

'A triggerfish,' I said.

'And a Chinese triggerfish,' responded Ned Land.

'Genus *Balistes*, family of Sclerodermi, order of plectognaths,' murmured Conseil.

Decidedly, Ned and Conseil would have made a brilliant naturalist between the two of them.

The Canadian was not mistaken. A school of triggerfish, with compact bodies and coarse-grained skin and armed with stings on their dorsal fins, were playing around the *Nautilus* while moving the four rows of spines that bristle on either side of their tails. Nothing could be more attractive than their skins, grey on top and white underneath with golden patches scintillating in the dark undertow of the waves. Amongst them some rays undulated, like tablecloths flapping in the wind, and I noticed to my great joy that they included the Chinese ray, yellowish on its upper part, a delicate pink on its stomach, and with three stings behind its eyes; a rare species, and even uncertain in Lacépède's time, who saw it only in Japanese sketches.

For two hours, a whole army of aquatic creatures escorted the *Nautilus*. During their games and their leaps, while they competed in beauty, colourfulness, and speed, I distinguished the green labrum, the Barbary mullet marked with two black stripes, the elytrous goby with rounded caudal fins, which is white with violet blotches on its back, the Japanese scombroid, the admirable mackerel of these seas, with a blue body and silver head, and brilliant azuries whose very name renders otiose any description, striped sparids picked out with black stripes on their caudal fins, zonifer sparids elegantly corseted in their six belts, *Aulostomi*, genuine snipefish or oystercatchers some of which reached one metre, Japanese newts, *Echidnae muraenae*, six-foot long serpents with small bright eyes and huge mouths bristling with teeth, and so on.

Our admiration was still at its peak. Our exclamations continued. Ned named the fish while Conseil classified them. I was in ecstasy at the brilliance of their appearance and the beauty of their forms. I had never before had the chance to observe living animals that could move around freely in their natural element.

I will not cite all the varieties that passed before our dazzled eyes, a whole collection from the seas of Japan and China.* These fish rushed up, more numerous than the birds in the air, undoubtedly drawn by the source of dazzling electric light.

Suddenly the light came on in the drawing-room. The metal panels closed again. The enchanting vision disappeared. But I continued to dream for a long time, until my eyes fell on the instruments hanging on the walls. The compass showed the direction as still north-north-east, the pressure-gauge read 5 atmospheres, corresponding to a depth of 50 metres, and the electric log gave a speed of 15 knots.

I expected to see Captain Nemo. But he didn't appear. The clock showed five p.m.

Ned and Conseil returned to their cabin. I went back to my room as well. My dinner was already there. It consisted of turtle soup made of the most delicate hawksbills, a red mullet with slightly flaky white flesh, whose separately prepared liver made a delicious dish, and fillets of emperor fish, whose flavour seemed better to me than salmon.

I spent the evening reading, writing, and thinking. Then, with my eyelids closing, I stretched out on my sea-wrack bed and fell into a deep sleep, while the *Nautilus* slid through the rapid current of the Black River.

15

A Written Invitation

THE following day, 9 November, I woke up after a sleep of twelve hours. Conseil came in as usual to find out 'how monsieur had slept' and to offer his services. He had left his friend the Canadian sleeping like a man who had never done anything else.

I let the good fellow chatter on as he wished, without bothering to reply much to him. I was preoccupied with Captain Nemo's absence during our viewing session the evening before, and I hoped to be able to see him again today.

Soon I had put on my byssus clothes. Once or twice Conseil commented on this material. I told him that it was made from the glossy silky threads which attach fan mussels to the rocks, these being a variety of shell very plentiful on the Mediterranean shores. It was formerly used to make fine materials like stockings and gloves, for it is very soft and warm. The crew of the *Nautilus* could therefore clothe themselves economically without needing cotton plants, sheep, or silkworms from the dry land.

Once dressed I went into the salon. It was deserted.

I plunged into studying the treasures of conchology assembled in the display cabinets. I also moved through vast herbariums filled with the rarest marine plants, maintaining their admirable colours, despite being dried. Among these precious hydrophytes, I noticed whorled *Cladostephi*, peacock's tails, caulerpas with vine leaves, graniferous *Callithamna*, delicate ceramiums in scarlet hues, fan-shaped agars, acetabulums like the caps of very low mushrooms, classified for a long time among the zoophytes, and finally a whole series of kelps.

The whole day went by without the honour of a visit from Captain Nemo. The panels of the salon did not open. Perhaps we were not meant to become too blasé about these beautiful things.

The direction of the *Nautilus* stayed at east-north-east, its speed 12 knots, its depth between 50 and 60 metres.

The following day, 10 November, the same abandonment, the same solitude. I saw nobody from the crew. Ned and Conseil spent most of the day with me. They too were astonished by the captain's baffling absence. Was the strange man ill? Was he planning to change his plans for us?

In any case, as Conseil pointed out, we enjoyed total freedom. We were exquisitely and copiously fed. Our host kept his side of the bargain. We had no grounds for complaint, and in any case the strangeness of our situation provided us with such superb compensation that we did not yet have the right to criticize it.

It was on that day that I began my diary of our adventures, which has allowed me to recount them with the most scrupulous accuracy; as a curious detail, I wrote my diary on paper made from sea-wrack.

Early on the morning of 11 November the fresh air coursing through the *Nautilus* told me that we had gone back up to the surface of the ocean to replenish our supply of oxygen. I headed for the central ladder, and climbed up to the platform.

It was six o'clock. I found the sky overcast, the sea grey but calm. Hardly any swell. Would Captain Nemo come? I was hoping to meet him here. But I found only the pilot, enclosed in his glass dome. Sitting on the bulge caused by the dinghy's hull, I breathed in the salty breeze with great pleasure.

Little by little, the mist dissipated due to the effect of the sun. The sun itself came up over the eastern horizon. The sea caught fire under its regard like a trail of powder. The clouds, scattered over the heights, took on all sorts of bright colours, with subtle shades and lots of 'mares' tails'[1] promising wind for the whole day.

But what difference did the wind make to the *Nautilus*, undaunted by storms?

I was admiring the cheerful sunrise, so joyful and so vivifying, when I heard somebody else climbing up to the platform.

I was getting ready to greet Captain Nemo, but it was his first officer who appeared—I had already seen him on the captain's first visit. He came forward on the platform, but did not seem to notice my presence. His powerful telescope at his eye, he studied every point of the horizon with extreme care. Then, having completed his examination, he went up to the hatch and pronounced the sentence containing the following words. I can remember it, as it was repeated every morning in identical circumstances. It went:

'Nautron respoc lorni virch.'*

What it meant, I could not say.

Having pronounced these words, the first officer went below again. I imagined that the *Nautilus* was going to continue its underwater navigation. So I went back down the hatch, along the gangway, and back to my room.

Five days went by like this, without the situation changing. Each morning I went up on the platform. The same phrase was pronounced by the same individual. Captain Nemo did not appear.

I had concluded that I would never see him again, when, on 16 November, going back into my room with Ned and Conseil, I found a note addressed to me on the table.

I opened it impatiently. It was written in clear bold handwriting, a little Gothic-looking and reminiscent of German writing.

The letter was couched in these terms:

---

[1] Small white clouds, light and with serrated edges.

16 November 1867

Dr Aronnax
On board the *Nautilus*

Captain Nemo invites Dr Aronnax on a hunting party which will visit his forests of Crespo Island tomorrow morning. He hopes that nothing will prevent Dr Aronnax from attending, and he would be pleased if his companions could join him.

Captain Nemo
Commander of the *Nautilus*

'Hunting!' exclaimed Ned.

'In the forests of Crespo Island!' added Conseil.

'So that individual does visit land sometimes?' enquired Ned Land.

'That seems clearly stated,' I said rereading the letter.

'Well we've got to accept,' answered the Canadian. 'Once on dry land, we can decide what to do. In any case, I wouldn't say no to a few hunks of fresh venison.'

Without trying to make sense of the discrepancy between Captain Nemo's manifest horror for landmasses and islands and his invitation to go hunting in forests, I merely replied:

'Let's see first of all what Crespo Island is.'

I consulted the planisphere, and at latitude 32° 40′ N and longitude 167° 50′ W I found a tiny island charted by Captain Crespo in 1801, that the old Spanish maps called Roca de la Plata,* meaning 'Silver Rock'. We were therefore about 1,800 miles from where we had started, and the *Nautilus* had changed direction somewhat and was now heading south-east.

I showed my companions the little rock lost in the middle of the Northern Pacific.

'If Captain Nemo sometimes goes ashore,' I said, 'at least he chooses islands which are utterly deserted.'

Land nodded without replying, and Conseil and he left the room. After supper, served to me by a silent and impassive steward, I went to bed, not without a slight feeling of worry.

When I woke up the following day, 17 November, I realized that the *Nautilus* was not moving at all. I quickly got dressed and went into the salon.

Captain Nemo was there. He had been waiting for me, and got

up, greeted me, and asked if it would be agreeable for me to accompany him.

As he made no reference to his absence over the last week, I did not mention it, and simply replied that my companions and I were ready to accompany him.

'But', I added, 'I will take the liberty of asking you one question.'

'Ask, Dr Aronnax, and if I can answer it, I will.'

'Well, captain, how does it happen that you own forests on Crespo Island, you who have broken all contact with the earth?'

'Sir, the forests I own need neither light nor heat from the sun. No lions, tigers, panthers, nor any other quadrupeds live there. I am the only person to know them. They grow for me alone. They are not terrestrial forests, but underwater ones.'

'Underwater ones!' I exclaimed.

'Yes, Dr Aronnax.'

'And you're offering to take me there?'

'Precisely.'

'On foot?'

'Yes, and without even getting our feet wet.'

'Whilst hunting?'

'Whilst hunting.'

'With guns in our hands?'

'With guns in our hands.'

I looked at the captain of the *Nautilus* with an expression that was not at all flattering for him.

'His brain must have gone,' I thought. 'He has had a fit which has lasted a week, and which is still continuing. What a pity! I liked him better when he was just strange rather than insane!'

This thought could clearly be read on my face, but Captain Nemo merely invited me to follow him, which I did like a man resigned to anything.

We arrived in the dining-room, where breakfast was already served.

'Dr Aronnax, please be so good as to share my breakfast without further formality. We can talk while we eat. I promised you a walk in a forest, but I did not promise to take you to a restaurant. So please eat your breakfast knowing that your dinner will probably be very late.'

I did justice to the meal. It was made up of various fishes and slices of sea slug, which is an excellent zoophyte, accompanied by very appetizing seaweeds such as *Porphyra laciniata* and *Laurencia pinnatifida*. We had perfectly clear water to drink, to which, following the captain, I added a few drops of an alcoholic beverage extracted from the seaweed known as waterleaf, as is customary in Kamchatka.

At first Captain Nemo ate without a word. Then he said:

'When I suggested that you accompany me to the forests of Crespo, you thought I was contradicting myself. When I informed you that they were underwater forests, you thought I was mad. Sir, you should never judge men too quickly.'

'But, captain, I assure you . . .'

'Please listen to me, and you will see if you should accuse me of madness or inconsistency.'

'I'm listening.'

'Sir, you know as well as I do that man can live underwater provided he takes with him a supply of air for breathing. While operating underwater, the workman wears watertight clothing and his head is enclosed in a metal capsule which receives air from the outside by means of force pumps and inflow valves.'

'Frogmen's suits.'

'Indeed, but in such conditions man is not free. He is tied to the pump which gives him the air through a rubber tube, a real chain riveting him to the land; and if we were bound to the *Nautilus* in such a way we would not go very far.'

'But how can one be free of this restriction?'

'By using the Rouquayrol–Denayrouze apparatus,* first developed by two of your compatriots, and which I have improved for my own use: it will allow you to try out new physiological conditions without your organs suffering in any way. It is comprised of a tank made of thick metal in which I store air at a pressure of 50 atmospheres. The tank is fastened to one's back by means of straps, like a soldier's haversack. Its upper section is an enclosure where air is kept in by a one-way mechanism, and can escape only at normal pressure. In the Rouquayrol apparatus, as normally used, two rubber pipes emerge from the container and lead to a type of round mouthpiece enclosing the user's mouth and nose; one pipe is used as an inlet for the air for breathing, the other for the escape of the used air, with one's tongue moving between the two tubes as one breathes in and out. But since I undergo considerable pressure at the bottom of the sea, I have had to enclose my head in a copper sphere, like those of frogmen's suits, with the tubes for breathing in and out leading to this sphere.'

'Fine, Captain Nemo, but the air you take with you must get used up quickly and as soon as the oxygen goes below 15 per cent, it becomes unbreathable.'

'Correct, Dr Aronnax. But as I mentioned, the *Nautilus*'s pumps allow me to store it at considerable pressure and so the tank can provide breathable air for up to nine or ten hours.'

'I have no more objections. I will simply ask you, captain: how do you manage to light your way on the ocean floor?'

'With the Ruhmkorff apparatus,* Dr Aronnax. Whereas the first apparatus is carried on one's back, this one is carried on the belt. It has a Bunsen battery which I activate, not containing potassium bichromate but sodium. An induction coil absorbs the electricity produced and directs it to a lantern of a special kind. In this lantern is a glass coil which contains a slight trace of carbon dioxide. When the apparatus is operating, the gas is luminous, providing a continuous white light. Thus equipped, I can breathe and I can see.'

'Captain Nemo, to all my objections you make such over-whelming replies that I no longer dare to doubt. However, although forced to accept the Rouquayrol and Ruhmkorff apparatuses, I must reserve my position regarding the rifle you are going to give me.'

'But the rifle does not work with powder,' said the captain.

'So it is an air gun?'

'Yes. How do you think I can manufacture powder on board my ship, since I have neither saltpetre, nor sulphur, nor charcoal?'

'But in any case,' I persisted, 'in order to be able to fire it under-water, in a medium 855 times as dense as air, you need to over-come considerable resistance.'

'That is no problem. There exist certain guns, following Fulton's design and improved by the Britons Phipps Coles and Burney, the

Frenchman Furcy, and the Italian Landi,* which are equipped with a special closing device and so can fire underwater. But I repeat: not having access to powder, I substituted compressed air, abundantly available from the *Nautilus*'s pumps.'

'But the air must get used up quickly?'

'Yes, but do I not have my Rouquayrol tank which can provide more as needed? All that is required is a suitable tap. In any case, Dr Aronnax, you will see for yourself that one does not use much air or ammunition in underwater hunting.'

'Nevertheless, in semi-darkness, immersed in this liquid which is much denser than air, shots can surely not carry very far and can rarely be fatal?'

'On the contrary sir. With this gun every shot is lethal: as soon as an animal is hit, however slightly, it falls down as if struck by lightning.'

'But I don't understand!'

'Because this gun does not fire ordinary bullets but small glass capsules, invented by the Austrian chemist Leniebroek,* and of which I have considerable supplies. These glass capsules, covered with steel casing and weighted with a lead ball, are exactly like miniature Leyden jars,* into which electricity has been forced at a very high voltage. They discharge at the slightest impact, and however powerful the animal, it falls down dead. I will add that these capsules are just .4 calibre, and that a fully loaded gun can contain up to ten.'

'I have no more objections,' I replied getting up from the table, 'and all I can do is take my rifle. Wherever you go, I will follow.'

Captain Nemo took me towards the stern of the *Nautilus*, and as I passed Ned and Conseil's cabin, I called to my two companions who immediately came and joined us.

We arrived at a compartment situated on the flank near the engine-room. This was where we were to put on our excursion clothing.

16

An Excursion over the Plains

THIS compartment was both the arsenal and the cloakroom of the *Nautilus*. A dozen frogmen's suits were hanging on the walls, ready for the excursionists.

When he saw them, Ned was visibly reluctant to put one on.

'But my good Ned,' I told him, 'the forests of Crespo Island are actually underwater forests!'

'Oh!' said the disappointed harpooner as his dreams of fresh meat vanished. 'What about you, Dr Aronnax, are you going to put one of those contraptions on?'

'We need to, Master Ned.'

'You can do as you wish, sir,' replied the harpooner, shrugging his shoulders. 'But I'm not going to put one on unless I'm forced to.'

'Nobody is forcing you Master Ned,' said Captain Nemo.

'And is Conseil going to take the risk?' enquired Ned.

'I follow wherever monsieur goes.'

At a sign from the captain, two of the crewmen came and helped us put on the heavy watertight suits, made of seamless rubber and designed to withstand considerable pressure. They were like coats of armour that were both elastic and strong. Each suit consisted of trousers and a jacket. The trousers ended in thick boots with heavy lead soles. The material of the jacket was kept in position by strips of copper which shielded the chest and so protected it from the water pressure, allowing the lungs to work freely; its sleeves finished in supple gloves which allowed one's hands free movement.

It will be seen that these much improved frogmen's suits were a far cry from the items of shapeless clothing invented and extolled in the eighteenth century, like the cork breastplates, the life-vests, the sea clothing, the buoys, etc.

Captain Nemo, one of his companions—a Hercules, who looked stupendously strong—Conseil, and I had soon put on our frogmen's suits. All we had to do now was to put the metallic spheres on our heads. But before doing this, I asked the captain if I could examine the rifles we would be using.

One of the *Nautilus*'s crewmen gave me a simple rifle with a relatively large butt made of hollowed-out steel plate. The butt served as a tank for the compressed air: a valve, operated by a trigger, allowed the air to escape into the metal tube. A container for the projectiles, hollowed out in the butt, held about 20 electric bullets* which a spring automatically placed in the barrel of the gun. As soon as one shot had been fired, another was ready to go off.

'Captain Nemo, this weapon is perfect and easy to use. Now all I want is to try it out. But how are we going to get to the ocean floor?'

'Dr Aronnax, the *Nautilus* is already resting on the bottom, 10 metres deep, and all we have to do is leave.'

'But how are we going to get out?'

'You will soon see.'

Captain Nemo put his head into his spherical helmet. Conseil and I did likewise, not before the Canadian had given us an ironical 'good hunting!' The top of our clothing had a collar of copper, incorporating a thread on to which the metal helmet could be screwed. Three holes, covered with thick glass, meant we could see in any direction merely by turning our heads inside the spheres. The Rouquayrol apparatuses began to work as soon as they had been placed on our backs, and I was able to breathe quite easily. With a Ruhmkorff lamp attached to my belt and a gun in hand, I was ready to leave. But to be honest, imprisoned in the heavy clothing and nailed to the deck by my lead soles, I wouldn't have been able to take a single step.

But this difficulty had been foreseen, for I could feel myself being propelled into a small room next to the cloakroom. My companions, similarly transported, followed behind. I heard a door fitted with seals closing behind us, and then we were in complete darkness.

After a few moments, a loud hissing sound reached my ears. A cold sensation started rising from my feet to my chest. Using a tap inside the ship, water had obviously been let in from the outside and was now completely filling the room. A second door then opened in the side of the *Nautilus*. A faint light came through. A few moments later our feet were treading the ocean floor.

And now, how can I possibly record the impression made on me by this excursion under the waters? Words are inadequate to recount such marvels! When even the artist's brush is incapable of depicting the unique effects of the liquid element, how could a pen begin to portray them?

Captain Nemo was walking ahead, his companion following a few steps behind us. Conseil and I stayed close together, as if we could talk through our metal shells. I no longer felt the weight of my clothing, my shoes, my air tank, nor the weight of the thick sphere in which my head was shaken around like an almond in its shell. All these objects, surrounded by water, lost a weight equal to the liquid displaced, and I felt very comfortable, thanks to the physical law discovered by Archimedes. I was no longer an inert object but could move quite freely.

The light astonished me with its penetration, for it lit up the ground as far as 30 feet below the surface. The sunlight traversed the aqueous substance easily but its colours dissipated. I could clearly see objects 100 metres away. Beyond that, the depths were tinted in fine shades of ultramarine, becoming bluer in the distance and fading into a sort of nebulous darkness. The water surrounding me was really a sort of air, denser than the terrestrial atmosphere but almost as clear. I could see the calm surface of the sea above my head.

We were walking over fine smooth sand, not rippled like beaches that retain the waves' imprint. This dazzling carpet reflected the sunlight with surprising intensity, almost like a mirror. Hence a widespread dazzle that filled the liquid molecules. Will I be believed if I say that at a depth of 30 feet, I could see as clearly as in the open air?

For a quarter of an hour, I walked over the glowing sand strewn with the impalpable dust of shells. Although the hull of the *Nautilus*, silhouetted like a long shoal, slowly disappeared, when night fell in the depth of the waters, its searchlight would help us find our way back on board, sending out its rays with perfect brilliance. This will be difficult to understand for anyone who has only seen those whitish and clear-cut beams on land. There the dust saturating the air gives the rays the appearance of a luminous mist; but on the sea's surface, and under it, the electric shafts are transmitted with incomparable purity.

We were proceeding over a sandy plain which seemed so vast as to be limitless. I was using my hands to push aside the liquid curtains which then closed up again behind me, and my footprints were being immediately erased by the pressure of the water.

Soon I could make out the shapes of a few objects, scarcely delineated in the distance. I observed a magnificent foreground of rocks, carpeted with the finest zoophytes, and I was immediately struck by an effect particular to this environment.

It was then ten in the morning. The sun's rays struck the surface of the waves at an oblique angle, and the light was decomposed by the refraction as if passing through a prism. It fell on the flowers, rocks, plantlets, shells, and polyps, and shaded their edges with all the colours of the solar spectrum. It was a marvel, a feast for the eyes, this interweaving of coloured tones, a true kaleidoscope of green, yellow, orange, violet, indigo, and blue, the complete contents of a crazy colourist's palette! Oh, why could I not tell Conseil the vivid sensations inebriating my brain and compete with him in making admiring exclamations! Why was I not able to convey my thoughts by that sign language used by Captain Nemo and his companion! For lack of better, I spoke to myself, I shouted out in the copper vessel on my head, perhaps using up more air in vain words than I should have.

On seeing this splendid spectacle, Conseil had stopped, as I had. Clearly the good chap, in the presence of these representatives of zoophytes and molluscs, was classifying, constantly classifying. Polyps and *Echinodermata* lay in profusion on the ground. The varied *Isidnae*, the *Cornularia* which lived in isolation, the clumps of virgin *Oculina* formerly called 'white coral', the fungus coral bristling like mushrooms, and the anemones adhering by their muscular discs—all constituted a flowerbed, spangled with porpoids and their involucres of blue-tinged tentacles, with starfish studded in the sand, and with verrucous asterophytons, a fine lace embroidered by naiads' hands and whose festoons swung in the slight undulations as we passed. I was unhappy that I had to crush under my feet the brilliant specimens of molluscs strewn in thousands over the ground, the concentric combshells, the hammer shells, the donaxes, veritable jumping shells, the top-shells, the red helmets, the angel-wing strombs, the aplesias, and so many other products of the inexhaustible ocean. But we could not stop, and headed on, whilst above our heads sailed the schools of Portuguese men-of-war trailing their ultramarine tentacles, jelly-fish whose opaline or delicate rose umbrellas festooned with sky-blue strakes shielded us from the sunlight, and pelagic panopea, which would have strewn our path with phosphorescent gleams, had it been dark!

I glimpsed all these marvels within a quarter of a mile, scarcely stopping as I followed Captain Nemo, gesturing me on. Soon the ground changed. The sandy plain was replaced by a layer of sticky mud that the Americans call 'ooze', composed exclusively of siliceous and limestone shells. Then we passed through a field of pelagic seaweed plants not yet torn away by the water and which were growing vigorously. These lawns of fine-woven material were soft under our feet and could be compared to the silkiest rugs made by man's hand.

But just as the vegetation stretched before our feet, our heads were also catered for. A trellis of marine plants, from the exuber-ant family of algae which has more than 2,000 known species, crisscrossed the surface of the water. I could see long floating ribbons of sea-wracks, some globular and some tubular: there were *Laurencia*, *Cladostephi* with slender foliage, and water leaves like cactus fans. I noticed that the green plants kept closer to the surface, whilst the red ones were at a medium depth, leaving the black or brown water-plants the task of forming the gardens and flowerbeds of the furthermost depths of the ocean.

These seaweeds are truly one of the wonders of creation, one of the marvels of the world's flora. This family produces both the smallest and the biggest vegetation on the globe. For if 40,000 of these imperceptible plantlets have been counted in 5 square mil-limetres, wracks have also been found whose length exceeds 500 metres.

We had left the *Nautilus* about an hour and a half before. It was nearly midday. I realized this from the perpendicularity of the sunlight, no longer refracted. The magical colours were slowly dis-appearing, and the emerald and sapphire nuances faded from our firmament. We were walking with a regular step that resonated on the ground with astonishing intensity. The slightest sounds were transmitted at a speed to which the ear is not accustomed on dry land. The reason is that water is a better conductor of sound than air, and transmits it four times as quickly.

At this point the ground went down more steeply. The light became a uniform colour. We had reached a depth of 100 metres, and were now at a pressure of 10 atmospheres. But my diving suit had been designed in such a way that I was not at all affected. I merely felt a certain stiffness in my fingers, and even this discomfort soon disappeared. As for the fatigue that should have been produced by a two-hour excursion kitted out in an unfamiliar way, it was non-existent. Helped by the water, I was moving with surprising ease.

Even at a depth of 300 feet, I could still see the sunlight, if faintly. Its intense brilliance had been replaced by a reddish twilight intermediate between day and night. But we could still see well enough to find our way, and did not yet need to switch on our Ruhmkorff lamps.

At this moment, Captain Nemo stopped. He waited for me to catch up, and pointed to some dark masses against the shadows not far away.

'These must be the forests of Crespo Island,' I thought. I was not mistaken.

17

An Underwater Forest

WE had finally reached the edge of the forest, doubtless one of the most beautiful in Captain Nemo's immense realm. He considered it his own, claiming the same rights over it as the first men in the first days of the world. In any case, who was there to dispute his possession of the underwater property? What braver pioneer could come, axe in hand, to cut down the dark undergrowth?

The forest was made of huge tree-like plants, and as soon as we went under their vast arches, our eyes were struck by the forms of their branches, remarkable forms I had never seen before.

None of the grasses carpeting the ground, none of the branches multiplying on the shrubs crept or drooped, and none stretched out horizontally. All rose towards the surface. There was not a single filament, not a single blade, however thin, which did not stand up as straight as iron stalks. The wracks and the creepers grew in rigid perpendicular lines determined by the density of the element that had given them birth. The plants were motionless, but when I shifted them with my hand, they immediately moved back to their original positions. It was the realm of the vertical.

I soon got used to this bizarre location and to the semidarkness surrounding us. The ground of the forest was studded with sharp rocks, difficult to avoid. The underwater flora seemed relatively complete, even richer perhaps than in a tropical or arctic region, where there is less variety. For a while, however, I involuntarily mixed up the kingdoms, taking zoophytes for hydrophytes, animals for plants. And who wouldn't have made such a mistake? Flora and fauna were so close in this submarine world!

I noticed that all the products of the vegetable kingdom were attached to the ground only superficially. Devoid of roots, indifferent to the fixed points they were attached to, whether sand, shells, tests, or pebbles, they merely needed them as a point of contact, not for their life. These plants were self-propagating, and the principle of their existence was in the water that bore them and nourished them. Most of them did not produce leaves but lamellas of fantastic shapes, although limited to a narrow range of colours: only pink, crimson, green, olive, fawn, and brown. I again saw, but this time not dried like the specimens in the *Nautilus*, *Padinae pavoni* in fans seeming to implore the breeze, scarlet rose-tangles, laminaria extending their edible young shoots, threadlike flexuous *Nereocystes* opening out to reach a height of 15 metres, clumps of acetabula with stems growing from the top, and many other pelagic plants all without flowers. 'A curious aberration,' one witty naturalist has said, 'where the animal kingdom flowers and the vegetable kingdom does not!'

Amongst the various shrubs as big as the trees of the temperate zones, or under their humid shade, grew genuine bushes with living flowers, hedges of zoophytes on which bloomed meandrine corals crisscrossed with complex furrows, yellowish *Caryophylli* with diaphanous tentacles, cespitose clumps of zoantharixans, and, to complete the illusion, fishflies flying from branch to branch like a swarm of humming birds, while yellow *Lepisanthes*, with bristling jaws and sharp scales, dactylopterous and Monocanthidae, rose from under our feet, like a flock of snipe.

At about one o'clock Captain Nemo gave the signal for a halt. For my part I was quite pleased, as we stretched out under a bower of aralias, whose long thin blades stood up like arrows.

I found this rest period delightful. The only thing missing was the charm of conversation. But it was impossible to talk, impossible to reply. I merely brought my big copper head close to Conseil's. I could see the worthy man's eyes shining with pleasure, and to show his satisfaction he moved about within his carapace in the most comical way imaginable.

After our four-hour march, I was astonished not to feel ravenous. Why my stomach behaved in such a way, I cannot say. But in contrast, I felt an uncontrollable desire to sleep, as happens with all divers. My eyes quickly closed behind the thick glass, and I fell into an irresistible slumber* that until then only the movement of walking had been able to overcome. I was in fact imitating Captain Nemo and his rugged companion who were already stretched out in the crystal limpidity, fast asleep.

How long I slept I could not calculate; but when I woke up again, the sun seemed to be already going down towards the horizon. Captain Nemo had already got up, and I was beginning to stretch when an unexpected sight suddenly brought me to my feet.

A few paces away, a monstrous sea spider, three feet high, was looking at me with its shifty eyes, ready to throw itself on me. Although my diving suit was thick enough to protect me from the animal's stings, I could not prevent a shudder of horror. Conseil and the sailor from the *Nautilus* woke up at this moment. Captain Nemo pointed out the hideous crustacean to his companion, and the animal was immediately beaten down with a single blow from the butt: I saw the monster's dreadful legs twisting in terrible convulsions.

This encounter made me realize that other, more redoubtable

animals surely haunted these dark depths, and that my diving suit would not protect me from their attacks. I hadn't thought of it until then, but decided to keep a watchful eye open. I imagined in any case that this halt was as far as our excursion would go; but I was mistaken for, instead of returning to the *Nautilus*, Captain Nemo continued with his daring venture.

The ground was still descending, its slope getting steeper and leading us into greater depths. It must have been about three o'clock when we reached a narrow valley between high vertical walls, at about 150 metres' depth. Thanks to the quality of our equipment, we had gone 90 metres further than the limit that nature seemed to have imposed until then on man's underwater excursions.

I say 150 metres, although no instrument allowed me to calculate the depth. But I did know that even in the clearest seas the sunlight could penetrate no further than this. Precisely then the darkness became intense. Nothing could be seen at a distance of ten paces. I was therefore groping my way along when I suddenly saw a bright white light. Captain Nemo had just switched on his electric lamp. His companion did likewise. Conseil and I followed their example. By turning a screw, I established contact between the coil and the glass spiral, and the sea, lit up by our four lanterns, was illuminated for 25 metres around.

Captain Nemo continued to force his way into the dark depths of the forest whose shrubs were growing scarcer and scarcer. I noticed that vegetable life was disappearing quicker than animal life. The pelagic plants were already abandoning the ground which had become arid, although an enormous number of animals could still be seen—zoophytes, articulates, molluscs, and fish.

While walking, I was thinking that the light from our Ruhmkorff lamps would automatically attract the inhabitants of these dark levels. But if they did come near, they kept at a distance that frustrated the huntsmen. Several times I saw Captain Nemo stopping and aiming his rifle; then, after a few moments of observation, he would get up again and resume his walking.

Finally, at about four o'clock, our marvellous expedition came to an end. A superb rock wall of imposing height rose up in front of us: a jumble of gigantic blocks, an enormous cliff of granite, with dark grottoes leading into it but no practicable way up. This was the coast of Crespo Island. This was land.

The captain suddenly stopped. His signal brought us to a halt, for however much I wanted to go beyond the wall, I too had to stop. Here Captain Nemo's realm finished. He did not wish to leave it. Beyond lay that portion of the globe where he would never again set foot.

We started back. Captain Nemo had taken the lead of our little troop once more, finding his way along without hesitating for a single moment. I thought I could see that we were not following the same path back to the *Nautilus*. The new route, very steep and thus very difficult, brought us quickly back up towards the surface. However, this return to the upper strata was not so sudden as to make decompression occur too quickly, for this would have caused grave disorders to our bodies, producing those internal injuries so fatal to divers. Very soon the light appeared and grew stronger, and since the sun was already low on the horizon, the refraction again gave the various objects a spectral ring.

At 10 metres' depth we were walking through a swarm of small fish of every sort, more numerous than the birds of the air, and more lively; but no aquatic game worth a gun-shot had yet appeared before our eyes.

All of a sudden, I saw the captain rapidly aiming his weapon and following an object moving amongst the shrubbery. The shot went off, I heard a faint hissing sound, and an animal fell stricken a few paces away.

It was a magnificent sea otter, an enhydra, the only quadruped that is exclusively marine. The five-foot otter was surely very valuable. Its skin, rich brown on top and silver underneath, was one of those admirable furs that are so sought after on the Russian and Chinese markets; the fineness and sheen of its coat meant it was worth at least 2,000 francs. I admired this curious mammal with its rounded head and short ears, round eyes, white whiskers like a cat's, webbed and clawed feet, and bushy tail. This precious carnivore, hunted and tracked down by fishermen, is becoming extremely rare, and it has taken refuge principally in the northern Pacific, where its species will probably soon become extinct.*

Captain Nemo's companion came and picked up the animal and loaded it over his shoulder, as we set off again.

For an hour the plain of sand stretched out before our feet. It often rose to less than 2 metres from the surface. I could then see our image clearly reflected upside-down: above us appeared an identical troop, reproducing all our movements and gestures, identical in every point except that they were marching with heads inverted and feet in the air.

Another effect to be noted. This was the passage of thick clouds which formed and disappeared very quickly; but on reflection, I realized that these so-called clouds were due merely to variations in the height of the long waves, and I also noticed the foaming white horses produced on the surface by the breaking crests. I was even able to follow the shadows of large birds passing over our heads as they produced a light quick trace on the surface.

It was then that I witnessed one of the finest gun shots ever to play on the heart-strings of a hunter. A big bird with a large wingspan, very clearly visible, was gliding towards us. Captain Nemo's companion aimed and shot at it when it was only a few metres above the waves.* The animal fell down dead, and dropped down within reach of the skilful hunter, who seized hold of it. It was an albatross of the finest sort, an admirable specimen of those pelagic birds.

Our progress had not been interrupted by this incident. For two hours we followed sandy plains alternating with seaweed-strewn prairies, very difficult to cross. Indeed, I could hardly take another step, when I noticed a vague glimmer interrupting the watery darkness about half a mile away. It was the *Nautilus*'s searchlight. Within twenty minutes we would be on board, and I would be able to breathe as I wished, for I felt that the air from my tank was no longer rich enough in oxygen. But I hadn't reckoned on an encounter which slightly postponed our arrival.

I had remained about twenty paces behind, when suddenly I saw Captain Nemo coming back towards me. With his strong hand he pushed me down, whilst his companion did the same with Conseil. I did not know what to make of this brusque attack, but felt reassured when I realized that the captain was lying down near me and remaining motionless.

I was stretched out on the ground in the shelter of a seaweed bush when, raising my head, I noticed some huge shapes moving noisily past, giving out phosphorescent gleams.

My blood froze in my veins! I had recognized the formidable sharks threatening us. They were a couple of blue sharks, terrible beasts with enormous tails and dull glassy eyes, which secrete a phosphorescent substance through holes near their muzzles. Monstrous fiery mouths* that can chew an entire man in their iron jaws! I was not aware whether Conseil was busy classifying them, but I know that for my part, I hardly studied their silver bellies and menacing mouths bristling with teeth from a scientific point of view, but more as a potential prey than as a naturalist.

Very fortunately, these voracious animals cannot see very well. They passed without noticing us, letting their brownish tails brush by us; and as if by a miracle we escaped this danger which is certainly greater than that of an encounter with a tiger in the heart of the jungle.

Half an hour later, guided by the electric beam, we reached the *Nautilus*. The outside door was still open, and Captain Nemo closed it as soon as we were back inside the first compartment. Then he pressed a button. I could hear the pumps working inside the ship, felt the water going down around me, and in a few moments the compartment was entirely empty. The inside door was opened, and we moved into the cloakroom.

There our diving suits were taken off, not without difficulty; and totally exhausted, faint from lack of food and sleep, I went back to my room—in a state of complete wonder at this extraordinary excursion over the ocean floor.

18

Four Thousand Leagues under the Pacific

THE following morning, 18 November, I had completely recovered from my tiredness of the day before. I went up on the platform just as the *Nautilus*'s first officer was enunciating his daily phrase. The idea then came to me that it concerned the state of the sea, and in particular that it meant 'we have nothing in sight'.

The ocean was indeed deserted. Not a sail in view. The heights of Crespo Island had disappeared during the night. The sea absorbed all the colours of the spectrum except blue, which it reflected in all directions, and so took on an admirable shade of indigo. A rainbow with long curves appeared regularly over the heaving waves.

I was admiring the magnificent sight when Captain Nemo appeared. He did not seem to notice my presence, and began a series of astronomical observations. Then, once his work was finished, he went to lean on the framework around the searchlight, and gazed abstractedly at the surface of the ocean.

Meanwhile about twenty sailors from the *Nautilus*, all strong, strapping men, had arrived on the platform. They had come to pull in the nets, left to drag during the night. The sailors clearly belonged to different countries, although the European type could be discerned in all of them. I recognized what were clearly Irish, French, a few Slavs, a Greek, and a Cretan.* These men were sparing of speech, and used amongst themselves only that bizarre language whose origin I could not begin to guess. Accordingly I had to give up hope of asking any questions.

The nets were pulled on board. These were trawls like those used on the Normandy coasts, huge pouches kept half-open by a floating yard and a chain threaded through the bottom meshes. The pouches, dragged along by their iron gantries, swept the bottom of the ocean and gathered in all its produce as they moved. That day, they brought in some curious specimens of these fishy waters: angler fish whose comic movements have given them the name of histrions, black Commerson's fish with antennae, undulating triggerfish with narrow red stripes, expanding-tetrodons with an extremely subtle venom, a few olive-hued lampreys, *macrorhini* covered in silvery scales, trichiures whose electric power is equal to that of the electric eel and electric ray, scaly notopterids with brown transversal stripes, greenish cod, several varieties of gobies, etc.; and finally a few fish of greater size, a metre-long scad with a prominent head, a few fine bonito mackerel bedecked in blue and silver, and three magnificent tuna whose speed of movement had not saved them from the trawl.

I estimated that this operation with the net was bringing in nearly half a ton of fish. It was a fine catch, but not unexpected. These nets had been dragging for several hours and had captured a whole aquatic world in their stranded prison. We were guaranteed food of excellent quality as many times as wished, thanks to the *Nautilus*'s speed and the attraction of its electric light.

These diverse products of the sea were immediately lowered down the hatch towards the storerooms, some to be eaten fresh and the others preserved.

Once the fishing was over and the air supplies renewed, I thought that the *Nautilus* would continue its underwater journey. I was getting ready to return to my room, when Captain Nemo turned to me and said without preamble:

'Look at this ocean, Dr Aronnax, is it not endowed with an authentic life of its own? Does it not have its angers and its moments of tenderness? Yesterday it went to sleep just like us, and now it is waking up again after a peaceful night!'

Neither good-day nor good morning! Wouldn't one have thought that this strange character was continuing a conversation already started?

'Look,' he continued; 'it is waking up in the sun's caresses! It is going to live its daily life again! How absorbing to study the full life of its organism! It has a pulse and arteries and it has spasms, and I fully support the scientist Maury, who discovered a circulation in it just as real as that of blood in animals.'

It was clear that Captain Nemo was not expecting a reply from me, and it seemed pointless to offer replies of 'clearly', 'yes, definitely', and 'you're quite right'. He was speaking mainly to himself, leaving a long gap after each sentence. He was thinking out loud.

'Yes,' he said, 'the ocean has an actual circulation, and to set it moving, all the Creator of all things had to do was to increase the caloric,* salt, and animalculae in it. The caloric produces different densities, which then create currents and counter-currents. Evaporation is negligible in the polar regions but very rapid in the tropical zones, and so produces a permanent interchange between the tropical and polar waters. I have also been able to detect currents going from top to bottom and back again, which form the ocean's real respiration. I have observed molecules of salt water heating up on the surface, descending towards the depths, reaching their maximum density at two degrees below zero, then cooling further and so becoming lighter and starting to move back up again. You will see the consequences of this phenomenon at the Poles,* and you will understand why, through this law of far-sighted nature, ice can form only on the surface of the waters!'

While Captain Nemo was finishing his sentence, I said to myself: 'The Pole! Does this intrepid being claim to be able to take us there?'

The captain had meanwhile fallen silent and was examining the element he so completely, so unceasingly studied. Then continuing:

'There are large quantities of salt in the sea, Dr Aronnax, and if you were to take out the dissolved salt it contains, you would have a mass of four-and-a-half million cubic leagues which, if spread out over the whole globe, would form a layer more than 10 metres high.* And do not think that the salt might be there due to a mere caprice of nature. No; it makes sea water less subject to evaporation, and so prevents the winds from carrying away too great a quantity of water vapour, which would then precipitate and submerge the temperate zones. A huge role, a role of stabilizer of the overall economy of the globe!'

Captain Nemo stopped, even got up and took a few steps across the platform, then came back towards me.

'As for the infusoria,' he continued, 'those billions of animal-culae, their role is no less important. The tiniest drop contains millions, and 800,000 are required to make 1 milligram. They absorb the sea salt, they assimilate the solid element of the water, they build the corals and the madrepores, and so they are the real constructors of the limestone landmasses! And then the drop of water, deprived of its mineral sustenance, becomes lighter, rises to the surface, absorbs salts left there by evaporation, grows heavier, descends again, and brings back down new elements for the ani-malculae to absorb. Hence a double current, rising and falling, and always movement, always life! Life more intense than on land, more exuberant, more immeasurable, blossoming in every part of the ocean, a deadly habitat for man, it has been said, a life-giving element for the myriads of animals—and for me!'

When Captain Nemo spoke in this way, he was completely transformed and he produced an extraordinary emotion in me.

'Here is real life!' he added. 'And I could imagine founding cities in the sea, agglomerations of underwater dwellings which, like the *Nautilus*, would come up to breathe on the surface of the oceans each morning, free cities if ever there were any, independent cities! And yet, who knows if some despot . . .'

Captain Nemo finished his sentence with a violent gesture. Then addressing me directly, as if to chase away some unhappy thought:

'Dr Aronnax,' he asked, 'do you know what the depth of the ocean is?'

'All I know, captain, is what the main soundings have taught us.'

'Could you please quote them, so that I can corroborate them as necessary?'

'Here are the few I can remember. If I am not mistaken, the average depth of the North Atlantic has been found to be 8,200 metres, and the Mediterranean, 2,500 metres. The deepest soundings have been made in the South Atlantic, near the 35th parallel, and gave 12,000 metres, 14,091 metres, and 15,149 metres.* In sum, it has been estimated that if all the water in the sea was levelled out, its average depth would be about 7 kilometres.'

'Very well, Dr Aronnax,' replied Captain Nemo. 'I hope we can show you better than that. As for the average depth of this part of the Pacific, I can tell you that it is only 4,000 metres.'

Having said that, Captain Nemo headed for the hatch and disappeared down the ladder. I followed him into the salon. The propeller immediately started to turn, and the log soon indicated a speed of 20 knots.

During the days and weeks that followed, Captain Nemo was very economical with his visits. I saw him only at rare intervals. His first officer took regular bearings, which I found marked on the map, so that I could follow the *Nautilus*'s course exactly.

Conseil and Land spent long hours with me. Conseil had related the marvels of our excursion to his friend, and the Canadian regretted not coming with us. But I hoped that there would be further opportunities in the future to visit the ocean forests.

Almost every day, the panels in the salon were opened for a few hours, and our eyes never grew tired of penetrating the mysteries of the underwater world.

The general direction of the *Nautilus* was south-east, and it stayed at a depth of between 100 and 150 metres. One day, however, through some mysterious caprice, it used its inclined planes to dive at an angle and reached water situated at 2,000 metres down. The thermometer indicated a temperature of 4.25°C which, at this depth, seems common to all latitudes.

At three a.m. on 26 November, the *Nautilus* cut the tropic of Cancer at longitude 172°. On the 27th it passed within sight of the archipelago of Hawaii, where Captain Cook* met his death on 14 February 1779. We had then covered 4,860 leagues from our starting-point. When I arrived on the platform that morning, I sighted Hawaii two miles to leeward, the biggest of the seven islands forming the archipelago. I could clearly make out the fields on its seaboard, the various mountain chains running parallel to the coast, and the volcanoes dominated by Mauna Kea rising 5,000 metres above sea-level. Amongst other specimens of these areas, the nets brought in pavonated fans, which are compacted polyps of a gracious form peculiar to this part of the ocean.

The *Nautilus* continued on its south-easterly course. It crossed the equator at longitude 142° on 1 December, and on the 4th of the same month, after a rapid and uneventful navigation, we sighted the Marquesas Islands. Three miles away at 8° 57′ S, 139° 32′ W I observed Cape Martin on Nuku Hiva, the main island in this group belonging to France. But I saw only the wooded mountains standing out above the skyline, for Captain Nemo did not like going near land. There the nets brought in fine specimens: dolphin fish with pale blue fins and golden tails, whose flesh is without equal in the world, *Hologymnosi* which have virtually no scales but an exquisite taste, *Ostorhinchi* with their bony jaws, and yellowish frigate mackerel which are just as good as bonito— all fish worthy of being classified in the ship's kitchen.

Having quit these charming islands under the protection of the

French flag, the *Nautilus* covered approximately 2,000 miles between 4 and 11 December. This navigation was noteworthy for an encounter with an enormous troop of calamar, curious molluscs closely related to the cuttlefish. French fishermen classify them as squid; and they belong to the class of cephalopods and family of dibranchiates, which also includes the cuttlefish and the argonaut. These calamar were particularly studied by the naturalists of classical times, and they provided numerous metaphors for the orators of the Agora, plus an excellent dish for the tables of the rich, if we are to believe Athenaeus,* a Greek doctor who lived before Galen.*

It was during the night of 9–10 December that the *Nautilus* encountered this army of molluscs of especially nocturnal habits. There were millions of them. They were migrating from the temperate to warmer zones, following the path of the herrings and sardines. Through the thick crystal windows, we watched them swimming backwards extremely fast by means of their locomotive tubes as they chased the fish and molluscs: eating the little ones, being eaten by the big ones, and waving in indescribable confusion the ten legs that nature has implanted on their heads, like a headdress of inflatable snakes. Despite its speed, the *Nautilus* sailed through the midst of this troop of creatures for several hours, and its nets brought in an uncountable number, amongst which I recognized the nine species that d'Orbigny* has classified as inhabiting the Pacific Ocean.

It can be seen that the ocean provided its most marvellous sights during this crossing, incessantly and without count. It varied them infinitely. The sea changed its backdrop and its scenery for our pleasure, and we were called on to contemplate the works of the Creator in the midst of the liquid element, but also to penetrate the most fearful mysteries of the ocean.

On 11 December I was reading in the salon. Ned Land and Conseil were observing the luminous waters through the half-open panels. The *Nautilus* was motionless. With tanks full, it lay at a depth of 1,000 metres, a sparsely inhabited region of the oceans, where only larger fish put in an occasional appearance.

The book I was reading was a charming one by Jean Macé* called *Les Serviteurs de l'estomac*, and I was savouring its sagacious lessons, when Conseil interrupted my reading.

'Would monsieur please come here for a moment?' he said in an unusual tone.

'What is it, Conseil?'

'Something monsieur should see.'

I got up, went to lean on the glass, and gazed.

In the full electric light, an enormous blackish object was suspended motionless in the midst of the waters. I observed it attentively, trying to identify the gigantic cetacean. But a thought suddenly crossed my mind.

'A ship!' I exclaimed.

'Yes,' replied Ned Land, 'a crippled ship which went straight down!'

He was correct. It was a ship with cut shrouds still hanging from their plates. Its hull seemed in good condition, and it could not have been wrecked for more than a few hours. The stumps of three masts, cut two feet above the deck, showed that the waterlogged ship must have sacrificed its masts. But it must have keeled sideways and filled up with water: it was still listing to port. A sad sight, this carcass lost beneath the waves; but sadder still, the sight of the deck where a few bodies still lay, made fast by ropes. I counted four—all men, with one of them still standing at the helm—then a woman half emerging through the deadlight in the poop, holding a child with both arms. It was a young woman. I was able to identify her features, brightly lit in the *Nautilus*'s lights and not yet decomposed by the water. In a supreme effort, she had raised the child above her head, a poor little being whose arms still clasped the neck of its mother! The positions of the four sailors were frightening, twisted as they were in convulsive movements, making a last effort to tear themselves from the ropes tying them to the ship. Only the helmsman, calmer, his face clear and serious, his greying hair stuck to his forehead, his hand tightly seizing the wheel, seemed still to be steering the wrecked three-master through the ocean depths.

What a scene! We stood silent, our hearts beating hard, at the sight of this shipwreck captured in mid-act, photographed as it were at its ultimate moment! And already I could see huge sharks advancing, their eyes ablaze, drawn by the lure of human flesh!

The *Nautilus* had been manœuvring around the submerged ship. For a brief moment I could read the board on its stern: The *Florida*, Sunderland.*

19

Vanikoro

THIS terrible sight inaugurated a series of maritime disasters that the *Nautilus* was to encounter on its route.* From the time it started travelling through more-frequented seas, we often sighted sunken hulls, completely rotten and hanging in the water, or, deeper, cannons, cannonballs, anchors, chains, and a thousand other iron objects being devoured by rust.

However, always carried on by this *Nautilus*, where we lived as if contagious, on 11 December* we sighted the Tuamotu Archipelago. This was Bougainville's* former Dangerous Archipelago, extending across 500 leagues from east-south-east to west-north-west, between 13° 30′ and 23° 50′ S, and 125° 30′ and 151° 30′ W, from Ducie Island to Matahiva. The archipelago covers an area of 370 square leagues, and is formed of about sixty island groups, amongst which can be noted the Gambier Islands, on which France has imposed its protectorate. These islands are coral producing. A slow but steady ascent, due to the work of the polyps, will one day join them all up. The new island will later attach itself to the neighbouring archipelagos, and a fifth continent will extend from New Zealand and New Caledonia all the way to the Marquesas.

The day I expounded this theory to Captain Nemo, he coldly replied:

'It is not new continents that the earth needs, but new men!'

The chances of navigation had brought the *Nautilus* near Reao, discovered in 1822 by Captain Bellingshausen of the *Mirny*,* and one of the most curious of the group. I was thus able to study the system of madrepores which built up the islands in this ocean.

Madrepores must not be confused with corals, for their structure is covered with a limestone crust; the changes in their structure led M. Milne-Edwards, my illustrious mentor, to classify them into five categories. The tiny animalculae which secrete this polypary live in billions inside their cells. Their limestone deposits create rocks, reefs, islets, and islands. Sometimes they form a circular ring, or lagoon, around a small inland lake, with gaps communicating with the open sea. Sometimes they produce barrier reefs like those off the coasts of New Caledonia and many of the islands of Tuamotu. In other cases, like Réunion and Mauritius, they form fringed reefs with high straight walls, where the ocean drops off very steeply.

While we worked our way along the shores of Reao at a distance of only a few cables, I admired the gigantic task completed by these microscopic workers. The walls were mainly the work of stony corals known as millepores, porites, astrea, and meandrines. These polyps develop particularly in the rough waters near the ocean surface, and consequently they start their foundations at the top, which then gradually sinks deeper together with the remains of the secretions. Such at least is the theory of Mr Darwin,* who explains in this way the formation of atolls—a better theory, in my view, than that which says that the madrepores build on the summits of mountains or volcanoes submerged a few feet below sea-level.

I was able to observe these curious walls very closely, for directly beside them our sound gave 300 metres' depth, and our electric current made this brilliant limestone sparkle.

Replying to Conseil, who had asked how long these colossal barriers took to grow, I astonished him greatly when I told him that scientists had calculated their growth to be an eighth of an inch per century.

'So to produce these walls, it must have taken . . .?'

'A hundred and ninety-two thousand years,* my good Conseil, thus uncommonly lengthening the biblical days. In any case the formation of coal—that is the mineralization of forests swamped by floods—required an even greater period. But I will add that the "days" of the Bible are simply eras and not the time between two sunrises for, according to the Bible itself, the sun does not date from the first day of creation.'

When the *Nautilus* came back to the surface, I could make out the whole of Reao, which was low and wooded. Its madreporic rocks had clearly been fertilized by storms and whirlwinds. One day a seed, carried by a hurricane from the neighbouring lands, fell on the limestone strata, covered with the decomposed remains of fish and marine plants forming the vegetable humus. A coconut, pushed by the waves, arrived on the new coast. The seed took root. The tree grew bigger and blocked the water vapour. A stream was born. Vegetation began to grow. A few animalculae, worms, and insects came ashore on tree-trunks brought in by the wind from other islands. Turtles came to lay their eggs. Birds nested in the young trees. In this way animal life developed and, drawn by the greenness and fertility, man appeared.* Thus these islands were formed, the enormous work of microscopic animals.

Towards evening, Reao melted into the distance and the *Nautilus* changed course noticeably. Having crossed the tropic of Capricorn at the 135th degree of longitude, it headed west-north-west, across the whole of the Tropics. Although the summer sun was generous with its rays, we did not suffer from the heat at all, for at 30 to 40 metres under the water the temperature never rose beyond 10 or 12 degrees.

On 15 December we passed to the west of the captivating archipelago of the Society Islands, with gracious Tahiti, the queen of the Pacific. In the morning I saw the high summits of this island a few miles to leeward. Its waters provided the ship's tables with excellent fish: mackerel, bonitos, albacores, and varieties of a sea snake called muraenophis.

The *Nautilus* had now covered 8,100 miles. The log indicated 9,720 miles when it passed through the archipelago of Tonga—the final resting-place for the crews of the *Argo*, the *Port-au-Prince*, and the *Duke of Portland*—and Samoa, where Captain de Langle, the friend of La Pérouse, was killed.* Then the Fijian archipelago was sighted, where the savages massacred Captain Bureau from Nantes,* commanding the *Aimable Joséphine*, and sailors of the *Union*.

This archipelago, which extends 100 leagues from north to south and 90 from east to west, is situated between 6° and 2°S and 174° and 179°W. It consists of a number of islands, islets, and reefs, notable amongst which are the islands of Viti Levu, Vanua Levu, and Kadavu.

It was Tasman* who discovered the group in 1643, the same year that Torricelli* invented the barometer and Louis XIV ascended the throne. I leave to the reader to decide which of these events was the most useful to mankind. Next came Cook in 1714, d'Entrecasteaux in 1793, and finally Dumont d'Urville* sorted out the geographical chaos of this archipelago in 1827. The *Nautilus* approached Vaileka Bay, where terrible adventures befell Captain Dillon, the first man to throw light on the mystery of La Pérouse's shipwreck.*

The bay was dredged several times, and provided us with excellent oysters in profusion. We ate immoderately, opening them at the table itself following Seneca's* precept. These molluscs belonged to the species known as *Ostrea lamellosa*, very common in Corsica. The bed at Vaileka was clearly very large; without multiple causes of destruction, the molluscs would end up filling the bays where they live, since as many as two million eggs have been found inside a single individual.

If on this occasion Master Ned had no reason to regret his gluttony, it was because the oyster is the only food which never causes indigestion. No less than sixteen dozen of these acephalous molluscs are needed to provide the 315 grams of nitrogen necessary for the daily sustenance of a single man.

On 25 December the *Nautilus* was sailing in the middle of the archipelago of Vanuatu, which Quiros* discovered in 1606, Bougainville explored in 1768, and to which Cook gave its present name in 1773. The group is made up of nine main islands, and forms a strip 120 leagues long from north-north-west to south-south-east, between 15° and 2°S, and 164° and 168°E. We passed quite close to the island of Aru; when we carried out our noon observations, it appeared as a mass of green forest surmounted by a very high peak.

It was Christmas Day, and it seemed to me that Land was very much missing the Anglo-Saxon Christmas, the big family festival which the Protestants are fanatically keen on.

I hadn't seen Captain Nemo for about a week, when on the morning of the 27th he came into the salon, again just like a man who has left you five minutes before. I was busy tracing the route of the *Nautilus* on the planisphere. The captain approached, put a finger on a point on the map, and said a single word:

'Vanikoro.'*

The name was magical. It was the name of the small islands where La Pérouse's vessels were wrecked. I stood up quickly.

'The *Nautilus* is taking us to Vanikoro?' I asked.

'Yes indeed.'

'And I will be able to visit those famous islands where the *Boussole* and the *Astrolabe* came to grief?'

'If that is your wish, monsieur.'

'When will we be in Vanikoro?'

'We are there now.'

With Captain Nemo following, I went up on to the platform and my eyes greedily scoured the horizon.

To the north-east emerged two volcanic islands of unequal size, surrounded by a coral reef measuring some 40 miles in circumference. We were near the island of Vanikoro itself, to which Dumont d'Urville gave the name of Île de la Recherche, and more precisely at the little haven of Vanu, situated at 16° 4′ S, 164° 32′ E. The island was covered with green vegetation from the beach up to the peaks of the interior, dominated by the 476-fathom-high Mount Kapogo.

Once the *Nautilus* had gone through a narrow pass in the outer ring of rocks, it was protected from the breakers, the sea being 30 to 40 fathoms deep. Under the verdant shade of the mangroves, I spotted a few savages who showed extreme surprise at our approach. And did they not see some formidable cetacean in this long blackish body, advancing almost submerged, fit to strike fear in their hearts?

Just then Captain Nemo asked me what I knew about La Pérouse's shipwreck.

'Only what everyone knows, captain.'

'And could you please tell me what everyone knows?' he asked in a slightly ironic tone.

'Certainly.'

I recounted what the last works by Dumont d'Urville had concluded, of which the following is a very brief summary:

In 1785 La Pérouse and his first officer Captain de Langle were sent by Louis XVI to circumnavigate the globe. They sailed off on board the corvettes the *Boussole* and the *Astrolabe*—but never came back.

In 1791, the French government, justifiably worried about the fate of the two corvettes, armed two large warships, the *Recherche* and the *Espérance*, which left Brest on 28 September under the command of Bruni d'Entrecasteaux. Two months later, it was stated in the declaration of a certain Bowen, captain of the *Albermarle*, that debris from wrecked ships had been seen on the coasts of New Georgia Island. But d'Entrecasteaux, not aware of this information—which was slightly suspect in any case—headed for the Admiralty Islands, indicated in a report by Captain Hunter* as where La Pérouse was shipwrecked.

His searches were in vain. The *Espérance* and the *Recherche* even went right past Vanikoro without stopping, and this voyage was generally very unfortunate, for d'Entrecasteaux lost his life in it, as did two of his officers and several of his sailors.

It was an old Pacific hand, Captain Dillon, who was the first to find incontrovertible traces of the shipwrecked men. On 15 May 1824 his ship, the *St Patrick*, passed near the island of Tikopia in Vanuatu. There a lascar accosted him in a dugout canoe and sold him a silver sword-handle with characters engraved on it with a burin. This character claimed that six years before, while staying on Vanikoro, he had seen two Europeans who had come from ships that had run aground on the island's reefs many years before.

Dillon conjectured that these were La Pérouse's ships, whose disappearance had stirred the whole world. He tried to go to Vanikoro, where his informant said there were many remains from the shipwreck still to be found, but the winds and currents prevented him.

Dillon went back to Calcutta. There he was able to interest the Royal Asiatic Society and the East India Company in his discovery. A ship, which he baptized the *Recherche*, was put at his disposal, and he left again on 23 January 1827, with a French agent on board.

Having put into port at several points in the Pacific, the *Recherche* anchored off Vanikoro on 7 July 1827, in the harbour of Vanu where the *Nautilus* was now floating.

There he collected numerous remains from the shipwreck: iron tools, anchors, strops from pulleys, swivel guns, an eighteen-pound cannonball, the remains of astronomical instruments, a piece of taffrail, and a bronze bell with the inscription, '*Bazin m'a fait*', the hallmark of the foundry of Brest Arsenal in about 1785. Doubt was no longer possible.

Dillon remained on the spot of the tragedy gathering extra information until October. Then he left Vanikoro, headed for New Zealand, then anchored in Calcutta on 7 April 1828, and finally returned to France, where he was very warmly received by Charles X.

But meanwhile Dumont d'Urville, not aware of the results of Dillon's work, had already left to seek the shipwreck elsewhere. The reason was that a whaling vessel had reported that medals and a St Louis cross had been found in the hands of savages in the Louisiades and New Caledonia.

Dumont d'Urville and the *Astrolabe* had therefore put to sea, and anchored in Hobart two months after Dillon left Vanikoro. There he learned of Dillon's findings, and also that a certain James Hobbs, first officer of the *Union* of Calcutta, had landed on an island situated at 8° 18′ S, 156° 30′ E and had noticed iron bars and some red material being used by the natives of those shores.

Dumont d'Urville was quite perplexed, not knowing whether to believe these tales reported in rather unreliable newspapers; so in the end he decided to pursue Dillon's traces instead.

On 10 February 1828 the *Astrolabe* arrived at Tikopia, took as guide and interpreter a deserter living on this island, headed for Vanikoro, sighted it on 12 February, skirted its reefs until the 14th, and finally on the 20th anchored inside the barrier, in the harbour of Vanu.

On the 23rd several officers travelled round the island, and brought back a few small pieces of wreckage. The natives, adopting a system of denials and false trails, refused to take them to the place where the accident had happened. Such suspicious behaviour implied that they had mistreated the shipwrecked men and, indeed, they seemed afraid that Dumont d'Urville had come to revenge La Pérouse and his unfortunate companions.

However, on the 26th, won over by presents and realizing that they had no reprisals to fear, they led the first officer, M. Jacquinot,* to the scene of the shipwreck.

At three or four fathoms deep, between the reefs of Pacu and Vanu, lay anchors, cannons, and iron and lead bars covered with limestone sediment. The dinghy and whaling-boat of the *Astrolabe* were sent to the spot and after considerable efforts their crew were able to raise an 1,800-pound anchor, a cast-iron eight-pound cannon, a lead bar, and two copper swivel guns.

Questioning the natives, Dumont d'Urville learned that La Pérouse had lost his two ships on the reefs of the island, had built a smaller vessel, but had then foundered a second time. Where? No one knew.

The captain of the *Astrolabe* then built a memorial to the celebrated navigator and his companions under a clump of mangrove trees. It was a simple four-sided pyramid on a coral base, constructed without any ironwork that might tempt the natives' light fingers.

Dumont d'Urville wanted to leave; but his crew were much weakened by the fevers of those unhealthy coasts and, very ill himself, he was unable to sail until 17 March.

Meanwhile the French government, fearing that Dumont d'Urville did not know about Dillon's work, had sent to Vanikoro a corvette stationed on the west coast of America called the *Bayonnaise*, commanded by Le Goarant de Tromelin.* The *Bayonnaise* anchored off Vanikoro a few months after the *Astrolabe* had left, found no new evidence, but observed that the savages had respected the memorial to La Pérouse.

That was the essence of the tale I recounted to Captain Nemo.

'So', he said, 'no one yet knows the last resting place of the third ship constructed by the shipwrecked sailors on the island of Vanikoro?'

'No one knows.'

Captain Nemo said nothing, but motioned to me to follow him into the salon. The *Nautilus* sank a few metres below the waves and the panels opened.

I rushed towards the window, and saw a coral accumulation covered with fungus coral, *Syphulina*, halcyons, and *Caryophylli*. Through the myriads of charming fish, rainbow wrasses, glyphisidons, pomfrets, diacopes, and soldierfish, I recognized pieces of wreckage that the grappling hooks had been unable to lift. There were iron stirrups, anchors, cannons, cannonballs, part of a capstan, a prow—all objects from wrecked ships, now carpeted with living flowers.

And whilst I was looking at this pathetic wreckage, Captain Nemo said in a grave voice:

'Captain La Pérouse left with his ships the *Boussole* and *Astrolabe* on 7 December 1785. He anchored first at Botany Bay, then visited Tonga and New Caledonia, headed for Santa Cruz, and put into Nomuka in the Haapai Group.* Then his ships arrived at the unknown reefs of Vanikoro. The *Boussole* was sailing in front, and hit the southern coast. The *Astrolabe* came to its help but also grounded. The first ship was destroyed almost immediately. Stranded to leeward, the second survived a few days. The natives gave a relatively warm welcome to the shipwrecked sailors; and they settled on the island to build a smaller vessel from the remains of the larger ones. A few sailors voluntarily remained on Vanikoro. The others, ill and weak, left with La Pérouse. They headed for the Solomon Islands and perished with all hands on the western coast of the main island of that group, between Capes Deception and Satisfaction.*

'But how do you know?' I exclaimed.

'This is what I found on the spot of that last shipwreck.'

Captain Nemo showed me a tin box stamped with the arms of France and completely corroded by salt-water. As he opened it, I saw a bundle of papers, yellowed but still legible.

These were the actual instructions from the Minister for the Navy to Captain La Pérouse, with marginal annotations written by Louis XVI!

'Ah, what a fine death for a sailor!' said Captain Nemo. 'A coral tomb provides a peaceful resting-place and may Heaven grant none other to my companions and me!'

20

Torres Strait

DURING the night of 27 to 28 December the *Nautilus* left the shores of Vanikoro at extraordinary speed. It headed south-westwards and within three days covered the 750 leagues from La Pérouse Island* to the south-eastern tip of New Guinea.

Very early on 1 January 1868, Conseil joined me on the platform.

'With monsieur's permission,' said the good fellow, 'I would like to wish him a Happy New Year.'

'What, Conseil, exactly as if I were in Paris in my study at the Jardin des Plantes? But I accept your wishes and thank you. I only ask what you mean by "a Happy New Year" in our present circumstances? Will this year bring an end to our imprisonment, or will it see a continuation of our strange voyage?'

'To be frank', answered Conseil, 'I do not really know how to reply to monsieur. There can be no doubt that we are witnessing curious things and that in two months we have not had the time to get bored. The latest marvel is always the most astonishing and if this progression continues, I do not know how it will all end. My view is that we will never have such an opportunity again.'

'Never again, Conseil.'

'In addition, Mr Nemo lives up to his Latin name, and does not bother us any more than if he did not exist.'

'As you say, Conseil.'

'I believe therefore, if monsieur pleases, that a happy new year would be one which would allow us to see everything.'

'Everything Conseil? That might be a very long year. But what does Ned Land think?'

'Ned thinks exactly the opposite to me,' replied Conseil. 'He is a positive spirit with an imperious stomach. Looking at fish and constantly eating them is not enough for him. The lack of wine, bread, and meat does not suit a pure Anglo-Saxon accustomed to steaks, and who appreciates his glass of brandy or gin!'

'For my part, Conseil, that is not what torments me, and I am managing very well on the diet on board.'

'So am I. I therefore wish to stay as much as Master Land wishes to escape. So if the new year is good for him, it will be bad for me, and vice versa. There will always be someone satisfied. In conclusion, I wish for monsieur whatever pleases monsieur.'

'Thank you Conseil. I merely ask if you can put off the question of presents, and replace them for the moment with a good handshake. That is all I have on me.'

'Monsieur has never been so generous.'

And the good fellow left me.

On 2 January we had covered 11,340 miles, that is 5,250 leagues from our starting-point in the Sea of Japan. Before the *Nautilus*'s prow stretched the perilous shores of the Coral Sea off the north-eastern coast of Australia. Our boat kept a few miles away from this dangerous reef where Cook's ships almost sank on 10 June 1770. His own ship hit a rock, and the only reason it did not go down was that a piece of coral broke off in the collision and stayed wedged in the hole in the hull.

I very much wanted to visit this 360-league long reef, against which a permanently squally sea breaks with terrible intensity like rolls of thunder. But just then the inclined planes of the *Nautilus* took us down to a great depth and I could no longer see anything of the high coral walls. I had to be content with the various specimens of fish brought up by our nets. I noted, amongst others, albacores, sorts of scombroid as large as tunas, with blueish flanks and transversal stripes which disappear when it dies. These fish accompanied us in schools and provided our table with a very delicate flesh. We also caught a large number of five-centimetre green-and-gold sparids with the taste of sea bream, and some flying pirapeds, genuine submarine swallows, which on dark nights streak both the airs and the waters with their phosphorescent gleams. Among the molluscs and zoophytes in the meshes of the dragnet, I found various species of alcyonarians, sea urchins, hammer-shells, spur-shells, solariums, cerites, and hyales. The flora were represented by lovely floating seaweed: oarweed and macrocystis soaked in mucilage sweating through their pores, and amongst which I collected an admirable *Nemostoma geliniaroida*, for placing among the natural curiosities of the ship's museum.

Two days after crossing the Coral Sea, on 4 January, we sighted the coast of New Guinea. At this juncture Captain Nemo told me he intended to enter the Indian Ocean via Torres Strait. He provided no other information. Ned was happy that this route was leading us nearer to the seas of Europe.

Torres Strait is considered dangerous because of the reefs with which it abounds, but also because of the savage inhabitants of its coasts. It separates Australia from the main island of New Guinea, also known as Papua.

New Guinea is 400 leagues long by 130 wide, with an area of 40,000 square leagues. It is situated between 0° 19′ and 10° 2′S and 128° 23′ and 146° 15′E. At noon when the first officer was measuring the altitude of the sun, I noticed the Arfak Mountains, rising in terraces and culminating in sharp peaks.

The island was discovered by the Portuguese Francisco Serrao in 1511, and successively visited by: don Jorge de Meneses in 1526, Grijalva in 1527, the Spaniard General Alvara de Saavedra in 1528, Iñigo Ortiz de Retes in 1545, the Dutchman Schouten in 1616, Nicholas Struyck in 1753, by Tasman, Dampier, Funnell, Carteret, Edwards, Bougainville, Cook, Forrest, and McCluer; and by d'Entrecasteaux in 1792, Duperrey in 1823, and by Dumont d'Urville in 1827.* According to M. de Rienzi, 'it is where the dark-skinned peoples who occupy the entire Malay Archipelago originally came from'; and I had no doubt that the hazards of our navigation would bring me face to face with the redoubtable Andamanese.*

The *Nautilus* was thus heading for the entrance of the most dangerous strait on the globe, one that the bravest captains hardly dare enter, the strait that Louis Vaez de Torres* braved when he came back from the Pacific to this part of Melanesia, and where in 1840 the grounded corvettes of Dumont d'Urville came close to going down with all hands. The *Nautilus*, superior to all the sea's dangers, was itself going to make acquaintance with the coral reefs.

Torres Strait is about 34 leagues wide, but is obstructed by an uncountable number of islands, islets, breakers, and rocks, making it virtually impossible to navigate. Consequently, to go through it, Captain Nemo took every possible precaution. The *Nautilus* remained on the surface of the water, moving forward at moderate speed. Like a whale's tail, its screw sluggishly beat the waves.

Profiting from the situation, my two companions and I had taken up position on the still-deserted platform. In front of us rose the pilot-house and, unless I am gravely mistaken, Captain Nemo was surely there as well, steering the *Nautilus* himself.

Before my eyes were the excellent maps of Torres Strait charted and designed by the hydrographic engineer Vincendon-Dumoulin and Ensign (now Admiral) Coupvent-Desbois* who were Dumont d'Urville's officers on his last voyage of circumnavigation. Together with Captain King's,* these are the maps that make best sense of the confusion in this narrow passage, and I was examining them with the closest attention.

Around the *Nautilus* the sea was boiling furiously. The current, bearing from south-east to north-west at a speed of two-and-a-half knots, was breaking over the coral tips emerging here and there.

'A bad sea!' said Ned.

'Very bad,' I answered, 'and not at all suited to a vessel like the *Nautilus*.'

'That damned captain', continued the Canadian, 'must be very sure of his route, because I can see clusters of coral that would tear his hull into a thousand pieces if it just grazed them!'

The situation was indeed highly dangerous but the *Nautilus* slid as if by enchantment through the furious reefs. It was not following the exact route of the *Astrolabe* and the *Zélée*, so fatal to Dumont d'Urville. It headed further north, round Murray Island, and then came back to the south-west heading for the Cumberland Passage. I thought it was going to enter this passage, when it headed north-west again, moving towards Tound Island and the Bad Channel through a large number of badly charted islands and islets.

I was already wondering whether Captain Nemo, reckless to the point of madness, intended to engage his ship in the pass where Dumont d'Urville's two corvettes had struck ground, when he changed direction for the second time, cut due west, and headed for Gueboroar Island.*

It was three p.m. The current was dying down; it was almost high tide. The *Nautilus* approached the island, with its remarkable coast of pandanuses, that I can still see today. We were following the shoreline at a distance of less than 2 miles.

Suddenly I was knocked over. The *Nautilus* had hit a reef; and remained motionless, listing slightly to port.

When I got up I saw that Captain Nemo and his deputy were on the platform. They studied the position of the ship, exchanging a few words in their incomprehensible idiom.

The situation was as follows. Gueboroar Island was visible two miles to starboard, its coastline stretching round from the north to the west like an enormous arm. To the south and east a few heads of coral were visible, already uncovered by the ebbing tide. We had gone aground at high tide in a sea where the tides are not large, an unfortunate circumstance for the chances of refloating the *Nautilus*. So solidly constructed was the ship, however, that its hull was not damaged in any way. But if it could neither sink nor be holed, it ran a high risk of remaining stuck on the reefs for ever, in which case Captain Nemo's submarine vessel was done for.

These thoughts were running through my mind when the captain, cool and calm and in command of himself as usual, came up, appearing neither upset nor annoyed.

'An accident?' I asked.

'No, an incident.'

'But an incident which will perhaps oblige you to dwell once more on the very land from where you have fled!'

Captain Nemo gave me a very strange look and made a negative sign. This told me quite clearly that nothing could ever force him to set foot on terra firma again. Then:

'Dr Aronnax, the *Nautilus* is far from finished: it will still carry you through the ocean's marvels. Our voyage is only just beginning, and I do not wish to deprive myself so quickly of the honour of your company.'

'However, Captain Nemo,' I said, ignoring the irony of his words, 'the *Nautilus* has run aground at high tide. The tides are not very large in the Pacific and if you cannot lighten the *Nautilus*, which seems probable, I do not see how it can be refloated.'

'The tides are not great in the Pacific, as you say. But in Torres Strait there are still one-and-a-half metres between high and low tide. Today is 4 January and in four days' time the moon will be full. So I would be very surprised if that kindly satellite does not raise this mass of water sufficiently to grant a favour that I wish to owe only to her.'

Upon which, Captain Nemo went back inside the *Nautilus* followed by his deputy. As for the vessel, it was no longer moving and remained as inert as if the coral polyps had already fixed it in their indestructible cement.

'Well sir?' said Ned Land, who came over after the captain had left.

'Well my good Ned, we shall calmly wait for high tide on the 9th, since it appears that the moon will be kind enough to refloat us.'

'Just like that?'

'Just like that.'

'And the captain is not going to drop his anchors, attach his engine to the chains, and do everything to pull off?'

'No need, because of the tide,' said Conseil.

The Canadian looked at Conseil, then shrugged his shoulders. This was the sailor in him talking.

'Monsieur,' he said, 'you can believe me when I tell you that this piece of iron will never sail under or over the seas again. It's worth only its weight in scrap, so I think the time has come to take leave of Captain Nemo.'

'My good Ned,' I replied, 'unlike you I have not given up hope for the valiant *Nautilus*: in four days' time we will see what the Pacific tides can do. In any case thinking of escape would be appropriate off the coast of England or the South of France, but the shores of New Guinea are different. We will have plenty of time to take those extreme measures if the *Nautilus* is unable to get free, which I would consider to be a serious situation.'

'But can't we at least try this land out? It's an island. On the island are trees. Under the trees, land animals, bearers of chops and beef which I would dearly like to sink my teeth into.'

'Here friend Ned is right,' said Conseil; 'I share his opinion. Could monsieur not ask his friend, Captain Nemo, to take us ashore, if only so that we can remain accustomed to setting foot on the solider parts of the planet?'

'I can ask him but he will refuse.'

'Monsieur should take that risk,' said Conseil; 'so we know where we stand with the captain.'

To my great surprise, Captain Nemo gave his permission, and did so with a great deal of grace and alacrity, without even extracting my promise to return on board. But an escape via New Guinea would have been highly dangerous, and I would not have advised Land to try it. It was better to be a prisoner on board the *Nautilus* than to fall into the hands of the Papuan natives.

The dinghy would be put at our disposal for the following morning. I did not try to find out if Captain Nemo was going to accompany us. I even felt sure that no crewman would be provided, and that Ned would have sole responsibility for directing the boat. The island was at most two miles away, and it would be a mere diversion for the Canadian to steer the light boat between the lines of reefs so fatal for larger vessels.

The following day, 5 January, the dinghy, with its cover off, was taken out of its cavity on the platform and launched into the sea. Two men were enough to perform this operation. The oars were in the boat and all we had to do now was to get in.

At eight o'clock we left the *Nautilus*, armed with rifles and axes. The sea was calm. A light breeze was blowing from the land. Conseil and I rowed vigorously while Ned steered us through the narrow channels between the breakers. The boat was easy to handle and moved quickly.

Ned Land could hardly contain his joy. He was a prisoner escaped from gaol, and he hardly thought that he had to go back inside again.

'Meat!' he kept repeating. 'We're going to eat meat, and what meat: real game! Not bread I tell you! I don't say that fish is a bad thing, but you can have too much of it, and a piece of fresh venison grilled on glowing coals will make a nice change from our usual fare.'

'Glutton,' replied Conseil, 'you are making my mouth water!'

'We still need to find out', I said, 'if the forests contain game and if the game is not sizeable enough to hunt the hunter.'

'Well,' said the Canadian, whose teeth seemed as sharp as a razor, 'I'll eat tiger—sirloin of tiger—if there are no other four-legged animals on the island.'

'Friend Ned is worrying me,' said Conseil.

'The first animal with four legs and no feathers, or with two legs and feathers,* will be greeted by my bullet, whatever sort it is.'

'So!' I replied. 'We're going to see hot-headed Master Land again!'

'Have no fear, Dr Aronnax, and row as hard as you can. I will only need 25 minutes to offer you a tasty dish.'

At half-past eight, the *Nautilus*'s boat had successfully negotiated the coral reef around Gueboroar and gently landed on a sandy beach.

21

A Few Days on Land

SETTING foot on land again made quite an impression on me. Ned Land tested the ground with his foot as if to take possession of it. All the same, it was only two months that we had been what Captain Nemo called 'the passengers of the *Nautilus*', in actual fact the prisoners of its commander.

Within a minute or two we were a rifle-shot away from the shore. The ground was almost entirely madreporic but some of the beds of the dried-up streams, strewn with pieces of granite, showed that the island had been formed in the primordial era. The horizon was entirely hidden behind a curtain of beautiful forest. The enormous trees, some reaching a height of 200 feet, were linked by garlands of creepers, true natural hammocks rocking in a slight breeze. There were mimosas, banyans, casuarinas, teaks, hibiscuses, pandanuses, and palm-trees, all mixed up in profusion; and beneath the shade of their verdant vault, at the foot of their gigantic trunks, grew orchids, leguminous plants, and ferns.

But without heeding any of these fine specimens of Papuan flora, the Canadian was combining serious business with pleasure. He spotted a coconut tree, knocked a few of its nuts down, and broke them open; we drank their milk and ate their flesh with a satisfaction that protested against the normal fare on board the *Nautilus*.

'Excellent!' pronounced Ned.

'Exquisite!' retorted Conseil.

'And I don't suppose', said the Canadian, 'that your Nemo could object to us bringing a cargo of coconuts back on board?'

'I'm sure not,' I replied, 'but he won't want any!'

'His loss,' said Conseil.

'And our gain. All the more for us.'

'Just a moment, Master Land,' I said as the harpooner began to attack another tree. 'Coconuts are all very well but before filling the boat with them, it would seem sensible to see whether the island produces some other substance just as useful. Fresh vegetables would be most welcome on board the *Nautilus*.'

'Monsieur is right,' said Conseil, 'and I propose we divide our boat into three parts, one for fruit, one for vegetables, and one for meat, of which I have not seen the slightest trace so far.'

'You should never give up, Conseil,' replied the Canadian.

'Let's continue on our way,' I said, 'but with our eyes peeled. Even if the island might appear uninhabited, it may contain individuals whose taste in game is less selective than ours.'

'Hey, hey!' voiced Land, with a meaningful move of his jaws.

'Ned!' said Conseil.

'Heck,' riposted the Canadian, 'I am beginning to understand the good side of cannibalism!'

'Ned, Ned, what are you saying?' said Conseil. 'You a cannibal? Then I will never be safe since I share your cabin! Am I to wake up one day half-eaten?'

'Dear Conseil, I like you a great deal, but not enough to eat you unless I really had to.'

'I can't count on that,' said Conseil. 'But let's get on with the hunting for we urgently need to shoot some game to satisfy this cannibal, or else one of these mornings monsieur will find only bits and pieces of his manservant to serve him.'

During this exchange, we had begun penetrating the dark vaults of the forest, and for two hours we crisscrossed it in every direction.

We were very lucky in our search for edible vegetables, and one of the most useful products of the Tropics was to provide us with precious food lacking on board.

I am referring to the breadfruit tree, in great supply on Gueboroar Island; I noticed mainly the seedless variety called *Rima* in Malay.*

It is different from other trees in having a straight trunk, 40 feet tall. Its top, which is gracefully round and formed of large, multi-lobed leaves, enables a naturalist to identify it as that same *Artocarpus* which has been so profitably introduced to the Mascarene Islands. Large round fruit stood out from the mass of greenery, ten centimetres across and with hexagonal swellings. They are a valuable example of the plants which nature has bestowed on regions lacking wheat, and though not requiring any cultivation, provide fruit eight months of the year.

Ned Land knew this fruit well. He had already eaten it on previous voyages, and knew how to prepare its edible part. Seeing it excited his desire so much that he was unable to hold on any longer.

'Sir, I'll die if I don't taste some of the dough from this breadfruit!'

'Go ahead, friend Ned, you can taste to your heart's delight. We're here to try things out, so feel free.'

'It won't take long,' said the Canadian.

Using a lens he lit a fire with some deadwood, which soon began crackling cheerfully. Meanwhile Conseil and I were choosing the best fruit from the *Artocarpus*. Some were not ripe enough, with their thick skin revealing a white, not very fibrous pulp. A large number of others, sticky and yellowish, were just waiting to be plucked.

There were no stones inside the fruit. Conseil carried about a dozen of them back to Ned, who cut them into thick slices and put them on the hot coals, repeating all the while:

'You will soon see, sir, how good it is!'

'Especially when you haven't had any for a long time!' said Conseil.

'It's no longer bread,' added the Canadian, 'it's delicate pastry. Have you ever had any sir?'

'No Ned.'

'Well get ready to taste something out of this world! If it doesn't knock you out, I'm not the king of harpooners!'

After a while the side of the fruit on the fire had turned completely black. Inside was a sort of dry white paste, or soft crumb, which tasted like artichoke.

I must admit that it was very good, and I ate with great pleasure.

'Unfortunately', I said, 'this dough can't be kept fresh, and so there seems little point in stocking up on board.'

'What are you saying!' exclaimed Ned. 'You are speaking as a naturalist, but I am going to act like a baker. Conseil, collect lots of these breadfruit which we'll pick up on our way back.'

'But how will you prepare them?' I asked him.

'By using the pulp to make a fermented dough which will keep indefinitely. When I want some, I'll just cook it in the kitchen, and you will find it excellent despite a slightly acidic taste.'

'So Master Ned, I can see that this bread is perfect . . .'

'No sir, it still needs a few fresh fruit or, failing that, vegetables.'

'Well then, let's go and look for some fruit and vegetables.'

Once our bread harvesting was over, we set off to complete this earthly meal.

Our search was not in vain, for by about midday we had gathered a generous supply of bananas. These delicious products of the tropical zone ripen the whole year round, and the Malays, who call them *pisang*, eat them uncooked. Along with the bananas we collected some enormous, very strong-tasting jackfruit, some delicious mangoes, and some pineapples of an incredible size. All this took a long time, but there was no reason to regret it.

Conseil was still observing Ned. The harpooner was walking ahead and as he worked his way through the forest, he was completing his provisions by collecting fine fruit with a sure hand.

'So now you have everything you want, friend Ned?'

'H'm.'

'Can you still be complaining?'

'All this fruit doesn't really make up a dinner. It's the end of the meal, the dessert. But what about the soup and the main course?'

'Indeed,' I said. 'Ned promised us chops, which now seem unlikely to materialize.'

'Sir, not only has the hunting not finished, but it hasn't even started yet. Patience! We'll certainly end up meeting some sort of animal with either feathers or hair, if not here, then somewhere else . . .'

'And if not today, then tomorrow,' added Conseil, 'for we should not wander too far. I even suggest returning to the boat.'

'What, already!'

'We have to be back before nightfall,' I said.

'So what time is it?'

'At least two o'clock,' replied Conseil.

'How time flies on dry land!' exclaimed Master Ned Land with a sigh of regret.

'Off we go!' said Conseil.

So back we went through the forest, completing our harvest by raiding the palm cabbage trees, whose palms need to be taken from the tops of the trees, and gathering some small beans, that I recognized to be what the Malays call *abrou*, and some yams of superior quality.

We were loaded down by the time we got back to the boat. But Ned still did not find his supplies sufficient, although luck was to favour him. Just as he was getting back in he spotted a few 25- or 30-foot trees, belonging to the palm tree family. This variety, as precious as the *Artocarpus*, is considered one of the most useful products in the Malay archipelago.

They were sago palms, which grow wild, similar to the mulberry in that they reproduce from their own offspring and their own seeds.*

Land knew how to deal with them. He took his axe, chopped with great vigour, and soon felled two or three sago palms: they were fully grown ones, as could be seen from the white powder speckling their leaves.

I watched him more as a naturalist than as a starving man. He cut a strip of bark one inch thick from each trunk and revealed a network of long fibres forming inextricable knots, gummed together with a sort of sticky flour. The flour was sago, an edible substance that is the principal diet of the Melanesians.

For the moment Ned merely chopped the trunks up, as if

making wood for burning: he thus postponed the job of extracting the flour, sifting it through cloth to separate out the fibrous parts, evaporating the liquid in the sun, and letting it harden in moulds.

We finally pushed off from shore at five o'clock, laden down with our booty, and half an hour later we drew up alongside the *Nautilus*. No one appeared. The enormous metal cylinder was as if deserted. Once the provisions were loaded on board, I went down to my room. I found my dinner ready. I ate, then went to bed.

The following day, 6 January, nothing had changed on board. No sound, no sign of life. The dinghy remained alongside where we had left it. We decided to go back to Gueboroar Island. Ned Land wanted to visit another part of the forest, hoping to have better luck hunting than the day before.

At dawn we were already on our way. The boat was carried along by the tide moving in towards the land, and we reached the island very quickly.

We got out and followed Ned Land, preferring to trust to his instinct, although his long legs nearly left us behind.

Ned headed westward along the coast, then forded a few streams, before reaching a plateau surrounded by splendid forests. A few kingfishers were stalking along the water-courses, but it was impossible to get near them. Their caution told me that these birds knew what to expect from bipeds like us, and I deduced that if the island was not actually inhabited, it was at least regularly visited.

Having crossed a rich plain, we arrived at the edge of a little wood brightened by the song and flight of a large number of birds.

'They're still only birds,' said Conseil.

'But some are edible.'

'On the contrary, dear Ned, I can see they're nothing but parrots.'

'My dear Conseil,' he solemnly replied, 'the parrot is the pheasant of those who have nothing else to eat.'

'And I will add', I said, 'that when properly prepared, the bird is worth sticking your fork into.'

And indeed, beneath the thick foliage, a large number of parrots were swooping from branch to branch, merely awaiting greater education to be able to speak a human tongue. For the moment they cackled together in the company of multicoloured parakeets and grave cockatoos apparently pondering some philosophical problem. All the while, brilliant red lories flew past like pieces of bunting carried away by the breeze, amongst noisy flights of kalaos, papuas painted in the finest shades of azure, and a whole collection of charming but generally inedible birds.

However, a bird particular to these regions and one which has never lived beyond the limits of the islands near Aru and Papua was missing from this collection, although chance was to allow me to admire one before long.

Having crossed a wood, we found a plain covered with bushes. Soon I saw some magnificent birds taking off. The way their long feathers were arranged meant they had to head into the wind to do so. Their undulating flight, the grace of their curves in the air, and the iridescence of their colours allured and charmed one's eyes. I had no difficulty in identifying them:

'Birds of paradise!'

'Order of Passeriformes, section of clystomores,' replied Conseil.

'Family of partridges?'

'I do not think so, Master Land. I am, nevertheless, counting on your skill to secure one of these charming products of the Tropics.'

'I'll have a go, sir, though I'm handier with a harpoon than a gun.'

The Malays, who trade a large number of these birds with the Chinese, have various methods for catching them that we could not employ. Sometimes they set snares at the tops of high trees where the birds of paradise like to live. Sometimes they capture them with a strong glue which stops them moving. Sometimes they even poison the springs where the birds like to drink. As for us, we were reduced to firing at them in flight, which left little chance of hitting them; and indeed we wasted much of our ammunition in vain.

By about 11 o'clock we had reached the foothills of the mountains in the centre of the island, and had still bagged nothing. Hunger spurred us on. The hunters in us had relied on the results of our own hunting, generally a mistake. But very fortunately

Conseil killed two birds with one stone, to his great surprise, and thus ensured lunch. He shot a white pigeon and a wood pigeon, which were quickly plucked, spitted, and grilled over a roaring deadwood fire. While these curious animals were cooking, Ned prepared some *Artocarpus*. Then the two pigeons were devoured down to the bones, and declared excellent. The nutmeg which they gorge themselves on flavours their flesh and makes it delicious.

'It's like chicken raised on truffles,' said Conseil.

'And now Ned, what else do you need?' I enquired.

'Some game with four legs, doctor,' he replied. 'All these pigeons and things are only hors-d'œuvres and nibbles! I won't be content until I've killed an animal with chops on it!'

'Nor me, Ned, until I catch a bird of paradise.'

'Let's continue then,' said Conseil, 'but heading back towards the coast. We are in the foothills of the mountains and it would seem sensible to return to the forest region.'

This was a good idea and was adopted. After an hour's walk we had reached a real forest of sago palms. A few harmless snakes fled from under our feet. Birds of paradise escaped as we approached, and I was really giving up being able to catch any, when Conseil, who was ahead, suddenly bent down, uttered a shout of triumph, and came back carrying a magnificent specimen.

'Congratulations!' I exclaimed.

'Monsieur is too kind.'

'But no, my good fellow, it was a master-stroke. To capture one of these birds alive, using one's bare hands!'

'If monsieur will study it closely he will see that my merit is not so great.'

'But why, Conseil?'

'Because this bird is drunk as a lord.'

'Drunk?'

'Yes monsieur, tipsy from the nutmeg it was eating under the nutmeg tree where I caught it. See, Ned, the terrible effects of intemperance.'

'My God! Considering how much gin I've drunk in the last two months, you can hardly talk.'

I examined the curious bird. Conseil was correct. The bird of paradise was drunk on the heady juice, totally incapacitated. It could not fly, it could hardly walk; but this didn't bother me, and I let it stew in its own nutmeg.

The bird belonged to the most beautiful of the eight species that have been observed in New Guinea and the neighbouring islands. It was the Great Emerald bird of paradise, one of the rarest.* It was a foot long. Its head seemed relatively small, with tiny eyes placed near the beak. But it had a wonderful collection of tints, with a yellow beak, brown feet and claws, hazel wings with purple tips, a pale-yellow head and back of neck, an emerald throat, and a rich brown stomach and breast. Two horned and downy frenums rose above its tail, with feathers that were very light and long and of a marvellous fineness, and these completed the array of that marvellous bird that the natives have poetically called 'the bird of the sun'.

I would have very much liked to take this superb bird of paradise back to Paris, and donate it to the Jardin des Plantes, which does not have a single living specimen.

'Is it that rare then?' asked the Canadian, in the tone of a hunter who hardly appreciates game from an aesthetic point of view.

'Very rare, my friend, and above all very difficult to capture alive; even dead these birds are the object of an important trade. As a result, the natives have ingeniously reconstructed them, just as pearls or diamonds are fabricated.'

'What!' exclaimed Conseil. 'They make fake birds of paradise?'

'Yes Conseil.'

'And does sir know how they go about it?'

'Perfectly. During the easterly monsoon season the birds of paradise shed their magnificent tail feathers, which the naturalists call subalary feathers. These are gathered by the bird-fakers, and carefully stitched on to some poor parakeet which has previously been mutilated. Then they dye the stitching, and varnish the bird, before sending the product of their singular industry to the museums and collectors of Europe.'

'Well,' said Ned, 'shame about the bird, but at least the feathers are okay, so unless you actually want to eat the creature, I don't see the problem.'

But if my desires were satisfied by catching this bird of paradise, the Canadian hunter's were not. Fortunately, at about two o'clock,

Ned shot a magnificent wild boar that the natives call *babi hutan*. The animal thus provided us with real quadruped meat, and was warmly welcomed. Land appeared very proud of his rifle shot. The pig, hit by the electric bullet, had fallen stone-dead.

The Canadian skinned and carefully gutted it, having extracted half a dozen chops to provide a grill for the evening meal. Then the hunting started again, soon to be marked by further exploits by Ned and Conseil.

The two friends had beaten the bushes, and thus set off a herd of kangaroos who hopped off on their elastic legs. But these animals did not flee quickly enough to escape being stopped by an electric capsule in full flight.

'Ah, sir!' exclaimed Ned Land, beginning to be affected by hunter's madness. 'What excellent game, especially when braised; what supplies for the *Nautilus*! Two, three, five on the ground, and when I think that we will guzzle all this meat ourselves and that those fools on board won't have a single scrap!'

I believe that carried away by his enthusiasm, the Canadian would have massacred the whole herd, at least if he had not spent so much time talking. But he satisfied himself with a dozen of these fascinating marsupials, which, as Conseil pointed out, form the first order of the aplacental mammals.

They were quite small. They belonged to a species of 'rabbit kangaroos' which normally live in the hollows of trees,* and can move very quickly. But if their size is not great, they do provide the best meat.

We were very pleased with the results of our hunting. A happy Ned suggested coming back the following day to this enchanted isle, which he wished to depopulate of all its edible quadrupeds; but events were to prove otherwise.

At six in the evening, we got back to the beach. Our boat was at its usual spot on the shore. The *Nautilus* emerged from the waves like a long reef two miles out.

Without further ado Ned got busy with the serious matter of cooking dinner. He knew his stuff. *Babi hutan* chops, grilled over the coals, were soon filling the air with a delicious aroma.

But I realize that I have become exactly like the Canadian. Here I am in ecstasy at freshly grilled pork! May I be forgiven, for the same reasons that I excused Master Land.

In the end, the dinner was very good indeed. Two wood pigeons completed our extraordinary menu. The sago paste, some bread-fruit from the *Artocarpus*, a few mangoes, half-a-dozen pine-apples, and the fermented milk from selected coconuts made our happiness complete. I even believe that the clearness of my worthy companions' brains left something to be desired.

'What about not going back to the *Nautilus* tonight?' said Conseil.

'What about never going back?' Ned Land rejoined.

At this moment a stone fell at our feet, interrupting the har-pooner's idea.

22

Captain Nemo's Lightning

We looked in the direction of the forest without getting up; my hand was suspended half-way to my mouth, although Land's reached its destination.

'Stones do not fall from the sky,' said Conseil; 'unless they are meteorites.'

A second stone, of carefully rounded shape, took a savoury wood pigeon's leg from Conseil's hand and lent support to his observation.

All three of us rose to our feet, guns on shoulders. We were ready for any attack.

'Is it monkeys?' exclaimed Ned.

'More or less,' said Conseil; 'savages.'

'To the boat!' I said, heading for the water.

It was indeed necessary to beat a retreat, since about twenty natives armed with bows and slings appeared on the edge of a thicket blocking the horizon less than a hundred paces to the right.

Our boat was on the shore, 10 fathoms away.

The savages approached, without running but making the most hostile gestures. Stones and arrows rained down.

Ned Land did not want to give up his provisions and in spite of the danger closing in, he picked up his pig with one hand,

and his kangaroos in the other, before decamping at a rate of knots.

A couple of moments later we were on the shore. Dropping the provisions and guns into the boat, pushing it out to sea, and starting the two oars going took only an instant. We had not gone any distance at all when a hundred savages, shouting and gesticulating, came waist-deep into the water. I watched to see if their arrival would bring anyone from the *Nautilus* on to the platform, but in vain. Lying in the distance, the enormous machine remained absolutely deserted.

Twenty minutes later we climbed on board. The hatches were lying open. We made the boat fast and went inside.

I went down to the salon, where music was being played. Captain Nemo was bent over his organ, deep in musical ecstasy.

'Captain?'

He did not hear.

'Captain!' I repeated, touching him.

He shivered, and turned round.

'Ah, it's you, doctor?' he said. 'Well how was your hunting? Did you gather any interesting plant specimens?'

'Yes, captain,' I replied. 'But unfortunately we also brought back a pack of bipeds, whose proximity worries me somewhat.'

'What sort of bipeds?'

'Savages.'

'Savages!' replied Captain Nemo in a sarcastic tone. 'And you're surprised, Dr Aronnax, that when you set foot on one of the lands of this globe, you find savages? Where are there not savages, and in any case, are those that you call savages any worse than the others?'

'But, captain . . .'

'For my part, sir, I have encountered them everywhere.'

'But', I replied, 'if you don't want to have them on board the *Nautilus* you should take some precautions.'

'Calm yourself, sir, there is nothing to worry about.'

'But there are a lot of natives.'

'How many did you see?'

'At least a hundred.'

'Dr Aronnax,' replied Captain Nemo, whose hands had gone back to the keyboard, 'even if all the natives of New Guinea were assembled on the beach, the *Nautilus* would have nothing to fear from their attack.'

The captain's fingers then ran over the instrument; I noticed that he only used the black keys, giving his melodies an essentially Scottish tonality. Soon he had forgotten I was there, and was deep in a reverie that I did not try to interrupt.

I went back to the platform. Night had already fallen, for at these latitudes the sun goes down quickly and there is no dusk. I could make out Gueboroar Island only vaguely now. But a large number of fires on the beach showed that the natives had not yet decided to leave.

I remained alone for several hours, sometimes musing about the natives, but without really being afraid of them. The captain's imperturbable confidence had won me over, and sometimes forgetting all about them and admiring the splendour of the tropical night, my memory flew back to France, following the stars in the sky which would shine over it in a few hours' time. The moon was radiant amid the constellations of the zenith. My thoughts then came back to this faithful and obliging satellite, which would come back to the same spot the day after tomorrow to raise the waves and pluck the *Nautilus* from its coral bed. At about midnight, seeing that everything was quiet on the darkened waves and beneath the trees on the shore, I returned to my cabin and fell into a deep sleep.

The night went by without incident. The Papuans were undoubtedly frightened by the mere view of the monster lying grounded in the bay, for its open hatches would have granted them easy access into the *Nautilus*.

At 6 a.m. on 8 January, I went back up to the platform. The shadows were lifting. Through the disappearing mists the island revealed its beaches and then its peaks.

The natives were still there, but more than the day before— perhaps five or six hundred. Some of them had taken advantage of the low tide to come forward on the coral heads to very near the *Nautilus*. I could easily make them out. They were true Papuans, men of athletic build and fine stock, with broad high foreheads, large noses, not flattened, and white teeth. Their woolly hair, dyed red, contrasted with their bodies, as black and shining as Nubians'. Their ear-lobes were cut and stretched, with bone beads hanging from them. These savages were generally naked. Amongst them I noticed a few women, clothed from the haunches to the knees with real grass skirts, held up by belts made of plants. Some of the chiefs had adorned their necks with crescents and necklaces of red and white glass beads. Nearly all of them were armed with bows, arrows, and shields, and carried on their shoulders a sort of net containing those rounded stones that they throw accurately with their slings.

One of the chieftains closest to the *Nautilus* was studying it with great attention. This was clearly a *mado* of high rank, for he was dressed in plaited banana leaves, finely worked on the edges and picked out in dazzling colours.

I could easily have shot this native, within close range, but I believed it better to wait for really hostile behaviour. When dealing with savages, it is better for the Europeans to riposte, rather than attack first.

During the whole of low tide the natives prowled near the *Nautilus*, but without making a great commotion. I heard them frequently repeating the word *assai*, and I understood from their gestures that they were inviting me to come ashore, an invitation I felt it better to decline.

So the dinghy did not leave the vessel that day, to the great displeasure of Master Land, unable to complete his provisions. The talented Canadian used the time to prepare the meat and flour he had brought back from Gueboroar. As for the savages, they went ashore again at about eleven in the morning, as soon as the tops of the coral began to disappear under the rising tide. But I could see that there were even more of them collecting on the beach. They had probably come from the neighbouring islands, or from New Guinea itself. I had not, however, noticed a single native dugout.

Having nothing better to do, I thought I would dredge these fine clear waters, where there could be seen a profusion of shells, zoophytes, and open-sea plants. This was in any case the last day the *Nautilus* was going to spend on these shores, that is if it floated at high tide the following day as Captain Nemo had promised.

I therefore called for Conseil, who brought me a small, light dredge, more or less like those used for collecting oysters.

'What about the savages?' asked Conseil. 'If monsieur pleases, they do not seem to me to be very ill-intentioned after all.'

'They *are* cannibals, my good fellow.'

'One can be a cannibal and a good man,' replied Conseil, 'just as one can be a glutton and honest. The one does not exclude the other.'

'All right, Conseil, I concede that they are honest cannibals, and that they eat their prisoners honourably. However, I do not wish to be devoured, even honestly, so I will remain on my guard, for the captain of the *Nautilus* does not seem to be taking any precautions. And now to work.'

For a couple of hours we worked hard at our fishing, but without bringing in anything rare. The dredge filled with Midas's ears, harp shells, *Melaniae*, but also the finest hammer shells I had ever seen. We also took some sea slugs, pearl oysters, and a dozen small turtles, which were set aside for the pantry.

But at the moment I least expected it, I found a marvel, or rather I should say, a very rarely encountered natural deformity. Conseil had just used the dredge, and his net was coming up loaded with various quite ordinary shells, when all of a sudden he saw me quickly plunge my arm into the net, pull a shell out, and give a conchologist's whoop, the most piercing cry the human throat is capable of.

'Is monsieur all right?' asked Conseil, startled. 'Has monsieur been bitten?'

'No my good fellow, but I would have willingly given a finger for my discovery.'

'What discovery?'

'This shell,' I said, showing the reason for my triumph.

'But it's simply a porphyry olive shell, of the genus *Oliva*, order of pectinibranchiates, class of gastropods, branch of molluscs . . .'

'Yes, Conseil, but instead of turning clockwise, this olive goes from left to right!'

'It can't do!'

'It can, my good fellow, it's a left-handed shell!'

'A left-handed shell?' repeated Conseil, his heart beating madly.

'Just look at its convolution!'

'Ah, monsieur can believe me,' said Conseil, taking the precious shell in his trembling hands, 'never have I experienced such emotion before.'

And there was good reason to be excited. As naturalists have pointed out, right-handedness is a law of nature. In their movements of translation and rotation, stars and their satellites move from right to left. Man uses his right hand more often than his left, and consequently his instruments and his machines, his staircases, locks, watch-springs, etc., are all designed to be used from right to left. Now Nature has generally followed this law in the winding of her shells. They are all right-handed, with rare exceptions; and when by chance their convolution *is* left-handed, collectors pay their weight in gold for them.

Conseil and I remained plunged in contemplation of our treasure, and I had promised to myself to enrich the Museum with it, when an ill-fated stone, projected by one of the natives, arrived and broke the precious object in Conseil's hand.

I uttered a cry of despair. Conseil threw himself on his gun, and took aim at a savage who was raising his sling about 10 yards away. I tried to stop him but the shot went off and broke the bracelet of amulets on the native's arm.

'Conseil,' I shouted. 'Conseil!'

'What, did monsieur not see that it was the cannibal's fault?'

'But a shell is not worth a man's life!' I said.

'Oh, the scoundrel! I would have preferred he broke my shoulder.'

Conseil was sincere, although I could not share his opinion. But the situation had changed during the last few moments without our noticing. About twenty dugout canoes had surrounded the *Nautilus*. These boats, hollowed out of tree-trunks, were long, narrow, and quite fast: they kept their balance by means of two bamboo outriggers floating on the surface. They had skilful half-naked paddlers in them, and it was not without trepidation that I saw them advancing.

It was evident that these Papuans had already had dealings with Europeans, and were familiar with their ships. But what could they possibly make of this long iron cylinder stretched out in the bay without either masts or funnels? Nothing good, for they had kept a respectful distance at first. But seeing it motionless, they slowly regained confidence, and were now trying to familiarize themselves with it. Now it was precisely this familiarity which needed to be prevented. Our guns, lacking detonations, could only make a moderate impression on these indigenous people, who only respect noisy devices. Lightning without peals of thunder would frighten people little, although the danger is in the lightning not the sound of thunder.

Suddenly the canoes came nearer the *Nautilus* and a cloud of arrows rained down on it.

'Good heavens, it's hailing,' said Conseil, 'and perhaps with poisoned hail!'

'We'd better go and tell Captain Nemo,' I said, disappearing down the hatch.

I went into the salon. No one was there. I ventured to knock on the door of the captain's bedroom.

I heard a 'Come in' and entered, finding Captain Nemo plunged in calculations filled with x's and algebraic signs.

'Am I disturbing you?' I said out of politeness.

'A little, Dr Aronnax,' replied the captain; 'but I assume that you must have a serious reason to want to see me.'

'Very serious. We are surrounded by native canoes, and will certainly be attacked by several hundred savages within a few minutes.'

'I see,' said Captain Nemo calmly; 'they have come with their canoes?'

'Yes, they have.'

'Well, all that is needed is to close the hatches.'

'Precisely, and I came to say . . .'

'Nothing could be simpler,' said Captain Nemo.

He pressed an electric button to transmit an order to the crew duty room.

'It's now taken care of,' he said after a pause, 'the dinghy is secured and the hatches closed. You are not afraid, I hope, that these gentlemen might attack the walls that your frigate's shells could not dent?'

'No, captain, but there is still a danger.'

'Yes?'

'Tomorrow, at the same time, we will need to open the hatches again to replenish the air inside the *Nautilus*.'

'That is true, since our vessel breathes like the cetaceans.'

'And if the Papuans are on the platform at that moment, I cannot see how you can prevent them coming in.'

'So, sir, you think they will venture on board?'

'I'm certain of it.'

'Well, doctor, let them. I can see no reason to prevent them. These Papuans are poor wretches after all, and I do not want my visit to Gueboroar Island to cost the life of a single one of these unfortunates!'

I was going to withdraw at that point, but Captain Nemo detained me and invited me to sit near him. He asked with interest about our land excursions and hunting, but did not seem to understand the need for meat that drove the Canadian. The conversation then touched on various other subjects, and Captain Nemo showed himself most kind, although not any more communicative.

Amongst other things, we got to talking about the *Nautilus*'s situation, aground at precisely the same spot where Dumont d'Urville got into great difficulties. Then, on this subject:

'D'Urville was one of your great sailors, he was one of your most intelligent navigators! He was France's Captain Cook. Unfortunate savant! To have braved the ice floes of the South Pole, the corals of the South Seas, the cannibals of the Pacific, only to perish miserably in a train accident! If this tireless man was able to reflect during the last few moments of his life, imagine what his last thoughts must have been.'

Speaking in this way Captain Nemo seemed moved, and his emotion was, I thought, to his credit.

Then, map in hand, we retraced what the French navigator had achieved: his voyages of circumnavigation; his two attempts to reach the South Pole, leading to the discovery of Adélie Land and Louis Philippe Land; and finally his hydrographic surveys of the main islands of the Pacific.

'What your d'Urville did on the surface of the seas,' Captain Nemo said, 'I have done in the interior of the oceans, but more easily, more completely than he could. The *Astrolabe* and the *Zélée*, always being pushed hither and thither by hurricanes, could not equal the *Nautilus*, a peaceful base for study, truly settled in the heart of the waters!'

'There is one point of resemblance, however, between Dumont d'Urville's corvettes and the *Nautilus*.'

'Which one is that, sir?'

'It is that the *Nautilus* has run aground like them!'

'The *Nautilus* is not aground!' Captain Nemo coldly replied. 'The *Nautilus* is designed to rest on the seabed; and I do not have to undertake the difficult work and manœuvres that d'Urville had to perform to refloat his corvettes. The *Astrolabe* and *Zélée* nearly perished, but my *Nautilus* is in no danger. At the said hour tomorrow, the tide will lift it calmly up, and it will continue its navigation through the seas.'

'Captain,' I said, 'I do not doubt . . .'

'Tomorrow,' Captain Nemo added as he got up, 'at 2.40 p.m., the *Nautilus* will float and will leave Torres Strait unharmed.'

Having pronounced these words in a slightly sharp tone, Captain Nemo bowed slightly. This was to take leave of me, and so I went back to my room.

There I found Conseil, keen to know the result of my conversation with the captain.

'My good fellow, when I inferred that his *Nautilus* was in danger from the Papuan natives, the captain replied very ironically. So I only have one thing to say to you: have confidence in him and go to sleep without worrying unduly.'

'Monsieur has no need of my services?'

'No, my friend. What is Ned Land doing?'

'With all due respect, monsieur,' replied Conseil, 'friend Ned is making a kangaroo pie that will be an absolute wonder.'

I remained alone and I went to bed, but slept quite badly. I could hear the savages, who were trampling about on the platform uttering deafening cries. The night went by in this way without the crew abandoning its usual inertia. They were no more worried by the presence of these cannibals than the soldiers inside a strong fort would have been by ants running over their fortifications.

I got up at 6 a.m. The hatches had not been opened, and so the air had not been renewed inside. But the tanks, designed to cope with any eventuality, were functioning properly, pumping a few cubic metres of oxygen into the thin atmosphere of the *Nautilus*.

I worked in my room until midday but without seeing Captain Nemo for a single moment. Apparently no preparations for leaving were being made on board.

I waited a while longer, then went into the salon. The clock read half-past two. In ten minutes the sea would have reached its maximum height, and if Captain Nemo had not made a rash promise, the *Nautilus* would immediately be freed. If not, many months would pass before it could leave its coral bed.

Soon a few preliminary vibrations could be felt in the hull of the vessel. I could hear its plates grinding against the hard limestone of the coral underneath.

At 2.35, Captain Nemo appeared in the salon.

'We're about to leave,' he said.

'Ah!' I said.

'I have given the order to open the hatches.'*

'But what about the Papuans?'

'The Papuans?' replied Captain Nemo, shrugging his shoulders slightly.

'Won't they come inside the *Nautilus*?'

'But how?'

'By coming down the hatches that you are opening.'

'Dr Aronnax,' he calmly replied, 'it is not that easy to enter the hatches of the *Nautilus*, even when they are open.'

I stared at the captain.

'You do not understand?'

'No, not at all.'

'Well come and you will see.'

I headed for the central stairwell. There, Ned and Conseil, puzzled and fascinated, were watching a few of the crewmen opening the hatches, whilst cries of anger and blood-curdling howls rang out outside.

The hatch covers were opened outwards. Twenty horrible faces appeared. But the first of these natives to put his hand on the guide-rail of the stairs* was thrown backwards by some invisible force and ran off, uttering awful cries and making exaggerated leaps.

Ten of his companions imitated him. Ten suffered the same fate.*

Conseil was in ecstasy. Land, carried away by his violent

instincts, rushed on to the staircase, but the moment he seized the guide-rail with his hands, he too was thrown back.

'My God!' he exclaimed. 'I've been struck by lightning!'

This explained everything. It was no longer a handrail, but a metal conductor completely charged with electricity from the vessel and culminating in the platform. Whoever touched it received a powerful shock, and this shock would have been fatal if the captain had put all the current from his apparatus into the conductor! Between his assailants and him, Nemo had extended an electric circuit that none could cross with impunity.*

The terrified Papuans had meanwhile retreated, crazed with terror. Half laughing, we massaged and consoled poor Ned, who was swearing like a madman.

Just then the *Nautilus*, raised by the last undulations of the tide, left its coral bed at that precise fortieth minute predicted by the captain. Its screw started beating the waters with majestic slowness. Its speed gradually increased, and sailing safe and sound on the ocean's surface, it left behind the dangerous passes of Torres Strait.*

23

Ægri Somnia*

THE following day, 10 January, the *Nautilus* continued its progress underwater, but with a remarkable speed that I cannot estimate to have been less than 35 knots. The speed of its screw was such that I could not see its revolutions, let alone count them.*

When I thought that the marvellous electrical agent not only gave movement, heat, and light to the *Nautilus*, but also protected it against external attacks, transforming it into a holy ark which no desecrator could touch without being struck by lightning, my admiration knew no limits; and this went from being directed to the machine back to the engineer who had built it.

We were heading due west, and on 11 January we rounded Cape Wessel, which is situated at longitude 135° and latitude 10°N, forming the eastern point of the Gulf of Carpentaria. There were still quite a number of reefs, but now more spread out and pinpointed on the chart with extreme precision. The *Nautilus* thus easily avoided the breakers of Money Reef to port and Victoria Reefs to starboard, situated at longitude 130° on the 10th parallel which we were following without deviating.

On 13 January Captain Nemo, having arrived in the Timor Sea, sighted the island of the same name at longitude 122°. This island, with an area of 1,625 square leagues, is governed by rajahs. These princes profess to be sons of crocodiles, that is issued from the highest origin to which human beings can claim. Accordingly, these scaly ancestors abound in the island's rivers, and are the subject of a particular veneration. They are protected, they are spoilt, they are adulated, they are fed, they are offered young maidens as fodder—and ill-fortune to the foreigner who lays a hand on the sacred lizards.*

But the *Nautilus* did not have to deal with these ugly animals. Timor was visible at noon for a mere moment, while the first officer was taking our position. In the same way, I caught only a glimpse of the little island of Roti, part of the same group, whose women have a firmly established reputation for beauty on the Malaysian markets.

Starting from that point, the direction of the *Nautilus*, which of course could go where it wanted, switched to the south-west. It headed for the Indian Ocean. Where were Captain Nemo's whims going to take us? Would he head back for the coasts of Asia again? Would he approach the shores of Europe? Such decisions seemed highly unlikely on the part of a man who fled the inhabited continents. Would he therefore go even further south? Would he round the Cape of Good Hope, then Cape Horn, and head for the South Pole? Would he finally come back to the waters of the Pacific, where his *Nautilus* could find easy and independent sailing? Time would tell.

Having coasted the last efforts of the solid element to withstand the liquid element, the reefs of Cartier, Hibernia, Seringapatam, and Scott, we were far from all land on 14 January. The speed of the *Nautilus* had markedly dropped, and it was highly capricious in its movements, sometimes sailing underwater, sometimes floating on the surface.

During this stretch of the voyage, Captain Nemo carried out

interesting experiments on the temperature of the water at different depths. Ordinarily, these measurements are obtained using quite complicated instruments, whose results are dubious or worse, either thermometric sounds whose glasses often break under the water-pressure or devices based on the change in the resistance of metal to electric currents. The results obtained in this way cannot be properly verified. In contrast, Captain Nemo was going to measure the temperatures of the sea depths using his own observation, and his thermometer, in direct contact with the various parts of the liquid, gave him the temperatures immediately and reliably.

Either by filling its tanks or by descending obliquely with its planes inclined, the *Nautilus* successively reached depths of 3,000, 4,000, 5,000, 7,000, 9,000, and 10,000 metres. The final conclusion of the experiments was that the sea possessed a constant temperature of $4\frac{1}{2}°$ at a depth of 1,000 metres, whatever the latitude.

I followed these experiments with inordinate interest. Captain Nemo showed a true passion for them. I often wondered why he made these observations. Was it to benefit his fellow beings? This seemed improbable, for his studies were destined to perish sooner or later with him in some unknown sea. Unless he was intending the results of his experiments for me. But that would mean he accepted that my strange voyage might come to an end, and this end, I could not yet see.

Whatever the reasons, Captain Nemo also told me of the various figures he had obtained, which established the relative densities of water in the main seas of the globe. From this information I drew a personal lesson which had nothing to do with science.

It was during the morning of 15 January. The captain, with whom I was strolling on the platform, asked me if I knew what the different densities of the oceans' waters were. I replied that I did not, and that science lacked rigorous observations on the subject.

'I have carried out such observations,' he said, 'and I can vouch for their accuracy.'

'Yes,' I replied. 'But the *Nautilus* is a world apart and its scientists' secrets do not reach dry land.'

'You are right, sir,' he said after a moment's silence. 'It is a world apart, as foreign to terra firma as the planets accompanying this globe around the sun, and we will never benefit from the studies of Saturn's or Jupiter's scientists. However, since chance has linked our two lives, I can communicate the results of my observations to you.'

'I am all ears, captain.'

'As you know, sea water is denser than fresh water, but its density is not uniform. If I take the density of fresh water as 1.000, I find 1.028 for the waters of the Atlantic, 1.026 for the Pacific, 1.030 for the Mediterranean . . .'

'Aha!' I thought. 'So he does venture into the Mediterranean.'

'. . . 1.018 for the Ionian Sea, and 1.029 for the waters of the Adriatic.'*

Decidedly the *Nautilus* did not avoid the frequented waters of Europe, and I deduced from this that it would bring us back towards more civilized landmasses, perhaps quite soon. I thought that Ned Land would be pleased to hear the news.

For a few days our time was spent entirely in experiments of all sorts concerning the salt content of water at different depths, its electric charge, its colour, its transparency, and in all these cases Captain Nemo employed an ingenuity which was equalled only by his good disposition towards me. Then I did not see him again for a few days, and remained as though quarantined on board his ship.

On 16 January, the *Nautilus* seemed to fall asleep only a few yards below the surface of the waves. Its electrical apparatus was no longer operating, and its motionless screw let it wander at the mercy of the currents. I supposed that the crew must be busy with internal repairs necessitated by the violence of the mechanical movements of the machine.

My companions and I were then witness to a curious scene. The panels of the salon were open, and as the searchlight of the *Nautilus* was not on, a dim darkness reigned amidst the waters. The stormy sky, covered with thick clouds, gave only the first depths of the ocean an insufficient light.

I observed the state of the sea in conditions where the largest fish appeared merely as faintly sketched shadows, when the *Nautilus* was suddenly surrounded by full light. At first I thought that the searchlight had been switched on again, and that it was projecting its electric brilliance through the liquid mass. I was wrong, as I realized with a quick glance.

The *Nautilus* was floating in a phosphorescent stratum, which was becoming dazzling in this darkness. It was produced by myriads of glowing animalculae, whose brightness increased as they slid over the metallic hull. I then noticed sparks in these luminous waters, as if produced by streams of molten lead in a fiery furnace or metallic bodies heated to red or white heat; as a result of the contrast certain radiant portions appeared as shadows in this burning environment, from which, however, all shades should logically have been banished. For this was no longer the even illumination of our normal lighting! A highly unusual vigour and movement were present. This light felt as if alive.

There was indeed an infinite agglomeration of pelagic infusoria and miliary noctilucents, actually globules of diaphanous jelly equipped with threadlike tentacles, of which 25,000 have been counted in 30 cubic centimetres of water. Their light was further increased by the distinctive gleams of jellyfish, starfish, *Aureliae*, piddocks, and other phosphorescent zoophytes, impregnated with the fertilizer of organic materials decomposed by the sea, and perhaps with mucus secreted by fish.

For several hours the *Nautilus* floated in these brilliant waves, with our admiration increasing when we saw large marine animals playing there like salamanders. In the midst of that fire which did not burn, I saw swift, elegant porpoises, the tireless clowns of the seas, as well as 3-metre sailfish, the intelligent forecasters of hurricanes, whose formidable swords sometimes struck the window of the salon. Small fishes also appeared, a variety of triggerfishes, jumping scombroids, wolf-unicorns, and a hundred others, streaking the luminous atmosphere as they swam.

The dazzling sight was an enchantment. Perhaps some atmospheric condition was increasing the effect of the phenomenon? Perhaps some storm was raging on the surface of the waves? But at a few metres' depth the *Nautilus* did not feel its fury as it swayed peacefully in the midst of the tranquil waters.

We continued on our way, constantly charmed by some new marvel. Conseil observed and classified the zoophytes, articulates, molluscs, and fish. The days went by quickly, and I no longer counted them. As was his wont, Ned attempted to vary the diet on board. Like true snails, we had got used to our shells, and I maintain that it is very easy to become a perfect snail.

This existence seemed easy and natural to us, and we could no longer imagine a different life on the terrestrial globe—when an event occurred to remind us of the strangeness of our situation.

On 18 January, the *Nautilus* was at longitude 105° and latitude 15°S. The weather was threatening, the sea hard and squally. There was a strong easterly wind. The barometer, which had been falling for several days, announced an approaching battle of the elements.

I climbed on to the platform while the first officer was taking his measurements of the hour angles. I waited for the sentence to be pronounced, following the daily habit, but that day it was replaced by another phrase, no less incomprehensible. I saw Captain Nemo appear almost immediately and his eye, equipped with a telescope, focus on the horizon.

For a minute or so the captain remained motionless, concentrating on the point captured in his field of vision. Then he lowered his telescope and exchanged about ten words with his deputy. The latter seemed to be in the sway of an emotion which he was trying in vain to control. Captain Nemo, more master of himself, remained cool. He seemed in any case to be raising objections, to which his deputy was replying with formal assurances. At least that is what I understood from the differences in their tones and gestures.

As for myself, I had carefully scrutinized the direction being observed, but without spotting anything. The sky and the water melted together in a horizonal line of perfect clarity.

Captain Nemo had started walking from one end of the platform to the other, without looking at me, perhaps without seeing me. His pace was assured, but less regular than usual. He stopped sometimes and examined the sea, his arms crossed on his chest. What could he be looking for in that immense space? The *Nautilus* was at that moment lying a few hundred miles from the nearest coast!

The first officer had picked his telescope up again, and was obstinately scrutinizing the horizon, coming and going, stamping his feet, his nervous agitation in contrast to his commander's calm.

In any case the mystery was necessarily going to be solved; for after a while, on an order from Captain Nemo, the engine increased its propulsive power and rotated the screw more quickly.

At this moment the first officer again drew his chief's attention to something. The captain stopped his pacing, and directed his telescope at the point indicated. He examined it for a long time. For my part, fascinated, I went down to the salon to fetch the excellent telescope I normally used. Then, leaning on the framework of the searchlight projecting at the front of the platform, I got ready to examine the whole line of sea and sky.

But my eye had not yet been applied to the glass, when the instrument was suddenly torn from my hands.

I turned round. Captain Nemo was before me, but I could hardly recognize him. His face was transfigured. His eyes, burning with a dark fire, stood out under his frowning eyebrows. His teeth were half bared. His stiff body, his clenched fists, and his head hunched on his shoulders demonstrated the violent hatred filling his whole person. He did not move. My telescope, dropping from his hand, rolled at his feet.

Had I inadvertently provoked this angry attitude? Did this bewildering character imagine that I had surprised some secret forbidden to the guests of the *Nautilus*?

No! I was not the object of the hatred, for he was not looking at me: his eyes remained implacably fixed on the invisible point of the horizon.

At long last, Captain Nemo regained his self-control. His face, which had been so deeply changed, recovered its usual calm. He said a few words in the foreign tongue to his first officer, and then he turned to me.

'Dr Aronnax,' he said, in rather an imperious tone, 'I want you to observe one of the engagements which bind you to me.'

'Yes, captain?'

'You must allow your companions and yourself to be locked up, until such time as I consider it appropriate to give you back your liberty.'

'You are the master,' I replied, gaping at him, 'but may I ask you a question?'

'You may not, sir.'

I could no longer question this, but merely obey, since all resistance would have been impossible.

I went down to the cabin Ned and Conseil occupied, and told them of the captain's decision. I leave it to the imagination how this information was greeted by the Canadian. But in any case there was no time for further explanation. Four crewmen were waiting at the door, and they led us to the cell where we had spent our first night on board the *Nautilus*.

Ned Land tried to protest, but the only reply was the door closing in his face.

'Could monsieur tell me what this means?' enquired Conseil.

I told my companions what had happened. They were as astonished as I was, and understood as little.

I fell into a deep reflection; the strange apprehension on Captain Nemo's face would not leave my mind. I felt incapable of putting two logical ideas together, and was getting lost in the most absurd hypotheses, when my concentration was interrupted by these words from Land:

'Look, lunch is served.'

The table was indeed ready. It was clear that Captain Nemo had arranged this at the same time as he had increased the speed of the *Nautilus*.

'Would monsieur allow me to make a suggestion?'

'Yes, my good fellow.'

'Well, monsieur should have lunch. It would only be sensible, because we do not know what might happen later.'

'You're right, Conseil.'

'Unfortunately', said Ned, 'we have only been given the normal menu on board.'

'Dear Ned,' said Conseil, 'what would you have said if there had been no food at all?'

This argument cut short the harpooner's protests.

We sat down. The meal was rather quiet. I did not eat very much. Conseil 'forced himself' through prudence, and Ned Land did not waste a mouthful, whatever his feelings. Then when lunch was finished, each of us rested in his corner.

Suddenly, the luminous globe lighting the cell went out, leaving us in total darkness. Ned Land soon went to sleep, and Conseil also allowed himself to fall into a heavy slumber, which astonished me. I was wondering what had caused his imperious need for sleep, when I felt my own brain being permeated with a thick torpor. My eyes, which I tried to keep open, closed despite my best efforts. I was prey to unhappy hallucinations. Sleeping tablets had clearly been added to the food we had eaten. Prison was not enough to hide Captain Nemo's activities from us, he also needed to employ sleep!

I heard the hatches being closed. The rocking of the sea, which caused a slight rolling movement, stopped. Had the *Nautilus* left the surface? Had it gone back down into the motionless depths?

I tried to resist sleep. It was impossible. My breathing grew weaker. I felt a deadly cold freezing my arms and legs, grown as heavy as if paralysed. My eyelids, exactly like leaden skull-caps, fell over my eyes. I could not lift them up. An unhealthy sleep, full of nightmares, took hold of my whole being. Then the visions disappeared, and left me completely prostrate.

24

The Coral Kingdom

THE following day I woke up with my head remarkably clear. To my great surprise I was in my room. My companions had undoubtedly also been put back in their cabin, without them realizing any more than I had. They would not know any more about what had happened during the night than I did, and I could only count on the hazards of the future to solve the mystery.

Next I thought about leaving the room. Was I free once again or still a prisoner? Entirely free. I opened the door, and went along the corridors, heading up to the central stairwell. The hatches, closed the day before, were now open again. I arrived on the platform.

Ned and Conseil were waiting for me. I asked them a few

questions. They knew nothing, having fallen into a heavy sleep which left them with no recollection, and had been very surprised to find themselves in their cabin.

As for the *Nautilus*, it seemed to us as peaceful and mysterious as ever. It was moving over the surface of the waves at a moderate speed. Nothing seemed changed on board.

Land examined the sea with his penetrating eyes. It was deserted. The Canadian could see nothing new at all on the horizon. Neither sails nor land. A westerly breeze was noisily blowing, and long waves, dishevelled by the wind, were making the vessel roll quite noticeably.

Once it had replenished its air, the *Nautilus* remained at an average depth of 15 metres, in order to be able to come up again quickly. Most unusually, this latter action was carried out several times during 19 January. The first officer went up to the platform on each occasion, and the accustomed phrase rang out through the ship.

As for Captain Nemo, he did not appear. Of those serving on board, I only saw the impassive steward, who served me with his usual precision and silence.

At about two o'clock I was busy sorting out my notes in the salon, when the captain opened the door and appeared. I greeted him. He gave me an almost imperceptible nod, without saying a word. I went back to my work, hoping that he would perhaps give me an·explanation of the events that had marked the previous night. He did nothing of the sort. I gazed at him. His face appeared tired, with reddened eyes that had not been refreshed by sleep. His face expressed a deep sadness, a real heartache. He walked up and down then sat down and got up again. He took a book at random, but put it down immediately. He consulted his instruments without taking his usual notes, and seemed unable to remain in one place for a single moment.

Finally he came up to me, and asked:

'Sir, are you a doctor?'

I expected this question so little that I looked at him for a time without replying.

'Are you a doctor?' he repeated. 'Several of your colleagues studied to be doctors: Gratiolet, Moquin-Tandon,* and others.'

'Yes, I am. I'm a doctor and a former hospital intern. I prac-tised for several years before joining the Museum.'

'Good.'

My reply had evidently satisfied Captain Nemo, but not knowing what the point of the conversation was, I waited for further questions, thus retaining the possibility of replying depending on circumstances.

'Dr Aronnax, would you consent to treat one of my men?'

'One of your men is ill?'

'Yes.'

'I am ready.'

'Please come this way.'

I will admit that my heart was pounding. For some reason, I could see a connection between this illness of a crewman and the events of the day before, and the mystery absorbed me at least as much as the sick man himself.

Captain Nemo took me to the stern of the *Nautilus*, and invited me to enter a cabin situated near the crew room.

On a bed lay a man about 40 years old with an energetic face, a typical Anglo-Saxon.

I leaned over him. He was not only ill, but wounded. His head was swathed in blood-stained dressing and resting on two pillows. I removed the dressing: the wounded man, staring with large eyes, allowed me to without a single complaint.

The wound was horrible. The cranium, shattered by a blunt instrument, revealed the brain laid bare, and the cerebral matter had undergone a deep abrasion. Blood clots had formed in the diffluent matter, which had turned maroon. There had been both contusion and concussion of the brain. The man's breathing was laboured, and a few spasms shook the muscles of his face. The cerebral phlegmasia was complete, and had produced a paralysis of sensation and movement.

I took the wounded man's pulse. It was intermittent. The extremities of the body were already becoming cold, and I could see that death was approaching, without it appearing possible to slow it down. Having seen to the poor man's wounds, I reapplied the dressings to his head; and turned to Captain Nemo.

'How did he get his wound?'

'What difference does it make!' the captain replied evasively. Then: 'A shock from the *Nautilus* broke one of the levers of the engine, which struck this man.* What is your diagnosis of his condition?'

I hesitated to give my view.

'You can speak freely,' said the captain. 'This man does not understand French.'

I looked at the wounded man one more time, and then said: 'This man will be dead within two hours.'

'Can nothing save him?'

'Nothing.'

Captain Nemo's hand tightened, and a few tears slipped from his eyes, which I did not believe capable of weeping.

For a few moments longer, I examined the dying man, as his life slowly ebbed away. He got paler and paler in the electric light bathing his deathbed. I looked at his intelligent head furrowed with premature wrinkles, which unhappiness, perhaps poverty, had hollowed out long before. I wanted to guess the secret of his life from the last words to escape his lips.

'You can retire now, Dr Aronnax,' Captain Nemo said.

I left the captain in the dying man's cabin and went back to my room, greatly moved by the scene. The whole day I was disturbed by sinister forebodings. That night I slept badly and, between my frequently interrupted dreams, I thought I could hear distant sighs and something like a funereal intoned psalm. Was this the prayer for the dead, murmured in that language I could not understand?

The following morning I went back on deck. Captain Nemo was already there. As soon as he saw me, he came up.

'Dr Aronnax, would you like an underwater excursion today?'

'With my companions?' I asked.

'If they wish.'

'They are at your command, captain.'

'Please put on your diving suits then.'

There was no discussion of the dying or dead man. I rejoined Ned Land and Conseil and told them of Captain Nemo's invitation. Conseil quickly accepted, and this time the Canadian agreed to accompany us.

It was then eight in the morning. At 8.30 we were fitted out for our second excursion, equipped with lighting and breathing apparatus. The double door opened, and accompanied by Captain Nemo, who was followed by about ten crewmen, we set foot on the solid ground where the *Nautilus* was resting at a depth of 10 metres.

A slight slope led to an uneven floor at about 15 fathoms. The bottom was completely different from the one I had visited on my first excursion under the waters of the Pacific Ocean. Here there was no fine sand, no underwater prairie, no pelagic forest. I instantly recognized the marvellous region which Captain Nemo was presenting to us that day. It was the coral kingdom.*

In the branch of the zoophytes, and in the class of the alcyonarians, one can observe the order of Gorgonacea, which includes the three groups of Gorgon heads, isidia, and corallines. It is to this latter group that coral belongs, a curious substance which has been classified in turn in the mineral, vegetable, and animal kingdoms. A medication for the ancients, a jewel for the moderns, it was only in 1694 that the Marseillais Peyssonel* definitively classified it in the animal kingdom.

Coral is a collection of animalculae united on a polypary of a stony and brittle nature. These polyps have a unique begetter which produces them by means of budding; they have their own existence while at the same time participating in communal life. They thus live a sort of natural socialism. I was aware of the latest studies carried out on this strange zoophyte, which becomes mineralized while arborizing, as the apposite terms of the naturalists would have it; and nothing could be of greater interest for me than to visit one of the petrified forests that nature has planted on the ocean floor.

The Ruhmkorff lamps were switched on and we followed a coral reef which was still being formed and which would, with the help of time one day, close off this portion of the Indian Ocean. The route was lined with labyrinthine bushes formed by the intermingling of small shrubs, covered with little starred flowers with white petals. But these arborescences fixed to the rocks on the ground were totally unlike the plants on earth, for all grew downwards.

The light produced a thousand charming effects when playing through the brightly coloured branches. I thought I could see the membranous and cylindrical tubes trembling in the movements of the water. I was tempted to gather their fresh corollas, adorned with delicate tentacles: some of them had just bloomed, while others which were hardly born had small fish with rapid fins grazing past them like flocks of birds. But if my hand approached these living flowers, these sensitive mimosae pudicae, the alert was immediately given throughout the colony. The white corollas moved back into their red sheaths, the flowers went out before my eyes, and the bush changed into a block of stony nipples.

Chance had placed me in the presence of the most valuable examples of this zoophyte. The coral was of similar quality to that collected on the Mediterranean coasts of France, Italy, and North Africa. Its brilliant shades justified its poetic names of *blood flower* and *foam of blood*, the names the trade gives to its finest products. Coral sells at up to 500 francs a kilogram, and the watery depths at this spot protected a fortune for a whole world of coral collectors. This precious matter, often mixed with other polyparies, formed compact inextricable groups called 'macciota', on which I noticed some admirable specimens of pink coral.

But soon the bushes grew smaller and the arborescences got larger. True petrified woods and the long aisles of a fantastic architecture opened up before our feet. Captain Nemo headed into a dark gallery, whose gentle slope led us to a depth of 100 metres. The light of our coils sometimes produced magical effects, clinging to the asperities of these natural arches and to pendentives hanging like chandeliers, where it picked out points of fire. Between the coral shrubs I noticed other polyps just as remarkable, mellites and irises with articulated ramifications, then some tufts of corallines, some green and some red: real wracks encrusted in their limestone salts, that the naturalists, after long debate, have definitively classified as belonging to the vegetable kingdom. But as one thinker has remarked,* 'perhaps this is the real point where life dimly rises from a sleep of stone, without yet cutting itself off from that rude starting-point'.

After two hours' march, we had finally reached a depth of about 300 metres, the furthest point where coral begins to form. But here there were no longer isolated bushes or modest copses of low trees. This was an enormous forest, with great mineral vegetation and enormous petrified trees bound together by garlands of elegant Plumalaria, those sea-creepers all offset by their tones and reflections. We passed freely under their high branches, lost in the shadow of the waves, whilst at our feet the tubipores, the mean-drines, the astrea, the mushroom corals, and the caryophyllenes formed a carpet of flowers strewn with dazzling gems.

Oh, what indescribable visions! Why could we not communicate our feelings? Why were we imprisoned in these glass and metal masks? Why were words to each other not possible? Why could we not live the life of the fish populating the liquid element, or even that of amphibians who can move for long hours through the dual realm of land and water as the whim takes them?

Meanwhile Captain Nemo had stopped. My companions and I interrupted our step, and when I turned round I saw that his men had formed a semi-circle around their leader. Looking closer, I noticed that four of them were carrying a long object on their shoulders.

We were now standing at the centre of a vast clearing, surrounded by the tall arborescences of the underwater forest. Our lamps projected a sort of dusky light over the space, inordinately lengthening the shadows on the ground. On the edge of the clearing, the darkness became immense, containing only the tiny sparks thrown out by the sharp edges of the coral.

Ned and Conseil were standing beside me. As we looked I understood that I was going to assist at a strange scene. When I examined the ground, I realized that it was swollen by slight extumescences encrusted with chalk deposits, laid out with a regularity that betrayed the hand of man.

In the middle of the clearing, on a pedestal of rocks roughly piled up, stood a coral cross, extending its long arms as if made of petrified blood.

On a sign from Captain Nemo, one of the men came forward, untied a pick from his belt, and began to dig a hole a few feet away from the cross.

Suddenly everything became clear! The clearing was a cemetery,* the hole a grave, the long object the body of the man who had died during the night! Captain Nemo and his men had come to bury their companion in this shared resting place on the bottom of the inaccessible ocean!

Never was my mind inflamed to such a point! Never was my brain invaded by more excited ideas! I did not want to see what my eyes could see!

Meanwhile the grave was slowly being dug. From time to time the fish would flee their disturbed sanctuary. I could hear the iron pick resounding on the chalky ground, sometimes producing sparks when it hit some flint lost at the bottom of the waters. The hole got longer and wider, and soon it was deep enough to admit the body.

The bearers approached. The body, wrapped in a cloth of white byssus, was lowered into the watery grave. Captain Nemo, arms crossed on chest, and all the friends of that man who had loved them, knelt in an attitude of prayer. My two companions and I had devoutly lowered our heads.

The grave was then covered with the fragments torn from the ground, forming a slight bulge.

When it was done, Captain Nemo and his men stood up. Approaching the grave, all knelt down again, and all stretched out their hands in a final farewell . . .

Then the funeral procession headed back to the *Nautilus*, passing once more under the arches of the forest in the midst of the woods, alongside the coral bushes, and continually climbing.

Finally the lights on board appeared. Their luminous trail guided us towards the *Nautilus*. At one o'clock we were back again.

As soon as I had changed my clothes, I went back up on the platform, and in the grip of a terrible obsession of ideas, I went and sat down beside the searchlight.

Captain Nemo joined me. I got up and asked him:

'So this man died during the night, as I foresaw?'

'Yes, Dr Aronnax.'

'And he is now resting beside his companions in that coral cemetery?'

'Yes, forgotten by all, but not by us! We have dug the grave and now the polyps have the task of sealing the dead in it for eternity!'

And in a sudden movement, hiding his face in clenched hands, the captain tried in vain to suppress a sob. Then he added:

'It's our cemetery there, peaceful, hundreds of feet below the surface of the waves.'

'At least your dead slumber tranquilly, captain, out of the reach of sharks.'

'Yes,' Captain Nemo replied gravely, 'sharks and men!'

PART TWO*

I

The Indian Ocean

HERE begins the second part of this voyage* under the seas. The first ended with that moving scene in the coral cemetery, which left such a deep impression on me. So was Captain Nemo's life spent completely in the bosom of the immense sea, where everything, even his tomb, was laid ready in its remotest chasms? There, not a single sea creature would come to trouble the final sleep of the inhabitants of the *Nautilus*, friends welded to each other in death as they were in life! 'Not a single man, either!' the captain had added.

Always the same defiance of human society, wild and implacable.*

For my part, I was no longer content with the hypothesis that satisfied Conseil. The worthy fellow persisted in seeing in the captain of the *Nautilus* merely one of those unrecognized scientists, who return humanity's indifference with mistrust. For him he was still a misunderstood genius, tired of the disappointments of the earth, who had had to take sanctuary in that inaccessible environment where he could freely exercise his abilities. But in my view this theory explained only one of Captain Nemo's sides.

The mystery of the previous night, when we had been shut up in prison and in slumber; the captain's violent precaution of tearing from my eye the telescope I was preparing to scour the horizon with; that man's fatal wound, caused by an inexplicable collision by the *Nautilus*: everything forced me in a single direction. No, Captain Nemo was not content merely to flee from mankind! His formidable machinery served not only his passion for freedom, but perhaps also the pursuit of some terrible sort of revenge.*

For the moment nothing is clear to me; I can only glimpse

gleams in the dark, and must limit myself to writing, so to speak, at the dictation of events.* But in any case nothing binds us to Captain Nemo. He knows that it is impossible to escape from the *Nautilus*. We are not even prisoners on our parole. No word of honour ties us. We are mere captives, prisoners disguised by being called guests, in a semblance of courtesy. However, Ned Land has not given up hope of recovering his liberty. It is clear that he will take the first opportunity chance offers him. I will undoubtedly do the same, and yet it will be a wrench to carry away with me what the captain's generosity has let us guess of the mysteries of the *Nautilus*. For is this man, all things considered, to be hated or admired? Is he a victim or a killer? Also, to be truthful, before leaving him for ever, I would like to finish off this tour of the submarine world whose beginnings have been so magnificent. I would like to study the marvels strewn under the seas of the globe in their entirety! I would like to finish seeing what no man has yet seen, even if I have to pay for this insatiable need to know with my life! What have I discovered to date? Nothing, or almost nothing, since we have covered only 6,000 leagues of the Pacific!

However, I know full well that the *Nautilus* is approaching inhabited shores, and that if some chance of escaping is offered to us, it would be cruel to sacrifice my companions to my passion for the unknown. I will have to follow, perhaps even guide them. But will an opportunity ever arise? Forcibly deprived of his free will, man longs for such an opportunity, but the scientist, the enquiring mind, fears it.

At noon that day, 21 January 1868, the first officer came to take the altitude of the sun. I went up on the platform, lit a cigar, and followed the operation. It seemed clear that this man could not understand French, for I made observations out loud several times which would have drawn some involuntary sign of attention from him if he had understood them, but he remained mute and impassive.*

Whilst the officer was carrying out his observations with the sextant, one of the *Nautilus*'s sailors—the vigorous man who had accompanied us to Crespo Island on our first underwater excursion—came to clean the glass of the searchlight. I studied the workings of the apparatus, whose power was multiplied a hundred times by rounded lenses like those on lighthouses, and which served to direct the light in the appropriate direction. The electric lamp was set up in such a way as to provide the maximum power of illumination. Thus its light was produced in a vacuum, which ensured it was both uniform and intense. The vacuum also economized on the graphite points creating the luminous arc. An important saving for Captain Nemo, who wouldn't easily have been able to renew his supply; but in these conditions they hardly ever wore out.

While the *Nautilus* got ready to continue its underwater travel, I went back down to the salon. The hatches closed again and we set sail due west.

We were ploughing the waves of the Indian Ocean, a vast liquid plain covering 550 million hectares, with waters so transparent that anyone looking down from the surface feels dizzy. The *Nautilus* was generally sailing at between 100 and 200 metres' depth. This carried on for a few days. To anyone else but me, with my immense love for the sea, the hours would undoubtedly have seemed long and monotonous, but my whole time was filled by daily excursions to the platform, where I got new strength from the invigorating ocean air, viewing the rich waters through the salon's windows, reading the books in the library, and writing my memoirs; and so did not leave a moment for tiredness or boredom.

The health of every one of us remained in a very satisfactory state. The diet on board suited us perfectly, and personally, I could easily have managed without the variety that Ned devoted his efforts to producing, through a spirit of protest. Even colds were not frequent in this constant temperature. In any case, there was a supply of the stony coral dendrophyllia on board, known in the South of France as sea fennel, which provided an excellent cough pastille in the shape of its polyps' melting flesh.

For a few days we saw many aquatic birds, palmipeds and sea-gulls of various sorts. Some were adroitly killed and when prepared in a certain way provided a very acceptable water-game. Amongst the great long-flight birds, winging at considerable distances from all land and resting on the waves from the fatigues of their flight, I noticed some magnificent albatrosses with discordant cries like donkeys' braying, birds belonging to the family of longipennates. Representatives of the family of totipalmates included rapid frigate birds which fished on the surface, and large numbers of boatswain birds or tropicbirds, including ones that were as large as pigeons with red ribbing and a white plumage shaded in pink tones which brought out the black colour of their wings.

The *Nautilus*'s nets brought in several kinds of turtle of the genus hawksbill, with curved backs and shells that are much appreciated. These reptiles are good at diving, and can stay underwater for a long time by closing the fleshy valves where their nasal tubes emerge. When they were caught, some of the hawksbills were still sleeping in their shells, safe from marine animals. The flesh of these turtles was generally mediocre, but their eggs produced a dish fit for kings.

As for the fish, they always startled us into admiration, as we surprised them in their secret aquatic life through the open panels. I observed several species that I had not had the opportunity to study until then.

I will cite principally ostracions, peculiar to the Red Sea, the Indian Ocean, and the tropical ocean regions off the coasts of America. These fish, like tortoises, armadillos, sea urchins, and crustaceans, are protected by an armour which is neither chalk nor stone but actual bone. Its armour is solid and is either triangular or quadrangular. Amongst the triangular ones, I noted some 5 centimetres long, with a health-giving flesh of an exquisite flavour, and brown tails and yellow fins; I recommend their acclimatization even in fresh water, to which a certain number of sea fish easily become accustomed. I will also cite the quadrangular ostracions with four large tubercules mounted on their backs; speckled ostracions with white points on their lower bodies, which can be domesticated like birds; trigonals fitted with spurs formed by the extension of their bony hides, whose bizarre groaning has given them the nickname of 'sea pigs'; and dromedaries with large conical humps and flesh that is hard and leathery.

I again pick out from the daily notes kept by Master Conseil two fish of the genus tetrodon peculiar to these seas: seven-inch Electridae of the brightest colours and bandtail puffers with red backs and white breasts and with three highly distinctive lengthwise rows of filaments. Next, from other genera: tail-less oviforms looking like black-brown eggs covered in white stripes; porcupine-fish, veritable sea porcupines armed with stings and able to swell up to form a ball bristling with darts; the sea-horses found in all oceans; flying pegasi with long snouts and very long pectoral fins arranged in the form of wings, thus allowing them, if not to fly, at least to spring into the air; spatulate pigeons whose tails are covered with many scaly rings; macrognathic fish with long jaws, fine 25-centimetre fish shining with the most pleasant colours; pale Callionymidae with rough heads; thousands of jumping blennies with black stripes and long pectoral fins gliding over the surface at tremendous speeds; delicious veliferous fish able to hoist their fins as if unfurling sails to catch favourable currents; splendid kutti on which Nature has lavished yellow, sky-blue, silver, and gold; trichoptera whose wings are formed of filaments; cotti always soiled with silt and which produce a rustling sound; gurnards whose livers are considered poisonous; *Bodiani* with moving eye-flaps; and finally souffies with long tubular snouts, the veritable fly-catchers of the ocean, armed with guns not designed by any Chassepot or Remington,* but which kill insects by simply hitting them with a drop of water.

In the 89th genus of fish classified by Lacépède, belonging to the second sub-class of osseous fish characterized by a gill cover and a bronchial membrane, I noticed the scorpion fish, whose head has stings on it and which has only one dorsal fin: depending on their subgenus, these creatures are either covered with small scales or devoid of them. The second subgenus provided us with specimens of didactyls thirty to forty centimetres long, with yellow stripes and fantastic-looking heads. It contains several specimens of that bizarre fish fittingly nicknamed the 'sea toad', a fish with a big head, sometimes hollowed out by deep sinuses, sometimes swollen with protuberances; it bristles with spurs and is studded with tubercules; it has hideous irregular horns; its body and tail are covered with callouses; its stings produce dangerous injuries; and it is vile and repugnant.

From 21 to 23 January, every 24 hours the *Nautilus* covered 250 leagues, or 540 miles, averaging 22 knots. If the various varieties of fish could be identified as they went past, this was because they were attracted by the electric light and tried to travel with us; most were left behind by the speed and quickly fell back; some, however, managed to keep up with the *Nautilus* for a while.

On the morning of the 24th, at latitude 12° 5′S and longitude 94° 33′E, we sighted Keeling Island, a madreporian upheaval covered with magnificent coconut trees that was visited by Mr Darwin and Captain Fitzroy.* The *Nautilus* followed the coasts of this desert island at a short distance. Its dredges brought in numerous specimens of polyps and echinoderms as well as curious tests from the branch of molluscs. A few precious examples from the species of delphinium added to Captain Nemo's treasures, to which I joined a punctiferous astrea, a sort of parasitic polypary often attached to a shell.

Soon Keeling Island disappeared over the horizon, and sail was set for the north-west, and the tip of the Indian subcontinent.

'Civilized lands,' Land said to me that day. 'Better than those islands of Papua, where there are more savages than deer! In India, Dr Aronnax, there are roads, railways, and British, French, and Indian towns. You cannot go five miles without meeting a compatriot. Hey, isn't this the time to take our leave from Captain Nemo?'

'No, Ned, no,' I answered in a very determined tone. 'Let it run, as you sailors say. The *Nautilus* is getting closer to the inhabited landmasses. It is heading towards Europe, let it take us there. Once we are back in our own seas, we can see about what we should do. In any case, I don't suppose that Captain Nemo will let us go hunting on the Malabar or Coromandel Coasts as he did in the forests of New Guinea.'

'Well, sir! Can't you try without his permission?'

I did not reply. I didn't want to talk about it. Deep down, I longed to see the hazards of destiny through to the end, the destiny that had cast me on board the *Nautilus*.

From Keeling Island onwards, our movements generally slowed down. They were also more changeable and often took us down to great depths. Several times we used the inclined planes, placed at an angle to the water-line by means of internal levers. In this way we descended two or three kilometres, but without ever probing the distant bottoms of the Indian Ocean, that sounds of 13,000 metres have not been able to touch. As for the temperature of the lower strata, the thermometer still invariably indicated

4 degrees above zero.* I observed only that the water of the upper strata was always colder when above shallows than in the open sea.

On 25 January the ocean was totally deserted, and the *Nautilus* spent the day on the surface, beating the waters with its powerful screw and making them spurt up to a great height. In these conditions, how could it not have been mistaken for a gigantic cetacean? I spent three-quarters of the day on the platform. I gazed at the sea. Nothing in view except, westerly at about 4 p.m., a long steamer, heading on the opposite tack. Its masts were visible for a while, but it could not sight the *Nautilus*, too flat and low in the water. I decided that the steamer had to belong to the Peninsular and Oriental Line, which goes from the island of Sri Lanka to Sydney, putting in at King George Sound and Melbourne.

At five o'clock, before that swift dusk which links day to night in the tropical zones, Conseil and I were marvelling at a curious sight.

There is one charming animal whose encounter is a promise of good luck, according to the ancients. Aristotle, Athenaeus, Pliny, and Oppian* studied its habits and exhausted the entire poetics of the scholars of Greece and Italy on it. They called it *Nautilus* or *Pompylius*. But modern science has not endorsed their terminology, and the mollusc is now known as the Argonaut.

Anyone consulting the worthy Conseil would have learned that the branch of molluscs is divided into five classes; that the first class, the cephalopods, whose members are sometimes exposed and sometimes testaceous, consists of two families, the *Dibranchia* and the *Tetrabranchia*; that these two families are distinguished by the number of their gills; that the *Dibranchia* has three genera, the argonaut, the calamar, and the cuttlefish; and that the *Tetrabranchia* only has one, the nautilus. If, following this nomenclature, a rebel spirit confused the argonaut, which is 'acetabuliform', that is equipped with suckers, with the nautilus, which is 'tentaculated' or equipped with tentacles, he would have no excuse for his mistake.

It was a school of these argonauts that was travelling over the surface of the ocean. We could count several hundred of them.

They belonged to the species of tuberculous argonauts, unique to the seas around India.

The gracious molluscs were using their locomotive tubes to move backwards by expelling through their tubes the water they had taken in. Of their eight tentacles, six were long and thin and floating on the water, and two were rounded into palmate shapes raised for the wind like light sails. I could see their spiral wavy shell perfectly, accurately compared by Cuvier to an elegant launch. A true vessel in fact. It transports the animal which has secreted it but isn't attached to it.

'Although the argonaut is free to leave its shell,' I said to Conseil, 'it never does.'

'Just like Captain Nemo,' he judiciously replied. 'Which is why he should have called his ship the *Argonaut*.'*

For another hour the *Nautilus* floated in the midst of this school of molluscs. Then some mysterious fright suddenly took hold of them. As if on a signal, all the sails were abruptly brought down, the arms retracted, the bodies contracted; the shells changed their centre of gravity and turned over, and the whole fleet disappeared under the waves. It happened instantaneously, and never did ships of a squadron manœuvre with more precision.

Night fell abruptly at this moment, as, hardly lifted by the breeze, the waves stretched peacefully out under the wales of the *Nautilus*.

The following day, 26 January, we cut the equator at the 82nd meridian, and returned to the northern hemisphere.*

During the day, a formidable pack of sharks formed a procession around us. Terrible animals, which abound in these seas and make them highly dangerous. They were *Heterodonti portusjacksonsi* with brown backs and whitish stomachs, armed with eleven rows of teeth, eyed sharks with necks marked with a large black spot surrounded by white resembling an eye, and Isabella sharks with round muzzles and dotted with dark points. Often these powerful animals would rush against the salon window with somewhat worrying violence. Ned Land was no longer in control of himself. He wanted to go back up to the surface and harpoon these monsters, especially certain dogfish sharks with jaws full of teeth laid out like a mosaic and great 5-metre striped sharks which provoked him with remarkable persistence. But soon the *Nautilus* would increase its speed and easily leave the fastest of these sharks behind.

On 27 January, at the opening of the vast Bay of Bengal, we encountered dead bodies floating on the surface on several occasions, a dreadful sight! These were the dead from Indian towns, washed down the Ganges and into the open sea, and which the vultures, the only grave-diggers of the country, had not finished eating. But there was no shortage of sharks to help them in their funereal work.

At seven in the evening, the half-submerged *Nautilus* was sailing through a sea of milk. As far as the eye could see, the ocean looked as if it had changed to milk. Was it the effect of the moon's rays? Hardly, since the moon was scarcely two days old and still hidden below the horizon in the rays of the sun. The whole sky, although lit up by the scintillations of the stars, seemed black in contrast with the whiteness of the waters.

Conseil could hardly believe his eyes, and asked me the reasons for this remarkable phenomenon. Fortunately I was in a position to reply.

'It is what is called a sea of milk,' I told him, 'a vast expanse of white water, often seen on the coasts of Amboina and the waters around.'

'But', asked Conseil, 'could monsieur inform me what produces such an effect, for I do not imagine that the water has actually changed to milk!'

'No, my good fellow, this whiteness which so surprises you is due merely to the presence of myriads of tiny infusoria creatures, types of tiny glow-worms of a gelatinous translucent appearance, the thickness of a hair, whose length is not greater than a fifth of a millimetre. Some of these creatures join together over a distance of several leagues.'

'Several leagues!'

'Yes my good fellow, and do not try to calculate the number of such infusoria. You would not get far, for navigators have apparently sailed on these seas of milk for more than 40 miles.'

I do not know if Conseil followed my recommendation, but he seemed plunged into deep thought, no doubt trying to calculate how many fifths of millimetres are contained in 40 miles square.

As for me, I continued to observe the phenomenon. For several hours, the *Nautilus*'s prow cut the whitish waves, and I noticed that it floated soundlessly over the silky water, as if sliding over those foamy areas sometimes produced in bays by the collision of currents and counter-currents.

At about midnight the sea suddenly resumed its normal colour, but behind us, as far as the eye could see, the sky reflected the whiteness of the waves for a long time as if filled with the dim gleams of an aurora borealis.

2

A New Suggestion by Captain Nemo

ON 28 February, when the *Nautilus* surfaced at noon at latitude 9° 4′ N, it was in view of land lying eight miles to the west. My eye was drawn to a range of mountains about 2,000 feet high, formed into very wild shapes. Once our position had been taken, I went back to the salon, and when it had been plotted on the map, I realized that we were in the environs of the island of Sri Lanka, that pearl hanging from the earlobe of the Indian subcontinent.

I went into the library to look for a book about the island, the most fertile on the globe. I found a volume by H. C. Sirr, Esq. entitled *Ceylon and the Cingalese*.* Returning to the salon, I first noted the co-ordinates of Sri Lanka, which antiquity called by so many different names. It was situated between 5° 55′ and 9° 49′ N and 79° 42′ and 82° 4′ E of the Greenwich meridian, its length was 275 miles, its maximum width 150 miles, its circumference 900 miles, and its area was 24,448 square miles, that is slightly smaller than Ireland.

Captain Nemo and his deputy appeared.

The captain glanced at the map, then turning to me:

'The island of Sri Lanka,' he said. 'A realm famous for its pearl fishing. Would it suit you, doctor, to visit one of the fishing grounds?'

'Most certainly, captain.'

'Good. It's easy to arrange. But if we can see the fishery, we won't be able to see the fishermen. The season has not started yet. No matter. I will give orders to head for the Gulf of Mannar, which we will reach during the night.'

The captain said a few words to his first officer, who immediately went out. Soon the *Nautilus* returned to its liquid element, and the pressure-gauge indicated that it was at a depth of 30 feet.

With the map in front of my eyes, I looked for the Gulf of Mannar. I found it on the ninth parallel, on the north-west coast of Sri Lanka. It was formed by a strip stretching out from the little island of Mannar. To reach the bay, we needed to work our way up the western coast of Sri Lanka.

'Dr Aronnax,' Captain Nemo continued, 'pearls are fished in the Bay of Bengal in the Indian Ocean, in the seas of China and Japan, in those of South America, in the Gulf of Panama, and in the Gulf of California; but it is Sri Lanka that has the best fishing. We are undoubtedly arriving a little early. The fishermen only assemble in the Gulf of Mannar during the month of March, where their 300 boats work for 30 days at the lucrative exploitation of the sea's treasures. Each boat has ten rowers and ten divers. The divers work in two groups, and dive alternately, going down to a depth of 12 metres by means of a heavy stone held between their feet and connected to the boat by a rope.'

'So this primitive method is still used?'

'It is,' said Captain Nemo, 'although the fisheries belong to the hardest-working people in the world, the British, to whom they were given by the Treaty of Amiens in 1802.'*

'It seems to me, nevertheless, that the diving suit, as you employ it, would be very useful in such an operation.'

'Yes, since the poor divers cannot remain underwater for very long. The Briton Percival,* in his journey to Sri Lanka, speaks of a 'Kafir' who spent five minutes without coming up to the surface. But this seems hardly credible to me. I know that some divers can stay as much as 57 seconds and very good ones, 87;* however, these are rare, and when these unfortunate beings come back on board, their noses and ears are dripping water tinted with blood. I believe that the average time these divers can manage is 30 seconds, during which time they rush to cram into a little net all the pearl oysters they can tear off; but generally these divers do not live to an old age: their sight diminishes; ulcerations break out on their eyes; wounds form on their bodies; and often they have strokes at the bottom of the sea.'

'Yes, a sad profession which serves only to satisfy a few caprices. But tell me, captain, how many oysters can a boat collect in a day?'

'About 40,000 to 50,000. It is even said that the British government carried out diving on its own account in 1814, and that its divers brought back 76 million oysters in 20 days' work.'

'Are these divers at least paid enough?'

'Scarcely. In Panama they earn only a dollar a week. Most of them only get one sol per pearl-bearing oyster, and how many they bring back with none inside!'

'A sol for the poor people who make their masters rich! It's odious.'

'So, doctor, you and your companions will visit the Bank of Mannar, and if by chance some early diver is already there, we will see him at work.'

'Agreed, captain.'

'Incidentally, Dr Aronnax, you're not afraid of sharks?'

'Sharks!' I exclaimed.

This question appeared senseless, or worse.

'Well?' said Captain Nemo.

'I must admit, captain, that I am not yet familiar with this sort of fish.'

'We are, and with time you will get used to them. In any case we will be armed, and as we follow our route perhaps we can bag a few sharks. It's interesting hunting. So, Dr Aronnax, until tomorrow, first thing.'

Having said that in a casual tone, Captain Nemo left the salon.

If you are invited to hunt bears in the mountains of Switzerland, you would say: 'Fine! Tomorrow we are going bear hunting.' If you are invited to hunt lions on the plains of the Atlas Mountains or tigers in the jungles of India, you would say: 'Oh! apparently we are going to try and bag a few tigers or lions!' But if you were invited to go hunting sharks in their natural element, you would perhaps request a few moments for reflection before accepting the invitation.

As for me, I passed a hand over my forehead, where a few drops of cold sweat were standing out.

'Let's reflect,' I said to myself, 'taking our time. Hunting for otter in the underwater forests as we did at Crespo Island is okay. But to run around the ocean floor, when one is more or less certain to bump into sharks, is another thing! I know full well that in certain countries, the Andaman Isles for example, the dark-skinned natives do not think twice about attacking sharks, dagger in one hand and noose in the other. But I also know that many of those who face the dreadful beasts don't come back alive! In any case I'm not a native, and even if I were, I do believe that some slight hesitation on my part would not be out of place.'

So there I was, dreaming of sharks, in a reverie of vast jaws armed with multiple rows of teeth and capable of cutting a man in two. I already felt the pain around my middle section. Also, I could not digest the casual way in which the captain had made the deplorable invitation! Wouldn't one have put it that way if we were going to track some inoffensive fox through the woods?

'Well!' I thought. 'Conseil will never want to come, and that will get me off going with the captain.'

As for Ned, I must admit that I did not feel as confident of his judgement. Dangers, however great, always held an attraction for his aggressive nature.

I started reading Sirr's book again, but I was turning the pages automatically.* Between the lines I could see jaws that were frighteningly open.

At this moment Conseil and the Canadian came in, with peaceful, even happy appearances. They did not know what was waiting for them.

'You know what, sir?' Ned Land said to me. 'Your Captain Nemo—cursed be his name!—has just made a very nice suggestion.'

'Ah,' I said, 'you know . . .'

'If monsieur pleases,' said Conseil, 'the captain of the *Nautilus* has invited us to visit the magnificent pearl fisheries of Sri Lanka tomorrow in monsieur's company. He did it in excellent terms, and behaved like a thorough gentleman.'

'He didn't say anything else to you?'

'Nothing, sir,' replied the Canadian. 'Except that he had spoken to you about this little excursion.'

'Just so, and did he give you any details about . . .'

'None. You will be coming with us, won't you?'

'Me . . .? I imagine so. I can see that you're looking forward to it, Master Land.'

'Yes it seems interesting, very interesting.'

'Dangerous, perhaps!' I added in an appealing tone.

'Dangerous?' replied Land. 'A mere excursion to an oyster bed?'

Captain Nemo had clearly not judged it useful to intimate the idea of sharks to my companions. As for me, I was looking at them with unfocused eyes, as if they were already missing a limb or two. Should I warn them? Undoubtedly, but I didn't know how to go about it.

'Monsieur,' Conseil said, 'would monsieur like to give us some details of pearl fishing?'

'About the fishing itself, or about the incidents which . . .'

'The fishing,' replied the Canadian. 'Before venturing on to terrain, it's useful to have some information about it.'

'Well sit down my friends, and I'll tell you everything that the Briton Sirr has just told me.'

Ned and Conseil sat down on the settee, and the Canadian started by asking:

'Sir, what is a pearl?'

'My good Ned, for the poet the pearl is a tear from the sea; for the Orientals it is a solidified dewdrop; for ladies it is a jewel of elongated form, of a hyalin lustre, made of mother-of-pearl, that they wear on their finger, ear, or neck; for the chemist it is a mixture of lime, phosphate, and carbonate with a little gelatine; and finally, for the naturalist it is merely an unhealthy secretion by the organ in certain bivalves that produces mother-of-pearl.'

'Branch of molluscs,' said Conseil, 'class of acephalics, order of testaceans.'

'Precisely, Professor Conseil. Now amongst these testaceans, pearls are produced by the earshell, iris, turbans, *Tridacnae*, and marine pinna, in a word by all those that secrete mother-of-pearl, the blue, bluish, violet, or white substance lining their valves.'

'Mussels as well?' asked the Canadian.

'Yes, the mussels of certain rivers in Scotland, Wales, Ireland, Saxony, Bohemia, and France.'

'Well, we'll have to be careful in future,' replied Ned.

'But', I continued, 'the mollusc which secretes pearls par excellence is the pearl-bearing oyster, the *Meleagrina margaritifera*, the precious pearl-oyster. The pearl is merely a mother-of-pearl accretion that takes on a globular form. Either it adheres to the shell of the oyster, or it encrusts itself in the creature's folds. On the valve, the pearl adheres; on the flesh, it is free. But its core is always a small hard body, either a sterile ovule or a grain of sand, around which the mother-of-pearl is successively deposited over several years in thin concentric layers.'

'Can several pearls be found in a single oyster?' asked Conseil.

'Yes my good fellow, there are certain pearl-oysters that are a true jewel-case. An oyster has even been cited, although I permit myself to doubt this, which contained no less than 150 sharks.'

'A hundred and fifty sharks!' exclaimed Ned.

'Did I say sharks!' I exclaimed quickly. 'I mean 150 pearls. Sharks would make no sense.'

'Indeed,' said Conseil. 'But will monsieur now tell us how the pearls are extracted?'

'There are several methods. When the pearls adhere to the valve, the fishermen often tear them off with pliers. But most frequently, the pearl-oysters are laid out on the mats of esparto grass covering the shore. They die in the open air, and after ten days they are at the appropriate degree of decay. They are plunged into vast tanks of sea water, and opened and washed. This is where the two stages of the gutters' work start. First they separate the sheets of mother-of-pearl, known in the trade as "true silver", "bastard white", or "bastard black", and pack them in boxes of 125 to 150 kilograms. Then they remove the parenchyma from the oyster and boil and sieve it, so as to separate out even the smallest pearls.'

'Does the price of pearls vary depending on their size?' asked Conseil.

'Not only depending on their size, but also their shape, their "water", or colour, and their "orient", or iridescent and variegated lustre which lends such charm to their appearance. The finest pearls form separately in the tissue of the mollusc; called virgin pearls or paragons, they are white, often opaque, but sometimes of an opaline transparency, and most commonly spherical or piriform. When spherical they form bracelets; piriform, drop-earrings and are sold individually, as they are the most precious. The other pearls adhere to the oyster's shell, and being more irregular, are sold by weight. Lastly, the small pearls known as seed pearls are classified in a low-grade class; they are also sold by weight and serve in particular for embroidery on church vestments.'

'But this work of separating the pearls according to size must be long and tedious?' asked the Canadian.

'No, my friend. The work is carried out by means of eleven sieves or colanders containing variable numbers of holes. The pearls that remain in the colanders containing 20 to 24 holes are of the first order. Those caught by the sieves with 100 to 800 holes are of the second order. The pearls from sieves with 900 to 1,000 holes form the seed.'

'Ingenious,' said Conseil, 'and now I understand how grading the pearls is carried out. But can monsieur tell us how much the work on the pearl-oyster beds brings in?'

'According to Sirr's book,' I replied, 'the pearl fisheries of Sri Lanka are leased for the sum of 3 million sharks per year.'

'Francs!' said Conseil.

'Yes, francs. Three million francs, but these pearl fisheries apparently no longer bring in what they used to. The same is true of the American ones, which produced 4 million francs in the reign of Charles V of France but at present, only two-thirds of that. In sum, the total turnover from pearls can be evaluated as being 9 million francs.'

'But', asked Conseil, 'have some pearls not been celebrated for being offered at a very high price?'

'Yes my good fellow. It is said that Caesar gave Servilia a pearl estimated to be worth about 120,000 francs of our money.'*

'I have even heard it told', said the Canadian, 'of a certain lady in ancient times who drank pearls in her vinegar.'

'Cleopatra,' said Conseil.

'I bet it tasted bad.'

'Awful, friend Ned,' replied Conseil; 'but at 1½ million francs a small glass of vinegar is highly priced.'

'I'm sorry I didn't marry that lady,' said the Canadian, moving his arm in a disquietening way.

'Ned Land, the husband of Cleopatra!' exclaimed Conseil.

'But I needed to get married, Conseil,' the Canadian replied seriously, 'and it was not my fault if it didn't actually work out. I even bought a necklace of pearls for Kat Tender,* my fiancée, who then married somebody else. Well that necklace only cost me a dollar and a half, and yet—Dr Aronnax should believe me—the pearls in it would not have passed through the colander with twenty holes.'

'My good Ned,' I said laughing, 'those were artificial pearls, mere globules of glass covered on the inside with essence of Orient.'

'Oh, that essence of Orient', replied the Canadian, 'must cost a great deal.'

'Virtually nothing! It is merely the silvery substance from the scales of a fish called bleak, collected underwater and preserved in ammonia. It has no value.'

'Perhaps that's why Kat Tender married someone else,' replied Master Land philosophically.

'But', I said, 'to come back to pearls of great value, I do not think that a king ever possessed one superior to Captain Nemo's.'

'This one?' said Conseil, pointing to a magnificent jewel displayed in a case.

'Yes, I believe I can assign it a value of 2 million . . .'

'Francs!' quickly said Conseil.

'Yes, 2 million francs, and it undoubtedly only cost the captain the effort of picking it up.'

'Hey!' exclaimed Ned Land. 'Maybe, we'll find another one tomorrow, on our excursion!'

'Bah!' said Conseil.

'And why not?'

'What would be the point of millions of francs on board the *Nautilus*?'

'On board there would be none,' said Ned, 'but elsewhere . . .'

'Oh, elsewhere!' said Conseil, shaking his head.

'In fact', I said, 'Master Land is right. If ever we bring a pearl worth several million back to Europe or America, it would lend both great authenticity and a great price to the story of our adventures.'

'Right,' said the Canadian.

'But', said Conseil, who always came back to the instructive side of things, 'is pearl fishing dangerous?'

'No,' I said quickly, 'especially if you take certain precautions.'

'What are the risks in that profession?' said Land. 'Swallowing a few mouthfuls of water!'

'As you say Ned. Incidentally,' I said, trying to adopt Captain Nemo's casual tone, 'are you afraid of sharks, my good Ned?'

'Me?' said the Canadian. 'As a professional harpooner, I am paid to laugh at them.'

'It is not a question of catching them with a swivel hook, hoisting them on the ship's deck, cutting their tails off with axes, opening up their stomachs, tearing out their hearts, and throwing them back into the sea!'

'Then, we're . . .?'

'Yes, precisely.'

'In the water?'

'In the water.'

'What the hell, with a good harpoon! You know sir, these sharks are quite poorly designed animals. They have to turn on to their stomach to bite you, and during that time . . .'

Ned Land had a way of saying the word *bite* that made cold shivers run down your spine.

'Well, and you, Conseil, what do you think of these sharks?'

'Me?' said Conseil. 'I will be frank with monsieur.'

'Here we go,' I thought.

'If monsieur can face such sharks,' said Conseil, 'I do not see why his faithful servant should not face them with him.'

3

A Pearl Worth Ten Million

NIGHT fell. I went to bed, and slept rather badly. Sharks played an important part in my dreams, and I found both very appropriate and very inappropriate the etymology which derives the French word for shark, *requin*, from the word *requiem*.*

I was woken at four in the morning by the steward that Captain Nemo had put at my personal service. I stood up quickly, got dressed, and went into the salon.

Captain Nemo was waiting there.

'Are you ready, Dr Aronnax?'

'I am.'

'Then please follow me.'

'And my companions, captain?'

'They have been informed, and are waiting for us.'

'Shouldn't we put on our diving suits?'

'Not yet. I haven't brought the *Nautilus* too close to the shore, and we are still some distance from Mannar Bank; but I have prepared the dinghy to take us to the exact spot for the diving, which will save us a long journey. The diving equipment is in the dinghy, and we can put it on when we actually begin our submarine exploration.'

Captain Nemo led the way to the central staircase leading up to the platform. There we found Ned and Conseil, delighted at the prospect of a 'pleasure party'. Five sailors from the *Nautilus*, oars at the ready, were waiting, tied up alongside.

The night was still dark. Patches of cloud covered the sky, revealing only the occasional star. I looked towards the land, but could see only an uncertain line masking the three-quarters of the horizon between the south-west and the north-west. Having worked its way up the western coast of Sri Lanka during the night, the *Nautilus* was now to the west of the bay, or rather of the gulf formed by Sri Lanka itself and Mannar Island. There, beneath the dark waters, lay the bank of pearl oysters, an inexhaustible source of pearls over twenty miles in length.

Captain Nemo, Conseil, Ned, and I took our places in the stern of the small boat. The coxswain took the tiller, his four companions leaned over their oars, the painter was cast off, and we pushed off.

The boat headed southwards. The rowers did not hurry. I noticed that while they pulled strongly, their strokes came at ten-second intervals, following the method generally used in national navies. As the boat coasted between strokes, the droplets pattered down on the dark waves like globules of molten lead. A slight swell, rolling in from the open sea, made the boat rock slightly, and the crests of a few waves lapped at the bow.

We were silent. What was Captain Nemo thinking? Perhaps about the land he was approaching, too near for his taste—unlike the Canadian, for whom it seemed still too far. As for Conseil, he was a mere spectator.

At about half-past five the first tints on the horizon showed the outline of the coast more clearly. It appeared to be somewhat flat on the eastern side, but undulating towards the south. We were still five miles away, and the coast blended into the misty waters. Between us and the shore the sea was deserted. Not a single diver or boat. A profound solitude reigned at the pearl-fishers' meeting place. As Captain Nemo had said, we were arriving in these waters a month too early.

At six o'clock the day broke with the abruptness characteristic of the Tropics, which do not have dawn or dusk. The sun's rays pierced the shoal of clouds piled up on the eastern horizon, and the radiant orb climbed rapidly.

I could now see the land distinctly, with a few trees scattered here and there.

The boat approached Mannar Island, whose rounded shape loomed to the south. Captain Nemo had risen from his seat, and was gazing over the sea.

At a sign from him the anchor was dropped, but the chain hardly ran, for just there was one of the highest points of the bed of pearl oysters and the depth was more than a metre. The boat swung round following the ebb-tide heading back out to sea.

'We're there, Dr Aronnax,' said Captain Nemo. 'You can see that the bay is well enclosed. In a month's time, large numbers of fishermen's boats will gather here, and the divers will boldly embark on their search in these waters. The bay is marvellously shaped for this kind of fishing. It is protected from strong winds, and the sea is never very high: highly favourable conditions for the divers' work. We will now put on our diving suits, and begin our excursion.'

I made no reply, and staring all the time at the suspect sea, was helped into my heavy sea suit by the sailors. Captain Nemo and my two companions also put on their suits. None of the men from the *Nautilus* were to accompany us on this new excursion.

We were soon enclosed in rubber garments up to the neck, with air equipment fastened on by shoulder straps. There was no sign of the Ruhmkorff lighting devices. Before placing my head in the copper helmet I mentioned this to the captain.

'They would be useless, as we shall not be descending to any great depth, and the sun will be enough to light our path. Besides, it would not be a good idea to carry an electric lamp in these waters. The light might accidentally attract some of the dangerous local inhabitants.'

As Captain Nemo spoke, I turned to Ned Land and Conseil. These two friends had already put their heads in the metal spheres, and could neither hear nor talk.

I had one last question for the captain.

'Our weapons?' I said. 'What about our guns?'

'Guns?' he said. 'What for? Do your mountaineers not attack bears with daggers in their hands? And is steel not safer than lead? Here is a faithful blade. Pass it through your waist and let's go.'

I looked at my companions. They were also armed like us and in addition Ned was brandishing an enormous harpoon which he had placed in the boat before we left the *Nautilus*.

Following the captain's example, I allowed the heavy copper sphere to be put on my head, and the air tanks immediately began to operate.

A moment later, the sailors let us gently down into the water one after another, and we set foot on a fine sand at about five feet depth. Captain Nemo made a sign to us. We followed him, descended a gentle slope, and disappeared under the waves.

The ideas which had obsessed me now left me. I became astonishingly calm. The ease with which I was able to move increased my confidence, and the unusual sights around me captured my imagination.

The sun was already producing enough light underwater. The smallest objects could be seen. After ten minutes' walk, we were about fifteen feet below the surface, and the ground became more or less level.

At our step, like flocks of snipe in a marsh, rose flights of curious fish, of the genus *Monoptera*, whose only fin is the tailfin. I recognized the Javanese, a real snake about 80 centimetres long with a pale stomach, which might easily have been taken for a conger eel, but for the gold lines on its sides. Amongst the stromatas, whose bodies are flattened and oval-shaped, I observed parus with brilliant colours and scythe-like dorsal fins, edible fish which, dried and marinated, make an excellent dish called *karawade*; I also saw Tranquebars belonging to the *Aspiphoroides*, whose bodies are covered with eight lengthwise sections of scaly armour.

The light grew stronger as the sun rose progressively higher. The ground gradually changed. The fine sand was replaced by an actual causeway of round stones covered with a carpet of molluscs and zoophytes. Amongst the specimens of these two branches, I noticed *Placuna* with thin unequal valves, an ostracod characteristic of the Red Sea and Indian Ocean, some orange Lucinae with orbicular shells, subulate terebra, some Persian murexes which provided the *Nautilus* with an excellent dye, some 15-centimetre horned murexes which stood up in the waves like hands trying to grasp hold of you, cornigerous *Turbinella* all bristling with spikes, ianthine ligules, *Anatinella*, edible shellfish consumed in Northern India, slightly luminous pelagic panopea, and lastly some beautiful flabelliform Oculinidae, magnificent fans which form some of the richest branching structures in these seas.

In the midst of these living plants, beneath these bowers of hydrophytes, ran awkward legions of articulates, chiefly the *Ramae dentalae*, whose carapace forms a slightly rounded triangle, birguses particular to these shores, and horrible *Parthenopes*, of repugnant appearance. A no less hideous animal, one that I encountered several times, was the enormous crab observed by Mr Darwin, on which nature has bestowed the instinct and strength required to live off coconuts. It climbs trees on beaches, knocks down the coconuts, making them fall and crack, and then prises them open with its powerful pincers.

Here beneath the transparent waves this crab scampered with inimitable agility, while green turtles, of the same species that frequent the Malabar Coast, moved slowly between the rocks strewn here and there.

At about seven we finally reached the beds on which the millions of pearl-oysters reproduced. These valuable molluscs adhered to the rocks, being strongly attached by a brown byssus which kept them immobile. In this respect, the oyster is inferior to the lowly mussel, which nature has given some powers of locomotion.

The pearl-oyster, *Meleagrina* or 'mother-of-pearl', whose valves are more or less equal, appears as a rounded shell with thick walls, very rough on the outside. Some of the shells were laminated and grooved with greenish bands starting at the top. These belonged to young oysters. Others, with rough black surfaces, ten years old or more, were as much as six inches across.

Captain Nemo pointed to the prodigious stockpile of pearl-oysters, and I understood that the supply was inexhaustible, for nature's creative power is beyond man's destructive bent. Land, faithful to his instinct, hastened to fill the net carried on his side with the finest oysters he could find.

But we could not tarry. We had to follow the captain, who seemed to be following paths known to him alone. The ground was rising appreciably, and sometimes, when I held my arm up, it rose above the surface of the water. But then the level of the beds would capriciously descend again. We often rounded high rocks worn into pyramid-like shapes. In their gloomy fissures enormous crustacea, standing on their long limbs like war-machines, looked at us with fixed eyes, while beneath our feet crawled myriapods, glycera, ariciae, and annelids, stretching out their exaggerated antennae and their groping tentacles.

A huge grotto now opened before us, excavated from a picturesque pile of rocks covered with tall ribbands of submarine flora. At first sight the grotto looked very dark indeed. The sun's rays seemed to gradually go out in it. Its vague transparency became nothing but drowned light.

Captain Nemo entered. We followed him. My eyes soon got used to the gloom. I realized that the springings of the arches were capriciously elaborate, and supported by natural pillars standing firmly on broad granite bases like the heavy columns of Tuscan architecture. Why was our guide leading us into this submarine crypt? I was to find out before long.

Having descended quite a steep decline, our feet were treading the bottom of a kind of circular pit. Here Captain Nemo stopped and pointed out to us something I had not yet noticed.

It was an oyster of a most extraordinary size, a gigantic *Tridacna*: a font able to hold an entire lake of holy water, a basin whose breadth was more than two yards and therefore larger than the one in the *Nautilus*'s sitting-room.

I approached the phenomenal mollusc.* It was fixed by its byssus to a granite slab, and there on its own it grew in the calm waters of the grotto. I estimated the weight of the *Tridacna* as 600 pounds. Now an oyster like this would contain about thirty pounds of flesh, and one would need the stomach of a Gargantua to swallow a few dozen of them.

The captain was aware of the bivalve's existence. It was obviously not the first time he had come here, and at first I thought that he had brought us only to show us this natural curiosity. I was mistaken. Captain Nemo had the specific motive of checking the *Tridacna*'s condition.

The two valves of the mollusc were half-open. The captain went over and thrust his dagger between the two halves so as to prevent the shell shutting again. He then used his hand to raise the membranous tissue with its fringed edges which formed the covering of the animal.

There, between the foliate folds, I saw a loose pearl of the size of a small coconut. Its globular form, its perfect transparency, its splendid water stamped it as a jewel of inestimable value. Carried away by curiosity, I stretched out my hand to take hold of it, to weigh it, to feel it. But the captain stopped me, shook his head, withdrew his dagger with a rapid movement, and let the shell suddenly close.

I then understood Captain Nemo's purpose. By leaving the pearl entombed in the *Tridacna*'s protection, he allowed it to grow imperceptibly. With each year the mollusc's secretion added new concentric rings. The captain alone knew of the grotto where this admirable fruit of nature was 'ripening'; he alone was raising it, so to speak, in order to put it in his priceless museum one day. Perhaps, after the fashion of the Chinese and the Indians, he had even brought the pearl into being by placing a piece of glass or metal in the folds of the mollusc, which by degrees became covered with the nacreous substance. In any case, comparing this pearl to those I already knew, and to those which gleamed in the captain's collection, I estimated its value to be at least ten million francs. It was more a magnificent natural curiosity than a luxurious jewel, for I am unaware of any ladies' ears capable of bearing it.

Our visit to the extravagant *Tridacna* was over. Captain Nemo left the grotto, and we returned again to the oyster beds, to the clear waters not yet disturbed by the divers' work.

We walked separately, just as if we were strollers, each of us stopping or wandering as our fancies dictated. For my part I no longer worried about the dangers that my imagination had so ridiculously exaggerated. The bottom was rising noticeably towards the surface, and my head soon rose above it as I stood in three feet of water. Conseil drew near me and, sticking his large capsule close to mine, said a friendly hello with his eyes. But this high ground only lasted a few yards and soon we were back in our own element. I believe I now have the right to call it that!

Ten minutes later, Captain Nemo suddenly stopped. I thought he was going to go back the way he had come. No—he motioned to us to crouch beside him, at the bottom of a large hollow. He pointed towards a particular spot in the liquid mass, and I looked steadily at it.

About six yards off a shadow appeared and fell over the ground. The worrying idea of sharks crossed my mind. But I was wrong and, once more, we were not dealing with ocean monsters.

It was a man—a living man, an Indian, a Black—a poor devil of a diver no doubt, who had come to glean some pickings before the main harvest. I saw the keel of his boat moored some feet above his head. He dived and rose repeatedly. A stone cut in the shape of a sugar loaf held with his feet helped him sink more quickly, while a rope secured him to the boat. That was his only equipment. As he reached the bottom at about 15 feet, he fell to his knees and filled his net with pearl-oysters collected at random. He then rose, emptied the bag, pulled up the stone, and started his operation over again, the whole lasting only thirty seconds.

The diver did not see us. We were hidden by the shadow of a rock. And besides, how could this poor Indian imagine that beings like himself were underwater watching his every movement, not losing a single detail of his fishing?

He dived and rose again many times. He only brought up about ten oysters each time, for he was obliged to tear some away from the bed they were attached to with their byssuses. And how many of the oysters had no pearls, although he was risking his life for them!

I watched him with great concentration. His movements were regular, and for half an hour no danger seemed to threaten him. I was getting used to watching this absorbing fishing, when suddenly, as the Indian was kneeling on the ground, I saw him make a sign of terror, stand up, and spring towards the surface.

I understood his terror. A gigantic shadow had appeared above the unfortunate diver. It was a large shark, swimming diagonally: eyes flaming and jaws wide open!

I was petrified with horror, unable to make a move.

The voracious fish, with a strong movement of its fins, accelerated towards the Indian. He threw himself aside, avoiding the shark's open jaws, but not the stroke of its tail, for he received a blow on his chest which laid him out on the ground.

This scene had taken only a few seconds. The shark came to attack again and, turning on its back, was about to cut the Indian in two, when Captain Nemo jumped up. His dagger in hand, he moved straight at the monster, ready for a hand-to-hand struggle.

The shark noticed this new adversary just as it was about to swallow the unfortunate diver. Turning on its belly, it went for the captain.

I can still see Captain Nemo's stance.

Coiled up on himself, he waited for the attack of this formidable shark with wonderful self-possession; when it rushed at him, the captain jumped aside with amazing agility, avoiding the impact and plunging his dagger into the brute's belly. But it was not over yet. A terrible struggle ensued.

The shark had 'roared' so to speak. The blood poured from its wounds in torrents. The sea was coloured red, and I could see nothing through this opaque liquid.

Nothing until, as it cleared away, I caught sight of the brave captain holding on to one of the shark's fins and striking blow after blow at its stomach with the dagger, unable, however, to place a mortal one to the centre of the heart. In its struggle the shark beat the water with fury, and the turbulence almost made me fall over.

I wanted to go to the captain's assistance. But I was frozen with horror, and could not move.

I looked on with a haggard eye. I saw the varying phases of the combat. The captain fell to the ground, overturned by the enormous mass weighing down on him. The shark's jaws opened inordinately, like industrial shears, and would have made an end of the captain, had Ned, as quick as thought, not thrust himself upon the shark, harpoon in hand, and driven the terrible weapon into its side.

The waters were filled with masses of blood. They shook as the shark beat them with indescribable fury. But Ned Land had struck home. It was the monster's last gasp. Pierced to the heart, it beat out its life in terrifying spasms, as the shock knocked Conseil down.

Ned Land had meanwhile freed the captain. On his feet and unharmed, Nemo rushed up to the Indian, quickly cut the cord which fastened the stone, took him in his arms, and then ascended with him to the surface with a vigorous kick.

We all followed, and a few moments later, miraculously preserved from death, we reached the diver's boat.

Captain Nemo's first care was to restore the unfortunate to life. I was afraid he might not succeed. But the chances were good, for the poor man's submersion had not lasted long, although the blow from the shark's tail could easily have been fatal.

Fortunately, after vigorous rubbing from Conseil and the captain, I saw the diver gradually regaining consciousness. He opened his eyes. How surprised he must have been to find four great copper heads leaning over him!

And still greater must have been his surprise when Captain Nemo took a string of pearls from a pocket in his clothing, and placed them in his hand. This magnificent generosity from the man of the seas was accepted by the poor Sinhalese with trembling hands. His startled eyes showed that he did not know to what superhuman being he owed his fortune and his life.

At a sign from the captain we returned to the oyster beds, retraced our steps, and reached the anchor of the *Nautilus*'s boat. Once in the boat, we got rid of the heavy copper carapaces with the sailors' assistance.

Captain Nemo's first words were addressed to the Canadian.

'Thank you, Master Land.'

'For services rendered,' said Ned. 'I owed you that one.'

A wan smile flitted across the captain's features, and that was all.

'To the *Nautilus*!' he cried.

The boat flew over the waves. A few minutes later we saw the body of the shark floating on the surface.

From the black markings on the ends of its fins, I recognized the terrible melanopterus of the Indian Ocean, belonging to the species of sharks in the strict sense. It was more than 25 feet long; and its enormous mouth filled a third of its body. It was an adult, as could be seen from the six rows of teeth arranged in its upper jaw in the shape of an isosceles triangle.

Conseil regarded it entirely from a scientific point of view, and I am sure he classified it, not incorrectly, amongst the cartilaginous animals—order of chondropterygians with fixed gills, family of selachians, genus sharks.

While I was looking at the inert mass, a dozen of its voracious relatives suddenly appeared around the boat; without worrying about us, they threw themselves upon the corpse and fought for the pieces.

At half-past nine we were on board the *Nautilus* again.

I began to reflect upon the incidents of our excursion to Mannar Bank. Two reflections inevitably followed. One was the outstanding bravery of Captain Nemo; the other his devotion to a fellow creature, a representative of the human race that he shunned under the seas. Whatever he might say, this strange man had not yet totally succeeded in killing his heart.

When I said as much to him he replied, with some little emotion:

'That Indian, doctor, is the inhabitant of an oppressed country. I am his compatriot, and shall remain so to my very last breath!'

4

The Red Sea

DURING 29 January the island of Sri Lanka disappeared below the horizon, and the *Nautilus*, moving at 20 knots, slid into the labyrinth of channels which separate the Maldives from the Laccadives. It even came close to Kiltan Island, a land of madreporic origin discovered by Vasco da Gama* in 1499, and one of the nineteen main islands of the Laccadive archipelago, situated between 10° and 14°30′S and 69° and 50°72′E.

We had now covered 16,220 miles, or 7,500 leagues, since our starting-point in the seas of Japan.

When the *Nautilus* surfaced on the following day, 30 January, there was no land in sight. It was moving north-north-west towards the Gulf of Oman, which is hollowed out between Arabia and the Indian subcontinent and serves as an outlet for the Persian Gulf.

This was obviously a cul-de-sac, without any way out at all. So where was Captain Nemo taking us? I had no idea. My ignorance did not satisfy the Canadian, who asked me where we were heading.

'We are heading, Master Ned, where the captain's whims take us.'

'His whims won't take us anywhere. The Persian Gulf has no way out; so if we go in, we'll be heading back out again in no time.'

'Well then, we will just head back, and if the *Nautilus* wishes to visit the Red Sea after the Persian Gulf, the strait of Bab el Mandeb will always be there to provide us a way through.'

'As you well know,' replied Ned, 'the Red Sea is just as closed as the Gulf, since the isthmus of Suez has not been cut through yet. And even if it had, a mysterious boat like ours couldn't venture into its canals with their regularly spaced lock gates. So the Red Sea is still not the route to take us back to Europe.'

'Which is why I didn't say we *were* going back to Europe.'

'So what do you imagine?'

'I imagine that after visiting the curious shores of Arabia and Egypt, the *Nautilus* will work its way back down the Indian Ocean, perhaps through the Mozambique Channel or past the Mascarene Islands, and hence reach the Cape of Good Hope.'

'And once at the Cape of Good Hope?' asked the Canadian with remarkable insistence.

'Well, we will enter the Atlantic, which is still unknown to us. Ah friend Ned, are you already tired of our journey under the seas? Are you already blasé about this constantly changing spectacle of submarine marvels? For my part, I would be most upset to come to the end of this voyage which so few men have had the chance to make.'

'But do you know, Dr Aronnax, that we've been imprisoned in the *Nautilus* for almost three months?'

'No, Ned, I didn't know, nor do I want to know, and I count neither the days nor the hours.'

'So what is the conclusion to all this?'

'The conclusion will come in its own good time. In any case, we can't do anything about it, so there is no point in discussing it. If you came and told me, "A chance of escape is available to us", I would talk it over with you, my good Ned. But such is not the case, and to be frank, I do not believe that Captain Nemo ever ventures into the seas of Europe.'

Through this short dialogue you will see that I had been reincarnated in the skin of the captain and had become a real *Nautilus* fanatic.

As for Ned, he concluded the conversation in the form of a soliloquy: 'All that is fine, but as far as I'm concerned, when you're not comfortable you just don't enjoy it any more.'

For four days, until 3 February, the *Nautilus* visited the Gulf of Oman at various speeds and depths. It seemed to be moving at random, as if hesitating as to the route to follow, but it never went further than the tropic of Cancer.

As we left this sea, we briefly sighted Muscat, the largest town in Oman. I admired its strange appearance, with its pale-coloured houses and forts standing out from the surrounding black rocks. I noticed the round domes of its mosques, the elegant points of its minarets, its fresh, green terraces. But this was just a vision, and soon the *Nautilus* plunged again under the dark waves of those shores.

It followed the Arabian coasts of Mahrah and Hadramaut at a distance of six miles, parallel to the undulating line of the mountains, relieved by a few ancient ruins. On 5 February we finally entered the Gulf of Aden, a funnel into the bottleneck of Bab el Mandeb that pours Indian waters into the Red Sea.

On 6 February the *Nautilus* was floating within sight of Aden, which is perched on a promontory with a narrow neck connecting it to the mainland. It forms an unassailable Gibraltar, whose fortifications the British have rebuilt since seizing them in 1839. I caught sight of the octagonal minarets of this town, which was once the richest and biggest trading entrepôt on the coast, according to the historian Idrisi.*

I firmly believed that, having reached this point, Captain Nemo would turn round; but to my great surprise, he did not.

The following day, 7 February, we entered the strait of Bab el Mandeb, which means 'Gate of Tears' in Arabic. Twenty miles wide, it is a mere 52 kilometres long, and it took hardly an hour for the *Nautilus* to cover it at full speed. I saw nothing, not even the island of Perim which the British government has used to strengthen the position of Aden. There were too many British and French steamers running lines between Suez and Bombay, Calcutta, Melbourne, Réunion, and Mauritius through this narrow passage for the *Nautilus* to attempt to show itself. So it remained prudently submerged.

Finally, at midday, we were ploughing the waves of the Red Sea.

That celebrated lake of biblical tradition is hardly freshened by rainwater, has no major river flowing into it, is constantly being reduced by evaporation, and loses a liquid layer one and a half metres high each year. The Red Sea is a remarkable gulf which would probably dry up entirely, if it were closed like a lake; it is worse off in this respect than its neighbours the Caspian or the Dead Sea, whose levels have only lowered to the point where their evaporation is equal to the sum of waters running into their basins.

The Red Sea is 2,600 kilometres long and 240 kilometres wide on average. At the time of the Ptolemies and the Roman emperors it was the main commercial artery in the world, and the cutting of the isthmus will give it back this classical importance, one which the railways of Suez have already partially brought back.*

I did not even try to understand the whim that had led Captain Nemo to bring us into this gulf. Rather I unreservedly approved the *Nautilus*'s entering it. It went at moderate speed, sometimes staying on the surface, at others diving to avoid a ship, so I was able to observe both the depths and the surface of this remarkable sea.

During the early hours of 8 February Mocha appeared to us, a town now in ruins, with walls that crumble at the mere sound of cannons and which is shaded here and there by green date trees. Formerly a major city, it has public markets, 26 mosques, and a three-kilometre-long city wall defended by fourteen forts.

Next the *Nautilus* drew close to the African shore where the sea is quite deep, and the water as clear as crystal. Through the open panels we were able to contemplate wonderful sprays of dazzling corals and huge slabs of rock covered with a splendid green fur of seaweeds and wracks. What indescribable sights, and what variety of places and scenery where the shoals and volcanic islands drop away offshore from the Libyan coast! But where the arborescences appeared in all their glory was near the eastern shores, which the *Nautilus* wasted no time in heading for. Off the coasts of Tehama, not only did the displays of zoophytes flourish below sea-level, but they also formed picturesque intertwinings unwinding 60 feet over its surface; the latter more capricious but less highly coloured than the former which used the water's vitality to maintain their freshness.

How many charmed hours I spent in this way at the window of the salon! How many new specimens of submarine flora and fauna I admired in the bright light of our electric lamp! I saw umbrella-shaped fungus coral, blue-grey sea anemones including

Thalassianthus aster, tubipores horizontal like flutes that waited only for the breath of the god Pan; shells particular to this sea, which settle in the madreporic excavations and whose bases are formed of short spirals; and finally a thousand specimens of a polypary that I had not yet observed, the common sponge.

The class of Porifera, the first of the group of polyps, was created for precisely this curious product, of such obvious usefulness. The sponge is not a vegetable, as a few naturalists still believe, but an animal of the lowest order, a polypary which is lower than coral. Its animal nature cannot be doubted, and one cannot support the ancients who considered it a being intermediate between the plants and the animals. I must say, however, that naturalists are not in agreement on how the sponge is organized. For some it is a polypary, and for others, such as M. Milne-Edwards, it is an isolated and unique individual.

The class of Porifera contains about 300 species, which are encountered in a large number of seas and even certain rivers where they have been described as 'fluviatile'. But their preferred waters are the Mediterranean, the Greek Islands, and the coasts of Syria and the Red Sea. There the fine soft sponges, which can fetch up to 150 francs each, reproduce and grow: the golden sponge of Syria, the hard sponge of Barbary, etc. But since I could not hope to study these zoophytes in the ports of the eastern Mediterranean, from which we were separated by the uncrossable isthmus of Suez, I satisfied myself with observing them in the waters of the Red Sea.

I called Conseil to my side, while the *Nautilus*, at an average depth of eight or nine metres, slowly skimmed over the beautiful rocks on the eastern coastline.

There grew sponges of all forms: pediculate, foliaceous, globular, and digitate. They aptly deserved their names of baskets, chalices, bulrushes, elkhorns, lions' feet, peacocks' tails, and Neptune's gloves, given them by fishermen, who are more poets than they are scientists. Little dribbles of water, after carrying life into each cell, were constantly being expelled by contraction from their fibrous material, covered with a sticky, semi-fluid substance. This substance disappears after the death of the polypary and putrefies while giving off ammonia. Nothing then remains apart from the hard or gelatinous fibres making up the domestic sponge, which takes on a reddish tint and is used for various purposes, depending on its degree of elasticity, permeability, and resistance to maceration.

These polyparies stuck to the rocks, to the shells of molluscs, and even to the stalks of hydrophytes. They filled the smallest gaps, some spreading out and others standing up or hanging down like coral growths. I informed Conseil that sponges were collected in two ways, either by net or by hand. The latter method, requiring the use of divers, is preferable,* for it leaves the polypary undamaged and so guarantees a much higher price.

The other zoophytes proliferating near the poriferans consisted mainly of jellyfish of a very elegant species; molluscs were represented by varieties of squid which d'Orbigny says are found only in the Red Sea; and reptiles by *virgata* turtles belonging to the genus of *Chelones*, which provided us with a healthy and delicate dish.

As for fish, they were numerous and often remarkable. The following were brought in most frequently by the nets of the *Nautilus*: rays, amongst them lymma with oval bodies of a dull red colour and irregular blue spots, recognizable from their twin serrated stings; Forsskål's stingrays with silvery backs; whip-tailed stingrays with dotted tails; bockats, huge two-metre-long cloaks undulating through the water; totally toothless aodons, which are a sort of cartilaginous fish closely related to the shark; dromedary *Ostracea* whose hump ends in a curved sting a foot and a half long; ophidians, which are actually moray eels with silver tails, blue backs, and brown pectorals edged with a grey border; fiatolae, species of stromateids zigzagged with narrow golden strips and decked out in the three colours of France; forty-centimetre-long gourami blennies; superb scads with seven transversal bands of a fine black tint, blue and yellow fins, and gold and silver scales; snooks; oriflamme mullets with yellow heads; parrot fish, labra, triggerfish, gobies, etc., and a thousand other fishes found in the oceans we had already visited.

On 9 February the *Nautilus* was floating in the broadest part of the Red Sea, between Suakin on the west coast and Al Qunfudhah on the east, where it is 190 miles wide.

At noon that day, once our position had been taken, Captain Nemo came up on the platform after me. I promised myself not to let him go down again without at least sounding him out on his plans for the future. He came up as soon as he spotted me, graciously offered me a cigar, and said:

'Well, monsieur, does the Red Sea please you? Have you seen enough of the marvels it holds, its fishes and zoophytes, its beds of sponges and its forests of corals? Have you seen the towns dotted along its shores?'

'Yes, captain, and the *Nautilus* lent itself marvellously to all this study. Ah, what an intelligent boat it is!'

'Yes, intelligent, audacious, and invulnerable! It fears neither the terrifying storms of the Red Sea, nor its currents, nor even its reefs.'

'This sea is indeed one of the worst, and if I am not mistaken, had an atrocious reputation in ancient times.'

'Yes indeed, Dr Aronnax. The Greek and Latin historians never speak well of it, and Strabo* says that it is particularly difficult during the Etesian winds and the rainy season. The Arab Idrisi, who calls it the Gulf of Colzoum, recounts that ships perished in great numbers on its sandbanks and that nobody ventured to navigate it at night. It is, he claims, a sea subject to terrible hurricanes, dotted with inhospitable islands, and "has nothing good" either in its depths or on its surface. The same views were held by Arrian, Agatharchidas, and Artemidorus.'*

'It is easy to see that these historians never sailed on the *Nautilus*.'

'Indeed,' the captain replied smiling, 'but in this respect, the moderns are little further advanced than the ancients. Many centuries were needed to discover the mechanical power of steam! Who knows if a second *Nautilus* will appear in the next 100 years! Progress is slow, Dr Aronnax.'

'Agreed,' I replied; 'your ship is a century ahead of its time, or perhaps several. What a shame that such a secret must die with its inventor!'

Captain Nemo did not reply. After a few moments of silence:

'You were speaking of the ancient historians' views on the dangers of navigating the Red Sea?'

'Yes, but were their fears not exaggerated?'

'Yes and no,' replied the captain, who seemed to be an expert on all aspects of 'his' Red Sea. 'What no longer poses a problem for a modern ship, well rigged, solidly constructed, in control of its direction thanks to obedient steam, offered all sorts of dangers to the vessels of the ancients. One must try to imagine those first navigators adventuring out on boats that were made of planks held together by ropes made of palm leaves, caulked with powdered resin, and waterproofed with tallow from dogfish. They didn't even have instruments to note their direction, and so sailed by dead reckoning in the midst of currents they hardly knew. In those conditions, shipwrecks were necessarily common. But in our time, the steamers plying between Suez and the South Seas no longer have anything to fear from the angers of this gulf, in spite of the contrary monsoons. Their captains and passengers do not prepare for departure with propitiary sacrifices, and, once back, they no longer adorn themselves with garlands and golden fillets to go and thank the gods in their neighbourhood temples.'

'Admittedly,' I said, 'and steam seems to have killed the skill of observation in sailors. But captain, since you seem to have specially studied this sea, can you tell me where the name comes from?'

'There are many explanations for it. Would you like to hear the ideas of a fourteenth-century chronicler?'

'Certainly.'

'This joker claimed that it got its name after the crossing by the Israelites, when the Pharaoh perished in the waves that closed up again on Moses' command:

> To miraculously portend
> The sea darkly redden'd
> And made them decree
> Call it then the Red Sea.'

'A poet's explanation, Captain Nemo, but insufficient to convince me. I would like to ask your personal opinion.'

'Here it is then. In my view, Dr Aronnax, the Red Sea's name should be seen as a translation of the Hebrew word "Edom",* and the ancients gave it this name because of the peculiar colour of its waters.'

'Until now, however, I have only seen waves which were clear, without any particular colour.'

'No doubt, but when we head for the end of the Gulf, you will notice their remarkable appearance. I remember seeing the Bay of Tur entirely red, like a sea of blood.'

'And you attribute this colour to the presence of microscopic algae?'

'Correct. There is a viscous purple matter produced by those sickly-looking plantlets known as *Trichodesma*, of which forty thousand are contained in a square millimetre. Perhaps you will observe some when we are at Tur.'

'So Captain Nemo, this is not the first time you have travelled through the Red Sea on the *Nautilus*?'

'No, monsieur.'

'Then, since you were speaking previously of the Crossing of the Red Sea and the drowning of the Egyptians, I would like to ask if you have found underwater traces of that great historic event?'

'No, and for a very good reason.'

'Namely?'

'That the spot where Moses crossed with all his people is so full of sand nowadays that camels can hardly bathe their legs there. My *Nautilus* would clearly not have enough water for it.'

'And this place . . .?'

'It's situated a little above Suez, in the arm of the sea that formed a deep estuary when the Red Sea stretched as far as the Bitter Lakes. Now whether their crossing was miraculous or not, the Jews did pass there on their way to the Promised Land, and the Pharaoh's army did perish at that spot. I deduce that excavations in those sands would uncover a great quantity of arms and tools of Egyptian origin.'

'Yes indeed,' I replied, 'and for the archaeologists' sake one must hope that such excavations will be carried out sooner or later, when new towns are built on this isthmus after the Suez Canal is opened. A canal which is totally useless for a ship like the *Nautilus*!'

'Undoubtedly, but useful for the world at large. The ancients full well understood the importance to their commercial affairs of creating a link between the Red Sea and Mediterranean; still they did not dream of digging a direct canal, but used the Nile as an intermediary instead. The canal connecting the Nile to the Red

Sea was very probably begun under Sesostris,* if tradition is to be believed. What is certain is that in 615 BC, Necho* began work on a canal drawing water from the Nile and going across the plains of Egypt opposite Arabia. This canal took four days to navigate, and was wide enough for two triremes to pass abreast. It was continued by Darius, son of Hystaspes, and probably finished by Ptolemy II.* Strabo saw it being used by ships; but the lack of gradient between its starting-point near Bubastis and the Red Sea meant that it was only navigable for a few months of the year. This canal served trade until the century of the Antonines; then it was abandoned, got silted up with sand, but was later restored on the orders of Caliph Umar.* But in AD 761 or 762 it was filled in once and for all by Caliph al-Mansur to prevent food reaching Mohammed ben Abdallah, who had rebelled against him.* During his expedition to Egypt, your General Bonaparte* rediscovered the traces of these works in the desert of Suez; but he was caught out by the tide, and almost died a few hours before reaching Hazeroth, the same place where Moses had camped 3,300 years before.'*

'Well captain, what the ancients did not dare undertake, namely a link which will connect two seas and reduce the distance from Cadiz to the Indies by 9,000 kilometres, M. de Lesseps* has done, and very shortly he will have made Africa into an enormous island.'

'Yes, Dr Aronnax, and you can justifiably be proud of your compatriot. He does more honour to his nation than the greatest of sea-captains! Like so many others, he began with obstacles and disappointments, but has triumphed because he has the necessary will-power. And it is sad to think that his works, which should have been international ones, enough to render illustrious an entire reign, succeeded in the end only through the energy of a single man. So all honour to M. de Lesseps!'

'Yes, all honour to this great citizen,' I replied, astonished by the intensity with which Captain Nemo had spoken.

'Unfortunately,' he continued, 'I cannot take you through the Suez Canal, but you will be able to catch a glimpse of the long breakwaters of Port Said the day after tomorrow, when we are in the Mediterranean.'

'In the Mediterranean!' I exclaimed.

'Yes, monsieur. Are you surprised?'

'What astonishes me is to think we will be there the day after tomorrow.'

'Really?'

'Yes, captain, although I ought not to be amazed by anything since arriving on board your ship!'

'But why the surprise?'

'Because of the frightful speed you will have to sail the *Nautilus* at to be in the Mediterranean the day after tomorrow, having circled Africa and the Cape of Good Hope!'

'But who says it is going to circle Africa, Dr Aronnax? Who said anything about rounding the Cape of Good Hope?'

'Nevertheless, unless the *Nautilus* can cross the isthmus by sailing over dry land . . .'

'Or under, Dr Aronnax.'

'Under?'

'Yes,' Captain Nemo replied calmly. 'A long time ago Nature made under that stretch of land what men are making today on its surface.'

'What, there is a passage!'

'Yes, an underground passage that I have called the Arabian Tunnel. It begins under Suez and finishes in the Bay of Pelusium.'

'But isn't the isthmus formed of moving sand?'

'Down to a certain depth. But at 50 metres there is only immovable bedrock.'

'And did you discover this passage by chance?' I asked, more and more surprised.

'By luck and reasoning, but more reasoning than luck.'

'I am listening, captain, but my ears won't believe what they can hear.'

'Ah, monsieur! *Aures habent et non audient** is of every period. Not only does this passage exist, but I have been through it several times. Without it, I wouldn't have ventured into this Red Sea cul-de-sac today.'

'Would it be indiscreet to enquire how you discovered the tunnel?'

'Monsieur,' replied the captain, 'there can be no secrets between people who are never to part.'

I did not react to his implication but waited for Captain Nemo's story.

'It was the simple reasoning of a naturalist that led me to discover the passage which I alone know about. I had noticed that in the Red Sea and the Mediterranean there are a number of fishes of absolutely identical species: ophidians, fiatola, rainbow wrasses, perches, horse-mackerel, and flying fish. Given this fact, I wondered if there might not be some link between the two seas. If it did exist, the underground current had to go from the Red Sea to the Mediterranean because of the difference in their levels. So I caught a large number of fish near Suez, put copper rings on their tails, and threw them back into the water again. A few months later, I caught a few specimens of my fish on the coast of Syria, together with their identification rings. That is how I demonstrated the link between the two seas. I looked for it with my *Nautilus*, found it, ventured in, and before long, monsieur, you too will have passed through my Arabian Tunnel!'

5

Arabian Tunnel

THAT same day, I told Conseil and Ned that part of the conversation which directly concerned them. When I informed them that within two days we would be in the waters of the Mediterranean, Conseil clapped his hands but the Canadian simply shrugged his shoulders.

'A submarine tunnel,' he exclaimed, 'a link between two seas! Who ever heard of such a thing?'

'Friend Ned,' replied Conseil, 'had you ever heard of the *Nautilus*? No. But it does exist. So do not shrug your shoulders so lightly, and do not reject things just because you have never heard of them.'

'We shall see!' exclaimed Land, shaking his head. 'After all, I would be only too pleased to believe in the captain's passage, and may God grant that it does lead us into the Mediterranean.'

That same evening, at 21°30′N, the *Nautilus* neared the Arabian coast, sailing on the surface of the sea. I spotted Jedda, the trading post for Egypt, Syria, Turkey, and India. I could quite clearly make out groups of buildings, ships tied up along the quays, and other ships whose draught forced them to anchor in the roads. The sun was quite low on the horizon and struck the houses of the town face on, bringing out their whiteness. Further out, a few reed and wooden sheds indicated the Bedouin quarter.

Soon Jedda faded into the shades of evening, and the *Nautilus* dived back down through the slightly phosphorescent water.

The following day, 10 February, several ships appeared, sailing on the opposite tack from us. The *Nautilus* resumed its submarine navigation; but at noon, the sea was deserted when we took our bearings, so it remained on its flotation line.

Accompanied by Ned and Conseil, I went to sit on the platform. The coast to the east was a bare outcrop totally blurred by the misty haze.

Leaning on the side of the dinghy, we were chatting about one thing and another, when Ned Land pointed at a spot on the ocean, and said:

'Can you see something there, Dr Aronnax?'

'No Ned, but I haven't got your eyes, you know.'

'Look carefully,' said Ned, 'there, starboard ahead, at about the same height as the searchlight. Can you see something moving?'

'Yes,' I said after careful observation. 'I can see something like a long black fish's body on the surface of the water.'

'Another *Nautilus*?' said Conseil.

'No,' replied the Canadian; 'unless I am gravely mistaken, it's some sort of marine animal.'

'Are there whales in the Red Sea?' asked Conseil.

'Yes, my good man,' I replied, 'they are sometimes encountered.'

'It isn't a whale,' said Ned not taking his eyes off the object. 'Whales and I are old friends, and I wouldn't make a mistake about the way they move.'

'Let's wait,' said Conseil. 'The *Nautilus* is heading in that direction, and it won't be long before we know what we're dealing with.'

The blackish object was soon only a mile away. It resembled a big reef stranded in the open sea. What was it? I was still unable to say for sure.

'Ah! It's moving! It's diving!' exclaimed Ned Land. 'Good Heavens! What can it be? It hasn't got a forked tail like a baleen or sperm whale and its fins are like cut-off limbs.'

'But then . . .' I said.

'Hey,' said the Canadian, 'it's on its back now and it's raising its breasts in the air!'

'It's a mermaid!' exclaimed Conseil. 'An authentic mermaid, with all due respect to monsieur.'

Conseil's term put me on the right track, and I realized that the animal belonged to the order of marine creatures which legend has made into mermaids, half women, half fish.

'No,' I said to him, 'it is not a mermaid, but a curious creature which has almost disappeared from the Red Sea. It is a dugong.'*

'Order of sirenians, group of pisciformes, sub-class monodelphians, class of mammals, branch of vertebrates,' replied Conseil.

And when Conseil had spoken, nothing more could be said.

Land was still staring. His eyes shone with cupidity at the sight of the animal. His hand seemed ready for the harpoon. He looked as though he was just waiting for the moment to throw himself into the sea and attack the animal in its element.

'Oh monsieur!' he said in a voice trembling with emotion. 'I have never killed one of "those".'

The whole harpooner was encapsulated in that one word.

At this moment, Captain Nemo appeared on the platform and noticed the dugong. He understood the feelings of the Canadian, and addressing him directly:

'If you were holding a harpoon, Master Land, wouldn't you be itching to use it?'

'Correct, sir.'

'And wouldn't you like to follow your trade of fisherman for a day, and add this cetacean to your tally?'

'Very much.'

'Well you can try!'

'Thank you sir,' replied Ned, his eyes blazing.

'Just one thing,' added the captain, 'I warn you not to miss the animal, for your own sake.'

'Is it dangerous to attack the dugong?' I asked, in spite of the Canadian's shrugging of his shoulders.

'Yes, sometimes. The animal comes back on its attackers and capsizes their boat. But with Master Land, there should be no fear. His eye is quick, his arm is sure. I am only saying he shouldn't miss the dugong because it is considered fine game, and I know that Master Land appreciates the finest cuts.'

'Oh,' said the Canadian, 'so that animal takes pleasure in being good eating as well, does it?'

'Yes, Master Land, its flesh is real meat. It is very highly esteemed, reserved for the tables of princes throughout Malaysia. This excellent animal is so fiercely hunted that, just like its congener, the manatee, it is becoming rarer and rarer.'

'And so, captain,' Conseil said seriously, 'if by chance this were the last of its race, would it not be better to spare it—in the interests of science?'

'Perhaps,' responded the Canadian; 'but in the interests of the table, it is better to hunt it.'

'So go ahead, Master Land,' replied Captain Nemo.

At this moment seven crewmen, as silent and impassive as always, climbed up to the platform. One was carrying a harpoon and line like those used by whalers. The boat's cover was taken off, and it was extracted from its recess and launched. Six oarsmen took their places on the seats as the coxswain sat down at the tiller. Ned, Conseil, and I sat at the back.

'Aren't you coming, captain?' I asked.

'No, monsieur, but I wish you good hunting.'

The boat shoved off and, carried forward by its six oars, headed quickly towards the dugong, floating at a distance of two miles from the *Nautilus*.

Once we were a few cables away from the cetacean, the oars were slowed and silently entered the quiet waters. Ned Land, harpoon in hand, went and stood at the front of the boat. The whaling harpoon is normally attached to a very long rope which unwinds quickly when the wounded animal drags it off. But here the rope was only about ten fathoms long, and its end was fastened to a small keg which would float to indicate where underwater the dugong was.

I had got up and could distinctly see the Canadian's adversary.

The dugong, also called the halicore, closely resembled a manatee. Its long, broad body ended in a greatly elongated caudal fin, and its side-fins in genuine fingers. The difference with the manatee was that its upper jaw was armed with two long, pointed teeth, which formed divergent tusks on each side.*

The dugong Ned Land was getting ready to attack was of colossal dimensions, more than seven metres in length. It was not moving and seemed to be asleep on the surface of the waves, making it easier to capture.

The boat carefully approached to within three fathoms of the animal. The oars remained suspended in their rowlocks. I half got up. Ned, his body leaning back a little, was brandishing his harpoon with an experienced hand.

Suddenly, there came a hissing sound and the dugong disappeared. The harpoon, thrown with some strength, had undoubtedly struck only water.

'Hell!' exclaimed the furious Canadian. 'I missed!'

'No,' I said, 'the animal is wounded—look at the blood—but your weapon did not lodge in its body.'

'My harpoon, my harpoon!' cried Land.

The sailors started rowing again, as the coxswain steered the boat towards the floating keg. Once the harpoon had been fished out of the water, the boat started pursuing the animal again.

The dugong came back up to the surface to breathe from time to time. Its wound had not unduly weakened it, for it was proceeding at great speed. The boat, rowed by strong arms, was flying along. Several times we got to within a few fathoms, but just as the Canadian got ready to strike, the dugong would suddenly dive, and so escape.

One can imagine the anger filling the impatient Ned Land. He threw the most vivid swear-words in the English language at the unfortunate creature. For my part, I had not got further than annoyance at seeing the dugong foil all our tricks.

We had pursued it without stopping for an hour, and I was beginning to believe that it would be very difficult to secure, when the animal had the unfortunate idea of revenge, which it was to regret. It came back at the boat to attack in its turn.

This trick was not lost on the Canadian.

'Careful!' he said.

The coxswain said a few words in his strange language, undoubtedly telling his men to stay on their guard.

The dugong, now only twenty feet from the boat, stopped and brusquely sniffed the air with its huge nostrils, not at the end but on the top part of its snout. Then, gathering momentum, it threw itself at us.

The boat could not avoid the collision; half capsized, it took on board one or two tons of water that needed to be bailed; but thanks to the coxswain's skill, it was hit at an angle rather than side on, and so did not turn over. Ned held tightly on to the prow and stabbed his harpoon at the gigantic animal; with its teeth enmeshed in the gunwales, it lifted the boat out of the water like a lion does a deer. We were thrown on top of each other, and I really do not know how the adventure would have finished, if the Canadian had not continued relentlessly attacking the animal, finally striking it to the heart.

I heard the grinding of teeth on metal as the dugong disappeared, taking the harpoon with it. But soon the keg came back up, and a few moments later the body of the animal appeared, lying on its back. The boat went alongside the dugong, and started towing it back to the *Nautilus*.

It was necessary to use heavy lifting gear to hoist the dugong on to the platform. It weighed 5,000 kilograms. The animal was cut up before the Canadian's eyes, who considered it essential to follow every detail of the operation. That same day, the steward served me for dinner a few slices of this flesh, skilfully prepared by the ship's cook. I found it excellent, superior even to veal, if not to beef.

The following day, 11 February, the *Nautilus*'s pantry was further enhanced with delicate game. A flock of sea-swallows settled down on the *Nautilus*. They were of a species of *Sterna nilotica* peculiar to Egypt, with black beaks, grey spotted heads, eyes surrounded with white dots, greyish backs, wings, and tails, white stomachs and throats, and red feet. We also caught a few dozen Nile ducks, wild birds with a gamey taste, whose necks and tops of the head are white flecked with black.

The *Nautilus*'s speed was moderate. It ambled along, so to

speak. I noticed that the water of the Red Sea was becoming less and less salty as we approached Suez.

At about five in the evening, we sighted the cape of Ras Muhammad to the north. It is this cape which forms the tip of Arabia Petraea, between the Gulf of Suez and the Gulf of Aqaba.

The *Nautilus* entered the strait of Jubail, which leads to the Gulf of Suez. I distinctly noticed a high mountain, above Ras Muhammad and between the two gulfs. This was Mount Horeb, the Sinai on whose summit Moses saw God face to face,* and which one imagines constantly crowned with lightning.

At six o'clock, the *Nautilus*, sometimes on the surface and at others submerged, passed Tur, at the end of a bay whose waters seemed dyed red, as remarked by Captain Nemo. Night fell to a heavy silence, broken occasionally by the cry of a pelican or a few night birds, the noise of surf hitting rocks, or the far-off groaning of a steamer beating the water of the gulf with its noisy blades.

From eight to nine o'clock the *Nautilus* remained a few metres underwater. According to my calculations, we were very close to Suez. Through the salon's panels, I could see the rocky floor brightly lit by our electric light. It seemed to me that the strait was getting narrower and narrower.

At a quarter past nine the boat had surfaced, and I went up on the platform. Very impatient to pass through Captain Nemo's tunnel, I felt quite restless, and wanted to breathe the fresh night air.

Amongst the shadows, I soon noticed a pale light half discoloured by the mist, shining about a mile away.

'A floating beacon,' somebody said close by me.

I turned round and found the captain.

'The buoy of Suez,' he continued. 'It will not be long before we enter the tunnel's mouth.'

'It can't be easy to get in?'

'No, monsieur. So it is my custom to direct the operation myself from the pilot's dome. And now, if you wish to go down, Dr Aronnax, the *Nautilus* is about to dive, and will only surface again at the other end of the Arabian Tunnel.'

I followed Captain Nemo. The hatch closed, the water tanks filled, and the vessel dived about ten metres.

Just as I was getting ready to return to my room, the captain stopped me.

'Dr Aronnax,' he said, 'would you like to accompany me to the pilot's dome?'

'I did not dare ask.'

'Please do come. You will see everything that can be seen of this channel which is both underground and underwater.'

Captain Nemo led me towards the central staircase. Half-way along the gangway he opened a door, followed the upper gangways, and arrived at the pilot's dome, which, as the reader knows, emerged at the end of the platform.

It was a cabin measuring six feet square, basically similar to those occupied by men at the helm of Mississippi or Hudson steamboats. In the middle was a vertical wheel which engaged the rudder-chains running to the aft of the *Nautilus*. Four glass-lens portholes in the walls of the cabin allowed the pilot to see in all directions.

The cabin was dark, but my eyes soon got used to it, and I noticed the pilot, a vigorous man, his hands resting on the spokes of the wheel. The sea outside was bright in the searchlight, beaming out from the other end of the platform behind the cabin.

'And now,' said Captain Nemo, 'let's look for the way through.'

Electric wires ran from the pilot's dome to the engine-room, enabling the captain to control both the direction and movement of his *Nautilus*. He pressed a metal button, and immediately the propeller slowed down markedly.

I silently examined the high, very rough wall that we were now running along and which formed the unshakeable foundation of the sandy massif of the coast. For an hour we followed it at a distance of only a few metres. Captain Nemo did not take his eyes off the compass suspended from its two concentric circles. With a single movement, the pilot was constantly changing the direction of the *Nautilus*.

I had taken up a position at the porthole, and could see magnificent substructures of corals, plus zoophytes, algae, and crustaceans waving their enormous legs as they stretched out of the hollows in the rocks.

At a quarter past ten, Captain Nemo took the wheel himself. A wide tunnel, black and deep, opened up in front of us. The *Nautilus* plunged boldly into it. An unusual rustling sound could be heard along its sides. This was the water of the Red Sea rushing towards the Mediterranean because of the slope of the tunnel. The *Nautilus* followed the torrent, as quick as an arrow in spite of the efforts of its engine to slow it down by means of the propeller in reverse.

On the narrow walls of the passage, I could no longer see anything but dazzling streaks, straight lines, fiery furrows traced by the speed and the electric light. My heart was beating wildly, as I compressed it with my hand.

At 10.35 Captain Nemo left the wheel and, turning to me, said: 'The Mediterranean.'

The *Nautilus*, carried on by the torrent, had crossed the isthmus of Suez in less than twenty minutes.

6

The Greek Islands

THE following day, 12 February, the *Nautilus* surfaced at daybreak. I rushed on to the platform. Three miles to the south the vague silhouette of Pelusium was outlined. A river had carried us from one sea to the other. But this tunnel, although easy to descend, had to be impossible to ascend.

At about seven o'clock, Ned and Conseil joined me. The two inseparable companions had slept peacefully, without bothering about the *Nautilus*'s feat.

'Well, monsieur the naturalist,' asked the Canadian in a slightly bantering tone, 'and what about the Mediterranean?'

'We're floating on its surface, friend Ned.'

'Eh!' said Conseil. 'During the night?'

'Yes, this very night we crossed that uncrossable isthmus in a few minutes.'

'I don't believe a word of it.'

'Well you had better, Master Land,' I said. 'That low rounded coast to the south is the Egyptian coast.'

'Try the other one,' replied the obstinate Canadian.

'But if monsieur says so,' Conseil told him, 'we have to believe monsieur.'

'In any case, Ned, Captain Nemo did me the honours of his tunnel, and I was beside him in the pilot's dome when he himself steered the *Nautilus* through that narrow passage.'

'Do you hear, Ned?' said Conseil.

'And since you have such good eyes,' I added, 'you can see the jetties at Port Said stretching out into the sea.'

The Canadian looked carefully.

'Actually,' he said, 'you are right, monsieur, and your captain is an outstanding individual. We are in the Mediterranean. Good. Let's now chat about our business, please, but in such a way that nobody can hear us.'

I could see what the Canadian was driving at. In any case, I thought it better to talk if he wanted to, so all three of us went and sat near the searchlight, where we were less exposed to the wet spray from the waves.

'Now, Ned, we are listening,' I said. 'What have you got to tell us?'

'What I have to tell you is very simple. We are now in Europe, and before Captain Nemo's whims take us off to the ends of the polar seas or back to Australasia, I would like to leave the *Nautilus*.'

I will admit that this discussion with the Canadian bothered me. I did not wish to fetter the freedom of my companions in any way, but nevertheless felt no desire to leave Captain Nemo. Thanks to him, thanks to his vessel, I was furthering my underwater studies each day, I was rewriting my book about the submarine depths in the very midst of that element. Would I ever again find such an opportunity to observe the marvels of the ocean? No, never! So I could not get used to the idea of abandoning the *Nautilus* before our cycle of investigation was over.

'Friend Ned,' I said, 'please reply frankly. Are you bored here? Do you regret the fate that threw you into Captain Nemo's hands?'

The Canadian remained silent for a few moments. Then, crossing his arms:

'Frankly,' he said, 'I don't regret this voyage under the sea. I will be pleased to have done it; but in order for me to have done it, it must be finished. That is how I see it.'

'It *will* finish, Ned.'

'Where and when?'

'Where, I don't know. When, I cannot say; or rather I imagine it will end when these oceans no longer have anything to teach us. Everything which starts necessarily has an end in this world.'

'I agree with monsieur,' replied Conseil; 'it is very likely that, having covered all the oceans of the globe, Captain Nemo will let all three of us go.'

'Go!' exclaimed the Canadian. 'He'll have a go at us, don't you mean?'

'Let's not exaggerate, Master Land,' I said. 'We have nothing to fear from the captain, but I do not share Conseil's ideas either. We are masters of the *Nautilus*'s secrets, and I have little hope that the captain will resign himself to giving us our freedom and letting the whole world know about them.'

'But then what do you hope for?' asked the Canadian.

'That circumstances will arise that we can—that we must—profit from, whether in six months' time or tomorrow.'

'Yeah!' said Ned Land. 'And where will we be in six months, do you think, monsieur the naturalist?'

'Perhaps here, perhaps in China. As you know, the *Nautilus* moves quickly. It crosses the oceans as swallows cross the air, or expresses the continents. It has no fear of busy seas. Who can say if it won't head right now for the coast of France, Britain, or America, where an escape could be attempted as easily as here?'

'Dr Aronnax,' replied the Canadian, 'your arguments are fundamentally flawed. You are speaking in the future: "We will be here! We will be there!" But I am speaking in the present: "We are here, and we must seize the opportunity."'

Land's logic was hemming me in; and I felt I was on very shaky ground. I no longer knew what argument to put forward in my favour.

'Monsieur,' he continued, 'let us suppose, by some remote chance, that Captain Nemo offered you freedom this very day, now. Would you accept?'

'I'm not sure.'

'And if he added that the offer he was making you today would not be repeated, would you accept?'

I did not reply.

'And what does friend Conseil think?' enquired Ned.

The worthy fellow calmly replied: 'Friend Conseil has nothing to say. He is totally disinterested in this question. Like his master, like his friend Ned, he is not married. Neither wife, nor parents, nor children are waiting for him back home. He is in monsieur's service, he agrees with monsieur, he speaks in unison with monsieur, and, to his great regret, he should not be counted on to form a majority. There are only two people here: monsieur on the one hand and Ned on the other. Having said that, friend Conseil is listening, and would be glad to keep the score.'

I couldn't help smiling to see Conseil annihilate his personality so completely. Deep down, the Canadian had to be delighted not to have him against him.

'So, monsieur,' said Ned Land, 'since Conseil does not exist, let's discuss this between the two of us. I have spoken, you have listened. What is your reply?'

It was clearly necessary to come to a conclusion, and I was not fond of subterfuges.

'Friend Ned,' I said, 'here is my reply. You are right, and my arguments do not hold against yours. We cannot count on Captain Nemo's goodwill. Elementary self-interest prevents him setting us free. Conversely, self-interest requires that we profit from the first opportunity for leaving the *Nautilus*.'

'Good, Dr Aronnax, wisely spoken.'

'But', I said, 'I have one remark to make, a single one. The opportunity must be a real one. Our first attempt to escape must succeed; because if it fails, we will not find another opportunity, and Captain Nemo will not forgive us.'

'All that is good,' replied the Canadian. 'But your remark applies to any attempt to escape, whether in two years' or in two days' time. So the conclusion remains the same: if a favourable occasion arises, we must take it.'

'Agreed. And now will you tell me, Ned, what you mean by a favourable occasion?'

'One which would bring the *Nautilus* close to a European coast on a dark night.'

'And would you try to escape by swimming?'

'Yes, if we were close enough to shore, and if the vessel was on the surface. No, if we were far away and the ship was underwater.'

'And in that case?'

'In that case, I would try to make use of the ship's dinghy. I know how it works. We could get inside, remove the bolts, and head back up to the surface, without even the pilot, who is for'ard, noticing our escape.'

'Well, Ned. Look out for this opportunity; but do not forget that one failure will ruin us.'

'I will not forget, monsieur.'

'And now Ned, do you want to know exactly what I think of your plan?'

'I do, Dr Aronnax.'

'Well I think—I do not say I hope—I think that this favourable opportunity won't arise.'

'Why?'

'Because Captain Nemo cannot hide from himself that we have not given up hope of recovering our liberty, and will remain on his guard, above all in the seas around Europe and in sight of the coast.'

'I agree with monsieur,' said Conseil.

'We shall see,' replied Ned Land, who was shaking his head in a determined manner.

'And now, Ned,' I added, 'let's stop there. Not a word of all this. The day that you are ready, you will tell us and we will follow you. I put myself completely in your hands.'*

Our conversation, which was later to have such grave consequences, finished there. I must say now that circumstances seemed to confirm what I had expected, to the Canadian's great despair. Did Captain Nemo not trust us in these busy seas, or did he merely wish to hide from the sight of the many ships of all nations ploughing the Mediterranean? I do not know, but most often he kept submerged and away from the coast. Either the *Nautilus* came up with only the pilot's dome showing, or it went down to great depths—for between the Greek Islands and Asia Minor we could not find the bottom at 2,000 metres.

Accordingly I did not sight the island of Kárpathos, one of the Sporades. But Captain Nemo quoted to me this line of Virgil about it, putting his finger on a point on the planisphere:

> *Est in Carpathio Neptuni gurgite vates*
> *Caeruleus Proteus . . .**

This was, indeed, the antique sojourn of Proteus, the old shepherd of Neptune's flocks, who kept watch over this island between Rhodes and Crete now called Scarpanto. But I only saw its granite foundations through the window of the salon.

The following day, 14 February,* I resolved to devote a few hours to studying the fish of the archipelago; but for some reason the panels remained tightly closed. Plotting the direction of the *Nautilus*, I noticed that it was heading for Candia, as Crete was formerly known. When I embarked on the *Abraham Lincoln*, the whole island had just rebelled against the Turkish despotism. But what had become of the insurrection since then, I had absolutely no idea.* And it was not Captain Nemo, deprived of any communication with dry land, who could have told me.

I accordingly made no allusion to that event when, that evening, I found myself alone with the captain in the salon. In any case, he seemed taciturn and preoccupied. Then, unlike his usual habit, he had the two panels of the salon opened, and going from one to the other, he attentively observed the water outside. With what aim? I could not guess, and for my part I used the time to study the fish passing before my eyes.

Amongst others, I noticed those aphid gobies cited by Aristotle, vulgarly known as 'sea slugs', which are especially encountered in the salty water around the Nile Delta. Near them meandered some half-phosphorescent sea bream, a type of sparid which the Egyptians considered sacred animals: their arrival in the waters of the river, whose fertile overflowing they heralded, was celebrated in religious ceremonies. I noticed also some *Cheilini* 30 centimetres long, bony fish with transparent scales whose pale colouring is marked with red spots; they are great devourers of marine vegetation, which gives them an exquisite taste. Accordingly these

Cheilini were very much sought after by the gourmets of ancient Rome, and their entrails, cooked with milt from moray eels, peacock brain, and flamingo tongues, made up that divine dish which delighted Vitellius.*

Another inhabitant of these seas caught my attention and brought back to my mind all my memories of antiquity. This was the remora, which travels attached to the bellies of sharks. According to the ancients, this small fish, attached to the keel of a ship, could stop it moving, and one of them held back Mark Antony's vessel in the Battle of Actium, so helping Augustus to victory.* On such things hang the destinies of nations! I also observed admirable *Anthias* from the order of Lutjani, fish sacred to the Greeks who attributed to them the power of expelling marine monsters from the waters they frequented; their name means *flowers*, which they justified with their shimmering colours, their reds going from scarlet to light pink to the brilliance of rubies, and with the fleeting tints moistening their dorsal fins. My eyes could not tear themselves away from the marvels of the sea— but were suddenly struck by an unexpected sight.

In the water itself a man appeared, a diver carrying a leather pouch on his belt. It was not a body abandoned to the waves. He was a living person, swimming with a vigorous stroke, disappearing sometimes to go and breathe on the surface, and diving down again immediately.

I turned to Captain Nemo, and exclaimed in an emotional voice:

'A man, someone shipwrecked! We must save him at all costs!'

The captain did not reply, but went and leaned against the window.

The man had come close and, with his face pressed against the panel, was looking at us.

To my profound stupefaction, Captain Nemo made a sign to him. The diver replied using his hand, immediately headed back up towards the surface, and did not appear again.

'Don't worry,' the captain said. 'That was Nicolas, from Cape Matapan, nicknamed the "Pesce". He is well known all over the Cyclades. A bold diver! The water is his element, and he lives here more than on land, continually going from one island to another, as far as Crete.'

'So you know him, captain?'

'And why not, Dr Aronnax?'

Having said that, Captain Nemo walked up to a cabinet placed near the port side of the salon. Near it I saw a trunk reinforced with iron bands; it had a copper plate bearing on it the monogram of the *Nautilus* and its motto *Mobilis in mobile*.

Without worrying about my presence, the captain opened the cabinet, a kind of safe containing a large number of bars.

They were gold bars. Where had this precious metal come from, representing as it did an enormous sum of money? Where did the captain get this gold, and what did he plan to do with it?

I did not say a word, but simply stared. Captain Nemo took the bars one by one and methodically arranged them in the trunk which he filled up entirely. I estimated that it then contained more than 1,000 kilograms of gold, that is nearly five million francs' worth.

The trunk was securely closed, and the captain wrote an address on its lid, using characters that looked as though they were modern Greek.*

Having done this, Captain Nemo pressed the button connected by wires to the crew room. Four men appeared, and with some effort they hauled the trunk out of the salon. Then I heard them moving it up the metal stairs using a hoist.

Suddenly Captain Nemo turned to me:

'You were saying, monsieur?'

'Nothing, captain.'

'Then, monsieur, you will allow me to say goodnight to you.'

And with this Captain Nemo left the salon.

I returned to my room highly intrigued, as can be imagined. I tried in vain to sleep. I endeavoured to find a connection between the appearance of the diver and the trunk full of gold. Soon I felt from the pitching and rolling that the *Nautilus* was leaving the lower strata to come back up to the surface of the water.

Then I heard the sound of feet on the platform. I understood that the dinghy was being removed and launched on to the sea. It struck the side of the *Nautilus*, and then all sound ceased.

Two hours later, the same sound and the same comings and goings happened again. The boat was hoisted on board, then fitted into its cavity, and the *Nautilus* dived under the waves once more.

The millions had been transported to their destination. To what part of the landmass? Who had Captain Nemo sent them to?

The following day, I recounted the night's events to Conseil and the Canadian, my curiosity excited to the highest possible degree. My companions were no less surprised than I.

'But where does he get it all?' asked Land.

To that, we had no answer. I went back to the salon after lunch, and set to work. Until five o'clock I wrote up my notes.* Suddenly—was it due to some personal indisposition?—I felt extremely hot, and had to take my byssus jacket off. This was incomprehensible, for we were not at high latitudes,* and in any case the *Nautilus*, submerged, should not have suffered from any rise in temperature. I looked at the pressure-gauge. It marked a depth of sixty feet, which heat from the atmosphere could not have got to.

I continued my work, but the temperature rose to the point of becoming unbearable.

Might there be a fire on board? I wondered.

I was just going to leave the salon, when Captain Nemo entered. He went to the thermometer, examined it, and turned to me:

'Forty-two degrees.'

'I had noticed, captain, and if this heat increases a little more, we won't be able to bear it.'

'Oh, monsieur, this heat will only increase if we want it to.'

'So you can vary it as you wish?'

'No, but I can move away from the source producing it.'

'It is coming from the outside, then?'

'Yes. We are floating in a stream of boiling water.'

'You're joking!'

'Look.'

The panels opened, and I saw that the sea was entirely white around the *Nautilus*. A smoky sulphurous vapour was unwinding through the current which was bubbling like water in a boiler. I leant my hand on one of the windows, but the heat was so intense I had to withdraw it.

'But where are we?'

'Near the island of Santorini, monsieur,' the captain replied. 'To be precise, in the channel separating Nea Kameni from Palea Kameni. I wanted to show you the curious sight of a submarine eruption.'

'I thought these new islands had finished forming.'

'Nothing is ever finished in the vicinity of volcanoes,' he replied, 'and the globe is still worked by underground fires. According to Cassiodorus* and Pliny, as early as the year 19 of our era a new island, Thira the divine, appeared on the same spot* where these small islands were recently formed. Then it disappeared under the waves, to appear again in 69, only to plunge down once more. From then until the modern era, the plutonic work ceased. But on 3 February 1866 a new piece of land, which was named George Island, emerged in the midst of sulphurous vapours near Nea Kameni and united with it on 6 February. A week later, on the 13th, Aphroessa Island appeared, leaving a channel of ten metres between it and Nea Kameni. I was in these seas when this happened, and was able to observe each of the phases. Aphroessa Island measured 300 feet in diameter by 30 feet high. It was composed of black vitreous lavas mixed with feldspathic fragments. Finally, on 10 March a small island called Reka appeared* near Nea Kameni, and since then these three little pieces of land have joined together, and now form a single island.'

'And the channel where we are now . . .?' I asked.

'Here,' replied Captain Nemo, showing me a map of the Greek Islands. 'You can see that I have traced the new lands on it.'

'But will this channel fill up one day?'

'It is possible, Dr Aronnax, for eight islets of lava have sprung up opposite St Nicolas Port on Palea Kameni since 1866. It is therefore evident that Nea and Palea will join up relatively soon. In the midst of the Pacific, it is the infusoria that form the land-masses, but here it is eruptive phenomena. Look, monsieur, look at the work going on under the waves.'

I came back to the window. The *Nautilus* was no longer moving. The heat was becoming intolerable. Previously white, the sea was now becoming red, due to the presence of an iron salt. In spite of the hermetically closed salon, an unbearable sulphurous smell was being given off, and I noticed scarlet flames whose vividness killed the brightness of the electricity.

I was dripping with perspiration, stifling, I felt I was going to cook. Yes, in truth, I felt myself cooking!

'We cannot remain in this boiling water any longer!' I said to the captain.

'No, it would not be prudent,' replied an impassive Nemo.

An order was given. The *Nautilus* went about and headed away from this furnace that it could not defy with impunity. A quarter of an hour later, we were breathing on the surface of the waves again.

The thought then occurred to me that if Ned had chosen these shores to carry out our escape, we would not have come out from this sea of fire alive.

The following day, 16 February, we left the basin between Rhodes and Alexandria, which has depths of 3,000 metres. The *Nautilus* passed Cerigo, doubled Cape Matapan, and left the islands of Greece.

7

The Mediterranean in Forty-Eight Hours

THE blue sea par excellence, the 'Great Sea' of the Hebrews, 'the Sea' of the Greeks, the *mare nostrum* of the Romans. Bordered by orange trees, aloes, cacti, maritime pines, embalmed in the perfume of myrtle trees, framed by severe mountains, saturated with a pure, transparent air, but constantly worked by the fires of the Earth—the Mediterranean is a veritable battlefield where Neptune and Pluto still fight for world domination. It is there, says Michelet, on its shores and in its waters that man bathes in one of the globe's most powerful climates.

But however beautiful, I was only able to catch a fleeting glimpse of this basin, which covers two million square kilometres. And nor was Captain Nemo's personal knowledge made available to me, as that enigmatic character did not appear once during our high-speed trajectory. I estimate the distance the *Nautilus* covered under the waves of this sea as about 600 leagues, and it finished the voyage in forty-eight hours. Having left the shores of Greece on the morning of 16 February, we had passed through the Strait of Gibraltar by sunrise on the 18th.

It was clear to me that the Mediterranean displeased Captain Nemo, pressed in as it was amongst the lands he wished to flee. Its waves and breezes brought too many memories back to him, perhaps too many regrets. Here he no longer had that freedom of movement, that manœuvrability which the other oceans gave him, and his *Nautilus* felt cramped between the narrow shores of Africa and Europe.

Accordingly, our speed was 25 knots, that is 12 leagues of 4 kilometres per hour. It goes without saying that Ned Land had to give up his escape plans, to his great annoyance. He could not use the dinghy while being transported at a speed of 12 or 13 metres a second. To have left the *Nautilus* would have been like jumping from a train moving at the same speed, a dangerous action if ever there was one. In addition, our vessel only surfaced in order to renew its supply of air at night, steering using the compass and information from the logline.

As a result I saw of the Mediterranean's depths merely what the traveller on an express glimpses of countryside passing before his eyes: far-off horizons, and not the close-ups which pass by in a flash. However, Conseil and I were able to observe some Mediterranean fishes whose powerful fins kept them alongside the *Nautilus* for a few moments. We remained on the lookout in front of the windows of the salon, and our notes allow me to summarize the ichthyology of that sea in a few words.

Of the various fishes living there, I saw some and glimpsed others, and many were whisked away from my eyes by the speeding *Nautilus*. Please permit me then to classify them according to this eccentric method. It will better depict my rapid observation.

Amidst the waters, brightly lit by the electric beams, snaked past some of those metre-long lampreys which are common in almost every climate. Oxyrhynchous creatures, kinds of five-foot wide rays with white stomachs and ash-grey spotted backs, appeared like huge shawls carried off by the currents. Other rays passed so quickly that I could not tell whether they deserved the title of eagle given them by the Greeks, or the epithets of rat, toad, and bat which modern fishermen give them. Dogfish sharks, twelve feet long and particularly feared by divers, raced each other. Marine foxes, eight feet long and endowed with a very fine sense of smell, appeared like great blue shadows. Dorados of the genus sparid, some measuring up to 1.3 metres, paraded in their circular banded silver and azure clothing, contrasting with the dark colours of their fins. These are fish devoted to Venus, with eyes highlighted by golden eyebrows: a precious species, at home in both fresh and salt water, living in the rivers, lakes, and oceans of all climates, adapting to every temperature. Their race goes back to the early geological periods of the Earth and has kept all its beauty from the first days. Travelling long distances, magnificent sturgeons of nine or ten metres struck the glass of the panels with their powerful tails and showed their bluish backs with small brown spots; they resembled sharks though they are not so powerful and are encountered in all seas; in the springtime they like to ascend the great rivers, fighting the currents of the Volga, Danube, Po, Rhine, Loire, and Oder. They live off herring, mackerel, salmon, and gadid; although they belong to the cartilaginous class they are delicate, are eaten fresh, dried, marinated, or salted, and were formerly carried in triumph to the table of Lucullus.* But of the various Mediterranean denizens, those that I could observe the most usefully when the *Nautilus* approached the surface belonged to the sixty-third genus of bony fish. These were scombrid tuna, with blue-black backs, silver stomachs, and dorsal combs radiating golden gleams. They have the reputation of following moving ships, seeking their fresh shadows under the fire of the tropical sky; and they lived up to their reputation, accompanying the *Nautilus* as they accompanied the ships of La Pérouse in times past. For long hours, they raced our vessel. I never grew tired of admiring animals so well designed for racing, with their little heads, their streamlined, slender bodies, in certain cases longer than three metres, their pectorals of remarkable strength, and their forked caudal fins. They swam in a triangular formation, like certain flocks of birds whose speed they matched, prompting the ancients to say that geometry and strategy were known to them. And yet they do not escape the pursuit of the Provençaux, who appreciate them as much as the inhabitants of the Sea of Marmara and Italy, for these precious animals throw themselves to perish blindly and silently by the thousand in the nets of Marseilles.

I will cite, from memory, the Mediterranean fishes that Conseil or I merely glimpsed. There were whitish fierasfers-knifefish passing like imperceptible vapours; conger *Muraenae*, three- or four-metre serpents, bright in their green, blue, and yellow shades; three-foot long cod-hakes, whose livers are a delicacy; taenia-bandfish floating like fine seaweed; gurnards that the poets call lyre-fish, and sailors whistler-fish, whose snouts are adorned with two triangular serrated blades that reproduce ancient Homer's instrument; swallow-gurnards swimming with the speed of the bird whose name they have taken; grouper-soldierfish with red heads and dorsal fins adorned with filaments; shad decorated with black, grey, brown, blue, yellow, and green spots, and which respond to the silvery sound of bells; splendid turbots, the pheasants of the sea, diamond-shaped with yellowish fins, dotted with brown, and whose upper left part is usually marbled with brown and yellow; and finally admirable shoals of grey mullet, veritable oceanic birds of paradise which the Romans bought at up to 10,000 sesterces each, and which they killed on their tables, so as to follow with cruel eyes the colour-changes from the cinnabar red of life to the pallid white of death.

And if I was not able to observe the *miraleti*, the trigger-fish, the tetrodons, the sea-horses, the jewel-fish, the trumpetfish, the blennies, the surmullets, the wrasses, the smelts, the flying fishes, the anchovies, the bream, the boops, the orfes, nor any of the main representatives of the order of Pleuronectes, namely the dab, flounders, plaice, soles, and flatfish common to the Atlantic and the Mediterranean, the blame should be put on the dizzying speed of the *Nautilus* through these rich waters.

As for marine mammals, near the opening of the Adriatic I believe I recognized two or three sperm whales of the genus physeter with dorsal fins, a few dolphins of the genus *Globicephala* particular to the Mediterranean with foreheads striped with small light lines, and a dozen seals with white stomachs and black coats, known as Mediterranean monk seals and which perfectly resemble three-metre long Dominicans.

For his part, Conseil thinks he saw a six-foot wide turtle adorned with three ridges running lengthwise. I regret not seeing this reptile, for I thought I recognized the leatherback from the description Conseil gave me—quite a rare species. For my part, I only noticed a few loggerhead turtles with their long carapaces.

As for the zoophytes, for a few moments I was able to appreciate a beautiful orange *Galeola* which attached itself to the window of the port panel; it formed a long fine filament, spreading into infinite branches and terminating in the finest lace ever spun by the rivals of Arachne.* Unfortunately, I was unable to catch this splendid specimen, and perhaps no other Mediterranean zoophytes would have offered themselves to my eyes if, on the evening of the 16th, the *Nautilus* had not markedly slowed down. This is what happened.

We were passing between Sicily and Tunisia. In the confined space between Cape Bon and the Strait of Messina, the sea floor rises very suddenly. A ridge is located there covered by only 17 metres of water, whilst on either side the depth is 170 metres. Accordingly the *Nautilus* had to manœuvre carefully in order to avoid the submarine barrier.

I showed Conseil this long reef on the map of the Mediterranean.

'With due respect, monsieur,' observed Conseil, 'it is like an isthmus connecting Europe and Africa.'

'Yes my good fellow,' I replied, 'it entirely blocks the Sicilian Channel, and Smyth's soundings prove that the two continents were formerly connected between Capes Boeo and Farina.'*

'I can easily believe it.'

'I will add that a similar barrier exists between Gibraltar and Ceuta, and completely closed the Mediterranean in earlier geological periods.'

'So what if one day a volcanic thrust were to lift the two barriers out of the waves!'

'It is hardly probable, Conseil.'

'But, if monsieur would allow me to finish, if this did happen, it would be quite annoying for M. de Lesseps, working so hard to cut his isthmus!'

'I agree, but I repeat that this phenomenon will not happen. The strength of the underground forces is constantly diminishing. Volcanoes, so numerous in the first days of the world, are gradually dying; their internal heat is reducing, for the temperature of the Earth's lower strata is lessening by a perceptible amount each century—and our globe will be the worse off for it, since this heat is life.'

'However, the sun . . .'

'The sun is insufficient, Conseil. Can it restore heat to a dead body?'

'I don't know about that.'

'Well my friend, the Earth will one day be a cold corpse. It will become uninhabitable and consequently uninhabited like the moon, which lost its vital heat a long time ago.'

'In how many centuries?' asked Conseil.

'In some hundreds of thousands of years, my good man.'

'Well then, we still have time to finish our voyage, provided, that is, Ned doesn't meddle with things!'

And Conseil, reassured, returned to his study of the shallow bottoms that the *Nautilus* was closely skimming over at a moderate speed.

There, on rocky and volcanic ground flourished a whole living flora of sponges, holothurians, hyaline Cydippes adorned with reddish tendrils giving off a slight phosphorescence, beroes, popularly known as sea cucumbers, bathing in the shimmerings of the solar spectrum, metre-wide itinerant comatulids whose purple tint reddened the waters, arborescent sea spiders of the greatest beauty, pavonaceous plants with long stalks, a large number of edible sea urchins of various species, and finally green sea anemones with brown discs on greyish trunks which disappeared amongst the olive-coloured hair of their tentacles.

Conseil worked hard at observing the molluscs and the articulates, and although the nomenclature is a little arid, I do not wish to upset the good fellow by omitting his personal observations.

In the branch of molluscs, he cites numerous pectiniform scallops, asses-foot thorny oysters piled up on each other, triangular donaxes, tridentate Hyalinae with yellow fins and transparent shells, orange pleurobranchiates, which are eggs with greenish dots or stippling, aplesias sometimes known as sea hares, small dolabriforms, plump aceres, umbrella shells specific to the Mediterranean, earshells whose shells produced a much sought after mother-of-pearl, flammulated scallops, beaked cockles that the Languedociens are said to prefer to oysters, the clam that is so dear to the Marseillais, fat white double clams, some of the kinds of clams so abundant on the coasts of North America and so quickly snapped up in New York, opercular pectens with varied colours, lithophaga hiding in their holes and whose peppery taste I greatly appreciated, furrowed heart cockles with bulging sides to their ventricose shells, *Cynthiae* bristling with scarlet tubers, *Carinariae* with curved points like delicate gondolas, crowned ferules, atlantas with spiral shells, grey tethys with white spots and fringed mantilla, eoliths like little slugs, Cavolines crawling on their backs, auriculae including the forget-me-not auricula in its oval shell, timid angel fish, periwinkles, Janthinae, cinerairia, petricola, Lamellariidiae, cabochons, Pandoridae, etc.

As for the articulates, Conseil's notes very accurately put them into six classes, of which three belong to the marine world. These are the crustaceans, cirripeds, and annelids.

The crustaceans are further divided into nine orders, of which the first one includes the decapods—that is creatures with heads and thoraxes usually welded together, mouth mechanisms composed of several pairs of jaws, and four, five, or six pairs of thoracic and ambulatory limbs. Conseil had followed the method of our master Milne-Edwards, who divides the decapods into three sections: the *Brachyura*, the *Macrura*, and the *Anomura*. The names are somewhat barbaric, but accurate and useful. Amongst the *Brachyura*, Conseil cites the *Amathiae* whose foreheads have two large divergent lumps, the Inachoid scorpions, which for some strange reason symbolized wisdom for the Greeks, amber massenes, amber spinimanes which had probably strayed into this shoal since they normally live at great depths, xanthos, *Pilumni*, rhombuses, granular *Calappae*—very easy to digest, according to Conseil—toothless corystes, *Ebalia*, cymopolias, woolly dorippes, etc. Amongst the *Macrura*—subdivided into five families: the armour-plated, the fossorials, the *Astacidae*, the prawns, and the *Ocypodidae*—Conseil cites common crayfish, the flesh of the female being very highly valued, scyllarian bears or sea cicadas, riparian decapods, and all sorts of other edible species; but he does not mention the subdivision of the *Astacidae* containing the lobsters, for the crayfish are the only lobsters found in the Mediterranean. Finally amongst the *Anomura*, he saw some common drocinas sheltering in some of those abandoned shells they take over, *Homolidae* with spiny foreheads, hermit crabs, hairy porcelain crabs,* and so on.

But there the work of Conseil stopped. There had been no time to conclude the class of shellfish by examining the *Stomapoda*, the *Amphipoda*, the homopods, the isopods, the *Trilobita*, the *Branchiapoda*, the *Ostracoda*, and the *Entomostraca*. Also, to end the study of the marine articulates properly, he should have cited the class of cirropods which contains the cyclops, and the arguluses, as well as the class of annelids that he would automatically have divided into the tubicolous and the dorsibranchiates. However, the *Nautilus* had got past the shallow bottoms of the Sicilian Channel, and resumed its normal speed in the deeper waters. Hence no more molluscs, no more articulates, no more zoophytes. Just a few big fish passing like shadows.

During the night of 16 to 17 February we entered the second Mediterranean basin, whose greatest depths reach 3,000 metres. Under the thrust of its propeller and sliding down on its inclined planes, the *Nautilus* plunged to the furthest parts of that sea.

There, although lacking in natural marvels, the mass of waters offered my eyes many moving and terrible scenes. We were crossing that part of the Mediterranean which is so rich in wrecks. From the Algerian coast to the shores of Provence, how many ships have been wrecked, how many vessels have disappeared! The Mediterranean is a mere lake compared to the vast liquid plains of the Pacific, but it is a capricious lake with changeable waves, today propitious and caressing for the frail tartan floating between the dual ultramarine of water and sky, tomorrow in a rage, tormented, dislocated by winds, breaking the strongest ships with its short waves which beat them with hurried blows.

In this rapid excursion through the lower strata, how many wrecks I spotted lying on the sea-floor, some already coated by coral, others covered only with a layer of rust; together with anchors, cannons, cannonballs, iron fittings, propeller blades, pieces of machinery, broken cylinders, stoved-in boilers; and finally in midwater, hulls floating suspended, some of them still upright and others upside down.

Some had perished in collisions, others by hitting a granite reef. I saw some ships that had sunk straight down, with their masts erect and their sails stiffened by the water. They seemed as if anchored in an enormous open roadstead waiting for the moment to depart. When the *Nautilus* passed amongst them and enveloped them with its electric beams it looked as though these ships were going to greet it with their signalling flags and send their registration numbers! But no, nothing but silence and death on the field of such disasters!

I observed that the Mediterranean floor became more crowded with the sinister wrecks as the *Nautilus* approached the Strait of Gibraltar. The coasts of Africa and Europe drew closer, and encounters in this narrow space were more frequent. I saw numerous iron carinas, fantastic ruins of steamers, some lying over, others upright like fierce animals. One of the boats presented a terrifying aspect, with its sides open, funnel bent, and only the frames of its paddle-wheels remaining, its helm separated from the stern post but still attached by an iron chain, and the rear name-board eaten away by marine salt! How many lives broken by these shipwrecks! How many victims carried down beneath the waves! Had some sailor on board survived to tell of the terrifying disaster, or did the waves still keep the secret of the accident? I do not know why the thought came to me that this boat lying buried under the sea could be the *Atlas*, which had disappeared with all hands twenty years before, and had never been heard of again! Ah, what a sinister history could be drawn from the Mediterranean floor, that vast bone cemetery, where so many treasures have been lost, where so many men have found death!

Meanwhile the *Nautilus*, fleet and indifferent, was moving through the ruins on full propeller. On 18 February, at about three in the morning, it arrived at the entrance to the Strait of Gibraltar.

There are two currents here: an upper current, known about for a long time, which brings the waters from the ocean into the Mediterranean basin; and a lower counter-current, whose existence has been demonstrated by hypothesis. The sum of the water of the Mediterranean, constantly increased by the current from the Atlantic and the rivers flowing into it, should raise its level each year, for the rate of evaporation is insufficient to re-establish equilibrium. But nothing of the sort happens, and so the existence has had to be posited of a lower current pouring the surplus through the Strait of Gibraltar from the Mediterranean into the Atlantic basin.

True indeed. It was this counter-current that the *Nautilus* was using to advance quickly through the narrow pass. For a moment I was able to glimpse the admirable ruins of the Temple of Hercules, sunken according to Pliny and Avienus,* together with the low island on which it stood, and then a few minutes later we were floating on the waves of the Atlantic Ocean.

8

Vigo Bay

THE Atlantic! That vast area of water covering 25 million square miles, 9,000 miles long by 2,700 miles wide on average. An important sea, almost unknown to the ancients except perhaps to the Carthaginians, those Dutchmen of antiquity, who travelled down the west coast of Europe and Africa looking for trade. An ocean whose parallel winding shores form an immense circumference channelling the world's largest rivers: the St Lawrence, the Mississippi, the Amazon, the Plata, the Orinoco, the Niger, the Senegal, the Elbe, the Loire, and the Rhine, bringing in waters from the most civilized countries and the most savage! A magnificent plain, continuously ploughed by ships of all nations, protected by the flags of the whole world, and terminating in those two terrible points so feared by sailors, Cape Horn and the Cape of Good Hope!

The *Nautilus* was slicing the waters with its cutwater, having covered nearly 10,000 leagues in three and a half months, a distance longer than two lines of longitude. Where would we go next, and what lay in store for us?

Having left the Strait of Gibraltar, the *Nautilus* made for the open sea. As it had surfaced we could once again enjoy our daily promenade on the platform.

I immediately went up, accompanied by Ned Land and Conseil. Cape St Vincent, the south-western point of the Iberian peninsula, appeared indistinctly twelve miles away. A southerly wind was blowing strongly. The sea was agitated and heaving, and was imparting a strong rolling motion to the *Nautilus*. It was almost impossible to stand up on the platform, continuously slammed by the huge sea. We went down again after taking a few mouthfuls of air.

I returned to my room. Conseil went to his cabin; but the Canadian, looking rather preoccupied, came with me. Our rapid journey through the Mediterranean had not allowed him to execute his plans and he did not hide his disappointment.

Once the door of my room was closed, he sat down and looked at me in silence.

'Friend Ned,' I said to him, 'I understand how you feel, but there is nothing you could have done. It would have been madness to leave from the *Nautilus* moving as it was.'

Land did not reply. His pursed lips and frowning eyebrows showed the violent obsession of a fixed idea at work in him.

'Look, we don't need to give up yet. We're moving up the coast of Portugal. Not far off are France and Britain where we could easily find refuge. Ah! if the *Nautilus* had sailed south after the Strait of Gibraltar, if it had carried us off into regions where there is no land, I would share your worries too. But we now know that Captain Nemo is not fleeing civilized seas, and I believe that in a few days you will be able to act with some degree of safety.'

Ned stared at me even more fixedly than before, and finally loosened his lips enough to say:

'It's for tonight.'

I stood up quickly. I admit I was not prepared for this. I would have liked to reply to the Canadian, but words failed me.

'We agreed to wait for an opportunity,' continued Ned Land. 'We now have that opportunity: this evening, while we are a few miles off the Spanish coast. The night will be dark with the wind blowing from the open sea. I have your word, Dr Aronnax, and I am counting on you.'

As I still did not utter a word, the Canadian got up, came up to me, and said:

'This evening at nine o'clock. I have told Conseil. At that time Captain Nemo will be shut in his room, probably asleep. Neither the engineers nor the crewmen will be able to see us. Conseil and I will head for the central staircase. You, Dr Aronnax, will remain in the library a few feet away from us, waiting for my signal. The oars, the mast, and the sail are in the dinghy. I've even managed to put a few supplies in. I've got hold of an adjustable spanner to undo the bolts holding the dinghy to the *Nautilus*'s hull. So everything's ready. See you tonight.'

'The sea is quite rough,' I said.

'Admittedly,' replied the Canadian, 'but we have to risk that. Freedom is worth paying for. In any case, it's a strong boat so a few miles with a following wind will not be much of a problem. Who knows if by tomorrow the submarine won't be a hundred leagues out to sea? So let's rely on luck, and by ten or eleven o'clock we'll either be on dry land or dead. So in God we trust, and till this evening!'

The Canadian withdrew, leaving me dumbfounded. I had imagined that given the right circumstances, I would have time to think and discuss the situation. My opinionated companion did not allow me this. But in any case what could I have said to him? Ned Land was 100 per cent right. It was a reasonable chance, and he was making the most of it. Could I now go back on my word and take responsibility for risking my companions' futures for completely selfish reasons? Might Captain Nemo not take us off tomorrow into the open seas far from any land?

At this point, a loud hissing sound told me that the tanks were being filled; and the *Nautilus* dived under the waves of the Atlantic.

I remained in my room. I wished to avoid the captain so that he could not see the emotion overwhelming me. So it was a sad day I spent, between my wish to regain freedom and my regret at saying goodbye to the marvellous *Nautilus* and leaving my underwater studies unfinished! To leave this ocean, 'my Atlantic' as I liked to call it, without having observed her every stratum and without uncovering her secrets, as the Indian and Pacific Oceans had been revealed to me! My novel was falling from my hands half-way through,* my dream was being interrupted at the vital moment! What terrible hours I spent, now seeing myself safe on land with my companions, now wishing, despite my rational side, that some unforeseen circumstance would prevent Ned's plans from unfolding.

Twice I went into the salon. I wanted to consult the compass. I wanted to see whether or not the *Nautilus* was really taking us towards the coast. The *Nautilus* was still in Portuguese waters. It was heading northwards following the coastline.

So I had to come to terms with my situation and get ready for an escape. My luggage was not very heavy. My notes, nothing else.

As for Captain Nemo, I wondered what he would think of our escape, what anxiety, what anguish it might cause him, and what he would do if our plans got out or if we did not succeed! Doubtless I had no reason to complain. Indeed, never had hospitality been more open than his. But I could not be accused of ingratitude for leaving him. No oath tied us to him: he counted only on the force of circumstances, and not on our word, to bind us to his company for ever. Moreover, all our attempts were justified because of his freely admitted claim to keep us prisoner on board his ship in perpetuity.*

I hadn't seen the captain since our visit to Santorini Island. Would chance make me meet him before our departure? I wanted and feared it at one and the same time. I listened out to see if I could hear him pacing in the room next to mine. No sound reached my ears. His bedroom was probably empty.

I wondered if this strange character was even still on board. Since that night when the dinghy had left the *Nautilus* on a mysterious errand, my ideas about him had changed a little. I believed that whatever Captain Nemo said, he must maintain relations of some sort with dry land. Did he ever leave the *Nautilus*? Entire weeks had often gone by without my seeing him at all. What did he do during this time? Whilst I had believed him to be in the grip of spells of misanthropy, could he not have been far away carrying out some secret mission of which I had no inkling?

All these ideas and a thousand others assailed me at the same time. Room for conjecture had to be infinite in the strange situation we found ourselves in. I felt an unbearable malaise. That day of waiting seemed to go on for ever. The hours chimed too slowly for my impatience.*

Dinner was served in my room as usual. I ate badly as I was so preoccupied. I left the table at seven o'clock. A hundred and twenty minutes—I was counting them—still lay before me until I was to meet Land. My agitation grew twice as bad. My pulse started throbbing violently. I couldn't stay in one place. I paced up and down, hoping to calm my troubled mind by moving around. The idea of perishing in our bold enterprise was the least of my worries; my heart beat much more wildly at the thought of our plan being discovered before we had left the *Nautilus*, of being taken to an angry Captain Nemo or, worse, one saddened by my abandonment.

I wanted to see the salon one last time. I went through the gangway to that museum where I had spent so many agreeable and useful hours. I looked at all the riches, all the treasures, as if on the day before an eternal exile, a leaving without any hope of return. I was going to give up for ever the marvels of nature and masterpieces of art amongst which my life had gone on for so long. I would have liked to examine the waters of the Atlantic through the windows of the salon; but the panels were hermetically closed and a cloak of metal separated me from that still-unfamiliar ocean.

While working my way round the salon, I arrived at the door in the triangular section which opened on to the captain's bedroom. To my great surprise, the door was slightly ajar. I involuntarily stepped back. If Captain Nemo was in his room, he might see me. Hearing no sound, however, I went closer. The room was empty. I pushed the door. I stepped inside. The same severe atmosphere, monk-like.

At that moment, my attention was caught by a few etchings on the walls that I had not noticed on my first visit. They were portraits of those great men of history whose lives were entirely devoted to a great human idea: Kosciusko, the hero who fell with the cry *Finis Poloniae*, Bozzaris, the Leonidas of modern Greece, O'Connell, the defender of Ireland, Washington, the founder of the American Union, Manin, the Italian patriot, Lincoln, who fell shot by a supporter of slavery, and finally John Brown,* that martyr to the freeing of the black race, hanging from his gallows, as so terribly drawn by Victor Hugo.

What link existed between these heroic souls and the soul of

Captain Nemo? Could I finally solve the mystery of his existence by this collection of portraits? Was he a champion of downtrodden peoples, a liberator of enslaved races? Had he taken part in the political and social upheavals that had recently marked the century? Had he been one of the heroes of that terrible American Civil War, that frightful but forever glorious battle . . . ?

Suddenly the clock struck eight. The first blow of the hammer tore me from my dreams. I trembled as if an invisible eye had penetrated my innermost thoughts, and rushed out of the room.

There my eyes stopped at the compass. We were still heading north. The logline indicated a moderate speed, the pressure-gauge a depth of about sixty feet. Circumstances were favouring the Canadian's plans.

I returned to my room. I dressed myself warmly in seaboots, sea-otter cap, and byssus jacket lined with sealskin. I was ready. I waited. Only the shuddering vibrations of the propeller broke the deep silence reigning on board. I listened out, my ears wide open. Would some ruckus suddenly tell me that Ned Land had been caught in his preparations for escape? A deadly fear took hold of me. I tried in vain to calm my nerves.

At a few minutes to nine, I put my ear against the captain's door. No sound. I left my room and went back to the salon: it was deserted and plunged into semi-darkness.

I opened the door communicating with the library. The same lack of light, the same solitude. I went and stood near the door opening on to the well of the central staircase. I waited for Ned's signal.

The vibrations of the propeller decreased noticeably, and then stopped altogether. Why the change in the *Nautilus*'s speed? Whether this halt helped or hindered Ned Land's plans, I could not say.

The silence was now broken only by the beating of my heart.

Suddenly I felt a bump. I realized that the *Nautilus* had come to rest on the ocean floor. My nervousness grew much worse. There was still no sign of the Canadian's signal. I wanted to go and find Land and urge him to put off his attempt. I was convinced there had been some change in our sailing.

At this point, the door of the main salon opened, and Captain Nemo appeared. He noticed me, and without further preamble:

'Ah, monsieur,' he said in a pleasant tone, 'I was looking for you. Do you know your history of Spain?'

Even if I had known the history of my own country off by heart, I would not have been able to quote a single detail of it under the circumstances, my mind troubled and my head empty.

'Well?' said Captain Nemo. 'Did you hear my question? Do you know the history of Spain?'

'Not at all well,' I replied.

'That's scientists for you, they don't know their history. Do sit down', he added, 'and I will relate to you a curious historical episode.'

The captain stretched himself out on a sofa and, mechanically, I took a place in the shadows near him.

'Monsieur,' he said to me, 'please listen carefully. This story will appeal to you as it answers a question that you have doubtless never been able to resolve.'

'I am listening, captain,' I said, not knowing where my interlocutor was heading, and wondering whether this incident had any connection with our ideas of escape.

'If you will permit,' said Captain Nemo, 'we will go back to 1702. You surely know that at that period your king Louis XIV, believing that a mere gesture from a potentate could make the Pyrenees disappear into the ground, imposed his grandson, the Duke of Anjou,* on the Spanish throne. This prince, who reigned more or less badly under the name Philip V, had to deal with strong external opposition.

'In fact, the previous year the royal houses of Holland, Austria, and England had signed a treaty of alliance at the Hague with the aim of removing the crown of Spain from Philip V and placing it on the head of an archduke, whom these countries prematurely called Charles III.

'Spain was obliged to resist this coalition. But she had practically no soldiers or sailors. However, she had plenty of money provided that her galleons, loaded with gold and silver from America, could enter her ports. Now in late 1702, Spain was expecting a rich convoy that France was escorting with a fleet of 23 vessels commanded by Admiral de Châteaurenault,* for the navies of the coalition were patrolling the Atlantic together.

'The convoy was to head for Cadiz, but the admiral learned

that the English fleet was cruising nearby, and resolved to head for a French port instead.

'The Spanish captains of the convoy protested against the decision. They wanted to be accompanied to a Spanish port, and if it could not be Cadiz, then Vigo Bay on the north-west coast of Spain, not blockaded at the time.

'Admiral de Châteaurenault was weak enough to obey these demands, and the galleons entered Vigo Bay.

'Unfortunately this bay formed an open roadstead which could not be defended. It was therefore necessary to unload the galleons quickly before the coalition fleet arrived: there would have been enough time for the disembarkation, if an unhappy question of rivalry had not suddenly emerged.

'Can you see how the events fit together?' Captain Nemo asked me.

'Perfectly,' I said, still not knowing for what reason this history lesson was being given.

'I'll continue then. This is what happened. The merchants of Cadiz had the right to receive all merchandise coming from the New World. Unloading the ingots from the galleons in Vigo port would have gone against their rights. They therefore complained to Madrid, and persuaded the weak Philip V that the convoy should remain sequestered in the roadstead of Vigo without unloading, until the enemy fleets had gone away again.

'Now while this decision was being taken, the English vessels arrived in Vigo Bay, on 22 October 1702. Although outnumbered, Admiral de Châteaurenault fought courageously. But when he saw that the convoy's riches were going to fall into the enemy's hands, he burned and scuppered the galleons and so sank them with their enormous treasure.'

Captain Nemo had stopped. I admit that I still could not see how his story concerned me.

'Well?' I asked.

'Well, Dr Aronnax, we are in Vigo Bay, and you are now in a position to penetrate its mysteries.'

The captain got up and asked me to follow him. I had had time to recover and did as he requested. The salon was dark, but the water sparkled through the clear windows. I looked.

Around the *Nautilus*, for a distance of half a mile, the waters appeared impregnated with electric light. The sandy bottom was clear and clean. Some of the crewmen in diving suits were busy salvaging half-rotten barrels and torn-open trunks in the midst of still-blackened wrecks. From these trunks and barrels escaped gold and silver bars, and cascades of pieces-of-eight and jewellery. The sand was strewn with them. Then, laden with their precious booty, the men were coming back to the *Nautilus*, depositing their burdens, and going back to continue their inexhaustible harvest of gold and silver.

I understood. This was the scene of the battle of 22 October 1702. On this very spot the galleons loaded for the Spanish government had sunk. Captain Nemo came here whenever he needed to take charge of the millions which he ballasted his *Nautilus* with. It was for him, and him alone, that America had given up its precious metals. He was the direct and only inheritor of the treasures taken from the Incas and others defeated by Hernando Cortez!*

'Did you know, monsieur,' he asked, smiling, 'that the sea contained so many riches?'

'I knew', I replied, 'that there are estimated to be two million tons of silver held in suspension in the water.'

'Doubtless, but the cost of extracting it would be greater than the profit. Here, in contrast, all I have to do is pick up what others have lost, not only in Vigo Bay but also at a thousand other shipwrecks noted on my submarine charts. Do you understand now why I am a multi-millionaire?'

'Yes indeed, captain. Allow me, however, to tell you that in making use of Vigo Bay, you are merely anticipating the work of a rival company.'*

'Which one?'

'A company which has received the right from the Spanish government to search for sunken galleons. The shareholders are attracted by a potentially enormous profit, for the value of these riches is estimated to be 500 million francs.'

'Five hundred million!' responded Captain Nemo. 'There used to be, but not any more.'

'So I gather. Accordingly, informing the shareholders would be a kind gesture. But who knows how the news would be received? What gamblers usually regret the most is losing not their money but their mad hopes. In the end, I pity them less than the thousands of wretches who could have benefited from so many riches if properly distributed, whilst now they will never be of any use to them at all!'

No sooner had I formulated this regret, than I felt it must have hurt Captain Nemo.

'Never be of any use!' he replied animatedly. 'What makes you believe, monsieur, that these riches must be considered wasted if I collect them? Do you think that it is for my own benefit that I take the trouble to gather these treasures? Who told you that I do not put them to good use? Do you think I am unaware there are suffering beings and oppressed races on this planet, wretches to be helped and victims to be avenged? Don't you understand . . .?'

Captain Nemo stopped with these last words, perhaps regretting having said too much. But I *had* understood. Whatever the reasons that had made him seek independence under the seas, he had above all remained a human being! He still felt the sufferings of humanity, and his great generosity extended to subjugated peoples as well as individuals!

I realized then for whom Captain Nemo's millions were destined, when the *Nautilus* was sailing through the waters of rebellious Crete!

9

A Vanished Continent

THE following morning, 19 February, the Canadian came into my room. I was expecting his visit. He seemed very disappointed.

'Well monsieur?' he said to me.

'Well Ned, luck was against us yesterday.'

'Yes, that damned captain had to stop at the exact moment we were going to escape from his boat!'

'Yes Ned, he was dealing with his banker.'

'His banker!'

'Or rather his bank. By which I mean this ocean where his riches are safer than they would be in the storerooms of a state.'

I then recounted the incidents of the day before, in the secret hope of bringing Ned round to the idea of not leaving the captain; but the only effect of my tale was that Ned expressed strong regrets he had not been able to visit the site of the Battle of Vigo.

'But in fact', he said, 'it's not over yet. It's just a harpoon-throw that went wide! We'll win next time, even tonight if need be . . .'

'In what direction is the *Nautilus* heading?'

'No idea,' replied Ned.

'Well at noon, we will see the position being taken.'

The Canadian went to rejoin Conseil. As soon as I was dressed, I made for the salon. The compass was not reassuring. The *Nautilus* was heading south-south-west. We were leaving Europe behind.

I waited impatiently for our position to be marked on the map. At about half-past eleven the tanks emptied and the vessel surfaced. I rushed on to the platform. Ned was already there.

No land in sight. Nothing but the immense sea. Just a few sails on the horizon, doubtless some of those which try to find favourable winds as far out as Cape São-Roque to be able to round the Cape of Good Hope. The sky was overcast. A squall was coming on.

In a rage, Ned tried to pierce the misty horizon. He still hoped that behind all the murk stretched the landfall he so eagerly sought.

At noon the sun appeared for a moment. The first officer used the bright spell to shoot the sun. Then, with the sea getting stormier, we went down again and the hatch was closed once more.

An hour later I consulted the map and saw that the position of the *Nautilus* was indicated as 33° 22′N, 16° 17′W, that is, 150 leagues from the nearest coast.* There was no way of even dreaming of an escape and I leave to your imagination how angry the Canadian was when I told him of our situation.

For my part, I was not too disappointed. It felt as though a weight bearing down on me had lifted, and I was able to resume my daily studies with relative calm.

At about eleven in the evening I received a very unexpected visit from Captain Nemo. With a great deal of grace, he asked me if I felt tired from staying up the night before. I replied in the negative.

'Then, Dr Aronnax, may I suggest a curious excursion?'

'Pray continue, captain.'

'You have still visited the submarine depths only in the daytime and in sunlight. Might it interest you to visit them on a dark night?'

'Yes indeed.'

'The excursion will be tiring, I warn you. We will need to march for a long time and climb a mountain. And the paths are not very well looked after.'

'What you say only increases my curiosity. I am ready when you are.'

'Please come, monsieur; we will put on our diving suits.'

When I got to the changing-room, I saw that neither my companions nor any of the crewmen were going to accompany us on our excursion. Captain Nemo had not even mentioned the possibility of taking Ned or Conseil.

We had soon put our equipment on. On our backs were tanks filled with plenty of air, but the electric lamps had not been got ready. I mentioned this to the captain.

'They would not be of any use to us,' he replied.

I thought I had misheard but could not repeat my question, for his head had already disappeared into its metallic container. I finished my preparations. I felt a reinforced stick being placed in my hand, and a few minutes later, after the usual procedure, we were walking at a depth of 300 metres on the floor of the Atlantic.

It was nearly twelve. The waters were very dark, but Captain Nemo pointed out a distant reddish point like a protracted gleam, glowing about two miles from the *Nautilus*. What this fire was, what materials fed it, how and why it was maintained in the liquid element, I could not have said. In any case it lit our path, albeit dimly; I soon got used to the peculiar gloom, and understood why the Ruhmkorff apparatus would not have helped in these conditions.

Captain Nemo and I walked close together, heading directly for the light he had indicated. The smooth ground climbed imperceptibly. We were taking long strides, helping ourselves along with our sticks; but progress was slow, for our feet sank down into the mud mixed with seaweed and dotted with flat stones.

While walking, I heard a sort of sizzling sound above my head. The noise sometimes got much louder and became a continuous crackling. I soon understood the reason. It was rain, pattering violently down on the surface of the water. Instinctively the thought came to me that I was going to get wet! Being rained on underwater: I couldn't help laughing at the strange idea! But to tell the truth, in the thick clothing of the diving suit I no longer had any sensation of being underwater, and only felt as if I was in an atmosphere slightly denser than on land.

After half an hour of walking the ground became rocky. Jellyfish, microscopic crustaceans, and pennatulaceous creatures lit it up slightly with their phosphorescent gleams. I caught glimpses of piles of stones, sometimes covered by millions of zoophytes and thickets of seaweed. My feet often slid on the sticky carpet of kelp, and without my iron-shod stick I would have fallen down more than once. Turning round, I could see the whitish searchlight of the *Nautilus* beginning to grow paler in the distance.

The stone piles I have just mentioned were laid out on the ocean floor with a certain regularity that I could not explain. I noticed gigantic furrows vanishing into the distant darkness and could not begin to guess how long they were. Other peculiarities also appeared which I could not understand. It seemed to me that my lead soles were heavily crushing a bed of bones which cracked with dry sounds. What was this vast plain that I was crossing? I would have liked to ask the captain, but I still could not understand the sign language he used to communicate with his companions while carrying out their submarine excursions.

Meanwhile the reddish glow which had been guiding us grew and soon inflamed the whole horizon. The existence underwater of this light intrigued me tremendously. Was I witnessing some outflow of electricity? Was I heading for some natural phenomenon that was still unknown to scientists on land? Or even—for the thought did cross my mind—did man perhaps have a part in this blaze? Was some hand fanning the fire? Would I meet companions or friends of Captain Nemo in these deep strata, living as strange an existence as him, and to whom he was paying a visit? Would I find a whole colony of exiles weary of the miseries of earth, who had sought independence on the bottom of the ocean— and found it? All these crazy, impossible ideas haunted me. In this frame of mind, over-stimulated by the new marvels from the bottom of the sea constantly passing before my eyes, I would not have been surprised to encounter one of those cities in the sea* that Captain Nemo had dreamed of!

Our path grew brighter and brighter. A whitening glow radiated out from the summit of a mountain of about 800 feet. But it was only a secondary image produced in the prism of those strata of water. The source of this inexplicable light, the focus, was located on the far side of the mountain.

Captain Nemo moved forward without hesitation through the stony mazes furrowing the bed of the Atlantic. He knew this dark route. Doubtless he had often walked it, and could not get lost. I followed him with perfect confidence. He appeared to me like some ocean spirit. While he was walking in front, I admired his tall build silhouetted in black against the luminous backdrop of the horizon.

It was now one o'clock in the morning. We had arrived at the first slopes of the mountain. But to start climbing them, we had to venture on to difficult paths leading through a huge thicket.

Yes, a thicket of dead trees, without leaves and without sap, trees mineralized by the water, dominated here and there by gigantic pines. It was like a seam of coal still standing, holding on to the sunken soil with its roots. Its branches, like fine cutouts of black paper, stood out clearly against the ceiling of the waters. Imagine to yourself a Hartz forest* clinging to the sides of the mountain, but a sunken forest. The paths were blocked with seaweed and wracks, amongst which teemed a whole world of crustaceans. I went on climbing the rocks, stepping over fallen trunks, breaking the sea creepers which swung from one tree to another, frightening away the fishes which flew from branch to branch. Carried away, I no longer felt tired. I followed my guide, who did not slacken his pace.

What a sight! How can I depict it! How can I paint the image of the woods and rocks in the liquid milieu, their dark and savage overhangs, their surfaces coloured by the red tones of this light increased by the refractive capacity of the water? We clambered over boulders which collapsed in great blocks, avalanching with heavy groans. To the right and left gaped dark tunnels whose ends could not be seen. Huge clearings looked as though they had been made by man's hand, and I wondered if some submarine inhabitant was not suddenly going to appear.

But Captain Nemo kept on climbing. I did not want to lose touch and so boldly followed him.* My stick proved very useful. Stumbling would have been dangerous on these narrow paths cut into the sides of chasms; but I walked with a firm tread and without feeling the intoxication of vertigo. Sometimes I jumped over a crevasse of a depth to make me recoil on land glaciers; sometimes I ventured on to wobbling tree-trunks thrown across one abyss after another, not looking under my feet, my eyes simply admiring the savage sights all around. Monumental rocks appeared, leaning on their irregularly cut bases, seeming to defy the laws of equilibrium. Between their stony knees, trees sprouted like jets under formidable pressure, and held up the same rocks that gave them root. Natural towers and broad rock faces, cut sheer like fortified walls, leaned at an angle that the laws of gravity would not have allowed on dry land.

I could certainly feel the difference made by the great density of the water when I scaled the inclines of impracticable slopes, despite my heavy clothing, copper head, and metal soles, when I climbed with the agility of a wild goat or chamois!

As I speak of this underwater expedition, I fully realize how unbelievable it all sounds! I am the recorder of things which may seem impossible but which are real and incontestable. I did not dream them. I felt and I saw them.

Two hours after leaving the *Nautilus* we crossed the tree-line, the mountain peak towered a hundred feet above our heads, its dazzling radiation projecting a shadow on to the slope below. A few petrified shrubs ran here and there in grimacing zigzags. Fish rose as one before our feet like birds surprised in tall grass. The rocky mass was hollowed out with impenetrable burrows, deep caverns, and pits at the bottom of which I could hear frightening things moving about. I blanched when I spotted an enormous antenna blocking my route, or terrifying claws clattering shut in the darkness of a cavity! Thousands of luminous points shone in the darkness. They were the eyes of huge crustaceans lurking in their dens, of gigantic lobsters standing to attention like halberdiers and waving their legs with metallic clanks, of titanic crabs set like cannon on their mounts, and of awe-inspiring squid* twisting their tentacles into a living brush of snakes.

What was this outrageous world I was still such an outsider to? These articulates for whom the rocks seeemed like a second carapace—which order did they belong to? Where had nature developed the secret of their brutish life, and for how many centuries had they been living in these furthermost recesses of the ocean?

But I could not stop. Captain Nemo, familiar with these terrifying animals, was no longer paying attention to them. We had arrived at a first plateau, where further surprises awaited me. Here picturesque ruins stood up, bearing the mark of man's hand and not that of the Creator.* They were vast accumulations, massed piles of stones where one could make out the vague forms of castles and temples, covered with a world of flowering zoophytes and over which, instead of ivy, seaweed and algae formed a thick vegetable cloak.

But what was this land sunk by cataclysms? Who had laid out these rocks and stones like the dolmens of prehistoric times? Where was I—what place had Captain Nemo chosen to bring me to?

I would have liked to ask him. Not able to, I stopped him. I seized hold of his arm. But he shook his head and pointed to the last summit of the mountain, seeming to say to me:

'Come! Further! Come with me!'*

I followed him in a last surge, and a few minutes later had reached the summit, about ten metres higher than the rest of the rocky mass.

I looked in the direction we had just come from. The mountain rose only about seven or eight hundred feet above the plain; but on the other side there was twice this drop to the bottom of the Atlantic. My eyes wandered into the distance, covering a vast space dazzlingly lit by the burning light. The mountain was a volcano. Fifty feet below the peak, in a rain of stones and volcanic slag, a large crater was vomiting torrents of lava, which spread out as a cascade of fire through the water. Like an enor-

mous torch, the volcano lit up the plain below to the farthest
points of the horizon.

I have said that the submarine crater was throwing out lava,
not flames. Flames need oxygen from the air, and cannot be produced underwater; but flows of lava, which already contain their
own incandescence, can be heated to white-hot, acting successfully against the liquid element and vaporizing it on contact.
Quick-flowing currents carried away all the resulting gases in diffusion as the lava torrents slid to the bottom of the mountain, like
the ejecta of Vesuvius in another Torre del Greco.*

Right there in front of my eyes—ruined, broken, collapsed—
appeared a city destroyed, its roofs fallen, its temples flattened, its
arches broken, its columns lying on the ground, but with the solid
proportions of a type of Tuscan architecture still discernible.
Further on lay a few remains of a gigantic aqueduct; here, the
silted bulge of an acropolis, with the floating forms of a
Parthenon; there a few traces of a quayside, as if some antique
port had once sheltered the merchant vessels and war triremes on
the shores of a long-lost ocean; further still, the long lines of
broken-down walls and broad deserted streets: a whole Pompeii
sunk beneath the waters,* that Captain Nemo was bringing back
to life before my very eyes!

Where was I? Where? I wanted to know at any cost, I wanted
to speak, I wanted to tear off the copper sphere imprisoning my
head.

But Captain Nemo came close to me and stopped me with a
sign. Then, picking up a chalky piece of stone, he went up to a
rock of black basalt and wrote a single word:

ATLANTIS

What a flash crossed my mind! Atlantis, that ancient Meropis
of Theopompus, the Atlantis of Plato, the continent denied by
Origen, Porphyry, Iamblichus, d'Anville, Malte-Brun, and
Humboldt, who all classified its disappearance as a legendary tale,
but accepted by Posidonius, Pliny, Ammianus Marcellinus,
Tertullian, Engel, Sherer, Tournefort, Buffon, and d'Avezac:* it
was there before my eyes, still bearing the irrefutable signs of the
catastrophe that struck it! So this was the sunken region that had
existed outside Europe, Asia, and Libya and beyond the Pillars of

Hercules, the land of the powerful Atlanteans* against whom ancient Greece had fought its first wars!

The historian who recorded the main events of those heroic times was Plato himself. His dialogue of *Timaeus* and *Critias* was, so to speak, dictated under the inspiration of Solon, poet and legislator.*

One day, Solon was talking with a few wise old men from Saïs, a town already 800 years old,* as shown by the annals engraved on the sacred walls of its temples. One of these old men recounted the story of another town 1,000 years more ancient. This first Athenian city, 900 centuries old, had been invaded and partly destroyed by the Atlanteans. The Atlanteans, he said, occupied an immense continent greater than Africa and Asia combined and covering an area between the twelfth degree and the fortieth degree north. Their domination stretched as far as Egypt. They wished to extend it even to Greece, but had had to retreat before the indomitable resistance of the Hellenes. The centuries went by. A cataclysm struck in the shape of floods and earthquakes. A night and a day were sufficient to destroy Atlantis, whose highest summits still emerge at Madeira, the Azores, the Canary Islands, and the Cape Verde Islands.

These were the historic memories that Captain Nemo's inscription brought to life in my mind. Led by the strangest of destinies, I was trampling one of the mountains of that continent, my hands were touching ruins hundreds of thousands of years old, contemporary with the early geological periods! I was walking on the same spot where the coevals of the first man had walked! I was crushing under my heavy soles skeletons of animals from those fabulous times, which the now mineralized trees used to cover with their shade!

Oh! why did I not have enough time? I longed to climb down the steep slopes of this mountain, cover every point of this immense continent which had doubtless connected Africa and America, and visit the great cities from before the Flood. There in front of my eyes, perhaps stretched Machimos the warlike and Eusebia the holy,* whose gigantic inhabitants lived entire centuries and were strong enough to pile up these blocks which still resisted the movements of the water. One day perhaps, some eruptive phenomenon would bring these sunken ruins back up to the surface of the ocean! Submarine volcanoes have often been recorded in this portion of the ocean, and ships have frequently felt extraordinary earthquakes while passing over the tormented deeps. Some vessels have registered dull sounds signalling turmoil between the elements in the deep; others have gathered volcanic cinders sent up from the sea. All this ground, as far as the equator, is still worked by plutonic forces. And who knows if in some far-off period, the summits of fire-breathing mountains will not one day be built up by the volcanic ejecta and successive strata of lava, and appear at the surface of the Atlantic!

While I was dreaming in this way, wanting to engrave in my memory all the details of this grandiose landscape, Captain Nemo, leaning on a mossy stele, remained motionless as if turned to stone in a silent ecstasy. Was he dreaming of the lost generations, was he asking them the secret of human destiny? Was it here that this strange being came to commune with history, to relive ancient life—he who wanted nothing to do with modern times? What I would have given then to know his thoughts, to share them, to understand them!

We remained at this place for an entire hour, contemplating the vast plain in the bright light from the lava which sometimes took on a surprising intensity. At times the interior boiling sent quick shivers through the crust of the mountain. Deep sounds, transmitted clearly in the liquid environment, reverberated with majestic amplitude.

The moon suddenly appeared for a moment through the mass of waters, sending a few pale rays down to the sunken continent. It was only a gleam, but produced an indescribable effect. The captain got up, looked on the huge plain one last time, then signalled to me to follow him.

We quickly descended the mountain. Once past the mineral forest, I saw the *Nautilus*'s searchlight shining like a star. The captain marched straight ahead; and we were back on board by the time the first tints of dawn came and whitened the surface of the ocean.

10

Underwater Coalmines

THE following day, 20 February, I woke up very late. The fatigue of the night had extended my sleep until eleven o'clock. I got up quickly. I was keen to know what direction the *Nautilus* was heading in. The instruments showed me that it was still sailing southwards at a speed of 20 knots and a depth of 100 metres.

Conseil came in. I recounted our nocturnal excursion to him; since the panels were open, he could still glimpse a part of the submerged continent.

The *Nautilus* was skimming only ten metres from the floor of the Atlantean plain. It was flying like a balloon carried off by the wind over the terrestrial prairies; but it would be more truthful to say that being in the salon was just like being in the compartment of an express train. The foreground before our eyes was made up of rocks cut into fantastic shapes and forests of trees that had changed from vegetable to animal, their motionless silhouettes grimacing under the waves. We saw masses of stones covered with carpets of axidias and anemones and bristling with long vertical hydrophytes, followed by blocks of curiously twisted lava bearing witness to the fury of the plutonic eruptions.

While these bizarre objects shone in our electric light, I narrated the history of the Atlantean inhabitants to Conseil, which, in a purely imaginary vein, inspired Bailly* to write so many charming pages. I told him about the wars of those heroic peoples. I discussed the question of Atlantis from a believer's point of view. But Conseil seemed distracted, and hardly listened to me; his indifference concerning historical questions was soon explained.

Numbers of fishes were drawing his eyes; when the fish passed, Conseil was carried off into the depths of classification, and left the real world. This being the case, my only choice was to follow him and to pursue again our ichthyological studies.

In fact, the fish of the Atlantic were not much different from those we had observed up till now. There were rays of gigantic dimensions, five metres long and with great muscular power that allows them to fly over the waves, plus sharks of various species. These included: a fifteen-foot glaucous with sharp triangular teeth whose transparency made it nearly invisible in the water, some brown sagrees, and some spine sharks shaped like prisms and reinforced with tubercular skin; as well as some sturgeons similar to their congeners in the Mediterranean and some yellowish-brown one-and-a-half-foot pipefish with small grey fins but without teeth or tongues, swimming past like thin, lithe snakes.

Amongst the osseous fishes, Conseil noted some blackish *Makairae*, three metres long and with a piercing sword in their upper jaws, some brightly coloured stingfish, known in Aristotle's time as sea dragons and very dangerous to touch because of the stings in their dorsals, then some dolphinfish with brown backs striped with blue lines framed in a golden edging, some lovely sea bream, some moonfish, like discs with azure reflections which when illuminated by the sunlight above seemed to form silver patches, and finally some eight-metre xiphoid swordfish moving in packs and equipped with yellowish fins cut into scythes and six-foot-long scimitars: these were intrepid animals, but herbivore rather than piscivore and, like well-trained husbands, obeyed the slightest signal from their females.

But while observing the diverse specimens of the marine fauna, I continued to examine the wide plains of Atlantis. Sometimes capricious changes in the ground forced the *Nautilus* to slow down, and it slid with the skill of a cetacean through the narrow bottlenecks of the hills. If the labyrinth became inextricable, then the machine would rise like a balloon, go over the obstacle, and continue its rapid progress a few metres above the seabed. A memorable and engrossing journey recalling the manœuvres of an aerostatic flight, with the difference that the *Nautilus* entirely obeyed its pilot's hand.

At about four in the afternoon the terrain, generally composed of thick mud mixed with mineralized branches, began to change: it became rockier and seemed strewn with conglomerates and basaltic tuffs, with a few sprinklings of lava and sulphurous obsidian. I thought that a mountain region would soon interrupt the broad plains and, indeed, during some of the *Nautilus*'s manœuvres, I caught a glimpse of the southern horizon blocked by a high wall apparently closing the way out. Its top part was clearly higher than the water level. This had to be a continent or at the very least an island, perhaps one of the islands of the Canaries or Cape Verde. Since the position had not been taken—on purpose perhaps—I did not know where we were.* But in any case such a wall seemed to mark the end of Atlantis, which we had actually only covered a tiny part of.

Night did not interrupt my observations. I remained alone, Conseil having gone back to his cabin. The *Nautilus* slowed down and cruised over the confused shapes on the sea-floor, sometimes pushing down past them as if it wished to land on them, sometimes capriciously surfacing. I caught glimpses then of a few bright constellations through the crystal of the waters, and particularly five or six stars which trail behind Orion's tail.

I would have stayed at my glass for a long time yet, admiring the beauties of the sea and the sky, but the panels suddenly closed. At this moment the *Nautilus* had just arrived at a high vertical wall. How it would manœuvre I could not guess. I went back to my room. The *Nautilus* was no longer moving. I fell asleep with the firm intention of waking up after a few hours' sleep.

But the following day it was eight o'clock before I returned to the living-room. I looked at the pressure-gauge. It told me that the *Nautilus* was afloat on the surface of the ocean. I could also hear footsteps on the platform. But there was no rolling to indicate the waves.

I headed up to the hatch. It was open. But instead of the daylight I expected, I found myself in total darkness. Where were we? Had I made a mistake? Was it still night? No! not a star shone, and the night is never of such absolute blackness.

I did not know what to think, when a voice said:

'Is that you, Dr Aronnax?'

'Ah! Captain Nemo,' I replied; 'where are we?'

'Underground, monsieur.'

'Underground!' I exclaimed. 'And the *Nautilus* is still afloat?'

'It is still afloat.'

'But I don't understand?'

'Wait a moment. Our searchlight is going to be switched on, and if you like clear situations, you'll be pleased.'

I stepped on to the platform and waited. The darkness was so complete that I could not see Captain Nemo at all. However, looking at the zenith exactly over my head, I thought I could detect an indeterminate gleam, like faint daylight through a circular aperture. But the searchlight suddenly came on, and its brilliance washed away the vague light.

For a moment my eyes were blinded by the dazzling electric jet, but then I looked again. The *Nautilus* was stationary. It was floating beside a shore converted to a quayside. The sea bearing it formed a lake imprisoned in a circus of walls measuring two miles in diameter, or about six miles right round. The water level—as indicated by the pressure-gauge—had to be the same as the external level, for there necessarily existed some means of communication between the lake and the ocean. The high walls were inclined at their bases, and converged to form a vault like an immense upside-down funnel five or six hundred metres high. At the summit was the circular orifice where I had detected the pale gleam, evidently coming from the sun.

Before examining the internal shape of the enormous cavern more attentively, and before deciding if it was the work of nature or man, I went straight up to Captain Nemo.

'Where are we?' I said.

'In the very centre of an extinct volcano, a volcano invaded by the sea following some convulsion of the earth. While you were sleeping the *Nautilus* entered this lagoon via a natural channel ten metres below the surface of the ocean. This is its home port, its safe haven: convenient, secret, and sheltered from the wind in every direction! Find me a harbour on the coasts of your landmasses or islands which is worth this refuge, guaranteed to be safe from the fury of hurricanes!'

'You're certainly safe here, Captain Nemo. Who could ever reach you at the centre of a volcano? But didn't I notice an opening at the top?'

'Yes, the crater; formerly filled with lava, steam, and flames, it now gives passage to this invigorating air we are breathing.'

'So what is this volcanic mountain then?'

'It forms one of the many small islands dotting the sea. A mere obstacle for other ships, but for us an enormous cavern. Chance led me to discover it, and so served me well.'*

'But couldn't someone enter the mouth of the crater of the volcano?'

'Not any more than I could climb up there. For about a hundred feet the internal slopes of this mountain are scalable but above that the walls overhang, and are no longer climbable.'

'I can see, captain, that nature serves you everywhere and on all occasions. You are in safety on this lake, and nobody but you can visit its waters. But what is the point of this refuge? The *Nautilus* does not need a port.'

'No, doctor, but it does need electricity to move, batteries to produce its electricity, sodium to feed its batteries, coal to make its sodium, and mines to furnish its coal. And just here, the sea covers entire forests swallowed up in earlier geological times: now mineralized and turned into coal, this seam I own is inexhaustible.'

'So your men work as miners, captain?'

'Precisely. The mine extends under the waves like those of Newcastle. Dressed in their frogmen's suits, pick and pickaxe in hand, my men go down here to extract the coal, with the result that I do not require any from the mines on land. When I burn it to manufacture sodium, the smoke escaping from the crater gives the mountain the appearance of an active volcano.'

'And will we see your companions at work?'

'No, at least not this time, I am in a hurry to continue our tour of the underwater world. I am merely going to draw from the sodium reserves I have already accumulated here. When we have loaded them on board, which will take just a day, we will continue our voyage. So if you wish to explore this cavern and go round the lagoon, please make use of this day, Dr Aronnax.'

I thanked the captain, and went in search of my two companions who had not yet left their cabin. I invited them to follow me without telling them where we were.

They went up on to the platform. Conseil, who was astonished by nothing, considered it natural to wake up under a mountain after going to sleep under the waves. But Ned Land's only idea was to search and see if the cavern had some way out.

After finishing breakfast at about ten o'clock, we climbed down to the shore.

'Here we are on dry land once more,' said Conseil.

'I do not call this "dry land",' replied the Canadian. 'And in any case, we are not on but under it.'

Between the foot of the mountain wall and the water of the lake stretched a sandy shore measuring 500 feet at its widest point. Following this shore, it was perfectly possible to go round the lake. But the base of the high wall itself was made up of fractured ground, on which lay volcanic blocks and enormous pumice stones in picturesque disorder. All these disaggregated masses, which subterranean fires had left with a polished glaze, scintillated as the electric stream from the searchlight flowed over them. The mica dust on the shore, kicked up by our feet, flew into the air in sparkling clouds.

The ground rose noticeably as it left the sandflats, and we soon arrived at long winding slopes, acting for us as mountain paths on which to climb little by little. But we needed to walk carefully over the uncemented conglomerates, as our feet slipped on the vitreous trachytes made of feldspar and quartz crystals.

The volcanic origin of this enormous pit was visible everywhere. I pointed it out to my companions.

'Can you imagine what this funnel must have been like when it was filling with boiling lava, when the level of the incandescent liquid reached the mouth of the mountain, like iron up the walls of a blast furnace?'

'I can imagine it perfectly,' replied Conseil. 'But will monsieur tell me why the great foundryman interrupted his work, and how it comes about that the oven has been replaced by the quiet waters of a lake?'

'Very probably because of the same convulsion that produced the underwater passage that let the *Nautilus* through. The waves of the Atlantic must have rushed inside the mountain. There was presumably a terrifying battle between the two elements, which ended to Neptune's advantage. But many centuries have passed since then, and the submerged volcano has now become a peaceful grotto.'

'Very well,' said Ned Land, 'I accept that explanation. But from our point of view, I'm sorry that the passage Dr Aronnax is talking about wasn't produced above sea level.'

'But, friend Ned,' said Conseil, 'if the passage hadn't been underwater, the *Nautilus* wouldn't have been able to come through!'

'And I would add, Master Land, that the water wouldn't have rushed under the mountain and the volcano would have remained a volcano. So your regrets are perhaps misplaced.'

Our climb continued. The incline grew steeper and steeper and narrower and narrower. Sometimes it was interrupted by crevasses which we had to cross. Overhangs needed to be worked around. We slid on our knees, we crept on our bellies. But with Conseil's skill and the Canadian's strength, we overcame all obstacles.

About a hundred feet up the terrain changed, but did not become any more easy-going. The conglomerates and trachytes gave way to black basalt, stretching out in strata full of blistered bumps; the conglomerates formed regular prisms lined up like a row of columns supporting the springs of an enormous vault, thus constituting an admirable example of natural architecture. Between the basalt sections snaked long torrents of solidified lava encrusted with bituminous spokes; at places wide carpets of sulphur stretched out. A more powerful light came in through the high crater, and washed a vague light over all these volcanic ejecta, entombed for ever in the heart of an extinct mountain.

But our climb was interrupted by insurmountable obstacles at a height of approximately 250 feet. The interior arch moulding changed into an overhang and our climb had to follow a circular route. At this height, the vegetable kingdom began to struggle for dominance with the mineral. A few shrubs and even trees emerged from the cracks in the rockface. I recognized some euphorbia oozing their caustic sap. Heliotropes were not living up to their name since the sunlight never reached them, and sadly displayed their bunches of flowers with half-faded colours and perfumes. Here and there, a few chrysanthemums grew timidly at the feet of aloes with long, sad, ill leaves. But between the lava flows I spotted some small violets, still slightly scented, and I must admit I breathed in their scent with great delight. Perfume is the soul of the flower, but the flowers of the sea, the splendid hydrophytes, have no souls!

We had arrived at the foot of a clump of robust dragon trees, pushing the rocks aside with their muscular roots, when Ned suddenly exclaimed:

'Ah! monsieur, a hive!'

'A hive!' I repeated, making a gesture full of incredulity.

'Yes a hive,' repeated the Canadian, 'with bees buzzing around.'

I went up to it and was forced to admit that it was true. Around a hole in the trunk of a dragon tree were several thousand of those ingenious insects, so common throughout the Canary Islands, where their products are so much sought after.

Quite naturally, the Canadian wished to make a provision of honey, and it would have been bad grace for me to oppose him. A quantity of dried leaves mixed with sulphur were lit using the spark from Ned's tinder-box lighter, and he began to smoke out the bees. The buzzing ceased little by little, before the eviscerated hive gave up several pounds of fragrant honey. Land filled his haversack with it.

'When I mix this honey with the breadfruit dough,' he said, 'I'll be able to cook you a delicious cake.'

'Parbleu!' said Conseil. 'Gingerbread?'

'A good idea,' I said. 'But let's continue our interesting walk.'

At bends in our path, the whole of the lake appeared before us. The searchlight lit up every part of its tranquil surface, not marred by a single ripple. The *Nautilus* remained perfectly still. The crewmen were moving briskly about the platform and the shore—black shadows neatly silhouetted in the luminous atmosphere.

We had reached the highest part of the first level of rocks holding up the vault. I realized that the bees were not the only representatives of the animal kingdom in the volcano. Birds of prey were gliding and turning here and there in the shadows, all descending from their nests perched on points of rock. There were sparrowhawks with white stomachs and screeching kestrels. Crashing down the slopes came fine fat bustards, carried down on their swift long legs. I will let the reader imagine if the Canadian's instinct was whetted by the sight of this savoury game, and whether he regretted not having a gun. He tried replacing shot with stones and, after several unsuccessful attempts, managed to wound one of the magnificent birds. To say that he risked his life twenty times trying to take hold of it is the simple truth, but he managed well enough, for the bustard eventually joined the honeycomb in his bag.

We had to climb down towards the shore again, for the crest was becoming impassable. Above us, the gaping crater appeared like the wide opening of a well. From where we were the sky could be made out quite clearly; I could see dishevelled clouds running from the west wind, leaving their misty rags behind on the summit of the mountain. They must have been at a low altitude, for the volcano did not rise more than eight hundred feet above sea level.

Half an hour after the Canadian's final exploit, we got back to the enclosed shore. Here the flora was represented by broad carpets of samphire, a small umbelliferous plant very good for preserving and making jam from, and which is also called saxifrage, glasswort, and sea fennel. Conseil gathered a few bunches. As for the fauna, this consisted of thousands of crustaceans of all sorts: lobsters, spider-crabs, palaemons, mysis, arachnids, *Galathea*, and a prodigious number of shells, including cowries, murexes, and limpets.

A magnificent cavern opened out at this point. My companions and I took pleasure in stretching ourselves out on its fine sand. Fire had polished its glazed and sparkling walls, all sprinkled with dust from the mica. Ned Land tested the walls, trying to find out how thick they were. I could not stop myself smiling. The conversation then turned to his perpetual plans for escape, and I thought I could give him some hope, without committing myself too much: namely that Captain Nemo had only come down south to renew his supply of sodium. I therefore hoped that he would now head for the coasts of Europe or America, and thus allow the Canadian to try again with greater success this time.

We had been stretched out in this charming cavern for about an hour. The conversation, lively at the beginning, was now languishing. A certain drowsiness took hold of us. As I could see no reason to resist sleep, I let myself fall into a deep slumber. I dreamed—one does not choose one's dreams—that my life was reduced to the vegetable life of a simple mollusc. The cavern seemed to form the double valve of my shell . . .

All of a sudden, I was woken by Conseil's voice.

'Danger! Look out!' shouted the good fellow.

'What's the matter?' I asked, half rising.

'There's water coming in!'

I got up. The sea was rushing into our shelter like a river, and, since we were decidedly not molluscs, we needed to move.

A few moments later, we were in safety above the cavern.

'So what's happening?' asked Conseil. 'Some new phenomenon?'

'No my friends,' I replied, 'it's the tide, only the tide which almost caught us out, just like Sir Walter Scott's hero!* The ocean is rising outside and through a completely natural law of equilibrium, the level of the lake is also rising. We've got out of it with half a bath. Let's go and change in the *Nautilus*.'

Three-quarters of an hour later, we had finished our circular tour and returned on board. The crew were finishing loading the supply of sodium, and the *Nautilus* could have left immediately.

However, Captain Nemo did not issue any instructions. Did he want to wait for night and leave his submarine passage under the cover of secrecy? Possibly.

Whatever the reason, the following day the *Nautilus* had left its home port and was sailing a few metres below the waves of the Atlantic, on the high seas far from any land.

11

The Sargasso Sea

THE direction of the *Nautilus* had not changed, so any hope of returning to European waters had to be put aside for the moment. Captain Nemo maintained a southerly course. Where was he taking us? I dared not think.

That day, the *Nautilus* crossed a remarkable region of the Atlantic Ocean. Everyone is aware of the existence of that great current of warm water known as the Gulf Stream. After leaving the Florida Strait, it heads towards Spitsbergen. But before reaching the Gulf of Mexico at about 44 degrees north, this current divides into two. The larger branch heads for the coasts of Ireland and Norway, whilst the second heads south starting from a point opposite the Azores; then, striking the African coast and describing an extended oval, it heads back towards the West Indies once more.

Now the warm water of this second branch—which is more like a necklace than a branch—surrounds that portion of the ocean which is cold, peaceful, and motionless and is called the Sargasso Sea.* A true lake in the middle of the Atlantic, which the waters of the great current take no less than three years to go round.

The Sargasso Sea, to be precise, covers the whole submerged area of Atlantis. Some authors have even claimed that the numerous grasses with which it is strewn are torn from the plains of the submerged continent. It is more probable, however, that the grasses, seaweeds, and wracks are taken from the shores of Europe and America and carried into this area by the Gulf Stream. This was one of the reasons that led Columbus to suppose that a new world existed. When the ships of the bold searcher arrived in the Sargasso Sea, they had problems sailing through the grasses which stopped their progress, to the great alarm of his crews, and they wasted three long weeks crossing them.

Such was the region that the *Nautilus* was now visiting. It was nothing less than a prairie, a tightly knit carpet of seaweeds, natans fucus, and bladder-wracks, so thick and compact that the prow of a vessel could barely tear through it. Captain Nemo did not wish to engage his screw in this grassy mass, and so kept a few metres below the surface of the waves.

The name Sargasso comes from the Spanish *sargazo** meaning 'sea-wrack'. This sea-wrack, floating varec, or gulfweed, is the main constituent of the immense bed. According to the scientist Maury, author of *The Physical Geography of the Sea*, such hydrophytes gather in this peaceful basin of the Atlantic:

'The explanation that can be given for this', he says, 'seems to result from an experiment everyone is familiar with. If pieces of cork or any other floating object are placed in a basin, and a circular movement is imparted to the water in this vase, the spread-out pieces will be seen to gather together in a group at the centre of the liquid surface, that is, at the least agitated point. In the phenomenon which concerns us, the basin is the Atlantic, the Gulf Stream the circular current, and the Sargasso Sea the central point where all the floating bodies come together.'

I share Maury's opinion, and have been able to study the phenomenon in that special environment which ships rarely enter. Above us floated bodies of every origin, piled up amongst the brownish grasses: tree-trunks torn from the Andes or the Rocky Mountains and carried down by the Amazon or the Mississippi, and numerous wrecks, either the remains of keels or hulls or stove-in sections so weighed down by shells and barnacles that they could no longer float on the surface. There is another idea of Maury's which will be proved one day: that this matter, accumulated for centuries, will mineralize in the action of the water and come to form inexhaustible coalmines. A precious reserve that far-sighted nature is laying down for the time when man has exhausted the mines on dry land.

In the midst of this inextricable fabric of grasses and fucus, I noticed charming star-shaped alcyonarians in pink colours, sea anemones that let their long tresses of tentacles drag in the current, green, red, and blue jellyfish, and especially the great rhizostomes described by Cuvier, with bluish umbrellas edged with violet frills.

The whole of 22 February was spent in the Sargasso Sea, where fish find abundant food among the marine plants and crustaceans. The following day, the ocean's appearance was back to normal.

From that moment on, for the eighteen days between 23 February and 12 March, the *Nautilus* kept to the North Atlantic, carrying us on at a constant speed of 100 leagues per 24 hours. Captain Nemo evidently wished to finish his submarine programme, and there was no doubt in my mind that he was planning to head back to the South Seas of the Pacific after rounding Cape Horn.

Ned had therefore been right to worry. In these wide seas, bereft of islands, we could not try to leave the vessel. Nor was there any way of opposing Captain Nemo's wishes. The only choice was to submit; but what we were unable to obtain using brute strength or ruse, I liked to think we could obtain by means of persuasion. Once the voyage was over, might Captain Nemo not agree to give us back our freedom if we swore never to reveal his existence? An oath of honour which we would have kept. But we needed to discuss this delicate question with the captain as soon as possible. Would I receive a warm reception if I asked for this freedom? Had he not declared, at the beginning and in formal fashion, that the secret surrounding his life demanded that we be kept imprisoned on board the *Nautilus* for ever? Would my silence over the last four months not appear to him to be tacit acceptance of the situation? Wouldn't raising the subject again cause suspicion which could hinder our plans if some favourable circumstance came up later? I weighed up all these questions, turned them over in my mind, and raised them with Conseil, but he remained just as undecided as I. The upshot was that, although not easily discouraged, I could see the chances of ever meeting my fellows again diminishing with each day, especially now that Captain Nemo was heading boldly towards the southern Atlantic!

During the eighteen days I mentioned above, no particular incident marked our voyage. I saw little of the captain. He was working. In the library I often found books he had left open, mainly books on natural history. My work on the submarine depths had been read by him, and the margin was covered with notes, sometimes contradicting my theories and my systems. But the captain satisfied himself with improving my work in this way, and it was rare for him to discuss it directly with me. Sometimes I heard the melancholy sounds of his organ, which he played with much expression, but only at night, in the midst of the most secret darkness, while the *Nautilus* was sleeping in the ocean wilderness.

During this part of the voyage, we sailed for entire days on the surface of the waves. The ocean was virtually empty—just a few sailing ships, loaded for the Indies and heading for the Cape of Good Hope. One day we were pursued by boats from a whaling ship which undoubtedly took us for an enormous whale of great value. But Captain Nemo did not wish to have these good men waste their time and effort, so he ended the chase by diving underwater. This incident seemed to greatly interest Ned Land. I believe I am correct in saying that the Canadian was sorry that our cetacean could not be killed by the fishermen's harpoons.

The fishes observed by Conseil and myself during this period differed little from those we had studied at other latitudes. They were mainly specimens from that terrible genus of cartilaginous fish, divided into three sub-genera and no less than thirty-two species: five-metre gallooned sharks, with squashed heads that are wider than their bodies, curved tail-fins, and backs bearing seven large black lengthwise stripes; and seven-gill sharks, cinder-grey with seven branchial openings and a single dorsal fin at approximately the middle of their body.

Large dogfish also passed, voracious fish if ever there were any. You can't give credit to fishermen's tales, but this is what they say. In one has been found a buffalo head and an entire calf; in another, two tuna fish and a uniformed sailor; in another, a soldier with his sword; and in a fourth, a horse and its rider. All this, to be frank, is not necessarily gospel truth. But as not one of these animals allowed itself to be caught in the *Nautilus*'s nets, I was not able to check exactly how voracious they are.

Elegant and playful schools of dolphins accompanied us for entire days. They went around in groups of five or six, hunting in packs like wolves in the countryside. They are no less voracious than the dogfish, so that I can believe a certain gentleman from Copenhagen who claims to have taken thirteen porpoises and fifteen seals from the stomach of one dolphin. It was, it is true, an orca, belonging to the biggest known species, that sometimes exceed 24 feet. This family of Delphinidae includes ten genera, and those that I saw belonged to the genus of *Delphinorhynchi*, remarkable for their extremely narrow snouts, four times as long as their heads. Their bodies, three metres long and black on top, were coloured pinkish-white underneath with very occasional small dots.

I will also cite curious specimens amongst these seas of fishes from the order of acanthopterygians and family of sciaenoids. A few authors—more poets than naturalists—have claimed that these fish sing harmoniously, and that their assembled voices form a concert that a choir of human voices could never equal. I am sure this is true, but to my regret, these sciaenas did not serenade us as we passed.

And finally, Conseil classified a great number of flying fish. Nothing was more engrossing than to watch the dolphins hunting them with ingenious skill. Whatever the range of their flight, whatever trajectory they described, even jumping right over the *Nautilus*, these unfortunate fish always found the mouth of a dolphin open to receive them. They were either pirapeds or red gurnards, and during the night their luminous mouths traced fiery tracks through the air that plunged into the dark waters like shooting stars.

Until 13 March, we continued on our course without change. That day, the *Nautilus* was employed in an experiment with soundings that interested me tremendously.

We had then covered 13,000 leagues since our starting-point in the open seas of the Pacific. Our position had been taken as 45° 37′ S, 37° 53′ W. These were the same waters where Captain Denham of the *Herald** had dropped 14,000 metres of sound without finding the bottom. There also, Lieut. Parker of the American frigate *Congress** was unable to reach the submarine floor at 15,140 metres.

Captain Nemo resolved to take the *Nautilus* to the greatest possible depth in order to investigate the different soundings. I got ready to note all the results of the experiment. The panels of the salon were opened and operations began for reaching those prodigious deeps.

You can easily see that diving by merely filling the tanks was out of the question. They would not have been able to increase the specific weight of the *Nautilus* sufficiently. But in any case, to have come up again, it would have been necessary to expel this water, and the pumps would not have been powerful enough to overcome the external pressure at those great depths.

Captain Nemo decided to head for the ocean floor by following a sufficiently oblique path, using his lateral planes placed at an angle of forty-five degrees to the *Nautilus*'s waterline. The propeller was also set at maximum speed, and its four blades soon began to thrash the water with indescribable violence.

Under this powerful impulse, the hull of the *Nautilus* trembled like a vibrating cord as it cut steadily into the waters. The captain and I, at our station in the salon, followed the rapidly descending needle of the pressure-gauge. Soon the inhabitable zone where most fish live had been left behind. Whilst there are some fish which can only live on the surface of the seas or rivers, there are a few which can survive at quite great depths. Amongst them, I observed the hexanchus, a sort of dogfish equipped with six respiratory slits, the telescope-fish with enormous eyes, the armoured gurnard with grey thoracic and black pectoral fins, with its plastron protected by light red bony plates, and finally a sort of grenadier, living at 1,200 metres and supporting a pressure of 120 atmospheres.

I asked Captain Nemo if he had observed fish at still greater depths.

'Fish?' he replied. 'Rarely. But do tell me: in the present state of science, what has been deduced, what do people really know?'

'The following, captain. It is known that when going towards the greatest depths of the ocean, vegetable life disappears more quickly than animal life. It is known that at points where animate life-forms are still encountered, there no longer lives a single hydrophyte. It is known that scallops and oysters live 2,000 metres down, and that McClintock, the hero of the polar seas,* drew a living starfish from a depth of 2,500 metres. It is known that the crew of the Royal Navy's *Bull-Dog* fished an asteria at 2,620 fathoms, or more than a league down. So Captain Nemo, how can you tell me that nothing is known?'

'I cannot monsieur,' he replied, 'I would not be so impolite. However, I would like to ask how you explain that these creatures can live at such depths?'

'I can give two explanations. First of all, the vertical currents caused by the differences in salt concentration and density of the water produce a movement which suffices to maintain a rudimentary life of crinoids and asterias.'

'Absolutely,' said the captain.

'And secondly, if oxygen is the basis of life, it is known that the quantity of oxygen dissolved in sea water actually increases with depth, since the pressure of the lowest depths helps to compress it.'

'Ah! that *is* known?' replied Captain Nemo, in a slightly surprised tone. 'Well, monsieur, people are right to assume that, because it is the truth. I would add that the swimming bladders of fish contain more nitrogen than oxygen when they are caught on the surface, but more oxygen than nitrogen when they are drawn from the great depths; which confirms your system. But let us continue our observations.'

My eyes turned to the pressure-gauge. It indicated a depth of 6,000 metres. We had been diving for an hour. The *Nautilus*, guided by its inclined planes, was still descending. The deserted waters were beautifully transparent, of an indescribable clarity. An hour later, we were at 13,000 metres—approximately three and a quarter leagues—and the bottom of the ocean was still nowhere in sight.

However, at 14,000 metres I noticed some dark peaks emerging from the waters, but these summits could belong to mountains as high as Mont Blanc or the Himalayas, higher even, for the depth of the chasms remained impossible to estimate.

The *Nautilus* descended lower still, in spite of the tremendous pressure it was undergoing. I could feel the plates trembling where their bolts were fixed; bars were bending; bulkheads were groaning; the windows in the salon seemed to be bending under the pressure of the water. And this robust machine would undoubtedly have given way if, as its captain had said, it had not been able to resist like a solid block.

Skimming over the slopes of these rocks lost under the waters, I noticed a few shells remaining, together with some serpula and living spirorbises, and a few starfish.

But soon these last representatives of animal life had disappeared and below three leagues* the *Nautilus* left behind the limits of submarine life, just as a balloon rises in the air above zones where breathing is possible. We reached a depth of 16,000 metres—four leagues—and the sides of the *Nautilus* were at this moment supporting a pressure of 1,600 atmospheres, that is 1,600 kilograms for every square centimetre of its surface!

'It's incredible!' I exclaimed. 'To roam these deep regions where man has never ventured! Look captain, look at the magnificent rocks, the uninhabited grottoes, the last areas of the globe where life is no longer possible! Can it be that all we will have to take with us are the memories of these yet-unseen sights?'

'Would it please you', Captain Nemo asked, 'to take back more than memories?'

'What do you mean?'

'I mean that nothing would be easier than to make a photographic record of this submarine region!'

I had not had time to express my surprise at this new suggestion, when, following a sign from Captain Nemo, a camera was brought into the salon. The electrically illuminated liquid element distributed a perfectly even light through the wide-open panels. No shadow, no obscuring shadows from artificial light. The sun could not have been more suited to tasks of this kind. The *Nautilus* was kept motionless by the thrust of its propeller working against the angle of its planes. The camera was aimed at the scene on the ocean floor, and within a few seconds we had obtained a very clear negative.

This is the print here. One can see: primordial rocks which have never known the light of day; the inferior granites which form the powerful bedrock of the globe; deep grottoes hollowed out in the rocky mass; profiles of an incomparable clarity whose extremities are picked out in black, as if by certain Flemish artists; then, beyond, a horizon of mountains, a superb undulating line which forms the background to the scene. I simply cannot describe this collection of shining rocks: polished black, without moss, without marks, in oddly cloven shapes, firmly anchored on the carpet of sand, sparkling in the beams of electric light.

Once Captain Nemo had finished the operation, he said to me:

'Let's go back up again, monsieur. We must not abuse this situation or expose the *Nautilus* to such pressures for too long.'

'Let's go up then,' I replied.

'Please hold on.'

Before I had had time to understand why the captain had given me this advice, I was thrown on to the carpet.

With its propeller engaged on a signal from the captain and its planes now at the vertical, the *Nautilus*, carried off like a balloon into the air, rose at a staggering speed. It raced through the waters. All details were blurred. In four minutes it covered the four leagues to the surface, emerged noisily like a flying fish, and fell back again, sending a wash soaring to a prodigious height.

12

Sperm Whales and Baleen Whales

DURING the night of 13 to 14 March, the *Nautilus* continued its route southwards. I thought that once at Cape Horn it would set sail for the west, in order to head for the seas of the Pacific and thus complete its journey around the world. It did nothing of the sort, and continued to head down towards the southern polar regions. Where did the *Nautilus* mean to go? To the Pole? That was crazy. I began to believe that Ned was right to fear the captain's recklessness.

The Canadian had not spoken to me for a long time about his plans to escape. He had become noticeably less communicative, almost silent. I could see how the long imprisonment was weighing down on him. I could feel how much anger was building up inside him. When he met the captain, his eyes would light up with a dark fire, and I always feared that his violent nature would lead him to take some extreme action.

That day, 14 March, he came with Conseil to find me in my room. I asked them the reason for their visit.

'A simple question to ask you, monsieur,' the Canadian said.

'Speak, Ned.'

'How many men do you believe there are on board the *Nautilus*?'

'I cannot say, my friend.'

'It seems to me', he continued, 'that it would not require a very large crew to run the *Nautilus*.'

'Just so,' I replied; 'at present, about ten men at most would be enough to operate things.'

'Exactly,' said the Canadian, 'why would there be more?'

'Why?' I repeated.

I stared at Land, whose plans were easy to guess.

'Because', I continued, 'if I follow my hunch and if I have properly understood the captain's life, the *Nautilus* is not only a ship, it must also be a place of refuge for those, like its captain, who have broken all ties with the land.'

'Perhaps,' said Conseil. 'But the *Nautilus* can only contain a finite number of men, and could monsieur not estimate what the maximum should be?'

'How could I do that, Conseil?'

'Through calculation. Given that monsieur knows the capacity of the ship, and consequently the quantity of air it contains; knowing also how much each man uses up in breathing; and comparing these figures with the *Nautilus*'s need to surface every 24 hours . . .'

Conseil's sentence did not seem to have an end, but I could see what he was getting at.

'I understand, but though that calculation is easy to make, I can only reach a very approximate figure.'

'It doesn't matter,' said Ned insistently.

'Here are the figures, then,' I replied. 'In an hour each man uses the oxygen in 100 litres of air, or in 24 hours the oxygen in 2,400 litres. We need, therefore, to find out how many times 2,400 litres goes into the air in the *Nautilus*.'

'Precisely,' said Conseil.

'Now', I continued, 'since the capacity of the *Nautilus* is 1,500 tons, and a ton is 1,000 litres, the *Nautilus* contains 1.5 million litres of air, which, divided by 2,400 . . .'

I quickly wrote down some calculations.

'. . . gives 625, which means that the air in the *Nautilus* could easily be sufficient for 625 men for 24 hours.'

'Six hundred and twenty-five!' exclaimed Ned.

'But take it from me that including passengers and sailors, as well as officers, we do not make up a tenth of that figure.'

'Still too many for three men!' murmured Conseil.

'So, my poor Ned, I can only advise patience.'

'More than patience,' replied Conseil; 'resignation.'

Conseil had indeed picked the appropriate term.

'But on the other hand,' he said, 'Captain Nemo cannot head south for ever. He will have to stop at some point, even if it's only at the ice-cap! He will then have to head towards more civilized seas! Then will be the time to execute Ned Land's plans.'

The Canadian shook his head, wiped his forehead with the back of his hand, and went out without replying.

'If I may be allowed to make an observation,' said Conseil,

'poor Ned is thinking about all the things he cannot have. Everything casts him back to his past life. Everything appears jaded to him, because everything is restricted. His former memories oppress him, and he is sore at heart. We need to understand him. What can he do here? Nothing. He is not a scientist like monsieur, and so is not able to take the same interest as us in the incredible things in the sea all about us. He would risk everything to be able to go to a tavern in his home country!'

It seemed clear that the monotony on board was unbearable to the Canadian, used as he was to a free and active life. There were few things he could take any interest in. However, that day something happened to remind him of his glory days as a harpooner.

At about eleven in the morning, being on the surface, the *Nautilus* fell in with a school of whales. An encounter which did not surprise me, for I knew that these animals, under outrageous pressure from hunting, have taken refuge in the higher latitudes.

The role played by the whale in the marine world and its influence on geographical discoveries have been considerable. The whale encouraged the Basques to follow it, then led on the Asturians of north-west Spain, the British, and the Dutch, hardened them to the dangers of the ocean, and took them from one end of the Earth to the other. Whales like to frequent the Arctic and Antarctic Oceans. Ancient legends even claim that these cetaceans led fishermen to a mere seven leagues from the North Pole. If the tale is false now, it will be true one day, for it will probably be while hunting a whale in the Arctic or Antarctic regions that men will reach those virgin points of the globe.

We were sitting on the platform in a calm sea. The equivalent of October in those latitudes gave us fine autumn days. It was the Canadian—never mistaken—who reported a whale on the eastern horizon. Looking carefully, one could see its blackish back rising and falling above the waves, about five miles away from the *Nautilus*.

'Ah!' exclaimed Ned Land, 'if I was on board a whaling ship, here is an encounter that would please me. It's a huge one. Look how high its blow-holes are sending columns of air and vapour! Damn! why do I have to be chained to this piece of steel!'

'What, Ned!' I replied. 'Have you not yet got over your old ideas of harpooning?'

'Can a whaler ever forget his former trade? Can you ever get tired of the feelings of the hunt?'

'Have you never been whaling in these seas, Ned?'

'Never, monsieur. Just the Arctic seas, and the Bering Strait as much as the Davis Strait.'

'Then you still haven't seen an Antarctic whale. It is the right whale that you have hunted until now, which never ventures into the warm waters of the equator.'

'Ah, monsieur, what are you trying to tell me?' replied the Canadian in an incredulous tone.

'I am telling you the facts.'

'You can't be! As I stand here, in '65, that's two and a half years ago, I boarded a whale near Greenland which still had in its side the stamped harpoon of a Bering whaling ship. Now I ask you, how could the animal have come and got itself killed east of America, since that was where it was killed, after it had been wounded west of America, unless it rounded either Cape Horn or the Cape of Good Hope and then crossed the equator?'

'I agree with friend Ned,' said Conseil, 'and await monsieur's reply.'

'Monsieur will reply by saying, my good friend, that each species of whale is particular to certain seas that it never leaves. And if one of these animals went from the Bering Strait to the Davis Strait, it must be because there is a passage from one to the other, round either the American or Asian coast.'

'Do we have to believe you?' asked the Canadian, winking.

'We have to believe monsieur,' said Conseil.

'So', continued the Canadian, 'since I have never been whaling in these waters, I don't know which whales live here?'

'That's what I told you, Ned.'

'All the more reason for getting acquainted with them,' replied Conseil.

'Look, look!' exclaimed the Canadian, emotion in his voice. 'It's getting nearer! It's coming at us! It's provoking me! It knows I can't do anything about it.'

Ned was stamping his foot. His hand was trembling as if holding an imaginary harpoon.

'These cetaceans, are they as big as those of the Arctic seas?'

'More or less Ned.'

'Because I have seen some big ones, monsieur. Whales up to 100 feet long! I've even been told that the *Hullamock* and the *Umgallick* of the Aleutians sometimes exceed 150 feet.'

'That seems exaggerated to me,' I replied. 'Those animals are only rorquals with dorsal fins, and like sperm whales, they are generally smaller than the right whale.'

'Ah!' exclaimed the Canadian, whose eyes did not leave the ocean, 'it's getting nearer, it's coming within reach of the *Nautilus*!'

Then, continuing his conversation:

'You speak of the sperm whale as a small animal! But gigantic sperm whales have been sighted. They are intelligent creatures. Some of them, it is said, cover themselves with seaweed and wracks. They are taken for small islands. People camp on them, they settle down and make fires . . .'

'They build houses,' said Conseil.

'Yes, joker,' replied Ned. 'Then one fine day the animal dives, and takes all its inhabitants to the bottom of the seas.'

'Like in the voyages of Sinbad the Sailor,'* I replied laughing. 'Ah! Master Land, you seem to like extraordinary stories! How wonderful your sperm whales are! I hope you do not really believe in them?'

'Mr Naturalist,' replied the Canadian seriously, 'you have to be able to believe anything where whales are concerned. Look how this one moves! Look how it swerves! It has been claimed that these animals can travel round the world in a fortnight.'

'I don't disagree.'

'But what you certainly don't know, Dr Aronnax, is that at the beginning of the world, whales could move still quicker.'

'Ah, really Ned! And why is that?'

'Because at that time their tails moved sideways like fish, that is they were totally vertical, and struck the water from left to right. But the Creator realized that they could move too quickly and so he twisted their tails, and since then they have beat the waves from top to bottom and cannot move so fast.'

'Well Ned,' I said, adopting one of the Canadian's expressions, 'do we have to believe you?'

'Not too much,' he replied, 'and not more than if I told you there are whales 300 feet long and weighing 50 tons.'*

'That's quite a lot to believe,' I said. 'However, it must be agreed that certain cetaceans grow to a considerable size, since it is said that they can provide up to 120 barrels of oil.'

'That I've seen,' said the Canadian.

'I can easily credit it, Ned, as I can believe that certain whales are the size of a hundred elephants. Think of the effect produced by such a mass travelling at full speed!'

'Is it true', asked Conseil, 'that they can sink ships?'

'Ships, I don't think so,' I replied. 'But it has been recounted that in 1820, in these same South Seas, a whale threw itself at the *Essex* and made it move backwards at a speed of four metres per second. Water came in aft, and the *Essex* sank almost immediately.'*

Ned looked at me sarcastically.

'For my part,' he said, 'I have received a blow from a whale's tail—in my boat, I mean. My companions and I were thrown to a height of six metres. But compared to monsieur's whale, mine was only a baby.'

'Do such animals live a long time?' asked Conseil.

'A thousand years,' replied the Canadian without hesitation.

'And how do you know, Ned?'

'Because people say so.'

'And why do people say so?'

'Because they know.'

'No, Ned, they do not know, they've worked it out. And here is the reasoning on which they base their arguments. Four hundred years ago, when fishermen first hunted whales, the animals were bigger than those caught today. It was therefore quite logically deduced that the smaller size of present-day whales is because they have not had time to reach their full size. This is what led Buffon to conclude that these cetaceans could—indeed had to—live a thousand years. Do you understand?'

Land did not understand. He was no longer listening. The whale was still approaching. He was devouring it with his eyes.

'Ah!' he exclaimed. 'It's not just one whale, it's ten, it's twenty—it's an entire school! And not to be able to do anything! To be here with my hands and feet tied!'

'But friend Ned,' said Conseil, 'why not go and ask Captain Nemo for permission . . .?'

Conseil had not finished his sentence, before Ned Land had galloped down the hatch and was running off in search of the captain. A few moments later, both men appeared on the platform.

Captain Nemo observed the school of cetaceans playing on the water a mile from the *Nautilus*.

'They're Antarctic whales,' he said. 'There are enough here to make the fortune of a whole fleet of whalers.'

'Well, monsieur!' asked the Canadian. 'Would it be all right to hunt them, if only to keep my hand in as harpooner?'

'What would be the point?' replied Captain Nemo. 'Hunting simply to destroy! We have no use for whale oil here on board.'

'Nevertheless, monsieur,' continued the Canadian, 'in the Red Sea you authorized us to chase a dugong!'

'We needed fresh meat for my crew. Here, it would be killing for killing's sake. I realize that it is one of man's privileges, but I cannot condone these murderous pastimes. By destroying the Antarctic whale like the right whale, inoffensive and good creatures as they are, your fellows commit a damnable action, Master Land. They have already emptied the whole of Baffin Bay, and will eventually destroy a class of useful animals. So leave the unfortunate whales in peace. They already have enough problems with their natural enemies, the sperm whales, the swordfish, and the sawfish, without you interfering.'

I leave to your imagination the expression on the Canadian's face during this lesson in morality. To reason with a hunter like this was to waste one's words. Ned looked at Captain Nemo and evidently did not understand what he was trying to say. Nevertheless the captain was right. The barbaric and unthinking relentlessness of the hunters will one day make the last whale disappear from the ocean.

Ned whistled *Yankee Doodle* between his teeth,* thrust his hands into his pockets, and turned his back on us.

Meanwhile Captain Nemo was observing the school of cetaceans, and addressing me:

'I was right to claim that, even without man, whales have enough natural enemies. These ones are going to have a battle to fight before long. Can you see those moving dark points eight miles to leeward, Dr Aronnax?'

'Yes, captain,' I replied.

'They are sperm whales, terrifying animals that I have some-times encountered in schools of two or three hundred! In their case, it is right to exterminate such cruel and evil-doing animals.'

At these words the Canadian quickly turned round.

'Well, captain,' I said, 'there is still time in the interests of the whales themselves . . .'

'No point in taking the risk, monsieur. The *Nautilus* will suffice to head off the sperm whales. It is armed with a steel ram, which is easily worth Master Land's harpoon, I think.'

The Canadian did not bother to conceal his shoulder-shrugging. Attacking cetaceans with blows from a cutwater! Who had ever heard of such a thing?

'You'll see, Dr Aronnax,' said Captain Nemo. 'We will show you some hunting you have not experienced yet. No pity for the ferocious cetaceans. They are only mouths and teeth!'

Mouth and teeth! There was no better way to depict the macro-cephalous being, which sometimes exceeds 25 metres in length. The enormous head of this cetacean occupies about a third of its body. Better armed than the whale, whose upper jaw is only equipped with bony plates, it has 25 huge teeth: 20 centimetres long, cylindrical but with conical ends, and weighing two pounds each. In the great cavities formed by the cartilage on the upper part of this enormous head are found three or four hundred kilo-grams of that precious oil called spermaceti. The sperm whale is a disgraceful animal, more tadpole than fish, as Frédol remarks.* It is poorly constructed, being a failure, so to speak, in the whole left-hand part of its framework, and hardly seeing except through its right eye.

Meanwhile the monstrous school was still approaching. They had spotted the baleen whales, and were getting ready to attack them. One could predict in advance the victory of the sperm whales, not only because they are better built for attack and their adversaries are inoffensive, but also because they can remain underwater longer without having to come and breathe on the surface.

It was time to go to the whales' help. The *Nautilus* dived under the water. Conseil, Ned, and I took our places at the windows in the salon. Captain Nemo went to join the pilot and to use his vessel as a destructive engine. Soon I could feel the throb of the propeller accelerating and our speed increasing.

The battle between the sperm whales and the whales had already begun when the *Nautilus* arrived. It manœuvred in such a way as to split the school of macrocephalous creatures in two. At first they appeared undisturbed at the sight of the new monster joining the battle, but soon they had to pay attention to its attacks.

What a battle! Ned Land himself quickly became enthusiastic, and finished up by clapping. In the captain's hands, the *Nautilus* had become a formidable harpoon. It threw itself at the fleshy masses, cutting right through them, and leaving behind two flailing halves of animal. The *Nautilus* was insensible to the frightening blows from the tails striking its sides. Nor did our vessel heed the impacts from its own efforts. Once one sperm whale had been killed, it chased after the next one, or turned on the spot so as not to miss its new prey: manœuvring backwards and forwards, obeying the helm, diving when a cetacean plunged into the depths, coming back up when it returned to the surface, striking it head-on or obliquely, cutting or tearing it, striking from all directions and at all speeds, to pierce it with the terrifying cutwater.

What a blood-letting! What a commotion on the surface of the waves! What high-pitched whistlings and distinctive bellowings came from the frightened animals. Their tails made great surges throughout these ordinarily peaceful waters.

This Homeric massacre, from which the sperm whales could not escape, continued for an hour. Several times, ten or twelve together tried to crush the *Nautilus* between their bodies. Through the windows we could see their enormous jaws paved with teeth and their formidable eyes. Land, no longer master of himself, threatened them and swore at them. We could feel them taking hold of our vessel like dogs worrying a young boar in undergrowth. But the *Nautilus*, increasing the power of its propeller, would carry them off, drag them down, or take them up to the surface, unhindered by their enormous weight or powerful embrace.

Finally the number of sperm whales began to reduce. The waves became calm once more. I could feel that we were moving up towards the surface. The hatch was opened, and we rushed on to the platform.

The sea was covered with mutilated bodies. A huge explosion could not have divided these fleshy masses or torn them to pieces with more violence. We were floating amongst gigantic bodies: bluish-backed, white-bellied, and completely covered with enormous protuberances. A few frightened sperm whales were still fleeing on the horizon. The waves were tinted red for a distance of several miles; the *Nautilus* was floating on a sea of blood.

Captain Nemo joined us.

'Well, Master Land?' he enquired.

'Well monsieur,' replied the Canadian, whose enthusiasm had diminished; 'it was a terrible sight indeed. But I am not a butcher, I am a hunter, and this was just butchers' work.'

'It was a massacre of evil animals,' said the captain, 'and the *Nautilus* is not a butcher's knife.'

'I prefer my harpoon.'

'To each his weapon,' replied the captain, staring at Ned.

I was afraid that Ned would allow himself to get carried away into some violent act, which would have had deplorable consequences. But his anger was distracted by the view of a whale that the *Nautilus* was drawing alongside at that moment.

The animal had not been able to escape the sperm whales' teeth. I recognized the Antarctic whale, with a depressed, entirely black head. Anatomically, it is distinguished from the right whale and the North-Caper by its seven cervical vertebrae being joined, and it also has two ribs more than its relatives. The unfortunate cetacean, lying on its side, its stomach perforated with bites, was dead. At the end of its mutilated fin still hung a small baby whale it had not been able to save from the massacre. Its open mouth allowed the water in and out, which murmured like a backwash through its bony plates.

Captain Nemo had brought the *Nautilus* near the animal's body. Two of his men climbed on to the flank of the whale, and I saw with astonishment that they were drawing from its breasts all the milk contained in them, that is two or three barrelfuls.

The captain offered me a cup of the still-warm milk. I could not prevent myself showing repugnance at this brew. He assured me that the milk was excellent, and no different from cows' milk.

I tasted it, and agreed with him. It was in fact a useful reserve for us, since this milk, in the form of salted butter or cheese, would bring pleasant variety to our ordinary fare.

From that day on, I noticed with anxiety that Ned Land's attitude towards Captain Nemo deteriorated steadily, and I resolved to keep as close an eye as possible on the behaviour of the Canadian.

13

The Ice-Cap

THE *Nautilus* had continued its imperturbable route southwards. It was following the 50th meridian at considerable speed. Did the *Nautilus* want to reach the Pole? I hardly thought so, because all attempts so far to get to that point of the globe had failed. In any case it was already late in the season, since 13 March in the Antarctic corresponds to 13 September in the Arctic, and ushers in the period of the equinox.

On 14 March I noticed pieces of ice floating at 55°S, mere pallid debris twenty to twenty-five feet long and forming reefs over which the sea broke. The *Nautilus* stayed on the surface. Ned Land, having already been whaling in the Arctic seas, was familiar with the spectacle of icebergs. Conseil and I admired them for the first time.

Hanging in the air above the southern horizon stretched a dazzling white strip. The British whalers have named it 'ice-blink'. However thick the clouds are, it can always be seen. It indicates the presence of pack-ice or an ice-shelf.

Larger blocks whose light changed depending on the caprices of the haze did in fact soon appear. Some of the masses were streaked with green veins, as if copper sulphate produced undulating lines in them. Touched as they were with bright limestone reflections, they would have been sufficient to construct a whole town of marble. Others were like enormous amethysts, allowing the light to penetrate and reflecting the sun's rays from the thousand facets of their crystals.

The further south we went, the more floating islands there were, and the larger they got. Polar birds nested on them in their thousands. There were petrels, black and white gulls, and puffins, all deafening us with their cries. Some of them took the *Nautilus* for the body of a whale, came and rested on it, and pecked at its metal with resounding taps.

During this navigation through the ice, Captain Nemo often stayed on the platform. He carefully scanned those lonely seas. I could see his calm regard sometimes becoming more intense. Was he saying to himself that in these polar seas, forbidden to man, he was at home, master of the uncrossable spaces? Perhaps. But he did not speak. He remained motionless, only interrupting his daydreaming when his instinct for action took control again. Then, steering his *Nautilus* with consummate skill, he would carefully avoid collision with the hulking masses, which occasionally measured several miles long by a height of between seventy and eighty metres. Often the horizon would seem to be entirely closed. At the 60th degree of latitude, indeed, all passes had disappeared. But Captain Nemo studied the situation, and soon found some narrow opening through which he audaciously slipped, knowing full well, however, that it would close up again behind him.

In this way the *Nautilus*, guided by his skilful hand, passed all the ice, which is classified by its form or size with a precision which enchanted Conseil: icebergs, literally meaning mountains; icefields, meaning unified, limitless areas; drift-ice, also called floating ice; and pack-ice, meaning broken pieces and called *patches* when the pieces are round and *streams* when they are longer.*

It was quite cold. The thermometer exposed to the external air measured two or three degrees below zero. But we were warmly dressed in furs from seals or sea bears. The interior of the *Nautilus*, constantly heated by its electrical devices, defied the most intense cold. In any case, it would have only had to dive a few metres below the waters to find a more bearable temperature.

Two months earlier we would have enjoyed permanent daylight

at this latitude, but night was already falling for three or four hours, and later it would throw six months of shadow over these circumpolar regions.

On 15 March* we passed the latitude of the South Shetlands and South Orkney. The captain told me that formerly numerous herds of seals had lived on these islands, but British and American whalers had massacred adults and pregnant females in a destructive rage, leaving the silence of death behind them in place of animated life.

On 16 March, at about eight in the morning, the *Nautilus*, which was following the 55th meridian, cut the Antarctic Circle. Ice surrounded us in every direction, closing the horizon. Nevertheless, Captain Nemo moved from pass to pass, always heading south.

'But where is he going?' I asked.

'Straight ahead,' replied Conseil. 'But he will stop when he is forced to.'

'I wouldn't swear to it!' I replied.

And to be frank, I have to admit that this adventurous expedition rather pleased me. I cannot express how the beauty of these new regions entranced me. The ice adopted fantastic attitudes. Here it seemed to form an oriental town with its countless minarets and mosques, there a city that had collapsed, thrown down by an earthquake. Views were constantly varied by the oblique sunlight, or became lost in the grey mists of snow dawns. From every direction, explosions, landslides, and great inversions of icebergs changed the view like the countryside in a diorama.

If the *Nautilus* was submerged when these equilibriums broke, the sound was transmitted underwater with frightening intensity, and the falling masses would create horrendous turbulence deep in the ocean. The *Nautilus* would then pitch and roll like a ship abandoned to the fury of the elements.

Often I could see no way out, and thought that we were definitely taken prisoner; but with his instinct guiding him, using the slightest sign, Captain Nemo would discover new passes. By observing the thin threads of bluish water streaking the icefields, he never faltered. I was convinced that he had already ventured into the Antarctic Ocean with the *Nautilus*.

However, on 16 March the ice completely blocked our route. It was not yet a single ice-cap, but many vast icefields stuck together by the cold. Such an obstacle could not stop Captain Nemo, and he threw himself at them with awesome violence. The *Nautilus* penetrated the crumbling mass like a wedge, breaking it up with terrifying cracking noises. It was the antique ram, but propelled by infinite power. Pieces of ice were thrown high into the air and fell back like hail around us. Our vessel was digging itself a canal by using its own momentum. Sometimes, carried on by inertia, it mounted the icefield and crushed it under its weight; sometimes, when swallowed up underneath, it would split the icefield in two merely by rolling and producing a large crack.

During these few days, violent squalls sometimes hailed down on us. When there were thick fogs we could not see each other from one end of the platform to the other, and the wind brusquely jumped around all the points of the compass. The snow would build up in layers so hard that they had to be broken up using a pick. At a temperature of just $-5°$ all the external parts of the *Nautilus* became covered in ice. Rigging could not possibly have functioned, for the falls would have been blocked in the grooves of the pullies. A vessel without sails, driven by an electric motor and without the need for coal, was the only one able to face such high latitudes.

In these conditions the barometer generally stayed very low. It even fell to $73\frac{1}{2}$ cm. Compass readings no longer meant very much. The maddened needles marked contradictory directions as they approached the Southern Magnetic Pole, not to be confused with the geographic pole. According to Hansteen,* the Magnetic Pole is actually situated at about 70°S, 130°E, and, according to Duperrey's observations, at 135°E and 70°30'S. Hence it was necessary to make repeated observations using the compasses at different places on the ship and then take their average. But often we relied on dead reckoning to calculate the route covered, a relatively unsatisfactory method in the sinuous passes with their constantly changing landmarks.

Finally, on 18 March, after twenty unsuccessful assaults, the *Nautilus* found itself finally blocked. It was no longer a question of streams, patches, or icefields, but an interminable and motionless barrier formed of mountains meshed together.

'The ice-cap!' the Canadian said.

I understood that for Ned, like all the navigators who had preceded us, this was an insuperable obstacle. Since the sun appeared for a moment at about midday, Captain Nemo was able to obtain a relatively precise observation which gave our position as 51° 30'W and 67° 39'S. We had already reached an advanced point in the Antarctic.

Before our eyes there was no longer any sign of sea or of any liquid surface. A vast tormented plain stretched beyond the cutwater of the *Nautilus*, tangled, confused blocks, with all the capricious chaos that characterizes the surface of a river some time before the ice starts to break up, but hugely magnified. Sharp peaks rose here and there like slender needles to a height of two hundred feet; also, a succession of cliffs, cut sheer and coloured with greyish tints, formed vast mirrors reflecting the few rays of sunlight, half drowned in the mist. Over this desolate nature loomed a savage silence, hardly broken by the beating of the wings of the petrels and the puffins. Everything was frozen, even sound.

The *Nautilus* was accordingly forced to halt its adventurous route through the fields of ice.

'Monsieur,' Land said to me that day, 'if your captain goes further . . .'

'Well?'

'Then he will be a master amongst men.'

'Why, Ned?'

'Because nobody can cross the ice-cap. Your captain is powerful, but hell! he is not as powerful as Nature, and you always have to stop when she has laid down her limits.'

'Right, Ned; and yet I would like to know what lies behind that icefield! Nothing annoys me more than a wall!'

'Monsieur is right,' said Conseil. 'Walls were invented to annoy scientists. There shouldn't be any walls.'

'Hey!' said the Canadian. 'Everybody knows what is behind the icefield.'

'And that is?' I asked.

'Ice, and yet more ice!'

'You seem certain of the fact, Ned,' I replied, 'but I personally am not so sure. That is why I would like to go and see for myself.'

'Well, please give up the idea. You have reached the ice-cap:

that is already enough, and neither you, your Captain Nemo, nor his *Nautilus* will go any further. Whether he wants to or not, we will eventually have to head back north, towards the realm of honest folk.'

I must admit that Ned Land was right, and until ships are made to navigate over icefields, they will have to stop in front of them.

The *Nautilus* was effectively immobilized, despite all its efforts, and despite the powerful methods used to break up the ice. Normally, anyone who can go no further is quite satisfied to turn round and go back; but here going back was as impossible as going forward, for the passes had closed up again behind us, and indeed if our vessel remained stationary it would not take long for us to become totally blocked. This is in fact what happened at about two in the afternoon, with the young ice forming on the sides with astonishing speed. I must say that Captain Nemo's behaviour appeared highly imprudent.

I was on the platform. The captain, who had been observing the situation for a while, said:

'Well, monsieur, what do you think?'

'I think that we are caught, captain.'

'Caught! And what do you mean by that?'

'I mean that we can go neither forwards nor backwards, nor in any other direction. This is, I believe, what people mean by "caught", at least in inhabited lands.'

'So, Dr Aronnax, you think the *Nautilus* will not be able to free itself?'

'With difficulty, captain, for the season is already too advanced for you to be able to count on the ice breaking up.'

'Ah, monsieur,' replied Captain Nemo in a sarcastic tone, 'you'll always be the same! You only see snags and obstacles! I can personally tell you that not only will the *Nautilus* free itself, but it will go still further!'

'Still further south?' I asked, looking at the captain.

'Yes, monsieur, to the Pole.'

'To the Pole!' I exclaimed, unable to restrain my incredulity.

'Yes!' the captain replied coldly. 'To the South Pole, to that unknown point where the meridians of the globe meet. You know that I can do what I want with the *Nautilus*.'*

Yes, I knew he could. I also knew that this man was courageous to the point of madness! Only the deluded mind of a madman could contemplate overcoming the obstacles around the South Pole, even less accessible than the North Pole, itself still not reached by the bravest navigators!

It suddenly occurred to me to ask Captain Nemo if he had already been to the Pole, untrodden by the foot of man.

'No, monsieur,' he replied; 'we will discover it together. Where others have failed, I will not. Never have I taken my *Nautilus* so far into the southern seas; but I repeat to you, it will go still further.'

'I want to believe you, captain,' I said in a sarcastic tone. 'I do believe you! Let's go forward! There are no obstacles for us! Let us break the ice-cap! Let's blow it up, and if it resists, give the *Nautilus* wings so that it can pass over!'

'Over?' replied Captain Nemo calmly. 'Not over, but under.'

'Under!' I exclaimed.

A sudden revelation had just filled my mind. I had finally understood the captain's project. The marvellous qualities of the *Nautilus* were going to serve it once again in this superhuman endeavour!

'I can see that we are beginning to understand each other,' the captain said to me, half smiling. 'You can already glimpse the feasibility—I would say the chance of a successful conclusion—of such an attempt. What is impossible for an ordinary ship is child's play for the *Nautilus*.* If there is a continent at the Pole, the *Nautilus* will stop at that continent. But if the Pole is open sea, the *Nautilus* will go to the Pole itself!'

'Exactly,' I said, carried away by the captain's reasoning; 'if the surface of the sea is frozen, its lower layers will be free, by that providential law which places the maximum density of sea water at a temperature above freezing. And if I am not mistaken, isn't the ratio of the underwater part of the icefield to the part above the water four to one?'*

'Approximately, monsieur. For each foot that icebergs stand out above sea level, they have three below. Now since these mountains of ice do not exceed a height of a hundred metres, they go no more than 300 into the water. Now what is 300 metres for the *Nautilus*?'

'Nothing monsieur.'

'It can even seek the uniform temperature of the marine waters at a greater depth, and there we can defy with impunity the thirty or forty degrees of cold on the surface.'

'Absolutely, monsieur, perfectly!' I exclaimed, getting excited.

'The only difficulty', continued Captain Nemo, 'will be to remain several days underwater without replenishing our reserves of air.'

'Is that all?' I replied. 'The *Nautilus* has vast tanks, we shall fill them up and they will provide us with all the oxygen we need.'

'Well thought out, Dr Aronnax,' the captain replied smiling. 'But not wishing to be accused of temerity, I am submitting all my objections to you in advance.'

'You still have some?'

'Only one more. If there is a sea at the South Pole, it is possible that this sea is entirely frozen, and consequently that we will not be able to surface.'

'All right monsieur, but have you forgotten that the *Nautilus* is armed with a redoubtable cutwater, which could break up these icefields if we launched it diagonally against them?'

'Well monsieur, we are having ideas today!'

'In any case, captain,' I added, getting more and more enthusiastic, 'what will stop us finding an open sea at the South Pole just like the North Pole? The actual poles and the Magnetic Poles of the Earth are not found at the same spot in either hemisphere, and until proved to the contrary, it has to be assumed that there is either a continent or an ocean free of ice at these two points of the globe.'

'I agree, Dr Aronnax,' replied Captain Nemo. 'I will only observe that after producing so many objections to my plan, you are now overwhelming me with arguments in its favour.'

Captain Nemo was right. I had got to the point of overtaking him in audacity. It was I who was carrying him off to the Pole! I was moving ahead of him. I was leaving him behind . . . But no, poor fool! Captain Nemo knew much better than you the pros and cons of the question, and was enjoying seeing you being carried away in fantastic reveries!

He did not waste a moment. On a signal, the first officer

appeared. The two men quickly spoke in their incomprehensible language, and either the deputy had been told about it before, or he saw no problem in carrying out the plan, for he showed no surprise at all.

However impassible, he did not exhibit the impassiveness that Conseil did when I announced to the worthy fellow that we were heading for the South Pole. An 'As monsieur pleases' was all that greeted my news, and I had to be content with that. As for Ned, if ever shoulders were shrugged, the Canadian's were.

'Can't you see?' he said. 'I pity you, and your Captain Nemo!'

'But we are going to the Pole, Master Ned.'

'Possibly, but we shan't be coming back!'

And Ned Land returned to his cabin, 'so as not to do something stupid,' he said as he left.

Meanwhile the preparations for the audacious attempt had begun. The *Nautilus*'s powerful pumps were forcing air into the tanks, storing it at high pressure. At about four o'clock Captain Nemo announced that the platform hatches were going to close. I cast a final look at the thick ice-cap we were going to go under. The weather was clear, the atmosphere perfectly pure, the cold very keen at −12°C. But the wind had dropped, and the temperature did not seem too intolerable.

About ten men armed with pickaxes climbed on to the sides of the *Nautilus*, broke the ice around the hull, and soon freed it. The operation did not take long, for the young ice was still thin. We all went inside. The tanks were filled up as usual using water kept free at the flotation line. Soon the *Nautilus* dived.

I sat in the salon with Conseil. Through the open window we watched the depths of the Southern Ocean. The thermometer was rising. The needle of the pressure-gauge oscillated on the dial.

At about 300 metres, and as Captain Nemo had predicted, we were moving under the undulating surface of the ice-cap, as the *Nautilus* dived still lower. It reached a depth of 800 metres. The temperature of the water, −12° on the surface, was now only −11. Two degrees already gained.* It goes without saying that the temperature of the *Nautilus*, raised by its heating devices, stayed at a much higher level. All these operations were carried out with extraordinary precision.

'We'll get through, if monsieur has no objection,' said Conseil.
'I'm counting on it!' I replied in a tone of deepest conviction.

In this unobstructed sea, the *Nautilus* had taken a route going
directly towards the Pole, and not deviating from the 52nd meridian. From 67° 30′ to 90°, 22½ degrees remained to be covered,
that is a little more than 500 leagues. The *Nautilus* maintained a
moderate speed of 26 knots, the velocity of an express train. If it
continued in the same way, 40 hours would be enough to reach
the Pole.

For part of the night, the novelty of the situation kept Conseil
and me at the window of the salon. The sea was illuminated by
the electric radiation of the searchlight, but seemed deserted. Fish
did not live in the imprisoned waters. They only made their way
through from the Antarctic Ocean to the open sea at the Pole. Our
progress was rapid. We could feel this from the tremblings of the
long steel hull.

At about two o'clock, I went to take a few hours' rest. Conseil
did the same. Going through the gangways, I did not meet Captain
Nemo. I supposed that he had stayed in the pilot's dome.

The following day, 19 March, I took up my position again in
the salon at five in the morning. The electric log told me that the
Nautilus had slowed down. It was moving towards the surface,
but carefully, slowly emptying its tanks.

My heart was beating. Were we going to come out and find the
free polar air once more?

No. A shock told me that the *Nautilus* had collided with
the lower surface of the ice-cap, still very thick to judge from
the dullness of the impact. We had 'touched', to employ the
marine expression, but in the other direction and at a depth of a
thousand feet: there were two thousand feet of ice above us, of
which a thousand emerged. The ice-cap thus reached a greater
height than we had noted at its edges. Not a very reassuring
fact.

During the day the *Nautilus* tried the experiment again several
times, and each time it came up against the ice forming a ceiling
above. At times the *Nautilus* encountered ice at 900 metres, which
implied 1,200 metres' thickness of which 200 rose above the
surface of the ocean. This was twice its height at the spot where
the *Nautilus* had dived under the waves.

I carefully noted these various depths, and thus obtained a submarine profile of the range jutting down into the waters.

By evening there was no change in our situation. The ice was between 400 and 500 metres deep. Definitely a reduction, but what a thickness still lay between us and the surface!

It was eight o'clock. According to the daily custom, the air should already have been renewed inside the *Nautilus* four hours previously. However, I did not suffer too much, although Captain Nemo had not yet called for extra oxygen from the tanks.

My sleep was troubled that night. Hope and fear besieged me in turn. I got up several times. The *Nautilus*'s gropings continued. At about three o'clock, I noted that we had touched the lower surface of the ice-cap at only 50 metres' depth. A hundred and fifty feet separated us from the surface of the water. The ice-cap was gradually becoming an isolated icefield. The mountain was changing into a plain.

My eyes no longer left the pressure-gauge. We were moving continuously upwards, at an angle, with the resplendent ice sparkling in the electric rays all the while. The ice-cap was getting thinner, both above and below. It was reducing mile after mile.

Finally at six in the morning on that memorable day of 19 March, the door of the salon opened. Captain Nemo appeared.

'The open sea!' he said.

14

The South Pole

I RUSHED on to the platform. Yes, the open sea! Just a few scattered ice-floes and floating icebergs. In the distance, a large sea; in the air, a world of birds; and myriads of fish in the water, which varied from deep blue to olive green depending on the depth. The thermometer marked +3°. In relative terms, this was like a spring enclosed behind the icefield, whose distant masses stood out on the northern horizon.

'Are we at the Pole?' I asked the captain, my heart beating wildly.

'I cannot tell. We will take our position at noon.'

'But will the sun appear through the mists?' I asked, staring at the beige sky.

'However little it appears, it will be enough for me.'

Ten miles to the south of the *Nautilus*, a solitary island rose to a height of 200 metres. We sailed towards it, but carefully, for the sea could be strewn with reefs.

An hour later we reached the island. Two hours after that we had finished going round it. It measured four or five miles in circumference. A narrow channel separated it from a considerable expanse of land, a continent perhaps, whose limits we were not able to gauge. The existence of land seemed to confirm Maury's hypothesis. The ingenious American noticed that between the South Pole and the 60th parallel, the sea is covered with floating ice blocks of enormous dimensions, rarely encountered in the North Atlantic. From this fact he drew the conclusion that the Antarctic Circle contains considerable land, since icebergs cannot form in the open sea but only on coasts. According to his calculations, the blocks of ice surrounding the South Pole form a huge ice-cap, whose width must reach 4,000 kilometres.

Fearing a collision, the *Nautilus* had stopped three cables away from the shore, which was dominated by a superb pile of rocks. The boat was launched. The captain, two of his men carrying instruments, and Conseil and I embarked. It was ten in the morning. I had not seen Land. Without doubt the Canadian was not ready to concede defeat in the face of the South Pole.

A few oar-strokes took the boat to the sand, where it ran aground. Just as Conseil was about to jump ashore, I held him back.

'Monsieur,' I said to Captain Nemo, 'the honour of being the first to set foot on this land belongs to you.'

'Indeed, monsieur,' replied the captain, 'it will bring me great joy to be the first man to leave footprints on this Polar ground.'

Having said that, he jumped lightly on to the sand. A strong emotion caused his heart to beat faster. He climbed a rock forming an overhang at the end of a little promontory, and there, with arms crossed, eyes gleaming, motionless and silent, he seemed to take possession of the southern regions.* After five minutes spent in this ecstasy, he turned towards us again.

'When you wish, monsieur,' he shouted to me.

I disembarked, followed by Conseil, and leaving the two crewmen in the boat.

The ground appeared to be a coloured tuff that spread into the distance, as if made of ground brick. It was covered in scoriae, lava-flows, and pumice stones. One could not mistake its volcanic origin. At places, a few slight exhalations produced a sulphurous smell, witness to still-active interior fires. Nevertheless, having climbed a high escarpment, I could not see any volcanoes within a radius of several miles. However, it is well known that James Ross* found the craters of Erebus and Terror in full activity in these Antarctic lands at the 167th meridian and 77° 32′ S.

The vegetation of this desolate continent seemed to be extremely limited. A few lichens of the species *Usmea melanox-antha* covered the black quartzose rocks. The meagre flora of the region was entirely composed of microscopic plantlets called rudimentary diatoms, forms of cells fitted between two quartzose shells, together with long purple and crimson wracks attached to little swimming bladders which the swell threw on to the coast.

The shore was dotted with molluscs: little mussels, limpets, smooth cockles shaped like hearts, and especially clios with oval-shaped membranous bodies and heads made up of two rounded lobes. I could also see myriads of three-centimetre southern clios of which a whale swallows a whole world with each mouthful. These charming pteropods, true sea butterflies, gave life to the open water near the shore.

Amongst other zoophytes appearing on the shallow bottoms were a few coral arborescences, which James Ross reports as living in the Antarctic seas at as deep as 1,000 metres, small dead man's fingers belonging to the species *Procellaria pelagica*, a large number of asterias peculiar to these climes, and some starfish studding the ground.

But where life was over-abundant was in the air. Thousands of birds of varied species flew and fluttered, deafening us with their cries. Others covered the rocks, watching us pass without fear and crowding familiarly under our feet. The latter were penguins: although clumsy and heavy on land, they are quite agile and supple in the water, where they have sometimes been confused with the fleet bonito. These ones produced raucous cries, and formed numerous assemblies; sober in gesture, but with much clamour.

Amongst the birds, I noticed sheathbills belonging to the family of waders, as big as pigeons: white in colour, with short conical beaks, and eyes surrounded with red circles. Conseil stocked up with them, for these birds make a pleasant dish when properly prepared. Murky albatrosses, with a wingspan of four metres, passed through the air; gigantic ospreys with curved wings, including some lammergeiers,* which are great devourers of seals, and are appropriately called the vultures of the sea; chequered gulls, like little ducks with the tops of their bodies coloured black and white; and finally a whole series of petrels, some of them verging on white with wings edged in brown, others blue and peculiar to the Antarctic seas. These petrels are 'so oily', as I said to Conseil, 'that the inhabitants of the Faeroe Islands merely add a wick before lighting them'.

'If they are so oily,' replied Conseil, 'they would indeed make perfect lamps! The only thing one could ask is that nature herself provide them with the wick!'

After about half a mile, the ground became completely covered with penguin 'nests', which are burrows for laying eggs in, and from which numerous birds were emerging. Later on, Captain Nemo had a few hundred hunted down, for their black flesh is highly edible. They produce a braying like a donkey's. These creatures are the size of a goose, their bodies slate-coloured turning white below and with ruffs of lemon piping, and they allowed themselves to be killed with stones without trying to escape.

Meanwhile the mist was not lifting, and at eleven o'clock the sun had still not appeared. Its absence continued to worry me. Without it, no observation was possible. How then could we determine whether or not we had reached the Pole?

When I joined Captain Nemo again, I found him silently leaning against a slab of rock and looking at the sky. He appeared impatient and annoyed. But what could he do? This audacious and energetic man did not command the sun as he did the sea.

Midday arrived without the sun showing itself for a single moment. It was not even possible to deduce where it was behind the curtain of cloud. And soon the cloud began to snow.

'Tomorrow,' the captain said simply, and we went back to the *Nautilus* through the windy swirls.

During our absence the nets had been spread, and I studied with interest the fish that had been hauled on board. The Antarctic seas serve as a refuge for a very great number of migrators, which flee the storms of the less elevated zones only to fall into the mouths of porpoises and seals. I noticed a few ten-centimetre southern bullheads, dull white cartilaginous animals, covered with pale strips and armed with spicules; and then some three-foot Antarctic chimaeras with very long silvery-white bodies and smooth skins, round heads, backs set with three fins, and snouts ending in trunks which curve back again towards their mouths. I tasted their flesh, but found it insipid, although Conseil appreciated it greatly.

The blizzard continued the following day. It was impossible to remain on the platform. From the salon, where I recorded the incidents of our excursion on to the polar continent, I heard the cries of the petrels and albatrosses sounding through the storm. The *Nautilus* did not remain where it was but headed about ten miles further south down the coast, through the half-light produced by the sun skimming above the edge of the horizon.

The following day, 20 March,* the snow had stopped. The cold was a little worse, with the thermometer marking 2°. The fog rose, and I hoped that we could make our observation today.

Since Captain Nemo had not yet appeared, the boat took Conseil and me to land. The ground was still volcanic in nature. Everywhere were traces of lava, scoriae, and basalt, although I was not able to locate the crater that had vomited them out. Here as before, myriads of birds animated the polar continent. But they shared this empire with vast herds of marine mammals, looking at us with their soft eyes. There were seals of various species, some stretched out on the shore, some lying on ice-floes, others climbing out of the sea or returning to it. They did not flee at our approach, never having had dealings with man, and I calculated that there were enough there to provision several hundred ships.

'Heavens,' said Conseil, 'what a good job Ned didn't come with us!'

'Why, Conseil?'

'Because the mad hunter would have killed everything.'

'That is going a little far, but I do believe we wouldn't have been able to stop our friend from harpooning a few of these magnificent cetaceans. And that would have upset Captain Nemo, for he never spills the blood of innocent creatures without good reason.'

'He is right.'

'Certainly, Conseil. But tell me, have you classified these superb specimens of marine fauna?'

'Monsieur knows full well that I have not had much practice. Monsieur needs to tell me the names of the animals first.'

'These are seals and walruses.'

'Genera of the family of pinnipeds,' hastened to say my learned Conseil, 'order of carnivores, group of unguiculates, sub-class of monodelphians, class of mammals, branch of vertebrates.'

'Good,' I replied. 'But these genera of seals and walruses also divide into species, and if I am not mistaken we will soon have an opportunity to observe them more closely. So let's take a walk.'

It was eight in the morning. There were still four hours to fill until the sun could usefully be observed. I headed towards a vast bay that cut into the granite cliff of the coast.

As far as the eye could see, the ground and ice-floes were covered with marine mammals, and I involuntarily looked for old Proteus, the mythological shepherd who watches over Neptune's enormous flocks. Seals were particularly numerous. The males and females formed distinct groups, the father watching over his family, the mother suckling her babes, while some stronger young ones were testing their independence a few feet away. When these mammals wanted to move they produced little jumps, contracting their bodies and helping themselves clumsily along with their imperfect fins, which form real forearms in their congeners, the manatees. I must say that in their natural element of water these animals swim admirably, with their flexible spines, narrow pelvises, short, close-set coats, and webbed feet. When resting on the shore, they adopt extremely graceful attitudes. Accordingly, when the ancients observed their soft faces, charming poses, and their deep, expressive, velvet eyes that the most beautiful woman would not be able to surpass,* they poeticized them in their own way, changing the males into Tritons and the females into Sirens.

I pointed out to Conseil the considerable development of the cerebral lobes in these intelligent cetaceans. No mammal except man has richer brain matter. Accordingly, seals are suited to receiving a degree of education. They are easily domesticated, and like certain other naturalists, I believe that if properly trained they could be of great service as fishing dogs.

Most were sleeping on the rocks or the sand. Amongst the seals in the strict sense, that is without external ears—differing in this respect from the otaries whose ears protrude—I observed several varieties of three-metre-long *Stenorhincus*. They had white hair, bulldog heads, and ten teeth in their jaw: four incisors at the top, four at the bottom, and two great canines standing out in the form of a fleur-de-lis. Between them slid a few sea elephants, a kind of seal with a short mobile trunk: the giant of the species has a girth of twenty feet and a length of ten metres. They did not move as we approached.

'Are these animals not dangerous?' asked Conseil.

'Not unless attacked. When seals defend their young, their fury is terrifying, and it is not uncommon for them to smash fishermen's boats into pieces.'

'They have the right to.'

'Perhaps so.'

Two miles further on, we had to stop at the headland which protected the bay from the south wind. This promontory fell sheer into the sea and its foot was foaming with swell. Beyond it could be heard some formidable roaring noises, like those made by a herd of ruminants.

'But', said Conseil, 'is it a bulls' concert?'

'No,' I said; 'walruses.'

'Are they fighting?'

'Fighting or playing.'

'With respect, we should go and see them.'

'Of course.'

And there we were, clambering over the black rocks, with the ground collapsing unexpectedly, working our way over stones made very treacherous by the ice. I slipped more than once, doing my back no good. Conseil, more cautious or more solidly built, never raised an eyebrow, but would simply say as he picked me up:

'If monsieur would be so good as to spread his weight more, monsieur would maintain his equilibrium better.'

Once at the top of the cape, I could see a vast white plain covered with walruses. They were playing together; the cries were of joy, not anger.

Walruses resemble seals in the shape of their bodies and the way their limbs are attached, but have no canines or incisors in their lower jaws; and their upper canines form tusks 80 centimetres long and 33 centimetres in circumference where they join the body. These teeth are very much sought after, being made of compact ivory without ridges, harder than elephants' and less prone to yellowing. As a result, walruses are excessively hunted, and will soon be destroyed down to the last since the hunters indiscriminately massacre the pregnant females and their young, destroying in fact more than four thousand of them each year.

Passing by these curious animals, I examined them at my leisure, for they did not bother to move. Their skin was thick and rough, of a fawn colour shading into red, and their coats, short and sparse. Some of them were as much as four metres long. Calmer and less fearful than their northern congeners, they did not appoint sentinels to watch the surroundings of their camp.

After examining this city of walruses, I thought of turning back. It was eleven o'clock, and if Captain Nemo found favourable conditions to make an observation, I wanted to be present when he did. However, I had little hope that the sun would show itself that day. Crushed clouds lying on the horizon hid it from our eyes. It was as if that jealous star did not wish human beings to take observations at this unreachable point of the globe.

All the same, I decided to go back to the *Nautilus*. We followed a narrow track along the summit of the cliff. By half-past eleven we were back on the landing strip. The boat had come ashore with the captain. I saw him standing on a block of basalt. His instruments lay near him and his eyes were fixed on the northern horizon, above which the sun was describing its flattened path.

I stood near him and waited in silence. Midday arrived: just as the day before, the sun did not appear.

Such was fate. We had still not made our observation. If we were not able to do so the next day, we would have to give up trying to measure our position.

It was 20 March. Tomorrow, the 21st, was the equinox, and if one ignored the refraction, the sun would vanish under the horizon for six months. With its disappearance the long polar night would begin. At the September equinox the sun had emerged from the northern horizon, rising in flattened spirals until 21 December. From that date, the summer solstice of these Antarctic regions, it had begun to fade once more; and tomorrow it was to send out its last rays.

I told Captain Nemo of my thoughts and fears.

'You are right, Dr Aronnax. If I cannot observe the height of the sun tomorrow, I will not be able to do so for another six months. But because the hazards of my navigation have brought me to these seas by 21 March, my position will be easy to take if the sun does show itself at noon tomorrow.'

'But why, captain?'

'Because when the celestial orb describes such flat spirals, it is difficult to measure its exact height above the horizon, and our instruments are prone to serious errors.'

'How will you proceed then?'

'I will just use my chronometer,' he said. 'If tomorrow, 21 March at noon, taking account of refraction, the sun's disc is exactly cut by the northern horizon, then I am at the South Pole.'

'Just so. Nevertheless, your affirmation cannot be mathematically rigorous because the equinox does not necessarily fall at noon.'

'Yes, monsieur, but the error will be less than a hundred metres, and that's all we need. Till tomorrow then.'

Captain Nemo returned on board. Conseil and I stayed until five o'clock, working our way up and down the beach, observing and studying. I did not find any curious objects except a penguin's egg of remarkable size, which a collector would have paid more than a thousand francs for. Its cream colour and stripes and its characters like hieroglyphics made it a rare curio. I put it into Conseil's hands, and the careful fellow, sure-footed and holding it like precious porcelain from China, got it back to the *Nautilus* in one piece.

There I deposited the rare egg behind one of the panes in the museum. I dined with gusto on an excellent piece of seal liver, which reminded me of pork. And then I went to bed, having invoked like a Hindu the favours of the radiant star.

The following day, 21 March, I went up on the platform as early as five o'clock. I found Captain Nemo already there.

'The weather is slightly clearer,' he said. 'I have high hopes. After breakfast, we'll head for land to choose an observation point.'

Having agreed on this issue, I went back in to look for Ned Land. I suggested he come with me but the obdurate Canadian refused, and I could see full well that his taciturnity and bad mood were getting worse by the day. But really, I did not regret his obstinacy under the circumstances. There were too many seals on shore, and I didn't want to lead the unreflecting fisherman into temptation.

After breakfast, I headed for land again. The *Nautilus* had moved a few miles further on during the night. It was now floating on the open sea a good league from the coast, which was dominated by a sharp peak four or five hundred metres high. In the boat were Captain Nemo and I and two crewmen, along with the instruments: a chronometer, a telescope, and a barometer.

During our crossing, I saw a large number of whales from the three species particular to the southern seas: the right whale, as the British call it, without a dorsal fin; the humpback or rorqual, with a wrinkled stomach and huge white fins, which do not form wings despite its French name, *baleinoptère*; and the finback, yellowish-brown in colour and the quickest of the three. This powerful animal can make itself heard at great distances when it sends columns of air and vapour up to considerable heights, turning into whorls of smoke. These various mammals were playing in schools in the peaceful waters, and I realized that this basin of the South Pole now served as a refuge for the cetaceans, too fiercely hunted by mankind.

I also saw long white-looking funicles belonging to salps, a type of aggregated mollusc, as well as jellyfish of great size rocking on the waves.

We reached land at nine o'clock. The sky was getting brighter, and the clouds were fleeing southwards.* Mists rose from the cold surface of the water. Captain Nemo headed for the peak, which he undoubtedly intended to be his observatory. It was hard going on the sharp lavas and pumice stones, through an atmosphere often filled with sulphurous air from the exhalations. For a man unused to walking on shore, the captain climbed the steepest slopes with a suppleness and agility that I could not equal and which a hunter of mountain goats would have envied.

It took us two hours to reach the summit of the peak, half made of porphyry and half basalt. From there, our eyes took in a vast sea, whose culmination towards the north coincided with the bottom of the sky. At our feet, dazzling fields of whiteness. Above our heads, unmisted pale blue. To the north, the sun's disc, like a ball of fire, already trimmed by the sharp edge of the horizon. From the heart of the water, hundreds of liquid jets falling in magnificent showers. In the distance, the *Nautilus* like a slumbering cetacean. Behind us, to the south and east, an immense land, a chaotic jumble of rocks and ice, whose limits could not be seen.

When Captain Nemo arrived at the peak itself, he carefully noted its height using the barometer, for he had to take account of it in his observation.

At a quarter to twelve the sun, now seen only by refraction, appeared like a golden disc and bestowed its last rays on this lonely continent, on these seas that man had never sailed.

Equipped with a reticle telescope which used a mirror to correct the refraction, Captain Nemo observed the heavenly body as it slowly sank beneath the horizon, following a very oblique course. I was holding the chronometer. My heart was beating wildly. If the disappearance of the sun's semicircle coincided with noon on the chronometer, we were at the Pole.

'Midday!' I exclaimed.

'The South Pole,' Captain Nemo announced in a grave voice, as he handed me the telescope showing the celestial orb cut in two equal portions by the horizon.

I watched the last rays crowning the peak and the shadows gradually climbing the slopes.

At this moment, Captain Nemo put his hand on my shoulder and said:

'Monsieur, in 1600 the Dutchman Gherritz,* carried off by currents and storms, reached 64°S and discovered the South

Shetlands. On 17 January 1773, the illustrious Cook, following the 38th meridian, arrived at 67°30′S, and on 30 January 1774, reached 71°15′S on the 119th meridian. In 1819, the Russian Bellingshausen found himself on the 69th parallel, and in 1821, on the 66th at 111°W. In 1820, the Briton Bransfield was stopped at the 65th degree. The same year, the American Morrell, whose tales are doubtful, discovered an open sea at 70°14′S while working his way along the 42nd meridian. In 1825, the Briton Powell was not able to go further than the 62nd degree. That same year, a mere sealer, the Briton Weddell, went as far as 72°14′S on the 35th meridian, and as far as 74°15′ on the 36th. In 1829, the Briton Foster, commanding the *Chanticleer*, took possession of the Antarctic continent at 63°26′S, 66°26′W. On 1 February 1831, the Briton Biscoe discovered Enderby Land at 68°50′S, Adelaide Island at 67°S on 5 February 1832, and Graham Land at 64°45′S on 21 February. In 1838, the Frenchman Dumont d'Urville, halted by the ice-cap at 62°57′S, took note of Louis-Philippe Land; on 21 January 1840, in a new push south, he named Adélie Land at 66°30′, and a week later, Clarie Coast at 64°40′. In 1838 the Briton Wilkes advanced to the 69th parallel on the 100th meridian. In 1839, the Briton Balleny* discovered Sabrina Coast, on the limit of the Antarctic Circle. Finally, on 12 January 1842 the Briton James Ross, commanding the ships the *Erebus* and the *Terror*, reached 76°56′S, 171°7′E, and discovered Victoria Land; on the 23rd of the same month, he noted the 74th parallel, the furthest point reached until then; on the 27th he was at 76°8′, on the 28th, 77°32′, on 2 February, 78°4′, and in 1842, he came back to the 71st degree, which he was not able to surpass. Well, on this 21st day of March 1868, I, Captain Nemo, have reached the South Pole and the 90th degree, and I take possession of this part of the globe, now comprising one-sixth of all the discovered continents.'

'In whose name, captain?'

'In my own, monsieur!'

And saying this, Captain Nemo unfurled a black flag, carrying a golden *N* quartered on its bunting.* Then turning to the sun, whose last rays were licking the sea at the horizon:

'Farewell, sun!' he exclaimed. 'Disappear, O bright orb. Take your sleep underneath this open sea, and let a night of six months cover my new realm* in its shadows!'

15

Accident or Incident?

THE following day, 22 March, preparations for departure began at six in the morning. The last gleams of dusk were melting into the night. There was a sharp cold. The constellations shone with surprising intensity. At the zenith sparkled the beautiful Southern Cross, the polar star of the Antarctic.

The thermometer marked −12° and when the wind freshened, it produced a sharp biting feeling. The ice-floes were multiplying on the open sea. The ocean was beginning to freeze everywhere. Numerous translucent black patches spreading over its surface announced that young ice was soon going to form. Clearly the southern basin, frozen for six months each winter, was totally inaccessible during that season. What did the whales do during that time? Undoubtedly they swam under the ice-cap to look for more comfortable seas. The seals and the walruses, used to living in the harshest climates, remained on the iced-over waters. These animals have an instinct for digging holes in the icefields and keeping them permanently open. It is at such holes that they come and breathe. When the birds, chased off by the cold, have emigrated north, these marine mammals remain the sole masters of the Antarctic.

Meanwhile the water-tanks had been filled, and the *Nautilus* was slowly descending. At a depth of 1,000 feet, it stopped. Its propeller began to beat the water, and it moved directly north-wards at a speed of fifteen knots. By evening time it was already floating under the immense frozen carapace of the ice-cap.

The panels of the salon had been closed as a safety measure, for the *Nautilus*'s hull might collide with some sunken block. Accordingly, I spent the day putting my notes in order. My mind was completely occupied by my memories of the Pole. We had reached that inaccessible point without fatigue, without danger, as if our floating compartment had slid along the tracks of a railway. And now our return was under way. Would it hold similar surprises for me? I thought it would, so inexhaustible are the submarine marvels! During the five and a half months that fate had kept us on board, we had covered 14,000 leagues, a distance longer than the terrestrial equator. How many curious and terrifying incidents had studded our voyage: hunting in the forests of Crespo, running aground in Torres Strait, the coral cemetery, fishing in Sri Lanka, the Arabian Tunnel, the fires of Santorini, the riches of Vigo Bay, Atlantis, and the South Pole! During the night, all these memories flitted from dream to dream, and would not release my mind into sleep for a single moment.

At three o'clock, I was fully woken by a violent shock. I had sat up on my bed and was listening out in the darkness, when I was suddenly thrown into the middle of the room. The *Nautilus* was now listing radically, and had clearly run aground.

I felt my way along the walls, and dragged myself through the gangways as far as the salon, still lit by the luminous ceiling. The furniture had fallen over. Fortunately the display cabinets, their feet solidly fixed, had not moved. With the vertical displaced, the starboard paintings were pressed hard against the wall coverings while the lower edges of the port ones were a foot away from them. The *Nautilus* was listing to starboard and lay completely motionless.

From inside I could hear sounds of feet and confused voices. But Captain Nemo did not appear. Just when I was about to leave the salon, Ned Land and Conseil came in.

'What's happened?' I immediately asked them.

'I was just coming to ask monsieur,' replied Conseil.

'Hell!' exclaimed the Canadian, 'I know! The *Nautilus* has hit ground, and judging from the angle we're listing at, I don't think we'll get out of this one like we did in Torres Strait.'

'But at least', I asked, 'it has gone back up to the surface, hasn't it?'

'We don't know,' replied Conseil.

'It's easy to find out.'

I consulted the pressure-gauge. To my great surprise it indicated a depth of 360 metres.

'What does that mean?' I exclaimed.

'We must ask Captain Nemo,' said Conseil.

'But where can we find him?' asked Ned.*

'Follow me,' I said.

We left the salon. In the library, nobody. On the central stair-case and in the crew-room, no one. I supposed that Captain Nemo had to be stationed in the pilot's dome. It was best to wait. The three of us came back to the salon.

I will skip over the Canadian's complaints. He enjoyed getting carried away. I let him vent his spleen as much as he wanted, without replying.

We had been in this situation for twenty minutes, trying to detect the slightest sound from the interior of the *Nautilus*, when Captain Nemo came in. He did not seem to see us. His face, usually so impassive, revealed a certain anxiety. He studied the compass and pressure-gauge in silence, and came and put his finger on a point of the planisphere, in the part showing the Southern Seas.

I did not want to interrupt him. But when he turned towards me a few moments later, I echoed an expression he had used in Torres Strait:

'An incident, captain?'

'No monsieur,' he said, 'an accident this time.'

'Serious?'

'Perhaps.'

'Is the danger immediate?'

'No.'

'Has the *Nautilus* run aground?'

'Yes.'

'And how did we run aground?'

'From a whim of nature, not from human error. There were no operational failures. However, we cannot prevent the effects of equilibrium. One can disdain human laws, but not resist natural ones.'

Captain Nemo had chosen a remarkable moment to indulge in such philosophical reflections. His answer left me totally in the dark.

'May I know, monsieur, what caused the accident?'

'An enormous block of ice, an entire mountain, turned over,' he replied. 'When icebergs are undermined at the bottom by warmer waters or by repeated collisions, their centre of gravity rises. They invert, they turn upside down. That is what happened this time. One such block swung over and hit the *Nautilus* sailing under it.

Then the iceberg slid under its hull and picked it up with irre-sistible force, and has now brought the *Nautilus* up to less dense strata, where it is at present lying on its side.'

'But can't we free the *Nautilus* by emptying its tanks to restore its equilibrium?'

'That is what is going on at the moment, monsieur. You can hear the pumps working. Look at the needle of the pressure-gauge. It indicates that the *Nautilus* is rising but the block of ice is also moving with it, and unless something stops it rising, our situation will not change.'

In actual fact, the *Nautilus* was still listing the same amount to starboard. It would undoubtedly come back to its normal position when the block came to a stop. But when it did, who knew if it wouldn't be because we had hit the upper part of the icefield, and were being frighteningly crushed between two icy surfaces.

I was thinking about the various implications of the situation. Captain Nemo did not take his eyes off the pressure-gauge. Since the collapse of the iceberg the *Nautilus* had climbed approxi-mately a hundred and fifty feet, but was still lying at the same angle.

Suddenly, we could feel a slight movement in the hull. The *Nautilus* was shifting slightly back to its normal position. The objects hanging in the salon began to move noticeably towards their normal position. The walls were approaching the vertical. Nobody spoke. With our hearts pumping, we could see, we could feel equilibrium returning. The floor was becoming horizontal under our feet again. Ten minutes went by like this.

'Finally we are straight again!' I exclaimed.

'Yes,' said Captain Nemo, heading for the door.

'But will we float?' I asked.

'Certainly,' he replied, 'since the tanks have not yet been emptied, for when they are empty, the *Nautilus* will have to surface again.'

The captain went out, and soon I saw that on his orders the *Nautilus*'s ascent had been stopped. It would soon have hit the lower part of the icefield, so it was better to remain submerged.

'That was a close shave!' said Conseil.

'Yes; we might have been crushed between blocks of ice, or at best imprisoned. And then, not able to renew our air . . . Yes, it was a close shave!'

'If it's finished,' murmured Ned.

I did not want to start a useless discussion with the Canadian, and so did not reply. In any case, the panels opened at that moment, and light surged in through the window from outside.

We were underwater, as I have said, but a dazzling wall of ice rose at a distance of ten metres on each side of the *Nautilus*. Above and below, a continuation of the same wall. Above, because the lower surface of the ice-cap arched over us like an enormous vault. Below, because the upturned block had slid little by little, and had found two points of support on the side walls, which maintained it in position. The *Nautilus* was imprisoned in a veritable tunnel of ice about twenty metres wide and filled with calm water. It was therefore easy for it to get out, either backwards or forwards, and then to continue its free movement under the ice-cap a few hundred metres further down.

The luminous ceiling had been switched off, and yet the salon was resplendent in intense light. The reason was the powerful illumination from the walls of ice, violently throwing back the searchlight's beams. I cannot depict the effect of the electric rays on these great, capriciously carved blocks, with each angle, each corner, each facet radiating a different effect, depending on the nature of the veins running through it. A dazzling mine of gems, especially sapphires, crisscrossing their blue jets with jets of emerald green. Here and there opaline shades of infinite subtlety ran through the shining points like fiery diamonds, dazzling the eye unbearably. The power of the searchlight was multiplied a hundred times, like that of a lamp through the lenses of a light-house of the first order.

'How beautiful it is! How beautiful!' exclaimed Conseil.

'Yes,' I said, 'it's a wonderful sight. Isn't it Ned?'

'Hell, yes,' riposted Land. 'It's superb! I hate to have to agree. We've never seen anything like it. But this sight may cost us dear. To be frank, I think that we're seeing things here that God wished to hide from man's eyes.'

Ned was right. It was too beautiful. Suddenly a shout from Conseil made me turn round.

'What's the matter?' I asked.

'Monsieur should close his eyes! Monsieur should not look.'

While saying this, Conseil was rubbing his eyelids vigorously.

'What's the matter, my fellow?'

'I am dazzled, blinded!'

My eyes turned involuntarily towards the window, but I was not able to bear the fire that devoured them.

I understood what had happened. The *Nautilus* had started moving very quickly. All the quiet reflections from the walls of ice had then changed into flashing rays. The fires from these myriads of diamonds worked together. The *Nautilus*, carried on by its propeller, was sailing through a sheath of lightning.

The panels of the salon closed. We put our hands over our eyes, still inundated with those concentric gleams which float in front of your retina when sunlight has struck them too violently. It took quite a while before our eyes recovered.

Finally we lowered our hands.

'Goodness, I would never have believed it,' said Conseil.

'And I still do not believe it!' replied the Canadian.

'When we are back on land, and take for granted so many of these brilliant works of nature's,' added Conseil, 'what will we think of the grey landmasses and insignificant works of art man has hand-crafted! No, the inhabited world is no longer worthy of us!'

Such words in the mouth of an impassive Fleming showed to what degree of turmoil our enthusiasm had reached. But the Canadian threw cold water on it as usual.

'The inhabited world,' he repeated, shaking his head. 'Calm down, friend Conseil, you'll never see it again!'

It was five in the morning. At that moment, a shock reverberated from the front of the *Nautilus*. I understood that its cutwater had hit a block of ice. This had to be an accident—the submarine tunnel between the blocks did not offer easy navigation. I thought that Captain Nemo would now change his route and either work his way round the obstacle or follow the windings of the tunnel. In any case, the forward motion would not be stopped. However, against my expectation, the *Nautilus* began moving backwards very fast.

'Have we changed direction?' said Conseil.

'Yes,' I replied, 'the tunnel must have no way out on this side.'

'But then . . .?'

'Then the implication is quite simple. We head back and we leave by the southern exit. That's all.'

Speaking like this, I wanted to appear more confident than I really was. The backwards movement of the *Nautilus* accelerated, and proceeding on reverse propeller, it carried us along with great speed.

'This will slow us down,' said Ned.

'What do a few hours more or less matter, provided we get out?'

'Yes,' said Ned, '*provided* we do get out.'

I spent a few moments walking around the salon and the library. My companions remained sitting without saying anything. I soon threw myself on to a sofa, and picked up a book, which my eyes began covering mechanically.

A quarter of an hour later, Conseil came up to me and said:

'Is monsieur reading something interesting?'

'Very interesting,' I replied.

'I agree. Monsieur is reading his own book.'

'My own book?'

I was indeed holding the work *The Ocean Deeps* in my hand. I had had no idea I was doing this. I closed the volume and continued my pacing. Ned and Conseil got up to go to bed.

'Please remain, my friends,' I said, retaining them, 'let's stay together until we have got out of this cul-de-sac.'

'As monsieur pleases,' replied Conseil.

A few hours went by. I often looked at the instruments on the salon walls. The pressure-gauge indicated that the *Nautilus* was staying at a constant depth of 300 metres, the compass, that it was still heading south, and the log-line, that it was moving at 20 knots, a very high speed in such an enclosed space. But Captain Nemo knew that he could not move too quickly, that minutes were in this case worth centuries.

At 8.25 there was a second shock. At the back this time. I turned pale. My companions had come close. I had taken Conseil's hand. We questioned each other with our eyes, more directly than if our thoughts were expressed in words.

At this moment, the captain entered the salon. I went up to him.

'So the route is blocked to the south?' I asked.

'Yes monsieur. When the iceberg overturned, it closed all ways out.'

'So we're trapped?'

'Yes, we are.'

16

Not Enough Air

So all around the *Nautilus*, above and below, was an impenetrable wall of ice. We were prisoners of the ice-cap. The Canadian struck the table with his awesome fist. Conseil remained silent. I looked at the captain. His face had resumed its customary impassiveness. He had crossed his arms reflectively. The *Nautilus* was no longer moving.

Then the captain spoke again:

'Messieurs,' he said in a calm voice, 'there are two ways of dying in the circumstances in which we find ourselves.'

The inexplicable character resembled a professor of mathematics carrying out a demonstration for his students.

'The first is to die through being crushed. The second is to die of asphyxiation. I do not mention the possibility of dying from hunger, for the provisions of the *Nautilus* will certainly last longer than we will. Let us therefore consider the probability of us being crushed and of us being asphyxiated.'

'As for being asphyxiated, captain,' I replied, 'there is little danger because our tanks are full.'

'True,' said Captain Nemo, 'but they will only provide us two days of air. We have been underwater for 36 hours, and already the heavy atmosphere of the *Nautilus* needs renewing. In 48 hours' time our reserves will also be exhausted.'

'Well captain, let's make sure we are safe within 48 hours!'

'We will at least try cutting through the wall surrounding us,' he replied.

'In which direction?' I asked.

'Carrying out soundings will tell us that. I am going to ground the *Nautilus* on the lower surface and my men in their diving suits will attack the iceberg at its least thick wall.'

'Can we open the panels of the salon?'

'Certainly. We are not moving.'

Captain Nemo went out. Soon hissing sounds told me that water was being let into the tanks. The *Nautilus* slowly sank and came to rest on the icy floor at a depth of 350 metres, the depth of the lower surface of ice.

'My friends,' I said, 'our situation is serious, but I am counting on your courage and energy.'

'Monsieur,' the Canadian replied, 'I will not trouble you with my recriminations at this point. I am ready to do anything for our collective safety.'

'Good, Ned,' I said, stretching out my hand to the Canadian.

'I will add that I am as good at using a pickaxe as a harpoon, and so I am at the captain's service if I can be of use.'

'He will not refuse your help. Come Ned.'

I took him to the room where the crew of the *Nautilus* were putting on their diving suits. I informed the captain of Ned's suggestion, which he accepted. The Canadian put on his sea-costume, and was soon as ready as his working companions. Each of them carried a Rouquayrol apparatus on his back, to which the tanks had provided a large amount of pure air. A considerable but necessary borrowing from the *Nautilus*'s reserves. As for the Ruhmkorff lamps, they were useless in the luminous waters filled with electric rays.

When Ned was ready I went back to the salon, where the windows were already uncovered, and positioned myself near Conseil to study the water around the *Nautilus*.

A few moments later, we saw a dozen crewmen stepping out on to the ice-shelf, Ned Land amongst them, recognizable from his larger size. Captain Nemo was also there.

Before proceeding to hollow out the walls, he had soundings made in order to ensure the work would be in the right direction. Long sounds were inserted into the side walls, but after 50 metres they were still stopped by the thick ice. It was useless to attack the top surface because this was the ice-cap itself, more than 400 metres thick above us. Captain Nemo then had the lower surface sounded. There, ten metres of wall separated us from the water.

We needed to cut a piece of sheet ice 30 feet thick and of the same surface area as the flotation line of the *Nautilus*. This meant cutting out about 6,500 cubic metres so as to make a hole through which we could descend to below the ice-cap.

The work began immediately, and carried on with unyielding single-mindedness. Instead of digging around the *Nautilus*, which would have been more difficult, Captain Nemo had a massive trench delineated eight metres from its port quarter. Then his men cut simultaneously into several points on its circumference. Soon pickaxes were vigorously attacking the compact matter, and large blocks emerging from the mass. Through a curious effect of specific gravity, the blocks were lighter than water, and flew up, so to speak, to the vault of the tunnel, which grew thicker at the top by the same amount it reduced at the bottom. But this hardly mattered, given that the lower wall was getting progressively thinner.

After two hours of hard work, Ned returned exhausted. He and his companions were replaced by new workers, whom Conseil and I joined. The first officer of the *Nautilus* directed us.

The water seemed remarkably cold, but I soon warmed up using the axe. My movements were very free, although produced at a pressure of thirty atmospheres.

When I returned after two hours of work to take some food and rest, I found a notable difference between the pure fluid that the Rouquayrol apparatus had been giving me and the atmosphere of the *Nautilus*, already full of carbon dioxide. The air had not been renewed for 48 hours, and its vivifying qualities were considerably reduced. Also, in a period of twelve hours we had only removed a slice of ice a metre thick from the designated area, that is about 600 cubic metres. Assuming the same amount of work was carried out every twelve hours, we still needed five nights and four days to finish.

'Five nights and four days,' I said to my companions, 'and we only have two days of air left in the tanks.'

'Without taking into account', replied Ned, 'that once we're out of this damned prison, we'll still be under the ice-cap without being able to reach the air.'

It was true. Who could calculate the minimum time needed for our deliverance? Would we not be suffocated and asphyxiated before the *Nautilus* got back up to the surface? Was the *Nautilus* destined to perish in this ice tomb with all those it contained? Such a prospect seemed terrifying, but everyone had clearly faced up to it and was resolved to do his duty until the end.

As I expected, a new layer one metre thick was removed from the enormous hole during the night. But when I put my diving suit on again in the morning, and entered the liquid mass at a temperature of six or seven degrees, I noticed the side wall was getting gradually closer. The layers of water furthest away from the trench were not being warmed by the work of the men or the action of their tools and so were subject to freezing. In the presence of this new and imminent danger, what were our chances of survival—how could we prevent the solidification of the liquid environment which might crush the walls of the *Nautilus* like glass?

I did not inform my two companions of this new danger. What was the point of running the risk of dampening their ardour for the difficult work of saving ourselves? But when I came back on board, I pointed out to Captain Nemo the additional serious complication.

'I know,' he said in that calm tone which the worst situations could not alter. 'It is an additional danger, but I can see no way of stopping it. The only chance of survival is to work more quickly than the solidification. We need to finish first, that's all.'

Finish first! But I suppose I should have been used to such forms of expression. For several hours that day I wielded the pickaxe with considerable stubbornness. The work bore me up. In any case, to work was to leave the *Nautilus* and to breathe the pure air supplied by the apparatus straight from the tanks. It was to leave an atmosphere which was impoverished and vitiated.

In the evening the trench was a metre deeper. When I returned on board, I was almost suffocated by the carbon dioxide filling the air. Ah, why did we not have some chemical means to eliminate this noxious gas? There was plenty of oxygen. All this water contained great quantities of the element, and decomposing it with our powerful batteries would have given us access to the life-giver. I had indeed thought of this, but what was the point, since the carbon dioxide we had breathed out had permeated every part of the ship? To absorb it, we would have needed containers filled with caustic potash, constantly shaken. But we had none on board, and nothing could replace it.

That evening, Captain Nemo had to open the taps of his tanks and send a few columns of pure air into the interior of the *Nautilus*. If he had not done so we would not have woken up again.

The following day, 26 March, I continued my miner's work and began on the fifth metre. The sides and ceiling of the ice-cap were getting visibly thicker. It was evident that they would join up before the *Nautilus* was able to free itself. Despair took hold of me for a moment. My pickaxe came near to falling from my hands. What was the point of digging if I was to suffocate to death, crushed by this water turning to stone, a torture that even the ferocity of savages could not have invented? I felt as if I was between the formidable jaws of a monster, ones which were inexorably closing shut.

At this moment Captain Nemo, directing the work and working himself, passed near me. I touched him with my glove, and showed him the walls of our prison. The port wall was now less than four metres from the *Nautilus*'s hull.

The captain understood, and signalled that I should follow him. We went back on board. Once my diving suit was off, I followed him into the salon.

'Dr Aronnax,' he said to me, 'we need to employ desperate measures, or else we are going to be sealed in this solidified water as if in concrete.'

'Yes,' I said, 'but what should we do?'

'Ah,' he exclaimed, 'if only my *Nautilus* was strong enough to bear this pressure without being crushed!'

'Well?' I asked, not really understanding his idea.

'Don't you understand that the freezing of the water would actually help us? Can you not see that the solidifying process would crack the walls of ice imprisoning us, as it cracks hard stones when they freeze! Can you not understand that it would then be an agent of survival instead of being one of destruction!'

'Yes captain, perhaps. But whatever resistance to being crushed the *Nautilus* has, it will not be able to bear such an awesome pressure, and would be made as flat as a sheet of metal.'

'I know monsieur. So we must not rely on help from nature, but only from ourselves. We must prevent the solidification, or at least slow it down. Not only are the sides closing in, but there remain only ten feet of water fore and aft of the *Nautilus*. The freezing is gaining on us in all directions.'

'How much time will the air from the tanks allow us to breathe on board?'

The captain looked me squarely in the face.

'The tanks will be empty the day after tomorrow!'

I was covered in a cold sweat, and yet how could I be surprised by his reply? The *Nautilus* had dived under the open seas of the Pole on 22 March. It was now the 26th. We had been living on the reserves for four days, and what breathable air remained needed to be kept for the workers. As I am writing these things, my impressions are still so vivid that my whole being is stricken with an involuntary terror and the air feels as if it is being tugged from my lungs!

However, Captain Nemo was reflecting, silent and motionless. An idea was visibly going through his mind, but he seemed to be rejecting it. He was responding negatively to himself. At last, words escaped his lips:

'Boiling water,' he murmured.

'Boiling water!' I exclaimed.

'Yes. We are enclosed in a relatively confined space. Would sending jets of boiling water continuously from the *Nautilus*'s pumps not raise the general temperature and so slow down the freezing?'

'We must try,' I said resolutely.

'Let's try then.'

The temperature outside read $-7°$. Captain Nemo took me to the kitchens, where vast distillation apparatuses produced drinking water by means of evaporation. They were now filled up with water, then all the heat from the electric batteries was sent through the liquid in the coils. In a few minutes the water reached $100°$. It was sent to the pumps while an equivalent amount of fresh water was introduced. The heat developed by the batteries was such that, merely by going through these apparatuses, cold water drawn from the sea arrived boiling at the pumping mechanisms.

Three hours after the pumping began, the thermometer showed −6° outside. We had gained one degree. Two hours later, the thermometer showed −4°.

'We're going to win,' I told the captain, after following the progress of this operation and accompanying it with numerous remarks.

'Probably,' he replied. 'We're not going to be crushed. We only have asphyxiation to worry about.'

During the night the temperature of the water went up to −1°. The pumping could not make it go up any further. But since sea water freezes only at −2°, I finally stopped worrying about the dangers of solidification.

The following day, 27 March, six metres of ice had been torn from the hole. There remained only four metres to go. This was still 48 hours of work. The air could not be renewed inside the *Nautilus*. Accordingly, the day got gradually worse and worse.

An unbearable heaviness came over me. At about three in the afternoon, the feeling of anguish in me grew to an overwhelming degree. Yawns dislocated my jaws. My lungs worked fast as they searched for the combustive gas indispensable for breathing, now more and more rarefied. A mortal torpor took hold of me. I was stretched out feeling very weak, almost unconscious. My good Conseil, undergoing the same symptoms, suffering the same suffering, did not leave me. He took my hand, he encouraged me, and I kept hearing him murmur:

'Ah, if only I could refrain from breathing in order to leave more air for monsieur!'

Tears came to my eyes when I heard him speak like this.

If the situation inside was intolerable for all of us, with what haste, with what joy we would put on our diving suits to take our turn to work. The pickaxes rang out on the frozen wall. Arms grew tired, hands blistered, but who cared about fatigue and pain! The vital air was entering our lungs! We were breathing, really breathing!

And yet no one extended his work underwater beyond the specified time. Once his task was over, each entrusted to his gasping companion the tank which would pour life into him. Captain

Nemo showed an example, submitting first to this severe discipline. Once the time had come, he gave his apparatus to another and returned to the ship's vitiated atmosphere, always calm, without a moment of weakness, without a murmur.

That day, the work was carried out with still more vigour. Only two metres remained to be removed from the area. Only two metres separated us from the open sea, but the tanks were almost empty. The little which remained had to be kept for the workers. Not an atom for the *Nautilus*!

When I returned on board, I half suffocated. What a night! I cannot depict it. Such suffering cannot be described. The following day my breathing was oppressed. I had headaches combined with stupefying vertigos, which made a drunkard of me. My companions experienced the same symptoms. A few crewmen were at their last gasp.

That day, the fifth of our imprisonment, Captain Nemo found the pick and pickaxe too slow, and resolved to attack the layer of ice still separating us from the liquid element. This man had kept his sang-froid and energy. He overcame his physical ills with moral force. He thought, he took himself in hand, he acted.

On his orders, the vessel was eased, that is removed from its frozen resting place by changing its specific weight slightly. While floating it was hauled until it was over the massive trench round its flotation line. Then its water tanks were opened slightly, it sank down again, and fitted into the hole.

The whole crew returned on board, and the double communication doors were closed. The *Nautilus* rested on the ice layer, less than a metre thick, pierced in a thousand places by the sounding holes.

The taps of the tanks were then opened wide, and 100 cubic metres of water rushed into them, increasing the weight of the *Nautilus* by 100,000 kilograms.

We waited, we listened, forgetting our suffering, still hoping. We were gambling our lives on a last attempt.

In spite of the murmuring sounds filling my head, I soon felt tremblings under the *Nautilus*'s hull. It shifted. The ice cracked with a bizarre sound like paper tearing and the *Nautilus* dropped down.

'We are going through!' Conseil murmured in my ear.

I was not able to reply. I grabbed his hand. I pressed it in the throes of an involuntary convulsion.

Suddenly, carried away by its massive overload, the *Nautilus* sank like a cannonball dropped in water—it fell as if in a vacuum. The whole electric force was then sent into the pumps, which immediately began to expel water from the tanks.

After a few minutes our fall stopped. Soon the pressure-gauge even indicated upward movement. The propeller, working at full speed, made the metal hull tremble down to the bolts themselves, and carried us off northwards.

But how long would this race under the ice-cap take until we reached the open sea? Another day? I would be dead by then.

Half stretched out on a sofa in the library, I was suffocating. My face was purple, my lips blue, my faculties suspended. I could no longer see, I could no longer hear. All idea of time had vanished from my mind. My muscles would not contract.

I could not count the hours that went by in this way, but I was conscious I was going into death-throes. I realized that I was about to die.

Suddenly I came to. A few mouthfuls of air had penetrated my lungs. Had we made it back up to the surface? Had we got through the icefield?

No! It was Ned and Conseil, my two good friends, depriving themselves to save me. A few atoms of air still remained at the bottom of an apparatus. Instead of breathing it themselves, they had kept it for me, and while themselves suffocating, they poured life into me drop by drop! I tried to push back the apparatus. But they held my hands, and for a few moments I breathed in with voluptuousness.

My eyes turned to the clock. It was eleven in the morning. It must have been 28 March. The *Nautilus* was slicing through the water at a speed of 40 knots.

Where was Captain Nemo? Had he succumbed? Were his companions dead with him?

The pressure-gauge indicated that we were only twenty feet away from the surface. A mere sheet of ice separated us from the air. Could we not break it?

In any case, the *Nautilus* was going to try. I could feel it manœuvring into an oblique position, lowering its stern and lifting its prow. Introducing some water had been enough to break the equilibrium. Then, pushed on by its powerful propeller, it ploughed up into the icefield like a formidable ram. It was breaking it up piece by piece, the *Nautilus* was withdrawing, then throwing itself at full speed against the field. The ice began to tear, and carrying through in a supreme thrust, it threw itself on to the icy surface, which it crushed under its weight.

The hatch was opened, or rather torn off, and pure air poured into every part of the *Nautilus*.

17

From Cape Horn to the Amazon

How I reached the platform I cannot say. Perhaps the Canadian took me there. But I was breathing, I was gulping down the invigorating sea air. My two companions beside me were drunk on the fresh air. Wretches who are deprived of food for too long cannot throw themselves unthinkingly on the first food they find. But we had no need to ration ourselves. We could breathe in great lungfuls of atmosphere, and the wind itself suffused us with this voluptuous intoxication!

'Ah,' said Conseil, 'how good oxygen is! Monsieur need not hold back from breathing it in. There is plenty for everyone.'

As for Ned, he was not speaking but had his mouth open to an extent that would have frightened a shark. And what powerful breathing! The Canadian was 'drawing' like a roaring stove.

Our strength soon came back, and when I looked around I realized that we were alone on the platform. No crew member, not even Captain Nemo. The strange sailors of the *Nautilus* satisfied themselves with the air circulating inside. Not one had come to refresh himself in the open air.

The first words I said were words of thanks to my two companions. Ned and Conseil had saved my life during the last hours of that long death-agony. All my gratitude was not too much to give for such devotion.

'Okay, monsieur!' Ned Land replied. 'Why talk about it? What did we have to do with it? Nothing. It was just a question of arithmetic. Your life was worth more than ours, so we had to save you.'

'No Ned,' I replied, 'it was not worth more, nobody is better than a man who is generous and good, and you are both of these!'

'Okay, okay!' said the embarrassed Canadian.

'And you, my good Conseil, you also suffered tremendously.'

'Not too much, to tell the truth monsieur. A few mouthfuls of air would not have gone astray, but I believe I would have got used to the situation. In any case, I saw monsieur fainting, and that did not give me the least desire to inhale. It took, as one says, my breath . . .'

Embarrassed to have launched himself into such banality, Conseil did not finish.

'My friends,' I replied, greatly moved, 'we are bound to each other for ever, and I am for ever in your debt.'

'Which I will draw on,' said the Canadian.

'Eh?' said Conseil.

'Yes,' continued Land, 'I will call on the right to drag you away with me when I leave this infernal *Nautilus*.'

'Come to mention it,' said Conseil, 'are we heading in the right direction?'

'Yes,' I replied, 'since we are moving towards the sun, and the sun is in the north here.'

'Agreed,' said Ned. 'But we still need to know whether we are heading for the Pacific or the Atlantic, that is for empty or for busy seas.'

I could not reply, being afraid that Captain Nemo was in fact taking us back to that vast ocean which bathes the coasts of both Asia and America. He would thus complete his submarine journey round the world, and return to the seas where the *Nautilus* found the most independence. But if we were going back to the Pacific, far from friendly shores, what would become of Ned Land's plans?

This important point would be settled before long. The *Nautilus* was moving quickly. The polar circle was soon crossed, and sail set for Cape Horn. We were off the extreme American point at seven in the evening on 31 March.

All our past suffering was forgotten. The memory of our icy imprisonment was fast fading from our memories. We only thought of the future. Captain Nemo did not appear either in the salon or on the platform. The position as measured by the first officer and plotted each day on the planisphere allowed me to follow the exact route of the *Nautilus*. And to my great satisfaction that evening it became evident that we were heading back north via the Atlantic.

I informed Ned and Conseil of the results of my deductions.

'Good news,' replied the Canadian, 'but where is the *Nautilus* actually going?'

'I cannot say, Ned.'

'Does the captain now wish to attack the North Pole having been to the South Pole, and return to the Pacific via the famous Northwest Passage?'

'We mustn't try and dissuade him even if he wants to do that,' replied Conseil.

'Well we'll part company from him before then!'

'In any case,' added Conseil, 'Captain Nemo is a remarkable man, and we will not regret having known him.'

'Above all when we've left him!' retorted Ned.

The following day, 1 April, the *Nautilus* surfaced a few minutes before noon, and we sighted a coast to the west. This was Tierra del Fuego, so called by the first navigators when they saw large amounts of smoke rising from the native huts. Tierra del Fuego forms a vast collection of islands more than eighty leagues in length by thirty leagues in width, between 53° and 56°S and 67° 50′ and 77° 14′ W. The coast seemed low, but high mountains rose in the distance. I even thought I glimpsed Mount Sarmiento, 2,070 metres above sea level. This is a block of schist in the shape of a pyramid with a very sharp summit, and whether it is covered in mists or is free of vapour 'predicts good or bad weather', as Ned Land told me.

'A wonderful barometer, my friend.'

'Yes, monsieur, a natural barometer which has always been right when I have navigated the passes of the Strait of Magellan.'

At that moment the peak appeared clearly etched against the background of the sky: in other words, a portent of good weather.

Diving again, the *Nautilus* approached the coast and worked its way along for a few miles. Through the salon windows I could see long creepers and gigantic wracks, those *pyrifera* kelps of which the open sea at the Pole had contained a few specimens. With their shiny, viscous filaments, they measured up to 300 metres long. Veritable cables, thicker than a thumb and very strong, they often serve for ships' mooring ropes. Another plant known as *Velpeaulia*, with four-foot leaves covered with coral accretions, carpeted the depths. It served as a nest and as food for myriads of crustaceans and molluscs like crabs and cuttlefish. Seals and otters indulged in splendid meals there, combining fish with marine vegetables, a bit like the British do.*

The *Nautilus* moved at great speed over the rich, luxuriant bottoms. In the evening it approached the Falkland Islands, whose rough summits I was able to see the following day. The sea was not very deep. I accordingly thought, with good reason, that the two main islands surrounded by a large number of smaller islands were formerly part of Magellanic lands. The Falklands were probably discovered by the celebrated John Davis,* who gave them the name of Davis Southern Islands. Later Richard Hawkins* called them Maidenland. At the beginning of the eighteenth century they were named the Malouines by fishermen from Saint-Malo, and finally the Falklands by the British, to whom they belong today.

On these shores, our nets brought in fine specimens of seaweeds, and particularly a certain wrack with roots laden with mussels that are the best in the world. Dozens of geese and ducks rained down on to the platform, and soon took their places in the sculleries. As regards fish, I particularly observed bony ones belonging to the goby genus, and above all twenty-centimetre double-spotted gobies, completely covered in white and yellow spots.

I also admired numerous jellyfish, particularly the most beautiful of their genus, the *Chrysaora*, peculiar to the seas off the Falklands. Sometimes they formed very smooth hemispherical parasols striped with reddish-brown lines, culminating in twelve regularly shaped scallops. Sometimes they became upside-down waste-paper baskets, from which grew gracious broad leaves and long red twigs. They swam by, waving their four foliaceous arms and allowing their opulent head of tentacles to drift behind. I would have liked to keep a few specimens of these delicate zoophytes; but they are only clouds, shadows, appearances, which melt and evaporate once outside their native element.

When the last hills of the Falklands had disappeared below the horizon, the *Nautilus* dived to between 20 and 55 metres and started following the American coast. Captain Nemo did not appear.

Until 3 April, sometimes below and sometimes on the surface, we did not leave the shores of Patagonia. The *Nautilus* went past the large estuary of the mouth of the Río de la Plata, and on 4 April was fifty miles off Uruguay. Its direction was still northerly as it followed the long curves of South America. We had now done 16,000 leagues since embarking in the seas of Japan.

At eleven in the morning we crossed the tropic of Capricorn on the 37th meridian, and passed by Cape Frio. To Ned's great displeasure, Captain Nemo obviously disliked the neighbourhood of these populated coasts of Brazil, for he moved with dizzying speed. Not even the quickest of fish or birds could keep up with us, and observing the natural curiosities of these seas was no longer possible.

This speed was maintained for several days, and in the evening of 9 April we sighted the easternmost point of South America, Cape São Roque.* But then the *Nautilus* moved away again, and went to seek greater depths in a submarine valley between this cape and Sierra Leone on the African coast. The valley divides off the West Indies, and finishes in the north in an enormous depression 9,000 metres deep. At that point, the geological cross-section of the ocean forms a cliff 6,000 metres high cut sheer as far as the Lesser Antilles, and, together with a similar wall off Cape Verde, encloses the whole of the sunken continent of Atlantis. The floor of this enormous valley is broken up by a few mountains which contribute to the picturesque views in the submarine depths. I speak about such matters on the basis of the hand-produced maps in the *Nautilus*'s library. Maps evidently drawn by Captain Nemo, based on his personal observations.

For two days we visited the deep deserted waters using the inclined planes on the *Nautilus* to make long diagonal descents, thus reaching all depths. But on 11 April we suddenly moved upwards, and sighted land again near the opening of the Amazon, a vast estuary delivering so much water that it desalinates the sea for a distance of several leagues.

We crossed the equator. Twenty miles to the west stood the Guyanas, a French possession* where we could easily have found refuge. But a strong wind was blowing up, and the furious waves would not have allowed a mere dinghy to confront them. Land undoubtedly understood this, for he did not say anything to me. For my part, I made no reference to his escape plans, because I did not wish to encourage some attempt which would inevitably have failed.

I easily filled the time with interesting studies. On 11 and 12 April the *Nautilus* did not leave the surface and its trawl brought in a miraculous draught of zoophytes, fish, and reptiles.

Some zoophytes had been swept up by the chains of the drag-nets. These were, for the most part, lovely *Phyllactina* belonging to the family of the actinias, and amongst other species the *Phyllactis protexta*: a native of this part of the ocean with a small cylindrical trunk, adorned with vertical lines, speckled with red points, and crowned with a spectacular blossoming of tentacles. As for the molluscs, they consisted of products that I had already observed: screw shells, porphyry olives with regular crisscrossing lines and red patches standing vividly out on a fleshy background, some fantastic scorpio shells like petrified scorpions, translucent hyales, argonauts, highly edible cuttlefish, and certain species of squid that the naturalists of antiquity classified amongst flying fishes and which serve mostly as bait for cod fishing.

Amongst the fish of these waters that I had not yet had the opportunity of studying, I noticed a number of other species. Amongst the cartilaginous fish were pike lampreys, a sort of fifteen-inch eel with greenish heads, violet fins, bluish-grey backs, brown and silver bellies dotted with bright patches, and circles of gold round the irises in their eyes: curious animals that the current of the Amazon must have carried down to the sea, for they live in fresh water; there were also tubercular rays with pointed snouts and long slender tails, armed with long toothed stings; small, one-metre sharks with grey milky skin and several rows of teeth curving backwards, commonly known as hammerheads;

vespertilian Lophiidae, sorts of reddish isosceles triangles half a metre long, with pectorals connected to fleshy extensions giving them the look of bats and with horny appendixes near their nostrils that have given them the popular name of sea-unicorns; and finally two species of triggerfish, the curassow whose dotted flanks shine with a vivid golden colour and the light-purple capriscus with iridescent nuances like a pigeon's throat. I will finish this very precise, albeit slightly dry, nomenclature with the series of bony fishes that I observed: ramblers from the genus of apteronots, which have a very blunt snout as white as snow, and a beautiful black body, and are equipped with a very long and very slender fleshy thong; prickly *Odontognathae*; thirty-centimetre long sardines resplendent in a bright silvery brilliance; *Scomberesox sauri* with two anal fins; two-metre long butterfly blennies in dark hues that are taken using burning torches, with plump firm white flesh, which when fresh tastes like eel and when dried, smoked salmon; half-red labra clothed in scales only as far as the base of their dorsal and anal fins; chrysopteri on which gold and silver mix their brilliance with ruby and topaz; golden-tail sparids whose flesh is extremely delicate and whose phosphorescence gives them away in the middle of the water; boops sparids with fine tongues and orange hues; Coro sciaenas with golden tail-fins; specimens of *Acanthurus nigricans*; four-eyed fish from Surinam, etc.

This 'etcetera' will not prevent me from quoting yet another fish Conseil will remember for a long while, and with good reason.

One of our nets had brought in a type of very flat ray which, without its tail, would have formed a perfect circle and which weighed about twenty kilograms. It was white underneath and verging on red on top, with large, round, deep-blue spots surrounded by black. Its very smooth skin ended in a bilobate fin. Stranded on the platform, it was convulsively struggling to turn itself over, and making so many attempts that a last somersault was about to carry it back into the sea. But Conseil, who was keen on his fish, threw himself on to it and took hold of it in both hands before I could stop him. He was on his back immediately, his legs in the air and half of his body paralysed, crying:

'Ah, my master, my master! Help me.'

This was the first time the poor fellow hadn't addressed me in the third person.

The Canadian and I picked him up. We rubbed him down with all our force, and when he was himself again, this persistent classifier murmured in a hesitant voice:

'Cartilaginous class, order of chondropterygians with fixed gills, suborder of selachians, family of rays, genus of torpedoes!'

'Yes, my friend,' I replied, 'it was a torpedo which put you in this deplorable state.'

'Ah, monsieur, believe me,' replied Conseil, 'I will take revenge on the animal!'

'But how?'

'By eating it.'

Which he did that very evening, but only out of revenge, for to tell the truth it was very tough.

The unfortunate Conseil had been attacked by a torpedo of the most dangerous species, the cumana. In a conducting environment like water, this bizarre animal shocks fish at several metres' distance, such is the power of its electric organ, whose two main surfaces cover as much as 27 square feet.

The following day, 12 April, the *Nautilus* approached the Dutch coast near the mouth of the Maroni. There several groups of manatees lived in families. These manatees, like the dugong and Steller's sea cow, belong to the order of sirenians. Six or seven metres long, these fine animals, peaceful and inoffensive, must have weighed at least 4,000 kilograms.* I told Ned Land and Conseil that far-seeing nature had given such mammals an important role. Like the seals, they graze on the submarine prairies and thus destroy the grass which accumulates and obstructs the mouths of tropical rivers.

'And do you know', I added, 'what happened when men almost entirely destroyed such useful species? Decaying grass poisoned the air, and the contaminated air produced yellow fever which is destroying these admirable countries. Poisonous vegetation has multiplied in the warm seas, and the damage has spread irresistibly from the mouth of the Río de la Plata to Florida!

'And if Toussenel* can be believed, this plague is nothing beside that which will strike our descendants when the seas are emptied of whales and seals. Crowded with squid, jellyfish, and calamar, they will become huge centres of infection because their waters will no longer contain the vast stomachs that God mandated to scour the surface of the seas.'

However, although not disdaining these theories, the crew of the *Nautilus* took half-a-dozen manatees. The aim was to supply the ship's kitchens with an excellent flesh, better than beef or veal. The hunting was not interesting. The manatees allowed themselves to be struck without defending themselves. Several tons of meat were taken on board for drying.

That same day, a remarkably conducted exercise in these seas so full of game increased the reserves of the *Nautilus* still further. The trawl nets had brought in a certain number of fish whose heads ended in oval plates with fleshy edges. They were echinoids, of the third family of malacopterygian subbrachials. Their flattened disc is made of transversal mobile cartilaginous laminae, which the animal can use to produce a vacuum, allowing it to stick to objects like a sucker.

The strata I had observed in the Mediterranean were also home to this species, but the ones here were *Echeneis osteochir*, particular to this sea. Each one that our sailors caught was put in a pail of water.

Once the fishing had been finished, the *Nautilus* approached the coast. A number of marine turtles were sleeping on the surface. It would have been difficult to take hold of the precious reptiles, for the least sound rouses them and their solid carapace resists harpoons. But the *Echeneis* were to perform the capture with extraordinary sureness and precision. The creatures were to act as living bait, which would have made any angler delighted at the method.

The men of the *Nautilus* fixed rings to the tails of these fishes that were wide enough not to get in the way of their movements, and the rings were attached to long cords, tied at the other end to the side.

The *Echeneis* were thrown into the sea, and immediately did their job by sticking to the plastrons of the turtles. So tenacious were they that they would have been torn to pieces rather than let go. They were hauled on board, together with the turtles to which they were stuck.

We thus took several loggerheads a metre wide and weighing 200 kilos. Their carapaces were covered with great flat corneas which were thin, transparent, and brown with white and yellow dots; and this made them very precious. In addition they were excellent from the point of view of comestibility, just like exquisite-tasting green turtles.

This fishing terminated our sojourn on the shores around the Amazon, and after nightfall the *Nautilus* headed out for the open sea once more.

18

Squid

FOR several days the *Nautilus* kept well away from the American coast. It clearly did not want to hang about the Gulf of Mexico or the Caribbean. Nevertheless, its keel would not have lacked water, for the average depth of these seas is 1,800 metres; but probably the waters dotted with islands and crisscrossed by steamers did not suit Captain Nemo.

On 16 April we sighted Martinique and Guadeloupe at a distance of about 30 miles. I caught a brief glimpse of their high peaks.

The Canadian was counting on implementing his plans in the Gulf, either by reaching a piece of land or by accosting one of the numerous boats which worked their way along the shores of the islands, and so he was very disappointed. Escape would have been practicable if Ned had managed to get hold of the boat without the captain knowing. But we could not even dream of doing this in mid-ocean.

Ned, Conseil, and I had quite a long conversation on the subject. We had been prisoners on board the *Nautilus* for six months. We had travelled 17,000 leagues and, as Ned pointed out, there was no reason to expect any change. He therefore made a suggestion which I was not expecting. This was that I categorically ask Captain Nemo: did he plan to keep us on board his vessel indefinitely?

Such a course of action did not appeal to me. In my view, it couldn't possibly succeed. We couldn't count on the captain of the *Nautilus*, only on ourselves alone and completely. Also, for some time the captain had become more sombre, withdrawn, and anti-social. He seemed to be avoiding me, as I only met him at rare intervals. Formerly, he had enjoyed explaining the underwater marvels to me; but now he left me to my studies and no longer came into the salon.

What change had come over him? What was he reacting to? I had done nothing to reproach myself with. Perhaps our very presence on board weighed on him? But in any case, he was certainly not the sort of man to give us back our freedom.

I therefore asked Ned to give me more time to think about the question. If his suggestion failed, it could wreck his plans by reviving the captain's suspicions, and make our situation very difficult. In addition, I had no arguments to offer concerning the state of our health. With the exception of the difficulties under the ice of the South Pole, we had never been in better health, Ned, Conseil, nor myself. The nourishing food, healthy atmosphere, regularity in our lives, and uniformity of temperature simply didn't allow illness to take hold. I could understand how a life like this would suit a man who had no regrets about leaving life on shore, a Captain Nemo who was at home here, who went where he wished, and who pursued goals that were mysterious to others and known only to himself; but as for the three of us, we had not been made to break with humanity. For my part, I did not wish my intriguing and original studies to be buried with me. I was now in a position to write the real book of the sea, and I wanted this book to appear sooner rather than later.

Through the open panel, ten metres below the surface of the West Indian waters, how many interesting specimens I could see for recording in my daily notes! Amongst other zoophytes, there were the Portuguese men-of-war known as pelagic men-of-war, which are thick oval-shaped bladders with a pearly sheen, spreading their membranes out to be blown in the current and letting their blue tentacles float like threads of silk, charming jellyfish to look at but authentic nettles to the touch for they secrete a corrosive liquid. Amongst the articulates there were one-and-half-metre long annelids, with pink trunks and 1,700 locomotive organs, which snaked through the water, going through all the colours of the rainbow as they passed by. In the branch of the fishes there were enormous cartilaginous Mobula mantas, ten feet long and 600 pounds in weight, with triangular pectoral fins, a slight swelling in the middle of the back, and fixed eyes on the edge of the front part of the head; floating like wrecked ships, they sometimes adhered to our window like dark shutters. There were American triggerfish for which Nature had mixed only white and black paint, long, fleshy, feathered gobies with yellow fins and prominent jaws, and 1.6-metre scombroids of the species of albacores with short sharp teeth and a fine covering of scales. Then red mullets appeared in clouds, enclosed from head to tail in golden stripes and waving their glorious fins; they are true masterpieces of jewellery that were formerly offered to Diana,* particularly sought out by rich Romans and the subject of the proverb: 'Those that catch them don't eat them!' Finally golden *Pomacentri* passed before our eyes, decked out in emerald strips and clothed in velvet and silk, like lords out of Veronese; sparina sparids fled using their swift thoracic fins; fifteen-inch clupeids produced an aura of phosphorescent gleams; grey mullets threshed the water with their large fleshy tails; red Coregonids seemed to scythe the sea with their sharp pectoral fins; and silvery Selenes justified their name by rising on the horizon of the waters with milky gleams like so many moons.

How many other marvellous specimens I would have observed, if the *Nautilus* hadn't gradually dropped down towards the lower strata! Its inclined planes carried it down to depths of 2,000 then 3,500 metres. The animal life now consisted only of crinoids, starfish, charming medusa-head pentacrinites whose straight stems supported small calyxes, top-shells, bloody dentalia, and fissurella, coastal molluscs of great size.

On 20 April we had come back up to an average depth of 1,500 metres. The closest land was the Bahamas, spread like cobblestones over the surface of the waters. High submarine cliffs rose, vertical walls of roughly hewn blocks resting on wide bases, with black holes opening up between them whose ends our electric rays could not penetrate.

The rocks were carpeted with huge grasses, giant laminarias, and enormous wracks: a true espalier of hydrophytes worthy of a world of Titans.

From these colossal plants, Conseil, Ned, and I naturally turned to listing the gigantic animals of the sea. Some of them were evidently destined to be the food of others. However, through the windows of the *Nautilus*, almost motionless, I could not yet see anything clinging to the long filaments except the principal articulates of the division of brachyurans: decapods with long limbs, purple crabs, and clios peculiar to the seas of the West Indies.

It was about eleven o'clock when Ned Land drew my attention to a formidable swarming moving through the large expanses of seaweed.

'Well,' I said, 'these are real squids' caves, and I would not be surprised to see a few monsters here!'

'What?' said Conseil. 'Calamar, mere calamar of the class of cephalopods?'

'No,' I said, 'giant squid. But friend Land is undoubtedly mistaken, for I can't see anything.'

'What a shame,' replied Conseil. 'I long to come face to face with one of those squid I have heard about so often, which can drag ships down to the bottom of the seas. Those beasts are called Krak . . .'

'Crackpots . . .' the Canadian interjected.

'Krakens,' continued Conseil, without paying attention to his companion's joke.

'I will never be able to believe', said Land, 'in the existence of such animals.'

'Why ever not? We ended up believing in monsieur's narwhal.'

'We were wrong, Conseil.'

'Undoubtedly, but others still believe in it.'

'Probably, Conseil, but for my part I have resolved to admit the existence of such monsters only after I have dissected them with my own hand.'

'So', Conseil asked, 'monsieur does not believe in giant squid?'

'Hey, who the hell has ever believed in them?' exclaimed the Canadian.

'Many people, friend Ned.'

'Not fishermen. Scientists perhaps!'

'With respect, Ned: fishermen and scientists.'

'But as I stand here,' said Conseil in the most serious tone, 'I can perfectly remember seeing a large ship being dragged under the waves by the arms of a cephalopod.'

'You have seen that?' asked the Canadian.

'Yes Ned.'

'With your own eyes?'

'With my own eyes.'

'Where, please?'

'At Saint-Malo,' Conseil replied imperturbably.

'In the port?' Ned asked sarcastically.

'No, in a church.'

'In a church!'

'Yes friend Ned. It was a painting of the said squid!'*

'So!' said Ned Land, bursting out laughing. 'Mr Conseil has been leading me on!'

'Actually, he is right,' I said. 'I have heard of the painting, but the subject of the picture is taken from legend, and you know what should be thought of legends in natural history!* When people start talking about monsters, their imaginations easily go off at a tangent. Not only has it been claimed that these squid can drag down ships, but a certain Olaus Magnus speaks of a mile-long cephalopod,* which seemed more like an island than an animal. It is also said that one day the Bishop of Nidaros erected an altar on an immense rock. Once his mass was over, the rock started moving and returned to the sea.* The rock was a squid.'

'And that's all?' asked the Canadian.

'No,' I replied. 'Another bishop, Pontoppidan of Bergen, also speaks of a squid on which a whole regiment of cavalry could manœuvre!'

'They didn't mess around, those bishops of olden days!' Ned remarked.

'Finally, the naturalists of antiquity cite monsters whose jaws resembled bays, and which were too big to get through the Strait of Gibraltar!'

'You don't say!'

'But what truth is there in all those tales?' asked Conseil.

'None, my friends, at least none amongst the parts which go beyond the limits of plausibility and become fable or legend.

However, if no cause is needed for the imagination of storytellers, some sort of pretext is. It cannot be denied that there are very big squid and calamar, even if they are smaller than whales. Aristotle observed the dimensions of a squid five cubits long, that is 3.10 metres. Our fishermen frequently see ones longer than 1.8 metres. The museums of Trieste and Montpellier contain skeletons of squid that are two metres long. What is more, the naturalists have calculated that an animal only six feet in length would have tentacles of twenty-seven feet, which is more than enough to make a formidable monster.'

'And are they still caught nowadays?' asked the Canadian.

'If they are not caught, at least sailors still see them. One of my friends, Captain Paul Bos of Le Havre,* has often told me that he encountered one such colossal monster in the Indian Ocean. And the most astonishing thing happened a few years ago, in 1861, which no longer allows the existence of these gigantic animals to be denied.'

'Go on,' said Ned Land.

'Thank you. In 1861, north-east of Tenerife, at the approximate latitude where we are now, the crew of the sloop *Alecton* sighted an enormous squid swimming in its wake. Captain Bouyer* closed on the animal and attacked it with harpoons and guns, but without great success, for bullets and harpoons passed through the soft flesh like unset jelly. After several unsuccessful attempts, the crew managed to put a slip knot round the mollusc's body. The knot slid as far as the tail-fins and stopped there. They then tried to haul the monster on board, but it was so heavy that the rope pulled the tail off, and deprived of this adornment, it disappeared under the water.'

'Finally we have a fact.'

'An indisputable fact, my good Ned. That was why it was proposed to call it "Bouyer's squid".'

'And how long was it?' he asked.

'Did it not measure about six metres?' said Conseil, standing at the window and examining the holes in the cliff.

'Precisely,' I replied.

'Was its head not crowned with eight tentacles, which waved in the water like a nest of serpents?'

'Absolutely.'

'Were its eyes not extremely prominent and large?'

'Yes Conseil.'

'And was its mouth not a real parrot's beak, a formidable one at that?'

'Indeed.'

'Well, if monsieur pleases,' calmly replied Conseil, 'if that isn't Bouyer's squid, then at least it must be one of its brothers.'

I gaped at him. Ned rushed to the window.

'What a frightening beast!' he exclaimed.

I looked in turn, and could not hide a movement of repulsion. In front of my eyes moved a horrible monster, worthy of appearing in any teratological legend.

It was a squid of colossal dimensions, eight metres in length. It was moving backwards at extreme velocity as it headed towards the *Nautilus*. It was staring with its enormous fixed eyes of sea-green hue. Its eight arms, or rather legs, were not only implanted on its head, thus giving these animals the name of cephalopods, but were twice as big as its body and waving around like the Furies' hair. We could distinctly see the 250 suckers in the form of hemispherical capsules on the inside of the tentacles. Sometimes these suckers were placed on the salon's windows and stuck there. The monster's mouth—a horny beak like a parrot's—was opening and closing vertically. Its tongue emerged oscillating from this pair of shears, and was made of a horny substance, itself equipped with several rows of sharp teeth. What a freak of nature: a bird's beak on a mollusc! Its body, cylindrical but swollen in the middle, formed a fleshy mass that had to weigh 20 to 25 tons. Its colour changed in quick succession according to the animal's irritation, and went progressively from pale grey to reddish-brown.*

What was the mollusc irritated at? Undoubtedly at the *Nautilus*, more formidable than it, and on which its sucking arms and mandibles could not really take hold. And yet what monsters these squid were, what vitality the Creator had endowed them with, and what vigour their movements had, since they possessed three hearts!

Chance had brought us to this squid, and I did not want to waste the opportunity of closely studying such a specimen of cephalopod. I overcame the horror its appearance caused me, picked up a pencil, and began to draw it.

'Perhaps it is the same one as the *Alecton* saw,' said Conseil.

'It can't be,' replied the Canadian, 'since the other one lost its tail and this one still has it.'

'Not necessarily,' I replied. 'The arms and tails of these animals form again by redintegration, and in seven years the squid's tail has undoubtedly had the time to grow again.'

'In any case,' replied Ned, 'if it's not this one, it's perhaps one of those!'

Other squid were indeed appearing at the starboard window. I counted seven of them. They formed a procession accompanying the *Nautilus*, and I could hear the grinding of their beaks on the metal hull. We had plenty on our plate.

I continued my work. These monsters stayed in our wake with such precision that they seemed motionless, and I could have traced them directly on to the window. We were in fact moving at moderate speed.

Suddenly the *Nautilus* stopped. The shock made its whole framework tremble.

'Have we hit something?' I asked.

'If we have,' replied the Canadian, 'then we're free again.'

The *Nautilus* was undoubtedly disengaged again, but was no longer moving. Its propeller blades were not cutting the waves. A minute passed before Captain Nemo, followed by his first officer, came into the salon.

I had not seen him for some time. He look sombre. Without speaking to us, perhaps without even seeing us, he approached the panel, looked at the squid, and said a few words to his first officer. His deputy went out.

Soon the panels were closed again. The ceiling was lit up. I approached the captain.

'A curious collection of squid,' I said, in the detached tone a visitor would use in front of the window of an aquarium.

'Right,' he replied, 'and we are going to fight them hand to hand.'

I looked at the captain. I thought I had misheard.

'Hand to hand?' I repeated.

'Yes, monsieur. The propeller has stopped. I think that the corneous mandibles of one of the squid have got caught in its blades, preventing us moving.'

'And what are you going to do?'

'Surface, and massacre all the vermin.'

'A difficult task.'

'Electric bullets are indeed powerless against this soft flesh, for they do not find enough resistance to explode. But we will attack them with axes.'

'And with harpoons, monsieur,' said the Canadian, 'if you will accept my help.'

'I accept, Master Land.'

'We're right behind you,' I said as Captain Nemo headed for the central staircase.

About ten men armed with grappling axes were standing ready for an attack. Conseil and I picked up two as well. Land seized a harpoon.

The *Nautilus* meanwhile had surfaced. One of the sailors, standing on the top steps, was unscrewing the bolts of the hatch. But the bolts were hardly free when the hatch suddenly shot open, clearly yanked up by the suckers on the arm of a squid.

Immediately one of those long arms slid like a snake into the opening as twenty others waved above. With a single axe blow, Captain Nemo severed the formidable tentacle, which then slid down the stairs, twisting.

While we were all rushing together towards the platform, two other arms, lashing through the air, landed on the sailor in front of Captain Nemo—and carried him off with irresistible force.

Captain Nemo exclaimed and rushed outside. We followed him as quickly as we could.

What a scene! The poor man, seized by the tentacle and glued to its suckers, was being rocked in the air at the whim of its enormous trunk. He was groaning as he suffocated, and he was shouting: 'Au secours! Au secours!' These words in French flabbergasted me. So I had a compatriot on board, perhaps several! I will hear his heartbreaking appeal in my ears till the end of my life.

The unfortunate man was lost. Who could possibly have

wrested him from that powerful embrace? However, Captain Nemo rushed at the squid, and with a single axe blow chopped off another arm. His first officer was angrily fighting other monsters crawling over the sides of the *Nautilus*. The crew were attacking them with their axes. The Canadian, Conseil, and I were plunging our weapons into the fleshy masses. A strong smell of musk filled the atmosphere. It was horrible.

For a moment I thought that the poor man enlaced by the squid could be rescued from its powerful suction. Seven arms out of eight had been severed. A single one, brandishing the victim like a quill, remained twisting in the air. But just as Captain Nemo and his deputy were rushing at the animal, it gave out a spurt of blackish liquid, secreted from a bursa in its abdomen.* We were blinded. By the time the cloud had cleared, the squid had vanished, carrying with it my unfortunate compatriot.*

Then our rage boiled over against the monsters. We were no longer in control of ourselves. Ten or twelve squid had invaded the platform and sides of the *Nautilus*. We were sliding around in the midst of the truncated serpents, tossing about on the platform in waves of blood and black ink. It was as if the viscous tentacles were coming back to life again like Hydra's heads. Ned Land's harpoons plunged repeatedly into the glaucous eyes of the squid, destroying them with each blow. But my brave companion was suddenly knocked down by the tentacles of a monster he could not avoid.

God! My heart leapt with revulsion and horror! The formidable squid's beak gaped open before Ned. The poor man was about to be cut in two. I rushed to help him. But Captain Nemo had got there before me and his axe disappeared between the two enormous jaws. Miraculously saved, the Canadian got up and drove his harpoon right through the triple heart of the squid.

'For services rendered!' Captain Nemo said.

Ned bowed without replying.

The battle had lasted for a mere quarter of an hour. The vanquished monsters, mutilated and terribly wounded, finally retreated and then disappeared under the waves.

Captain Nemo, red* with blood, motionless near the searchlight, examined the sea which had swallowed up one of his companions, as large tears flowed from his eyes.

19

The Gulf Stream

NONE of us will ever forget that terrible scene of 20 April. I wrote about it under the imprint of powerful emotions. Since then, I have re-examined the narrative and read it to Conseil and Ned. They found it factually correct, but too pallid. To paint such a picture would take the pen of the most illustrious of our poets, the author of *Les Travailleurs de la mer*.*

I said that Captain Nemo was weeping as he regarded the waves. His grief was immense. This was the second companion he had lost since we had arrived on board, and what a death! This friend had been crushed, suffocated, and broken by the formidable arms of the squid, then ground in its iron jaw, and so would not be able to rest with his companions in the peaceful waters of the coral cemetery!

As for me, it was the cry of despair the wretch uttered in the midst of the battle which had torn my heart. The poor Frenchman had forgotten his conventional language and had gone back to speaking the tongue of his country and his mother to issue his ultimate appeal.* Amongst the crew of the *Nautilus*, tied to Captain Nemo body and soul, like him fleeing contact with humanity, I had a compatriot! Was he the only one representing France in this mysterious association clearly composed of individuals of different nationalities? This was yet another of the unanswerable questions constantly surfacing in my mind.

Captain Nemo went back to his room, and I did not see him for some time. But how clearly sad, desperate, and irresolute he was, if I can judge the st. 'e of his soul from our ship, which reflected all his moods! The *Nautilus* no longer maintained a fixed course. It came, it went, it drifted like a plaything of the waves. Its propeller had been freed, and yet was hardly used. The *Nautilus* was sailing at random, unable to tear itself away from the scene of its great battle, the sea which had swallowed up one of its members!

Ten days went by in this way. It was only on 1 May that the

Nautilus again set a clear course for the north, after sighting the Bahamas at the opening of the Old Bahama Channel. We were following the current of the sea's largest river, with its own banks, its own fish, and its own temperature. I refer to the Gulf Stream.

It is indeed a river, flowing freely through the middle of the Atlantic, but without mixing with the surrounding ocean's water. It is a salt river, saltier than the surrounding sea. Its average depth is 3,000 feet, and width, 60 miles. At places it moves at a speed of 4 kilometres an hour. The unchanging volume of its water is larger than all the rivers of the globe put together.

The true source of the Gulf Stream, discovered by Commander Maury, its starting-point so to speak, is the Golfe de Gascogne. There its pale water, still cool, begins to collect. It heads southwards, runs down equatorial Africa, warms its water under the rays of the Tropics, crosses the Atlantic, reaches Cape São Roque on the Brazilian coast, and then splits into two branches, with one heading off to replenish itself in the warm molecules of the Caribbean. Then the Gulf Stream begins its role as moderator, for it is designed to re-establish the equilibrium between temperatures and to mix the water of the Tropics with the northern waters. Superheated in the Gulf of Mexico, it heads north along the American coast, reaches as far as Nova Scotia, changes direction under the impact of the cold current from the Davis Strait, and heads back out into the ocean. Following a line of latitude, the loxodromic line, it splits in two at about the 43rd degree, with one branch, helped by the north-east trade wind, returning to the Golfe de Gascogne and the Azores, and the other, having slightly warmed the shores of Ireland and Norway, heading past Spitsbergen, where it falls to 4° and joins the open sea of the Pole.*

It was on this oceanic river that the *Nautilus* was sailing. When it leaves the Old Bahama Channel, which is over fourteen leagues wide and 350 metres deep, the Gulf Stream moves at 8 kilometres an hour, but this speed decreases constantly as it heads north. Indeed, we have to hope that this regularity is maintained; for if its speed and direction were ever to change, as some people believe is happening already, the climate of Europe will undergo changes of an unforeseeable nature.

At about midday I was on the platform with Conseil. I

explained to him the peculiarities of the Gulf Stream. When my explanation was over, I asked him to put his hand in the current. Conseil obeyed, and was astonished to feel a sensation of neither cold nor warmth.

'This is because the water of the Gulf Stream when it leaves the Gulf of Mexico is at almost blood-temperature. The Gulf Stream is a huge reservoir of heat, allowing the coasts of Europe to clothe themselves in permanent foliage, and if Maury can be believed, the heat of this current would provide enough calorific value to maintain in fusion a river of molten iron as big as the Amazon or the Missouri.'

At this point the Gulf Stream was moving at 2.25 metres a second. Its current is so distinct from the surrounding sea that its water clearly stands out from the cold water of the rest of the ocean. Darker and with a greater concentration of saline matter, its pure indigo stands out from the green water around it. Such indeed is the clearness of the line of demarcation, that off the Carolinas the *Nautilus* visibly had its cutwater in the Gulf Stream, while its propeller was still beating the ocean.

This current held a whole universe of living beings within it. The argonauts, so common in the Mediterranean, sailed here in numerous schools. Amongst the cartilaginous fish, the most remarkable were the rays, whose slender tails made up about a third of their bodies, in vast rhomboids 25 feet long. We also saw some small, metre-long sharks, with big heads, short rounded snouts, several rows of pointed teeth, and bodies apparently covered in scales.

Amongst the bony fish, I noted some dusky labra particular to these seas; some lane sparids with irises shining like fires; some metre-long sciaenas with large jaws bristling with tiny teeth, and which produce a slight cry; some of the *Acanthurus nigricans* mentioned above; blue dolphinfish picked out in gold and silver; parrot fish, true oceanic rainbows competing in colour with the most beautiful birds of the Tropics; naked blennies with triangular heads; bluish rhombuses without scales; Batrachoidids with a crossways yellow strip representing a Greek *t*; swarms of small *Gobiosomae bosc* covered with brown blotches; lungfish with silvery heads and yellow tails; various examples of Salmonids;

mullets with slender waists and dazzling soft lustres, fish which Lacépède dedicated to his good lady wife; and finally a beautiful fish, the American *Eques lanceolatus* decorated with all the orders and bedecked with all the ribbons, which frequents the shores of that great nation where ribbons and orders are so little valued.

I will add that during the night, the phosphorescent water of the Gulf Stream competed with the electric beam from our searchlight, especially in the stormy weather that frequently assailed us.

On 8 May we were still off Cape Hatteras, opposite North Carolina. The width of the Gulf Stream is 75 miles here, and its depth, 210 metres. The *Nautilus* continued to wander as it wished. It was as if there was no lookout on board. I will admit that an escape would have been possible in these conditions. There were populated shores offering easy refuge everywhere. The sea was constantly crossed by numerous steamers between New York and Boston and the Gulf of Mexico, and was full day and night of the little schooners plying between various points on the American coast. We could hope to be picked up. It was in sum a perfect opportunity, despite the 30 miles between the *Nautilus* and the coast of the Union.

But an unfortunate circumstance scuppered the Canadian's plans. The weather was very bad. We were approaching waters where there were frequent storms, the home of waterspouts and cyclones generated by none other than the Gulf Stream. To confront an often raging sea in a frail boat was to face certain death. Even Ned Land agreed. So he reined in his terrible homesickness, that only escape could cure.

'Monsieur,' he said that day, 'it's got to finish. I have to know what's what. Your Nemo is steering clear of land and heading north, but I tell you I have already had enough of the South Pole, and am not going with him to the North Pole.'

'What can we do, Ned, since escape is impossible for the moment?'

'I come back to my original idea. The captain needs to be confronted. You said nothing when we were in your home seas. I want to speak now that we are in mine. When I think that in a few days' time the *Nautilus* is going to be off Nova Scotia, that a large bay opens out there near Newfoundland, and that the St Lawrence empties into that same bay! When I think that the St Lawrence is my own river, the river of my home town, Québec; when I think of all this, I get very angry. My hair stands on end. Look monsieur, I would prefer to throw myself into the sea! I can't stay here! I'm suffocating!'

The Canadian was clearly at the end of his tether. His energetic personality could not get used to our extended imprisonment. His physiognomy was changing from day to day. His personality was getting gloomier and gloomier. I knew how much he was suffering for I too was feeling homesick. It was nearly seven months since our last news from land. In addition, Captain Nemo's isolation, his taciturnity, and especially his changed mood since the battle with the squid—all this made things appear in a different light to me. I no longer felt the same enthusiasm as at the beginning. One had to be a Fleming like Conseil to accept an environment designed for whales and sea creatures. Truly, if this good fellow had had gills instead of lungs, I think he would have made a very good fish.

'Well monsieur?' Land asked again, seeing that I was not going to reply.

'Well Ned, do you want me to ask Captain Nemo what his intentions are?'

'Yes monsieur.'

'Even though he has already told us?'

'Yes, I want to be doubly certain. Say it's from me, from me alone if you want.'

'But I rarely meet him. He even seems to be avoiding me.'

'All the more reason for going and seeing him.'

'I will ask him.'

'When?' asked the Canadian insistently.

'When I next meet him.'

'Dr Aronnax, do you want me to go and see him myself?'

'No, let me do it. Tomorrow . . .'

'Today.'

'All right. I will see him today,' I replied to Ned, who would certainly have ruined everything if he had acted on his own.

I remained alone; having decided to put our case, I resolved to get it over with immediately. I like things that are done more than things still to do.

I returned to my own room. From there I could hear steps in Captain Nemo's. The opportunity of seeing him had to be seized. I knocked on his door. There was no reply. I knocked again, then turned the knob. The door opened.

I went in. The captain was there. Bent over his desk, he had not heard me. Determined not to leave until I had spoken to him, I went up to him. He raised his head, frowned brusquely, and said to me in an abrupt tone:

'You here! What do you want?'

'To speak to you, captain.'

'But I am busy, monsieur, I am working. Will you not give me the same freedom to remain alone that I give to you?'

This reception was hardly encouraging. But I was determined to hear him out so I could respond to everything he said.

'Monsieur,' I said coldly, 'I have to speak to you of a matter which will suffer no delay.'

'Which matter monsieur?' he replied sarcastically. 'Have you made some discovery which has slipped my attention? Has the sea yielded you some new secret?'

We were still a long way off the point. Before I could reply, he showed me a manuscript open on his desk, and said to me in a graver tone:

'This, Dr Aronnax, is written in several languages. It contains a summary of my studies on the sea, and God willing, it will not perish with me. This manuscript, signed with my name and containing the story of my life, will be enclosed in a small floating container.* The last survivor from among us on board the *Nautilus* will cast the container into the sea, and it will go wherever the waves carry it.'

The name of this man! His own story written by himself! Would his mystery be unveiled one day? But at this moment,* I only saw what he said as a way of broaching my subject.

'Captain,' I replied, 'I can only approve your intentions. The results of your studies must not be lost. But the means you employ seem slightly crude to me. Who knows where the wind will send the container, into whose hands it will fall? Why don't you or one of your men . . .?'

'Never, monsieur!' said the captain, sharply interrupting me.

'But my companions and I would be prepared to keep this manuscript secret, and if you gave us back our freedom . . .'

'Your freedom!' repeated Captain Nemo, getting up.

'Yes monsieur, and it is this subject that I wanted to speak to you about. We have been on board your vessel seven months, and I wish to ask you today, in my name and my companions', if your intention is to keep us here for ever.'

'Dr Aronnax,' said Captain Nemo, 'I will answer you today as I answered you seven months ago: he who enters the *Nautilus* is destined never to leave it again.'

'But you are inflicting slavery on us!'

'Give it whatever name you wish.'

'But everywhere you go the slave retains the right to regain his freedom! And no holds are barred in how he attempts to do this!'

'Who is depriving you of that right?' replied Captain Nemo. 'Have I ever thought of binding you with oaths?'

The captain was staring at me with his arms crossed.

'Monsieur,' I said to him, 'covering this same ground a second time would be to neither your taste nor mine. So since this subject has been opened, let's make sure we close it. I repeat, I am not the only one concerned. For me, study is a support, a powerful diversion, an absorption, a passion which can help me forget everything. Like you, I can live ignored and obscure in the fragile hope of some day leaving the results of my work to the future, in a risky container entrusted to the winds and waves of chance. In short, I admire you and happily follow you in your role, part of which I can understand. But there are other aspects of your life I have caught glimpses of, which remain shrouded in confusion and mystery, and in which my companions and I have no part. Even on the occasions when our hearts have gone out to you, moved by some of your pain or your acts of genius or courage, we have had to hide all signs of the sympathy that comes from the sight of what is fine and good, whether displayed by friend or enemy. Well, it is this feeling that we are foreign to everything that concerns you which makes our position untenable. An impossible one even for me, but doubly impossible for Ned. Every human being, by the very fact of being human, is worthy of respect. Have you ever asked yourself what plans of vengeance could be engendered by the love of freedom and hatred of slavery in a nature like the Canadian's, what he could think or do . . .?'

I fell silent. Captain Nemo got up.

'Ned Land can think or do as he wishes. What difference does it make to me? It was not I who sought out his company. It is not for my own pleasure that I keep him on board my vessel! As for you, Dr Aronnax, you are acute enough to understand anything, even silence. I have nothing more to say to you. May this first time that you have raised this subject be also the last; I will not even be able to listen to you a second time.'*

I withdrew. Starting from that day, our relationship was very tense. I relayed the conversation to my two companions.

'We now know', said Ned, 'that there is nothing to be expected from this man. The *Nautilus* is approaching Long Island. We will try to escape, whatever the weather.'

But the sky was becoming more and more threatening. Signs of a hurricane were approaching. The air was turning pale white, even milky. The fine sheaves of cirrus on the horizon were being replaced by strata of nimbo-cumulus. Other low-lying clouds were quickly fleeing. The sea was roughening as it rolled in in long swells. The birds were disappearing, with the exception of the petrels, which revel in storms. The barometer was lowering markedly, showing an exceptional amount of moisture in the air. The contents of the storm-glass were decomposing with the electricity filling the air. A battle of the elements was nigh.

The storm broke on that same 18 May,* when the *Nautilus* was off Long Island and a few miles from the passes into New York. I am able to describe this battle of the elements, because Captain Nemo had an inexplicable caprice and decided to face it on the surface, instead of fleeing to the depths of the sea.

The wind was blowing from the south-west, first as a near gale, namely at 15 metres a second, and then increasing to 25 at about three in the afternoon. In other words, a storm had blown up.

Captain Nemo, unshakeable in the blasts, had taken position on the platform. He had made himself fast at the waist, to resist the huge wash of the waves. I had hoisted myself up and attached myself as well, dividing my admiration between the storm and the incomparable man defying it.

The unchained sea was being swept by large shreds of clouds that dipped into the waves. I could no longer see any of those small intermediate waves that form at the bottom of big troughs. Nothing but long fuliginous undulations, whose crests were so firm that they did not break. Mutually aroused by each other, their height grew. Now lying on its side, now erect like a mast, the *Nautilus* was pitching and rolling frighteningly.

At about five o'clock, a torrential rain fell, but did not suppress the wind or sea. A hurricane unleashed itself at a speed of 45 metres a second, that is nearly 40 leagues an hour. In such conditions it tears tiles from roofs and smashes them into doors, breaks iron grilles, knocks down houses, and bodily moves 24-calibre cannon. And yet even in the midst of the storm the *Nautilus* bore out the words of a wise engineer: 'There is no well-constructed hull that cannot withstand the sea!' This was not a fixed rock, that the waves would have demolished, but a mobile and obedient steel cylinder, without rigging or masts, and so able to resist the fury without suffering any damage.

I carefully examined the unleashed waves. They measured up to 15 metres high by 150 to 175 metres long, and their speed was 15 metres a second, or half that of the wind. Their volume and power increased with the depth of the water. I understood then the role of the waves, capturing air and sending it down to the bottom of the sea, together with life-giving oxygen. It has been calculated that their pressure reaches the enormous figure of 3,000 kilograms per square foot of surface they batter. It was waves like this which moved a block in the Hebrides weighing 42 tons. It was they that, having flattened part of Tokyo in Japan in the storm of 23 December 1864, went and broke on the shores of America the very same day, having crossed at 700 kilometres an hour.

The intensity of the tempest increased as dusk fell. The barometer dropped to 710 millimetres, as happened during a cyclone in 1860 in Réunion. As the day ended, I saw a large ship passing on the horizon and struggling with great difficulty. It lay to at low steam in order to remain head-on to the wind. It was clearly one of the lines from New York to Liverpool or Le Havre. It soon disappeared into the darkness.

At ten o'clock the sky appeared to be on fire. The air was sundered by powerful flashes of lightning. I could not stand the light, but Captain Nemo contemplated them face on, as if drawing the soul of the storm into him. A terrifying sound filled the air, a complex sound composed of the roar of crushed waves, moans from the wind, and peals of thunder. The wind turned to all points of the compass, as the cyclone, which had started from the east, went back there after turning through north, west, and south, having rotated the opposite way from the storms of the southern hemisphere.

Ah, the Gulf Stream! It fully justified its name of Ruler of Storms! It is the Gulf Stream which creates these frightening cyclones from the temperature difference between the air strata and its own currents.

The drops had become a fiery rain. The tiny points of water had changed into exploding crests. It was exactly as if Captain Nemo, desiring a death worthy of him, was endeavouring to be struck by lightning. In a terrible movement of pitching, the *Nautilus* erected its steel ram into the air like the point of a lightning conductor, and I could see long sparks spurting from it.

Exhausted, with no strength left, I crawled on my stomach to the hatch. I opened it, and climbed back down again to the salon. The storm was now reaching its maximum strength. It was impossible to stand up inside the *Nautilus*.

Captain Nemo came in about midnight. I could hear the tanks filling gradually as the submarine gently sank below the surface of the waves.

Through the open windows of the salon, I could see great frightened fish, passing like ghosts through the fiery waters. A few were struck by lightning in front of my eyes.

The *Nautilus* was still going down. I thought that it would find calm water at a depth of fifteen metres. But the upper strata were being shaken too violently. It needed to seek repose at fifty metres within the bowels of the sea.

But what calm there, what silence, what peace! Who could have thought that a terrifying hurricane was being unleashed at that moment on the surface of the same ocean?

20

47° 24′ N, 17° 28′ W

AFTER this storm we were pushed eastwards. All hope disappeared of escaping to the landfalls of New York or the St Lawrence. Poor Ned, desperate, shut himself away like Captain Nemo. Conseil and I never left each other's company.

I have said that the *Nautilus* headed east. More precisely, I should have said north-east. For several days it wandered, now beneath the surface, now on top amongst those fogs that are so feared by navigators. They are mainly caused by ice melting, which produces a very high degree of humidity in the atmosphere. How many ships have been lost in these waters just when they were about to sight the glimmering lights of the coast! How many wrecks due to these opaque blankets! How many impacts on reefs whose undertow was hidden by the sound of the wind! How many collisions between ships, in spite of their position lights and the warnings of their whistles and alarm bells!

As a result, the floor of the sea resembled a battle-scene, where still lay all the vanquished of the ocean: some old and already coated, others young and reflecting the light from our searchlight on their copper fittings and hulls. Amongst them, how many vessels lost with all hands and their community of immigrants on the dangerous spots of Cape Race, St Paul Island, the Strait of Belle Isle, and the St Lawrence estuary, notorious in the accident statistics! And in just the last few years, how many victims have been added to those funereal annals by the Royal Mail, Inman, and Montreal lines! How many ships: the *Solway*, the *Isis*, the *Parramatta*, the *Hungarian*, the *Canadian*, the *Anglo-Saxon*, the *Humboldt*, and the *United States*, all wrecked; the *Arctic* and the *Lyonnais*, sunk in a collision; and the *President*, the *Pacific*, and the *City of Glasgow*,* all vanished, cause unknown: sombre debris, amongst which the *Nautilus* navigated as though inspecting the dead!

On 15 May we were at the southern tip of the Bank of Newfoundland. This bank is the product of considerable amounts of marine alluvion, an accumulation of organic waste brought either from the equator by the current of the Gulf Stream or from the North Pole by the counter-current of cold water running down the American coast. Erratic blocks of disintegrating ice were piled up on one another, and a vast bone cemetery of billions of dead fish, molluscs, and zoophytes had built up.

The sea is not very deep at the Bank of Newfoundland, a few hundred fathoms at most. But to the south, a deep depression suddenly drops, a 3,000-metre hole. There the Gulf Stream grows wider and its current spreads out. But in losing speed and temperature, it becomes a sea.

Amongst the fish that the *Nautilus* frightened as it passed, I will cite the metre-long cyclopteroid with a black back and orange stomach, providing an example of conjugal fidelity rarely followed by its congeners, a huge Forsskål's stingray, a sort of emerald moray eel which has an excellent taste, big-eyed carracks whose heads resemble dogs', blennies viviparous like snakes, 20-centimetre dusky frillgobies or black gudgeons, and *Macrura* with long tails and shining with a silvery glitter: quick fish that had ventured far from the hyperborean seas.

The nets also brought in a fish that is daring, audacious, energetic, muscly, and armed with spines on its head and spurs on its fins, a real two- or three-metre scorpion, the relentless enemy of the blennies, gadids, and salmon: this was the cottus of the southern seas, with a brown tuberculous body and red fins. The fishermen of the *Nautilus* found it difficult to seize hold of this animal, which uses the shape of its opercula to protect its respiratory organs from the drying effect of the atmosphere and so can live some time out of water.

I will cite—for the record—naked blennies, which are small fish that accompany ships in the northern seas, oxyrhynchous whitebait found only in the northern Atlantic, and scorpion fish; and so I reach the gadids, principally from the species of cod, which I surprised in their favourite waters on that inexhaustible Bank of Newfoundland.

These cod can be said to be mountain fish, for Newfoundland is really a submarine mountain. While the *Nautilus* opened up a route for itself through their crowded battalions, Conseil could not refrain from making an observation:

'Are those cod?' he said. 'But I thought that cod were flat like dab or sole?'

'Fool!' I exclaimed. 'Cod are only flat at the grocer's shop, where they are slit open and spread out. But in the water, they are spindle-shaped like mullet, and perfectly adapted for swimming.'

'I can well believe monsieur,' replied Conseil. 'What a swarm, what an ant-heap!'

'Eh, my friend, there would be more without their enemies, namely scorpion fish and men! Do you know how many eggs have been found in a single female?'

'Let's not be stingy. Five hundred thousand.'

'Eleven million, my friend.'

'Eleven million! I will never believe it until I have counted them myself.'

'Count them, Conseil. But it would be quicker if you believed me. In any case, the French, British, Americans, Danes, and Norwegians catch thousands of cod. They are consumed in tremendous quantities, and without the astonishing fecundity of these fish, the seas would soon be emptied of them. In Britain and America alone, 5,000 ships with 75,000 men work at cod fishing. Each ship brings back 40,000 fish on average, which makes a total of 25 million.* On the coasts of Norway, the same again.'

'Well, I will trust monsieur, and not count them.'

'Pardon?'

'The eleven million eggs. But I will simply make a remark.'

'Yes?'

'That all the eggs hatched by four cod would be sufficient to feed Britain, America, and Norway.'

While we were skimming over the bottom of the Bank of Newfoundland, I could easily see the hundreds of long lines, each with two hundred hooks, deployed by each boat. The lines, dragged along using small clips, were stopped from sinking by lines fixed to cork buoys. The *Nautilus* had to manœuvre carefully through this submarine network.

But in any case we did not remain long in these busy waters. The *Nautilus* moved up to the 42nd degree of latitude. This was off St John's, Newfoundland, and the port of Heart's Content, where the transatlantic cable ends.

Instead of continuing northwards, the *Nautilus* headed east, as if wanting to follow the telegraphic plateau on which the cable rests, and whose relief has been mapped out with extreme precision by large numbers of soundings.

It was on 17 May, approximately 500 miles from Heart's Content and at a depth of 2,800 metres, that I first spotted the cable lying on the ground. I had not warned Conseil, and initially he took it for a gigantic sea serpent, and was about to classify it according to his usual method. But I soon enlightened the worthy fellow, and to make up for his disappointment, told him various details of the laying of the cable.

The first one was laid in 1857–8; but it stopped working after transmitting about 400 telegrams. In 1863 the engineers constructed a new cable, measuring 3,400 kilometres and weighing 4,500 tons, and loaded it on to the *Great Eastern*. This attempt also failed.

On 25 May the *Nautilus* was at 3,836 metres' depth, and at the precise spot where the first break happened that halted the enterprise. It occurred 638 miles from the coast of Ireland. It was realized at two o'clock one afternoon that communication with Europe had been interrupted. The electricians on board decided to cut the cable before bringing it up again, and by eleven o'clock they had brought up the damaged parts. A join and splice were made; and then the cable was let down again. But a few days later it broke once more and could not be retrieved from the depths.

The Americans were not discouraged. The audacious Cyrus Field,* the promoter of the enterprise, who was risking his entire fortune, launched a new subscription. It was immediately snapped up. Another cable was installed taking greater precautions. The cluster of conducting wires was insulated in an envelope of gutta-percha, but also protected by a covering of textile matter, in turn contained in a metal casing. The *Great Eastern* sailed off again on 13 July 1866.

This time the operation worked well. However, one incident did occur. Several times while unrolling the cable, the electricians noticed that nails had recently been driven into it so as to damage its core. Captain Anderson* and his officers and engineers held a meeting, discussed the problem, and put up notices saying that if the guilty party were found, he would be thrown into the sea without further sentencing. From that moment on, the criminal acts did not reoccur.

On 23 July the *Great Eastern* was only 800 kilometres off Newfoundland, when the news of the armistice between Prussia and Austria after Sadowa* was telegraphed to it from Ireland. On the 27th it sighted Heart's Content through the fog. The enterprise had succeeded, and in its first telegram, young America sent old Europe wise words which are so rarely understood: 'Glory to God in the highest, and on earth peace, good will towards men.'*

I did not expect to find the electric cable in the same state as when it came out of the workshops. The long serpent, covered with the remains of shells and bristling with foraminifers, had indeed become encrusted in a stony coat, thus protecting it from the perforators of molluscs. It rested calmly, sheltered from the movements of the sea, at a pressure suitable for the transmission of the electric spark, which goes from America to Europe in 0.32 seconds. The life of this cable will undoubtedly be infinite, for it has been observed that its gutta-percha covering actually improves from being kept in salt water.

In addition, this plateau is very well chosen, and the cable is never submerged so deep that it could break. The *Nautilus* followed it to its lowest point at 4,431 metres, where it was still lying without undue stretching. Then we approached the spot where the 1863 accident happened.

The ocean floor formed a valley 120 kilometres wide: Mont Blanc could have been put in it without emerging from the surface of the water. This valley is enclosed to the east by a vertical wall 2,000 metres high. We arrived there on 28 May; the *Nautilus* was only 150 kilometres away from Ireland.

Was Captain Nemo going to head north, so that he could land in the British Isles? No; to my great surprise, he went back down south again, heading for the seas of Europe. While we were working our way around the Emerald Isle, I briefly glimpsed Cape Clear and Fastnet lighthouse which provides light for thousands of ships from Glasgow and Liverpool.

An important question then arose in my mind. Would the *Nautilus* dare to venture into the English Channel? Ned Land had reappeared since we had come close to land, and never stopped asking me. How could I answer? Captain Nemo remained invisible. Having let the Canadian catch a glimpse of the shores of America, was he now going to show me the coasts of France?

The *Nautilus* was still heading south. On 30 May it came within sight of Land's End, and passed between that extreme point of England and the Scilly Isles, on the starboard side.

If it wanted to go into the Channel, it would have to cut sharply to the east. It did not do this.

During the whole of 31 May the *Nautilus* described a series of circles on the surface, greatly intriguing me. It seemed to be looking for a spot which it had difficulty in finding. At noon, Captain Nemo came to measure the position himself. He did not speak to me. He seemed more sombre than ever. What could be making him so unhappy? Was it being so close to European shores? Did he have memories of his abandoned homeland? In that case, what did he experience—remorse or regret? For a long time such thoughts filled my mind, and I had a hunch that chance would shortly betray the captain's secrets.

The following day, 1 June, the *Nautilus* performed the same manœuvres. It was clear that it was trying to identify a precise point in the ocean. As on the day before, Captain Nemo came to take the height of the sun. The sea was fine, the sky pure. Eight miles to the east, a large steam-driven ship stood out on the line of the horizon. No flag was visible on its gaff and I could not identify its nationality.

A few moments before the sun passed the meridian, Captain Nemo took his sextant and made extremely precise observations. The absolute stillness of the water facilitated his operation, since the *Nautilus* lay motionless, neither pitching nor rolling.

I was on the platform. When he had taken our position, the captain said only these words:

'It is here!'

He went back down through the hatch. Had he seen the vessel, which now changed direction and seemed to be coming nearer? I cannot say.

I went back to the salon. The hatch was closed, and I could hear the hissing of water in the tanks. The *Nautilus* began to sink—straight down, for its propeller was not operating and so did not affect its movement.

A few minutes later, it stopped at a depth of 833 metres, and came to rest on the ocean floor.

The salon's luminous ceiling went out, the panels opened, and through the windows I could see the sea brightly lit up by the searchlight for half a mile around.

I looked to port, but could see nothing but the immensity of the calm water.

On the seabed to starboard appeared a large extumescence which drew my attention. It resembled ruins buried under a coating of whitish shells like a cloak of snow. When I examined the shape more carefully, I thought I recognized the thickened forms of a ship without masts, which must have sunk bow first. The wreck certainly dated from a long time before. Its hull must have spent many years on the ocean floor to be so encrusted by limestone from the water.

What was this ship? Why was the *Nautilus* coming to visit its tomb? Was it not some shipwreck that had sunk the vessel?

I did not know what to think, when near me I heard Captain Nemo saying in a slow voice:

'Formerly this ship was called the *Marseillais*. It carried 74 cannons and was launched in 1762. On 13 August 1778, commanded by Lapoype-Vertrieux, it fought bravely against the *Preston*. On 4 July 1779, it took part in the capture of Grenada with the fleet of Admiral d'Estaing. On 5 September 1781, it participated in the fighting in Chesapeake Bay with the Count of Grasse. In 1794, the French Republic gave the ship a new name. On 16 April of the same year, it joined the fleet of Villaret de Joyeuse in Brest, charged with escorting a convoy of wheat from America under the command of Admiral Vanstabel.* On 11 and 12 *Prairial* of the year II, this fleet encountered British vessels. Monsieur, it is today 13 *Prairial*, 1 June 1868. Seventy-four years ago to the day, on this same spot of 47° 24′ N, 17° 28′ W, this ship lost two of its three masts in a heroic battle; it had taken on water and a third of its crew were out of action. It preferred to scuttle itself with its 356 crew rather than surrender. Nailing its flag to the poop, it disappeared under the waves with the cry "Long live the Republic!"'

'The *Vengeur*!'* I exclaimed.

'Yes, monsieur.* The *Vengeur*! A fine name!'* said Captain Nemo, crossing his arms.

21

A Massacre

THE way he spoke, the unexpectedness of the scene, the recounting of the story of the patriotic ship, and the vehemence with which this strange character had pronounced the last words about the *Vengeur*, leaving me in no doubt about his meaning: everything combined to make a deep impression on me. My eyes no longer left the captain. With his arm stretched out towards the sea, he was studying the glorious wreck* with glowing eyes. Perhaps I would never know who he was, where he came from, where he was going, but I could see the man more and more distinctly from the scientist. It was not common misanthropy that had enclosed Captain Nemo and his companions in the flanks of the *Nautilus*, but a monstrous or sublime hatred that time could not diminish.*

Was this hatred still seeking revenge? The future would soon show me.

Meanwhile the *Nautilus* was moving slowly up to the surface, and I could see the indistinct forms of the *Vengeur* disappearing little by little. Soon a slight rolling told me that we were floating in the open air.

At this moment a dull explosion sounded. I looked at the captain. He did not move.

'Captain?' I said.

He did not reply.

I left him and went up to the platform. Conseil and the Canadian were there before me.

'Where did that explosion come from?' I asked.

'From the firing of a cannon,' replied Ned.

I looked in the direction of the ship that I had seen. It had got nearer and was clearly sailing at full steam. It was now six miles away.

'What sort of vessel is it, Ned?'

'From its rigging and its low masts, I would bet that it is a warship. I hope it comes at us and sinks us if need be, our damned *Nautilus*!'

'Friend Ned,' replied Conseil, 'what harm can it do to the *Nautilus*? Will it come and attack it underwater? Will it shell it at the bottom of the seas?'

'Tell me Ned,' I said, 'can you see the nationality of the vessel?'

The Canadian screwed up his brows, lowered his eyelids, concentrated his vision at their edges, and stared for a few moments at the ship with all the power of his eyes.

'No monsieur, I can't see what nation it belongs to. Its flag is not hoisted. But I can tell that it is a warship, for there is a long pennant at the end of the mainmast.'

For a quarter of an hour we continued to observe the ship as it steamed towards us. I could not accept, however, that it had recognized the *Nautilus* at such a distance, still less that it knew what this submarine machine was.

Soon the Canadian announced to me that the vessel was a great warship with a cutwater: an armour-plated double-decker. Thick black smoke was pouring from its two funnels. Its furled sails could not be distinguished from the yard line. Its gaff bore no flag. The distance still stopped the colours of its pennant from being identifiable, for they hung down in a thin ribbon.

It was coming nearer quickly. If Captain Nemo allowed it to approach, we stood a chance of being saved.

'Monsieur, if this ship passes within a mile, I am going to throw myself into the sea, and I urge you to do the same.'

I did not reply to the Canadian's proposal, but continued to watch the ship as it got larger. Whether British, French, American, or Russian, it was certain that it would pick us up, if only we could reach it.

'Monsieur should be so kind as to remember', interjected Conseil, 'that we have some experience of swimming. He can entrust to me the task of towing him to the ship, if it suits him to follow friend Ned.'

I was going to reply, when white smoke spurted out from the

stern of the warship. A few seconds later, the water was disturbed by the impact of a heavy body, splashing the stern of the *Nautilus*. Shortly afterwards, an explosion struck my ear.

'What! Are they firing at us?' I exclaimed.

'Good for them,' murmured Ned.

'So they are not taking us for shipwrecked people clinging to a wreck!'

'With respect, monsieur . . . oh!' said Conseil, shaking off the water that a new shell had splashed on to him. 'With respect, monsieur, they have seen a narwhal and they are firing their cannon at the narwhal.'

'But they must see full well', I expostulated, 'that they are dealing with people!'

'Perhaps for that very reason!' said Land staring at me.

A sudden revolution took place in my mind. The existence of the so-called monster must have been cleared up. When the Canadian struck it with his harpoon during the encounter with the *Abraham Lincoln*, Captain Farragut must have realized that the narwhal was a submarine boat, more dangerous than any supernatural cetacean.

Yes, that had to be the case, and this terrible machine of destruction was clearly being pursued over every ocean!

It would indeed be terrible if Captain Nemo was using the *Nautilus* for the sake of revenge, as now seemed clear! During that night in the middle of the Indian Ocean when he had locked us up in that cell, had he not attacked some ship?* That man buried in the coral cemetery, had he not been a victim of the collision caused by the *Nautilus*? Yes, I repeat: it had to be so. Part of Captain Nemo's mysterious life had been unveiled, and if his identity was still not clear, at least the coalition of nations against him were no longer pursuing a fantastic being, but a man who had sworn implacable hatred against them!

All this formidable past appeared before my eyes. Instead of encountering friends on the approaching ship, we could only find merciless enemies.

Meanwhile the shells were increasing around us. Some of them hit the surface of the sea, bounced off, and went considerable distances. But none hit the *Nautilus*.

The armour-plated ship was no more than three miles away

now. In spite of the violent cannon attack, Captain Nemo did not appear on the platform, and yet if one of those conical projectiles had squarely struck the hull of the *Nautilus*, it would have been fatal.

The Canadian then said:

'Monsieur, we must try everything to get out of this situation we're in. Let's make signals! Heck! Perhaps they will realize that we are honest men!'

Ned Land took out his handkerchief and waved it in the air. But he had hardly raised it when, despite his tremendous strength, he was floored by an iron hand and cast to the deck.

'Wretch!' exclaimed the captain. 'Do you want me to nail your miserable carcass to the cutwater of the *Nautilus* when it launches itself at that ship!'

Captain Nemo, terrible to hear, was yet more terrifying to behold. His face had grown pale: his heart must have undergone spasms and stopped beating for a moment. His pupils were highly contracted. His mouth was no longer speaking, it was roaring. With his body bent forward, he was twisting the Canadian's shoulders in his hands.

Then, letting him go and turning again to the man-of-war, whose shells were raining down around him:

'Ah, you know who I am, ship of an accursed nation!'* he declaimed in a powerful voice. 'As for me, I do not need your colours to identify you! Look, I am going to show you mine!'

And Captain Nemo unfurled a black flag at the front of the platform, identical to the one he had planted on the South Pole.

At that moment, a shell obliquely struck the hull of the *Nautilus*, but without making a hole, ricocheted near the captain, and finished up in the sea.

Captain Nemo shrugged his shoulders. Then, addressing me:

'Go inside,' he said curtly. 'Go inside, you and your companions.'

'Monsieur!' I exclaimed. 'Are you going to attack this ship?'

'I'm going to sink it.'

'You are not!'

'I am,' he coldly replied. 'Do not take it on yourself to judge me, monsieur. Fate is showing you what you should not have seen.

The attack has come* and the response will be terrible. Go back down.'

'What ship is this?'

'You do not know? Well so much the better! Its nationality will remain a secret for you. *Go down.*'*

The Canadian, Conseil, and I could only obey. About fifteen sailors from the *Nautilus* stood around the captain, staring with implacable hatred at this ship bearing down on them. The same thought of revenge was clearly driving all of their souls.

I went back in just as another projectile grazed the *Nautilus*'s hull. I could hear the captain exclaiming:

'Strike, crazy ship! Waste your useless shells. You will not escape the *Nautilus*'s ram. But it is not on this spot that you shall perish! I do not want your ruins to sully the remains of the *Vengeur*!'

I went back to my room. The captain and his deputy remained on the platform. The propeller started up. The *Nautilus* moved away at speed, and was soon out of reach of the vessel's shells. But the pursuit continued, with Captain Nemo content merely to maintain his distance.

At about four in the afternoon, unable to contain the impatience and worry devouring me, I returned to the central staircase. The hatch was open. I ventured out on to the platform. The captain was still agitatedly pacing up and down. He was looking at the ship, five or six miles to leeward. He was moving back and forth like a wild animal, as he allowed himself to be pursued and so drew it eastwards. However, he did not attack. Perhaps he was still hesitating?

I tried to intervene one last time, but I had hardly addressed Captain Nemo before he imposed silence on me.

'I am the law, I am the justice!'* he said. 'I am the oppressed, and they are the oppressor! It is because of them that everything I loved, cherished, venerated—country, wife, children, parents— perished as I watched!* Everything I hate is there! Keep quiet!'*

I threw a last glance at the warship, which was straining at full steam. Then I joined Ned and Conseil again.

'We're going to escape!' I exclaimed.

'Well,' said Ned, 'what ship is it?'

'I don't know, but whatever it is, it will be sunk before night-fall. It would be better to perish with it than to become involved in reprisals, whose fairness we cannot judge.'

'That is also my opinion,' Ned coldly replied. 'Let's wait for darkness.'

Night came. A deep silence reigned on board. The compass showed that the *Nautilus* had not changed direction. I could hear the beating as its propeller struck the waves with a quick rhythm. It remained on the surface and the slight rolling took it now to one side, now to the other.

My companions and I resolved to try to escape as soon as the vessel was close enough for us to make ourselves heard or seen, for it was three days before the full moon, and the light was bright. Once on board the ship, if we could not prevent it being attacked, at least we would have tried everything that circumstances allowed us to do. Several times I thought that the *Nautilus* was getting ready for an assault, but it would merely let its adversary come closer, and then shortly afterwards accelerate away again.

Part of the night went by without incident. We watched out for a chance to act. We said little, for we were too much on edge. Ned would have liked to throw himself into the sea. I forced him to wait. I thought the *Nautilus* would surely attack the double-decker on the surface of the waves, and it would then be not only possible but easy to escape.

At three in the morning, feeling rather worried, I went back up to the platform. Captain Nemo was still there. He was standing at the front near his flag, which a slight breeze unfurled above his head. His eyes no longer left the vessel. His extraordinarily intense gaze seemed to be attracting it, beguiling it, dragging it in more surely than if he had towed it!

The moon was at its highest point. Jupiter was rising in the east. In the midst of this peaceful nature, sky and ocean vied in calmness, and the sea offered the moon the most beautiful mirror that had ever reflected it.

But when I thought of the deep calm of the elements compared to all the angers growing in the flanks of the imperceptible *Nautilus*, I felt my whole being quake.

The vessel remained two miles away from us. It had come closer, moving towards that phosphorescent light which indicated the *Nautilus*'s presence. I could see its green and red position lights and its white navigation light on the main foresail stay. A vague glow lit up its rigging, and showed that the boiler was being pushed to its very limit. Sheaves of sparks and cinders of burning coal escaped from its funnels, producing stars in the air.

I remained thus until six a.m., without Captain Nemo seeming to have noticed me. The vessel stayed a mile and a half away, and as soon as the first gleams of daylight began to appear, it started firing its cannons again. The time could not be far off when the *Nautilus* would start attacking its adversary, and my companions and I would leave for ever this man that I dared not judge.*

I was getting ready to go down and tell them, when the first officer climbed up on to the platform. Several sailors were with him. Captain Nemo did not see them, or perhaps did not want to. Preparations were being made which could be called the action stations of the *Nautilus*. They were very simple. The jackstay forming the handrail around the platform was lowered. The domes for the searchlight and pilot-house slid into the hull so as to form a unified line with it.* The surface of the long metal cigar no longer offered a single point that could interfere with its operation.

I went back down to the salon. The *Nautilus* was still on the surface. A few morning gleams were slipping into the liquid strata. As some of the waves went by, the windows were lit up by the red of the rising sun. That terrible day of 2 June was just beginning.

At five o'clock* the log told me that the *Nautilus* was slowing down. I realized that it was allowing itself to be approached.* The explosions were getting louder. The shells were ploughing into the surrounding water, moving through it with a curious hissing sound.

'My friends,' I said, 'the time has come. Let's shake hands and may God protect us!'

Ned Land was determined, Conseil calm, and I, on edge and hardly able to control my nerves.

We went into the library. Just as I opened the door giving on to the well of the central staircase, I heard the hatch slam shut.

The Canadian rushed towards the steps, but I held him back. A familiar hissing sound told me that water was flooding into the tanks. In a few seconds, the *Nautilus* had sunk a few metres below the surface.*

I understood then what was happening. It was too late to do anything. The *Nautilus* was not planning to strike the impenetrable armour of the double-decker, but the section below its flotation line, where a metal cover no longer protected the planking.

We were prisoners once more—forced witnesses of the sinister drama being prepared. In any case, we hardly had time to think. Taking refuge in my room, we looked at each other without a single word. A profound stupor had taken hold of my mind. My brain had stopped working. I found myself in that uncomfortable state of waiting for a frightening explosion. I waited and listened, my sense of hearing the only part of me alive!

Meanwhile the speed of the *Nautilus* had noticeably increased as it gathered momentum. Its hull trembled.

Suddenly, I gave a cry. A shock had occurred, but a relatively slight one. I could feel the strength of penetration of the steel cutwater. I could hear scraping noises. The *Nautilus*, carried on by its propulsive force, was passing clean through the vessel, like a sailmaker's needle through canvas!

I could no longer keep still. Mad, bewildered, I rushed out of my room and into the salon.

Captain Nemo was there. Silent, sombre, implacable, he was watching the port window.

An enormous object was sinking into the water; and, so as to follow every detail of its death-throes, the *Nautilus* was descending into the abyss too. Ten metres away from me, I could see a hull torn open, with water rushing in with the sound of thunder, then the double line of cannons and bulwarks. The deck was covered with black shadows, all moving around.

The water was rising. The wretches rushed into the rigging, clung on to the masts, were twisted under the waters. It was a human ant-heap caught out by the invasion of a sea.

Paralysed, stiff with anguish, my hair standing on end, my eyes unnaturally wide, hardly able to breathe, without air, without voice, I was watching too! An irresistible attraction glued me to the glass.

The enormous vessel was slowly sinking. The *Nautilus* followed it, watching for its slightest movements. Suddenly, an explosion occurred. The pressure made the decks of the vessel fly off, as if fire had broken out in its hold. The thrust of the water was such that the *Nautilus* was pushed aside.

Now the unhappy ship sank more quickly. Its crow's nests, laden with victims, went down, next its crosstrees, bending under the weight of clusters of men, and finally the tip of its main-mast.*
Then the sombre mass disappeared, and with it the crew of bodies carried down in a formidable undertow . . .

I turned to Captain Nemo. That terrible lawgiver, that archangel of hate, was watching still. When everything was finished, Captain Nemo headed for the door of his room, opened it, and went in. My eyes followed him.

On the far wall, below the pictures of his heroes, I could see the portrait of a woman, still young, with two small children. Captain Nemo looked at them for a few moments, stretched out his arms to them, and then knelt down sobbing.*

22

Captain Nemo's Last Words

THE panels had closed again on this frightening vision, but the light had not been switched on again in the salon. Inside the *Nautilus* was only darkness and silence. It was leaving that place of destruction a hundred feet beneath the water at prodigious speed. In what direction was it heading? North or south? Where was this man fleeing after his terrible reprisal?*

I had returned to my room where Ned and Conseil were silently waiting. I felt an invincible horror for Captain Nemo. Whatever he had suffered at the hands of men, he did not have the right to inflict punishment in this way. He had made me the witness of his acts of revenge, if not the accomplice. That was already too much.

At eleven o'clock the electric light came on again. I went into the salon. It was deserted. I consulted the various instruments. The *Nautilus* was fleeing north at a speed of 25 knots, sometimes on the surface of the water, sometimes 30 feet below.

While noting our position on the map, I realized that we were passing near the end of the English Channel, and that our movement was taking us towards the Arctic seas at unsurpassed speed.*

I could barely identify the quickly passing long-nosed sharks, hammerhead sharks, or spotted dogfish frequenting these waters; nor the great sea-eagles, the clouds of sea-horses like knights in chess sets, the eels oscillating like firework squibs, the armies of crabs fleeing obliquely while crossing their pincers over their shells, nor finally the schools of porpoise racing the *Nautilus*. I did not even think of observing, studying, or classifying them.

By evening, we had covered 200 leagues of the Atlantic. Shadows fell, and the sea was covered with darkness; but then the moon rose.*

I went back to my room. I could not sleep. I was assailed by nightmares. The terrifying scene of destruction was repeating over and over in my mind.

Starting from that day, who could have said where the *Nautilus* took us through that basin of the North Atlantic? Always at a speed that could not be guessed! Always through the Arctic fogs. Did it put in at the tip of Spitsbergen, or on the shores of Novaya Zemlya? Did it go through those unknown seas, the White Sea, the Kara Sea, the Gulf of Ob, the Lyakhov Islands, or along the unexplored shores of the Asian coast? I could not say. Time went by without me being able to calculate it. The time of the clocks on board had been suspended.* As in the polar regions, day and night no longer seemed to be following their regular course. I felt myself carried off into the realm of the extra-natural, where Poe's overworked imagination moved at ease. At each moment I expected to see, like the fabulous Gordon Pym, 'a shrouded human figure, very far larger in its proportions than any dweller among men, thrown across the cataract which defends the approaches to the Pole'!*

I estimate—but am perhaps mistaken—that this wild movement of the *Nautilus* carried on for two or three weeks; and I do not know how long it would have lasted if it had not been for the catastrophe that terminated our voyage. Of Captain Nemo there was no longer any sign. Of his first officer either. Not one crew member was visible for a single moment. The *Nautilus* navigated almost permanently underwater. When it went up to the surface again to replenish its air, the hatches opened and closed automatically.* The position was no longer plotted on the planisphere. I had no idea where we were.

I must also say that the Canadian was at the end of his patience and tether, and no longer left his cabin. Conseil could no longer drag a single word out of him, and feared that he might kill himself in a fit of madness or under the effect of devastating homesickness. He devotedly watched over him every second of the day.

It will be understood that in such circumstances the situation was no longer tenable.*

One morning—on what date I cannot say—I had started dozing during the first few hours of the day. An uncomfortable and unhealthy doze. When I woke up, I found Land leaning over me and saying in a low voice:

'We're going to escape!'

I sat up.

'When?'

'Tonight. All surveillance seems to have vanished from the *Nautilus*. There seems to be a total stupor on board. Will you be ready?'

'I will. But where are we?'

'In sight of some land that I glimpsed through the fog this morning, twenty miles east.'

'What land?'

'I don't know, but whatever country it is, we will find shelter there.'*

'Yes, Ned! We will try to escape tonight, even if the sea does swallow us up!'

'The sea is stormy, the wind violent, but covering twenty miles in the *Nautilus*'s boat does not frighten me. I have been able to put some food and a few bottles of water in without the crew realizing.'*

'I will follow you.'

'In any case, if I am caught, I will fight back, I will get myself killed.'

'We will die together, friend Ned.'

I was ready for anything. The Canadian left me. I went up on the platform, although I could scarcely stand up due to the rocking from the waves. The sky was threatening, but since there was land behind that fog, we had to try to escape. We could not wait a day or even an hour.*

I went back to the salon, fearing and desiring at the same time that I would meet Captain Nemo, wanting and not wanting to see him. What could I say to him? Would I be able to hide the involuntary horror he inspired in me? No, better not to come face to face with him! Better to forget him! And yet!

How this day dragged on, the last one I was ever to spend on board the *Nautilus*! I remained alone. Ned and Conseil avoided speaking to me for fear of giving themselves away.

At six o'clock I dined, but did not feel hungry. In spite of my distaste I forced myself to eat, wishing to maintain my strength.

At half-past six, Ned Land came into my room:

'We will not see each other again before we leave. At ten o'clock, the moon will not yet be up. The darkness will help us. Come to the boat. Conseil and I will be waiting for you there.'

Then the Canadian went out without giving me time to reply.

I wanted to know the *Nautilus*'s direction. I made for the salon. We were heading north-north-east at a frightening speed and at fifty metres' depth.

I cast a last look at the marvels of nature and treasures of art amassed in the museum, at this unrivalled collection destined to perish one day at the bottom of the seas, together with the man who had assembled it. I wanted to engrave in my mind a last memory of it. I remained an hour thus, bathed in the emanations from the luminous ceiling, reviewing the resplendent treasures behind the panes. Then I returned to my room.

I put on strong sea clothing. I gathered my notes together, and tied them with great care to my body. My heart was beating violently. I could not make it throb less. My trouble and unease would certainly have given me away before Captain Nemo.

What was he doing at this moment? I listened at the door of his room. I heard footsteps, telling me that Captain Nemo was there. He had not gone to bed.* With each step I thought he was going to appear and ask me why I wanted to escape. Feelings of alarm kept on gripping me. My imagination magnified them. The impression became so strong that I wondered if it would not be better to march into the captain's room, look him in the face, and defy him with my attitude and my eyes!

It was the promptings of a madman. Fortunately I held myself back, and went to stretch out on my bed so as to reduce the agitation in my body. My nerves calmed down a little, but in a rapid vision in my overexcited brain I relived my whole life on board the *Nautilus*, all the happy and unhappy incidents that had marked it since my disappearance from the *Abraham Lincoln*: the submarine hunting, Torres Strait, the savages of Papua, the running aground, the coral cemetery, the route under Suez, the island of Santorini, the Cretan diver, Vigo Bay, Atlantis, the ice-cap, the South Pole, the imprisonment in the ice, the battle with the squid, the storm on the Gulf Stream, the *Vengeur*, and that terrible scene of the sinking of the vessel with all hands. All these events passed before my eyes like minor scenes taking place in the backdrop of the stage. Then against this strange setting Captain Nemo grew out of all proportion. His character was accentuated and took on superhuman dimension. He was no longer a fellow human, but a marine being, a spirit of the seas.

It was half-past nine. I took my head in my hands to stop it exploding. I closed my eyes. I no longer wanted to think. Still half an hour to wait! Half an hour of a nightmare that might send me mad!

Suddenly I heard distant chords from the organ, the sad harmony of an indefinable tune, the veritable complaint of a soul wishing to break all ties with earth. I listened with all my senses, hardly breathing, plunged like Captain Nemo into musical ecstasies that carried him beyond the limits of this world.

Then a thought suddenly terrified me. Captain Nemo had obviously left his room. He was in that salon that I had to cross to escape. There I would meet him one last time. He would see me, perhaps even speak to me! A sign from him could destroy me, a single word chain me to his ship!

Meanwhile ten o'clock was about to strike. The time had come to leave my room and join my companions.

There was no time to hesitate, even were Captain Nemo to surge up before me. I carefully opened my door. And yet it seemed to me that as it moved on its hinges, it made a frightening sound. Perhaps the sound existed only in my imagination!

I crawled forward through the dark gangways of the *Nautilus*, stopping after each step to compress the beatings of my heart.

I arrived at the angled door to the salon. I opened it slowly. The room was plunged into deep darkness. The chords of the organ were still faintly echoing. Captain Nemo was there. He did not see me. I think that even in full light he would not have noticed me, so much did his ecstasy absorb him.

I dragged myself over the carpet, avoiding the slightest contact whose sound might have betrayed my presence. It took me five minutes to reach the far door leading into the library.

I was going to open it, when a sigh from Captain Nemo nailed me to the spot. I realized that he was getting up. I even caught sight of him, for a few rays of light from the lit-up library were filtering as far as the salon. He came towards me, his arms crossed, silently gliding rather than walking, just like a ghost. His oppressed breast heaved with sobbings, and I could hear him murmuring. The closing words reached my ear:

'God almighty! Enough! Enough!'*

Was it an avowal of remorse, escaping thus from the conscience of this man . . . ?

Bewildered, I rushed into the library. I climbed the central staircase, followed the upper gangway, and reached the boat. I went through the opening which had already allowed access to my two companions.

'Let's go! Let's go!' I exclaimed.

'Straightaway,' replied the Canadian.

The opening in the metal plate of the *Nautilus* was closed and bolted using an adjustable spanner Ned had brought with him. The opening in the boat itself was also closed, and the Canadian began to unscrew the bolts still attaching us to the submarine vessel.

Suddenly a sound could be heard inside. Voices were sharply replying to each other. What was it? Had our escape been discovered? I could feel Ned Land sliding a knife into my hand.

'Yes,' I murmured, 'we are ready to die!'

The Canadian had stopped his work. But one word, repeated many times, a terrifying word, told me the reason for the agitation spreading through the *Nautilus*. It was not us the crew were upset with.

They were exclaiming 'Maelstrom! Maelstrom!'*

The Maelstrom! Could a more frightening word sound in our ears in a more desperate situation? Were we in its dangerous waters off the Norwegian coast? Was the *Nautilus* being sucked down into that vortex at the very moment our boat had been about to cast off?

It is known that, at the greatest flow, the waters caught between the Faeroes and the Lofoten Islands move with irresistible violence. They form a whirlpool from which no ship has ever been able to escape.* Monstrous waves rush in from all points of the horizon. They form a funnel fittingly called the 'navel of the ocean', with a power of attraction stretching over a distance of fifteen kilometres. Not only are ships sucked in, but also whales and even polar bears from the Arctic.

It was here that the *Nautilus* had involuntarily—or perhaps voluntarily—been engaged by its captain.* It was describing a spiral whose radius was decreasing all the time. The boat, still attached to its side, was also being transported at a dizzying speed. I could feel it. I was experiencing the turning feeling caused by a rotation that goes on for too long. We were in a state of terror! Terror to the highest degree! Our blood was no longer circulating. Our nervous systems were deadened. We were covered with cold sweat, as if on a death-bed. What a noise around our frail boat! What moanings echoed from miles around! What a din from the waters broken on the sharp rocks of the bottom, where the hardest bodies break up, where tree-trunks wear themselves out, where they produce a 'fur of hair', as the Norwegian expression has it!*

What a situation! We were being shaken frightfully. The *Nautilus* was fighting like a human being. Its steel muscles were cracking. Sometimes it stood up, and us with it.*

'We need to hold on', said Ned, 'and screw the bolts back in. If we stay attached to the *Nautilus*, we can still get out alive . . . !'*

He had not finished speaking, when a cracking sound could be heard. The bolts gave way; and the dinghy was torn from its hole and launched into the midst of the whirlpool like a stone from a sling.

My head struck an iron spar; and because of this violent impact I lost consciousness.

23

Conclusion

THIS is the conclusion of our journey under the seas. What happened that night, how the boat escaped from the formidable undertow of the Maelstrom, how Ned, Conseil, and I emerged from the deep, I cannot say. But when I came to, I was lying in the hut of a Lofoten Islands fisherman. My two companions were safe and sound beside me, squeezing my hands. We embraced warmly.*

At this moment, we cannot think of returning to France.* There are not many means of transport between the north and south of Norway. I am therefore forced to wait for the steamship which makes the fortnightly run to North Cape.

So it is here, in the midst of the good people who saved us, that I am revising the tale of these adventures.* It is scrupulously accurate. Not a single fact has been omitted, not the slightest detail exaggerated. It is the faithful narration of an incredible expedition through an element inaccessible to man, although progress will open it up one day.

Will I be believed? I do not know, but it is not that important. What I can proclaim now is my right to speak of the seas through which I covered twenty thousand leagues in less than ten months; and to speak of that submarine journey around the world, which has revealed so many of the marvels of the Mediterranean and Red seas and of the Pacific, Indian, Atlantic, Arctic, and Antarctic oceans!

But what became of the *Nautilus*?* Did it resist the embrace of the Maelstrom? Is Captain Nemo still alive?* Is he continuing his terrifying reprisals under the ocean, or did he stop at his last massacre? Will the waves one day wash up the manuscript containing the entire story of his life?* Will I finally discover his name? Will the nationality of the vessel sunk tell us Captain Nemo's own nationality?

I hope so. I also hope that his powerful vessel overcame the sea's most terrifying deep and that the *Nautilus* survived where so many ships have perished!* If this is the case, if Captain Nemo does still inhabit his adopted oceanic homeland, may hate die down in that wild heart! May the contemplation of so many marvels extinguish his desire for revenge! May the lawgiver disappear and the scientist continue his peaceful exploration of the seas! If his destiny is strange, it is also sublime. Do I not understand it myself? Have I not lived ten months of that extra-natural existence? So, to that question which the Book of Ecclesiastes posed 6,000 years ago, 'hast thou walked in the search of the depth?',* two men, amongst all men, now have the right to reply. Captain Nemo and I.*

THE END

APPENDIX

SOURCES OF IDEAS ON SUBMARINE NAVIGATION

It is important to establish the state of knowledge concerning submarines when Verne created the *Nautilus*.

His basic ideas were not original. *Nautile* and *Nautilus* were common names for diving-bells and submarines in the nineteenth century, as Verne himself pointed out in a letter to his editor on 13 November 1894. The novelist had already set the opening chapter of *Captain Hatteras* on a ship called the *Nautilus* floating in Liverpool docks. Also, at least twenty-five manned vessels had dived before 1869. A slightly miscellaneous list might include: Alexander the Great who was reported to have used a glass diving-bell; William Bourne who introduced immersion tanks (1578); Cornelius Van Drebbel who built a leather-covered rowing boat (1620) that he claimed could remain underwater for hours; David Bushnell's *Turtle* (1776), with a depth-gauge and one hand-cranked propeller for forward movement and another for vertical, which made an unsuccessful attack on a British ship in New York Harbour; the Coëssin brothers' probably unsteerable *Nautile* (1809, 1819); the *Cyclops* (1854—mentioned in Maury) and *Bull-Dog* (1855) which explored the Atlantic; Winans' cigar-shaped 'roller ships' (1858, 1864); Laubeuf's *Narval*; Wood's *Stromboli*; Alstitt's vessel (1862) introducing the electric motor; Halstead's *Intelligent Whale* tested in 1865–6; the 79-by-15-metre monitor *Miantonomon*, exhibited in Marseilles in 1867; and the *Lightning* (1868). Many submarines were ultimately designed to attack British warships.

More directly related to Verne, and in any case more fully documented, are: Fulton's *Nautilus* (1801—see note to p. 105 below); the Confederate *Hunley*, which blew up the *Housatonic* in Charleston Harbor in 1864 but itself sank, killing its nine crew; Petit's submarine used in the Baie de la Somme, and in which he died in 1834; a 'cigar-boat' produced by Verne's mathematics teacher, Villeroi (1832, successfully tested in Philadelphia Harbor in 1862–3), which had a hatch, pumps to rise and descend, and a mechanical propeller; the *Pilote* built by Conseil, a friend of Verne's, complete with a viewing chamber, automatic aeration valves, a screw, and diving fins (1858—see note to p. 17 below); and the *Ictineo*, with a double hull, ballast tanks, steam-driven drill for piercing hulls, and chemical plant for producing oxygen for breathing, tested by Monturiol in Barcelona in 1862 and in France in 1868. Verne certainly visited Hallet's *Nautilus* (1857—see note to p. 22 below) and Brun's *Plongeur* (1863, 1867—see note to p. 22 below) at the Universal Exposition in 1867. Riou's illustrations for the original French edition show the influence of Brun's vessel.

One major problem for all these vessels was that of stability, and they often went straight to the bottom. Also, none of them contained a usable optical periscope, for this was invented only in 1870. But their biggest problem was lack of power underwater, since no source of sufficient oxygen for engines was available.

Verne probably got some of his ideas from previous writings on the subject, including a description of Villeroi's cigar-boat and the *Ictineo* in Louis Figuier's *Les Merveilles de la science* (1869), 666. Three titles on submarines published before 1870 were: Captain Mérobert (pseudonym of Clément-Jules Briois), *Voyage au fond de la mer* (1845); Léon Sonrel (1839–70), *Le Fond de la mer* (1868); and Henri de La Blanchère, *Le Club des toqués, aventures sous-marines, sublunaires et autres* [1869?]. According to Jean Jules-Verne (p. 143), 'as early as 1867 [Verne] read the book by Renard and Margolet [*sic*]' on submarine navigation. However, this seems to be mixing up as many as three authors and three books published by Hetzel which were important sources for Verne: Frédéric Zurcher and Élie Margollé, *Histoire de la navigation* (1867) and *Le Monde sous-marin* (1868); and Léon Renard, *Le Fond de la mer* (1868). In a letter to his editor dated 30 April (1868), Verne writes 'the identical chapters of the books of MM. Renard and Margollé are the history of the submarine cable [and] the history of submarine boats; in any case, I will give you more details on Monday' (quoted by MD, p. 66). MD points out that *Le Fond de la mer* covers such ideas visible in *Twenty Thousand Leagues* (*20TL*) as underwater fishing, byssus clothing, Fulton's *Nautilus*, Conseil's submarine, and others; and that *Le Monde sous-marin* describes soundings of the great deeps, currents, the Maelstrom, species of fish, aquariums, atolls, and Atlantis.

More generally, works claimed to be Verne's sources for the marine sections of the novel include: Scott's *The Pirate* (1822), Fenimore Cooper's *The Pilot* (1823), and Théophile Gautier's *Fortunio* (1838), *Les Deux étoiles* (1848), and *Partie carrée* (1848, 1851). Indisputable sources are: Homer's *Odyssey*, Maury's *The Physical Geography of the Sea* (1855), Michelet's *La Mer* (1861), Figuier's *Articulés, poissons, reptiles et zoophytes, mollusques*, Hugo's *Les Travailleurs de la mer* (1866), Henri de La Blanchère's *La Pêche et les poissons* (with a Preface by A. Duméril and '1,100 illustrations ... based on photographs' [1868]), Larousse's *Grand dictionnaire universel du XIXe siècle* (1866–76), Arthur Mangin's *Les Mystères de l'océan* (1864, 1868), and various works by Poe.

But as early as 1861 Verne himself had created a submersible. The climax of his short story 'San Carlos', published only in 1993, involves customs boats pursuing a vessel 'of bizarre construction'. It is completely watertight thanks to an internal metal hull; and is 'spacious' inside, carrying a whole world of clothing, 'hams, butter, fine wines, oil, tobacco, madder, soap, and metals'. When finally surrounded by his pursuants, the eponymous hero and his companions simply 'open a valve in the bottom, and so escape by sinking to a depth of ten fathoms'. They then use a 'submarine current' to move away. The boat is one of 'those mysterious vessels that are kept submerged at a constant depth by means of forward and rear sections filled with air'. San Carlos's submersible thus prefigures the *Nautilus* in many ways. Additional similarities with *20TL* are the hero's Spanish nationality, his outlaw condition, and his predilection for tax-free cigars and volcanoes.

As for Verne's ideas after *20TL*, submarines also occur in his *Mathias Sandorf* (1885), *For the Flag* (1896), and *The Master of the World* (1904); but they bear little comparison with Nemo's invention, being mere means of locomotion, lacking in flair or imagination. The *Nautilus* does come back in *The Mysterious Island* (1873), but is a pale shadow of itself (see note to p. 380 below).

An article under Jules Verne's name (but probably by his son Michel, according to Gondolo della Riva), entitled 'Future of the Submarine: Author of the *Nautilus* says its use will be confined to war and it will bring peace', appeared in *Popular Mechanics* in June 1904. It says 'I am not in any way the inventor of submarine navigation, and reference will show that many years [. . .] before [. . .], the Italians were at work upon submarine war vessels, and other nations were busied with them too [. . .]. The *Nautilus*, as I have written of it, will never be, I think, an actual fact.'

EXPLANATORY NOTES

5 *Cuvier ... Quatrefages*: French naturalists. *Cuvier*: Georges (Baron de) (1769–1832), geologist and zoologist; a founder of comparative anatomy and palaeontology, and the creationist, catastrophist, and anti-evolutionist author of *De l'histoire naturelle des cétacés* (1804) and *Discours sur les révolutions de la surface du globe* (1825). Many of the marine lists of *20TL* seem to be drawn directly from Cuvier, but with the adjectives added by Verne. *Lacépède*: Bernard-Germain-Étienne de la Ville (Comte de) (1756–1825). A disciple of Cuvier and Buffon, he wrote *Histoire naturelle des poissons* (1803) and *Histoire naturelle des cétacés* (1804). *M. Duméril*: (Verne: 'M. Dumeril') Henri-André (1812–70), or possibly his father André-Marie-Constant (1774–1860), specialists in reptiles and fish. *M. de Quatrefages*: Jean-Louis-Armand de Quatrefages de Bréau (1810–92), naturalist and anthropologist, anti-Darwinist, and author of *Histoire de l'homme* (1867). He appears prominently in the prehistoric section added with the seventh edition of *Journey to the Centre of the Earth* (1867).

6 *the Calcutta and Burma Steam Navigation Company, had encountered this moving object five miles east of the Australian coastline*: (Verne: 'the Calcutta and Burnach [. . .]') became the British India Steam Navigation Company in 1869. MS2 has '500 miles'.

two columns of water: this sighting of the sea monster is presaged in *Journey to the Centre of the Earth*, where Axel and Lidenbrock see a 'cetaceous monster which Cuvier and Blumenbach never dreamed of [. . .] motionless as if asleep [and a] water-column, rising to a height of 500 feet'. The creature turns out to be an island, and the column a geyser. MS2 has the water rising only '50 feet into the air'.

the 'Helvetia' of the French Line and the 'Shannon' of the Royal Mail: the French Line was also known as the French Transatlantic Company; *Around the World* says that the British and North American Royal Mail Steam Packet Company was another name for the Cunard Line (cf. note on Cunard below).

the 'kulammak' and the 'umgullick': these two words are later spelled 'Hullamock [. . .] Umgallick' (I 12) (MS2: 'Hullamack' and 'Umgullick').

the Inman Line: (Verne: 'Iseman'; *MÉR*: 'Inman') the informal name of the Inman and International Steamship Company. Verne writes 'Inmann' in II 20.

7 *the white whale, that terrible 'Moby Dick'*: (*MÉR*: 'Maby Dick'; MS2: 'Moby(?) Dick') *Moby-Dick; or, the Whale* (1850) by Herman Melville

(1819–91) presents Captain Ahab's obsession for vengeance on the whale that took his leg off, culminating in his death and the sinking of his ship. Ray Bradbury (1962) finds important parallels between *Moby-Dick* and *20TL*. Certainly, they have the theme of revenge in common, as well as a remarkable number of elements. Thus we find in Melville: Ecclesiastes, Leviathan, Seneca, Cleopatra, Dampier, Darwin, Maury, Agassiz, Albermarle, the Maelstrom, the Battle of Actium, the sea of milk, cannibalism, the *Argo*, the sinking of the *Essex* by a whale, the narwhal as a 'sea-unicorn' or variety of whale, shells, the rewarding of the first seaman to sight the monster, the deliberate drawing down of an electrical storm on to the ship, 'the great Kraken of Bishop Pontoppodan [*sic*]'—presumed to be the 'great live squid', 'a vast pulpy mass, furlongs in length and breadth', with 'innumerable long arms radiating from its centre, and curling and twisting like a nest of anacondas, as if blindly to catch at any hapless object within reach'—and 'Aristotle; Pliny [. . .] Linnaeus [. . .] Lacépède [. . .] Cuvier [and] John Hunter' (ch. 32)—all ideas which appear in Verne's volume, together with many of Melville's localities. Melville's vessel goes down in the deep trench off eastern Japan—where Verne's first emerges. Both endings feature a whirlpool which swallows up the vessel, followed by a short posterior epilogue quoting the Book of Job; and each closes with a reference to the sea, respectively 'five' and 'six thousand years ago'. The first edition of *Moby-Dick* had on its title page: 'There Leviathan, | Hugest of living creatures, in the deep | Stretch'd like a promontory sleeps or swims, | And seems a moving land; and at his gills | Draws in, and at his breath spouts out a sea. | *Paradise Lost*': all elements visible in *20TL*. However, *Moby-Dick* was translated into French only in 1941, and Verne could not read English (although he may have had access to reviews or summaries). Accordingly, although Melville and Verne undoubtedly share a common vision, direct influence must still remain an open question.

7 *Kraken*: sea monsters that lived off the coast of Norway and crushed ships with their tentacles, undoubtedly derived from giant squid (which can grow up to 60 feet and weigh 2 tonnes). Verne's *Les Histoires de Jean-Marie Cabidoulin* (1901) features kraken prominently (with some of its monsters curiously resembling . . . the *Nautilus*).

Aristotle . . . Egede: published works on sea monsters. *Aristotle*: (384–322 BC), philosopher and author of 'Auscultationes mirabiles' about Atlantis and a *History of Animals* containing the first major biological classification. *Pliny*: the Elder, Gaius Plinius Secundus (AD 23–79); author of a 37-volume *Natural History*, including: 'The Indian Sea breedeth the most and the biggest fishes that are: among which the Whales and Whirlpooles called Balæne, take up as much in length as four acres or arpens of land' (IX. ii. 4, quoted in *Moby-Dick*). Pliny also describes a 700-pound 'polyp', apparently a squid, with a head as big as a cask, arms 30 feet long, and evil-smelling breath, which came ashore in Carteia, Spain, tormented dogs, and climbed over a fence before being overpowered. He also writes of 'more than 300 monsters, astonishingly varied in shape and size' thrown up on a coast and of 'elephants and rams, with horns as white as snow, and many Nereids [sea-nymphs]' thrown up at Santoña (IX. v). *Bishop Pontoppidan*: Erik Pontoppidan (1698–1764), bishop of Bergen, theologian, and author of *Natural History of Norway* (1752). He describes a monster 'whose back, or upper part, which seems an English mile and a half in circumference, looks at first like a number of small islands', with arms or tentacles reaching out of the sea, a strong smell, and able to discharge a muddy fluid. One was caught in the cleft of a rock in 1680: the bishop concludes that it resembles a 'polyp' (probably a squid). *Paul Egede*: (Verne: 'Heggede') (1708–89), Norwegian missionary and specialist in Greenlandic, author of the journal *Eftererretninger om Grønland* (1789), which describes a monster: 'its head reached as high as a mainmast [. . .]. It had a long pointed snout, and spouted like a whale-fish [. . .] great broad paws; the body seemed covered with shell-work [. . .]. The under part of its body was shaped like an enormous huge serpent.'

Captain Harrington: although the reports of 1866–7 are fictional, what Captain Harrington and 20 others saw in 1857 was recorded in a formal report to the Admiralty. About 10 miles from St Helena he observed a creature swimming towards the land: it was about 200 feet long, with a head shaped like a barrel and crowned with a wrinkled crest. It resembled a serpent 'of a dark colour about the head, and was covered with several white spots'. PC (p. 281) notes that George Henry Harrington's observation on 12 December 1857 was reported in *The Times* of 16 February 1858 and the *Zoologist* of 1858 (p. 5989).

that enormous serpent . . . the pages of the old 'Constitutionnel': a liberal periodical (1815–1914) which serialized George Sand, Eugène Sue, and Dumas *père*, and was suppressed and revived five times. PC (p. 282) reports that it was accused by a rival of inventing the story of a sea serpent, but was cleared by an enquiry in 1891. Such was the frequency of stories of sea serpents that by the 1880s the word had come to mean any controversy (*OED*). Verne is in fact 'de-metaphorizing' a standard metaphor, since 'the sea serpent of the old *Constitutionnel*' was a well-known cliché meaning the periodical's support for a British-style parliamentary regime in France.

the 'Indian Archipelago' . . . 'Petermanns Mitteilungen': contemporary periodicals. 'The Indian Archipelago': probably the *East India Association* (London, 1867–71). *Abbé Moigno's 'Cosmos'*: François-Napoléon Moigno (1804–84), mathematician and ex-Jesuit; he founded *Le Cosmos* in 1852. '*Petermanns Mitteilungen*': (Verne: 'Petermann's *Mittheilungen*') or *Petermanns geographische*

Mitteilungen (Gotha, 1860–1915), founded by August Petermann (1822–78), cartographer and geographer, described by Professor Lidenbrock in *Journey to the Centre of the Earth* as his 'friend'.

7 *Linnaeus's*: Carolus Linnaeus (1707–78), Swedish botanist who devised the binomial method of animal and plant classification based on evolutionary relationships, and believed in Kraken.

8 '*Nature does not produce idiots*': 'la nature ne fait pas de sots', a pun on 'la nature ne fait pas de sauts' ('Nature does not make leaps') (Linnaeus's *Philosophia Botanica* (1750), sec. 77).

an article for a much-feared satirical newspaper: MS2: 'an article in the *Figaro*', an interesting variant showing that Verne's acerbic comments are in reality directed at the French press.

pushed his spurs in like Hippolytus: the son of Theseus in Greek mythology. Theseus calls on Poseidon, the god of the sea, to take Hippolytus' life and Poseidon sends a sea monster to frighten Hippolytus' horses, causing him to be dragged to his death.
   Verne seems to be deliberately producing a mixed metaphor that reverses the roles of the monster and Hippolytus; his message is that the journalist is being too bold.

the 'Moravian' of the Montreal Ocean Company was sailing at 27° 30′N, 72°15′W: MS2 has 'the *Lafayette* of the French Line, responsible for the postal service between Saint-Nazaire and Veracruz' and adds, 'Its laden displacement was 5,800 tons'. It was forgotten to change the co-ordinates: a ship coming from Canada would not sail at 27°30′N.

dry dock: MS2 adds 'of Saint-Nazaire'. The deletion of the French references is presumably due to Hetzel's sensitivity about anything that might be remotely controversial.

9 *British shipowner Cunard*: Sir Samuel (1787–1865), Canadian founder of the British and North American Royal Mail Steam Packet Company (1840), officially renamed the Cunard Line in 1878.

In 1853 . . . the 'Great Eastern': the date in fact only applies to the first-named Cunard ship; *the 'Arabia'*: Cunard's last wooden paddle-ship; *the 'Persia'*: one of his first iron ships (1856); *the 'China'*: (which Phileas Fogg narrowly misses in New York) launched in 1862; *the 'Scotia'*: Cunard's last paddle-driven ship. It held the transatlantic record until 1869, at 8 days 22 hours (WJM and FPW); *the 'Java'*: built 1865; *the 'Russia'*: (MS2: 'the *Prussia*'!) built 1867; *the 'Great Eastern'*: Verne saw Brunel's ship (then called the *Leviathan*) being constructed in Greenwich in 1859. By far the largest ship in the world, it was equipped with a single screw propeller, paddlewheels, *and* a full set of sails. In 1867 Napoleon III chartered it to carry Americans to the Universal Exposition. Verne himself travelled on the *Great Eastern* to New York and back in March and April 1867, describing it in a letter to Hetzel as 'an eighth wonder of the world' and writing the semi-fictional *A Floating City* (1871) about his trip.

10 *Captain Anderson*: this dynamic fictional figure is presumably based on the forceful real-life Captain Anderson of the *Great Eastern* described in Part Two.

Bureau Veritas: 1828– , rival to the *International Lloyd's Register*. The figure of '3,000 ships whose losses are recorded each year' seems a little high.

11 *lecturer*: Aronnax is stated to be a modest 'lecturer' ('professeur suppléant'), and not a professor, as has been the usual translation to date.

12 *'submarine' vessel*: ('bateau "sous-marin"') the first use of 'submarine' as a noun meaning 'vessel' was in 1896 in French and in about 1898 in English.

chassepot rifles . . . underwater rams: contemporary armaments: *chassepot rifles*: breech-loading rifles used in the French army from 1866 to 1874, invented by Antoine Chassepot (1833–1905); *floating mines*: Verne's 'torpilles' may mean stationary mines, not 'torpedoes' in the modern sense. Fulton (cf. note to p. 105 below) demonstrated floating mines off Brest in 1801, and Robert Whitehead invented a submerged self-propelling version between 1864 and 1869; *underwater rams*: the phrase was first used about the *Merrimac* (cf. following note).

'Monitor': the *Monitor* and the *Virginia* (ex-*Merrimac*) fought the first battle between ironclads, in 1862 in the American Civil War. A major innovation of the *Monitor* was the turret, allowing its cannon to fire in different directions. More generally, a 'monitor' was a heavily iron-clad warship with a low flat deck, operating nearly submerged, invented by Swedish-American John Ericsson (1803–89).

13 *Pierre Aronnax*: the illustration of Aronnax in the French edition, with arms folded, is a portrait of Verne himself.

In MS1A, he is 'Oyonnax'. In MS2, the name is written 'Arronax' or 'Arronnax'—except on the first occurrence, 'Aronnax', which apparently caused this form to be retained. Oyonnax is a village in the Ain, near Lyon, the confluence of the remarkably named Sarsouille and Ange ('S + Knave' and 'Angel'). Aron and Oyon are attested names, both more or less Jewish, and may point, respectively, to A. Oyon, author of *Une Véritable cité ouvrière* (1865) and Émile Aron (born 1829), a revolutionary poet.

a Giant Narwhal: Verne constructs his mystery by mixing legend (the unicorn's curved horn, often brought back to Europe, was the narwhal's) and exaggeration (the maximum size of the narwhal, which lives only near the Arctic, is about 16 feet). Aronnax is here distinctly creationist.

15 *that sea which never changes, unlike the terrestrial core which is almost continually being modified*: Verne delights in inverting opposites, especially in describing the sea in terrestrial terms and vice versa, a persistent metaphor in *20TL*.

The 'Shipping & Mercantile Gazette and Lloyd's List', the 'Paquebot', and the 'Revue maritime et coloniale': (Verne: '*Shipping and Mercantile Gazette* and *Lloyd's*') respectively: London, 1836–1916; 'Journal of Navigation and Sea-Voyages', Paris, 1866–July 1869; and Paris, 1861–   .

Captain Farragut: the name comes from David G. Farragut (1801–70), the Unionist admiral who produced the famous 'Damn the torpedoes—full speed ahead!' (1864). WJM and FPW report that he visited France in 1867.

this sharp customer had stopped some telegram on its way across: Verne is constantly laying traps for the unwary (on occasion false traps!). In the light of what we later know, and given that the transatlantic cable is in fact subsequently visited by Aronnax, the wag's suggestion is not as implausible as all that.

16 *a steamer of the San Francisco–Shanghai line*: the MÉR edition (but not MS2) has 'the *Tampico*, a steamer of the [. . .]'. MS2 has the date as '2 July'.

Fifth Avenue Hotel: Verne stayed there twice in 1867 (*A Floating City*, chs. 34 and 39). Other elements of America shared between the two 1871 books include the *Great Eastern*, the hotel lift, the 20-franc cab ride to the 'pier' (in English), the Hudson, the East River, Broadway, Brooklyn, Sandy Hook, Napoleon, Agassiz, and George Sand. Some biographers report that a 'Professor Arronax [*sic*]', newly arrived from the Nebraska Badlands, stayed in the Fifth Avenue Hotel at the same time as Verne.

J. B. Hobson: possibly the J. B. Hobson who spoke before the House Committee on Mines and Mining in 1892. In 1867 the Navy Secretary was Gideon Welles.

17 *Conseil*: this surname is taken from Jacques-François Conseil, a friend of Verne's who tested a 3-tonne ellipsoid submarine in 1858 at Le Tréport. Similar in many ways to Verne's vessel, it had a hatch, a small chamber for viewing the exterior, valves that opened automatically on the surface for aeration, a propeller, and four horizontal fins for diving. Conseil published a brochure about it entitled *Bateau de sauvetage, dit 'Pilote'* (1863).

the whole hierarchy of phyla, divisions, classes, sub-classes, orders, families, genera, sub-genera, species, and varieties: the narrator is using Linnaeus's hierarchy; for example, Dog is: animal kingdom; phylum Chordata; class Mammalia; order Carnivora; family Canidae; genus *Canis*; and species *familiaris*.

18 *Archaeotheria . . . Chaeropotami*: extinct mammals. *Archaeotheria*: (Verne: 'les archiotherium') huge warthog-like animals (N. America). *Hyracotheria*: or *Eohippi*: genus of very small horse, found in Wyoming and Utah. *Oreodons*: genus intermediate between hog, deer, and camel that lived near the Rockies. *Chaeropotami*: genus close to *Hyracotherium*.

'monsieur's live babirusa': why is Aronnax travelling across the USA with a wild pig found only in the East Indies?

19 *The hotel lift*: the lift in the Fifth Avenue Hotel, installed in 1859, was famous for its innovative engineering, being raised and lowered by a vertical screw.

20 *the half-open slide valves*: Miller (1976) states that Verne read John Griffiths, *Marine and Naval Architecture* (1844), and Nat Bowditch, *The American Practical Navigator* [. . .] (3rd edn. 1809); but this is improbable since these volumes were not translated and Verne could not read English.

21 *the frigate followed the splendid right bank of the river, the New Jersey side crowded with villas, and passed between the forts*: the last part of the Hudson leading to Forts Wadsworth and Hamilton is New York State on both sides.

with the 39 stars: WJM and FPW point out that the American flag had 37 stars in 1867, and reached 39 only in 1889.

Leviathan: a monstrous sea creature in the Old Testament, later identified with the whale: a 'sword shall punish Leviathan the piercing serpent [. . .] Leviathan that crooked serpent; and he shall slay the dragon that is in the sea' (Isaiah 27: 1; cf. Job 41: 1 and Psalms 104: 26).

22 *Knight of Rhodes*: a member of a military religious order, also known as the Knights Hospitallers or the Knights of St John, Jerusalem, and Malta.

Dieudonné of Gozo: (d. 1353), delivered Rhodes from a monstrous serpent (Mickel, p. 110).

the 'Argus': Argus was a giant with a hundred eyes set to guard Io; hence a watchful person.

latest model of breech-loading cannon: although this is an American one, Verne must also be thinking of Krupp's great cannon, the Big-Will, seen at the Universal Exposition.

due to be exhibited at the 1867 Universal Exposition: it opened on the Champ-de-Mars on 1 April, and had 43,000 exhibits and 6.8 million visitors. Michel reports that the Rouquayrol–Denayrouze diving apparatus won a gold medal at it. Verne went to it, probably in June, and saw such important inspirations as the Big-Will and Hallet's submarine *Nautilus* (1857), with its riveted sheet-metal, side tanks, and magnifying panes. He also saw section and complete models of Siméon

Bourgeois and Charles-Marie Brun's *Plongeur*, a 146-foot, 80-horse-power metal submarine launched in Rochefort in 1863 and relaunched in 1867. It measured a slender 6 metres by 42, weighed 410 tonnes, and, like Verne's vessel, had a flat deck, a recessed lifeboat, a spur, inclined planes, and observation windows, and used compressed air for breathing and to expel the water from its ballast tanks.

Aronnax is speaking in July 1867, which does not seem to make sense, for the Universal Exposition had already opened.

23 *Ned Land*: from *land* of course, but perhaps also from Tommaso Landi (see note to p. 105 below).

24 *whose depths are still hidden from human eyes*: the present tense implies that, even at the end of the story, no one will have seen the depths.

incredible comets crossing space or prehistoric monsters living inside the Earth ... such fantasies: Verne is being ironic at the expense of his own *Hector Servadac* (1877) and *Journey to the Centre of the Earth* (1864, 1867).

27 *'because it's not true,' he replied, unwittingly echoing a celebrated riposte of Arago's*: according to Michel Ardan in *From the Earth to the Moon*, 'Arago borrowed from Plutarch' the quotation 'Perhaps the stories are not true!' Jacques Arago (1790–1855) was a friend of Verne's and author of *Voyage autour du monde* (1844).

On 30 June: they were off Patagonia on 30 July. This '30 June' and the following '3 July' and '6 July' should logically be in about the second week of August.

28 *after a chase of only a few minutes*: much of the information about hunting whales in *20TL* seems to come from 'Whaling', *Le Magasin pittoresque* (1834), 6–8 and 65–6.

30 *in a state of permanent erethism*: erethism is the 'abnormal sensitivity of an organ to stimulation'!

36 *When the huge narwhal came to the surface to breathe*: why is the submarine making such a noise at two in the morning and why is it sending jets of water to a height of 120 feet?

41 *Byron or Poe, who are masters*: the present tense either indicates the age of Verne's sources or anticipates Nemo's view that 'The great masters are ageless'. Byron (1788–1824) swam the Hellespont (now the Dardanelles) in 1810 to prove that the mythological Leander could have done it. Poe (1809–49), for his part, claimed that as a youth he would have thought nothing of Byron's feat (PC, p. 283).

45 *'The boat hasn't moved?'*: if Conseil and Aronnax fell into the sea at the same spot as Land, and have been swimming for three hours, why do they finish up in the same place?

47 *'Mobilis in Mobile'*: in Latin 'Mobilis' means 'nimble, mobile, lively; shifting, varying, changeable; inconstant, or fickle', and thus 'Mobilis

in mobile' can be translated as 'Mobile in the mobile element' or 'Changing within change'. One source could be the phrases 'mobilis res' and 'mobilis bona', which Verne surely came across during his legal studies.

Considerable discussion has been generated about the correct Latin form and the attempts over the three editions to correct its six occurrences. Given that 'Mobile' is here a substantivized adjective, both the ablative noun 'Mobile' and the ablative adjective 'Mobili' may be considered correct. However, it was clearly intended to amend all instances of 'Mobili', although this was still only partially successful in the 1871 edition, for the monogram itself continued to read 'Mobili'. According to Mickel (p. 44), the shape of the monogram was also changed from two semi-circles surrounding the *N* in the 1869 edition, to the single semi-circle of 1871.

48 *'Maybe they can hear us'*: the captain does seem to be able to read Aronnax and Ned's minds, and his entrances do have uncanny timing. Furthermore, the 'We have nothing in sight' must be communicated from the platform by some means. Finally, in the closing chapters Aronnax remarks: 'Ned Land and Conseil avoided speaking to me for fear of giving themselves away.' Is there perhaps some secret listening (or watching) device on board? Or is the pilot-house used to lip-read?

49 *Diderot*: Denis (1713–84), novelist, philosopher, and editor of the *Encyclopédie* (1751–80).

prosopopoeia, metonymy, and hypallage: classical figures of speech. In prosopopoeia, an imaginary or absent person is represented as speaking or acting; in metonymy, an idea replaces a related one, as in 'bottle' for 'strong drink'; in hypallage, the normal relation between two words is reversed, as in 'her beauty's face'.

A pupil of Gratiolet or Engel would have read his physiognomy like an open book: Dr Pierre-Louis Gratiolet (1815–65) worked as an anatomist and naturalist, and published extensively on physiognomy. Dr Josef Engel (1816–99) was an Austrian anatomist and specialist in hydrotherapy who published from 1840 to 1865.

50 *how he penetrated your very soul! How he could pierce the liquid depths*: Verne is equating seeing into the depths of the mind and into the depths of the sea—pre-Freudian ideas of the subconscious.

51 *Draw from your bag the best English ever spoken by an Anglo-Saxon*: is Ned Land a native speaker of English or of French? Of course some of his characteristics may reflect his Canadian origin, such as his being simultaneously 'half French' and 'American' and his directness and litigiousness. But his name is English, his ancestry French, he is apparently an 'Anglo-Saxon' and swears in English, although his culture is francophone.

Aronnax does not say what language is used by the four main

characters, but it must be French—even when Nemo is declaiming to himself!

51 *invoked 'habeas corpus' . . . unlawfully keeping us prisoners*: the legal language throughout this paragraph reflects Verne's training.

52 *neither the language of Arago nor that of Faraday*: François Arago (1786–1853), astronomer and physicist, studied electromagnetism (his brother Jacques—see note to p. 27 above—was an explorer friend of Verne's). Michael Faraday (1791–1867), British physicist, laid the foundations of classical field theory, developed the first dynamo, and formulated Faraday's Laws. An article by Sainte-Claire Deville in vol. 4 of the *MÉR* (1865–6) praises him.

53 *He brought us clothing*: the narrator omits to mention that he and Conseil have been virtually naked since their swim (and the illustrations in the French edition loyally avoid depicting them).

    the Adelphi Hotel in Liverpool: Verne stayed in the Queen's Hotel on his impecunious 1859 visit to Liverpool, but at the Adelphi in 1867 (18–20 March).

54 *a natural reaction after the interminable night in which we had fought with death*: Aronnax is being slightly duplicitous: we later learn that Nemo seems to administer drugs to his passengers when it suits his purposes; also, two paragraphs above, the *N* may easily stand for the vessel as well as for its captain.

56 *the 'aerifery'*: ('l'"aérifère"')—although the adjective 'aérifère' is established in French, the noun is not attested.

61 *'Calmez-vous, maître Land, et vous, monsieur le professeur, veuillez m'écouter!'*: 'Calm yourself, Master Land, and you, Dr Aronnax, please listen to me!'

62 *Was it unintentionally that Master Land here struck me with his harpoon?*: the captain's use of 'me' for 'my submarine' shows his passionate identification with the vessel—and his antipathy for Ned.

63 *in the same way as Oedipus must have looked at the Sphinx*: the Sphinx proposed a riddle to all travellers, and killed them if they answered incorrectly; but when Oedipus solved the riddle, the Sphinx killed herself instead.

65 *But no promise binds us to the master of this ship*: the captain's 'condition' is that of 'passive obedience' in being 'confine[d] to [. . .] cabins', which Aronnax accepts on behalf of the three men. The 'question asked' concerning the 'choice between life and death' seems to be simply whether they accept to live in the submarine (rather than go back overboard); to which, as Aronnax says, 'no reply is possible' (or indeed given). In sum a promise *has* been made ('passive obedience'), but not a promise to stay. Nemo later says: 'I want you to observe one of the engagements which bind you to me.' But he is mistakenly using

a plural; he has them locked up in the prison cell, not their cabins; and he is abusing the ambiguity of Aronnax (at least) being 'bound' to the captain: bound by his promise or unable to leave?

The explanation of the three discrepancies is to be found in MS2: ' "You are therefore my guests, I do not say my prisoners [. . .] I will impose only three conditions [. . .] they will bind you only within certain limits and their sole aim is to safeguard the mystery of my existence. | "First, you will never seek to know who I used to be, nor who I am, what I used to do nor what I am doing, why I chose to live in these conditions nor why I still live in them. As for the events which take place on my ship and which you will witness, I leave them to your discretion and do not ask you to keep them secret. You will be able to repeat what you have seen, heard, or understood, if ever you return to your fellows [. . .]" | In sum, this first condition was fair; the stranger left us every freedom compatible with the particular demands of his ship and forbade only investigations concerning his person. | "Secondly," he continued, "you will never try to leave my ship without my authorization and even if certain circumstances seemed to you to be favourable to an escape, I do not want you to flee without my consent [. . .] I alone will judge the circumstances in which we will come to separate. Months, years may go by without circumstances being appropriate and you will patiently wait for the time to be ripe to take up again that unbearable yoke of the Earth which men call freedom. Do you accept?" | "We accept," I replied [. . .] this second condition explicitly made us prisoners on our parole.' (MD, pp. 66–7).

This passage is revealing. The idea was for Nemo, who in this version already has a mysterious past, to impose two extra conditions on his 'guests': secrecy and not attempting to return to their 'fellows' (as if the submariners were no longer 'terrestrials'), in return for which he holds out the possibility of releasing them one day. All these ideas will greatly exercise Aronnax's mind over the coming months, with frequent echoes of Nemo's deleted speech (e.g. 'We are not even prisoners on our parole.') Some of Aronnax's musings about Nemo, and even the terrible anguish he feels on leaving, may in sum make more sense after reading this passage.

In line with the MS2 version, in I 11 below MS1 has 'I have promised not to try to find out who you are' in place of the published 'without trying to discover who you are'. Later, instead of 'how your domestic arrangements will be taken care of on board the *Nautilus*', it reads '[. . .] during the indeterminate stay(?) which you will make here'. Similarly, the 1871 'since you will never leave this submarine [. . .]' replaces the MS1 ' "I do not know whether you will ever see dry land again. It is possible that the opportunity will not arise. And if ever you do see it again [. . .] you will have permission xxxxxxx [. . .]" | There was no xxxxx on the possibility of a departure and in any case it was not the right time. We resumed our stroll through the gangway and I returned to the marvellous museum. I sat down again on a divan.'

66 *I will merely be Captain Nemo for you*: in much of MS1A, the commandant is 'Captain x', and he is also called 'the stranger' more often; he is 'Captain Juan Nemo' three times in I 15–16, and thereafter 'Captain Nemo' or baldly 'Nemo'. 'Juan Nemo' would of course make him Spanish, with resonances of Don Juan; and would also make 'Nemo' a surname (cf. Conseil's 'Mr Nemo').

'Nemo' on its own has the advantage of concealing any nationality, and is probably an allusion to many sources. First, Nemo, 'no one', is the Latin equivalent of the Greek 'Outis', the name Ulysses takes on meeting Polyphemus the Cyclops, the son of Poseidon in the *Odyssey*. This alias allows him to use the grammatical pun 'Nemo/No one is killing me' to dupe the Cyclops. Ulysses is later imprisoned by Atlas's daughter for seven years in Ogygia, 'the navel of the seas' (as Verne calls the Maelstrom in II 22); Ogygia was also called 'the island of Atlas', often associated with Atlantis.

Nemo is, secondly, the assumed name of the dead opium addict at the beginning of Dickens's *Bleak House* (1853). The word also occurs in 'Nemo me impune lacessit' ('No one assails me with impunity'), the motto of the Scottish Crown reproduced in the Edinburgh Coat of Arms, which Verne must have seen frequently during his 1859 visit; it is quoted in Poe's 'The Cask of Amontillado' (1846). Many other Latin quotations contain 'nemo', including one that fits the captain: 'Nemo repente fuit turpissimus' ('No man ever became very wicked all at once').

There might also be echoes of the 'admirable' 'floating and sweating seaweed' Nemo*stoma* cited in the text and of the Lago di *Nem*i near Rome (cited by Byron in *Childe Harold*), ancient Lacus *Nemo*rensis, located in the crater of an extinct volcano drained by a 2-mile tunnel. In the fifteenth century a classical statue was raised from Lake Nemi during an attempt to salvage two Roman ships; and a primitive diving-suit was used in sixteenth-century explorations of the lake.

The illustration of Nemo, described by Verne as 'the most energetic imaginable', is based on Hetzel, but especially on Colonel Jean-Baptiste Charras (1810–65): a junior war minister, friend of Hetzel's, and author of *Histoire de la Campagne de 1815: Waterloo* (1857). He was banished from France from 1852 until his death.

the 'Nautilus': a nautilus (< Latin < Greek 'sailor') is a cephalopod mollusc of the genus *Nautilus*, especially the *N. pompilius* found in the Indian and Pacific oceans. It has a spiral, mother-of-pearl-lined shell with air-filled chambers that regulate ascent and descent, plus grasping tentacles surrounding a sharp beak. Maury says: 'The tiny nautilus rides out the hurricane, and weathers storms in which the stoutest men-of-war have foundered' (sec. 1028); and American author

Oliver Wendell Holmes (1809–94) wrote a poem called 'The Chambered Nautilus' (1858), which also mentions sea-sirens and coral reefs. The symbolism is of course in the self-sufficiency and security of the shell and the dual mode of locomotion (paddling and sailing). Its form, *nauti-* plus a masculine ending, combines scientific and mythological resonances, and is Latin and so non-localized, like its inventor. The name itself had regularly been used for submarines before 20TL, especially Fulton's and Hallet's.

67 *Neptune's old shepherd*: Neptune was the Roman god of the sea; his shepherd was Proteus, a minor sea-god and herdsman of the flocks of the sea, with the power to take on many shapes.

68 *a cuttlefish or squid*: the vocabulary of 'byssus [. . .] aplesias [. . .] sea-wrack [. . .] cuttlefish or squid' is taken from *La Mer* (1861) by Jules Michelet (1798–1874), author of a 17-volume *Histoire de la France* (1833–67). Chelebourg says the same source also provides: the remark that coral is perhaps 'the real point where life dimly rises from a sleep of stone, without yet cutting itself off from that rude starting-point'; the idea of whale sightings proving the existence of the Northwest and Northeast Passages; some of the details of Atlantis; the sea of milk, the Black River, the open sea at the South Pole, the animalculae, the madrepores as makers of worlds, the 'blood flower' coral, and the submarine forests; the Mediterranean being 'one of the globe's most powerful climates'; the harpooner as bold hero confronting monstrous whales on a fragile skiff; the (incorrect) idea of the killer squid; the giant crustaceans wearing armour; the idea that volcanoes were more active in the early geological periods (II ii, I iv, III iv, II iii, II v, II iv, II iv, IV ii, III i, III i, II x); and, according to WJM and FPW, the probably incorrect idea of sperm whales attacking baleen whales.

a living infinity, as one of your poets has said: MS2 reads, 'as your illustrious Michelet said'. This whole paragraph is found in II 2 in MS2, with, however, the less accurate 'four-fifths' for 'seven-tenths', lists of creatures in the various groupings, and the phrase 'Here I am master'.

69 *It was a library*: MS1: 'It was a library and smoking-room.'

70 *it is very thin in comparison with yours*: MS1 has instead: 'never did it offer me such a precious collection of books.'

free use of them: MS1 adds: 'for all the time that circumstances will force me to keep you in this prison.'

Homer . . . Sand: writers. *Xenophon*: (430?–355? BC), historian, philosopher, and author of the *Anabasis*, which contains the quotation 'The sea! The sea!' (IV. vii. 24), central to Verne's 'Edom' (1910). *Victor Hugo*: (1802–85), poet, dramatist, and author notably of *The Hunchback of Notre Dame* (1831), *Les Misérables* (1862), and *The Toilers of the Sea* (1866). *Rabelais*: François (c.1490–1553), author of

the four books of *Gargantua and Pantagruel* (1535–52). *Mme Sand*:
George, pseudonym of Amandine-Aurore-Lucie Dupin (Baronne)
Dudevant (1804–76), novelist; on 25 July 1865 she had written to
Verne: 'I hope that you will soon take us into the depths of the sea
and that you will have your characters travel in those divers' machines
which your scientific knowledge and imagination will permit themselves to improve', an inspiration for *20TL* that Verne confirmed in an
interview with Brisson in 1897.

Despite the phrase 'everything that humanity has produced of greatest beauty in history, poetry, the novel'. Hugo and Sand are the only
nineteenth-century novelists or poets mentioned in *20TL*. Verne's lists
are instead scientists, painters, and musicians; he may be reacting to a
ferocious remark of Hetzel's in the margin of a list of writers in *Paris
in the Twentieth Century*: 'I find all this review puerile.' Hugo and
Sand both figured amongst Hetzel's best-sellers; and Michelet also had
regular contacts with the publisher.

MS2 adds 'from Aeschylus to Dumas *fils*.' Aeschylus (525–456 BC)
wrote accounts of an eruption of Etna, plus, notably, *The Persians* (472
BC), about Athens' naval victory over Persia. Concerning Alexandre
Dumas *fils* (1824–95), the novelist and playwright of *La Dame aux
camélias* (1848, 1852), Verne told Sherard in 1893: 'the friend to
whom I owe the deepest debt of gratitude and affection is Alexandre
Dumas the younger, whom I first met at the age of twenty-one. We
became chums almost at once [. . .] he was my first mentor. [. . .] He
introduced me to his father [. . .] we wrote together a play called *Pailles
rompues* [1849] [. . .] and a comedy called *Onze jours de siège* [1850].'
Was the reason for the deletion perhaps a disagreement between the
two?

MS1 has 'of greatest beauty, ~~from the holy scriptures~~ [. . .]'.

70 *Humboldt . . . Agassiz*: scientists. *Humboldt*: Alexander (Baron von)
(1769–1859), naturalist, statesman, and traveller; his *Aspects of
Nature* is quoted by Maury, and he wrote about Atlantis in *Kosmos*
and in *Examen critique de l'histoire de la géographie du nouveau continent* (1836) (I 167). *Arago*: see note to p. 52 above. *Foucault*: Léon
(1819–68), physicist, invented the gyroscope and studied refraction in
water. *Henri Sainte-Claire Deville*: (1818–81), chemist and educator,
studied the thermal disassociation of compounds and aluminium (his
brother Charles (1814–76) was a geologist and friend of Verne's); his
pupil Fouqué examined Santorini (cf. II 6) in 1865. *Chasles*: Michel
(1793–1880), mathematician, specialist in geometry. *Milne-Edwards*:
Henri (1800–85), French zoologist, an anti-Darwinian who worked on
molluscs and crustaceans, and was apparently the first scientist to dive
under the sea (in 1844 off Sicily, with Quatrefages); in 1861 he found
invertebrates attached to a submarine cable at 1,800 metres; Aronnax
later refers to him as 'my illustrious mentor' (I 19). *Tyndall*: John
(1820–93), British physicist, studied the scattering of light by suspended particles.

Faraday: see note to p. 52 above. *Berthelot*: Marcellin (1827–1907), organic chemist and public official. *Abbé Secchi*: Angelo (1818–78), astronomer; pioneered classifying stars by means of their spectra. *Commander Maury*: Matthew Fontaine (1806–73), US and Confederate naval officer and hydrographer; author of *The Physical Geography of the Sea* (translated into French by P. A. Terquem (1855); translated again by Zurcher and Margollé (Hetzel, 1866)), discovered the Gulf Stream and the system of ocean circulation, was the first to sound the Atlantic, and invented an electric torpedo. Verne's 'The sea has its rivers like the continents' is taken from him, as is the idea of low barometer readings in the Antarctic (WJM and FPW). *Agassiz*: Louis (1807–73), Swiss-American zoologist and geologist, anti-Darwinian author of a five-volume *Research on Fossil Fish* (1833–44), four-volume *Contributions to the Natural History of the United States* (1857–62), and *Voyage au Brésil* (1868), which inspired Verne's *The Giant Raft* (1881). A footnote in the recently discovered manuscript of *Journey to the Centre of the Earth*, deleted in the published editions, reads, 'Professor Lidenbrock is here using the classification proposed for fish by Professor Agassiz which is based on the layout, nature, and form of the scales': Agassiz, in other words, is the unsuspected source for the first living creatures found underground.

MS1 has a much shorter list, but preceded by 'On a table could be seen, half leafed through, works by Milne Eddvard [*sic*] [. . .]'.

amongst the books of Joseph Bertrand, 'Les Fondateurs de l'astronomie': Joseph Bertrand (1822–1900) taught at the École Normale Supérieure and wrote *Arago et sa vie scientifique* (1865) and *Les Fondateurs de l'astronomie moderne, Copernic, Tycho Brahé, Képler, Galilée, Newton* (Hetzel, 1865), described in *From the Earth to the Moon* as a 'fine book by M. J. Bertrand of the Institute', and advised Verne for that and other works; Verne's first cousin, Henri Garcet, a mathematics teacher at the Lycée Henri IV who also contributed to Verne's novels, was Bertrand's assistant.

the fitting out of the 'Nautilus' did not date from after that: Verne means the opposite.

71 *an enormous, magnificently lit salon*: in December 1868 Verne wrote, 'I have received Riou's sketches [. . .]. I think he should make the characters much smaller and the salons much bigger. These are mere corners of the salon which do not give any idea of the *Nautilus*'s marvels.' The final illustrations show a huge hall of a room.

72 *a Madonna by Raphael . . . Vernet*: unspecified works from the western European canon: *a Madonna by Raphael* (1483–1520), Italian Renaissance painter, whose works include a number of famous Madonnas; *a Virgin by Leonardo da Vinci*: (1452–1519), Florentine Renaissance engineer, scientist, and painter of *The Virgin of the Rocks* (1483–5 and 1490s to 1508); *a nymph by Correggio*: real name

Antonio Allegri (1489?–1534), Renaissance painter; *a woman by Titian*: originally Tiziano Vecellio (1488?–1576), Venetian artist of *The Assumption of the Virgin* (1518); *an Adoration by Veronese*: Paolo, originally Paola Caliari (1528–88), painter of the Venetian school; *an Assumption by Murillo*: Bartolomé Esteban (1617–82), Spanish artist of genre scenes, portraits, and religious subjects; *a portrait by Holbein*: Hans, the Elder (1465?–1524), or Hans, the Younger (1497?–1543), German-born painters of religious works; *a monk by Velázquez*: Diego Rodríguez de Silva y (1599–1660), Spanish painter of portraits, still lifes, and genre and historical scenes; *a martyr by Ribera*: José or Jusepe de (1588–1652), Spanish baroque painter; *a country fair by Rubens*: Peter Paul (1577–1640), Flemish baroque painter of portraits and allegorical, historical, and religious scenes; *two Flemish landscapes by Teniers*: David, the Younger (1610–90), landscapes and religious and genre scenes; *Gerrit Dou*: (1613–75), Dutch pupil of Rembrandt; *Metsu*: Gabriel (1629–67), Dutch painter, probably a pupil of Dou; *Paul Potter*: (1625–54), Dutch painter of landscape and animal scenes; *Géricault*: Théodore (1791–1824), painted *The Raft of the Medusa* (1819), a major source for *The Chancellor*; *Prud'hon*: Pierre-Paul (1758–1823), foreshadowed the romantic style; *Backhuysen*: Ludolphe (1631–1709), Dutch painter of ships; *Vernet*: Joseph (1714–89), painter of shipwrecks, sunsets, and conflagrations, including *Jonas sortant de la Baleine* and *Vue intérieure du Vésuve*.

It is no coincidence that the last name in the list should be a J. Vernet with a strong interest in the sea, ships, monsters, the interiors of volcanoes, and eruptions (*Five Weeks in a Balloon* also places a 'Werne' in a prominent position).

MS2 is again revealing (MD, p. 67). The Virgin was a 'half-dressed woman', 'the woman by Titian', 'a courtesan'; and the Veronese, Murillo, Velázquez, and Ribera were originally absent: in other words, all the religious paintings! If the naked flesh tenuously survives, in the illustrations to *The Mysterious Island*, the Christian pictures seem out of character for a Nemo who has deleted the holy scriptures from his library—and may be a sign of Hetzel's imposition of 'moral' values.

72 *Delacroix ... Daubigny*: modern artists. *Delacroix*: Eugène (1798–1863), romantic painter of *Liberty Leading the People* (1831). *Ingres*: Jean-Auguste-Dominique (1780–1867), painter of classical and mythological works. *Decamps*: Alexandre (1803–60), introduced oriental themes, and painted animal subjects. *Troyon*: Constant (1813–65), painter of landscapes and animals. *Meissonier*: Jean-Louis-Ernest (1815–91), painter of genre and military scenes. *Daubigny*: Charles-François (1817–78), painter of landscapes which influenced the Impressionists. It will be noted that all the moderns are French, as are the three most recent old masters.

'Daubigny' was added in the 1871 edition. MS2 is again quite different (MD, p. 68). The following are present, without it being clear why they were deleted: Scheffer (Ary, 1795–1858, French portraitist, including a famous one of Arago); Delaroche (Paul, 1797–1856, historical painter); Courbet (Gustave, 1819–77, portrait and landscape painter); Rosa Bonheur (1822–99, farm and rustic scenes); Fromentin (Eugène, 1820–76, oriental scenes); and Millet (Jean-François, 1814–75, landscapes). MS1 has 'Daubigny' back in again; but only Courbet and Fromentin from the above list.

Weber . . . Gounod: western European composers. *Weber*: Carl Maria von (1786–1826), German. *Rossini*: Gioacchino Antonio (1792–1868). *Mozart*: Wolfgang (1756–91), Austrian. *Beethoven*: Ludwig van (1770–1827), German. *Haydn*: (Franz) Joseph (1732–1809), Austrian. *Meyerbeer*: Giacomo (1791–1864), German who lived in France after 1824; his opera *L'Africaine* opened in 1865. *Hérold*: Louis-Joseph-Ferdinand (1791–1833), comic opera. *Wagner*: Richard (1813–83), German. *Auber*: Daniel-François-Esprit (1782–1871), operatic works. *Gounod*: Charles-François (1818–93), the opera *Roméo et Juliette* (1867). Wagner is the only non-French contemporary. Verne's interest in opera is perhaps connected with his own libretto *La Mille et deuxième nuit* (1850).

'Massé' also appeared in the 1869 edition (WJM and FPW). Victor Massé (1822–84), often quoted by Verne in the same phrase as Wagner, composed comic opera, and was a member of Verne's mid-1850s dining club the 'Onze-sans-femmes' ('The Womenless Eleven'). He is described in *Paris in the Twentieth Century* as 'the last musician with sentiment and feeling, whose *Indienne* was the masterpiece of the period'.

Orpheus: mythological musician and one of the Argonauts; visited the underworld.

MS1 has: 'a Delacroix, an Ingres are merely for me contemporaries of Apelles or Xerxes, and it seems to me that this world has not survived them very long.' Apelles was a fourth-century BC Greek painter. Xerxes I (c.519–465 BC), king of Persia, is said to have cut a canal through the isthmus of Mount Athos; he defeated Leonidas (one of Nemo's heroes) at Thermopylae.

73 *Captain Nemo fell silent and seemed lost in a deep reverie*: immediately before this sentence, MS1 has: '"Contemporaries of Orpheus, whose success they never equalled in the stone age." | "But you love their works." | "Yes, but there is a music I prefer to the music of all the ancient and modern artists." | "Which music, captain?" | "My own, sir." | This reply explained to me the vague sounds I had heard during the first night spent on the hull of the *Nautilus*.'

This dialogue perhaps also explains why Aronnax, who identifies paintings at a mere glance, is never able to place the music Nemo is playing; and why Nemo's denial that he is an 'artist' seems slightly equivocal. Verne's reference to 'the stone age' fits in with his dramatically shortened time-scales, since he has not totally given up the date of Genesis as 4004 BC; it was only in about 1865 that opinion was convinced that man had existed in prehistoric times. The Stone Age is now reckoned to have generally finished in about 4000 BC; the term was first used in the 1860s.

75 *Tavernier*: Jean-Baptiste (1605–89), traveller, trader, and author of *Six voyages en Turquie, en Perse et aux Indes* (1676–7).

searched: MS1 adds: 'You can see that the casket of the sea is inexhaustible.'

No museum in Europe possesses a comparable collection of marine products: this sentence is missing from the 1869 edition.

76 *almost hermit-like appearance*: MS1 adds 'less comfortable perhaps than mine'.

Only the barest of necessities: the whole of the introduction to the *Nautilus* is drawn from Verne's seminal visit to a mansion house in 'Ockley' (Oakley in Fife) in 1859. Thus Verne's first book, *Backwards to Britain*, parallels *20TL* in that it describes a difficult sea-journey, climbing up a ladder, a surprising welcome in French, a change into dry clothes, and an attendant speaking a mysterious language. The guests enter the habitation 'without even being able to study its external form', and find 'assembled all the discoveries of modern luxury': perfumed bedrooms and 'a magnificent salon' with angled seats, display cabinets, and windows 'allowing extensive views in all directions'. The walls are covered with 'magnificent canvases from the Italian school [. . .] and a few masterpieces from the Flemish school'; and the salon leads into an 'austere and peaceful library and a natural history room'. There is even artificial illumination of the exterior, a 'plaintive melody', and a 'platform' on the top with a 'powerful telescope' for viewing the whole horizon. In sum, the guests are 'flabbergasted to find such luxury in the middle of the half-wild countryside'. The identity in every detail is remarkable; if the autobiographic text had been written after *20TL*, one would suspect direct borrowing *from* the novel. Even the Gothic toilets in Fife anticipate Nemo's perfect plumbing.

A visit I made to Oakley in September 1996 reveals further surprises. The description of *Backwards to Britain* is scrupulously exact, with the stone jetty of Crombie Point (Verne: 'Cramby') and above all Inzievar House, ancestral seat of the Seligos, identical in every respect to Verne's description, down to the 'phenomenal' vine, the 'platform' and every architectural feature. If we accept Inzievar as the surprising origin for the *Nautilus*, further research into its floor-plan, furnishing, and paintings may well reveal vital additional information about the inspiration of *20TL*.

on the surface: MS1 adds, 'You can see that I am amply equipped', surely an intentional *double entendre*.

77 *That agent is electricity*: this sentence is replaced in MS1 by: 'it steers me, it charges my rifles.'

78 *I could have established a circuit between wires sunk at different depths, and hence obtained electricity from the difference in temperature between them*: in other words, Nemo does not employ the innovative idea of deriving electricity directly from the water. However, in *Master of the World* (1904) Verne incorrectly says that electricity 'was drawn from the surrounding water by the celebrated Captain Nemo, when he launched his *Nautilus* through the depths of the Ocean'.

Bunsen: Robert Wilhelm (1811–99), chemist who contributed to the invention of the zinc-carbon battery and the spectroscope, and improved the Bunsen burner.

Dr Aronnax, you will see me at work: although we do hear more about the captain's underwater mines (an idea drawn from Verne's Scottish visit), we never in fact see him working there.

79 *wind, water, and steam*: MS1 adds 'and will on its own meet all humanity's needs'.

The total length was about 115 feet: from centre to end, as confirmed by Nemo's figure of 'exactly 70 metres' a page later. In the opening chapters, Aronnax had rejected 200 feet as the length, and 'reliable' sources had given 350 feet.

81 *But its door was closed*: MS1: '[. . .] a score of men, and indeed no more than this [. . .] were needed to operate the *Nautilus*. I thought therefore that the crew of this strange ship were limited to that number. About ten seamen were busy working, and did not seem to notice my presence in the room.'

Ruhmkorff: Heinrich Daniel (1803–77), physicist.

up to 120 revolutions per second: Nemo means per minute!

A speed of 50 knots: MS1: '30 knots'; MS2: '35 knots'.

82 *It is an elongated cylinder with conical ends*: MS1: 'It is long so as to go fast.' In addition to the serious scientific point, Verne is being scurrilous again.

83 *its volume 1,500.2 m³*: a misprint for '1,507.2 m³' (which is correct in MS1). The '1,356.48 m³' of the following paragraph should also be about '1,350 m³'. On the other hand, the weights of '1,500' and '1,507' tons are clearly rounded-down figures.

961.62 tons, which, when added to the 394.96, gives . . . 1,356.48 tons: in fact 1,356.58. MS1 has the area as '1,011.49 m²'.

84 *100 atmospheres*: Gagneux points out that variations in temperature and salinity have a much greater effect than the pressure on water density.

86 *I love it like the flesh of my flesh*: Genesis 2: 23–4: 'And Adam said [. . .] "[The] flesh of my flesh: she shall be called Woman, because she

was taken out of Man" [who] shall cleave unto his wife: and they shall be one flesh.' Nemo's relationship to his submarine is both paternal and carnal.

86 *the Dutchman Jansen*: Marin Henry (1817–93), Dutch translator of Maury (see note to p. 91 below) and the author of *Een brug over den oceaan* (1869) as well as works on measuring sea temperatures and on the East Indies, referred to frequently in Maury.

87 *Le Creusot . . . Hart Brothers of New York*: manufacturing companies. *Le Creusot*: the Schneider iron and steel mills and munition factories (founded 1837) at Le Creusot, Saône-et-Loire. *Penn and Co. of London*: (Verne: 'Pen') John Penn & Sons, of Greenwich; constructed the first treadmill (1817) and patented an important improvement to the screw-propeller (1854). *Laird's of Liverpool*: (Verne: 'Leard') Laird Brothers, in fact of Birkenhead, possibly constructed the first iron vessel (1829). *Scott & Co. of Glasgow*: shipbuilders, in fact of Greenock. In *Captain Hatteras*, following the detailed designs of a mysterious and anonymous captain, this same company had already constructed an exceptional ship with a sort of a spur, destined for a unique expedition. *Cail and Co. of Paris*: steel works in Denain, near Lille, founded by Jean-François Cail (1804–71); constructed locomotives, etc. *Krupp in Prussia*: family of steel manufacturers including Alfred (1812–87) and Friedrich Alfred (1854–1902). *Motala in Sweden*: a small town producing naval and electrical equipment. *Hart Brothers of New York*: no trace has been found of this company.

88 *1,687,000 francs*: in fact 1,687,500. Is the number of Nemo's mistakes a sign that he is showing off a little?

    the ten billion francs of France's debts: 1869: 'twelve billion francs' (WJM and FPW).

    383,255,800 square kilometres, or more than 38 million hectares: modern estimates give 361 million square kilometres; and given that 100 hectares are a square kilometre, the second figure should read 'thirty-eight *billion*'. Also, the '2,250 million cubic miles' must mean cubic *kilometres*, for modern estimates give 322 million cubic miles. Finally, 'a sphere sixty leagues in diameter' would only give about 40 million cubic miles.

89 *its metal plates overlapped slightly*: this seems to contradict the earlier 'The blackish surface I was standing on was smooth and polished, and had no overlapping sections'.

90 *37° 15´*: this should be '137° 15″'.

91 *Galileo*: Galileo Galilei (1564–1642), astronomer and physicist who developed the telescope, observed sunspots, and discovered that all bodies fell at the same speed. In 1633 the Inquisition made him renounce his support of Copernican theory. Verne often quotes him as a model of the misunderstood scientist.

Maury: American oceanographer, featured in Nemo's library; wrote *The Physical Geography of the Sea* (1855), a major source for Verne. A brief selection of information clearly taken from Maury would include: the references to Wilkes, Ehrenberg, Humboldt, Faraday, Captains King and Fitzroy, Franklin, Parker, Denham, Dumont d'Urville, and Ross; 'ooze', the expansion undergone by freezing water, the role of undercurrents, the proof of the Northwest Passage by finding whales with stamped harpoons in them on the other side, the idea that right whales cannot pass the warm waters of the equator, the use of British miles, information about burials at sea, messages-in-bottles, sounding techniques, and the transatlantic cable over the 'telegraphic plateau'; the associated bringing up of specimens, the idea of life on the seabed and the pressure there, the calm in the deeps, jellyfish as nettles, the sea of milk, luminescence, the salinity of the sea, animalculae, and the nautilus shell; the idea of driftwood coming down the Mississippi (not tree-trunks down the Missouri, as Verne implausibly claims), the difference in the level between the Red Sea and Mediterranean, the Sargasso Sea, the Gulf Stream, the 'Kuro-Siwo' (*sic*) or Black Stream, the idea of the large Antarctic landmass needed to produce the icebergs, and many of the localities. It is clear that Verne owes a large debt to Maury.

Kuro-Scivo of the Japanese, the Black River, which leaves the Bay of Bengal: the *Kodansha Encyclopedia* gives 'Kuroshio', 'Black Stream', or 'Japan Current', and says it originates east of the Philippines.

92 *Hôtel du Sommerard*: a museum in the rue Sommerard in the Latin Quarter, devoted mainly to medieval France; now known as the Cluny Museum.

93 *Ehrenberg*: (Verne: 'Erhemberg') Dr Christian Gottfried (1795–1876), naturalist specializing in coral, author of 'Passat-Staub und Blut-Regen', quoted by Maury; worked with Humboldt.

97 *the seas of Japan and China*: it was presumably near this point in the text that Hetzel made one of his more catastrophic suggestions/instructions, in line with his wish to make Verne's books more commercial. His letters, found by Gondolo della Riva, have unfortunately not been published to date. However, the following, probably written in 1868 or 1869, is an exception: 'Sunday—3 a.m. [. . .] save some little Chinese kidnapped by Chinese pirates. They are not dangerous. They are funny, they are to be taken home in the dinghy. They are completely taken in [*sic*]. Nemo cannot worry about them [*sic*]. One could be kept on board. No one understands him, he understands no one. He would cheer the *Nautilus* up. But that is your business.'

100 *'Nautron respoc lorni virch'*: (MS1: '[. . .] restoll loui [. . .]') Soriano (p. 350) points out that lorni may connote *lorgner* ('look (with desire)'); *respoc*, *corps* ('body'); and *virch*, *vir* ('man')—producing

'look at man's body', with strong homosexual overtones. But it could equally be argued that *Nautron* contains the root *naut-*, and that *respoc* is an anagram of *Crespo* (see following note), or even gives *re-spoc*, 'look again' (WJM and FPW). Aronnax later deduces that the phrase means 'We have nothing in sight', but it is not clear which words mean what.

101 *Captain Crespo ... Roca de la Plata*: (Verne: 'Rocca') Roca de la Plata/Crespo Island is invented, apparently together with its discoverer, although it is not clear why Verne does not simply choose an existing island. 'Roca de la Plata' is possibly derived from Río de la Plata in South America.

103 *Rouquayrol–Denayrouze apparatus*: Benoît Rouquayrol (1826–75), engineer, and naval Lieut. Auguste Denayrouze (1838–83). Michel reports that the automatic regulation of incoming air pressure for a given depth was invented by Rouquayrol in 1860; and that the compressed air-tank worn on one's back, the direct ancestor of the modern aqualung, was finished in 1864, and sold to navies worldwide. The most sophisticated version allowed an hour's diving at 10 metres, or half an hour at 40 metres: much less than Nemo's version. PC reports that air was forced into the reservoir by a pipe from the surface, which could be disconnected if wished.

104 *Ruhmkorff apparatus*: this device plays a prominent role in *Journey to the Centre of the Earth* ('The Ruhmkorff apparatus consists of a Bunsen battery [...] an induction coil [...] and a glass coil under vacuum [...] producing a continuous white light').

105 *Fulton ... Landi*: inventors of naval armaments. *Fulton*: Robert (1765–1815), American inventor and engineer. He designed the first commercially successful steamboat (1807); and built two different submarines called *Nautilus*, designed to launch explosives against British ships. He successfully demonstrated his three-man 21-foot candle-lit craft on the Seine in Paris in 1800–1. The *Nautilus* had a spindle shape, a folding sail, a ballast pump, a conning tower with glass ports, rudders/diving planes for vertical and horizontal control, compressed air to supply oxygen, a hand-powered four-blade propeller, and a torpedo charge on a trailing rope. His *Nautilus* was also successfully tested by the French Navy at Brest in 1802, but they considered its methods unfair, and in the end Fulton destroyed his *Nautilus*. *Britons Phipps Coles and Burney*: (Verne: 'Philippe Coles and Burley') Captain Cowper Phipps Coles (1819–70), author of *Iron-Clad Sea-Going Ships* [1863?] and *Letters from Captain C. Coles to the Secretary of the Admiralty on Sea-Going Turret-Ships* [1865?]; probably William Burney (1762–1832), editor of *A New and Universal Dictionary of the Marine* (1830), containing an appendix on French naval terminology; *the Frenchman Furcy*: no trace has been found; *the Italian Landi*: Tommaso (dates unknown), author of *Nouveau procédé pour l'immersion du câble télégraphique sous-marin* [...] [1860s].

the Austrian chemist Leniebroek: WJM and FPW write 'Leinebroch' but no trace of either name has been found.

Leyden jars: electrical condensers with a glass jar as a dielectric between sheets of tin foil (1745).

107 *about 20 electric bullets*: two pages earlier, Nemo had said 'a fully loaded gun can contain up to ten' electric capsules.

113 *an irresistible slumber*: Mickel claims that the Rouquayrol–Denayrouze apparatus requires the tongue to move back and forth between the in and out tubes, meaning that one cannot sleep, an idea he seems to have borrowed from Miller (1976). WJM and FPW, however, admit that the argument applies only to 'the Rouquayrol apparatus, *as normally used*' (I 15), and not necessarily to Nemo's improved version.

115 *its species will probably soon become extinct*: sea otters were indeed almost hunted to extinction, but are now protected. Verne's own opposition to hunting is clearly stated on numerous occasions, so it is possible that Nemo's behaviour (plus his companion's a page below, and even the unjustified over-fishing in I 18) is being criticized, if not by Aronnax, at least by the author.

116 *shot at it when it was only a few metres above the waves*: WJM and FPW are ironical about the difficulty of shooting while compensating for the refraction: however, no compensation is necessary if the bird is vertically overhead.

117 *Monstrous fiery mouths*: 'fire flies' ('mouches à feu') in the 1869, 1871, and Livre de Pouche editions seems to be an error for 'fiery mouths' ('bouches à feu'). Ellis says that such sharks do not have 'glassy eyes' or a 'phosphorescent substance', but in fact at least one species of dogfish shark is luminescent.

118 *I recognized what were clearly Irish, French, a few Slavs, a Greek, and a Cretan*: Aronnax has an amazing, almost racist, ability to discern the different nationalities; but the men's appearance is the only way the narrator can indicate their varied origins and hence the scale of Nemo's social experiment.

119 *caloric*: an indestructible, all-pervading, undetectable fluid formerly believed to be responsible for the transfer of heat.

120 *You will see the consequences of this phenomenon at the Poles*: Aronnax will see only one Pole (II 13).

four-and-a-half million cubic leagues . . . a layer more than 10 metres high: the first figure is much too large, and the second much too small.

121 *15,149 metres*: the great depths quoted in 20TL are based on faulty sounding techniques, and some are more than double the correct figure. The deepest point is now calculated, using sonar, to be about 10,900 metres.

122 *Cook*: Captain James (1728–79), navigator. He explored the coasts of Australia and New Zealand, and is credited with preventing scurvy through proper diet.

123 *Athenaeus*: scholar and doctor (flourished third century AD), founder of the Pneumatic sect, author of *Deipnosophistai* ('Men learned in the arts of the banquet').

Galen: Claudius Galen (AD 130?–200), Greek physician and anatomist.

d'Orbigny: Alcide-Charles-Victor-Dessalines (1802–57), creationist geologist who published an eight-volume *Paléontologie française* (1840–54), ordering rock strata by their fossil content and thus dividing the past into visible stages (the metaphor that generates *Journey to the Centre of the Earth*).

Jean Macé: (1815–94), publicist and author of *Les Serviteurs de l'estomac* (1864). He founded the *Magasin d'Éducation et de Récréation* with Hetzel in 1864 (Verne also directed it from 1866); its inaugural issue started the serialization of *Captain Hatteras*. In *Paris in the Twentieth Century*, Verne calls him 'the most ingenious of scientific popularizers'.

125 *The 'Florida', Sunderland*: the name is highly unusual for a British ship: it must be borrowed from the Confederate *Florida* which sank 37 Northern ships in just over a year, and was at the centre of the *Alabama* Affair, mentioned several times in Verne's correspondence and works (see following note).

a series of maritime disasters that the 'Nautilus' was to encounter on its route: given the suspicious coincidence of meeting the *Florida* and the tragic ending of *20TL*, Nemo has at the very least an unhealthy interest in wrecked ships and may actually be sinking them himself! But in any case, this incident may be an anticipatory hint as to national groups which Nemo will attack in Part Two: the Confederates and/or the British.

on 11 December: it was already 11 December at the end of the previous chapter. Has Verne forgotten; or else is he subtly marking the sinking of the *Florida* as at Tuamotu, in the centre of the huge area of the Pacific owned by the French and an unlikely place to meet a British ship?

Bougainville's: Louis Antoine de Bougainville (1729–1811), explorer, naturalist, and geographer. He fought in the American War of Independence, rediscovered the Solomon Islands, and wrote a *Voyage Around the World* (1771–2).

Captain Bellingshausen of the 'Mirny': (Verne: 'Captain Bell of the *Minerve*') Fabian Gottlieb von Bellingshausen (1778–1852), admiral and explorer. He skirted round Antarctica and discovered Peter I and Alexander I Islands. He is mentioned again (Verne: 'Bellinghausen') in the Antarctic episode.

126 *Mr Darwin*: Charles Robert (1809–82), British naturalist. From data
accumulated on a circumnavigation on the *Beagle* (1831–6), he formulated the modern concept of evolution in *On the Origin of Species*
(1859, French translation 1862) and *The Descent of Man* (1871).
Verne's mention of him here is his first. Although on this occasion
approval is given to Darwin's writings on coral reefs or the ocean
depths (which were translated in the periodical *Le Tour du monde* in
1860), on evolution itself Verne remained silent until 1901, when he
said: 'I am far from arriving at Darwin's conclusion, whose ideas I
have absolutely no sympathy with.' Elsewhere Verne announced 'the
conclusions I shall put forward [in *The Village in the Treetops* (1901)]
are those of a believer, and entirely opposed to the theories of Darwin'.
A central theme of *Edom* (1910) is human evolution, or rather its
repeated absence.

A hundred and ninety-two thousand years: the figures quoted in fact
give about 10 million years. WJM and FPW point out that the rate of
growth of coral is incorrect by a factor of about 50.

127 *In this way animal life developed and . . . man appeared*: throughout
this paragraph Verne's deadpan narrative describes the successive
stages of the population of empty landmasses, without providing any
adverbs or extended clauses. There is no causal link or time-frame, and
thus the feat is performed of reconciling biblical and biological
accounts of the past. Verne's description of the arrival of man, in particular, scrupulously avoids any question of where he came from. His
source is Michelet, who has, however, much less detail: 'the solid
coconut [. . .] pushed by the waves [. . .] germinates, grows, and is now
a tree, a robust coconut tree. [. . .] Soon palm trees can be seen. From
the water vapour that they stop comes a stream.'

Tonga . . . killed: historical events in the South Pacific. *the final resting-
place for the crews of the 'Argo', the 'Port-au-Prince', and the 'Duke
of Portland'*: the *Argo* was an Australian brig wrecked on Argo Reef,
south-east Fiji, in January 1800; the *Port-au-Prince* was a Liverpool
privateer seized on 23 November 1806 by natives of the Lefuka
Islands; and the *Duke of Portland* was an American ship seized at
Tongataboo in the Friendly Islands in June 1802: in all three cases the
majority of the survivors were killed by the natives. *Captain de Langle,
the friend of La Pérouse*: Paul de Langle (1744–87), captain of the
Astrolabe, killed on 11 December 1787 on Tutuila in the Samoan
group. Jean-François de Galaup (Comte de) La Pérouse (1741–88)
was an explorer who died on Vanikoro in 1788 (see below, note to p.
129).

Captain Bureau from Nantes: possibly Louis-Marcellin (born *c*.1800).
The incident happened in July 1834.

128 *Tasman*: Abel Janszoon (1603–59), Dutch navigator and explorer, discovered Tasmania and New Zealand, and circumnavigated Australia,
thus proving it an island.

128 *Torricelli*: Evangelista (1608–47), mathematician and physicist, disciple of Galileo.

Cook in 1714, d'Entrecasteaux in 1793, and finally Dumont d'Urville: Cook in fact visited Fiji in 1774. Antoine-Raymond-Joseph de Bruni (Chevalier) d'Entrecasteaux (1737–93): his search for La Pérouse is described in *Voyage de Dentrecasteaux* [sic], *envoyé à la recherche de La Pérouse: Rédigé par M. de Rossel* (1808). Jules-Sébastien-César Dumont d'Urville (1790–1842), explorer who studied terrestrial magnetism, charted the South Atlantic, South Pacific, and Antarctic, and discovered Adélie and Clarie Coasts.

Captain Dillon, the first man to throw light on the mystery of La Pérouse's shipwreck: Peter Dillon (1785?–1847), Irish captain; given a French state pension for his work. He wrote *Narrative [. . .] of a voyage in the South Seas [. . .] to ascertain the actual fate of La Pérouse* (1829, French translation 1830). Vaileka was also known as 'Dillon's Rock'.

Seneca's: Lucius Annaeus Seneca, the Younger (*c*.4 BC–AD 65), Stoic philosopher, writer, and politician. Verse 375 of his *Medea* reads: 'Centuries will come, in the old age of the Earth, when the Ocean will give things back their freedom, when the land will stretch immense, when Tethys will uncover new continents, and when Thule will no longer be the end of the world.'

Quiros: Admiral Pedro-Fernandez de (1560?–1614), Portuguese navigator.

129 *Vanikoro*: or Vanikolo, in the Santa Cruz Islands, south-east Solomon Islands.

130 *a report by Captain Hunter*: John Hunter (1738–1821), later governor of New South Wales. He explored the Furneaux Islands and Bass Strait, showed that Tasmania was an island, and wrote *An Historical Journal [. . .] with an Abridged Account of the New Discoveries in the South Seas* (1793).

132 *M. Jacquinot*: Charles-Hector (1796–1879), admiral; he edited Dumont d'Urville's *Voyage au Pôle sud et dans l'Océanie [. . .]* (1842–54) after his death.

the 'Bayonnaise', commanded by Le Goarant de Tromelin: (Verne: 'Legoarant de Tromelin') Louis-François-Marie-Nicolas Le Goarant de Tromelin (1786–1867), later rear admiral. The *Bayonnaise* was a corvette in fact sent to report on the political situation in Hawaii, and thence, via Tikopia and Vanikoro (17 June 1828), back to France.

133 *visited Tonga and New Caledonia, headed for Santa Cruz, and put into Nomuka in the Haapai Group*: Tonga in fact includes the Haapai Group.

Satisfaction: in this paragraph Verne is weaving fact and fiction, with the story up to and including the departure ('northwards') in the cannibalized ship being what Captain Dillon learned from the islanders. The wreck of the *Boussole* was located only in 1964, 500 metres north-west of the *Astrolabe*. The rest still remains an unsolved mystery, although it has been surmised that the ship finished up at Simbo. Verne's tin box and location are invented—or borrowed from a different story.

134 *La Pérouse Island:* Verne has 'le groupe de La Pérouse', but modern texts refer to La Pérouse Island, Vanikoro.

136 *the Portuguese Francisco Serrao ... Dumont d'Urville in 1827:* all the authorities quoted by Verne are indeed reported, with various degrees of reliability, to have visited New Guinea; *the Portuguese Francisco Serrao in 1511:* (Verne 'Serrano') despatched by Albuquerque from Malacca to the Moluccas; *don Jorge de Meneses in 1526:* (Verne: 'don José de Meneses') captain-designate of the Moluccas, but was blown off course *en route*: it is not certain that he found New Guinea; *Grijalva in 1527:* Juan de (1489?–1527), Spanish navigator and explorer of Mexico; *the Spanish general Alvar de Saavedra in 1528:* (d. 1529), relative and friend of Cortez, who sent him to the South Seas in 1527; it is in fact conjectural which landmass he sighted; *Iñigo Ortiz de Retes in 1545:* (Verne: 'Juigo Ortez') despatched from the Moluccas; *the Dutchman Schouten in 1616:* (Verne: 'Shouten') Willem (1567?–1625), mariner, discovered the Admiralty Islands, and was the first to sail round Cape Horn, named after his birthplace Hoorn; *Nicholas Struyck in 1753:* (Verne: 'Nicolas Sruick') (1687–1769), author of geographical works; *Dampier:* William (1652–1715), British buccaneer and explorer who reported sea serpents. He sailed around the world three times, and was on the privateering expeditions when Alexander Selkirk, the model for Robinson Crusoe, was marooned on Juan Fernandez and then rescued; *Funnell:* (Verne: 'Fumel') William (dates unknown), mate who served with Dampier on the *St George*; author of *A Voyage Round the World* (1707); *Carteret:* Philip (d. 1796), British rear admiral, explorer, and map-maker, sailed around the world (1766–9); *Edwards:* Captain Edwards of the *Pandora*, despatched to the Pacific to apprehend the *Bounty* mutineers; *Forrest:* Thomas (1729?–1802?), captain and author of *A Voyage to New Guinea, Moluccas* [. . .] (1774–6) and *A Treatise on the Monsoons in the East Indies* (1782); *McCluer ... in 1792:* (Verne: 'Mac Cluer') John (d. 1794?), British explorer and surveyor; *Duperrey in 1823:* Louis-Isidore (1786–1865), navigator, geographer, and author of *Voyage autour du monde* [. . .] *dans la corvette* [. . .] *'La Coquille'* (1826) (the same ship, re-baptized the *Astrolabe*, took part in La Pérouse's ill-fated expedition).

According to M. de Rienzi, 'it is where the dark-skinned peoples [Noirs] who occupy the entire Malay Archipelago originally came from' ... the redoubtable Andamanese: Grégoire-Louis Domeny de Rienzi (1789–1843), navigator and author of *Dictionnaire usuel et* scientifique de géographie (1841) and Océanie, ou cinquième partie du monde (1836–8). *Captain Grant's Children* (II 16) quotes his racist views as follows: 'M. de Rienzi understandably proposed classifying [the Australian aborigines] as a separate race which he called "pithecomorphs", i.e. "men in the form of monkeys".' Rienzi is the only dead person in *20TL* to be dignified with 'M.'. We may note the strange terminology here, perhaps explained by Verne's obsession with cannibalism. The 'Andamanese' especially, whether or not referring to the inhabitants of the Andaman Islands near India, are similarly characterized in *Around the World* as 'beings placed on the lowest rung of the human scale, although it is not correct to say that they are cannibals'! However, many writers of the period (including J. S. Mill) made disparaging remarks about the Andamanese.

136 *Luis Vaez de Torres*: (Verne: 'Louis Paz de Torrès') Spanish navigator who flourished in 1606: he served under Quiros (see note to p. 128 above).

137 *the hydrographic engineer Vincendon-Dumoulin and Ensign (now Admiral) Coupvent-Desbois*: Clément-Adrien Vincendon-Dumoulin (1811–58) wrote *Îles Marquises, ou Nouka Hiva* (1843), *Îles Taïti* (1844), and *Hydrographie du voyage au Pôle sud et dans l'océanie, par Dumont d'Urville* (1843–5). Auguste-Élie-Aimé Coupvent-Desbois (1814–92) was co-author with Vincendon-Dumoulin of *Physique* (1850). The maps Verne is referring to are *Cartes des Îles Salomon* [. . .] (1841).

Captain King's: Philip (Gidley) King (1758–1808), published books on the South Sea islands, and was governor of New South Wales, 1800–6.

Gueboroar Island: no trace has been found of this archetypal Robinson Crusoe and Swiss Family Robinson-inspired desert island (or of the Tound Island and Bad Channel in the previous paragraph). Given that the reefs in the following paragraph seem to be the Warrior Reefs, it may possibly be Gabba Island. But in any case Gueboroar itself is invented, given the variety of fauna and of 'mountains' and 'plains', absent in reality from the low-lying islands around.

141 *with two legs and feathers*: allusion to Plato's definition of man as a 'featherless biped'.

143 *'Rima' in Malay*: no trace of Verne's Malay words, 'rima', 'abrou', 'mado', or 'assai', has been found; his 'bari-outang' is a misprint for 'babi-outang', modernized here as 'babi hutan' ('jungle pig').

145 *they reproduce from their own offspring and their own seeds*: Verne often delights in allusions to non-standard sexual behaviour—here the biblical 'spilling one's seed'.

149 *Great Emerald bird of paradise, one of the rarest*: given Verne's description, this must be the Magnificent Bird of Paradise; in contrast

with Verne's 'eight species', more than 40 species of birds of paradise have now been identified.

150 *a species of 'rabbit kangaroos' which normally live in the hollows of trees*: either tree kangaroos, hare wallabies, or forest wallabies.

160 *I have given the order to open the hatches*: why? They will be on the open sea in a couple of hours. This scene seems therefore badly timed: if the *Nautilus* had been marooned for longer, it would have had to open its hatches to breathe before moving off.

the guide-rail of the stairs: the corresponding illustration confirms that this is a free-standing staircase, despite the description in I 12 of 'an iron ladder ['échelle'], fixed firmly to the wall'.

Ten suffered the same fate: MS2A has perhaps its most significant variant here (MD, p. 68): '~~"The Papuans?" Captain Nemo replied, shrugging his shoulders slightly. [. . .] He pressed the [sic] switch. A blood-curdling cry was heard outside. I was pale with fright. The panels had been opened. I looked at Captain Nemo, still impassive, and rushed out of the salon. I arrived on the platform. Twenty canoes were fleeing, a hundred dead bodies lay along the flanks of the Nautilus. I understood: the platform, insulated by some unknown method and charged with all the electricity on board, had produced the same effect as a huge battery. The savages crowding on to it had been struck by lightning!~~'

161 *Between his assailants and him, Nemo had extended an electric circuit that none could cross with impunity*: the vocabulary and the plot seem perfectly designed to illustrate the 'Nemo me impune lacessit' central to the captain's character.

it left behind the dangerous passes of Torres Strait: MS2 contains a description of a three-master observed as the submarine leaves Torres Strait, but this was deleted at Hetzel's request (MD, p. 64).

'Ægri Somnia': 'bad dreams'.

I could not see its revolutions, let alone count them: not surprising, since Aronnax is inside the submarine.

162 *the sacred lizards*: crocodiles are not, of course, lizards. However, the crocodile may owe its name to a resemblance to a lizard, *krokodilos*, that lived in Ionia; according to Herodotus, its name derived in turn from *krok* ('pebble') and *drilos* ('circumcised man'), again due to a resemblance. Verne's inaccuracy would then fit in with a general tendency to smuggle crude sexual imagery into his works.

Verne's facts are authentic, with virgins sacrificed to crocodiles in Timor until at least 1790.

164 *1.018 for the Ionian Sea, and 1.029 for the waters of the Adriatic*: given that the other densities are at least 1.026, '1.018' may be a misprint.

170 *Moquin-Tandon*: Horace-Benedict-Alfred (1804–63), botanist and doctor, author of *Histoire naturelle des mollusques* [. . .] (1855) and *Le Monde de la mer* (1865, under the pseudonym Alfred Frédol). The paragraph below on ostracions (II 1) is taken from his 1865 work.

172 *which struck this man*: *MÉR* adds, 'The first officer was at his side. He [the injured man] threw himself foward to prevent the blow. . . . A brother getting himself killed for his brother, a friend for his friend, what could be simpler! That is the law for everyone on the Nautilus.' This passage, which also appeared in the 1869 edition, does not make it clear how the blow was to be prevented. It is the only real interaction we observe between Nemo's crew members, and illustrates the high ideals prevailing. It may have been suppressed since the man is not yet dead when Nemo is speaking. It also contains a slight allusion to Dumas *père*'s 'One for all, and all for one!' Other ideas probably taken from *The Count of Monte Cristo*—to which Verne dedicated his *Mathias Sandorf* (1885)—include Xenophon, Lucullus, and 'Château-Renaud' (Verne uses the same spelling in MS2); the Mediterranean boat called a 'tartan', 'the famous sea serpent of the *Constitutionnel*', and a large, multilingual library; the notions of Greek liberation from the Turks, of fashioning pen and ink from fish remains in prison, of cruelly watching dying fish change colour as they die on the dining table, of the hero keeping a portrait of a young woman on his bedroom wall; and a parading of artists, including Meyerbeer, Delacroix, Decamps, Potter, Dow, Murillo, and Raphael.

173 *the coral kingdom*: the *Musée des familles*, to which Verne contributed regularly, contained an article by Bertsch on coral reefs (March 1863), as well as one on Hallet's trials of the *Nautilus* on the Seine (July 1858), written by Verne's friend and co-author Pitre-Chevalier.

it was only in 1694 that the Marseillais Peyssonel: (Verne: 'Peysonnel') Claude-Charles de (1727–90), author of *Traité du corail* (London, 1756: Verne's date is erroneous).

174 *But as one thinker has remarked*: Michelet, in *La Mer*.

175 *The clearing was a cemetery*: Verne borrows elements of the powerful burial scene from his own description of the funeral of one of the sailors similarly killed by machinery on board the *Great Eastern* (*A Floating City*, ch. 30).

178 *PART TWO*: the division is an important one, especially as MS2A was revised before MS1B was. There was also a gap of a year between the book publication of the two parts, leading Verne to write: 'Paris, 27 December 1869 | My dear father [. . .] I haven't tried to obtain articles [reviews] for *Twenty Thousand Leagues under the Seas*. I'm waiting for the second volume to appear, as the first alone cannot give an idea of the work.'

Here begins the second part of this voyage: MS1 adds, slightly obscurely: 'Not that it cannot deviate, either through the space we have covered, or through the time spent covering it.'

Always the same defiance of human society, wild and implacable: MS2 has the stronger: 'Always the same defiance [. . .] ~~of the human race, or rather the same hatred, xxxxxxxx and permanent,~~ wild and implacable. ~~I That was the true mystery surrounding him, the key to his enigmatic existence. Yes, it was in this hate that the secret was to be sought.~~' Five lines lower, MS1 reads, '[. . .] the wound of that man, most certainly struck in a violent battle': another hint of Nemo's secret agenda.

some terrible sort of revenge: the reader's mystification at this stage is no doubt intentional. But even with the benefit of hindsight, it is hard to see how Aronnax deduces Nemo's mission of vengeance from a wounded man.

179   *writing, so to speak, at the dictation of events*: Aronnax claims to be writing without the benefit of hindsight; and the mixture of tenses in these opening pages is a sign of the resulting tensions. He presumably writes notes every day or at the first opportunity—but has to conceal information (and conceal his concealment). By the time he is able to write up the underwater excursion, for instance, he knows that it is a funeral, but chooses not to reveal this until the end.

but he remained mute and impassive: MS1 adds: 'and yet I sometimes saw his lips purse and his eyes sparkle under their lids': a rare sign of passion in Nemo's crewmen.

182   *Remington*: Philo (1816–89), American inventor of the breech-loading rifle, in collaboration with his father Eliphalet Remington (1793–1861); also developed the typewriter from about 1873.

183   *Captain Fitzroy*: (later vice-admiral) Robert (1805–65), hydrographer and meteorologist, captain of the *Beagle* on Darwin's 1831–6 trip and editor of *Narrative of the Surveying Voyages of His Majesty's Ships 'Adventure' and 'Beagle'* (1839). MS1 says Darwin's visit to Keeling Island was 'in 1858'.

184   *the thermometer still invariably indicated 4 degrees above zero*: modern studies indicate a minimum of 1 degree.

Oppian: Greek poet born in Cilicia (flourished second century AD), author of a five-volume *Halieutica* ('On Fishing').

185   *he should have called his ship the 'Argonaut'*: throughout the novel there is play on the term 'argonaut': a modern *Argo* is mentioned by Verne, alluding to Jason's *Argo* in the *Odyssey*; and *naut* occurs frequently, in *nautique* but also in the daily 'Nautron [. . .]'. In his correspondence Verne refers to 'the Aragonautes' (Jacques and François Arago).

185 *and returned to the northern hemisphere*: MS1 adds, 'which we had not in fact left very much since our refuging ['refugiement'] on board the *Nautilus*.' Verne is perhaps obliquely hinting at Nemo's predilection for the shipping lanes.

187 *a volume by H. C. Sirr, Esq. entitled 'Ceylon and the Cingalese'*: (Verne and MS2: '*Ceylan and* [. . .]'; MS1: '*Ceylon*') Henry Charles Sirr (1807–72): his book was published in 1850, with a chapter on the Mannar pearl fishery.

188 *Treaty of Amiens in 1802*: between Britain and Napoleonic France.

　　Percival: (Verne: 'Perceval'; MS1: 'Percival') Robert (1765–1827), author of *An Account of Ceylon* [. . .] (1803).

　　some divers can stay as much as 57 seconds and very good ones, 87: these figures seem very low.

190 *I was turning the pages automatically*: starting from about 1867, Verne's writing includes vocabulary of 'automatically', 'instinctively', and even 'subconsciously', signs of an interest in the hidden workings of the mind. Some influence may be due to William Carpenter (1813–85), referred to in the 1867 edition of *Journey to the Centre of the Earth*. Carpenter was not only a writer on the ocean depths and the law of oceanic circulation, but the author of *Zoology* [. . .] *and Fossil Remains* (1857, 1866), *The Unconscious Action of the Brain* (1866–71), and 'Is Man an Automaton?' (1875). At least one of his works was translated by Abbé Moigno, cited in I 1.

193 *Caesar gave Servilia a pearl estimated to be worth about 120,000 francs of our money*: Servilia was the mother of Brutus, one of Caesar's assassins (44 BC). It was this gift, reported by Suetonius in *Lives of the Twelve Caesars*, which encouraged the rumour that Brutus was Caesar's illegitimate son (Mickel, p. 299).

194 *Kat Tender*: phonetically close to 'qu'attendre?' ('what to expect?'), although Soriano interprets it as 'chatte tendre' ('tender pussy').

196 *the etymology which derives the French word for shark, 'requin', from the word 'requiem'*: Robert says that 'requin' seems to be derived either from *requiem* or from 'quien' ('chien (de mer)').

201 *the phenomenal mollusc*: the giant clam (*Tridacna gigans*) does reach a few feet in size, can weigh 440 lbs, and can trap divers. However, it has been pointed out that pearls are not clear but milky, that such big oysters cannot snap shut, that the biggest pearl found to date (in Palawan in the Philippines) is only the size of a golf ball, and that huge pearls are in any case of little commercial value.

206 *Vasco da Gama*: (1469?–1524), Portuguese explorer; the first European to travel to India by sea (1497–9).

208 *Idrisi*: (1099?–1164?), Arabian geographer, scientist, and poet. His monumental *Kitab Rujjar* (1154) contains a description of the entire known Earth.

209 *this classical importance, one which the railways of Suez have already partially brought back*: the 204-mile Cairo-to-Suez railway was finished on 7 December 1858. The British (as reported in *The Times* of 7 April 1858) considered it a triumph for their imperial communications and a slap in the face for the French. They subsequently opposed each stage of the building of the Suez Canal.

211 *The latter method, requiring the use of divers, is preferable*: only a few pages previously, Aronnax/Verne had castigated pearl fishing for its cruel effect on divers' health.

212 *Strabo*: (63? BC–AD 24?), Greek historian, philosopher, vulcanologist, and firm believer in monsters in the Mediterranean. He was the author of a 17-volume *Geographia*, which Verne praises in *The Great Journeys* [. . .] (1878–80): 'This work, together with Ptolemy's, forms the most important monument that Antiquity has left to modern geographers.'

Arrian . . . Artemidorus: Greek thinkers. *Arrian*: or Flavius Arrianus, historian of the second century AD, author of the *Anabasis*, a life of Alexander the Great, and the *Indica*. *Agatharchidas*: flourished 177 BC, general in the Peloponnesian War and author of *On the Erythraean Sea*. *Artemidorus*: flourished 100 BC, author of a systematic geography in eleven volumes.

213 *the Hebrew word 'Edom' [meaning 'red' sea]*: the 1869 and 1871 editions and MS2 all have 'Edrom', but this misprint has been corrected here to 'Edom', following the *MÉR* edition. 'Edom' certainly means 'red(dish-brown)' in Hebrew, but the 'Red Sea' in the English Bible is the translation of 'Yam Suf' (literally 'sea of reeds'), not now believed to be the modern Red Sea.

The posthumous story 'Eternal Adam', of unparalleled brilliance and ascribed mainly to Michel Verne, is entitled 'Edom' in manuscript form. The word is therefore of considerable significance as a link between the two works. Edom was Esau's other name (Genesis 36: 8); and Esau/Edom's second-millennium BC outcast descendants were also known as Edom, as was the wilderness they lived in, south-east of ancient Israel.

215 *Sesostris*: probably in fact Sesostris III (1878–1843 BC), the legendary fifth ruler of the twelfth dynasty of Egypt.

Necho: twenty-sixth-dynasty pharaoh (ruled 609–593 BC), mentioned in the Bible (2 Chronicles 35: 20, 22; 36: 4). He sent Phoenicians on an expedition that may have circumnavigated Africa.

Darius . . . Ptolemy II: ancient rulers. *Darius*: Darius I (the Great) (*c.*558–486 BC), king of Persia, defeated at the Battle of Marathon (490 BC). *Hystaspes*: satrap of Parthia (*c.*522 BC). *Ptolemy II*: (*c.*308–246 BC), king of Egypt (285–246 BC); married his sister Arsinoe.

215 *until the century of the Antonines . . . Caliph Umar*: the Antonines were the Roman emperors Antoninus Pius (AD 86–161) and Marcus Aelius Aurelius Antoninus (121–80 BC). Caliph Umar ibn al-Khattab (c.586–644), or Umar I, was the second caliph, who expanded the Muslim empire and probably instituted the *haj* to Mecca.

filled in once and for all by Caliph al-Mansur to prevent food reaching Mohammed ben Abdallah, who had rebelled against him: Abu Jaafer Abdullah al-Mansur (712?–75), caliph (754–75); it seems to have been in fact in 775 that he filled in the canal. Mohammed ben Abdallah (d. 764), now called Abdulla ibn Ali, was al-Mansur's uncle and governor of Syria; his rebellion apparently took place in 754.

General Bonaparte: Napoleon Bonaparte (1769–1821), emperor of France (1804–14 and 1815); reformed the French administration and conquered most of Europe; exiled in Elba and St Helena. In 1799 a survey he ordered concluded that building a direct sea-level canal between the Mediterranean and Red Sea was impractical.

Hazeroth, the same place where Moses had camped 3,300 years before: Verne writes 'Hadjaroth' (Hazeroth in English), but in Exodus 14: 2 Moses is clearly enjoined: 'encamp before Pihahiroth, between Migdol and the sea, over against Baalzephon'.

M. de Lesseps: Ferdinand-Marie (Vicomte) (1805–94), French diplomat who built the Suez Canal (17 November 1869), described in *Around the World* as 'the magnificent work of M. de Lesseps'. Verne's Cross of the Légion d'honneur in 1870 was proposed by Lesseps.

216 *'Aures habent et non audient'*: 'they have ears and do not hear' (Mark 8: 18).

219 *dugong*: Ned's 7-metre, 5,000-kilogram dugong is exceptional, for the maximum size in real life is 4.5 metres and the weight slightly over a tonne. This paragraph is derived from Arthur Mangin's *Les Mystères de l'océan* (1864, 1868): 'In all the countries inhabited by the Malay race, the flesh of the dugong is so esteemed that it is reserved for the tables of princes, and this cetacean is undergoing a war of extermination which will eventually make it disappear.' Also taken from Mangin is the vocabulary of 'sirenian', 'siren', and 'half woman, half fish', as well as the statistics and the comparison with beef and veal three pages below.

Many other paragraphs in *20TL* are derived from Mangin, including perhaps those about sea monsters. Even Aronnax's title *The Mysteries of the Ocean Deeps* shows its influence. In addition, information about the laying of the transatlantic cable is probably taken from Mangin's article 'Le *Great-Eastern* et le câble transatlantique' in the *Musée des familles* (no. 33 (Sept. 1866), 366–8). Miller (1976; p. 321) says that it was Arthur Mangin of the French Academy who helped discredit the *Alecton*'s report (see note to p. 343 below), arguing that it was a case of mass hysteria and that 'the giant squid

[. . .] would be some sort of contradiction of the great laws of harmony and equilibrium that rule over living nature'.

221 *which formed divergent tusks on each side*: WJM and FPW point out that tusks indicate a male dugong, and so Ned could not have seen its breasts two pages previously. Ellis points out that dugongs do not have 'fingers', and describes as 'ludicrous' the comparison with a lion attacking a deer, but erroneously implies that these two animals never share the same habitat. He also points out that dugongs are usually inoffensive; and that 'one or two tons' is a lot of water for a small boat.

223 *Mount Horeb, the Sinai on whose summit Moses saw God face to face*: Mount Horeb/Sinai was indeed where Moses received the Ten Commandments, but its location is not certain, and Moses was not allowed to look on God: 'thou shalt see my back parts: but my face shall not be seen' (Exodus 33: 23).

229 *I put myself completely in your hands*: in MS2 this is preceded by an insincere 'I know you to be a prudent and skilful man'.

230 *'Est in Carpathio Neptuni gurgite vates | Caeruleus Proteus . . .'*: 'In Neptune's Carpathian flood there dwells a seer, Proteus, of sea-green hue' (Virgil, *Georgics*, iv. 387–8). The poem then continues: 'who traverses the mighty main in his car drawn by fishes', an idea borrowed in an early piece ascribed to Verne, 'Submarine Locomotives' in the *Musée des familles* (1857).

The following day, 14 February: logically this should be '13'. Similarly '19 March' seems to occur on two different days (II 13).

what had become of the insurrection since then, I had absolutely no idea: the Cretan revolt against Turkish rule broke out in 1866, and continued on and off until 1869, when statesmen met in Paris to discuss it.

231 *Vitellius*: (AD 15–69), briefly Roman emperor in the 'year of the four emperors' (AD 69).

Mark Antony's vessel in the Battle of Actium, so helping Augustus to victory: Mark Antony (83?–30 BC) and Cleopatra were defeated at the Battle of Actium in western Greece (31 BC), leading to the crowning in 29 BC of Octavian, the first Roman emperor, who took the name Augustus in 27 BC.

232 *the captain wrote an address on its lid, using characters that looked as though they were modern Greek*: MS2 has Nemo writing 'in black ink' 'an address in copper-plate as follows:', followed by a page break; in other words it was planned to include the actual address (and for Aronnax to be able to read modern Greek). MS1 has '1,100' for the weight of the gold, together with an important variant: Nemo writes to 'A. P. Leader of the Cretan Insurrection'. MD (p. 64) suggests this is Petropoulaki, the leader of the Greek voluntary corps.

It was argued in the *Sunday Times* of 5 March 1978 that Nemo is based on Gustave Flourens, a French revolutionary, supporter of the 1866 Cretan revolt, and close friend of Mrs Karl and Miss Jenny Marx. Further investigation shows that Flourens (1838–71) fought in both the Polish Insurrection (1863) and the Cretan uprising, supported the Irish nationalists, lived in exile in London and Belgium, and wrote distinguished volumes, like *Histoire de l'homme* (1863) and *Science de l'homme* (1865), as well as political works (1863, 1864). He was very much in view in France as 20TL was being completed, for he was imprisoned for holding a political meeting on 25 March 1869, fought a duel for defamation on 5 August, declared the government illegal on 7 February 1870, and was implicated in Beaury's arrest on 20 April 1870.

Similarities clearly exist with Nemo's scientific and revolutionary activities, and with his romantic rebellion, but would perhaps not be conclusive on their own. However, a vital clue is provided by *Paris in the Twentieth Century*, which describes the hero in 1960 as 'pass[ing] in front of the Sorbonne where M. Flourens was still giving his lectures with the greatest success, still keen, still young' (he occupied a chair at the Natural History Museum at the age of 25). Nemo is therefore probably based on Flourens.

233 *Until five o'clock I wrote up my notes*: if earlier Aronnax referred to the existence of his notes, now he is referring to his own writing. There are in fact three distinct levels: the events he describes in the notes, the meta-event of noting them, and the meta-meta-event of noting the noting. Aronnax has nearly entered a self-depicting loop, from which there is no escape. But further levels also exist. Thus Aronnax's 'sorting out [of his] notes' constitutes a fourth level; recasting them in past-tense, personal-memoir style a fifth; submitting the result to Ned and Conseil a sixth; publishing it a seventh; having it severely criticized and annotated by Nemo, an eighth; and putting out a revised edition, a ninth. If Aronnax's two works do not occupy all these levels, he himself sometimes seems to mix the two up in his mind. It is presumably while rewriting that he slips in '[. . .] what the future held for me' and other allusions to later events.

we were not at high latitudes: a slip for 'at low latitudes'.

234 *Cassiodorus*: Flavius Magnus Aurelius (*c.* AD 490–*c.*585), statesman and historian.

on the same spot: there were indeed a succession of volcanic explosions in about 1620–1500 BC on Thira in the Santorini archipelago. An enormous crater opened in the middle of the island and caused a 100-foot tidal wave which swept the coast of Crete and the whole of the eastern Mediterranean, a possible origin of the Atlantis legend. A small volcano appeared from the sea at (Palea) Kameni in 197 BC; Nea Kameni itself emerged in 1707. Verne's main source of information may be Strabo, who refers to Plato's *Timaeus* on tidal waves and volcanoes and transcribes Posidonius' observations on the birth of Thira in Santorini (Book 7, ch. 2).

Finally on 10 March, a small island called Reka appeared: to know the name, Nemo must either have launched his submarine after 10 March 1866, or still have some contact with dry land.

237 *Lucullus*: Lucius Licinius Lucullus (110?–56? BC), wealthy Roman noble who helped defeat Mithridates.

239 *Arachne*: (Greek for 'spider') Arachne wove a tapestry depicting the gods' amorous activities. When Athena tore it up out of jealousy, Arachne hanged herself, but was turned into a spider.

it entirely blocks the Sicilian Channel, and Smyth's soundings prove that the two continents were formerly connected between Capes Boeo and Farina: (Verne: 'Boco [. . .] Furina') Verne's 'Strait of Libya', where 'Libya' meant most of North Africa, seems to correspond to the modern Sicilian Channel. Although the reference to 'Smyth's' soundings (Verne: 'Smith's') is extremely general, fortunately Maury's introduction identifies him as Rear Admiral William Henry Smyth, author of *The Mediterranean* (1854).

242 *hairy porcelain crabs*: a sexual imagery is visible in *20TL*, with 'plump' 6- or 8-inch 'queues' ('tails' but also 'pricks') or 'porcellanes' ('hairy porcelain crabs' or 'cowry shells', but also 'sows' vulva'); Verne also slips in such ideas as cooking in 'milt' (fish semen), which he calls 'divine'.

244 *Avienus*: Rufius Festus, fourth-century AD poet. He wrote *Ora Maritima*, translated as *Description de la Terre, régions maritimes* (1843), a wild account of the Mediterranean and other areas. It gives details (xv, 9) of Himilco's search for Atlantis in the South Atlantic, where he is driven southwards and becalmed in masses of seaweed, before coming back via the Azores, Madeira, and an active volcano (probably Tenerife).

246 *My novel was falling from my hands half-way through*: is Aronnax thinking of novel-reading in general or is he referring to the book of his own adventures? *20TL* is in any case the story of its own writing. Aronnax was originally an obscure academic, the author of *The Mysteries* [. . .]. On this basis, he is invited to write his article for the *New York Herald*, which in turn produces the written invitation to hunt the monster. Once on the submarine, Nemo refers to Aronnax's future writing, using a whalebone pen and squid ink—and shortly afterwards Aronnax dutifully starts. Nemo later admits that he too has kept a record, and may entrust it to the waves as a message-in-a-bottle. At the end, Aronnax will reveal that his new 'study' of the sea has become a 'narrative', and is magically complete. His book thus ends up coinciding with Verne's novel.

247 *in perpetuity*: instead of the words following 'gratitude', MS2 has '~~No, however, for the captain was exceeding his rights in claiming to be able to keep us on board his ship in perpetuity.~~'

my impatience: MS2: 'my impatiences'; like Zola and the realists, Verne often invents plurals of abstract nouns.

248 *Kosciusko . . . John Brown*: heroes who generally died defending a liberal or patriotic cause. The list includes one Pole, two Greeks, one anti-Austrian, two anti-Confederates, and three anti-Britons: probably all ideas considered by Verne for Nemo's own vendetta. *Kosciusko*: Thaddeus (1746–1817), Polish general. He fought for American independence, and in 1794 led an unsuccessful rebellion against Russian and Prussian control of Poland. *Bozzaris, the Leonidas of modern Greece*: Marco (1786–1823), fought in the war of independence against the Turks, and died in the defence of Missolonghi. *Leonidas*: king of Sparta who died defending the Pass of Thermopylae with 300 men (480 BC) in the Second Persian War. *O'Connell, the defender of Ireland*: Daniel, 'the Liberator' (1775–1847), political leader who worked for Irish independence. *Washington, the founder of the American Union*: George (1732–99), commander-in-chief in the War of Independence and first president (1789–97). *Manin, the Italian patriot*: Daniele (1804–57), led the Venetians against Austrian rule in 1848 and headed a short-lived republic. *Lincoln, who fell shot by a supporter of slavery*: Abraham (1809–65), sixteenth US president (1861–5). He maintained the Union in the Civil War and made the Emancipation Proclamation (1863). *John Brown*: (1800–59), American abolitionist celebrated in the song *John Brown's Body*. He attempted to use force to liberate Southern slaves, but was defeated and hanged.

Verne wrote to Hetzel, 'The incident of John Brown [of which no trace is known] pleased me by its concise form, but in my view, it diminishes the captain. His nationality needs to be kept vague, together with the causes which cast him into his strange existence. In addition the incident of an *Alabama* or a false *Alabama* is unacceptable and inexplicable; if Nemo wanted to take revenge on the slavers, he only had to serve in Grant's army and everything was settled.' (Jules-Verne, p. 149; 'Monday' (March 1869)). The *Alabama*, which claimed to have sunk 75 merchantmen, was destroyed by the Unionist *Kearsarge* off Cherbourg on 11 June 1864, and commemorated in a famous painting by Manet. This battle has clear connections with Nemo's final attack, also in the English Channel.

250 *Louis XIV . . . imposed his grandson, the Duke of Anjou*: historical events. *Louis XIV*: (1638–1715), the Sun King (ruled 1643–1715), built the Palace of Versailles. *The Duke of Anjou*: (1683–1746), ruled Spain as Philip V (1700–46).

Admiral de Châteaurenault: (Verne: 'Château-Renault'; MS2: 'Chateau-Renaud') François-Louis de Rousselet de (1637–1716).

Despite the various problems, he was congratulated by Louis XIV. Nemo's account is misleading, for Châteaurenault was not able to scuttle the whole fleet.

252 *Hernando Cortez*: (1485–1547), Spanish explorer who conquered the Aztecs.

the work of a rival company: following searches by Ernest Bazin, a society was founded to recover the galleons from the Bay of Vigo in 1869, meaning that Aronnax cannot in fact know of its founding.

254 *33° 22′N, 16° 17′W, that is, 150 leagues from the nearest coast*: these co-ordinates are very close to Madeira. Is it a deliberate mistake by Aronnax to prevent Ned's escape?

257 *one of those cities in the sea*: ('villes sous-marines') a reference to Poe's poem 'The City in the Sea' (1831), with its 'The waves have now a redder glow'—hence Aronnax's observation of 'a distant reddish point' and a 'reddish glow'. Nemo's idea of the city *rising* each day to the surface to breathe possibly ironically echoes Poe's 'Down, down that town shall settle hence'.

a Hartz forest: *Moby-Dick* (ch. 42) refers to 'the old fairy tales of Central Europe [and] "the tall pale man" of the Hartz forests, whose changeless pallor unrustlingly glides through the green of the groves [. . .] this phantom'. We may note the appositeness to underwater conditions of Melville's 'unrustlingly', and the description two paragraphs previously of Nemo as a 'tall' 'ocean spirit'. The context in Melville's tale is a discussion of why whiteness can be so frightening; whereas Verne is in this scene self-consciously playing on the effect of blackness. The spelling itself is another link between the two novels, for the normal form is 'Harz'. However, the theme, based on legends of witches' covens associated with the Harz Mountains in Central Germany, was a common one in nineteenth-century literature, with Heinrich Heine's *Harzreise* (*The Harz Journey*) (1826) and Goethe's *Faust* (1832) just two examples. Once again, then, the similarity between Melville and Verne is troubling, but not absolutely conclusive.

258 *and so boldly followed him*: MS2 adds the interesting '~~and due to a purely physical effect, the more I climbed towards the top strata, the heavier I felt~~'.

259 *awe-inspiring squid*: MS2 has 'giant squid'; the same paragraph in MS2 has 'crustaceans, lurking like tigers' and 'crabs [. . .] ready to pounce'.

not that of the Creator: MS2: 'not that of nature'.

seeming to say to me: 'Come! Further! Come with me!': this imaginary conversation is unique in that Nemo is using the intimate form ('Viens!'), perhaps in response to Aronnax's seizing of his arm; it thus heralds the tremendous discovery. In MS2 it is Nemo who initiates the contact by taking Aronnax's arm when pointing out the reddish glow.

260 *like the ejecta of Vesuvius in another Torre del Greco*: a port and valley below Mount Vesuvius, destroyed many times, and further damaged by an earthquake in 1857.

a whole Pompeii sunk beneath the waters: Pompeii was destroyed by the eruption of Vesuvius in AD 79 and rediscovered in 1748. Some of the details of Verne's Atlantis may perhaps be taken from it.

that ancient Meropis of Theopompus ... d'Avezac: believers and disbelievers in Atlantis: *that ancient Meropis of Theopompus*: Theopompus (*c.*378/376–after 323 BC), Greek historian. According to the *Varia Historia* (iii. 18) of Aelianus (flourished early second century AD), Theopompus writes of a conversation Midas, king of Phrygia, has with the aged satyr Silenus, who tells him of the continent of Meropis (*mer + opis* ('over or near')), considerably larger than the known world. *Plato*: (427?–347? BC), Greek philosopher, author of *The Republic*. *Origen*: or Origines Adamantius (AD 185?–254?), Christian philosopher who castrated himself to ensure his celibacy. *Porphyry*: (*c.* AD 232–*c.*305), philosopher who helped found Neoplatonism. *Iamblichus*: (d. *c.*330), Syrian-born Greek mystic philosopher, author of *De Mysteriis* ('On Mysteries'). *d'Anville*: Jean-Baptiste Bourguignon d'Anville (1697–1782), geographer and cartographer. *Malte-Brun*: either Conrad (1775–1826), Danish geographer, founder of the Société de géographie (of which Verne was a member), or his French son, Victor-Adolphe (1816–89), secretary-general of the Société de géographie. Conrad Malte-Brun's *Précis de la géographie universelle* (1810–28, revised regularly until the 1870s) is lyrically referred to in Verne's *Backwards to Britain*, and his son's *Nouvelles annales* of August 1869 refer to an article entitled 'Around the World in Eighty Days', the origin of Verne's novel. *Posidonius*: (135–50 BC), Greek stoic philosopher, vulcanologist, polymath, and partial believer in Atlantis. *Ammianus Marcellinus*: (*c.* AD 325/330–*c.*395), historian who wrote about Atlantis as a historical fact. *Tertullian*: Quintus Septimus Florens (*c.* AD 160–*c.*230), Carthaginian church father, founder of the schismatic Tertullianists. *Sherer*: Jean-Benoît (dates unknown), author of *Recherches historiques et géographiques sur le Nouveau-monde* (1787), about the origins of the American Indians compared with the races of Europe and America. *Tournefort*: Joseph Pitton de (1656–1708), botanist and author of *Voyage au Levant* (1717), containing sections on history and archaeology and discussing Atlantis. *Buffon*: George-Louis-Leclerc (Comte de) (1707–88), French pre-evolutionary naturalist. His works include a 44-volume *Histoire naturelle* (1749–1804), with an illustration of a cephalopod embracing a frigate, and a *Discours sur le style*. His theories of a central fire led Bailly to locate Atlantis at a North Pole with a tropical climate. *d'Avezac*: Armand (1800–75), geographer and author of *Les Îles fantastiques de l'océan occidental* (1845).

261 *the land of the powerful Atlanteans*: the Atlantis idea has gripped generations of writers. Normally taken as being west of the Pillars of Hercules, it has often been suggested that Atlantis was part of Thira (modern Santorini, discussed in note to p. 234 above) and sank in the volcanic eruption of about 1615 or 1500 BC. Thira's Bronze Age ruins were first explored by the French in the 1860s, when pumice was being quarried to build the Suez Canal.

Although now converted into a tourist attraction, Atlantis is considered seriously in Verne's *L'Agence Thompson et Co.* (1907): 'Peaks, mountains, and volcanoes still emerge. The Azores, Madeira, the Canaries, and the islands of Cape Verde cannot be anything else. The rest was swallowed up.' Atlantis is also central to 'Edom' (1910), where remains of 'columns and pottery, such as we had never seen' prove to survivors of a future cataclysm that they formed merely part of an indefinite number of civilizations that have risen and fallen.

His dialogue of 'Timaeus' and 'Critias' was, so to speak, dictated under the inspiration of Solon, poet and legislator: Plato used Atlantis to illustrate his theory of human history as a cyclical rise and fall. His *Timaeus* describes a large island containing a Utopia, in 'the western sea' on the 'other' side of the Pillars of Hercules: 'There occurred violent earthquakes and floods; and in a single day and night of misfortune all your warlike men in a body sank into the earth, and the island of Atlantis in like manner disappeared into the depths of the sea. For which reason the sea in those parts is impassable and impenetrable, because there is a shoal of mud in the way' (trans. Benjamin Jowett).

The information reported in Verne's next paragraph is taken mainly from Plato's *Critias*. But whereas Verne describes the Athenian town as '900 centuries old' (and his own description refers to 'ruins that were hundreds of thousands of years old!'), Plato says '9,000 years'. *Solon*: (c.639–c.559 BC), statesman whose constitutional reforms became the basis of the Athenian state.

Saïs, a town already 800 years old: Saïs, at the fork in the Nile, was the ancient capital of Lower Egypt, with an important temple complex. WJM and FPW report that Verne's '800 years' is a misquoting of Plato's '8,000 years', which would be consistent with the figures of 1,000 and 9,000 years.

Machimos the warlike and Eusebia the holy: (Verne: 'Makhimos [. . .] Eusebès') the source for these two localities is Aelianus, whose *Varia Historia* (iii. 18) reports that the great towns of 'Machimos (the warlike) and [. . .] Eusebia (the holy)' are in Meropis. He continues that the inhabitants of Machimos 'formerly wished to penetrate our islands [Greece] and, having crossed the ocean with 10 million men, reached the Hyperboreans [a people living in a perpetually warm land found north of the source of the north wind]'. Machimos may possibly be derived from Michmash (or Mukhmas) near Mount Ephraim in Israel, the scene of a biblical battle (1 Samuel 14: 1–46); and Eusebia may perhaps be connected with Eusebia (modern Kayseri) in Turkey, close to the third-millennium BC Hittite-Assyrian city of Kanesh.

263 *Bailly*: Jean-Sylvain (1736–93), scholar and politician, author of *Lettres sur l'Atlantide de Platon* [. . .] (London, 1779), president of the States-General (1789), and mayor of Paris (1790); guillotined. *Captain Hatteras* (II 24) refers to the 'French astronomer, Bailly, who maintained that the Atlanteans, the disciplined lost race of which Plato speaks, lived here [at the North Pole]'.

265 *I did not know where we were*: the position is, however, vital, indicating as it does the location of both Atlantis and Nemo's home port. Nemo's invitation to visit the lost continent was issued at 16° 17′ W, 33° 22′ N, just beside Madeira. Then from dawn until 4 p.m. the *Nautilus* sails 'southwards' at '20 knots', presumably covering about 200 miles, until it nears 'a continent or at the very least an island, perhaps one of the islands of the Canaries or of Cape Verde'. Aronnax is again being duplicitous, for this must be the Canary Islands, with Cape Verde a good 1,000 miles further on. The submarine then continues on into the night more slowly, covering about 100 miles, and reaches another 'high vertical wall', presumably Nemo's base. (Verne drops heavy hints when he has Aronnax discover bees on it, 'so common throughout the Canary Islands'.) The Canaries are perfect for the captain, since they are actively volcanic (thus hiding his smoke), partly deserted, and Spanish, an appropriate home port for 'Juan Nemo'. But in any case, MS1 gives the game away, for it entitles this chapter 'The Coalmines of Tenerife', that is in the Canaries.

266 *served me well*: MS2 adds 'Here I am master of the lake!', an allusion to Scott's *Lady of the Lake* (1810). Sir Walter Scott (1771–1832), referred to at the end of this chapter, was a major inspiration for Verne's *Backwards to Britain*.

272 *Sir Walter Scott's hero*: presumably Darcie Latimer in *Redgauntlet* (1824), who is nearly cut off by the tide on the Solway Firth ('Letter IV').

273 *Sargasso Sea*: the calm centre of the clockwise rotation of the North Atlantic. Nautical lore referred to vessels trapped within dense seaweed (Maury says 'the speed of vessels [. . .] is often much retarded' (Miller 1976; p. 260)). In fact the floating masses posed no obstacle to ships, and the area was avoided because of the lack of wind. Modern maps indicate it as a relatively small area in the western Atlantic, but Verne is following Maury's Plate VI, 'Gulf Stream and Drift', which shows the main Sargasso Sea as centred on 30° W, south-west of the Canaries, with the area around 'the Bermudas' as an extension.

the name Sargasso comes from the Spanish 'sargazo': (Verne: '*sargazzo*') in fact from the Portuguese.

In the following paragraph, Verne quotes (approximately) from Maury. To ensure a faithful translation of Verne, it is the French version which has been translated back into English.

277 *Captain Denham of the 'Herald'*: (cf. Maury, sec. 688) Captain Sir Henry Mangles Denham (1800–87), naval surveyor, later admiral; he prepared accurate navigational charts of the Fijian archipelago (1855–6), and wrote a pamphlet *Abstract of his marine surveying services* [. . .] (n.d.).

Lieut. Parker of the American frigate 'Congress': (Verne: 'Parcker') quoted by Maury (secs. 466, 688) as Lieut. J. P. Parker in 1852. WJM and FPW point out that the '15,140 metres' in this paragraph was '15,149 metres' in I 18.

278 *McClintock, the hero of the polar seas*: (Verne: 'Mac Clintock') Leopold, later Sir, author of *The Voyage of the 'Fox' in the Arctic Seas* [. . .] (1859). McClintock's *Fox*, fitted out by Lady Franklin, discovered a cairn in 1859 which proved that Sir John Franklin had died in 1847. The *Bull-Dog* of the following sentence dived in 1855.

279 *below three leagues*: the submarine had previously been at a depth of 'three and a quarter leagues'.

285 *Sinbad the Sailor*: in *The Thousand and One Nights* he makes seven voyages, encounters sea monsters and the Old Man of the Sea, and is carried aloft by a giant roc.

286 *50 tons*: WJM and FPW point out that this would more logically be '500 tons'. 'October' (p. 283) is also a slip.

the 'Essex' sank almost immediately: the attack and sinking of the *Essex* are also related in *Moby-Dick*, similarly forming a prelude to the final crescendo, although Verne describes a '(baleen) whale' and Melville, a sperm whale. Melville's cited source is *Narrative* [. . .] *of the Whale-Ship 'Essex'* [. . .] (1821) by Owen Chase, the first mate, whose account of the 1820 incident has the sperm whale stopping the ship dead at three knots rather than pushing it backwards, as in Verne.

287 *Ned whistled 'Yankee Doodle' between his teeth*: despite his own colonial origin, Ned's subtext is apparently anti-colonial, but possibly also designed to annoy Nemo by being anti-upper class. In *From the Earth to the Moon* Verne describes 'Yankee Doodle' as the American 'national anthem' and compares it to the Revolutionary 'Marseillaise'.

288 *as Frédol remarks*: Alfred Frédol, pseudonym of Moquin-Tandon (see note to p. 170 above).

292 *pack-ice, meaning broken pieces and called 'patches' when the pieces are round and 'streams' when they are longer*: (Verne: 'palchs') the OED quotes an 1850 source: 'If the field is broken up into a number of pieces, none of which are more than forty or fifty yards across, the whole is called a *pack*, if the pieces are broad they are called a *patch*; and when long and narrow a *stream*.'

293 On 15 March: MS2 has '~~16~~ March' (and '~~17~~ March' in the next para-
    graph); it also writes 'Sethland' and initially has 'two or three degrees
    above zero'. At the end of the chapter, '~~22~~ March' will become '19' in
    1871.

294 Hansteen: (Verne: 'Hansten') Christophe (1784–1873), Norwegian
    astronomer, physicist, researcher in terrestrial magnetism, and
    author.

296 I can do what I want with the 'Nautilus': MS2 has 'I do what I say.',
    more revealing of Nemo's self-image.

297 child's play for the 'Nautilus': MS2 has 'child's play for *Nautilus*', as
    if it were an animate being.

    four to one: (MS2: 'one to four') neither this ratio, nor Nemo's three
    to one, nor even simple operations, are accurate in many of the fol-
    lowing calculations.

299 Two degrees already gained: in fact one. Nor does a water tempera-
    ture of $-12°$ seem plausible.

302 he seemed to take possession of the southern regions: MS2: 'he
    appeared as the spirit of the southern regions'.

303 James Ross: Sir James (Clark) Ross (1800–62), explorer and admiral.
    He helped locate the North Magnetic Pole in 1831; and discovered the
    Ross Sea, Ross Ice Shelf, and Victoria Land (1839–43). The informa-
    tion in this paragraph is taken from Maury (sec. 468), who says
    however that Mount Terror is extinct.

304 ospreys with curved wings, including some lammergeieres: Verne has
    'quebrante-huesos' (*sic* for *quebrantahuesos*, as in MS1); it is not clear
    why he is using the Spanish term.

305 The following day, 20 March: this should logically be 21.

306 that the most beautiful woman would not be able to surpass: MS2 has
    the more misogynist 'to equal'. Ellis points out that walruses are not
    found in the Antarctic. (Nor are the puffins seen in I 13.)

310 southwards: throughout this polar episode, Verne has forgotten that
    south and north have become increasingly arbitrary as they approach
    the Pole.

311 in 1600 the Dutchman Gherritz: or Gerritsz (Verne: 'Ghéritk'), Dirck
    or Derk, navigator. He was swept south from South America in a
    storm, in fact in 1599, and discovered high snow-covered mountains,
    thought to be the South Shetlands.

    Verne's 'semi-structured' list of the successive latitudes reached by
    the Antarctic explorers is an echo of his anti-hero Captain Hatteras,
    whose only thought is the distance from the North Pole, an obsession
    which will lead to his madness and death. But the origin of the
    compass-direction fixation in the entire *Extraordinary Journeys* is
    Backwards to Britain, where the focus of all Verne's dreams is the
    Highlands, and the northwards pull a leitmotiv to every chapter.

312 *In 1820, the Briton Bransfield ... the Briton Balleny*: explorers. *Bransfield*: (Verne: 'Brunsfield') Lieut. Edward (*c.*1795–1852). He is generally thought to have been the first to have sighted the Antarctic mainland. However, recent cartographic studies have shown that the continent may have been known as early as the sixteenth century; *Morrell*: (Verne: 'Morrel') Captain Benjamin (1795–1835), author of *A Narrative of Four Voyages [...] to the South Seas [...] and Antarctic Ocean* (1832). He was not in fact in the Antarctic in 1820; *Powell*: George (dates unknown); apparently a sealer, he discovered the South Orkneys; *Weddell*: (Verne: 'Weddel') James (1787–1834). He discovered the Weddell Sea and the surrounding area. His southwards record was in fact achieved in 1823; *Foster, commanding the 'Chanticleer'*: (Verne: 'Forster') Henry (1796–1831), author of *Narrative of a Voyage to the Southern Atlantic Ocean* (1834); *Biscoe*: (Verne: 'Biscoë') John (1794–1843), RN, discovered Enderby Land and the Biscoe Islands (1830–2); *Wilkes*: (in fact American) Lieut. Charles (1798–1877), led the six-ship US Exploration Expedition (1838–42) and discovered Wilkes Land; *Balleny*: John (b. *c.*1790), whaling captain, discovered Balleny Island. WJM and FPW point out that '76° 56"' in the following sentence is an error for '70° 56"'.

a black flag, carrying a golden 'N' quartered on its bunting: an allusion to Napoleon, whose *N* adorns many French buildings and bridges. The black flag is traditionally a pirate flag; and black is also the colour of anarchists. The black colour on the white ice is in addition a textual metaphor. But much of the power of the colour image derives from the gold of the sun's rays before the blackness of the six-month night.

my new realm: a footnote to Verne's *An Antarctic Mystery* (1897) reads: 'someone had already set foot on this point of the globe, on 21 March 1868' (II 10). The authorial voice summarizes the approach by 'that mysterious character' and describes the Antarctic scene, before concluding: 'And at the moment that the horizon, just to the north, cut the solar disc in two equal parts, he took possession of that continent in his own name, and unfurled a flag of bunting embroidered with a golden N. Offshore floated a submarine boat called *Nautilus* whose commander was called Captain Nemo. J. V.'

314 *'But where can we find him?' asked Ned*: Ned and Conseil do not know their way around the library or dining-room (they eat in their cabin).

332 *a bit like the British do*: Verne may possible be thinking of a general tendency to mix dishes. In *Backwards to Britain* (ch. 23), he writes: 'A soup was served, a mixture of meat and stock', naming it as the Scottish 'hotchpotch' (which is consonant with 'hotpot').

John Davis: (*c.*1550–1605), discovered the Davis Strait and Baffin Bay while attempting to find a Northwest Passage.

332 *Richard Hawkins*: Sir (1562–1622), admiral; commanded an expedition to South America (1583–97), where he was imprisoned by the Spanish.

333 *the easternmost point of South America, Cape São Roque*: although Cape São Roque is the point closest to Africa, it is not the furthest east.

334 *the Guyanas, a French possession*: French Guyana in fact coexisted with British and Dutch Guyana, as Verne himself implies a page later when he writes, misleadingly, of 'the Dutch coast near the mouth of the Maroni'.

336 *at least 4,000 kilograms*: in fact the maximum size of the manatee is about 5 metres and 700 kilograms. Ellis points out that the illustration mistakenly shows manatees resting on rocks, whereas in reality they never leave the water.

Toussenel: Alphonse (1803–85), author of *L'Esprit des bêtes: Le Monde des oiseaux* (1847, reprinted many times) and of the illustrated *L'Esprit des bêtes: Mammifères de France*, with a preface by P.-J. Stahl (pseudonym of Hetzel) (Hetzel, 1868).

340 *Diana*: the virgin goddess of hunting and of childbirth, associated with the moon.

342 *a painting of the said squid*: Ellis says that the church referred to is St Thomas's Chapel; and that the painting is an *ex-voto* from sailors grateful for surviving the incident described in Montfort's book (see note to p. 347 below).

and you know what should be thought of legends in natural history!: MS2 has '*ex-votos*' instead of 'legends': not only anti-clerical but showing the connection with St Thomas's Chapel and Montfort.

but a certain Olaus Magnus speaks of a mile-long cephalopod: (Verne: 'Olaüs Magnus') (1490–1557), Swedish scholar and archbishop of Uppsala, an expert on runes and author of a work translated as *Histoire des pays septentrionaux* (1560, 1561). In fact, his monsters are only about 200 feet long.

one day the Bishop of Nidaros erected an altar on an immense rock. Once his mass was over, the rock started moving and returned to the sea: (Verne: 'Nidros') Eric Falkendorff, archbishop of Nidaros (now Trondheim), wrote a letter to Pope Leo X about this mass. Larousse's *Grand dictionnaire universel du XIX* siècle reads: 'Olaüs Magnus recounts the heroic deeds of a colossal cephalopod at least a mile long, which resembled an island in the midst of the waters more than an animal. The bishop of Nidaros discovered one of these gigantic animals peacefully sleeping in the sun and took it for an immense rock. He had an altar erected on its back and duly celebrated mass. The kraken remained motionless while the ceremony was continuing; but scarcely had the bishop regained the shore than it dived back down into the sea.'

343 *Captain Paul Bos of Le Havre*: no trace has been found.

MD (p. 66) says that a possible influence on *20TL* was Gustave Lennier, director of the Muséum d'histoire naturelle of Le Havre, where Verne visited an exhibition in June 1868 that Lennier had organized, including African and American fish; its catalogue was published as *Les Merveilles de l'aquarium de l'exposition du Havre* (1868).

Captain Bouyer: (Verne: 'Commander Bouguer') Frédéric (dates unknown), author of *L'Amour d'un monstre: Scènes de la vie créole* (1866) (the title may be an allusion to the 1861 incident) and *La Guyane française; notes et souvenirs d'un voyage exécuté en 1862–1863* (1867), with illustrations by Riou, one of the illustrators of *20TL*. Vierne (1986; p. 375) reports that a letter to the *Figaro* of 21 August 1871 indicated Verne's misspelling, which was not however corrected in subsequent reprints. The incident Aronnax relates took place on 30 November 1861: it is certified in a letter written to the French Academy of Sciences by Sabin Berthelot, French consul at Tenerife: 'the steam despatch-boat *Alecton* [. . .] encountered a monstrous polyp [. . .] 16–18 feet in length without counting the eight formidable arms, covered with air-holes [. . .] eyes [of] a frightful fixity. Its mouth like a parrot's beak [. . .] about two tons [. . .] a strong odour of musk.' The tail apparently weighed 40 lb. The story was much criticized, including the impracticability of trying to haul a two-ton mass on to a small ship using a single rope, the strange behaviour of the creature in swimming under the boat and remaining on the scene for two or three hours, and the lack of information about the tail. However, in the 1870s a whole series of similar creatures were washed up on Newfoundland, with enormous eyes, parrot-like beaks, and tentacles reportedly up to 35 feet long. Modern authorities indicate maximum total lengths of 50 feet and weights of two tonnes.

344 *reddish-brown*: Ellis claims that this description is worse than 'wrong', arguing that 'blue-green eyes' and a 'hornlike' tongue are errors and that an eight-metre squid could not weigh 20,000 kilograms. But 'blue-green' is in fact a mistranslation and Verne may possibly be indicating the length of the body *without* the tentacles.

Verne's mention of the Furies (the terrible winged goddesses with serpentine hair) is surely motivated by the name of the first Fury, Alecto, also the name of Bouyer's vessel.

347 *a spurt of blackish liquid, secreted from a bursa in its abdomen*: some of the symbolism of this battle scene may derive from the 'black ink' and the 'quill' mentioned in it, perhaps referring to the struggle of writing and hence to Nemo's remark to Aronnax that his 'ink will be the liquid secreted by a cuttlefish or squid'.

with it my unfortunate compatriot: the musk smell and dark liquid are similar to descriptions going back to Pontoppidan and Pliny. But this scene bears a close resemblance to what a Captain Jean Magnus Dens told Pierre Denys (de) Montfort (director of the Natural History Museum, cited by Hugo, but apparently later convicted of forgery). Montfort's *Histoire naturelle, générale et particulière des mollusques* (1802–5), states that 'poulpes' can sink ships, and reports that Dens's men were scraping their ship between St Helena and Cape Negro, when a huge animal rose from the water and threw a giant tentacle round two of them. Another arm seized a third man, who shouted for help. The crew cut off the monster's arm with axes and knives, and several harpoons were driven into the monster, but to little effect, and it eventually carried off the two sailors. The third man was delirious and died the following night. The arm cut off was 25 feet long, as thick as a mizzen yard, and had suckers as big as saucepan lids. In reality, although little is known about the giant squid, there are very few authentic accounts of squid attacking ships or people. But Dens's story (perhaps together with Bouyer's monster) is surely a source for Verne's dramatic episode.

347 *red*: MS2 has 'red and black', a clear reference to Stendhal's novel, but also a striking conjunction of blood and ink.

348 *the author of 'Les Travailleurs de la mer'*: Hugo depicts a battle with an octopus ('pieuvre') (II iv. 2–3). Despite similarities with Verne, such as the colour change, there are also considerable differences: Hugo emphasizes the tough skin, the phosphorescence when mating, the fact that the mouth and the anus are combined, and so on.

It has often been pointed out that Verne's squid has 'eight arms' (like an *octo*pus), whereas squid in fact have ten. WJM and FPW claim that Aronnax's 'triple heart' is 'really three modified blood vessels'—but Ellis says 'squid do indeed possess three hearts'.

his ultimate appeal: MS2 adds 'to his companions', implying that there are other French-speakers amongst the crew.

349 *the open sea of the Pole*: all the information in this paragraph is taken from Maury, although rewritten considerably. Verne quotes two different maximum speeds for the Gulf Stream, possibly due to a confusion between miles and kilometres.

353 *in a small floating container*: MS2 has '~~bottle~~ cask' (the final chapter in MS2 also has 'bottle'). The idea that Nemo will include his name and the story of his life is added in the margin.

at this moment: Verne writes 'en ce moment', unusual accompanying the preterite, for it indicates a high degree of presentness. Instead of this phrase, MS2 has '~~I shut up the thoughts inside me~~': in other words a posterior narrator analysing Aronnax-the-character. In the next paragraph, MS2 has '~~risky~~' in place of 'crude'.

355 *a second time*: the six paragraphs ending here were added in the margin of MS2. They replace: ' ~~"But finally, by what right are you holding us?" | "By the right that I assume," said the captain firmly. "I~~

~~have already given you my reasons, and am astonished to see you~~
~~coming back to the subject."~~ | "But you are inflicting slavery on us!"
| "Give it the name you wish." | ~~"But we have the right to regain our~~
~~freedom by any means."~~ | ~~"Regain it. I have not asked for your word~~
~~that you will never leave the vessel without my authorization."~~ | ~~"We~~
~~would not have given it you, sir!"~~ | ~~Captain Nemo looked at me, his~~
~~arms proudly crossed.~~ | ~~"May this first time that you have raised the~~
~~subject be also the last."~~'

This final conversation between Nemo and Aronnax illuminates
their relationship. Behaviour between nineteenth-century gentlemen
demanded that one kept one's word and maintained some level of courtesy (just as men-of-war conventionally gave warning before attacking). The MS2 dialogue is more forthright concerning the limits of
what either side can do. But the 1871 version adds Aronnax's important assessment of Nemo, of their position on board, of his own
obscure hopes of a perhaps posthumous fame, and of his incompre-
hension of the captain's life, almost in terms a quarrelling couple might
use. Despite his closing threat of what Ned might do, his arguments
are essentially subjective, amounting to an appeal for mercy. Nemo
easily crushes Aronnax by referring to his absolute power, and by
saying (again like a quarrelling couple) that it was not him who got
them into this situation. His only concession is the flattery he uses of
his interlocutor's ability to 'understand anything': untrue, for Aronnax
has just said exactly the opposite.

that same 18 May: a misprint; the date must be about 11 May.

358 *the 'Solway' . . . 'City of Glasgow'*: lost ships. *the 'Solway'*: (constructed 1841) 20 miles west of Corunna, 7 April 1843, 35 lives lost;
the 'Isis': (1842) off Bermuda, 8 October 1842, no lives lost; *the
'Hungarian'*: Sable Island, 20 February 1860, 237 lives lost; *the
'Canadian'*: Belle Isle Strait, 4 June 1861, 35 lives lost; *the 'Anglo-
Saxon'*: (1856) near Cape Henry, 27 April 1863, 238 lives lost; *the
'United States'*: Bird Rocks, Gulf of St Lawrence, 25 April 1861, all
lives lost; *the 'President'*: last seen on 11 March 1841, with 136 people
on board; *the 'City of Glasgow'*: (1850) sailed for Delaware on 1
March 1854, and never seen again.

360 *which makes a total of 25 million*: in fact 20 million. (Five lines lower,
'four cod' should similarly read 'three'.)

361 *Cyrus Field*: Cyrus (West) Field (1819–92), American merchant
and financier. The first Atlantic Cable of 1858 failed after three
weeks, but the 1866 one was successful. Field crossed the Atlantic on
the *Great Eastern* again in 1867, with Verne present on the same
trip.

Captain Anderson: ch. 3 of *A Floating City* presents a flattering portrait of this real-life personnage, who was still captain of the *Great
Eastern* on Verne's own crossings.

362 *the armistice between Prussia and Austria after Sadowa*: village in North Czechoslovakia, site of the final Prussian victory in the Seven Weeks War (1866).

'*Glory to God in the highest, and on earth peace, good will towards men.*': Luke 2: 14. Allotte de la Fuÿe reports that this telegram was sent by the American president to Queen Victoria.

364 *the 'Marseillais' . . . Admiral Vanstabel*: naval officers. *Lapoype-Vertrieux*: (Verne: 'La Poype-Vertrieux') Jean-François, Marquis de Lapoype (1758–1851); *Admiral d'Estaing*: Charles Hector (Comte) (1729–94), French naval commander; guillotined; *Count of Grasse*: François-Joseph-Paul, Marquis de Grasse-Tilly (1722–88), admiral. His blockade of Chesapeake Bay cut off Cornwallis's retreat in the War of Independence and so proved decisive; *Villaret de Joyeuse*: (Verne: 'Villaret-Joyeuse') Louis-Thomas (1750–1824), admiral who fought courageously in the battle Verne describes, and was later able to escort the convoy of wheat into Brest. In 1802, however, the same officer refused Fulton's request for his *Nautilus* to be allowed to attack a British warship positioned off Brest; *Admiral Vanstabel*: (Verne: 'van Stabel') Pierre-Jean (1746–97), French admiral.

The 'Vengeur'!: the main message of this episode is Nemo's Republicanism, as indicated by his use of the revolutionary calendar and his 'Long live the Republic!' The captain chooses an incident which was a defeat for France and involved the suicide of up to 356 men, even though the campaign as a whole was a success; thus showing his late-romantic attraction towards 'glorious losers'.

   Surprisingly, Verne omits to mention that the submarine is off the coasts of France and England. WJM and FPW point out that a British nationality for Nemo's victims is here hinted at (the later sinking will also take place near the English Channel).

365 *Yes, monsieur*: MS2 has: '~~But give it back its real name:~~ Le Vengeur ~~du peuple~~!' Nemo further emphasizes his support for 'the people', namely for the underdog, Republicanism, and left-wing values. He is in sum opposed to all the great powers; with definite indications of anti-Turk, anti-Confederate, anti-Russian, and anti-British sentiments. Indeed, as Aronnax says, there is a '*coalition* of nations against him' and Nemo has 'sworn implacable hatred against *them*'.

A fine name!: Verne often inserts anagrams of his surname; here 'Vengeur' gives 'verne' and 'gu' with a soft *g*: a fine name indeed!

the glorious wreck: MS2 has 'the ~~Republican~~ wreck'. The deletion of the R word is in line with Hetzel's editorial policy, for it is absent from Verne's major works, even though the novelist was elected to Amiens Council on a Republican list.

a monstrous or sublime hatred that time could not diminish: Hetzel insisted on radical changes to the manuscript, especially the ending. We know that he also imposed drastic alterations on *Captain Hatteras*,

The Mysterious Island, and *Hector Servadac*, in each case inserting an implausible happy ending that altered the meaning of the whole novel.

Verne protested, writing an important account of Nemo's character and motives: 'I can see full well that you're picturing a very different fellow from mine. . . . We have agreed on two main points: 1. to change the horror that the captain inspires in xx after his great execution, in the character's interest. 2. to speed up the action after the sinking of the double-decker. This will be done, but, for the rest, all I need to do is to justify the captain's terrible action in terms of the provocation he undergoes. Nemo doesn't run after ships and sink them every five minutes, he responds to attacks. But nowhere, whatever your letter says, have I made him a man who kills for killing's sake. He has a generous nature and his feelings are sometimes brought into play in the environment he lives in. His hatred of humanity is sufficiently explained by what he has suffered, both he and his family . . . I now arrive at the part of your letter which informs me that the second volume is very different from the first, in the sense that the man shows himself more violent. This proves to me that you don't sufficiently remember the first, for I am sure I have followed a very natural crescendo. There *are* generous sentiments, *especially* in the second volume and only the force of events makes our hero become a sombre law-maker. . . . Now please take good note, my dear Hetzel: when you read this second volume you were very pleased at the improvement it had undergone and it was the last few pages that appalled you; you are right about the effect produced on Arronnax [*sic*], and I will change it. But *vis-à-vis* Captain Nemo it's not the same, and when you explain him in a different way you change him to the point that I can't recognize him. | What I mean is that if he was a fellow to be done again—which I feel perfectly incapable of, for I've been living with him for two years, I couldn't imagine him otherwise—it wouldn't be a day that needed to be spent in Paris, but a month . . . In sum, your letter has tortured me' (Jules-Verne, pp. 148–9; March 1869).

Reading this letter, one can sympathize with the author, for the subtleties of Nemo's character seem to have been lost on the publisher, who falls into the trap of 'judging' Nemo's actions in isolation. The climax is so much a product of the previous 600 pages that Hetzel's quick-fix changes do seem of a nature to 'torture' his author. But Verne agrees to change 'the effect produced on Arronnax'.

367 *had he not attacked some ship?*: MS2 has '~~of a certain nation which he pursued with his hate~~'. This version, unlike the final one, implied that all Nemo's attacks were against ships from one country. In that case, given the nationality of the *Vengeur's* enemies, and unlike still earlier versions, it would probably have been Britain.

Amidst these questions, the reader may not notice apparent

inconsistencies in Nemo's behaviour. Why is Aronnax drugged and imprisoned for the first incident, whereas on the other occasion the panels are not even closed? Further, if Nemo only ripostes when attacked, does this apply to the *Florida*, presumably not even a warship? Furthermore, if a correlation between drugs and attacks is established, it leads to other questions. Why does Nemo administer drugs when Aronnax first arrives—was he perhaps already attacking some ship? And what ship was in the vicinity, apart from . . . the *Abraham Lincoln*?

368 *ship of an accursed nation*: the correspondence shows that originally Nemo was Polish, and his enemies Russian. Although this would have been popular in France, Hetzel vetoed it as he did not want to upset the Russian government. Verne protested in at least four letters: 'suppose Nemo to be a *Pole*, and the ship sunk a *Russian* one, would there be the shadow of an objection to raise? No, a hundred times no! . . . the first idea of the book, true, logical, complete: a Pole—Russia. But since we cannot say it . . . let's imagine that it can be *that*.' (Jules-Verne, p. 146; April 1869?). 'But, to be frank, I regret my Pole, I had got used to him, we were good friends, and what is more, it was more straightforward, more sincere' (C.-N. Martin, p. 171; Spring 1867?)

369 *The attack has come*: MS2 has Aronnax saying '~~It would be the act of a barbarian.~~'; producing the response ' "Keep quiet, ~~sir~~," replied the captain in an irritated tone, "~~Keep quiet, sir~~ [. . .] ~~When I confined you to that cell,~~ [. . .] The attack has come! ~~from them!~~ [. . .]" ' The '~~from them~~' emphasizes Nemo's leitmotiv of only riposting, like Aronnax and the 'savages', of ensuring that no one assails him with impunity. The published version of this dialogue shows Nemo's considerable restraint *vis-à-vis* Aronnax, perhaps a sign of his disdain.

Go down: MS2: 'Go down~~, I tell you~~.'

    In a letter from Le Crotoy dated 'Thursday', Verne promises Hetzel that he will take out 'the horror that Nemo inspires in Aronnax at the end, and take out that attitude of hate that Nemo has on seeing the ship being sunk, and will not even make him assist at this "sinking" ' (Jules-Verne, p. 145).

I am the law, I am the justice: a mocking, anarchistic echo of 'I am the first, I am the last' (Isaiah 44: 6) and 'I am the way, and the truth, and the life' (John 14: 6) at the Last Supper, in response to 'doubting Thomas' (John 14: 5–6), a phrase Verne uses in I 2. 20*TL* is unique in Verne's output in its density of biblical reference, including: Leviathan, Edom, the unicorn as a symbol of virile strength or freedom, the 'archangel of hatred', the 'days' of Genesis being 'eras', Jonah and references to being 'in a belly' ('Jonah was in the belly of the fish three days and three nights', Jonah 1: 17), the 'draught of the fishes' (Luke 5: 9), the ark (Genesis 6–7), the crossing of the Red Sea (Exodus 14: 21–31), the 'fiery furnace' (Daniel 3: 6), 'they have ears and do not hear' (Mark 8: 18), the 'fire which did not burn' ('the bush burned with fire, and the bush [was] not consumed', Exodus 3: 2), and the final 'hast thou walked in the search of the depth?'

country, wife, children, parents—perished as I watched!: this is perhaps the biggest hint about Nemo's nationality in the published version. By speaking of his country ('patrie'), he possibly implies that it is a European one which has 'perished', since many other areas of the globe were not considered as nations. Poland would be the most obvious example.

'I refuse to write the letter in question concerning Captain Nemo if I cannot explain his hatred, or I will remain silent about the reason for the hero's hatred and life, his nationality, etc. Or, if necessary, I will change the ending. . . . You say: but he performs an evil act! I reply no; imagine again—this was the original idea for the book—a Polish nobleman whose daughters have been raped, wife killed with an axe, father killed with a knout [a whip with leather thongs, used on Russian criminals], a Pole whose friends all die in Siberia and whose nationality will soon disappear from Europe under the Russian tyranny. If that man does not have the right to sink Russian frigates everywhere he encounters them, then revenge is nothing but an empty word. In such a situation, *I* would sink without hesitation. In order not to feel as I do on this matter, one would have to have never hated. . . . I have no wish to indulge in politics, a subject I am ill-suited to and since politics has no connection with all that. | After all this, I repeat I will act for the best, and if necessary, I will change the ending of the sunk ship' (C.-N. Martin, pp. 174–5; Le Crotoy, end of May 1869).

Verne is referring to the Polish insurrection of 1863 against Russian despotism. Presumably he was being told to write a letter to the press to 'explain' Nemo's behaviour—a strange idea after 600 pages of justification.

WJM and FPW suggest that Nemo is Indian. It is true that previous hints had included: the ambiguous 'That Indian, Professor, is an inhabitant of an oppressed country. I am his compatriot, and shall remain so to my very last breath!' (II 3); Aronnax's speculation that Nemo was 'born in the lower latitudes' (I 8); and the location of the two previous encounters (the *Florida* was sunk at Tuamotu; I 23 took place between the Cocos Islands and Java). However, Nemo's art collection, preferred composers, and other cultural references are exclusively western European or Greek—there is little trace of oriental influence in his allusions. Given the name of the *Florida*, apparently taken from the notorious Confederate vessel, and the attack on the *Abraham Lincoln*, one could just as plausibly argue that Nemo was anti-American. Also, the correspondence and the manuscripts seem to preclude any specific interpretation. In sum, although traces remain of anti-British, anti-Russian, anti-Turkish, anti-American, and even anti-Austrian crusades, Nemo's own nationality is left open. In the same letter, Verne himself wrote 'Readers will suppose what they want, depending on their character'.

369 *Keep quiet!*: MS2: ' ~~"Keep quiet, sir," he exclaimed. "Do you know who you are imploring? A man expelled from his country, despotically exiled, xxxx from his wife, xxxx from his children whom the pain killed, and whom he was not allowed to see again [. . .] For the last time, keep quiet!"~~ ' The MS2 version is less courteous, less subtle, and less literary, but does not involve Nemo's wife and children being killed as he watched, and does not mention his parents.

371 *leave for ever this man that I did not dare judge*: MS2 has 'leave for ever ~~the Nautilus~~'.

so as to form a unified line with it: MS2 has ' ~~to my great surprise~~'.

five o'clock: this is inconsistent with the earlier 'six a.m.' (WJM and FPW).

it was allowing itself to be approached: Hetzel suggested that Nemo 'back the *Nautilus* into a cul-de-sac from which he cannot escape except by sinking the ship'. Verne riposted that the *Nautilus* was too quick and too strong to allow that to happen; and that if it *was* cornered, that would mean there wasn't enough water to sink the ship in (Jules-Verne, p. 145).

372 *a few metres below the surface*: Gagneux asks why the submarine submerges, as its ram will then probably pass clean under the ship.

373 *the tip of its main-mast*: MS2 adds: ' ~~There, in a last convulsion a poor little cabin boy, as if chained in the pale flame, twisted himself in a last convulsion.~~ ', with echoes of the pathos of the sinking *Florida*.

knelt down sobbing: for these two paragraphs, MS2 reads 'I turned to Captain Nemo. ~~He was watching still. His eyes shining, fixed to one side, his teeth uncovered under his raised lip, his body stiff, his fingers clenched, his head hunched in his shoulders. A veritable statue of hatred, such as I ha as he had already appeared to my eyes in the seas of India~~'. After 'Nemo' an addition is made in the margin: 'This sombre lawgiver, veritable archangel of hatred, as he had already appeared to me in the seas of India, was watching'; with the four published sentences added in the margin after the word 'still'. The striking portrait of Nemo is presumably omitted because it is identical to the one in the Indian Ocean, apart from the fixity of the eyes.

his terrible reprisal: MS2: 'his bloody execution'.

374 *at unsurpassed speed*: MS2 has 'I saw that we ~~had entered the English Channel, which couldn't help but reassure me. At this phase of the moon, the tides already had some reef [sic]. Their current which is 75 centimetres per second between Ouessant and Land's End, must have been 2.50 metres [per second], and carried us on still more quickly. | The bottom of the Channel is 170 metres deep on average. It is rela-~~

~~tively flat, it forms a sandy valley, still(?) between Britain and France.~~
~~That day, the *Nautilus* kept quite close to the coast of north-west~~
~~France.~~' Verne cannot resist taking his submarine near his birthplace
and demonstrating his familiarity with the Channel.

then the moon rose: MS2: 'The state of my mind would not have
allowed it. | By evening, we had covered ~~the whole of the Channel~~
~~between Brest and the mouth of the Seine. The clock read eight seven~~
~~o'clock, when the lights of la Hève sent us their electric brilliance. I~~
~~recognized the magnificent cliffs of Cap d'Antifer, which took on a fan-~~
~~tastic appearance as night fell: their limestone strata, dotted with small~~
~~patches of grass, produced an interminable procession of strange~~
~~figures, queens of the middle ages arranged with the roughness of the~~
~~old painters, a Cimabue or a Marekgun(?), bishops in long high~~
~~mitres blessing lords in helmets and armour, ladies with long head-~~
~~dresses on their xxxx, with broad folds, squires standing behind vast~~
~~feast-tables; fortified castles with turrets and machicolations, but too~~
~~small and not in proper perspective, as in the bas-reliefs in old cathe-~~
~~drals. | Then night fell, the vision melted into the mists of the evening.~~
Night fell, and the sea was covered by darkness until the moon rose.'
Verne shows his knowledge of the area round Le Havre (Cap d'Antifer
will later be alluded to in the title *Captain Antifer*). He also reveals his
powerful visual imagination, stimulated by paintings but also by
natural complexities: in *Captain Hatteras*, he often imagines whole
scenes from glimpses of icefields. Cimabue (JV: 'Crinabuë') (1240?–
1302?) was an Italian painter of New Testament frescoes.

The time of the clocks on board had been suspended: an allusion to
Lamartine's 'Oh time! Suspend your flight!', and presumably meaning
that the clocks have actually stopped—Verne often takes metaphors
literally. Since the Atlantic, the time of narration has accelerated radically; indications of date have also become more infrequent as Aronnax becomes more distraught, and will soon disappear altogether.

*At each moment I expected to see, like the fabulous Gordon Pym, 'a
shrouded human figure . . . which defends the approaches to the
Pole'!*: Verne is apparently quoting Baudelaire's translation at the end
of the main section of Poe's *The Narrative of Arthur Gordon Pym of
Nantucket* (1838). However, Poe does not have the phrase 'thrown
across the cataract which defends the approaches to the Pole', the final
words being: 'And the hue of the skin of the figure was of the perfect
whiteness of the snow.' In addition, Baudelaire's translation is misleading, for Poe speaks of a 'human figure', meaning something like
'human form', whereas Baudelaire and Verne have 'figure humaine,'
which would usually mean 'human face' (especially in conjunction
with 'voilée').

Verne wrote only one literary study: 'Edgar Poe et ses œuvres' (*Le
Musée des familles* (April 1864), 193–208). This article explores 'A
Descent into the Maelström' ('a vertiginous excursion attempted by

fishermen from Lofoten') and especially *Arthur Gordon Pym*, referring to Baudelaire's translation and preface. His *An Antarctic
Mystery* (1897) is a sort of interpretation, adaptation, and sequel to
Poe's novel.

375 *When it went up to the surface again to replenish its air, the hatches
['panneaux'] opened and closed automatically*: Verne generally uses
'panneaux' for both the panels covering the windows and the hatches
for entering the submarine or dinghy. Here he is probably thinking of
the hatches; and presumably 'automatically' means 'without visible
human effort' or even 'by electrical means'. However, this creates other
mysteries: why did we not know about this before? And why was it
not used to keep the Papuans and the squid out?

no longer tenable: the last four paragraphs, starting from 'in my mind',
appear in the margin of MS2, replacing a visit to the bay on which Le
Crotoy is located: '~~At about midnight, we passed near the Baie de la
Somme whose 10,000 hectares of sand are covered by the rising tide.~~'

find shelter there: MS2 omits 'One morning—what date I cannot say',
but has instead 'Ned Land who was watching for me to wake up'.
Aronnax then replies to Ned, '~~"We must seize the opportunity."~~ | "Will
you be ready monsieur?" | "Yes. But where are we?" | ~~"We're past the
Strait of Dover. We've sighted the lights of Great Yar(?) and North(?)
Foreland(?). We're moving into the North Sea. No time to be lost!
Who knows if we will be carried off."~~'

without the crew realizing: MS2 adds: 'Depending on the wind, we
will land in Scotland or Holland.' Scotland does not really seem to be
on their route, but just as in several other novels, Verne cannot resist
the idea, however implausible, of heading back to his beloved
Scotland.

376 *a day or even an hour*: instead of these two sentences MS2 has: 'The
Nautilus was floating a few miles from land, which was lying to starboard. A hot day was in store. The sky was white, the air calm. Not
a breath of wind. On the sea small regular ripples created intersecting
diamond shapes. The sun picked them out in sparkling points. The
water, like liquid emerald, heaved in broad waves that the *Nautilus*
did not even feel. In the quivering haze, a few far-off fishing boats and
two or three coasting luggers with flaccid sails faded indistinctly away.
The smoke from a steamer traced a motionless cloud against the backdrop of the sky. | The weather looked as though it was going to help
us. The *Nautilus* kept close to land as it headed northwards.
Unfortunately it was moving fast. Would it engage the narrow passes
of the Kattegat or the Sound? Would it enter that Baltic Sea which has
no way out? I did not know what to think. But I imagined that it would
in fact move up the west coast of Norway. | Yes. Ned was right. We
should not waste a day or even an hour. | After the bearings at noon,
the *Nautilus* dived again. I went back [. . .]' Verne is again painting a

picture, possibly based on one of the artists he mentions. And again, while the pace of this chapter has to be maintained, we can greatly regret the fine vision of a *Nautilus* moving over a tranquil and harmonious European sea.

'Crotoy, 15 May 1869 . . . I agree with you. The end of the voyage through the English Channel between Calais, Boulogne, and Dover is crowded out. It needs redoing. You mustn't know where you are. It would be dreadful and the bombshell of the Maelstrom even more dreadful. | As for a slaver, corsair, or pirate ship, you know full well that these ships don't exist any more. And if we are sticking as much as possible to contemporary reality, it would be unwise to assume the existence of things which do not in fact exist. I'm constantly telling you this, arguing from logic. | The best idea was Nemo battling against the whole of society. A fine situation but difficult to make people believe in, since there was no motive for such a fight. | Less good, there was the battle of the outlaw against those who had made him an outlaw, a Pole against Russia. That was forthright. We rejected it for purely commercial reasons. | But if it is now just a battle by Nemo against an implausible enemy who is as mysterious as him, it's not a duel between two individuals any more. It singularly diminishes the whole thing. | No, as you say, we need to keep it vague, and we'll manage to.' 'Implausible' refers to the idea of slavers or pirates; but it is not clear who the other 'individual' would have been.

He had not gone to bed: MS2 adds the equivocal 'I would have preferred him to be in bed.'

378 *God almighty! Enough! Enough!*: MS2 has ~~'Enough! Enough! Enough!'~~: more obsessive, but less religious.

379 *Maelstrom!*: Pontoppidan, quoted twice in *20TL*, describes the Maelstrom (I 77). Verne's episode may also show a slight influence from the ending of Poe's 'MS. Found in a Bottle' (1833) (which also mentions the 'slumbers of the kraken'). But it demonstrates significant borrowing from 'A Descent into the Maelström' (1841), including such features as the terrifying effect of the name itself, the manner of escape (Poe's first-person narrator lashes himself to a barrel), the period of unconsciousness, and the rescue by Lofoten Islands fishermen. Where Poe writes 'Large stocks of firs and pine *trees* [. . .] rise again *broken and torn* to such a degree as if *bristles* grew upon them. This plainly shows the *bottom* to consist of *craggy rocks*', Verne has 'the *sharp rocks* of the *bottom*, where the hardest bodies break up, where *tree-trunks* wear themselves out and produce a *"fur of hair"*': a clear borrowing.

a whirlpool from which no ship has ever been able to escape: the whirlpool is about 5 miles wide, with a current reaching 13 knots, although the strong local winds can make it more dangerous.

379 *engaged by its captain*: MS2 adds 'It was jibbing at a dizzy speed.'

In addition to the obvious man-machine comparison and phallic and childbirth symbolism, the whole of this paragraph is written in the imperfect tense in French. This produces an unusual effect, which combines with the contrast between the previously open space and a circular, introjective one ('navel', 'spiral'). Above all, the imperfect tense helps to create two opposed but interacting times-of-events: on the one hand, the succession of events is emphasized, as is typical in the adventure novel; but on the other, time is hardly moving at all, giving the impression of being ethereal, non-spatial, or drugged, as in the best Romantic tradition.

as the Norwegian expression has it: Verne often has to resort to quotation to get his more daring passages through (e.g. the erotic description in *Around the World*, pp. 70–1). Given the similarity with Poe, we may doubt his quoted source, epecially as MS2 has '~~a Norwegian author poet has said~~'.

and us with it: MS2 adds '~~How long this torture went on, I could not say. What happened, I could not recount. A single incident has remained in my mind.~~'

we can still get out alive . . . !: MS2: ' "We need ~~to do something!" said Ned. | "Yes!" I exclaimed. "Go on, Ned! Undo the last bolt! And let us die far from the Nautilus!" | The bolts were undone, and following a violent shock I lost consciousness.~~' In the original version, in other words, the three deliberately entered the Maelstrom in a frail boat—Aronnax's suicidal impulse is a further sign of the horror that he now feels for the *Nautilus*.

380 *We embraced warmly*: MS2 adds 'I was in a bad state.'

we cannot think of returning to France: the narrator is playing a delicate balancing act here, with narrative and fictional time precariously converging. Since he is now using the present, what events can he narrate, how can the future be recounted, how can the narration present its own demise? This is undoubtedly a problem of much fiction, but seems to be more acute here because of Aronnax's revision of the manuscript describing his adventures. The present tense, in other words, constitutes the sign of a stagnation, a self-consciousness, and a self-referentiality that the narrator usually avoids.

I am revising the tale of these adventures: MS2: 'I revised'. Aronnax has become the author of *20TL*, although he does not name the book.

But what became of the 'Nautilus'?: Verne's submarine and its inventor will have many imitators over the following century. These include Conan Doyle's *The Maracot Deep* (1929) and Paul Eluard, with Georges Perec and Philippe Sollers both making direct reference to *20TL*. Arthur Rimbaud's 'Le Bateau ivre', begun in August 1871, is also derived from this novel, with heavy borrowing of imagery and themes. A brief summary of images and quotations taken straight from Verne would include 'monitors', 'phosphorescence', 'wake [...] of cotton', 'lactescent', 'Floridas', 'may my keel explode', 'sea bream', 'conserve', 'singing fishes', 'Maelstrom', the Sargasso Sea, and sinking corpses.

Is Captain Nemo still alive?: Nemo reappears in *The Mysterious Island* (1873), complete with the *Nautilus*, as the agent who has secretly been protecting the settlers from the dangers of the desert island; and eventually dies. The 'true' nationality of Nemo and all his crew is 'revealed' to be Indian (although at least one of them had previously been French). His victims were, it seems, British after all; and so on. But this Nemo bears no resemblance to the Nemo we know; and the most basic facts do not tally. His age, for instance, is wildly off; and he claims, in a strange echo of Hetzel's implausible suggestion, that he sank the warship 'in a narrow, shallow bay—I needed to get through'.

The Mysterious Island is therefore of little help in understanding the true Nemo. Even his actions to help the settlers seem suspect, for they destroy the validity of their utopian experiment. In addition, recent discoveries about Hetzel's interventions have further undermined the validity of the 1873 novel. In the published version, but not in the manuscript, we read of Nemo's deathbed remorse and of Smith's pompous assessment of his life as a 'mistake'. In the book version of *The Mysterious Island*, Nemo gives the settlers a trunk of jewellery, whereas in the manuscript they get the giant pearl he had so carefully nurtured in *20TL*. The captain's dying words, the absurd 'God and my country!', were brutally, criminally, imposed by Hetzel. The manuscript had instead 'Independence!'

Voyage à travers l'impossible (1882), published under Verne and Adolphe d'Ennery's joint names, goes even further in betraying Verne's thought. 'Nemo', for example, has become a reactionary and a bigot, and declaims: 'you will see emboldened criminals multiplying indefinitely [...] and assassins telling themselves: "We can kill without fear; we will not be executed! [...] remorse is a vain word, for God does not exist! [etc.]"' This Colonel Blimp-like diatribe shows the absurdity of some of the literary works to which Verne's name was attached, and cannot be taken seriously. In sum, it is preferable to forget the two commercially inspired sequels which travesty the man we know. *20TL* must remain the only authorized version of the mysterious captain. Nemo the restless anarchist is still prowling the ocean deeps.

381 *the manuscript containing the entire story of his life*: 'Edom' (1910) consists mainly of a manuscript left to fate, recounting a similarly unique experience. In fact, parallels with *20TL* appear systematic. A select list of them would include: the pleasure of smoking; an allusion to the battle between the *Merrimac* and the *Monitor*; an overwhelming dominance of the oceans and an exclusive diet of sea-food; the

incorporation of biblical language into the text; an interest in archae-
ological remains as a way of investigating the truth of legends; a fas-
cination for the lost continent of Atlantis, destroyed by volcanic action,
with descriptions of its arches and broken columns giving rise to heady
contemplations on human destiny; the idea of the ruins being brought
up from the depths by volcanic activity; an interest in the word 'Edom';
an invented language containing teasing hints of both European and
non-European languages; a new and totally masculine society; a surprising re-emergence of French to convey a heartfelt message; and the
contrast between a scientific composition, written by men of superior
learning but destined to be lost, and a personal narration, composed
by a slow-witted and self-centred author but surviving many vicissi-
tudes to great effect. 'Edom' is therefore a brilliantly appropriate
sequel to Nemo's life story.

381 *survived where so many ships have perished*: MS2 originally read 'I
also believe, I fear that his powerful machine has overcome the sea's
most terrifying abyss and that his *Nautilus* has survived where so many
ships have perished!' This is different from the published version in
using the subjunctive form, in implying that the submarine probably
did escape, and above all in considering such an outcome undesirable.
An addition to MS2 complicates matters further: the words '~~yet
more~~—for must I hope so?—' are inserted after 'fear'; and the subjunctive *ait* is crossed out and replaced with . . . *ait* again. In sum, the
complexities of Aronnax's feelings are reflected in the mood of the verb
and the hesitation between believing, fearing, and hoping in the successive versions of the sentence.

*that question which the Book of Ecclesiastes posed 6,000 years ago,
'hast thou walked in the search of the depth?'*: Verne has, 'Qui a jamais
pu sonder les profondeurs de l'abîme?', clearly meant to quote 'hast
thou walked in the search of the depth?' (Job 38: 16), but literally
translatable as 'Who has ever been able to sound the depths of the
abyss?' But he may also be thinking of 'That which is far off, and
exceeding deep, who can find it out?' (Ecclesiastes 7: 24) and 'Who
shall descend into the deep?' (Romans 10: 7), or even of 'Hast thou
entered into the springs of the sea?' (Job 38: 16).

The title page of Zurcher and Margollé's *Le Monde sous-marin*
(Hetzel, 1868) contains a remarkably similar epigraph: 'Qui sondera
les mystères de l'Abîme? Job' ('Who will sound the mysteries of
the Abyss? Job'). Furthermore, Renard's *Le Fond de la mer* (also
Hetzel, 1868) again begins with the words 'Qui pénètrera les mystères
de l'Océan?' ('Who will penetrate the mysteries of the Ocean?'), as-
cribing it however to the Wisdom of Solomon. MD (p. 65) points out
that only the Zurcher and Margollé quotation and attribution are
correct, meaning that the other two authors probably copied from
them.

The 'Epilogue' of *Moby-Dick* has as epigraph a remarkably similar quotation from the same book of the Bible ('And I only am escaped alone to tell thee.'—Job 1: 19).

Since the seventeenth century, the date of the Creation had been calculated as 4004 BC; and Verne's '6,000 years' implies that he ascribes to Ecclesiastes the same age. But throughout the nineteenth century, especially following the discovery of ancient fossil remains, doubt was cast on the traditional age of Creation, and in any case modern scholarship dates the Book of Ecclesiastes as third century BC.

Captain Nemo and I: MS1 is radically different: 'But what became of the *Nautilus*? Did it perhaps succumb. [*sic*] But perhaps also its formidable construction allowed it to resist and to get out of the abyss. And what became of Captain Nemo? I do not think anyone will ever know. Perhaps he died? As for the sunken frigate, it will easily be discovered which government has lost it and so its nationality will be known [. . .] As for me, who have assisted at so many [scenes?], how can I forget him, if he is still living with his *Nautilus* and his companions, the Man of the Waters, entirely free!' (MD, pp. 64–5). Unlike the published version, this draft implies that if Nemo does survive he will cease his revenge, and will not put the manuscript of his life and works into a bottle. It does not criticize his actions, and indeed closes with support of his way of life.

MS2 reads 'Vengeances' for 'vengeance': both a reification and a multiplication. It ends with 'Is he not the only man who can reply "I have!" to that question of the Book of Ecclesiastes, "hast thou walked in the search of the depth?"' The published text is then substituted in the margin, apart from two variants: it reads 'secrets of the abyss' rather than 'depths of the abyss'; and 'loudly and clearly' rather than the published 'now'. MD claims that the phrase 'but, one should take careful note, he is unassailable ['imprenable']' is first added on folio 133 and then crossed out; but this must in fact be in MS1.

Several comments should be made. The quotation from Job in MS2 is closer to the original. Also, having Nemo take the curtain solo, without Aronnax (or Ned or Conseil), is perhaps aesthetically preferable. And finally, the idea of Nemo's 'unassailability' or 'impregnability', perhaps deleted because of Aronnax's bourgeois values, sounds very much like an ultimate defiance thrown at Hetzel and all conformists.

The Oxford World's Classics Website

www.worldsclassics.co.uk

- Information about new titles
- Explore the full range of Oxford World's Classics
- Links to other literary sites and the main OUP webpage
- Imaginative competitions, with bookish prizes
- Peruse the Oxford World's Classics Magazine
- Articles by editors
- Extracts from Introductions
- A forum for discussion and feedback on the series
- Special information for teachers and lecturers

www.worldsclassics.co.uk

American Literature

British and Irish Literature

Children's Literature

Classics and Ancient Literature

Colonial Literature

Eastern Literature

European Literature

History

Medieval Literature

Oxford English Drama

Poetry

Philosophy

Politics

Religion

The Oxford Shakespeare

A complete list of Oxford Paperbacks, including Oxford World's Classics, Oxford Shakespeare, Oxford Drama, and Oxford Paperback Reference, is available in the UK from the Academic Division Publicity Department, Oxford University Press, Great Clarendon Street, Oxford OX2 6DP.

In the USA, complete lists are available from the Paperbacks Marketing Manager, Oxford University Press, 198 Madison Avenue, New York, NY 10016.

Oxford Paperbacks are available from all good bookshops. In case of difficulty, customers in the UK can order direct from Oxford University Press Bookshop, Freepost, 116 High Street, Oxford OX1 4BR, enclosing full payment. Please add 10 per cent of published price for postage and packing.